PRAISE FOR THIS NEW EDITION OF MALCOLM

"[Malcolm] is an amazing masterpiece, and it has been held back or turned away by so many people simply because of MacDonald's usage of what to many people seems to be an undecipherable and in some cases, uncanny language. In his explaining of the Scottish accents and jargons to our minds, David Jack is...making George MacDonald's works open to us that we too may benefit from them."

Douglas Gresham
Stepson of C. S. Lewis
Series Producer, *The Chronicles of Narnia*

"For many readers, the use of the Doric dialect in MacDonald's Scottish writings has resulted in the misunderstanding, misinterpretation, or abandonment of these captivating novels altogether. In this edition of *Malcolm*, David Jack does a masterful job not only preserving the original meaning and nuance within his interpretation, but also respecting the original text by including it intact. This volume would be a welcome addition to any George MacDonald reader, scholar or layman alike."

Dean Hardy
Teacher of Christian Philosophy and Apologetics at
Charlotte Christian School and the author of
*Waking the Dead: George MacDonald as
Philosopher, Mystic, and Apologist*

"Like many, I was put off for years reading my great-great-grandfather's "Scottish" novels, many of which feature extensive dialogue by characters who speak Scots. I tried on numerous occasions, but, I am ashamed to say, gave up! So I welcome the Scots-English Editions, like this one for *Malcolm*, which place English translations side-by-side with the original text. Without doubt translator David Jack came along at just the right time! David has a love of George, and a love for Scotland, so does not simply popularize passages, but gives them deep thought and care to reflect aspects of character, and occasionally plot, which the author was trying to get across. I hope these newly available works will increase interest in George, and in his message for all of us."

Christopher MacDonald,
Great-great-grandson of George MacDonald

I commend this new and vigorous edition of *Malcolm*. You, the reader, will journey into the foothills of imaginative literature, with its pleasing panoramas of gentle valleys and calm rivers. Your undertaking will be blessed and give you the strength to carry on into

the higher uplands. By following in the footsteps of the Inklings, the reader will safe-
guard the insight that Coleridge, that early explorer, strove so hard to bring back when
he gave us his understanding of imagination as the highest human ability "as a vessel by
which divinity passes down into humanity". Prepare yourself for the ongoing war against
positivism, every 'good-book' read and step taken along this path is a battle won. Only you
can fight it, the calling is to you.

Owen A. Barfield
Grandson & Trustee, Owen Barfield Literary Estate

CORAGE GOD MEND AL
EX LIBRIS
GEORGE
MACDONALD

MALCOLM

GEORGE MACDONALD

TRANSLATED BY
DAVID JACK

INTRODUCTION BY
DOUGLAS GRESHAM

ILLUSTRATED BY
CARRIE STOUT

Malcolm is an independent production by David Jack

The redesigned replica of George MacDonald's bookplate inside the front cover was provided by Michael Phillips, who notes that "it shows an old man entering his tomb through the door of death, and emerging from it with a new body of strength into the light of eternity."

Scots dialogue translated by David Jack
Translator's Preface by David Jack
Cover art, design, and interior illustrations by Carrie Stout
Introduction by Douglas Gresham

Paperback ISBN: 978-1-7385314-0-0

MacDonald's Scottish Novels

David Elginbrod

Alec Forbes of Howglen

Robert Falconer

Malcolm

The Marquis of Lossie

Sir Gibbie

Castle Warlock

Donal Grant

What's Mine's Mine

The Elect Lady

Heather and Snow

Salted With Fire

GEORGE MACDONALD'S SCOTTISH NOVELS:
THE SCOTS-ENGLISH EDITIONS

The man who loves the antique speech...of his childhood, and knows how to use it, possesses therein a certain kind of power over the hearts of men, which the most refined and perfect of languages cannot give, inasmuch as it has travelled farther from the original sources of laughter and tears.

-Sir Gibbie

"George MacDonald writes of homely things and simple people who saw, in the stuff of a shepherd's cottage or a fisherman's arduous work on the cold sea, the love of God."

-Elisabeth Elliot

"All his life he continued to love the rock from which he had been hewn. All that is best in his novels carries us back to that 'kaleyard' world of granite and heather, of bleaching greens beside burns that look as if they flowed not with water but with stout, to the thudding of wooden machinery, the oatcakes, the fresh milk, the pride, the poverty, and the passionate love of hard-won learning."

-C S Lewis

"Among the many men of genius Scotland produced in the nineteenth century, there was only one...who really represented what Scottish religion should have been, if it had continued the colour of the Scottish medieval poetry. In his particular type of literary work, he did indeed realise the apparent paradox of a St. Francis of Aberdeen."

-G K Chesterton

"While MacDonald's current reputation rests largely on his mythopoeic genius, the reader who would truly know him cannot afford to neglect the twelve novels set in his native Scotland. Full of the spiritual wisdom characterising all his work, there is a further element of oracular power drawn from the very soil itself, so strong was his bond to the land that reared him. As soon might we separate Dickens from London, Hardy from Wessex, or Tolstoy from the heart of Russia, as think of George MacDonald without picturing the Aberdeenshire he brought to life in these stories."

-David Jack

CONTENTS

Publisher's Acknowledgements xv
Translator's Preface xvi
Introduction by Douglas Gresham xxi
Malcolm Cast Of Characters xxiii

CHAPTER I   MISS HORN 1
CHAPTER II   BARBARA CATANACH 6
CHAPTER III   THE MAD LAIRD 11
CHAPTER IV   PHEMY MAIR 15
CHAPTER V   LADY FLORIMEL 19
CHAPTER VI   DUNCAN MACPHAIL.. 28
CHAPTER VII   ALEXANDER GRAHAM 38
CHAPTER VIII   THE SWIVEL... 47
CHAPTER IX   THE SALMON TROUT 56
CHAPTER X   THE FUNERAL.. 68
CHAPTER XI   THE OLD CHURCH... 74
CHAPTER XII   THE CHURCHYARD.. 80
CHAPTER XIII   THE MARQUIS OF LOSSIE..................................... 87
CHAPTER XIV   MEG PARTAN'S LAMP 95
CHAPTER XV   THE SLOPE OF THE DUNE.................................... 100
CHAPTER XVI   THE STORM 110
CHAPTER XVII   THE ACCUSATION 117
CHAPTER XVIII   THE QUARREL.. 125
CHAPTER XIX   DUNCAN'S PIPES 134
CHAPTER XX   ADVANCES 147
CHAPTER XXI   MEDIATION 154
CHAPTER XXII   WHENCE AND WHITHER? 162
CHAPTER XXIII   ARMAGEDDON 169
CHAPTER XXIV   THE FEAST 178
CHAPTER XXV   THE NIGHT WATCH 188
CHAPTER XXVI   NOT AT CHURCH 198
CHAPTER XXVII   LORD GERNON 207
CHAPTER XXVIII A FISHER WEDDING.. 212

CHAPTER XXIX FLORIMEL AND DUNCAN 216

CHAPTER XXX THE REVIVAL 228

CHAPTER XXXI WANDERING STARS 242

CHAPTER XXXII THE SKIPPER'S CHAMBER 249

CHAPTER XXXIII THE LIBRARY 261

CHAPTER XXXIV MILTON, AND THE BAY MARE 270

CHAPTER XXXV KIRKBYRES 275

CHAPTER XXXVI THE BLOW 286

CHAPTER XXXVII THE CUTTER 292

CHAPTER XXXVIII THE TWO DOGS 296

CHAPTER XXXIX COLONSAY CASTLE 303

CHAPTER XL THE DEIL'S WINNOCK 312

CHAPTER XLI THE CLOUDED SAPPHIRES 318

CHAPTER XLII DUNCAN'S DISCLOSURE 334

CHAPTER XLIII THE WIZARD'S CHAMBER 344

CHAPTER XLIV THE HERMIT 350

CHAPTER XLV MR CAIRNS AND THE MARQUIS 358

CHAPTER XLVI THE BAILLIES' BARN 367

CHAPTER XLVII MRS STEWART'S CLAIM 377

CHAPTER XLVIII THE BAILLIES' BARN AGAIN 390

CHAPTER XLIX MOUNT PISGAH 398

CHAPTER L LIZZY FINDLAY 409

CHAPTER LI THE LAIRD'S BURROW 415

CHAPTER LII CREAM OR SCUM? 420

CHAPTER LIII THE SCHOOLMASTER'S COTTAGE 424

CHAPTER LIV ONE DAY 432

CHAPTER LV THE SAME NIGHT 443

CHAPTER LVI SOMETHING FORGOTTEN 447

CHAPTER LVII THE LAIRD'S QUEST 450

CHAPTER LVIII MALCOLM AND MRS STEWART 457

CHAPTER LIX AN HONEST PLOT 463

CHAPTER LX THE SACRAMENT 473

CHAPTER LXI MISS HORN AND THE PIPER 481

CHAPTER LXII THE CUTTLE FISH AND THE CRAB 487

CHAPTER LXIII MISS HORN AND LORD LOSSIE 493

CHAPTER LXIV THE LAIRD AND HIS MOTHER 508

CHAPTER LXV	THE LAIRD'S VISION	511
CHAPTER LXVI	THE CRY FROM THE CHAMBER	518
CHAPTER LXVII	FEET OF WOOL	526
CHAPTER LXVIII	HANDS OF IRON	534
CHAPTER LXIX	THE MARQUIS AND THE SCHOOLMASTER	540
CHAPTER LXX	END OR BEGINNING?	547
APPENDIX	LITERAL ENGLISH TRANSLATION OF MR GRAHAM'S POEM (CHAPTER XLII)	557

PUBLISHER'S ACKNOWLEDGEMENTS

George MacDonald's extensive use of Scots in several of his greatest novels has been a stumbling block for many potential readers. This series of Scots-English translations offers unique assistance to all who wish to read the original, unabridged texts (read by C S Lewis, G K Chesterton, et al.) by retaining, in its entirety, the authentic Scots speech, and placing a parallel English column alongside MacDonald's dialogue.

This new edition of Malcolm is the fifth in the series, following on from Robert Falconer, Castle Warlock, Sir Gibbie, and Donal Grant. It would not have been possible without help from the following contributors, to whom I would like to express my deepest thanks: my wife Jessica, for creating the original two-column format; Carrie Stout, for her beautiful illustrative work; Douglas Gresham, for his excellent introduction; and Adriana Tonello, for the map of Scotland which follows my preface.

TRANSLATOR'S PREFACE

> "A prince can mak a belted knight,
> A marquis, duke, an a' that!
> But an honest man's aboon his might –
> Guid faith, he mauna fa' that!
> For a' that, an a' that,
> Their dignities, an a' that,
> The pith o' sense an pride o' worth,
> Are higher rank than a' that."

BURNS

If any reader of this series, remembering the supposedly unexampled length of its recent fourth instalment,[1] should weigh the present volume in their hand and find it heftier still, it is possible they will be a little puzzled, and feel that the thing needs some explaining. Since I have no wish to make a mystery, I may point out that the former story is indeed longer when measured by word count, but that here we come up against a much more dialogue-driven work–or rather a novel which is fuller than the other of its author's native Scots. This has naturally led to its impressive "doorstop" size; and while the narrative itself is only *rather* long, the 550 plus pages provide a feast of language and a unique chance to luxuriate.

This linguistic richness has been achieved in the simplest of ways. All of the lengthier Scottish works, including *Malcolm*'s sequel, contain episodes in Aberdeen or in London, or other broadenings of their characters' horizons which necessitate the speaking of English. The sole exception is the present tale,[2] whose entire plot unfolds in the small north-eastern fishing village of "Portlossie." By this means, MacDonald has been able to create, at least for the non-Scottish reader, the feeling of a world set apart, and to acquaint us with the children of his invention through the constant utterance of their shared mother-tongue. The English-speaking Lady Florimel and her father (both incomers to the region) seem to have Doric dinned in their ears from all sides; and though old Duncan makes shift to speak their language, he does so always after his own Gaelicised fashion, so that the veil of unrecognition still remains unlifted.

What strikes us more familiarly, at least at first glance, is the coincidence of title and hero's name. Such "doubling up" has been seen three times already in our series, in the case of *Robert Falconer*, of *Sir Gibbie*, and of *Donal Grant*; and with *David Elginbrod* and *Alec Forbes*

---

1 *Donal Grant*, the sequel to *Sir Gibbie*, and the longest of all George MacDonald's novels.

2 *What's Mine's Mine* is only a partial exception, for though the location remains constant, this entails no transition, since English is spoken throughout.

still to come, half the works on our list can be similarly accounted for. Even the omission of a surname might, in the current instance, have less to do with an attempt at uniqueness than with the preservation of a close-kept secret. But it does seem that Malcolm is an especially apt title, and an especially apt name, even compared with the others I have briefly mentioned. Its literal meaning is "servant," or "disciple,"[3] and it was the second most common name for Scottish monarchs before the Union of the Crowns. It is this blend of nobility and self-negation which is embodied in the person of our hero, and which appears (helpfully for my purpose) in the very first of MacDonald's *Unspoken Sermons*:

> "What is the kingdom of Christ? A rule of love, of truth—a rule of service. The king is the chief servant in it...It is *like king like subject* in the kingdom of heaven. No rule of force, as of one kind over another kind. It is the rule of *kind*, of *nature*, of deepest nature—of *God*. If, then, to enter into this kingdom, we must become children, the spirit of children must be its pervading spirit throughout, from lowly subject to lowliest king."[4]

Since Malcolm has been given two long novels to himself (this one, and *The Marquis of Lossie*) we shall, if we wish, have him by the creelful, and have plenty of opportunity to discover what stuff he is made of. But before his creator uproots him and alters his destiny, he shows him to us first *in situ*: that is, in the local fishing community where he is widely known, and in the house of his old, blind "daddy."

As to his home, it is as humble as his occupation, and would appear sufficiently plain even compared to the dwellings of the upper town; for not only Lossie House, but even Miss Horn's modest parlour is described as a sort of wonder beside it. Yet if a character like Sir Gibbie scarcely knew that his origins were humble, Malcolm, knowing full well, is positively proud: the thought of a marquisate would not move him, nor an earldom elevate–except insofar as either might secure his place by Lady Florimel, and give him further opportunities to serve her. But it is his relationship and interplay with Duncan, far more than any scenes with his young mistress, that truly show him to advantage. The "fisher lad" himself is of course a type of Christ (at different points he is wounded in hand and foot) and his elder a kind of Pictish patriarch–a walking anachronism, full of eulogies and execrations and an ancient unreserve which makes us privy to them all. We feel in Malcolm's presence as if we are standing on holy ground, but with Duncan we are staggered at the genius that could ever have conceived him. To say that he is peerless may be to sully his sublimity with weak wordplay, but I can think of no other way to sum him up: his place is with the immortals.

One final remark ought to be made touching Malcolm MacPhail and his world, before leaving both to the reader, that they might be allowed to speak for themselves. In one of

---

3 Specifically, "disciple of Columba"
4 *Unspoken Sermons*, series 1, *The Child in the Midst*

G K Chesterton's more *recherché* literary essays,[5] he has drawn a comparison between the fisherman and Curdie the miner. On Chesterton's view they are one and the same, and while he was referring to the two sequels (*The Marquis of Lossie* and *The Princess and Curdie*) his general point remains: all of MacDonald's fiction is pregnant with the marvellous, and to those who have read his myths it has been granted to understand the mystery of his melodramas. To a great extent, I share his conviction that Malcolm is Curdie, but if this is so, it is as clear from the first part of his adventures as from the second. We have only to replace the goblin mines with the North Sea; their hordes of gems with hordes of fishes, and the mystery unfolds itself: Malcolm even helps us to the discovery with all his talk about the battle of Armageddon, and his wish that he might *make songs as weapons for going about his work*. There are hints of other fairy-tales too, for Bawby Catanach, as well as being a possible tribute to Mrs Gamp,[6] is equally reminiscent of the witch Makemnoit[7] — and who can fail to think of *The Golden Key*'s aëranths, when they read the following lines?

"it's jist a gradation o' services, an' the highest en' o' ony animal is to contreebute to the life o' ane higher than itsel'; sae that it 's the gran' preevilege o' the fish we tak, to be aten by human bein's, an' uphaud what's abune them."	"it's just a gradation of services, and the highest end of any animal is to contribute to the life of one higher than itself; so that it's the grand privilege of the fish we take, to be eaten by human beings, and sustain what's above them."

*****

TRANSLATING THE DORIC

Writing to his friend Arthur Greeves in 1946, C S Lewis affirmed MacDonald's "Scotch" usage–it let him (said Lewis) "say strongly and racily things he w[oul]d spoil in English."[8] I do not think he was guilty of overstating the case: in fact the spoliation can be said to go with the territory, and to keep it to a minimum is a cause for triumph. Such has been my modest endeavour here, in the fifth of our Scots/English editions, though admittedly the task becomes more important given the vast quantities of Scots involved. Perhaps the right hand column may surpass itself at times, and rise above this meagre level; and I have certainly been pleased by the approbation which has met my former endeavours. But the stakes are inevitably raised for a project like this one, as *Malcolm* is such a firm favourite in MacDonald circles–so if I approached it, some months ago, with a degree of fear and trembling, there are many of whose sympathy I ought to be secure.

---

5 *George MacDonald and His Work* (1901)

6 Sarah Gamp, also a midwife, is one of the highlights of Dickens' *Martin Chuzzlewit*

7 In MacDonald's fairy tale, *The Light Princess*

8 Extract by C S Lewis © copyright C S Lewis Pte Ltd

One factor at least has been strongly in my favour. I had decided, as early as book two, that since Scots and English are the two *languages* concerned, I would only translate the first, and would leave any dialects of the latter tongue completely undisturbed. This has largely solved the problem of Duncan, for it is always English he speaks,[9] however much he subjects it to his own Gaelic filter. I have, however, relaxed my rule by a fraction in his case, altering the "translated" column subtly, so as to preserve the look and feel of the original, while smoothing out the thornier words unclarified by context. Mostly, this has been done by swapping single letters–changing "p" back to "b" for example, when the old man refers to his "poy" or his "pible," but I have not always meddled even this far, and have generally rather felt my way through difficulties than observed any strict or consistent rule. None of the essential *Duncanisms* have been removed, and if one can remember his continual preference for the third person feminine it will be an aid to understanding and a great point gained.

The remaining passages of speech (English always excepted) are in Doric; and these unquestionably come thick and fast upon us: from the first *tête-à-tête* between Mistress Mellis and Miss Horn to the hero's denunciation of the *howdie* wherewith the action closes. Translation here has been relatively straightforward and if I have often been almost gunwale under in terms of sheer volume, there have been no particularly unusual obstacles to take me out of my course. If anything, the process has been (though laborious) quite refreshing; for with nearly everyone but Duncan speaking Scots–and he usually in conference with Malcolm–there have been fewer of those annoying alternations that can interrupt a translator's rhythm. Occasionally, it has made sense to leave Scots in both columns, such as when Lord Lossie (on p.346) tells Malcolm to "Leave your beastly gibberish"; or when Mrs Catanach makes a pun out of the delightful word "gowkmey" (p.58.) Mister Graham's poem (p.337) I have rendered in English *after* the Scots original, with slight modifications to keep the rhyme intact, but the spirit I hope I have duly honoured.

Arguably the most evocative single line of Scots–of the "mother tongue" one might say, but for the tragic irony–is the plaint of the mad laird, "I dinna ken whaur I cam frae," which runs through *Malcolm* like a refrain. This I have usually translated, but once or twice have left alone: partly because the translation "I don't know where I came from" will by that time have become familiar, and partly because I trust that most will be able to decipher it unaided.

* * * * *

Translator's note: The reader who takes an interest in the locales of these tales will search in vain for "Portlossie" on a map of Scotland—see overleaf. The setting however is real, and can be found in eastern Morayshire (just on the border of MacDonald's native Aberdeenshire) under the name of Cullen. I more than suspect that the fictional name was inspired by another north-east community: my own childhood home of Lossiemouth, at no great distance from Cullen, and hugging the same coastline.

---

9 Or at least never Scots. When particularly animated, he does break out into the odd line of Gaelic.

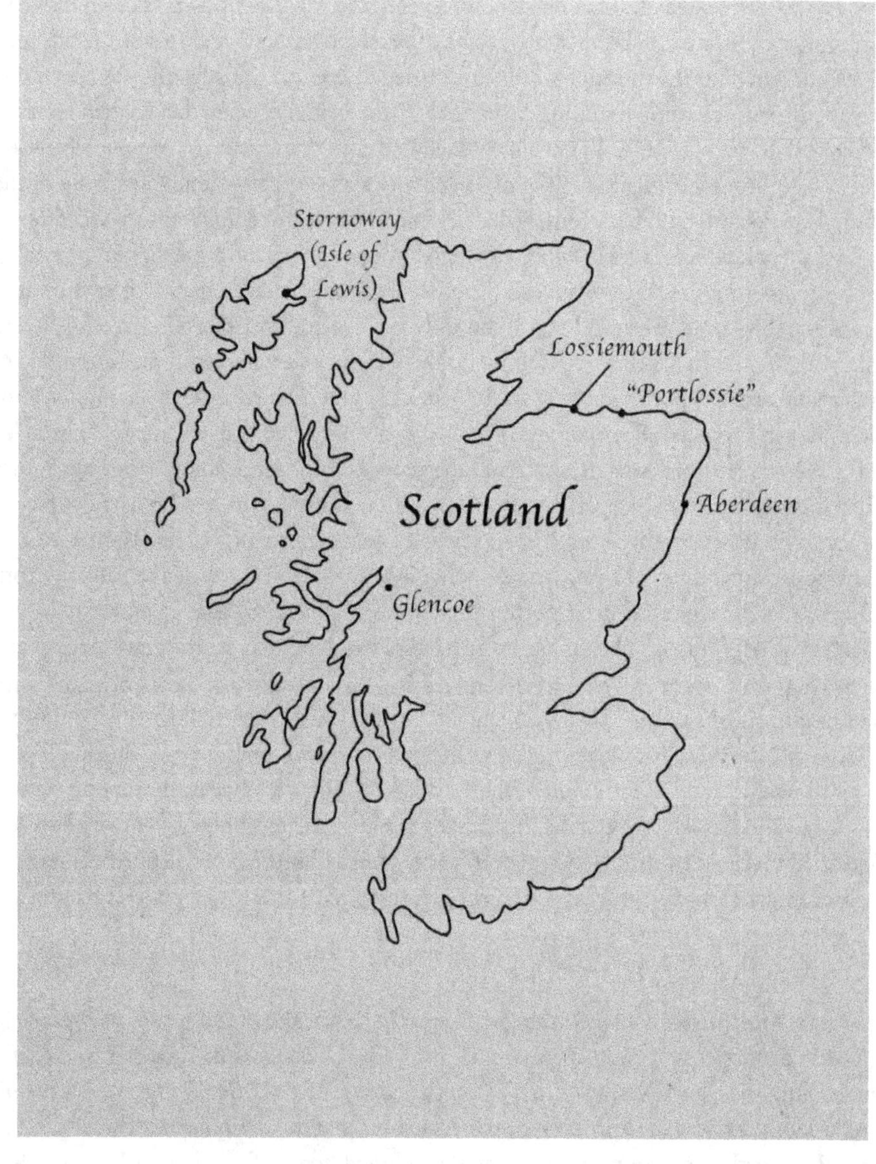

Stornoway
(Isle of
Lewis)
Lossiemouth
"Portlossie"
Scotland
Aberdeen
Glencoe

INTRODUCTION

BY DOUGLAS GRESHAM

"Malcolm" is one of George MacDonald's best books. Indeed, I am convinced my Stepfather's using the title "Letters To Malcolm" for one of his books, is in tribute to George MacDonald's usage of the name in this one.

This is a book that can lead us to where we may not want to go, but know that we must. And MacDonald makes it easy rather than difficult. It is a book that is rife with a variety of Scottish local accents and forms, and one very determined Highlander who speaks the Scots Gaelic and is very naturally proud of it. A variety of Scottish accents are used throughout the book. This makes "Malcolm" rather difficult for many of us to read. Had I not had my Stepfather to teach me how to read and understand much of the Doric and other Scottish local tones, I too might be unable to read "Malcolm" to this very day. But this particular linguistic malady has now been treated and indeed, cured, by David Jack. It is a task he has already taken on for several other works of that noble and brilliant author George MacDonald. And I have read them and have enjoyed the ability to look across the pages to look up any particular phrases or words that I have missed or forgotten in the past.

MacDonald was no ordinary writer, he was a man whose books have entranced and gathered into a large congregation, people all over the world who have had the good fortune to have been born and raised in Scotland and been brought up reading, and fluently at that, in the varying Scottish accents. But now, David Jack has devised a way of filling his books with both the Modern English translation and the original Doric. He places the Doric and its counterparts, in its own column to the left of the columns of the English translation. Thus anyone who reads English can now delightedly read MacDonald's "Malcolm".

The book itself is an amazing masterpiece, and it has been held back or turned away by so many people simply because of MacDonald's usage of what to many people seems to be an undecipherable and in some cases, uncanny language.

MacDonald wrote not merely for money (though he did need it) but for the well-being, physical, emotional and spiritual of his readers. He was a man who understood fear, pain and deep sorrow and he wrote in part, to help us to dismiss those rabid intruders which tear at our souls. He had lost four of his eight children and one granddaughter to that insidious intruder tuberculosis. He knew and understood how the enemy can tear at our minds, our hearts and our souls, and in his literature he fought back valiantly! This great and humble man was not fighting for himself, but for us, for you and me and I, for one, owe him humble thanks as do all who read his books.

In his explaining and opening of the Scottish accents and jargons to our minds, David Jack is doing something similar, and making George MacDonald's works open to us that we too may benefit from them.

Blessings,
Douglas Gresham.

MALCOLM CAST OF CHARACTERS

THE SEATON

MALCOLM MACPHAIL: A young fisherman, and the hero of the novel
DUNCAN MACPHAIL: Malcolm's "daddy," the town piper
MEG PARTAN/"THE PARTANESS":[1] The MacPhails' termagant neighbour
LIZZIE FINDLAY: Meg's daughter

THE NEW TOWN

MISS HORN: A spinster, and third cousin to the deceased Griselda Campbell
JEAN: Miss Horn's servant/housekeeper
BARBARA/"BAWBY" CATANACH: Jean's friend, a scheming midwife
MISTRESS MELLIS: The draper's wife, who lives opposite Miss Horn
WATTY WITHERSPAIL: The local undertaker

THE "ALTON"/OLD TOWN

MR GRAHAM: The local schoolmaster, and Malcolm's mentor
MR CAIRNS: The local parish minister

LOSSIE HOUSE

LORD LOSSIE:[2] A middle-aged nobleman who has recently become marquis
LADY FLORIMEL: Lord Lossie's beautiful young daughter
MRS COURTHOPE: Their English housekeeper
MR CRATHIE: The factor
JOHNNY BYKES: An officious gatekeeper
LADY BELLAIR A guest at The House during some part of the novel
LORD MEIKLEHAM: Lady Bellair's nephew, another guest

---

1 Otherwise Mrs Findlay
2 Also known as the Marquis of Lossie

MALCOLM CAST OF CHARACTERS (CONT'D)

KIRKBYRES/THE STEWARTS

MRS STEWART: The Lady of Kirkbyres
STEPHEN STEWART/ "THE MAD LAIRD": Her estranged son, a hunchback

SCAURNOSE

JOSEPH MAIR/"BLUE PETER": A fisherman-friend of Malcolm's
ANNIE MAIR: Blue Peter's wife
PHEMY MAIR: Their young daughter, the "mad laird's" closest friend
JANET MAIR: Blue Peter's elder sister
BOW O' MEAL & JEAMES GENTLE: Two more Scaurnose fishermen
MISTER MACLEOD: Another fisherman, who is brought back to the village from Stornoway, and instigates a religious revival

DUFF HARBOUR

MR BIGG: A local minister
MISS FORSYTH: Miss Horn's friend/her hostess when she visits the town
MR SOUTAR: Another friend of Miss Horn's, a lawyer

MISCELLANEOUS

MR MORRISON: A justice of the peace
MR GLENNIE: Lord Lossie's Aberdeen lawyer
"SHELTIE," "MAPPY," "PEERY," & "POOCHY" Pupils of Mr Graham

CHAPTER I

MISS HORN

"Na, na; I hae nae feelin's, I'm thankfu' to say. I never kent ony guid come o' *them*. They're a terrible sicht i' the gait."

"Naebody ever thoucht o' layin' 't to yer chairge, mem."

"'Deed, I aye had eneuch adu to du the thing I had to du, no to say the thing 'at naebody wad du but mysel'. I hae had nae leisur' for feelin's an' that," insisted Miss Horn.

But here a heavy step descending the stair just outside the room attracted her attention, and checking the flow of her speech perforce, with three ungainly strides she reached the landing.

"Watty Witherspail! Watty!" she called after the footsteps down the stair.

"Yes, mem," answered a gruff voice from below.

"Watty, whan ye fess the bit boxie, jist pit a hemmer an' a puckle nails i' your pooch to men' the hen-hoose door. The tane maun be atten't till as weel's the tither."

"The bit boxie" was the coffin of her third cousin Griselda Campbell, whose body lay on the room on her left hand as she called down the stair. Into that on her right Miss Horn now re-entered, to rejoin Mrs Mellis, the wife of the principal draper in the town, who had called ostensibly to condole with her, but really to see the corpse.

"Na, na; I have no feelings, I'm thankful to say. I never knew any good come of *them*. They do nothing but get in the way."

"Nobody ever thought of laying them to your charge, ma'am."

"Indeed, I always had enough trouble to do the thing I had to do, not to say the thing that nobody would do but myself. I haven't had time to waste on feelings," insisted Miss Horn.

But here a heavy step descending the stair just outside the room attracted her attention, and checking the flow of her speech perforce, with three ungainly strides she reached the landing.

"Watty Witherspail! Watty!" she called after the footsteps down the stair.

"Yes, ma'am," answered a gruff voice from below.

"Watty, when you fetch the bit boxie, just put a hammer and some nails in your pocket to mend the hen-house door. The one must be seen to as well as the other."

"The bit boxie" was the coffin of her third cousin Griselda Campbell, whose body lay on the room on her left hand as she called down the stair. Into that on her right Miss Horn now re-entered, to rejoin Mrs Mellis, the wife of the principal draper in the town, who had called ostensibly to condole with her, but really to see the corpse.

"Aih! she was taen yoong!" sighed the visitor, with long-drawn tones and a shake of the head, implying that therein lay ground of complaint, at which poor mortals dared but hint.

"No that yoong," returned Miss Horn. "She was upo' the edge o' aucht an' thirty."

"Weel, she had a sair time o' 't."

"No that sair, sae far as I see—an' wha sud ken better? She's had a bien doon-sittin', and sud hae had as lang's I was to the fore. Na, na; it was nowther sae young nor yet sae sair."

"Aih! but she was a patient cratur wi' a' flesh," persisted Mrs Mellis, as if she would not willingly be foiled in the attempt to extort for the dead some syllable of acknowledgment from the lips of her late companion.

"'Deed she was that!—a wheen ower patient wi' some. But that cam' o' haein mair hert nor brains. She had feelin's gien ye like—and to spare. But I never took ower ony o' the stock. It's a pity she hadna the jeedgment to match, for she never misdoobted onybody eneuch. But I wat it disna maitter noo, for she's gane whaur it's less wantit. For ane 'at has the hairmlessness o' the doo in this ill-wulled warl', there's a feck o' ten 'at has the wisdom o' the serpent. An' the serpents mak sair wark wi' the doos—lat alane them 'at flees into the verra mou's o' them."

"Weel, ye're jist richt there," said Mrs Mellis. "An' as ye say, she was aye some easy to perswaud. I hae nae doubt she believed to the verra last he wad come back and mairry her."

"Aih! She was taken young!" sighed the visitor, with long-drawn tones and a shake of the head, implying that therein lay ground of complaint, at which poor mortals dared but hint.

"Not that young," returned Miss Horn. "She was nearly thirty-eight."

"Well, she had a hard time of it."

"Not that hard, as far as I see—and who should know better? She's had a comfortable home here, and should have had as long as I was around. Na, na; it was neither so young nor yet so hard."

"Aih! but she was a patient creature with all flesh," persisted Mrs Mellis, as if she would not willingly be foiled in the attempt to extort for the dead some syllable of acknowledgment from the lips of her late companion.

"She was that, indeed!—a deal too patient with some. But that came of having more heart than brains. She had feelings if you like—and to spare. But I never took over any of the stock. It's a pity she hadn't the judgement to match, for she never suspected anybody enough. But indeed it doesn't matter now, for she's gone where it's less wanted. For one that has the harmlessness of the dove in this ill-willed world, there's half a score of others that have the wisdom of the serpent. And the serpents make sad work with the doves—let alone those that fly into their very mouths."

"Well, you're just right there," said Mrs Mellis. "And as you say, she was always quite easy to persuade. I have no doubt she believed to the very last he would come back and marry her."

"Come back and mairry her! Wha or what div ye mean? I jist tell ye Mistress Mellis—an' it 's weel ye're named—gien ye daur to hint at ae word o' sic clavers, it's this side o' this door o' mine ye s' be less acquant wi'."

As she spoke, the hawk-eyes of Miss Horn glowed on each side of her hawk nose, which grew more and more hooked as she glared, while her neck went craning forward as if she were on the point of making a swoop on the offender. Mrs Mellis's voice trembled with something like fear as she replied:

"Gude guide 's, Miss Horn! What hae I said to gar ye look at me sae by ordinar 's that?"

"Said!" repeated Miss Horn, in a tone that revealed both annoyance with herself and contempt for her visitor. "There's no a claver in a' the countryside but ye maun fess 't hame aneth yer oxter, as gin 't were the prodigal afore he repentit. Ye s' get sma thanks for sic like here. An' her lyin' there as she'll lie till the jeedgment day, puir thing!"

"I'm sure I meant no offence, Miss Horn," said her visitor. "I thocht a' body kent 'at she was ill about him."

"Aboot wha, i' the name o' the father o' lees?"

"Ow, aboot that lang-leggit doctor 'at set oot for the Ingies, an' dee'd afore he wan across the equautor. Only fouk said he was nae mair deid nor a halvert worm, an' wad be hame whan she was merried."

"It's a' lees frae heid to fit, an' frae hert to skin."

"Come back and marry her! Who or what do you mean? I just tell you Mistress Mellis—and it's well you're named[1]—if you dare to hint at one word of such gossip, I won't be so quick to open my door to you again."

As she spoke, the hawk-eyes of Miss Horn glowed on each side of her hawk nose, which grew more and more hooked as she glared, while her neck went craning forward as if she were on the point of making a swoop on the offender. Mrs Mellis's voice trembled with something like fear as she replied:

"Good gracious, Miss Horn! What have I said to make you give me such a look?"

"Said!" repeated Miss Horn, in a tone that revealed both annoyance with herself and contempt for her visitor. "There's not a scrap of idle talk for miles around but you must fetch it home under your arm, as if it were the prodigal before he repented. You'll get small thanks here for your pains. And her lying there as she'll lie till the judgement day, poor thing!"

"I'm sure I meant no offence, Miss Horn," said her visitor. "I thought everyone knew that she was ill about[2] him."

"About who, in the name of the father of lies?"

"Oh, about that long-legged doctor that set out for the Indies, and died before he crossed the equator. Only folk said he was no more dead than a sliced-up worm, and would be home when she was married."

"It's all lies from head to foot, and from heart to skin."

---

1 MISTRESS MELLIS…NAMED: The Scots word *mell* and the English *meddle* are rough counterparts.
2 ILL ABOUT: the Scots ought to be rendered "fond of"; but the literal translation preserves the double-meaning in Mistress Mellis' words

"Weel, it was plain to see she dwyned awa efter he gaed, an' never was hersel' again–ye dinna deny that?"

"It's a' havers," persisted Miss Horn, but in accents considerably softened. "She cared na mair aboot the chield nor I did mysel'. She dwyned, I grant ye, an' he gaed awa, I grant ye; but the win' blaws an' the water rins, an the tane has little to du wi' the tither."

"Weel, weel; I'm sorry I said onything to offen' ye, an' I canna say mair. Wi' yer leave, Miss Horn, I'll jist gang an' tak' a last leuk at her, puir thing!"

"'Deed, ye s' du naething o' the kin'! I s' lat nobody glower at her 'at wad gang an spairge sic havers about her, Mistress Mellis. To say 'at sic a doo as my Grizel, puir, saft-hertit, winsome thing, wad hae lookit twice at ony sic a serpent as him! Na, na, mem! Gang yer wa's hame, an' come back straucht frae yer prayers the morn's mornin'. By that time she'll be quaiet in her coffin, an' I'll be quaiet i' my temper. Syne I'll lat ye see her—maybe.—I wiss I was weel rid o' the sicht o' her, for I canna bide it. Lord, I canna bide it."

These last words were uttered in a murmured aside, inaudible to Mrs Mellis, to whom, however, they did not apply, but to the dead body. She rose notwithstanding in considerable displeasure, and with a formal farewell walked from the room, casting a curious glance as she left it in the direction of that where the body lay, and descended the stairs as slowly as if on every step she deliberated whether the next would bear her weight. Miss Horn, who had followed her to the head of the stair, watched her out of sight below the landing, when she turned and walked back

"Well, it was plain to see she pined away after he went, and never was herself again–you don't deny that?"

"It's all nonsense," persisted Miss Horn, but in accents considerably softened. "She cared no more about him than I did myself. She failed, I grant you, and he left, I grant you; but the wind blows and the water runs, and the one has little to do with the other."

"Well, well; I'm sorry I said anything to offend you, and I can't say more. With your leave, Miss Horn, I'll just go and take a last look at her, poor thing!"

"Indeed, you'll do no such thing! I'll let nobody glower at her that would go and spread such nonsense about her, Mistress Mellis. To say that such a dove as my Grizel, poor, soft-hearted, winsome thing, would have looked twice at any such a serpent as him! Na, na, ma'am! You go home, and come back straight from your prayers tomorrow morning. By that time she'll be quiet in her coffin, and I'll be quiet in my temper. Then I'll let you see her—maybe.—I wish I was well rid of the sight of her, for I can't stand it. Lord, I can't stand it."

These last words were uttered in a murmured aside, inaudible to Mrs Mellis, to whom, however, they did not apply, but to the dead body. She rose notwithstanding in considerable displeasure, and with a formal farewell walked from the room, casting a curious glance as she left it in the direction of that where the body lay, and descended the stairs as slowly as if on every step she deliberated whether the next would bear her weight. Miss Horn, who had followed her to the head of the stair, watched her out of sight below the landing, when she turned and walked back once more into the parlour, but with a lingering look towards the opposite room, as if she saw through the closed door what lay white on the white bed.

"It's a God's mercy I hae no feelin's," she said to herself. "To even my bonny Grizel to sic a lang kyte-clung chiel as yon! Aih, puir Grizel! She's gane frae me like a knotless threid."

once more into the parlour, but with a lingering look towards the opposite room, as if she saw through the closed door what lay white on the white bed.

"It's a God's mercy I have no feelings," she said to herself. "To pair my bonny Grizel with such a stalky, half-fed fellow as that! Aih, poor Grizel! She's gone from me like a knotless thread."

CHAPTER II

BARBARA CATANACH

Miss Horn was interrupted by the sound of the latch of the street door, and sprung from her chair in anger.

"Canna they lat her sleep for five mee-nutes?" she cried aloud, forgetting that there was no fear of rousing her any more.– "It'll be Jean come in frae the pump," she reflected, after a moment's pause; but, hearing no footstep along the passage to the kitchen, concluded–"It's no her, for *she* gangs aboot the hoose like the fore half o' a new-shod cowt;" and went down the stair to see who might have thus presumed to enter unbidden.

Miss Horn was interrupted by the sound of the latch of the street door, and sprung from her chair in anger.

"Can't they let her sleep for five min-utes?" she cried aloud, forgetting that there was no fear of rousing her any more.– "It'll be Jean come in from the pump," she reflected, after a moment's pause; but, hearing no footstep along the passage to the kitchen, concluded– "It's not her, for *she* goes about the house like the front end of a new-shod colt;" and went down the stair to see who might have thus presumed to enter unbidden.

In the kitchen, the floor of which was as white as scrubbing could make it, and sprinkled with sea-sand—under the gaily painted Dutch clock, which went on ticking as loud as ever, though just below the dead—sat a woman about sixty years of age, whose plump face to the first glance looked kindly, to the second, cunning, and to the third, evil. To the last look the plumpness appeared unhealthy, suggesting a doughy indentation to the finger, and its colour also was pasty. Her deep-set, black-bright eyes, glowing from under the darkest of eyebrows, which met over her nose, had something of a fascinating influ-ence—so much of it that at a first interview one was not likely for a time to notice any other of her features. She rose as Miss Horn entered, buried a fat fist in a soft side, and stood silent.

"Weel?" said Miss Horn interroga-tively, and was silent also.

"I thocht ye micht want a cast o' my callin'," said the woman.

"Well?" said Miss Horn interroga-tively, and was silent also.

"I thought a bit of my help might be wanted," said the woman.

"Na, na; there's no a han' 'at s' lay finger upo' the bairn but mine ain," said Miss Horn. "I had it a' ower, my lee lane, afore the skreigh o' day. She's lyin' quaiet noo–verra quaiet–waitin' upo' Watty Witherspail. Whan he fesses hame her bit boxie, we s' hae her laid canny intill 't, an' hae dune wi' 't."

"Weel, mem, for a leddy-born, like yersel', I maun say, ye tak it unco composed!"

"I'm no awaur, Mistress Catanach, o' ony necessity laid upo' ye to say yer min' i' this hoose. It's no expeckit. But what for sud I no tak' it wi' composur'? We'll hae to tak' oor ain turn er lang, as composed as we hae the skiel o', and gang oot like a lang-nibbit can'le–ay, an lea' jist sic a memory ahin' some o' 's, Bawby."

"I kenna gien ye mean me, Miss Horn," said the woman; "but it 's no that muckle o' a memory I expec' to lea' ahin' me."

"The less the better," muttered Miss Horn; but her unwelcome visitor went on:

"Them 'at 's maist i' *my* debt kens least aboot it; and then mithers canna be said to hae muckle to be thankfu' for. It's God's trowth, I *ken* waur nor ever I *did*, mem. A body in my trade canna help fa'in' amo' ill company whiles, for we're a' born in sin, an' brocht furth in ineequity, as the Buik says; in fac', it's a' sin thegither: we come o' sin an' we gang for sin; but ye ken the likes o' me maunna clype. A' the same, gien ye dinna tak the help o' my han', ye winna refuse me the sicht o' my een, puir thing!"

"There's nane sall luik upon her deid 'at wasna a pleesur' till her livin'; an' ye ken weel eneuch, Bawby, she cudna thole the sicht o' *you.*"

"Na, na; there's not a hand shall lay finger upon the child but my own," said Miss Horn. "I had it all over, by myself, before the day broke. She's lying quiet now–very quiet–waiting on Watty Witherspail. When he brings home her box, we'll have her laid decently into it, and have done with it."

"Well, ma'am, for a lady-born, like yourself, I must say you take it very calmly!"

"I'm not aware, Mistress Catanach, that you're under any necessity of speaking your mind in this house. It's not expected. But why shouldn't I take it calmly? We'll have to take our own turn soon enough, with as much composure as we can manage, and go out like a long-wicked candle–ay, and leave just such a memory behind some of us, Bawby."

"I don't know if you mean me, Miss Horn," said the woman; "but it's not that much of a memory I expect to leave behind me."

"The less the better," muttered Miss Horn; but her unwelcome visitor went on:

"Those most in *my* debt know least about it; and then mothers can't be said to have much to be thankful for. It's God's truth, I *know* worse than ever I *did*, ma'am. A body in my trade can't help mingling in bad company at times, for we're all born in sin, and brought forth in iniquity, as the Book says; in fact, it's all sin together: we come of sin and we go for sin; but you know the likes of me mustn't tell tales. All the same, if you don't take the help of my hand, you won't refuse me the sight of my eyes, poor thing!"

"There's none shall look upon her dead that wasn't a pleasure to her living; and you know well enough, Bawby, she couldn't stand the sight of *you.*"

"An' guid rizzon had she for that, gien a' 'at gangs throu' my heid er I fa' asleep i' the lang mirk nichts be a hair better nor ane o' the auld wives' fables 'at fowk says the holy buik maks sae licht o'."

"What mean ye?" demanded Miss Horn, sternly and curtly.

"I ken what I mean mysel', an' ane that's no content wi' that, bude ill be a howdie. I wad fain hae gotten a fancy oot o' my heid that's been there this mony a lang day; but please yersel', mem, gien ye winna be neebourly."

"Ye s' no gang near her—no to save ye frae a' the ill dreams that ever gethered aboot a sin-stappit bowster!" cried Miss Horn, and drew down her long upper lip in a strong arch.

"Ca cannie! ca cannie!" said Bawby. "Dinna anger me ower sair, for I *am* but mortal. Fowk tak a heap frae you, Miss Horn, 'at they'll tak frae nane ither, for your temper's weel kent, an' little made o'; but it's an ill-faured thing to anger the howdie—sae muckle lies upo' *her*; an' I'm no i' the tune to put up wi' muckle the nicht. I wonner at ye bein' sae oonneebourlike—at sic a time tu, wi' a corp i' the hoose!"

"Gang awa—gang oot o't: it's *my* hoose," said Miss Horn, in a low, hoarse voice, restrained from rising to tempest pitch only by the consciousness of what lay on the other side of the ceiling above her head. "I wad as sune lat a cat intill the deid-chaumer to gang loupin' ower the corp, or may be waur, as I wad lat yersel' intill 't Bawby Catanach; an' there's till ye!"

"And good reason she had for that, if all that goes through my head before I fall asleep in the long dark nights has more to it than one of the old wives' fables that folk say the Bible takes so lightly."

"What do you mean?" demanded Miss Horn, sternly and curtly.

"I know what I mean myself, and one that's not content with that could hardly follow my calling. I would fain have rid myself of a fancy I've had this many a long day; but please yourself, ma'am, if you won't be neighbourly."

"You shan't go near her—not to save you from all the bad dreams that ever gathered about a sin-stuffed bolster!" cried Miss Horn, and drew down her long upper lip in a strong arch.

"Gently! gently, now!" said Bawby. "Don't anger me too much, for I *am* but mortal. Folk take a lot from you, Miss Horn, that they'll take from no one else, for your temper's well known, and little heeded; but it's a bad business angering the midwife—so much lies upon *her*; and I'm not in the mood to put up with much tonight. I wonder at you being so unneighbourly—at such a time too, with a corpse in the house!"

"Go away—go out of it: it's *my* house," said Miss Horn, in a low, hoarse voice, restrained from rising to tempest pitch only by the consciousness of what lay on the other side of the ceiling above her head. "I would as soon let a cat into the death-chamber to go leaping over the corpse, or maybe worse, as I would let you into it, Bawby Catanach; and so I tell you!"

At this moment the opportune entrance of Jean afforded fitting occasion to her mistress for leaving the room without encountering the dilemma of either turning the woman out—a proceeding which the latter, from the way in which she set her short, stout figure square on the floor, appeared ready to resist—or of herself abandoning the field in discomfiture: she turned and marched from the kitchen with her head in the air, and the gait of one who had been insulted on her own premises.

She was sitting in the parlour, still red-faced and wrathful, when Jean entered, and, closing the door behind her, drew near to her mistress, bearing a narrative, commenced at the door, of all she had seen, heard, and done, while "oot an' aboot i' the toon." (out and about in the town.) But Miss Horn interrupted her the moment she began to speak.

"Is that wuman furth the hoose, Jean?" she asked, in the tone of one who waited her answer in the affirmative as a preliminary condition of all further conversation.

"She's gane, mem," answered Jean—adding to herself in a wordless thought, "I'm no sayin' *whaur*."

"She's a wuman I wadna hae ye throng wi', Jean."

"I ken no ill o' her, mem," returned Jean.

"She's eneuch to corrup' a kirkyaird!" said her mistress, with more force than fitness.

Jean, however, was on the shady side of fifty, more likely to have already yielded than to be liable to a first assault of corruption; and little did Miss Horn think how useless was her warning, or where Barbara Catanach was at that very moment. Trusting to Jean's cunning, as well she might; she was in the dead-chamber, and standing over the dead. She had folded back the sheet—not from the face, but from the feet—and raised the night dress of fine linen in which the love of her cousin had robed the dead for the repose of the tomb.

"Has that woman left the house?" she asked, in the tone of one who waited her answer in the affirmative as a preliminary condition of all further conversation.

"She's gone, ma'am," answered Jean—adding to herself in a wordless thought, "I'm not saying *where*."

"She's a woman I wouldn't have you friendly with, Jean."

"I know no ill of her, ma'am." returned Jean.

"She's enough to corrupt a church-yard!" said her mistress, with more force than fitness.

Jean, however, was on the shady side of fifty, more likely to have already yielded than to be liable to a first assault of corruption; and little did Miss Horn think how useless was her warning, or where Barbara Catanach was at that very moment. Trusting to Jean's cunning, as well she might; she was in the dead-chamber, and standing over the dead. She had folded back the sheet—not from the face, but from the feet—and raised the night dress of fine linen in which the love of her cousin had robed the dead for the repose of the tomb.

"It wad hae been tellin' her," she muttered, "to hae spoken Bawby fair! I'm no used to be fa'en foul o' that gait. I s' be even wi' her yet, I'm thinkin'—the auld speldin'! Losh! and Praise be thankit! there it 's! It's there!—a wee darker, but the same–jist whaur I could ha' laid the pint o' my finger upo' 't i' the mirk!—Noo lat the worms eat it," she concluded, as she folded down the linen of shroud and sheet—"an' no mortal ken o' 't but mysel' an' him 'at bude till hae seen 't, gien he was a hair better nor Glenkindie's man i' the auld ballant!"[4]

"It would have been better for her," she muttered, "to have spoken Bawby fair! I'm not used to being fallen foul of that way. I'll be even with her yet, I'm thinking—the old spelding![3] Lord! and thank heaven! there it is! It's there!—a little darker, but the same—just where I could have laid the point of my finger upon it in the dark!—Now let the worms eat it," she concluded, as she folded down the linen of shroud and sheet—"and no mortal know of it but myself and him that must have seen it, if he was a hair better than Glenkindie's man in the old ballad!"[4]

The instant she had rearranged the garments of the dead, she turned and made for the door with a softness of step that strangely contrasted with the ponderousness of her figure, and indicated great muscular strength, opened it with noiseless circumspection to the width of an inch, peeped out from the crack, and seeing the opposite door still shut, stepped out with a swift, noiseless swing of person and door simultaneously, closed the door behind her, stole down the stairs, and left the house. Not a board creaked, not a latch clicked as she went. She stepped into the street as sedately as if she had come from paying to the dead the last offices of her composite calling, the projected front of her person appearing itself aware of its dignity as the visible sign and symbol of a good conscience and kindly heart.

---

3 SPELDING (Scots): a haddock or other small fish split open and dried in the sun.

4 GLENKINDIE'S MAN...BALLAD: The ballad of Glenkindie tells of a treacherous serving-man who personates his master in order to bed his mistress in the dark. The implication here is that Griselda Campbell's lover, by not resorting to such measures, must have seen the same mark on her body which Mistress Catanach has just identified.

CHAPTER III

THE MAD LAIRD

When Mistress Catanach arrived at the opening of a street which was just
opposite her own door, and led steep toward the sea-town, she stood, and
shading her eyes with her hooded hand, although the sun was far behind her,
looked out to sea. It was the forenoon of a day of early summer. The larks were many and
loud in the skies above her—for, although she stood in a street, she was only a few yards
from the green fields—but she could hardly have heard them, for their music was not for
her. To the northward, whither her gaze—if gaze it could be called—was directed, all but
cloudless blue heavens stretched over an all but shadowless blue sea; two bold, jagged
promontories, one on each side of her, formed a wide bay; between that on the west and
the sea town at her feet, lay a great curve of yellow sand, upon which the long breakers,
born of last night's wind, were still roaring from the northeast, although the gale had now
sunk to a breeze—cold and of doubtful influence. From the chimneys of the fishermen's
houses below, ascended a yellowish smoke, which, against the blue of the sea, assumed
a dull green colour as it drifted vanishing towards the southwest. But Mrs Catanach was
looking neither at nor for anything: she had no fisherman husband, or any other rela-
tive at sea; she was but revolving something in her unwholesome mind, and this was her
mode of concealing an operation which naturally would have been performed with down-
bent head and eyes on the ground.

While she thus stood a strange figure drew near, approaching her with step almost as
noiseless as that with which she had herself made her escape from Miss Horn's house. At
a few yards' distance from her it stood, and gazed up at her countenance as intently as she
seemed to be gazing on the sea. It was a man of dwarfish height and uncertain age, with a
huge hump upon his back, features of great refinement, a long thin beard, and a forehead
unnaturally large, over eyes which, although of a pale blue, mingled with a certain mot-
tled milky gleam, had a pathetic, dog-like expression. Decently dressed in black, he stood
with his hands in the pockets of his trowsers, gazing immovably in Mrs Catanach's face.

Becoming suddenly aware of his presence, she glanced downward, gave a great start
and a half scream, and exclaimed in no gentle tones:

"Preserve 's! Whaur come *ye* frae?"   "Preserve us! Where do *you* come from?"

It was neither that she did not know the man, nor that she meant any offence: her words were the mere embodiment of the annoyance of startled surprise; but their effect was peculiar.

Without a single other motion he turned abruptly on one heel, gazed seaward with quick flushed cheeks and glowing eyes, but, apparently too polite to refuse an answer to the evidently unpleasant question, replied in low, almost sullen tones:

"I dinna ken whaur I come frae. Ye *ken* 'at I dinna ken whaur I come frae. I dinna ken whaur *ye* come frae. I dinna ken whaur onybody comes frae."

"I don't know where I come from. You *know* that I don't know where I come from. I don't know where *you* come from. I don't know where anybody comes from."

"Hoot, laird! nae offence!" returned Mrs Catanach. "It was yer ain wyte. What gart ye stan' glowerin' at a body that gait, ohn telled them 'at ye was there?"

"Heavens, laird! no offence!" returned Mrs Catanach. "It was your own fault. What made you stand glowering at me that way, without telling me you were there?"

"I thocht ye was luikin' whaur ye cam frae," returned the man in tones apologetic and hesitating.

"I thought you were looking where you came from," returned the man in tones apologetic and hesitating.

"'Deed I fash wi' nae sic freits," said Mrs Catanach.

"Indeed, I don't fret myself with such fancies," said Mrs Catanach.

"Sae lang's ye ken whaur ye're gaein' till," suggested the man.

"So long as you know where you're going to," suggested the man.

"Toots! I fash as little wi' that either, and ken jist as muckle about the tane as the tither," she answered with a low oily guttural laugh of contemptuous pity.

"Bah! I bother as little with that either, and know just as much about the one as the other," she answered with a low oily guttural laugh of contemptuous pity.

"I ken mair nor that mysel', but no muckle," said the man. "I dinna ken whaur I cam frae, and I dinna ken whaur I'm gaun till; but I ken 'at I'm gaun *whaur* I cam frae. That stan's to rizzon, ye see; but they telled me 'at *ye* kenned a' about whaur we a' cam frae."

"I know more than that myself, but not much," said the man. "I don't know where I came from, and I don't know where I'm going to; but I know that I'm going *where* I came from. That stands to reason, you see; but they told me that *you* knew all about where we all came from."

"Deil a bit o' 't!" persisted Mrs Catanach, in tones of repudiation. "What care I whaur I cam frae, sae lang's—"

"Devil a bit of it!" persisted Mrs Catanach, in tones of repudiation. "What care I where I came from, so long as—"

"Sae lang's what, gien ye please?" pleaded the man, with a childlike entreaty in his voice.

"So long as what, if you please?" pleaded the man, with a childlike entreaty in his voice.

"Weel—gien ye *wull* hae't—sae lang's I cam frae my mither," said the woman, looking down on the inquirer with a vulgar laugh.

"Well—if you *will* know—so long as I came from my mother," said the woman, looking down on the inquirer with a vulgar laugh.

The hunchback uttered a shriek of dismay, and turned and fled; and as he turned, long, thin, white hands flashed out of his pockets, pressed against his ears, and intertwined their fingers at the back of his neck. With a marvellous swiftness he shot down the steep descent towards the shore.

"The deil's in't 'at I bude to anger him!" said the woman, and walked away, with a short laugh of small satisfaction.

The hunchback uttered a shriek of dismay, and turned and fled; and as he turned, long, thin, white hands flashed out of his pockets, pressed against his ears, and intertwined their fingers at the back of his neck. With a marvellous swiftness he shot down the steep descent towards the shore.

"The devil's in it that I had to anger him!" said the woman, and walked away, with a short laugh of small satisfaction.

The style she had given the hunchback was no nickname. Stephen Stewart was laird of the small property and ancient house of Kirkbyres, of which his mother managed the affairs—hardly *for* her son, seeing that, beyond his clothes, and five pounds a year of pocket money, he derived no personal advantage from his possessions. He never went near his own house, for, from some unknown reason, plentifully aimed at in the dark by the neighbours, he had such a dislike to his mother that he could not bear to hear the name of mother, or even the slightest allusion to the relationship.

Some said he was a fool; others a madman; some both; none, however, said he was a rogue; and all would have been willing to allow that whatever it might be that caused the difference between him and other men, throughout the disturbing element blew ever and anon the air of a sweet humanity.

Along the shore, in the direction of the great rocky promontory that closed in the bay on the west, with his hands still clasped over his ears, as if the awful word were following him, he flew rather than fled. It was nearly low water, and the wet sand afforded an easy road to his flying feet. Betwixt sea and shore, a sail in the offing the sole other moving thing in the solitary landscape, like a hunted creature he sped, his footsteps melting and vanishing behind him in the half-quick sand.

Where the curve of the water line turned northward at the root of the promontory, six or eight fishing boats were drawn up on the beach in various stages of existence. One was little more than half built, the fresh wood shining against the background of dark rock. Another was newly tarred; its sides glistened with the rich shadowy brown, and filled the air with a comfortable odour. Another wore age-long neglect on every plank and seam; half its props had sunk or decayed, and the huge hollow leaned low on one side, disclosing the squalid desolation of its lean-ribbed and naked interior, producing all the phantasmic effect of a great swampy desert; old pools of water overgrown with a green scum, lay in the hollows between its rotting timbers, and the upper planks were baking and cracking in the sun. Near where they lay a steep path ascended the cliff, whence through grass and ploughed land, it led across the promontory to the fishing village of Scaurnose, which lay on the other side of it. There the mad laird, or Mad Humpy, as he was called by the baser sort, often received shelter, chiefly from the family of a certain Joseph Mair, one of the most respectable inhabitants of the place.

But the way he now pursued lay close under the cliffs of the headland, and was rocky and difficult. He passed the boats, going between them and the cliffs, at a footpace, with his eyes on the ground, and not even a glance at the two men who were at work on the unfinished boat. One of them was his friend, Joseph Mair. They ceased their work for a moment to look after him.

"That's the puir laird again," said Joseph, the instant he was beyond hearing. "Something's wrang wi' him. I wonder what's come ower him!"

"I haena seen him for a while noo," returned the other. "They tell me 'at his mither made him ower to the deil afore he cam to the light; and sae, aye as his birthday comes roun', Sawtan gets the pooer ower him. Eh, but he's a fearsome sicht whan he's ta'en that gait!" continued the speaker. "I met him ance i' the gloamin', jist ower by the toon, wi' his een glowerin' like uily lamps, an' the slaver rinnin' doon his lang baird. I jist laup as gien I had seen the muckle Sawtan himsel'."

"Ye nott na hae dune that," was the reply. "He's jist as hairmless, e'en at the warst, as ony lamb. He's but a puir cratur wha's tribble's ower strang for him—that's a'. Sawtan has as little to du wi' him as wi' ony man I ken."

"That's the poor laird again," said Joseph, the instant he was beyond hearing. "Something's wrong with him. I wonder what's come over him!"

"I haven't seen him for a while now," returned the other. "They tell me that his mother made him over to the devil before he was born; and so, whenever his birthday comes round, Satan has the power over him. Eh, but he's a fearsome sight when he's taken that way!" continued the speaker. "I met him once in the gloaming, just over by the town, with his eyes glowering like oil lamps, and the slaver running down his long beard. I gave a jump as if I had seen the great Satan himself."

"You needn't have done that," was the reply. "He's just as harmless, even at the worst, as any lamb. He's but a poor creature whose trouble's too much for his strength—that's all. Satan has as little to do with him as with any man I know."

CHAPTER IV

PHEMY MAIR

With eyes that stared as if they and not her ears were the organs of hearing, this talk was heard by a child of about ten years of age, who sat in the bottom of the ruined boat, like a pearl in a decaying oyster-shell, one hand arrested in the act of dabbling in a green pool, the other on its way to her lips with a mouthful of the seaweed called *dulse*. She was the daughter of Joseph Mair just mentioned—a fisherman who had been to sea in a man of war (in consequence of which his to-name or nickname was Blue Peter), where having been found capable, he was employed as carpenter's mate, and came to be very handy with his tools: having saved a little money by serving in another man's boat, he was now building one for himself.

He was a dark-complexioned, foreign-looking man, with gold rings in his ears, which he said enabled him to look through the wind "ohn his een watered." (without his eyes watering.) Unlike most of his fellows, he was a sober and indeed thoughtful man, ready to listen to the voice of reason from any quarter; they were, in general, men of hardihood and courage, encountering as a mere matter of course such perilous weather as the fishers on a great part of our coasts would have declined to meet, and during the fishing season were diligent in their calling, and made a good deal of money; but when the weather was such that they could not go to sea, when their nets were in order, and nothing special requiring to be done, they would have bouts of hard drinking, and spend a great portion of what ought to have been their provision for the winter.

Their women were in general coarse in manners and rude in speech; often of great strength and courage, and of strongly-marked character. They were almost invariably the daughters of fishermen, for a wife taken from among the rural population would have been all but useless in regard of the peculiar duties required of her. If these were less dangerous than those of their husbands, they were quite as laborious, and less interesting. The most severe consisted in carrying the fish into the country for sale, in a huge creel or basket, which when full was sometimes more than a man could lift to place on the woman's back. With this burden, kept in its place by a band across her chest, she would walk as many as twenty miles, arriving at some inland town early in the forenoon, in time to dispose of her fish for the requirements of the day. I may add that, although her eldest child was probably born within a few weeks after her marriage, infidelity was almost unknown amongst them.

In some respects, although in none of its good qualities, Mrs. Mair was an exception from her class. Her mother had been the daughter of a small farmer, and she had well-to-do relations in an inland parish; but how much these facts were concerned in the result it would be hard to say: certainly she was one of those elect whom Nature sends into the world for the softening and elevation of her other children. She was still slight and graceful, with a clear complexion, and the prettiest teeth possible; the former two at least of which advantages she must have lost long before, had it not been that, while her husband's prudence had rendered hard work less imperative, he had a singular care over her good looks; and that a rough, honest, elder sister of his lived with them, whom it would have been no kindness to keep from the hardest work, seeing it was only through such that she could have found a sufficiency of healthy interest in life. While Janet Mair carried the creel, Annie only assisted in making the nets, and in cleaning and drying the fish, of which they cured considerable quantities; these, with her household and maternal duties, afforded her ample occupation. Their children were well-trained, and being of necessity, from the narrowness of their house accommodation, a great deal with their parents, heard enough to make them think after their faculty.

The mad laird was, as I have said, a visitor at their house oftener than anywhere else. On such occasions he slept in a garret accessible by a ladder from the ground floor, which consisted only of a kitchen and a closet. Little Phemy Mair was therefore familiar with his appearance, his ways, and his speech; and she was a favourite with him, although hitherto his shyness had been sufficient to prevent any approach to intimacy with even a child of ten.

When the poor fellow had got some little distance beyond the boats, he stopped and withdrew his hands from his ears: in rushed the sound of the sea, the louder that the caverns of his brain had been so long closed to its entrance. With a moan of dismay he once more pressed his palms against them, and thus deafened, shouted with a voice of agony into the noise of the rising tide: "I dinna ken whaur I come frae!" ("I don't know where I come from!") after which cry, wrung from the grief of human ignorance, he once more took to his heels, though with far less swiftness than before, and fled stumbling and scrambling over the rocks.

Scarcely had he vanished from view of the boats, when Phemy scrambled out of her big mussel-shell. Its upheaved side being toward the boat at which her father was at work, she escaped unperceived, and so ran along the base of the promontory, where the rough way was perhaps easier to the feet of a child content to take smaller steps and climb or descend by the help of more insignificant inequalities. She came within sight of the laird just as he turned into the mouth of a well-known cave and vanished.

Phemy was one of those rare and blessed natures which have endless courage because they have no distrust, and she ran straight into the cave after him, without even first stopping to look in.

It was not a very interesting cave to look into. The strata of which it was composed, upheaved almost to the perpendicular, shaped an opening like the half of a Gothic arch divided vertically and leaning over a little to one side, which opening rose to the full height of the cave, and seemed to lay bare every corner of it to a single glance. In length it was only about four or five times its width. The floor was smooth and dry, consisting of hard rock. The walls and roof were jagged with projections and shadowed with recesses, but there was little to rouse any frightful fancies.

When Phemy entered, the laird was nowhere to be seen. But she went straight to the back of the cave, to its farthest visible point. There she rounded a projection and began an ascent which only familiarity with rocky ways could have enabled such a child to accomplish. At the top she passed through another opening, and by a longer and more gently sloping descent reached the floor of a second cave, as level and nearly as smooth as a table. On her left hand, what light managed to creep through the tortuous entrance was caught and reflected in a dull glimmer from the undefined surface of a well of fresh water which lay in a sort of basin in the rock: on a bedded stone beside it sat the laird, with his head in his hands, his elbows on his knees, and his hump upheaved above his head, like Mount Sinai over the head of Christian in the Pilgrim's Progress.

As his hands were still pressed on his ears, he heard nothing of Phemy's approach, and she stood for a while staring at him in the vague glimmer, apparently with no anxiety as to what was to come next.

Weary at length—for the forlorn man continued movelessly sunk in his own thoughts, or what he had for such—the eyes of the child began to wander about the darkness, to which they had already got so far accustomed as to make the most of the scanty light. Presently she fancied she saw something glitter, away in the darkness—two things: they must be eyes!—the eyes of an otter or of a polecat, in which creatures the caves along the shore abounded. Seized with sudden fright, she ran to the laird and laid her hand on his shoulder, crying,

"Leuk, laird, leuk!"

He started to his feet and gazed bewildered at the child, rubbing his eyes once and again. She stood between the well and the entrance, so that all the light there was, gathered upon her pale face.

"Whaur do ye come frae?" he cried.

"I cam frae the auld boat," she answered.

"What do ye want wi' me?"

"Naething, sir; I only cam to see hoo ye was getting' on. I wadna hae disturbit ye, sir, but I saw the twa een o' a wullcat, or sic like, glowerin' awa yonner i' the mirk, an' they fleyt me 'at I grippit ye."

"Look, laird, look!"

He started to his feet and gazed bewildered at the child, rubbing his eyes once and again. She stood between the well and the entrance, so that all the light there was, gathered upon her pale face.

"Where do you come from?" he cried.

"I came from the old boat," she answered.

"What do you want with me?"

"Nothing, sir; I only came to see how you were getting on. I wouldn't have disturbed you, sir, but I saw the two eyes of a wildcat, or suchlike, glowering away yonder in the dark, and I gripped you from fear at them."

"Weel, weel; sit ye doon, bairnie," said the mad laird in a soothing voice; "the wullcat sanna touch ye. Ye're no fleyt at *me*, are ye?"

"Na!" answered the child. "What for sud I be fleyt at you, sir? I'm Phemy Mair."

"Eh, bairnie! it's you, is't?" he returned in tones of satisfaction, for he had not hitherto recognised her. "Sit ye doon, sit ye doon, an' we'll see about it a'."

"Well, well; have a seat, child," said the mad laird in a soothing voice; "the wildcat shan't touch you. You're not afraid of *me*, are you?"

"Na!" answered the child. "Why should I be afraid of you, sir? I'm Phemy Mair."

"Eh, child! it's you, is it?" he returned in tones of satisfaction, for he had not hitherto recognised her. "Sit you down, sit you down, and we'll see about it all."

Phemy obeyed, and seated herself on the nearest projection. The laird placed himself beside her, and once more buried his face, but not his ears, in his hands. Nothing entered them, however, but the sound of the rising tide, for Phemy sat by him in the faintly glimmering dusk, as without fear felt, so without word spoken.

The evening crept on, and the night came down, but all the effect of the growing darkness was that the child drew gradually nearer to her uncouth companion, until at length her hand stole into his, her head sank upon his shoulder, his arm went round her to hold her safe, and thus she fell fast asleep. After a while, the laird gently roused her and took her home, on their way warning her, in strange yet to her comprehensible utterance, to say nothing of where she had found him, for if she exposed his place of refuge, wicked people would take him, and he should never see her again.

CHAPTER V

LADY FLORIMEL

All the coast to the east of the little harbour was rock, bold and high, of a grey and brown hard stone, which after a mighty sweep, shot out northward, and closed in the bay on that side with a second great promontory. The long curved strip of sand on the west, reaching to the promontory of Scaurnose, was the only open portion of the coast for miles. Here the coasting vessel gliding past gained a pleasant peep of open fields, belts of wood and farm houses, with now and then a glimpse of a great house amidst its trees. In the distance one or two bare solitary hills, imposing in aspect only from their desolation, for their form gave no effect to their altitude, rose to the height of over a thousand feet.

On this comparatively level part of the shore, parallel with its line, and at some distance beyond the usual high-water-mark, the waves of ten thousand northern storms had cast up a long dune or bank of sand, terminating towards the west within a few yards of a huge solitary rock of the ugly kind called conglomerate, which must have been separated from the roots of the promontory by the rush of waters at unusually high tides, for in winter they still sometimes rounded the rock, and running down behind the dune, turned it into a long island. The sand on the inland side of the dune, covered with short sweet grass, browsed on by sheep, and with the largest and reddest of daisies, was thus occasionally swept by wild salt waves, and at times, when the northern wind blew straight as an arrow and keen as a sword from the regions of endless snow, lay under a sheet of gleaming ice.

The sun had been up for some time in a cloudless sky. The wind had changed to the south, and wafted soft country odours to the shore, in place of sweeping to inland farms the scents of seaweed and broken salt waters, mingled with a suspicion of icebergs. From what was called the *Seaton*, or seatown, of Portlossie, a crowd of cottages occupied entirely by fisherfolk, a solitary figure was walking westward along this grass at the back of the dune, singing. On his left hand the ground rose to the high road; on his right was the dune, interlaced and bound together by the long clasping roots of the coarse bent, without which its sands would have been but the sport of every wind that blew. It shut out from him all sight of the sea, but the moan and rush of the rising tide sounded close behind it. At his back rose the town of Portlossie, high above the harbour and the Seaton, with its houses of grey and brown stone, roofed with blue slates and red tiles. It was no highland town—scarce one within it could speak the highland tongue, yet down from its high streets on the fitful air of the morning now floated intermittently the sound of bagpipes—borne winding from street to street, and loud blown to wake the sleeping inhabitants and let them know that it was now six of the clock.

He was a youth of about twenty, with a long, swinging, heavy-footed stride, which took in the ground rapidly—a movement unlike that of the other men of the place, who always walked slowly, and never but on dire compulsion ran. He was rather tall, and large-limbed. His dress was like that of a fisherman, consisting of blue serge trowsers, a shirt striped blue and white, and a Guernsey frock, which he carried flung across his shoulder. On his head he wore a round blue bonnet, with a tuft of scarlet in the centre.

His face was more than handsome—with large features, not finely cut, and a look of mingled nobility and ingenuousness—the latter amounting to simplicity, or even inno-cence; while the clear outlook from his full and well-opened hazel eyes indicated both courage and promptitude. His dark brown hair came in large curling masses from under his bonnet. It was such a form and face as would have drawn every eye in a crowded thoroughfare.

About the middle of the long sandhill, a sort of wide embrasure was cut in its top, in which stood an old-fashioned brass swivel-gun: when the lad reached the place, he sprang up the sloping side of the dune, seated himself on the gun, drew from his trowsers a large silver watch, regarded it steadily for a few minutes, replaced it, and took from his pocket a flint and steel, wherewith he kindled a bit of touch paper, which, rising, he applied to the vent of the swivel. Followed a great roar.

Its echoes had nearly died away, when a startled little cry reached his keen ear, and looking along the shore to discover whence it came, he spied a woman on a low rock that ran a little way out into the water. She had half risen from a sitting posture, and apparently her cry was the result of the discovery that the rising tide had overreached and surrounded her. There was no danger whatever, but the girl might well shrink from plunging into the clear beryl depth in which swayed the seaweed clothing the slippery slopes of the rock. He rushed from the sandhill, crying, as he approached her, "Dinna be in a hurry, mem; bide till I come to ye," ("Don't be in a hurry, ma'am; wait till I come to you,") and running straight into the water struggled through the deepening tide, the distance being short and the depth almost too shallow for swimming. In a moment he was by her side, scarcely saw the bare feet she had been bathing in the water, heeded as little the motion of the hand which waved him back, caught her in his arms like a baby, and had her safe on the shore ere she could utter a word; nor did he stop until he had carried her to the slope of the sandhill, where he set her gently down, and without a suspicion of the liberty he was taking, and filled only with a passion of service, was proceeding to dry her feet with the frock which he had dropped there as he ran to her assistance.

"Let me alone, pray," cried the girl with a half-amused indignation, drawing back her feet and throwing down a book she carried that she might the better hide them with her skirt. But although she shrank from his devotion, she could neither mistake it nor help being pleased with his kindness. Probably she had never before been immediately indebted to such an ill-clad individual of the human race, but even in such a costume she could not fail to see he was a fine fellow. Nor was the impression disturbed when he opened his mouth and spoke in the broad dialect of the country, for she had no associations to cause her to misinterpret its homeliness as vulgarity.

"Whaur's yer stockin's, mem?" he said.

"You gave me no time to bring them away, you caught me up so– rudely," answered the girl half querulously, but in such lovely speech as had never before greeted his Scottish ears.

"Where's your stockings, ma'am?" he said.

"You gave me no time to bring them away, you caught me up so– rudely," answered the girl half querulously, but in such lovely speech as had never before greeted his Scottish ears.

Before the words were well beyond her lips he was already on his way back to the rock, running, as he walked, with great, heavy-footed strides. The abandoned shoes and stockings were in imminent danger of being floated off by the rising water, but he dashed in, swam a few strokes, caught them up, waded back to the shore, and, leaving a wet track all the way behind him but carrying the rescued clothing at arm's length before him, rejoined their owner. Spreading his frock out before her, he laid the shoes and stockings upon it, and, observing that she continued to keep her feet hidden under the skirts of her dress, turned his back and stood.

"Why don't you go away?" said the girl, venturing one set of toes from under their tent, but hesitating to proceed further in the business.

Without word or turn of head he walked away.

Either flattered by his absolute obedience, and persuaded that he was a true squire, or unwilling to forego what amusement she might gain from him, she drew in her half-issuing foot, and, certainly urged in part by an inherent disposition to tease, spoke again.

"You're not going away without thanking me?" she said.

"What for, mem?" he returned simply, standing stock-still again with his back towards her.

"You needn't stand so. You don't think I would go on dressing while you remained in sight?"

"I was as guid's awa', mem," he said, and turning a glowing face, looked at her for a moment, then cast his eyes on the ground.

"What for, ma'am?" he returned simply, standing stock-still again with his back towards her.

"You needn't stand so. You don't think I would go on dressing while you remained in sight?"

"I was as good as gone, ma'am," he said, and turning a glowing face, looked at her for a moment, then cast his eyes on the ground.

"Tell me what you mean by not thanking me," she insisted.

"They wad be dull thanks, mem, that war thankit afore I kenned what for."

"For allowing you to carry me ashore, of course."

"Be thankit, mem, wi' a' my hert. Will I gang doon o' my knees?"

"No. Why should you go on your knees?"

"'Cause ye're 'maist ower bonny to luik at stan'in', mem, an' I'm feared for angerin' ye."

"Don't say ma'am to me."

"What am I to say, than, mem?—I ask yer pardon, mem."

"Say *my lady*. That's how people speak to me."

"I thocht ye bude to be somebody by ordinar', my leddy! That'll be hoo ye're so terrible bonny," he returned, with some tremulousness in his tone. "But ye maun put on yer hose, my leddy, or ye'll get yer feet cauld, and that's no guid for the likes o' you."

The form of address she prescribed, conveyed to him no definite idea of rank. It but added intensity to the notion of her being a lady, as distinguished from one of the women of his own condition in life.

"And pray what is to become of *you*," she returned, "with your clothes as wet as water can make them?"

"The saut water kens me ower weel to do me ony ill," returned the lad. "I gang weet to the skin mony a day frae mornin' till nicht, and mony a nicht frae nicht till mornin'—at the heerin' fishin', ye ken, my leddy."

"Tell me what you mean by not thanking me," she insisted.

"They would be dull thanks, ma'am, that were given before I knew what for."

"For allowing you to carry me ashore, of course."

"Be thanked, ma'am, with all my heart. Will I go down on my knees?"

"No. Why should you go on your knees?"

"Because you're almost too bonny to look at standing, ma'am, and I'm afraid I'll anger you."

"Don't say ma'am to me."

"What am I to say then, ma'am?—I ask your pardon, ma'am."

"Say *my lady*. That's how people speak to me."

"I thought you must be somebody special, my lady! That'll be why you're so terribly bonny," he returned, with some tremulousness in his tone. "But you must put on your stockings, my lady, or you'll get your feet cold, and that's not good for the likes of you."

The form of address she prescribed, conveyed to him no definite idea of rank. It but added intensity to the notion of her being a lady, as distinguished from one of the women of his own condition in life.

"And pray what is to become of *you*," she returned, "with your clothes as wet as water can make them?"

"The salt water knows me too well to do me any harm," returned the lad. "I go wet to the skin many a day from morning to night, and many a night from night to morning—at the herring fishing, you know, my lady."

One might well be inclined to ask what could have tempted her to talk in such a familiar way to a creature like him—human indeed, but separated from her by a gulf more impassable far than that which divided her from the thrones, principalities, and powers of the upper regions? And how is the fact to be accounted for, that here she put out a dainty foot, and reaching for one of her stockings, began to draw it gently over the said foot? Either her sense of his inferiority was such that she regarded his presence no more than that of a dog, or, possibly, she was tempted to put his behaviour to the test. He, on his part, stood quietly regarding the operation, either that, with the instinct of an inborn refinement, he was aware he ought not to manifest more shamefacedness than the lady herself, or that he was hardly more accustomed to the sight of gleaming fish than the bare feet of maidens.

"I'm thinkin', my leddy," he went on, in absolute simplicity, "that sma' fut o' yer ain has danced mony a braw dance on mony a braw flure."

"How old do you take me for then?" she rejoined, and went on drawing the garment over her foot by the shortest possible stages.

"Ye'll no be muckle ower twenty," he said.

"I'm only sixteen," she returned, laughing merrily.

"What *will* ye be or ye behaud!" he exclaimed, after a brief pause of astonishment.

"Do you ever dance in this part of the country?" she asked, heedless of his surprise.

"No that muckle, at least amo' the fisherfowks, excep' it be at a weddin'. I was at ane last nicht."

"And did you dance?"

"'Deed did I, my leddy. I danced the maist o' the lasses clean aff o' their legs."

"What made you so cruel?"

"Weel, ye see, mem,—I mean my leddy,—fowk said I was ill aboot the bride; an' sae I bude to dance 't oot o' their heids."

"I'm thinking, my lady," he went on, in absolute simplicity, "that small foot of yours has danced many a fine dance on many a fine floor."

"How old do you take me for then?" she rejoined, and went on drawing the garment over her foot by the shortest possible stages.

"You won't be much over twenty," he said.

"I'm only sixteen," she returned, laughing merrily.

"What *will* you be when you're grown!" he exclaimed, after a brief pause of astonishment.

"Do you ever dance in this part of the country?" she asked, heedless of his surprise.

"Not that much, at least among the fisherfolk, except it be at a wedding. I was at one last night."

"And did you dance?"

"Indeed I did, my lady. I danced most of the lasses clean off their legs."

"What made you so cruel?"

"Well, you see, ma'am—I mean my lady,—folk said I was keen on the bride; and so I had to dance it out of their heads."

"And how much truth was there in what they said?" she asked, with a sly glance up in the handsome, now glowing face.

"Gien there was ony, there was unco little," he replied. "The chield's walcome till her for me. But she was the bonniest lassie we had.—It was what we ca' a penny weddin'," he went on, as if willing to change the side of the subject.

"And what's a penny wedding?"

"It's a' kin' o' a custom amo' the fishers. There's some gey puir fowk amon' 's, ye see, an' when a twa o' them merries, the lave o' 's wants to gie them a bit o' a start like. Sae we a' gang to the weddin' an' eats an' drinks plenty, an' pays for a' 'at we hae; and they mak' a guid profit out o' 't, for the things doesna cost them nearhan' sae muckle as we pay. So they hae a guid han'fu' ower for the plenishin'."

"And what do they give you to eat and drink?" asked the girl, making talk.

"Ow, skate an' mustard to eat, an' whusky to drink," answered the lad, laughing. "But it's mair for the fun. I dinna care muckle about whusky an' that kin' o' thing mysel'. It's the fiddles an' the dancin' 'at I like."

"You have music, then?"

"Ay; jist the fiddles an' the pipes."

"The bagpipes, do you mean?"

"Ay; my gran'father plays *them*."

"But you're not in the Highlands here: how come you to have bagpipes?"

"It's a stray bag, an' no more. But the fowk here likes the cry o' 't well eneuch, an' hae 't to wauk them ilka mornin'. Yon was my gran'father ye heard afore I fired the gun. Yon was his pipes waukin' them, honest fowk."

"And how much truth was there in what they said?" she asked, with a sly glance up in the handsome, now glowing face.

"If there was any, there was very little," he replied. "The man's welcome to her for me. But she was the bonniest lassie we had.—It was what we call a penny wedding," he went on, as if willing to change the side of the subject.

"And what's a penny wedding?"

"It's a sort of custom among the fishers. There's some very poor folk among us, you see, and when two of them marry, the rest of us want to give them something of a start. So we all go to the wedding and have plenty to eat and drink, and pay for it all; and they make a good profit out of it, for the things don't cost them nearly as much as we pay. So they have a good handful left over for fitting out their home."

"And what do they give you to eat and drink?" asked the girl, making talk.

"Oh, skate and mustard to eat, and whisky to drink," answered the lad, laughing. "But it's more for the fun. I don't care much about whisky and that kind of thing myself. It's the fiddles and the dancing that I like."

"You have music, then?"

"Ay; just the fiddles and the pipes."

"The bagpipes, do you mean?"

"Ay; my grandfather plays *them*."

"But you're not in the Highlands here: how come you to have bagpipes?"

"It's a stray bag, and no more. But the folk here like the cry of it well enough, and have it to wake them every morning. That was my grandfather you heard before I fired the gun. That was his pipes waking them, honest folk."

"And what made you fire the gun in that reckless way? Don't you know it is very dangerous?"

"Dangerous mem—my leddy, I mean! There was naething intill 't but a pennyworth o' blastin' pooder. It wadna blaw the froth aff o' the tap o' a jaw."

"It nearly blew me out of my small wits, though."

"I'm verra sorry it frichtit ye. But, gien I *had* seen ye, I bude to fire the gun."

"I don't understand you quite; but I suppose you mean it was your business to fire the gun."

"Jist that, my leddy."

"Why?"

"'Cause it 's been decreet i' the toon cooncil that at sax o' the clock ilka mornin' that gun's to be fired—at least sae lang's my lord, the marquis, is at Portlossie Hoose. Ye see it's a royal brugh, this, an' it costs but aboot a penny, an' it's gran' like to hae a sma' cannon to fire. An' gien I was to neglec' it, my gran'father wad gang on skirlin'–what's the English for *skirlin'*, my leddy–skirlin' o' the pipes?"

"I don't know. But from the sound of the word I should suppose it stands for *screaming*."

"Aye, that's it; only *screamin's* no sae guid as *skirlin'*. My gran'father's an auld man, as I was gaein' on to say, an' has hardly breath eneuch to fill the bag; but he wad be efter dirkin' onybody 'at said sic a thing, and till he heard that gun he wad gang on blawin' though he sud burst himsel.' There's naebody kens the smeddum in an auld hielan' man!"

"And what made you fire the gun in that reckless way? Don't you know it is very dangerous?"

"Dangerous ma'am—my lady, I mean! There was nothing in it but a pennyworth of blasting powder. It wouldn't blow the froth off the top of a sea wave."

"It nearly blew me out of my small wits, though."

"I'm very sorry it frightened you. But, supposing I *had* seen you, I still had to fire the gun."

"I don't understand you quite; but I suppose you mean it was your business to fire the gun."

"Just that, my lady."

"Why?"

"Because it's been decreed in the town council that at six o'clock every morning that gun's to be fired–at least so long as my lord, the marquis, is at Portlossie House. You see it's a royal borough, this, and it costs but about a penny, and it's grand-like to have a small cannon to fire. And if I was to neglect it, my grandfather would go on skirling–what's the English for *skirling*, my lady–skirling of the pipes?"

"I don't know. But from the sound of the word I should suppose it stands for *screaming*."

"Aye, that's it; only *screaming's* not so good as *skirling*. My grandfather's an old man, as I was about to tell you, and has hardly breath enough to fill the bag; but he would drive his dirk into the man that said so, and till he heard that gun he would go on blowing though he should burst himself. Nobody knows the spirit in an old highland man!"

By the time the conversation had reached this point, the lady had got her shoes on, had taken up her book from the sand, and was now sitting with it in her lap. No sound reached them but that of the tide, for the scream of the bagpipes had ceased the moment the swivel was fired. The sun was growing hot, and the sea, although so far in the cold north, was gorgeous in purple and green, suffused as with the overpowering pomp of a peacock's plumage in the sun. Away to the left the solid promontory trembled against the horizon, as if ready to dissolve and vanish between the bright air and the lucid sea that fringed its base with white. The glow of a young summer morning pervaded earth and sea and sky, and swelled the heart of the youth as he stood in unconscious bewilderment before the self-possession of the girl. She was younger than he, and knew far less that was worth knowing, yet had a world of advantage over him—not merely from the effect of her presence on one who had never seen anything half so beautiful, but from a certain readiness of surface thought, combined with the sweet polish of her speech, and an assurance of superiority which appeared to them both to lift her, like one of the old immortals, far above the level of the man whom she favoured with her passing converse. What in her words, as here presented only to the eye, may seem *brusqueness* or even forwardness, was so tempered, so toned, so fashioned by the *naïveté* with which she spoke, that it sounded in his ears as the utterance of absolute condescension. As to her personal appearance, the lad might well have taken her for twenty, for she looked more of a woman than, tall and strongly built as he was, he looked of a man. She was rather tall, rather slender, finely formed, with small hands and feet, and full throat. Her hair was of a dark brown; her eyes of such a blue that no one could have suggested grey; her complexion fair—a little freckled, which gave it the warmest tint it had; her nose nearly straight, her mouth rather large but well formed; and her forehead, as much of it as was to be seen under a garden hat, rose with promise above a pair of dark and finely-pencilled eyebrows.

The description I have here given may be regarded as occupying the space of a brief silence, during which the lad stood motionless, like one awaiting further command.

"Why don't you go?" said the lady. "I want to read my book."

He gave a great sigh, as if waking from a pleasant dream, took off his bonnet with a clumsy movement which yet had in it a grace worthy of a Stuart court, and descending the dune walked away along the sands towards the sea-town.

When he had gone about a couple of hundred yards, he looked back involuntarily. The lady had vanished. He concluded that she had crossed to the other side of the dune; but when he had gone so far on his way to the village as to clear the eastern end of the sandhill, and there turned and looked up its southern slope, she was still nowhere to be seen. The old highland stories of his grandfather came crowding to mind, and, altogether human as she had appeared, he almost doubted whether the sea, from which he had thought he rescued her, were not her native element. The book, however, not to mention the shoes and stockings, was against the supposition. Anyhow, he had seen a vision of some order or other, as certainly as if an angel from heaven had appeared to him, for the waters of his mind had been troubled with a new sense of grace and beauty, giving an altogether fresh glory to existence.

Of course no one would dream of falling in love with an unearthly creature, even an angel; at least, something homely must mingle with the glory ere that become possible; and as to this girl, the youth could scarcely have regarded her with a greater sense of *far-off-ness* had he known her for the daughter of a king of the sea—one whose very element was essentially death to him as life to her. Still he walked home as if the heavy boots he wore were wings at his heels, like those of the little Eurus or Boreas that stood blowing his trumpet for ever in the round open temple which from the top of a grassy hill in the park overlooked the Seaton.

"Sic een!" he kept saying to himself; "an' sic sma' white han's! an' sic a bonny fut! Eh hoo she wad glitter throu' the water in a bag net! Faith! gien she war to sing 'come doon' to me, I wad gang. Wad that be to lowse baith sowl an' body, I wonner? I'll see what Maister Graham says to that. It's a fine question to put till 'im: 'Gien a body was to gang wi' a mermaid, wha they say has nae sowl to be saved, wad that be the loss o' his sowl, as weel's o' the bodily life o' 'im?'"

"Such eyes!" he kept saying to himself; "and such small white hands! and such a bonny foot! Eh how she would glitter through the water in a bag net! Faith! if she were to sing 'come down' to me, I would go. Would that be to lose both soul and body, I wonder? I'll see what Mister Graham says to that. It's a fine question to put to him: 'If a man was to go with a mermaid, who they say has no soul to be saved, would that be to lose his soul, as well as his bodily life?'"

CHAPTER VI

DUNCAN MACPHAIL

The sea-town of Portlossie was as irregular a gathering of small cottages as could be found on the surface of the globe. They faced every way, turned their backs and gables every way—only of the roofs could you predict the position; were divided from each other by every sort of small, irregular space and passage, and looked like a national assembly debating a constitution. Close behind the Seaton, as it was called, ran a highway, climbing far above the chimneys of the village to the level of the town above. Behind this road, and separated from it by a high wall of stone, lay a succession of heights and hollows covered with grass. In front of the cottages lay sand and sea. The place was cleaner than most fishing villages, but so closely built, so thickly inhabited, and so pervaded with "a very ancient and fishlike smell," that but for the besom of the salt north wind it must have been unhealthy. Eastward the houses could extend no further for the harbour, and westward no further for a small river that crossed the sands to find the sea—discursively and merrily at low water, but with sullen, submissive mingling when banked back by the tide.

Avoiding the many nets extended long and wide on the grassy sands, the youth walked through the tide-swollen mouth of the river, and passed along the front of the village until he arrived at a house, the small window in the seaward gable of which was filled with a curious collection of things for sale—dusty looking sweets in a glass bottle; gingerbread cakes in the shape of large hearts, thickly studded with sugar-plums of rainbow colours, invitingly poisonous; strings of tin covers for tobacco pipes, overlapping each other like fish-scales; toys, and tapes, and needles, and twenty other kinds of things, all huddled together.

Turning the corner of this house, he went down the narrow passage between it and the next, and in at its open door. But the moment it was entered it lost all appearance of a shop, and the room with the tempting window showed itself only as a poor kitchen with an earthen floor.

"Weel, hoo did the pipes behave themsels the day, daddy?" said the youth as he strode in.

"Well, how did the pipes behave themselves today, daddy?" said the youth as he strode in.

"Och, she'll pe peing a coot poy today," returned the tremulous voice of a grey-headed old man, who was leaning over a small peat-fire on the hearth, sifting oatmeal through the fingers of his left hand into a pot, while he stirred the boiling mess with a short stick held in his right.

"Och, she'll be being a coot boy today,"[5] returned the tremulous voice of a grey-headed old man, who was leaning over a small peat-fire on the hearth, sifting oatmeal through the fingers of his left hand into a pot, while he stirred the boiling mess with a short stick held in his right.

It had grown to be understood between them that the pulmonary conditions of the old piper should be attributed not to his internal, but his external lungs—namely, the bag of his pipes. Both sets had of late years manifested strong symptoms of decay, and decided measures had had to be again and again resorted to in the case of the latter to put off its evil day, and keep within it the breath of its musical existence. The youth's question, then, as to the behaviour of the pipes, was in reality an inquiry after the condition of his grandfather's lungs, which, for their part, grew yearly more and more asthmatic: notwithstanding which Duncan MacPhail would not hear of resigning the dignity of town-piper.

"That's fine, daddy," returned the youth. "Wull I mak oot the parritch? I'm thinkin ye've had eneuch o' hingin' ower the fire this het mornin'."

"That's fine, daddy," returned the youth. "Will I finish making the porridge? I'm thinking you've had enough of hanging over the fire this hot morning."

"No, sir," answered Duncan. "She'll pe perfectly able to make ta parritch herself, my poy Malcolm. Ta tay will tawn when her poy must make his own parritch, an' she'll be wantin' no more parritch, but haf to trink ta rainwater, and no trop of ta uisgebeatha to put into it, my poy Malcolm."

"No, sir," answered Duncan. "She'll be perfectly able to make ta porridge herself, my boy Malcolm. Ta day will dawn when her boy must make his own porridge, and she'll be wantin' no more porridge, but haf to drink ta rainwater, and no drop of ta uisgebeatha (whisky) to put into it, my boy Malcolm."

His grandson was quite accustomed to the old man's heathenish mode of regarding his immediate existence after death as a long confinement in the grave, and generally had a word or two ready wherewith to combat the frightful notion; but, as he spoke, Duncan lifted the pot from the fire, and set it on its three legs on the deal table in the middle of the room, adding:

His grandson was quite accustomed to the old man's heathenish mode of regarding his immediate existence after death as a long confinement in the grave, and generally had a word or two ready wherewith to combat the frightful notion; but, as he spoke, Duncan lifted the pot from the fire, and set it on its three legs on the deal table in the middle of the room, adding:

---

5 N.B. while the columns have been retained whenever Duncan speaks, this is only to modify (very slightly) his Highland mode of utterance. Since he is speaking English, not Scots, no full "translation" has been deemed necessary. Note also that he refers to himself in 3rd person feminine.

"Tere, my man—tere's ta parritch! And was it ta putter, or ta traicle, or ta pottle o' peer, she would be havin' for kitchie tis fine mornin'?"

This point settled, the two sat down to eat their breakfast; and no one would have discovered, from the manner in which the old man helped himself, nor yet from the look of his eyes, that he was stone blind. It came neither of old age nor disease—he had been born blind. His eyes, although large and wide, looked like those of a sleep-walker—open with shut sense; the shine in them was all reflected light—glitter, no glow; and their colour was so pale that they suggested some horrible sight as having driven from them hue and vision together.

"Haf you eated enough, my son?" he said, when he heard Malcolm lay down his spoon.

"Ay, plenty, thank ye, daddy, and they were richt weel made," replied the lad, whose mode of speech was entirely different from his grandfather's: the latter had learned English as a foreign language, but could not speak Scotch, his mother tongue being Gaelic.

As they rose from the table, a small girl, with hair wildly suggestive of insurrection and conflagration, entered, and said, in a loud screetch—"Maister MacPhail, my mither wants a pot o' bleckin', an' ye're to be sure an' gie her't gweed, she says."

"Fery coot, my chilt, Jeannie; but young Malcolm and old Tuncan hasn't made teir prayers yet, and you know fery well tat she won't sell pefore she's made her prayers. Tell your mother tat she'll pe bringin' ta blackin' when she comes to look to ta lamp."

"Tere, my man–tere's ta porridge! And was it ta butter, or ta treacle, or ta bottle o' beer, she would be havin' for kitchie (condiment) tis fine mornin'?"

This point settled, the two sat down to eat their breakfast; and no one would have discovered, from the manner in which the old man helped himself, nor yet from the look of his eyes, that he was stone blind. It came neither of old age nor disease—he had been born blind. His eyes, although large and wide, looked like those of a sleep-walker—open with shut sense; the shine in them was all reflected light—glitter, no glow; and their colour was so pale that they suggested some horrible sight as having driven from them hue and vision together.

"Haf you eated enough, my son?" he said, when he heard Malcolm lay down his spoon.

"Ay, plenty, thank you daddy, and you did a grand job making it," replied the lad, whose mode of speech was entirely different from his grandfather's: the latter had learned English as a foreign language, but could not speak Scotch, his mother tongue being Gaelic.

As they rose from the table, a small girl, with hair wildly suggestive of insurrection and conflagration, entered, and said, in a loud screetch—"Mister MacPhail, my mother wants a pot of blacking, and you're to be sure and give her the best, she says."

"Fery coot, my child, Jeannie; but young Malcolm and old Tuncan hasn't made their prayers yet, and you know fery well tat she won't sell pefore she's made her prayers. Tell your mother tat she'll be bringin' ta blackin' when she comes to look to ta lamp."

The child ran off without response. Malcolm lifted the pot from the table and set it on the hearth; put the plates together and the spoons, and set them on a chair, for there was no dresser; tilted the table, and wiped it hearthward—then from a shelf took down and laid upon it a bible, before which he seated himself with an air of reverence. The old man sat down on a low chair by the chimney corner, took off his bonnet, closed his eyes and murmured some almost inaudible words; then repeated in Gaelic the first line of the hundred and third psalm—

O m' anam, beannuich thus' a nis—

and raised a tune of marvellous wail. Arrived at the end of the line, he repeated the process with the next, and so went on, giving every line first in the voice of speech and then in the voice of song, through three stanzas of eight lines each. And no less strange was the singing than the tune—wild and wailful as the wind of his native desolations, or as the sound of his own pipes borne thereon; and apparently all but lawless, for the multitude of so-called grace-notes, hovering and fluttering endlessly around the centre tone like the comments on a text, rendered it nearly impossible to unravel from them the air even of a known tune. It had in its kind the same liquid uncertainty of confluent sound which had hitherto rendered it impossible for Malcolm to learn more than a few of the common phrases of his grandfather's mother-tongue.

The psalm over, during which the sightless eyeballs of the singer had been turned up towards the rafters of the cottage—a sign surely that the germ of light, "the sunny seed," as Henry Vaughan calls it, must be in him, else why should he lift his *eyes* when he thought upward?—Malcolm read a chapter of the Bible, plainly the next in an ordered succession, for it could never have been chosen or culled; after which they kneeled together, and the old man poured out a prayer, beginning in a low, scarcely audible voice, which rose at length to a loud, modulated chant. Not a sentence, hardly a phrase, of the utterance, did his grandson lay hold of; but there were a few inhabitants of the place who could have interpreted it, and it was commonly believed that one part of his devotions was invariably a prolonged petition for vengeance on Campbell of Glenlyon, the main instrument in the massacre of Glenco.

He *could* have prayed in English, and then his grandson might have joined in his petitions, but the thought of such a thing would never have presented itself to him. Nay, although, understanding both languages, he used that which was unintelligible to the lad, he yet regarded himself as the party who had the right to resent the consequent schism. Such a conversation as now followed was no new thing after prayers.

"I could fery well wish, Malcolm, my son," said the old man, "tat you would be learnin' to speak your own lancuach. It is all fery well for ta Sassenach podies to read ta Piple in English, for it will be pleasing ta Maker not to make tem cawpable of ta Gaelic, no more tan monkeys; but for all tat it's not ta vord of God. Ta Gaelic is ta lancuach of ta carden of Aiden, and no doubt but it pe ta lancuach in which ta Shepherd calls his sheep on ta everlastin' hills. You see, Malcolm, it must be so, for how can a mortal man speak to his God in *anything put* Gaelic? When Mr Craham—no, not Mr Craham, ta coot man; it was ta new Minister—he speak an' say to her: 'Mr MacPhail, you ought to make your prayers in Enclish,' I was fery wrathful, and I answered and said: 'Mr Downey, do you tare to suppose tat God doesn't prefer ta Gaelic to ta Sassenach tongue!'—'Mr MacPhail,' says he, 'it'll pe for your poy I mean it. How's ta lad to learn ta way of salvation if you speak to your God in his presence in a strange tongue? So I was opedient to his vord, and ta next efening I tid kneel town in Sassenach and I tid make begin. But, ochone! she wouldn't go; her tongue would be cleafing to ta roof of her mouth; ta claymore would be sticking rusty in ta scappard; for her heart she was ashamed to speak to ta Hielan'man's Maker in ta Sassenach tongue. You must pe learning ta Gaelic, or you'll not pe peing worthy to pe her nain son, Malcolm."

"But daddy, wha's to learn me?" asked his grandson, gayly.

"I could fery well wish, Malcolm, my son," said the old man, "tat you would be learnin' to speak your own lancuach. It is all fery well for ta Sassenach *(Saxon, i.e., non-Celtic)* bodies to read ta Bible in English, for it will be pleasing ta Maker not to make tem capable of ta Gaelic, no more tan monkeys; but for all tat it's not ta word of God. Ta Gaelic is ta lancuach of ta garden of Eden, and no doubt but it be ta lancuach in which ta Shepherd calls his sheep on ta everlastin' hills. You see, Malcolm, it must be so, for how can a mortal man speak to his God in *anything but* Gaelic? When Mr Graham–no, not Mr Graham, ta coot man; it was ta new Minister–he speak an' say to her: 'Mr MacPhail, you ought to make your prayers in English,' I was fery wrathful, and I answered and said: 'Mr. Downey, do you dare to suppose tat God doesn't prefer ta Gaelic to ta Sassenach tongue!'–'Mr MacPhail,' says he, "it'll be for your boy I mean it. How's ta lad to learn ta way of salvation if you speak to your God in his presence in a strange tongue? So I was obedient to his vord, and ta next efening I did kneel down in Sassenach and I did make begin. But, alas! she wouldn't go; her tongue would be cleafing to ta roof of her mouth; ta claymore would be sticking rusty in ta scabbard; for her heart she was ashamed to speak to ta Highlandman's Maker in ta Sassenach tongue. You must be learning ta Gaelic, or you'll not be being worthy to be her own son, Malcolm."

"But daddy, who's to teach me?" asked his grandson, gayly.

"Learn you, Malcolm! Ta Gaelic is ta lancuach of Nature, and wants no learning. *I nefer did pe learning it, yat I nefer haf to say to myself 'What is it she would be saying?'* when I speak ta Gaelic; put she always has to set ta tead men—that is ta vords—on their feet, and put tem in pattle-array, when she would pe speaking ta dull mechanic English. When she opens her mouth to it, ta Gaelic comes like a spring of pure water, Malcolm. Ta plenty of it *must* run out. Try it now, Malcolm. Shust oppen your mouth in ta Gaelic shape, and see if ta Gaelic will not pe falling from it."

Seized with a merry fit, Malcolm did open his mouth in the Gaelic shape, and sent from it a strange gabble, imitative of the most frequently recurring sounds of his grandfather's speech.

"Hoo will that du, daddy?" he asked, after jabbering gibberish for the space of a minute.

"It will not be paad for a peginning, Malcolm. She cannot say it shust pe vorts, or tat tere pe much of ta sense in it; but it pe fery like what ta pabes will say pefore tey pekin to speak it properly. So it 's all fery well, and if you will only pe putting your mouth in ta Gaelic shape often enough, ta sounds will soon pe taking ta shape of it, and ta vorts will be coming trough ta mists, and pefore you know, you'll pe peing a creat credit to your cranfather, my boy, Malcolm."

A silence followed, for Malcolm's attempt had not had the result he anticipated: he had thought only to make his grandfather laugh. Presently the old man resumed, in the kindest voice:

"Learn you, Malcolm! Ta Gaelic is ta lancuach of Nature, and wants no learning. *I nefer did be learning it, yet I nefer haf to say to myself 'What is it she would be saying?'* when I speak ta Gaelic; but she always has to set ta dead men–that is ta words–on their feet, and put them in battle-array, when she would be speaking ta dull mechanic English. When she opens her mouth to it, ta Gaelic comes like a spring of pure water, Malcolm. Ta plenty of it *must* run out. Try it now, Malcolm. Shust oppen your mouth in ta Gaelic shape, and see if ta Gaelic will not be falling from it."

Seized with a merry fit, Malcolm did open his mouth in the Gaelic shape, and sent from it a strange gabble, imitative of the most frequently recurring sounds of his grandfather's speech.

"How will that do, daddy?" he asked, after jabbering gibberish for the space of a minute.

"It will not be baad for a beginning, Malcolm. She cannot say it shust be words, or tat tere be much of ta sense in it; but it be fery like what ta babes will say before tey begin to speak it properly. So it's all fery well, and if you will only be putting your mouth in ta Gaelic shape often enough, ta sounds will soon be taking ta shape of it, and ta words will be coming through ta mists, and before you know, you'll be being a creat credit to your cranfather, my boy, Malcolm."

A silence followed, for Malcolm's attempt had not had the result he anticipated: he had thought only to make his grandfather laugh. Presently the old man resumed, in the kindest voice:

"And tere's another thing, Malcolm, tat's much wanting to you: you'll never pe a man—not to speak of a pard like your cranfather—if you'll not pe learning to play on ta bagpipes."

"And tere's another thing, Malcolm, tat's much wanting to you: you'll never be a man–not to speak of a bard like your cranfather–if you'll not be learning to play on ta bagpipes."

Malcolm, who had been leaning against the *chimley-lug* (fireside) while his grandfather spoke, moved gently round behind his chair, reached out for the pipes where they lay in a corner at the old man's side, and catching them up softly, put the mouthpiece to his lips. With a few vigorous blasts he filled the bag, and out burst the double droning bass, while the youth's fingers, clutching the chanter as by the throat, at once compelled its screeches into shape far better, at least, than his lips had been able to give to the crude material of Gaelic. He played the only reel he knew, but that with vigour and effect.

At the first sound of its notes the old man sprung to his feet and began capering to the reel—partly in delight with the music, but far more in delight with the musician, while, ever and anon, with feeble yell, he uttered the unspellable *Hoogh* of the Highlander, and jumped, as he thought, high in the air, though his failing limbs, alas! lifted his feet scarce an inch from the floor.

"Aigh! aigh!" he sighed at length, yielding the contest between his legs and the lungs of the lad—"aigh! aigh! She'll die happy! she'll die happy! Hear till her poy, how he makes ta pipes speak ta true Gaelic! Ta pest o' Gaelic, tat! Old Tuncan's pipes 'll not know how to be talking Sassenach. See to it! see to it! He had put to blow in at ta one end, and out came ta reel at the other. Hoogh! hoogh! Play us ta Righil Thulachan, Malcolm, my chief!"

"Aigh! Aigh!" he sighed at length, yielding the contest between his legs and the lungs of the lad— "aigh! aigh! She'll die happy! she'll die happy! Hear to her boy, how he makes ta pipes speak ta true Gaelic! Ta best o' Gaelic, tat! Old Tuncan's pipes 'll not know how to be talking Sassenach. See to it! see to it! He had but to blow in at ta one end, and out came ta reel at the other. Hoogh! hoogh! Play us ta Righil Thulachan, Malcolm, my chief!"

"I kenna reel, strathspey, nor lilt, but jist that burd alane, daddy."

"I don't know reel, strathspey, nor lilt, but just that single one, daddy."

"Give tem to me, my poy!" cried the old piper, reaching out a hand as eager to clutch the uncouth instrument as the miser's to finger his gold; "hear well to me as I play, and you'll soon be able to play pibroch or coronach with the best piper between Cape Wrath and ta Mull o' Cantyre."

"Give tem to me, my boy!" cried the old piper, reaching out a hand as eager to clutch the uncouth instrument as the miser's to finger his gold; "hear well to me as I play, and you'll soon be able to play pibroch or coronach with the best piper between Cape Wrath and ta Mull of Kintyre."

He played tune after tune until his breath failed him, and an exhausted grunt of the drone—in the middle of a coronach, followed by an abrupt pause, revealed the emptiness of both lungs and bag. Then first he remembered his object, forgotten the moment he had filled his bag.

"Now, Malcolm," he said, offering the pipes to his grandson; "you play tat after."

He had himself of course, learned all by the ear, but could hardly have been serious in requesting Malcolm to follow him through such a succession of tortuous mazes.

"I haena a memory up to that, daddy; but I s' get a haud o' Mr Graham's flute music, and maybe that'll help me a bit.— Wadna ye be takin' hame Meg Partan's blackin' 'at ye promised her?"

"Surely, my son. She should always be keeping her promises."

He played tune after tune until his breath failed him, and an exhausted grunt of the drone—in the middle of a coronach, followed by an abrupt pause, revealed the emptiness of both lungs and bag. Then first he remembered his object, forgotten the moment he had filled his bag.

"Now, Malcolm," he said, offering the pipes to his grandson; "you play tat after."

He had himself of course, learned all by the ear, but could hardly have been serious in requesting Malcolm to follow him through such a succession of tortuous mazes.

"I haven't the memory for it, daddy; but I'll get a hold of Mr Graham's flute music, and maybe that'll help me a bit.— Won't you be taking home Meg Partan's blacking that you promised her?"

"Surely, my son. She should always be keeping her promises."

He rose, and getting a small stone bottle and his stick from the corner between the projecting *inglecheek* and the window, left the house, to walk with unerring steps through the labyrinth of the village, threading his way from passage to passage, and avoiding pools and projecting stones, not to say houses, and human beings. His eyes, or indeed perhaps rather his whole face, appeared to possess an ethereal sense as of touch, for, without the slightest contact in the ordinary sense of the word, he was aware of the neighbourhood of material objects, as if through the pulsations of some medium to others imperceptible. He could, with perfect accuracy, tell the height of any wall or fence within a few feet of him; could perceive at once whether it was high or low or half tide, and that merely by going out in front of the houses and turning his face with its sightless eyeballs towards the sea; knew whether a woman who spoke to him had a child in her arms or not; and, indeed, was believed to know sooner than ordinary mortals that one was about to become a mother.

He was a strange figure to look upon in that lowland village, for he invariably wore the highland dress: in truth, he had never had a pair of trowsers on his legs, and was far from pleased that his grandson clothed himself in such contemptible garments. But, contrasted with the showy style of his costume, there was something most pathetic in the blended pallor of hue into which the originally gorgeous colours of his kilt had faded—noticeable chiefly on weekdays, when he wore no sporran; for the kilt, encountering, from its loose construction, comparatively little strain or friction, may reach an antiquity unknown to the garments of the low country, and, while perfectly decent, yet look ancient exceedingly. On Sundays, however, he made the best of himself, and came out like a belated and aged butterfly—with his father's sporran, or tasselled goatskin purse, in front of him, his grandfather's dirk at his side, his great grandfather's *skene-dhu*, or little black hafted knife, stuck in the stocking of his right leg, and a huge round brooch of brass—nearly half a foot in diameter, and, Mr Graham said, as old as the battle of Harlaw—on his left shoulder. In these adornments he would walk proudly to church, leaning on the arm of his grandson.

"The piper's gey brokken-like the day," said one of the fishermen's wives to a neighbour as he passed them—the fact being that he had not yet recovered from his second revel in the pipes so soon after the exhaustion of his morning's duty, and was, in consequence, more asthmatic than usual.

"I doobt he'll be slippin' awa some cauld nicht," said the other: "his leevin' breath's ill to get."

"Ay; he has to warstle for't, puir man! Weel, he'll be missed, the blin' body! It's exterordinor hoo he's managed to live, and bring up sic a fine lad as that Malcolm o' his."

"Weel, ye see, Providence has been kin' till *him* as weel 's ither blin' craturs. The toon's pipin' 's no to be despised; an' there's the cryin', an' the chop, an' the lamps. 'Deed he's been an eident cratur— an' for a blin' man, as ye say, it 's jist exterordinar."

"Div ye min' whan first he cam' to the toon, lass?"

"Ay; what wad hinner me min'in' that? It's nae sae lang."

"Ma'colm 'at's sic a fine laad noo, they tell me wasna muckle bigger nor a gey haddie."

"But the auld man was an auld man than, though nae doobt he's unco' failed sin syne."

"A dochter's bairn, they say, the laad."

"Ay, they say, but wha kens? Duncan could never be gotten to open his mou' as to the father or mither o' 'im, an' sae it weel may be as they say. It's nigh twenty year noo, I'm thinkin' sin he made's appearance. Ye wasna come frae Scaurnose er' than."

"Some fowk says the auld man's name's no MacPhail, an' he maun hae come here in hidin' for some rouch job or ither 'at he's been mixed up wi'."

"I s' believe nae ill o' sic a puir, hairmless body. Fowk 'at maks their ain livin', wantin' the een to guide them, canna be that far aff the straucht. Guid guide 's! we hae eneuch to answer for, oor ainsels, ohn passed jeedgment upo ane anither."

"I was but tellin' ye what fowk telled me," returned the younger woman.

"Ay, ay, lass; I ken that, for I ken there was fowk to tell ye."

"A daughter's child, they say, the lad."

"Ay, they say, but who knows? Duncan could never be made to open his mouth as to his father or mother, and so it well may be as they say. It's nearly twenty years now, I'm thinking, since he first appeared. You hadn't yet come from Scaurnose at the time."

"Some folk say the old man's name's not MacPhail, and he must have come here in hiding for some rough job or other that he's been mixed up with."

"I'll believe nothing bad of such a poor, harmless body. Folk that make their own living, without their eyes to guide them, can't be that far from the straight road. My goodness! we have enough to answer for, our own selves, without passing judgement upon one another."

"I was only telling you what folk told me," returned the younger woman.

"Ay, ay, lass; I know that, for I know there were folk to tell you."

CHAPTER VII

ALEXANDER GRAHAM

As soon as his grandfather left the house, Malcolm went out also, closing the door behind him, and turning the key, but leaving it in the lock. He ascended to the upper town, only, however, to pass through its main street, at the top of which he turned and looked back for a few moments, apparently in contemplation. The descent to the shore was so sudden that he could see nothing of the harbour or of the village he had left—nothing but the blue bay and the filmy mountains of Sutherlandshire, molten by distance into cloudy questions, and looking, betwixt blue sea and blue sky, less substantial than either. After gazing for a moment, he turned again, and held on his way, through fields which no fence parted from the road. The morning was still glorious, the larks right jubilant, and the air filled with the sweet scents of cottage flowers. Across the fields came the occasional low of an ox, and the distant sounds of children at play. But Malcolm saw without noting, and heard without heeding, for his mind was full of speculation concerning the lovely girl, whose vision appeared already far off:—who might she be? whence had she come? whither could she have vanished? That she did not belong to the neighbourhood was certain, he thought; but there was a farm-house near the sea-town where they let lodgings; and, although it was early in the season, she might belong to some family which had come to spend a few of the summer weeks there; possibly his appearance had prevented her from having her bath that morning. If he should have the good fortune to see her again, he would show her a place far fitter for the purpose—a perfect arbour of rocks, utterly secluded, with a floor of deep sand, and without a hole for crab or lobster.

His road led him in the direction of a few cottages lying in a hollow. Beside them rose a vision of trees, bordered by an ivy-grown wall, from amidst whose summits shot the spire of the church; and from beyond the spire, through the trees, came golden glimmers as of vane and crescent and pinnacled ball, that hinted at some shadowy abode of enchantment within; but as he descended the slope towards the cottages the trees gradually rose and shut in everything.

These cottages were far more ancient than the houses of the town, were covered with green thatch, were buried in ivy, and would soon be radiant with roses and honeysuckles. They were gathered irregularly about a gate of curious old ironwork, opening on the churchyard, but more like an entrance to the grounds behind the church, for it told of ancient state, bearing on each of its pillars a great stone heron with a fish in its beak.

This was the quarter whence had come the noises of children, but they had now ceased, or rather sunk into a gentle murmur, which oozed, like the sound of bees from a straw-covered beehive, out of a cottage rather larger than the rest, which stood close by the churchyard gate. It was the parish school, and these cottages were all that remained of the old town of Portlossie, which had at one time stretched in a long irregular street almost to the shore. The town cross yet stood, but away solitary on a green hill that overlooked the sands.

During the summer the long walk from the new town to the school and to the church was anything but a hardship: in winter it was otherwise, for then there were days in which few would venture the single mile that separated them.

The door of the school, bisected longitudinally, had one of its halves open, and by it outflowed the gentle hum of the honeybees of learning. Malcolm walked in, and had the whole of the busy scene at once before him. The place was like a barn, open from wall to wall, and from floor to rafters and thatch, browned with the peat smoke of vanished winters. Two thirds of the space were filled with long desks and forms; the other had only the master's desk, and thus afforded room for standing classes. At the present moment it was vacant, for the prayer was but just over, and the Bible-class had not been called up: there Alexander Graham, the schoolmaster, descending from his desk, met and welcomed Malcolm with a kind shake of the hand. He was a man of middle height, but very thin; and about five and forty years of age, but looked older, because of his thin grey hair and a stoop in the shoulders. He was dressed in a shabby black tailcoat, and clean white neckcloth; the rest of his clothes were of parson grey, noticeably shabby also. The quiet sweetness of his smile, and a composed look of submission were suggestive of the purification of sorrow, but were attributed by the townsfolk to disappointment; for he was still but a schoolmaster, whose aim they thought must be a pulpit and a parish. But Mr Graham had been early released from such an ambition, if it had ever possessed him, and had for many years been more than content to give himself to the hopefuller work of training children for the true ends of life: he lived the quietest of studious lives, with an old housekeeper.

Malcolm had been a favourite pupil, and the relation of master and scholar did not cease when the latter saw that he ought to do something to lighten the burden of his grandfather, and so left the school and betook himself to the life of a fisherman—with the slow leave of Duncan, who had set his heart on making a scholar of him, and would never, indeed, had Gaelic been amongst his studies, have been won by the most laboursome petition. He asserted himself perfectly able to provide for both for ten years to come at least, in proof of which he roused the inhabitants of Portlossie, during the space of a whole month, a full hour earlier than usual, with the most terrific blasts of the bagpipes, and this notwithstanding complaint and expostulation on all sides, so that at length the provost had to interfere; after which outburst of defiance to time, however, his energy had begun to decay so visibly that Malcolm gave himself to the pipes in secret, that he might be ready, in case of sudden emergency, to take his grandfather's place; for Duncan lived in constant dread of the hour when his office might be taken from him and conferred on a mere drummer, or, still worse, on a certain ne'er-do-weel cousin of the provost, so devoid of music as to be capable only of ringing a bell.

"I've had an invitation to Miss Campbell's funeral—Miss Horn's cousin, you know," said Mr Graham, in a hesitating and subdued voice: "could you manage to take the school for me, Malcolm?"

"Yes, sir. There's naething to hinner me. What day is 't upo'?"

"Yes, sir. There's nothing to hinder me. What day will it be?"

"Saturday."

"Saturday."

"Verra weel, sir. I s' be here in guid time."

"Very well, sir. I'll be here in good time."

This matter settled, the business of the school, in which, as he did often, Malcolm had come to assist, began. Only a pupil of his own could have worked with Mr Graham, for his mode was very peculiar. But the strangest fact in it would have been the last to reveal itself to an ordinary observer. This was, that he rarely contradicted anything: he would call up the opposing truth, set it face to face with the error, and leave the two to fight it out. The human mind and conscience were, he said, the plains of Armageddon, where the battle of good and evil was for ever raging; and the one business of a teacher was to rouse and urge this battle by leading fresh forces of the truth into the field—forces composed as little as might be of the hireling troops of the intellect, and as much as possible of the native energies of the heart, imagination, and conscience. In a word, he would oppose error only by teaching the truth.

In early life he had come under the influence of the writings of William Law, which he read as one who pondered every doctrine in that light which only obedience to the truth can open upon it. With a keen eye for the discovery of universal law in the individual fact, he read even the marvels of the New Testament practically. Hence, in training his soldiers, every lesson he gave them was a missile; every admonishment of youth or maiden was as the mounting of an armed champion, and the launching of him with a *God-speed* into the thick of the fight.

He now called up the Bible-class, and Malcolm sat beside and listened. That morning they had to read one of the chapters in the history of Jacob.

"Was Jacob a good man?" he asked, as soon as the reading, each of the scholars in turn taking a verse, was over.

An apparently universal expression of assent followed; halting its wake, however, came the voice of a boy near the bottom of the class:

"Wasna he some dooble, sir?"

"Wasn't he quite double sir?"

"You are right, Sheltie," said the master; "he *was* double. I must, I find, put the question in another shape:—Was Jacob a bad man?"

Again came such a burst of yesses that it might have been taken for a general hiss. But limping in the rear came again the half-dissentient voice of Jamie Joss, whom the master had just addressed as Sheltie:

"Pairtly, sir."

"You think, then, Sheltie, that a man may be both bad and good?"

"I dinna ken, sir. I think he may be whiles ane an' whiles the ither, an' whiles maybe it wad be ill to say whilk. Oor collie's whiles in twa min's whether he'll du what he's telled or no."

"That's the battle of Armageddon, Sheltie, my man. It's aye ragin', ohn gun roared or bayonet clashed. Ye maun up an' do yer best in't, my man. Gien ye dee fechtin' like a man, ye'll flee up wi' a quaiet face an' wide open een; an' there's a great Ane 'at 'll say to ye, 'Weel dune, laddie!' But gien ye gie in to the enemy, he'll turn ye intill a creepin' thing 'at eats dirt; an' there 'll no be a hole in a' the crystal wa' o' the New Jerusalem near eneuch to the grun' to lat ye creep throu'."

As soon as ever Alexander Graham, the polished thinker and sweet-mannered gentleman, opened his mouth concerning the things he loved best, that moment the most poetic forms came pouring out in the most rugged speech.

"I reckon, sir," said Sheltie, "Jacob hadna fouchten oot his battle."

"You are right, Sheltie," said the master; "he *was* double. I must, I find, put the question in another shape:—Was Jacob a bad man?"

Again came such a burst of yesses that it might have been taken for a general hiss. But limping in the rear came again the half-dissentient voice of Jamie Joss, whom the master had just addressed as Sheltie:

"Partly, sir."

"You think, then, Sheltie, that a man may be both bad and good?"

"I don't know, sir. I think he may be sometimes one and sometimes the other, and sometimes it would be hard to tell which. Our collie's in two minds sometimes about whether he'll do what he's told or not."

"That's the battle of Armageddon, Sheltie, my man. It's always raging, though no gun should roar, nor bayonet clash. You must join in and do your best in it, my man. If you die fighting like a man, you'll fly up with a quiet face and wide open eyes; and there's a great One that'll say to you, 'Well done, laddie!' But if you give in to the enemy, he'll turn you into a creeping thing that eats dirt; and there won't be a hole in all the crystal wall of the New Jerusalem near enough to the ground to let you creep through."

As soon as ever Alexander Graham, the polished thinker and sweet-mannered gentleman, opened his mouth concerning the things he loved best, that moment the most poetic forms came pouring out in the most rugged speech.

"I reckon, sir," said Sheltie, "Jacob hadn't fought out his battle."

"That's jist it, my boy. And because he wouldna get up and fecht manfully, God had to tak him in han'. Ye've heard tell o' generals, when their troops war rinnin' awa', haein' to cut this man doon, shute that ane, and lick anither, till he turned them a' richt face aboot and drave them on to the foe like a spate! And the trouble God took wi' Jacob wasna lost upon him at last."

"An' what cam o' Esau, sir?" asked a pale-faced maiden with blue eyes. "He wasna an ill kin' o' a chield—was he, sir?"

"No, Mappy," answered the master; "he was a fine chield, as you say; but he nott mair time and gentler treatment to mak onything o' him. Ye see he had a guid hert, but was a duller kin' o' cratur a'thegither, and cared for naething he could na see or hanle. He never thoucht muckle aboot God at a'. Jacob was anither sort—a poet kin' o' a man, but a sneck-drawin' cratur for a' that. It was easier, hooever, to get the slyness oot o' Jacob, than the dulness oot o' Esau. Punishment tellt upo' Jacob like upon a thin-skinned horse, whauras Esau was mair like the minister's powny, that can hardly be made to unnerstan' that ye want him to gang on. But o' the ither han', dullness is a thing that can be borne wi': there's nae hurry aboot that; but the deceitfu' tricks o' Jacob war na to be endured, and sae the tawse cam doon upo' *him*."

"An' what for didna God mak Esau as clever as Jacob?" asked a wizened-faced boy near the top of the class.

"That's just it, my boy. And because he wouldn't get up and fight manfully, God had to take him in hand. You've heard tell of generals, when their troops were running away, having to cut this man down, shoot that one, and lick another, till he turned them all right face about and drove them onto the foe like a spate! And the trouble God took with Jacob wasn't lost upon him at last."

"And what became of Esau, sir?" asked a pale-faced maiden with blue eyes. "He wasn't a bad sort of a man—was he, sir?"

"No, Mappy," answered the master; "he was a fine fellow, as you say; but he needed more time and gentler treatment to make anything of him. You see he had a good heart, but was a duller kind of creature altogether, and cared for nothing he couldn't see or handle. He never thought much about God at all. Jacob was another sort—a poet kind of a man, but a sly character for all that. It was easier, however, to get the slyness out of Jacob, than the dullness out of Esau. Punishment told upon Jacob like upon a thin-skinned horse, whereas Esau was more like the minister's pony, that can hardly be made to understand that you want him to go on. But on the other hand, dullness is a thing that can be borne with: there's no hurry about that; but the deceitful tricks of Jacob weren't to be endured, and so the tawse (leather strap) came down upon *him*."

"And why didn't God make Esau as clever as Jacob?" asked a wizened-faced boy near the top of the class.

"Ah, my *Peery!*" said Mr Graham, "I canna tell ye that. A' that I can tell is, that God hadna dune makin' at him, an' some kin' o' fowk tak langer to mak oot than ithers. An' ye canna tell what they're to be till they're made oot. But whether what I tell ye be richt or no, God maun hae the verra best o' rizzons for't, ower guid maybe for us to unnerstan'—the best o' rizzons for Esau himsel', I mean, for the Creator luiks efter his cratur first ava'.—And now," concluded Mr Graham, resuming his English, "go to your lessons; and be diligent, that God may think it worth while to get on faster with the making of you." In a moment the class was dispersed and all were seated. In another, the sound of scuffling arose, and fists were seen storming across a desk.

"Andrew Jamieson and Poochy, come up here," said the master in a loud voice.

"*He* hittit me first," cried Andrew, the moment they were within a respectful distance of the master, whereupon Mr Graham turned to the other with inquiry in his eyes.

"He had nae business to ca' me Poochy."

"No more he had; but you had just as little right to punish him for it. The offence was against me: he had no right to use my name for you, and the quarrel was mine. For the present you are Poochy no more: go to your place, William Wilson."

The boy burst out sobbing, and crept back to his seat with his knuckles in his eyes.

"Ah, my *Peery!*" said Mr Graham, "I can't tell you that. All that I can tell is, that God hadn't done making him, and some kind of folk take longer to finish than others. And you can't tell what they're to be till they *are* finished. But whether what I tell you be right or not, God must have the very best of reasons for it, too good perhaps for us to understand—the best of reasons for Esau himself, I mean, for the Creator looks after his creature first of all.—And now," concluded Mr Graham, resuming his English, "go to your lessons; and be diligent, that God may think it worth while to get on faster with the making of you." In a moment the class was dispersed and all were seated. In another, the sound of scuffling arose, and fists were seen storming across a desk.

"Andrew Jamieson and Poochy, come up here," said the master in a loud voice.

"*He* hit me first," cried Andrew, the moment they were within a respectful distance of the master, whereupon Mr Graham turned to the other with inquiry in his eyes.

"He had no business to call me Poochy."

"No more he had; but you had just as little right to punish him for it. The offence was against me: he had no right to use my name for you, and the quarrel was mine. For the present you are Poochy no more: go to your place, William Wilson."

The boy burst out sobbing, and crept back to his seat with his knuckles in his eyes.

"Andrew Jamieson," the master went on, "I had almost got a name for you, but you have sent it away. You are not ready for it yet, I see. Go to your place."

With downcast looks Andrew followed William, and the watchful eyes of the master saw that, instead of quarrelling any more during the day, they seemed to catch at every opportunity of showing each other a kindness.

Mr Graham never used bodily punishment: he ruled chiefly by the aid of a system of individual titles, of the mingled characters of pet-name and nickname. As soon as the individuality of a boy had attained to signs of blossoming—that is, had become such that he could predict not only an upright but a characteristic behaviour in given circumstances, he would take him aside and whisper in his ear that henceforth, so long as he deserved it, he would call him by a certain name—one generally derived from some object in the animal or vegetable world, and pointing to a resemblance which was not often patent to any eye but the master's own. He had given the name of *Poochy*, for instance to William Wilson, because, like the kangaroo, he sought his object in a succession of awkward, yet not the less availing leaps—gulping his knowledge and pocketing his conquered marble after a like fashion. *Mappy*, the name which thus belonged to a certain flaxen-haired, soft-eyed girl, corresponds to the English *bunny*. *Sheltie* is the small Scotch mountain-pony, active and strong. *Peery* means *pegtop*. But not above a quarter of the children had pet names. To gain one was to reach the highest honour of the school; the withdrawal of it was the severest of punishments, and the restoring of it the sign of perfect reconciliation. The master permitted no one else to use it, and was seldom known to forget himself so far as to utter it while its owner was in disgrace. The hope of gaining such a name, or the fear of losing it, was in the pupil the strongest ally of the master, the most powerful enforcement of his influences. It was a scheme of government by aspiration. But it owed all its operative power to the character of the man who had adopted rather than invented it—for the scheme had been suggested by a certain passage in the book of the Revelation.

Without having read a word of Swedenborg, he was a believer in the absolute correspondence of the inward and outward; and, thus long before the younger Darwin arose, had suspected a close relationship—remote identity, indeed, in nature and history, between the animal and human worlds. But photographs from a good many different points would be necessary to afford anything like a complete notion of the character of this country schoolmaster.

Towards noon, while he was busy with an astronomical class, explaining, by means partly of the blackboard, partly of two boys representing the relation of the earth and the moon, how it comes that we see but one half of the latter, the door gently opened and the troubled face of the mad laird peeped slowly in. His body followed as gently, and at last— sad symbol of his weight of care—his hump appeared, with a slow half-revolution as he turned to shut the door behind him. Taking off his hat, he walked up to Mr Graham, who, busy with his astronomy, had not perceived his entrance, touched him on the arm, and, standing on tiptoe, whispered softly in his ear, as if it were a painful secret that must be respected,—

"I dinna ken whaur I cam frae. I want to come to the school."

"I don't know where I came from. I want to come to the school."

Mr Graham turned and shook hands with him, respectfully addressing him as Mr Stewart, and got down for him the armchair which stood behind his desk. But, with the politest bow, the laird declined it, and mournfully repeating the words, "I dinna ken whaur I cam frae," took a place readily yielded him in the astronomical circle surrounding the symbolic boys.

This was not by any means his first appearance there; for every now and then he was seized with a desire to go to school, plainly with the object of finding out where he came from. This always fell in his quieter times, and for days together he would attend regularly; in one instance he was not absent an hour for a whole month. He spoke so little, however, that it was impossible to tell how much he understood, although he seemed to enjoy all that went on. He was so quiet, so sadly gentle, that he gave no trouble of any sort, and after the first few minutes of a fresh appearance, the attention of the scholars was rarely distracted by his presence.

The way in which the master treated him awoke like respect in his pupils. Boys and girls were equally ready to make room for him on their forms, and any one of the latter who had by some kind attention awakened the watery glint of a smile on the melancholy features of the troubled man, would boast of her success. Hence it came that the neighbourhood of Portlossie was the one spot in the county where a person of weak intellect or peculiar appearance might go about free of insult.

The peculiar sentence the laird so often uttered was the only one he invariably spoke with definite clearness. In every other attempt at speech he was liable to be assailed by an often recurring impediment, during the continuance of which he could compass but a word here and there, often betaking himself in the agony of suppressed utterance, to the most extravagant gestures, with which he would sometimes succeed in so supplementing his words as to render his meaning intelligible.

The two boys representing the earth and the moon, had returned to their places in the class, and Mr Graham had gone on to give a description of the moon, in which he had necessarily mentioned the enormous height of her mountains as compared with those of the earth. But in the course of asking some questions, he found a need of further explanation, and therefore once more required the services of the boy sun and boy moon. The moment the latter, however, began to describe his circle around the former, Mr Stewart stepped gravely up to him, and, laying hold of his hand, led him back to his station in the class: then, turning first one shoulder, then the other to the company, so as to attract attention to his hump, uttered the single word *Mountain*, and took on himself the part of the moon, proceeding to revolve in the circle which represented her orbit. Several of the boys and girls smiled, but no one laughed, for Mr Graham's gravity maintained theirs. Without remark, he used the mad laird for a moon to the end of his explanation.

Mr Stewart remained in the school all the morning, stood up with every class Mr Graham taught, and in the intervals sat, with book or slate before him, still as a Brahmin on the fancied verge of his re-absorption, save that he murmured to himself now and then,

"I dinna ken whaur I cam frae."   "I don't know where I came from."

When his pupils dispersed for dinner, Mr Graham invited him to go to his house and share his homely meal, but with polished gesture and broken speech, Mr Stewart declined, walked away towards the town, and was seen no more that afternoon.

CHAPTER VIII

THE SWIVEL

Mrs Courthope, the housekeeper at Lossie House, was a good woman, who did not stand upon her dignities, as small rulers are apt to do, but cultivated friendly relations with the people of the Sea Town. Some of the rougher of the women despised the sweet outlandish speech she had brought with her from her native England, and accused her of *mim-mou'dness*, or an affected modesty in the use of words; but not the less was she in their eyes a great lady,—whence indeed came the special pleasure in finding flaws in her—for to them she was the representative of the noble family on whose skirts they and their ancestors had been settled for ages, the last marquis not having visited the place for many years, and the present having but lately succeeded.

Duncan MacPhail was a favourite with her; for the English woman will generally prefer the highland to the lowland Scotsman; and she seldom visited the Seaton without looking in upon him so that when Malcolm returned from the Alton, or Old Town, where the school was, it did not in the least surprise him to find her seated with his grandfather. Apparently, however, there had been some dissension between them; for the old man sat in his corner strangely wrathful, his face in a glow, his head thrown back, his nostrils distended, and his eyelids working, as if his eyes were "poor dumb mouths," like Caesar's wounds, trying to speak.

"We are told in the New Testament to forgive our enemies, you know," said Mrs Courthope, heedless of his entrance, but in a voice that seemed rather to plead than oppose.

"Inteet she will not be false to her shief and her clan," retorted Duncan persistently. "She will *not* forgife Cawmil of Glenlyon."

"But he's dead long since, and we may at least hope he repented and was forgiven."

"She'll be hoping nothing of the kind, Mistress Kertope," replied Duncan. "But if, as you say, God will be forgifing him, which I do not belief;—let that pe enough for ta greedy blackguard. Sure, it matters but small whether poor Tuncan MacPhail will be forgifing him or not. Anyhow, he must do without it, for he shall not haf it. He is a tamn fillain and scounrel, and so she says, with her respecs to *you*, Mistress Kertope."

His sightless eyes flashed with indignation; and perceiving it was time to change the subject, the housekeeper turned to Malcolm.

"Could you bring me a nice mackerel or whiting for my lord's breakfast tomorrow morning, Malcolm?" she said.

"Certaintly, mem. I s' be wi ye in guid time wi' the best the sea 'll gie me," he answered.

"If I have the fish by nine o'clock, that will be early enough," she returned.

"I wad na like to wait sae lang for *my* brakfast," remarked Malcolm.

"You wouldn't mind it much, if you waited asleep," said Mrs. Courthope.

"Can onybody sleep till sic a time o' day as that?" exclaimed the youth.

"You must remember my lord doesn't go to bed for hours after you, Malcolm."

"An' what can keep him up a' that time? It's no as gien he war efter the herrin', an' had the win' an' the watter an' the netfu's o' waumlin craturs to haud him waukin'."

"But he's dead long since, and we may at least hope he repented and was forgiven."

"She'll be hoping nothing of the kind, Mistress Kertope," replied Duncan. "But if, as you say, God will be forgifing him, which I do not belief;—let that be enough for ta greedy blackguard. Sure, it matters but small whether poor Tuncan MacPhail will be forgifing him or not. Anyhow, he must do without it, for he shall not haf it. He is a tamn fillain and scounrel, and so she says, with her respecs to *you*, Mistress Kertope."

His sightless eyes flashed with indignation; and perceiving it was time to change the subject, the housekeeper turned to Malcolm.

"Could you bring me a nice mackerel or whiting for my lord's breakfast tomorrow morning, Malcolm?" she said.

"Certainly, ma'am. I'll be with you in good time with the best the sea will give me," he answered.

"If I have the fish by nine o'clock, that will be early enough," she returned.

"I wouldn't like to wait so long for *my* breakfast," remarked Malcolm.

"You wouldn't mind it much, if you waited asleep," said Mrs Courthope.

"Can anybody sleep till such a time of day as that?" exclaimed the youth.

"You must remember my lord doesn't go to bed for hours after you, Malcolm."

"And what can keep him up all that time? It's not as if he were after the herring, and had the wind and the water and the netfuls of writhing fish to stay wakeful for."

"Oh! he reads and writes, and sometimes goes walking about the grounds
after everybody else is in bed," said Mrs
Courthope, "he and his dog."

"Well, I wad rather be up ear'," said
Malcolm; "a heap raither. I like fine to be
oot i' the quaiet o' the mornin' afore the
sun's up to set the din gaun; whan it's a'
clear but no bricht–like the back o' a bonny
sawmon; an' air an' watter an' a' luiks
as gien they war waitin' for something–
quaiet, verra quaiet, but no content."

Malcolm uttered this long speech, and
went on with more like it, in the hope of
affording time for the stormy waters of
Duncan's spirit to assuage. Nor was he
disappointed; for, if there was a sound on
the earth Duncan loved to hear, it was the
voice of his boy; and by degrees the tempest sank to repose, the gathered glooms
melted from his countenance, and the
sunlight of a smile broke out.

"Hear to him!" he cried. "Her poy will
be a creat pard some tay, and sing pefore
ta Stuart kings, when they come pack to
Holyrood!"

Mrs Courthope had enough of poetry
in her to be pleased with Malcolm's quiet
enthusiasm, and spoke a kind word of
sympathy with the old man's delight as she
rose to take her leave. Duncan rose also,
and followed her to the door, making her
a courtly bow, and that just as she turned
away.

"It 'll pe a coot 'oman, Mistress Kertope," he said as he came back; "and it 'll no
pe to plame her for forgifing Glenlyon, for
he did not kill *her* creat crandmother. Put
it'll pe fery paad preeding to request her
nainsel, Tuncan MacPhail, to be forgifing

"Oh! he reads and writes, and sometimes goes walking about the grounds
after everybody else is in bed," said Mrs
Courthope, "he and his dog."

"Well, I would rather be up early," said
Malcolm; "far rather. I like well to be out in
the quiet of the morning before the sun's
up to set the din going; when it's all clear
but not bright–like the back of a bonny
salmon; and air and water and all look as
if they were waiting for something–quiet,
very quiet, but not content."

Malcolm uttered this long speech, and
went on with more like it, in the hope of
affording time for the stormy waters of
Duncan's spirit to assuage. Nor was he
disappointed; for, if there was a sound on
the earth Duncan loved to hear, it was the
voice of his boy; and by degrees the tempest sank to repose, the gathered glooms
melted from his countenance, and the
sunlight of a smile broke out.

"Hear to him!" he cried. "Her boy will
be a creat bard some day, and sing pefore
ta Stuart kings, when they come back to
Holyrood!"

Mrs Courthope had enough of poetry
in her to be pleased with Malcolm's quiet
enthusiasm, and spoke a kind word of
sympathy with the old man's delight as she
rose to take her leave. Duncan rose also,
and followed her to the door, making her
a courtly bow, and that just as she turned
away.

"It 'll be a coot woman, Mistress Kertope," he said as he came back; "and it 'll no
be to blame her for forgifing Glenlyon, for
he did not kill *her* creat crandmother. But
it'll be fery baad breeding to request her
nainsel, Tuncan MacPhail, to be forgifing ta

ta rascal. Only she'll pe put a voman, and it'll not pe knowing no petter to her.—You'll be minding you'll be firing ta cun at six o'clock exackly, Malcolm, for all she says; for my lord peing put shust come home to his property, it might be a fex to him if tere was any mistake so soon. Put inteed, I vonder he hasn't been sending for old Tuncan to be gifing him a song or two on ta peeps; for he'll pe hafing ta oceans of fery coot highland plood in his own feins; and his friend, ta Prince of Wales, who has no more rights to it than a maackerel fish, will pe wearing ta kilts at Holyrood. So mind you pe firing ta cun at sax, my son."

rascal. Only she'll be but a woman, and it'll not be knowing no better to her.—You'll be minding you'll be firing ta gun at six o'clock exackly, Malcolm, for all she says; for my lord being but shust come home to his property, it might be a fex to him if tere was any mistake so soon. But inteed, I wonder he hasn't been sending for old Tuncan to be gifing him a song or two on ta peeps; for he'll be hafing ta oceans of fery coot highland blood in his own feins; and his friend, ta Prince of Wales, who has no more rights to it than a maackerel fish, will be wearing ta kilts at Holyrood. So mind you be firing ta gun at sax, my son."

For some years, young as he was, Malcolm had hired himself to one or other of the boat proprietors of the Seaton or of Scaurnose, for the herring fishing—only, however, in the immediate neighbourhood, refusing to go to the western islands, or any station whence he could not return to sleep at his grandfather's cottage. He had thus on every occasion earned enough to provide for the following winter, so that his grandfather's little income as piper, and other small returns, were accumulating in various concealments about the cottage; for, in his care for the future, Duncan dreaded lest Malcolm should buy things for him, without which, in his own sightless judgment, he could do well enough.

Until the herring-season should arrive, however, Malcolm made a little money by line fishing; for he had bargained, the year before, with the captain of a schooner for an old ship's boat, and had patched and caulked it into a sufficiently serviceable condition. He sold his fish in the town and immediate neighbourhood, where a good many house-keepers favoured the handsome and cheery young fisherman.

He would now be often out in the bay long before it was time to call his grandfather, in his turn to rouse the sleepers of Portlossie. But the old man had as yet always waked about the right time, and the inhabitants had never had any ground of complaint—a few minutes one way or the other being of little consequence. He was the cock which woke the whole yard: morning after morning his pipes went crowing through the streets of the upper region, his music ending always with his round. But after the institution of the gun signal, his custom was to go on playing where he stood until he heard it, or to stop short in the midst of his round and his liveliest *rêveillê* the moment it reached his ear. Loath as he might be to give over, that sense of good manners which was supreme in every highlander of the old time, interdicted the fingering of a note after the marquis's gun had called aloud.

When Malcolm meant to go fishing, he always loaded the swivel the night before, and about sunset the same evening he set out for that purpose. Not a creature was visible on the border of the curving bay except a few boys far off on the gleaming sands whence the tide had just receded: they were digging for sand-eels—lovely little silvery fishes—which, as every now and then the spade turned one or two up, they threw into a tin pail for bait. But on the summit of the long sandhill, the lonely figure of a man was walking to and fro in the level light of the rosy west; and as Malcolm climbed the near end of the dune, it was turning far off at the other: halfway between them was the embrasure with the brass swivel, and there they met.

Although he had never seen him before, Malcolm perceived at once it must be Lord Lossie, and lifted his bonnet. The marquis nodded and passed on, but the next moment, hearing the noise of Malcolm's proceedings with the swivel, turned and said— "What are you about there with that gun, my lad?"

"I'm jist ga'in' to dicht her oot an' lod her, my lord," answered Malcolm.

"And what next? You're not going to fire the thing?"

"Ay—the morn's mornin', my lord."

"What will that be for?"

"Ow, jist to wauk yer lordship."

"Hm!" said his lordship, with more expression than articulation.

"Will I no lod her?" asked Malcolm, throwing down the ramrod, and approaching the swivel, as if to turn the muzzle of it again into the embrasure.

"Oh, yes! load her by all means. I don't want to interfere with any of your customs. But if that is your object, the means, I fear, are inadequate."

"It's a comfort to hear that, my lord; for I canna aye be sure o' my auld watch, an' may weel be oot a five minutes or twa whiles. Sae, in future, seein' it 's o' sic sma' consequence to yer lordship, I s' jist let her aff whan it 's convenient. A feow minutes winna maitter muckle to the bailie bodies."

There was something in Malcolm's address that pleased Lord Lossie—the mingling of respect and humour, probably—the frankness and composure, perhaps. He was not self-conscious enough to be shy, and was so free from design of any sort that he doubted the good will of no one.

"I'm just going to clean her out and load her, my lord," answered Malcolm.

"And what next? You're not going to fire the thing?"

"Ay–tomorrow morning, my lord."

"What will that be for?"

"Oh, just to wake your lordship."

"Hm!" said his lordship, with more expression than articulation.

"Will I not load her?" asked Malcolm, throwing down the ramrod, and approaching the swivel, as if to turn the muzzle of it again into the embrasure.

"Oh, yes! load her by all means. I don't want to interfere with any of your customs. But if that is your object, the means, I fear, are inadequate."

"It's a comfort to hear that, my lord; for I can't always be sure of my old watch, and may well be out by five or ten minutes at times. So, in future, seeing as it's of such small consequence to your lordship, I'll just let her off when it's convenient. A few minutes won't matter much to the bailies."

There was something in Malcolm's address that pleased Lord Lossie—the mingling of respect and humour, probably—the frankness and composure, perhaps. He was not self-conscious enough to be shy, and was so free from design of any sort that he doubted the good will of no one.

"What's your name?" asked the marquis abruptly.

"Malcolm MacPhail, my lord."

"MacPhail? I heard the name this very day! Let me see."

"My gran'father's the blin' piper, my lord."

"Yes, yes. Tell him I shall want him at the House. I left my own piper at Ceanglas."

"I'll fess him wi' me the morn, gien ye like, my lord, for I'll be ower wi' some fine troot or ither, gien I haena the waur luck, the morn's mornin': Mistress Courthope says she'll be aye ready for ane to fry to yer lordship's brakfast. But I'm thinkin' that'll be ower ear' for ye to see him."

"I'll send for him when I want him. Go on with your brazen serpent there, only mind you don't give her too much supper."

"Jist look at her ribs, my lord! *she* winna rive!" was the youth's response; and the marquis was moving off with a smile, when Malcolm called after him.

"Gien yer lordship likes to see yer ain ferlies, I ken whaur some o' them lie," he said.

"What do you mean by *ferlies?*" asked the marquis.

"Ow! keeriosities, ye ken. For enstance, there's some queer caves alang the cost—twa or three o' them afore ye come to the Scaurnose. They say the water bude till ha' howkit them ance upon a time, an' they maun hae been fu' o' partans, an' lobsters, an' their frien's an' neebours; but they're heigh an' dreigh noo, as the fule said o' his minister, an' naething intill them but foumarts, an' otters, an' sic like."

"What's your name?" asked the marquis abruptly.

"Malcolm MacPhail, my lord."

"MacPhail? I heard the name this very day! Let me see."

"My grandfather's the blind piper, my lord."

"Yes, yes. Tell him I shall want him at the House. I left my own piper at Ceanglas."

"I'll bring him with me tomorrow, if you like, my lord, for I'll be over with some fine trout or other, if my luck holds, tomorrow morning: Mistress Courthope says she'll always be ready to fry one for your lordship's breakfast. But I'm thinking that'll be too early for you to see him."

"I'll send for him when I want him. Go on with your brazen serpent there, only mind you don't give her too much supper."

"Just look at her ribs, my lord! *she* won't burst!" was the youth's response; and the marquis was moving off with a smile, when Malcolm called after him.

"If your lordship likes to see your own ferlies, I know where some of them lie," he said.

"What do you mean by *ferlies?*" asked the marquis.

"Oh! curiosities, you know. For instance, there's some queer caves along the coast—two or three of them before you come to the Scaurnose. They say the water must have hollowed them out once upon a time, and they must have been full of crabs, and lobsters, and their friends and neighbours; but they're high and dry now, as the fool said of his minister, and nothing inside them but pole-cats, and otters, and suchlike."

"Well, well, my lad, we'll see," said his lordship kindly and turning once more, he resumed his walk.

"At yer lordship's will," answered Malcolm in a low voice as he lifted his bonnet and again bent to the swivel.

The next morning, he was rowing slowly along in the bay, when he was startled by the sound of his grandfather's pipes, wafted clear and shrill on a breath of southern wind, from the top of the town. He looked at his watch: it was not yet five o'clock. The expectation of a summons to play at Lossie House, had so excited the old man's brain that he had waked long before his usual time, and Portlossie must wake also. The worst of it was, that he had already, as Malcolm knew from the direction of the sound, almost reached the end of his beat, and must even now be expecting the report of the swivel, until he heard which he would not cease playing, so long as there was a breath in his body. Pulling, therefore, with all his might, Malcolm soon ran his boat ashore, and in another instant the sharp yell of the swivel rang among the rocks of the promontory. He was still standing, lapped in a light reverie as he watched the smoke flying seaward, when a voice, already well known to him said, close at his side:

"What *are* you about with that horrid cannon?"

Malcolm started.

"Ye garred me loup, my leddy!" he returned with a smile and an obeisance.

"You told me," the girl went on emphatically, and as she spoke she disengaged her watch from her girdle, "that you fired it at six o'clock. It is not nearly six."

"Didna ye hear the pipes, my leddy?" he rejoined.

"Yes, well enough; but a whole regiment of pipes can't make it six o'clock when my watch says ten minutes past five."

"Eh, sic a braw watch!" exclaimed Malcolm. "What's a' thae bonny white k-nots about the face o' 't?"

"Pearls," she answered, in a tone that implied pity of his ignorance.

"Jist look at it aside mine!" he exclaimed in admiration, pulling out his great old turnip.

"Well, well, my lad, we'll see," said his lordship kindly and turning once more, he resumed his walk.

"At your lordship's will," answered Malcolm in a low voice as he lifted his bonnet and again bent to the swivel.

"What *are* you about with that horrid cannon?"

Malcolm started.

"You made me jump, my lady!" he returned with a smile and an obeisance.

"You told me," the girl went on emphatically, and as she spoke she disengaged her watch from her girdle, "that you fired it at six o'clock. It is not nearly six."

"Didn't you hear the pipes, my lady?" he rejoined.

"Yes, well enough; but a whole regiment of pipes can't make it six o'clock when my watch says ten minutes past five."

"Eh, such a fine watch!" exclaimed Malcolm. "What are all those bonny white knots about its face?"

"Pearls," she answered, in a tone that implied pity of his ignorance.

"Just look at it beside mine!" he exclaimed in admiration, pulling out his great old turnip.

"There!" cried the girl; "your own watch says only a quarter past five."

"Ow, ay! my leddy; I set it by the toon clock 'at hings i' the window o' the Lossie Airms last nicht. But I maun awa' an' luik efter my lines, or atween the deil an' the dogfish my lord'll fare ill."

"You haven't told me why you fired the gun," she persisted.

Thus compelled, Malcolm had to explain that the motive lay in his anxiety lest his grandfather should over-exert himself, seeing he was subject to severe attacks of asthma.

"He could stop when he was tired," she objected.

"Ay, gien his pride wad lat him," answered Malcolm, and turned away again, eager to draw his line.

"Have you a boat of your own?" asked the lady.

"Ay; yon's her, doon on the shore yonner. Wad ye like a row? She's fine an' quaiet."

"Who? The boat?"

"The sea, my leddy."

"Is your boat clean?"

"O' a' thing but fish. But na, it's no fit for sic a bonny goon as that. I winna lat ye gang the day, my leddy; but gien ye like to be here the morn's mornin', I s' be here at this same hoor, an' hae my boat as clean's a Sunday sark."

"You think more of my gown than of myself," she returned.

"There's no fear o' yersel', my leddy. Ye're ower weel made to blaud. But wae's me for the goon or it had been an hoor i' the boat the day!—no to mention the fish comin' walopin' ower the gunnel ane efter the ither. But 'deed I *maun* say good mornin', mem!"

"There!" cried the girl; "your own watch says only a quarter past five."

"Oh, ay! my lady; I set it by the town clock that hangs in the window of the Lossie Arms last night. But I must go and look after my lines, or between the devil and the dogfish my lord will fare ill."

"You haven't told me why you fired the gun," she persisted.

Thus compelled, Malcolm had to explain that the motive lay in his anxiety lest his grandfather should over-exert himself, seeing he was subject to severe attacks of asthma.

"He could stop when he was tired," she objected.

"Ay, if his pride would let him," answered Malcolm, and turned away again, eager to draw his line.

"Have you a boat of your own?" asked the lady.

"Ay; that's her, down on the shore yonder. Would you like a row? She's fine and quiet."

"Who? The boat?"

"The sea, my lady."

"Is your boat clean?"

"Of everything but fish. But na, it's not fit for such a bonny gown as that. I won't let you go today, my lady; but if you like to be here tomorrow morning, I'll be here at this same hour, and have my boat as clean as a Sunday shirt."

"You think more of my gown than of myself," she returned.

"There's no fear of yourself, my lady. You're too well made to spoil. But woe's me for the gown before it had been an hour in the boat today!—not to mention the fish coming walloping over the gunnel one after the other. But indeed I *must* say good morning, ma'am!"

"By all means. I don't want to keep you a moment from your precious fish."

"By all means. I don't want to keep you a moment from your precious fish."

Feeling rebuked, without well knowing why, Malcolm accepted the dismissal, and ran to his boat. By the time he had taken his oars, the girl had vanished.

His line was a short one; but twice the number of fish he wanted were already hanging from the hooks. It was still very early when he reached the harbour. At home he found his grandfather waiting for him, and his breakfast ready.

It was hard to convince Duncan that he had waked the royal burgh a whole hour too soon. He insisted that, as he had never made such a blunder before, he could not have made it now.

"It's ta watch 'at 'll pe telling ta lies, Malcolm, my poy," he said thoughtfully. "She was once pefore."

"But the sun says the same 's the watch, daddy," persisted Malcolm.

Duncan understood the position of the sun and what it signified, as well as the clearest-eyed man in Port Lossie, but he could not afford to yield.

"It was peing some conspeeracy of ta cursit Cawmills, to make her loss her poor pension," he said. "Put never you mind, Malcolm; I'll pe making up for ta plunder ta morrow mornin'. Ta coot peoples shall haf teir sleeps a whole hour after tey ought to be at teir works."

"It's ta watch 'at 'll be telling ta lies, Malcolm, my boy," he said thoughtfully. "She was once before."

"But the sun says the same as the watch, daddy," persisted Malcolm.

Duncan understood the position of the sun and what it signified, as well as the clearest-eyed man in Port Lossie, but he could not afford to yield.

"It was being some conspeeracy of ta cursed Cawmills, to make her loss her poor pension," he said. "But never you mind, Malcolm; I'll be making up for ta blunder ta morrow mornin'. Ta coot peoples shall haf teir sleeps a whole hour after tey ought to be at teir works."

CHAPTER IX

THE SALMON TROUT

Malcolm walked up through the town with his fish, hoping to part with some of the less desirable of them, and so lighten his basket, before entering the grounds of Lossie House. But he had met with little success, and was now approaching the town gate, as they called it, which closed a short street at right angles to the principal one, when he came upon Mrs Catanach—on her knees, cleaning her doorstep.

"Weel, Malcolm, what fish hae ye?" she said, without looking up.

"Hoo kent ye it was me, Mistress Catanach?" asked the lad.

"Kent it was you!" she repeated. "Gien there be but twa feet at ance in ony street o' Portlossie, I'll tell ye whase heid's abune them, an' my een steekit."

"Hoot! ye're a witch, Mistress Catanach!" said Malcolm merrily.

"That's as may be," she returned, rising, and nodding mysteriously; "I hae tauld ye nae mair nor the trowth. But what garred ye whup's a' oot o' oor nakit beds by five o'clock i' the mornin', this mornin', man! That's no what ye're paid for."

"Deed, mem, it was jist a mistak' o' my puir daddy's. He had been feart o' sleepin' ower lang, ye see, an' sae had waukit ower sune. I was oot efter the fish mysel'."

"But ye fired the gun 'gen the chap o' five."

"Ow, ay! I fired the gun. The puir man wod hae bursten himsel' gien I hadna."

"Well, Malcolm, what fish have you?" she said, without looking up.

"How did you know it was me, Mistress Catanach?" asked the lad.

"Know it was you!" she repeated. "If there be but two feet at once in any street of Portlossie, I'll tell you whose head's above them, with my eyes shut."

"Heavens! you're a witch, Mistress Catanach!" said Malcolm merrily.

"That's as may be," she returned, rising, and nodding mysteriously; "I have told you no more than the truth. But what possessed you to whip us all out of our naked beds by five o'clock in the morning, this morning, man! That's not what you're paid for."

"Indeed, ma'am, it was just a mistake of my poor daddy's. He had been afraid he'd oversleep, you see, and so he woke up too soon. I was out after the fish myself."

"But you fired the gun on the stroke of five."

"Oh, ay! I fired the gun. The poor man would have burst himself if I hadn't."

"Deil gien he *had* bursten himsel'–the auld heelan' sholt!" exclaimed Mrs Catanach spitefully.

"Ye sanna even sic words to my gran'father, Mrs Catanach," said Malcolm with rebuke.

She laughed a strange laugh.

"*Sanna!*" she repeated contemptuously. "An' wha's your gran'father, that I sud tak tent hoo I wag my tongue ower *his* richtousness?"

Then, with a sudden change of her tone to one of would-be friendliness—

"But what'll ye be seekin' for that bit sawmon trooty, man?" she said.

As she spoke she approached his basket, and would have taken the fish in her hands, but Malcolm involuntarily drew back.

"It's gauin' to the Hoose to my lord's brakfast," he said.

"Hoots! ye'll jist lea' the troot wi' me.— Ye'll be seekin' a saxpence for 't, I reckon," she persisted, again approaching the basket.

"I tell ye, Mistress Catanach," said Malcolm, drawing back now in the fear that if she once had it she would not yield it again, "it's gauin' up to the Hoose!"

"Hoots! there's naebody there seen 't yet. It's new oot o' the watter."

"But Mistress Courthope was doon last nicht, an' wantit the best I cud heuk."

"Mistress Courthope! Wha cares for her? A mim, cantin' auld body! Gie *me* the trootie, Ma'colm. Ye're a bonny laad, an' it s' be the better for ye."

"Deed I cudna du 't, Mistress Catanach—though I'm sorry to disobleege ye. It's bespoken, ye see. But there's a fine haddie, an' a bonny sma' coddie, an' a goukmey."

─────

6 SHOLT (variant of "Sheltie"): a Shetland pony

"What though he *had* burst himself– the old highland sholt!"[6] exclaimed Mrs Catanach spitefully.

"You shan't speak so of my grandfather, Mrs Catanach," said Malcolm with rebuke.

She laughed a strange laugh.

"*Shan't!*" she repeated contemptuously. "And who's your grandfather, that I should heed how I talk of *his* character?"

Then, with a sudden change of her tone to one of would-be friendliness—

"But what price will you be wanting for that salmon trout, man?" she said.

As she spoke she approached his basket, and would have taken the fish in her hands, but Malcolm involuntarily drew back.

"It's going to the House for my lord's breakfast," he said.

"Heavens! you'll just leave the trout with me.—You'll be wanting a sixpence for it, I reckon," she persisted, again approaching the basket.

"I tell you, Mistress Catanach," said Malcolm, drawing back now in the fear that if she once had it she would not yield it again, "it's going up to the House!"

"Heavens! there's nobody there has seen it yet. It's new out of the water."

"But Mistress Courthope was down last night, and wanted the best I could catch."

"Mistress Courthope! Who cares for her? A prim, canting old body! Give *me* the trout, Malcolm. You're a bonny lad, and it'll be the better for you."

"Indeed, I couldn't do it, Mistress Catanach–though I'm sorry to disoblige you. It's bespoken, you see. But there's a fine haddock, and a bonny small cod, and a goukmey (gray gurnard.)"

"Gae 'wa' wi' yer haddies, an' yer goukmeys! Ye sanna gowk *me* wi' them."

"Weel, I wadna wonner," said Malcolm, "gien Mrs Courthope wad like the haddie tu, an' maybe the lave o' them as weel. Hers is a muckle faimily to haud eatin.' I'll jist gang to the Hoose first afore I mak ony mair offers frae my creel."

"Ye'll lea' the troot wi' *me*," said Mrs Catanach imperiously.

"Na; I canna du that. Ye maun see yersel' 'at I canna."

The woman's face grew dark with anger. "It s' be the *waur* for ye," she cried.

"I'm no gauin' to be fleyt at ye. Ye're no sic a witch as that comes till, though ye *div* ken a body's fit upo' the flags! My blin' luckie deddy can du mair nor that!" said Malcolm, irritated by her persistency, threats and evil looks.

"Daur ye *me?*" she returned, her pasty cheeks now red as fire, and her wicked eyes flashing as she shook her clenched fist at him.

"What for no?" he answered coolly, turning his head back over his shoulder, for he was already on his way to the gate.

"Ye s' ken that, ye misbegotten funlin'!" shrieked the woman, and waddled hastily into the house.

"What ails her?" said Malcolm to himself. "She micht ha' seen 'at I bude to gie Mrs Courthope the first offer."

"Go away with your haddocks, and your gowkmeys! You shan't gowk (fool) *me* with them."

"Well, I wouldn't wonder," said Malcolm, "if Mrs Courthope would like the haddock too, and maybe the rest of them as well. Hers is a great family to feed. I'll just go to the House first before I make any more offers from my creel."

"You'll leave the trout with *me*," said Mrs Catanach imperiously.

"Na; I can't do that. You must see yourself that I can't."

The woman's face grew dark with anger. "It'll be the *worse* for you," she cried.

"I'm not going to let you frighten me. You're not such a witch as that comes to, though you *do* know a body's foot upon the flags! My blind grandfather can do more than that!" said Malcolm, irritated by her persistency, threats and evil looks.

"Dare *me*, will you?" she returned, her pasty cheeks now red as fire, and her wicked eyes flashing as she shook her clenched fist at him.

"Why not?" he answered coolly, turning his head back over his shoulder, for he was already on his way to the gate.

"I'll let you know why not, you misbegotten foundling!" shrieked the woman, and waddled hastily into the house.

"What's got into her?" said Malcolm to himself. "She might have seen that I had to give Mrs Courthope the first offer."

By a winding carriage-drive, through trees whose growth was stunted by the sea-winds, which had cut off their tops as with a keen razor, Malcolm made a slow descent, yet was soon shadowed by timber of a more prosperous growth, rising as from a lake of the loveliest green, spangled with starry daisies. The air was full of sweet odours uplifted with the ascending dew, and trembled with a hundred songs at once, for here was a very paradise for birds. At length he came in sight of a long low wing of the house, and went to the door that led to the kitchen. There a maid informed him that Mrs Courthope was in the hall, and he had better take his basket there, for she wanted to see him. He obeyed, and sought the main entrance.

The house was an ancient pile, mainly of two sides at right angles, but with many gables, mostly having corbel steps—a genuine old Scottish dwelling, small-windowed and gray, with steep slated roofs, and many turrets, each with a conical top. Some of these turrets rose from the ground, encasing spiral stone stairs; others were but bartizans, their interiors forming recesses in rooms. They gave the house something of the air of a French chateau, only it looked stronger and far grimmer. Carved around some of the windows, in ancient characters, were Scripture texts and antique proverbs. Two time-worn specimens of heraldic zoology, in a state of fearful and everlasting excitement, stood rampant and gaping, one on each side of the hall door, contrasting strangely with the repose of the ancient house, which looked very like what the oldest part of it was said to have been—a monastery. It had at the same time, however, a somewhat warlike expression, wherein consisting it would have been difficult to say; nor could it ever have been capable of much defence, although its position in that regard was splendid. In front was a great gravel space, in the centre of which lay a huge block of serpentine, from a quarry on the estate, filling the office of goal, being the pivot, as it were, around which all carriages turned.

On one side of the house was a great stone bridge, of lofty span, stretching across a little glen, in which ran a brown stream spotted with foam—the same that entered the frith beside the Seaton; not muddy, however, for though dark it was clear—its brown being a rich transparent hue, almost red, gathered from the peat bogs of the great moorland hill behind. Only a very narrow terrace-walk, with battlemented parapet, lay between the back of the house, and a precipitous descent of a hundred feet to this rivulet. Up its banks, lovely with flowers and rich with shrubs and trees below, you might ascend until by slow gradations you left the woods and all culture behind, and found yourself, though still within the precincts of Lossie House, on the lonely side of the waste hill, a thousand feet above the sea.

The hall-door stood open, and just within hovered Mrs Courthope, dusting certain precious things not to be handled by a housemaid. This portion of the building was so narrow that the hall occupied its entire width, and on the opposite side of it another door, standing also open, gave a glimpse of the glen.

"Good morning, Malcolm," said Mrs Courthope, when she turned and saw whose shadow fell on the marble floor. "What have you brought me?"

"A fine salmon troot, mem. But gien ye had hard hoo Mistress Catanach flytit at me 'cause I wadna gie 't to her! You wad hae thocht, mem, she was something no canny—the w'y 'at she first beggit, an' syne fleecht, an syne a' but banned an' swore."

"A fine salmon trout, ma'am. But if you had heard how Mistress Catanach scolded me because I wouldn't give it to her! You would have thought, ma'am, she was something not canny–the way she first begged, and then flattered, and then all but banned and swore."

"She's a peculiar person, that, Malcolm. Those are nice whitings. I don't care about the trout. Just take it to her as you go back."

"I doobt gien she'll take it, mem. She's an awfu' vengefu' cratur, fowk says."

"You remind me, Malcolm," returned Mrs Courthope, "that I'm not at ease about your grandfather. He is not in a Christian frame of mind at all—and he is an old man too. If we don't forgive our enemies, you know, the Bible plainly tells us we shall not be forgiven ourselves."

"I'm thinkin' it was a greater nor the Bible said that, mem," returned Malcolm, who was an apt pupil of Mr Graham. "But ye'll be meanin' Cawmill o' Glenlyon," he went on with a smile. "It canna maitter muckle to him whether my gran'father forgie him or no, seein' he's been deid this hunner year."

"It's not Campbell of Glenlyon, it's your grandfather I am anxious about," said Mrs Courthope. "Nor is it only Campbell of Glenlyon he's so fierce against, but all his posterity as well."

"They dinna exist, mem. There's no sic a bein' o' the face o' the yearth, as a descendant o' *that* Glenlyon."

"It makes little difference, I fear," said Mrs Courthope, who was no bad logician. "The question isn't whether or not there's anybody to forgive, but whether Duncan MacPhail is willing to forgive."

"That I do believe he is, mem; though he wad be as sair astonished to hear 't as ye are yersel'."

"I don't know what you mean by that, Malcolm."

"She's a peculiar person, that, Malcolm. Those are nice whitings. I don't care about the trout. Just take it to her as you go back."

"I doubt if she'll take it, ma'am. She's an awfully vengeful woman, folk say."

"You remind me, Malcolm," returned Mrs Courthope, "that I'm not at ease about your grandfather. He is not in a Christian frame of mind at all—and he is an old man too. If we don't forgive our enemies, you know, the Bible plainly tells us we shall not be forgiven ourselves."

"I'm thinking it was a greater than the Bible that said that, ma'am," returned Malcolm, who was an apt pupil of Mr Graham. "But you'll be meaning Campbell of Glenlyon," he went on with a smile. "It can't be any great matter to him whether my grandfather forgives him or not, seeing he's been dead these hundred years."

"It's not Campbell of Glenlyon, it's your grandfather I am anxious about," said Mrs Courthope. "Nor is it only Campbell of Glenlyon he's so fierce against, but all his posterity as well."

"They don't exist, ma'am. There's no such being on the face of the earth, as a descendant of *that* Glenlyon."

"It makes little difference, I fear," said Mrs Courthope, who was no bad logician. "The question isn't whether or not there's anybody to forgive, but whether Duncan MacPhail is willing to forgive."

"That I do believe he is, ma'am; though he would be as sore astonished to hear it as you are yourself."

"I don't know what you mean by that, Malcolm."

"I mean, mem, 'at a blin' man, like my gran'father, canna ken himsel' richt, seein' he canna ken ither fowk richt. It's by kennin' ither fowk 'at ye come to ken yersel, mem—isna't noo?"

"Blindness surely doesn't prevent a man from knowing other people. He hears them, and he feels them, and indeed has generally more kindness from them because of his affliction."

"Frae some o' them, mem; but it's little kin'ness my gran'father has expairienced frae Cawmill o' Glenlyon, mem."

"And just as little injury, I should suppose," said Mrs Courthope.

"Ye're wrang there, mem: a murdered mither maun be an unco skaith to oye's oye. But supposin' ye to be richt, what I say's to the pint for a' that. I maun jist explain a wee.—When I was a laddie at the schule, I was ance tell't that ane o' the loons was i' the wye o' mockin' my gran'father. Whan I hard it, I thocht I cud jist rive the hert o' 'im, an' set my teeth in't, as the Dutch sodger did to the Spainiard. But whan I got a grip o' 'im, an' the rascal turned up a frichtit kin' o' a dog-like face to me, I jist could *not* drive my steikit neive intil't. Mem, a face is an awfu' thing! There's aye something luikin' oot o' 't 'at ye canna do as ye like wi'. But my gran'father never saw a face in's life—lat alane Glenlyon's 'at's been dirt for sae mony a year. Gien he war luikin' intil the face o' that Glenlyon even, I do believe he wad no more drive his durk intill him—"

"Drive his dirk into him!" echoed Mrs Courthope, in horror at the very disclaimer.

"I mean, ma'am, that a blind man, like my grandfather, can't have a true knowledge of himself, because he hasn't that knowledge of other folk. It's by knowing other folk that you come to know yourself, ma'am—isn't it now?"

"Blindness surely doesn't prevent a man from knowing other people. He hears them, and he feels them, and indeed has generally more kindness from them because of his affliction."

"From some of them, ma'am; but it's little kindness my grandfather has experienced from Campbell of Glenlyon, ma'am."

"And just as little injury, I should suppose," said Mrs Courthope.

"You're wrong there, ma'am: a murdered mother must be a great injury to grandson's grandson. But supposing you were right, what I say is to the point for all that. I must explain a bit, though.–When I was a lad at the school, I was once told that one of the boys had taken to mocking my grandfather. When I heard it, I thought I could just tear his heart out, and set my teeth in it, as the Dutch soldier did to the Spaniard. But when I got a grip of him, and the rascal turned up a frightened kind of a dog-like face to me, I just could *not* drive my clenched fist into it. Ma'am, a face is an awful thing! There's always something looking out of it that you can't do as you like with. But my grandfather never saw a face in his life—let alone Glenlyon's that's been dirt for so many years. If he were looking into even *that* face, I do believe he would no more drive his dirk into him—"

"Drive his dirk into him!" echoed Mrs Courthope, in horror at the very disclaimer.

"No, I'm sure he wad *not*," persisted Malcolm, innocently. "He micht not tak him oot o' a pot, but he wad neither durk him nor fling him in. I'm no that sure he wadna even rax him a han'. Ae thing I *am* certain o',—that by the time he meets Glenlyon in haven, he'll be no that far frae lattin' byganes be byganes."

"Meets Glenlyon in heaven!" again echoed Mrs Courthope, who knew enough of the story to be startled at the taken-for-granted way in which Malcolm spoke. "Is it probable that a wretch such as your legends describe him should ever get there?"

"Ye dinna think God's forgien him, than, mem?"

"I have no right to judge Glenlyon, or any other man; but, as you ask me, I must say I see no likelihood of it."

"Hoo can ye compleen o' my puir blin' grandfather for no forgiein' him, than?—I hae ye there, mem!"

"He *may* have repented, you know," said Mrs Courthope feebly, finding herself in less room than was comfortable.

"In sic case," returned Malcolm, "the auld man 'ill hear a' aboot it the meenit he wins there; an' I mak nae doobt he'll du his best to perswaud himsel'."

"But what if he shouldn't get there?" persisted Mrs Courthope, in pure benevolence.

"Hoot toot, mem! I wonner to hear ye! A Cawmill latten in, and my gran'father hauden oot! That wad be jist yellow-faced Willie ower again!⁷—Na, na; things gang anither gait up there. My gran'father's a rale guid man, for a' 'at he has a wye o' luikin' at things 'at's mair efter the law nor the gospel."

"No, I'm sure he would *not*," persisted Malcolm, innocently. "He mightn't lift him out of a pit, but he would neither stab him nor fling him in. I'm not that sure that he wouldn't reach a hand to him. One thing I *am* certain of—that by the time he meets Glenlyon in heaven, he won't be that far from letting bygones be bygones."

"Meets Glenlyon in heaven!" again echoed Mrs Courthope, who knew enough of the story to be startled at the taken-for-granted way in which Malcolm spoke. "Is it probable that a wretch such as your legends describe him should ever get there?"

"You don't think God's forgiven him, then, ma'am?"

"I have no right to judge Glenlyon, or any other man; but, as you ask me, I must say I see no likelihood of it."

"How can you complain of my poor blind grandfather for not forgiving him, then?—I have you there, ma'am!"

"He *may* have repented, you know," said Mrs Courthope feebly, finding herself in less room than was comfortable.

"In which case," returned Malcolm, "the old man will hear all about it the minute he arrives; and I make no doubt he'll do his best to persuade himself."

"But what if he shouldn't get there?" persisted Mrs Courthope, in pure benevolence.

"Good heavens, ma'am! I wonder to hear you! A Campbell let in, and my grandfather kept out! That would be just yellow-faced Willie over again!⁷—Na, na; things follow a different rule up there. My grandfather's one of the true sort, for all that there's more of law than of gospel in how he looks at things."

---

7 Lord Stair, the prime mover in the Massacre of Glenco.

Apparently Mrs Courthope had come at length to the conclusion that Malcolm was as much of a heathen as his grandfather, for in silence she chose her fish, in silence paid him his price, and then with only a sad *Good-day*, turned and left him.

He would have gone back by the river-side to the sea-gate, but Mrs Courthope having waived her right to the fish in favour of Mrs Catanach, he felt bound to give her another chance, and so returned the way he had come.

"Here's yer troot, Mistress Cat'nach," he called aloud at her door, which generally stood a little ajar. "Ye s' hae't for the saxpence—an' a guid bargain tu, for ane o' sic dimensions!"

"Here's your trout, Mistress Catanach," he called aloud at her door, which generally stood a little ajar. "It's yours for sixpence—and a good bargain too, when you see the size of it!"

As he spoke, he held the fish in at the door, but his eyes were turned to the main street, whence the factor's gig was at the moment rounding the corner into that in which he stood; when suddenly the salmon trout was snatched from his hand, and flung so violently in his face, that he staggered back into the road: the factor had to pull sharply up to avoid driving over him. His rout rather than retreat was followed by a burst of insulting laughter, and at the same moment, out of the house rushed a large vile-looking mongrel, with hair like an ill-used door-mat and an abbreviated nose, fresh from the ashpit, caught up the trout, and rushed with it towards the gate.

"That's richt, my bairn!" shouted Mrs Catanach to the brute as he ran: "tak it to Mrs Courthope. Tak it back wi' my compliments."

"That's right, my child!" shouted Mrs Catanach to the brute as he ran: "take it to Mrs Courthope. Take it back with my compliments."

Amidst a burst of malign laughter she slammed her door, and from a window sideways watched the young fisherman.

As he stood looking after the dog in wrath and bewilderment, the factor, having recovered from the fit of merriment into which the sudden explosion of events had cast him, and succeeded in quieting his scared horse, said, slackening his reins to move on,

"You sell your fish too cheap, Malcolm."

"The deil's i' the tyke," rejoined Malcolm, and, seized at last by a sense of the ludicrousness of the whole affair, burst out laughing, and turned for the High Street.

"You sell your fish too cheap, Malcolm."

"The devil's in the dog," rejoined Malcolm, and, seized at last by a sense of the ludicrousness of the whole affair, burst out laughing, and turned for the High Street.

"Na, na, laddie; the deil's no awa' in sic a hurry: he bed," said a voice behind him.

"Na, na, laddie; the devil's not away in such a hurry: he stayed," said a voice behind him.

Malcolm turned again and lifted his bonnet. It was Miss Horn, who had come up from the Seaton.

"Did ye see yon, mem?" he asked.

Malcolm turned again and lifted his bonnet. It was Miss Horn, who had come up from the Seaton.

"Did you see that, ma'am?" he asked.

"Ay, weel that, as I cam up the brae. Dinna stan' there, laddie. The jaud 'll be watchin' ye like a cat watchin' a mouse. I ken her! She's a cat-wuman, an' I canna bide her. She's no mowse. *She's* in secrets mair nor guid, I s' wad. Come awa' wi' me; I want a bit fish. I can ill eat an' her lyin' deid i' the hoose—it winna gang ower; but I maun get some strength pitten intil me afore the berial. It's a God's mercy I wasna made wi' feelin's, or what wad hae come o' me! Whaur's the gude o' greetin? It's no worth the saut i' the watter o' 't, Ma'colm. It's an ill wardle, an micht be a bonny ane—gien't warna for ill men."

"'Deed, mem! I'm thinkin' mair aboot ill women, at this prasent," said Malcolm. "Maybe there's no sic a thing, but yon's unco like ane. As bonny a sawmon troot 's ever ye saw, mem! It's a' I'm cawpable o' to haud ohn cursed that foul tyke o' hers."

"Hoot, laddie! haud yer tongue."

"Ay will I. I'm na gaun to du 't, ye ken. But sic a fine troot 's that—the verra ane ye wad hae likit, mem!"

"Never ye min' the troot. There's mair whaur that cam frae. What anger't her at ye?"

"Naething mair nor that I bude to gie Mistress Courthope the first wale o' my fish."

"The wuman's no worth yer notice, 'cep to haud oot o' her gait, laddie; an' that ye had better luik till, for she's no canny. Dinna ye anger her again gien ye can help it. She has an ill luik, an' I canna bide her.—Hae, there's yer siller. Jean, tak in this fish."

"Ay, well enough, as I came up the hill. Don't stand there, laddie. The jade'll be watching you like a cat watching a mouse. I know her! She's a cat-woman, and I can't stand her. She's not safe. *She's* in secrets more than good, I'll wager. Come away with me; I want some fish. I can't eat with her lying dead in the house—I can't get it down; but I must get some strength put into me before the burial. It's a God's mercy I wasn't made with feelings, or what would have come of me! Where's the good of crying? It's not worth the salt in the water of it, Malcolm. It's a bad world, and might be a bonny one—if it weren't for bad men."

"Indeed, ma'am! I'm thinking more about bad women, at this moment," said Malcolm. "Maybe there's no such thing, but she's very like one. As bonny a salmon trout as ever you saw, ma'am! It's all I can do to keep from cursing that foul tyke of hers."

"Heavens, laddie! hold your tongue."

"Ay, I will. I'm not going to do it, you know. But such a fine trout as that–the very one you would have liked, ma'am!"

"Never you mind the trout. There's more where that came from. What angered her at you?"

"Nothing more than that I had to give Mistress Courthope the first choice of my fish."

"The woman's not worth your notice, except to keep out of her way, laddie; and that you had better do, for she's not canny. Don't you anger her again if you can help it. She has an evil look, and I can't stand her.–Here's your money. Jean, take in this fish."

During the latter part of the conversation they had been standing at the door, while Miss Horn ferreted the needful pence from a pocket under her gown. She now entered, but as Malcolm waited for Jean to take the fish, she turned on the threshold, and said:

"Wad ye no like to see her, Ma'colm?—A guid frien' she was to you, sae lang's she was here," she added after a short pause.

The youth hesitated.

"I never saw a corp i' my life, mem, an' I'm jist some feared," he said, after another brief silence.

"Hoot, laddie!" returned Miss Horn, in a somewhat offended tone.—"That'll be what comes o' haein' feelin's. A bonny corp 's the bonniest thing in creation,—an' that quaiet!—Eh! sic a heap o' them as there *has* been sin' Awbel," she went on—"an ilk ane o' them luikin', as gien there never had been anither but itsel'! Ye *oucht* to see a corp, Ma'colm. Ye'll hae't to du afore ye're ane yersel', an' ye'll never see a bonnier nor my Grizel."

"Be 't to yer wull, mem," said Malcolm resignedly.

During the latter part of the conversation they had been standing at the door, while Miss Horn ferreted the needful pence from a pocket under her gown. She now entered, but as Malcolm waited for Jean to take the fish, she turned on the threshold, and said:

"Wouldn't you like to see her, Malcolm?—A good friend she was to you, so long as she was here," she added after a short pause.

The youth hesitated.

"I never saw a corpse in my life, ma'am, and I'm a bit frightened," he said, after another brief silence.

"Heavens, laddie!" returned Miss Horn, in a somewhat offended tone.—"That'll be what comes of having feelings. A bonny corpse is the bonniest thing in creation,—and that quiet!—Eh! such a heap of them as there *has* been since Abel," she went on—"and each of them looking as if there never had been another but itself! You *ought* to see a corpse, Malcolm. You'll have to before you're one yourself, and you'll never see a bonnier than my Grizel."

"So be it, ma'am," said Malcolm resignedly.

At once she led the way, and he followed her in silence up the stair and into the dead-chamber.

There on the white bed lay the long, black, misshapen thing she had called "the bit boxie:" and with a strange sinking at the heart, Malcolm approached it.

Miss Horn's hand came from behind him, and withdrew a covering; there lay a vision lovely indeed to behold!—a fixed evanescence—a listening stillness,—awful, yet with a look of entreaty, at once resigned and unyielding, that strangely drew the heart of Malcolm. He saw a low white forehead, large eyeballs upheaving closed lids, finely-modelled features of which the tightened skin showed all the delicacy, and a mouth of suffering whereon the vanishing Psyche had left the shadow of the smile with which she awoke. The tears gathered in his eyes, and Miss Horn saw them.

"Ye maun lay yer han' upo' her, Ma'colm," she said. "Ye sud aye touch the deid, to haud ye ohn dreamed aboot them."

"I wad be laith," answered Malcolm; "she wad be ower bonny a dream to miss.—'Are they a' like that?" he added, speaking under his breath.

"Na, 'deed no!" replied Miss Horn, with mild indignation. "Wad ye expec' Bawby Cat'nach to luik like that, no?—I beg yer pardon for mentionin' the wuman, my dear," she added with sudden divergence, bending towards the still face, and speaking in a tenderly apologetic tone; "I ken weel ye canna bide the verra name o' her; but it s' be the last time ye s' hear 't to a' eternity, my doo." Then turning again to Malcolm— "Lay yer han' upon her broo, I tell ye," she said.

"I daurna," replied the youth, still under his breath; "my han's are no clean. I wadna for the warl' touch her wi' fishy han's."

"You must lay your hand upon her, Malcolm," she said. "You should always touch the dead, to keep you from dreaming about them."

"I'd hardly like to," answered Malcolm; "she would be too bonny a dream to miss.—Are they all like that?" he added, speaking under his breath.

"Indeed they are not!" replied Miss Horn, with mild indignation. "Would you expect Bawby Catanach to look like that?—I beg your pardon for mentioning the woman, my dear," she added with sudden divergence, bending towards the still face, and speaking in a tenderly apologetic tone; "I'm well aware you can't stand the very name of her; but it'll be the last time you'll hear it to all eternity, my dove." Then turning again to Malcolm—"Lay your hand upon her brow, I tell you," she said.

"I daren't," replied the youth, still under his breath; "my hands aren't clean. I wouldn't for the world touch her with fishy hands."

The same moment, moved by a sudden impulse, whose irresistibleness was veiled in his unconsciousness, he bent down, and put his lips to the forehead.

As suddenly he started back erect with dismay on every feature.

"Eh, mem!" he cried in an agonised whisper, "she's dooms cauld!"

"What sud she be?" retorted Miss Horn. "Wad ye hae her beeried warm?"

He followed her from the room in silence, with the sense of a faint sting on his lips. She led him into her parlour, and gave him a glass of wine.

"Ye'll come to the beerial upo' Setterday?" she asked, half inviting, half enquiring.

"I'm sorry to say, mem, 'at I canna," he answered. "I promised Maister Graham to tak the schule for him, an' lat him gang."

"Eh, ma'am!" he cried in an agonised whisper, "she's dreadfully cold!"

"What should she be?" retorted Miss Horn. "Would you have her buried warm?"

He followed her from the room in silence, with the sense of a faint sting on his lips. She led him into her parlour, and gave him a glass of wine.

"You'll come to the burial on Saturday?" she asked, half inviting, half enquiring.

"I'm sorry to say, ma'am, that I can't," he answered. "I promised Mister Graham to take the school for him, and let him go."

"Weel, weel! Mr Graham's obleeged to ye, nae doobt, an' we canna help it. Gie my compliments to yer gran'father."

"I'll du that, mem. He'll be sair pleased, for he's unco gratefu' for ony sic attention," said Malcolm, and with the words took his leave.

"Well, well! Mr Graham's obliged to you, no doubt, and we can't help it. Give my compliments to your grandfather."

"I'll do that, ma'am. He'll be mighty pleased, for he's very grateful for any such attention," said Malcolm, and with the words took his leave.

CHAPTER X

THE FUNERAL

That night the weather changed, and grew cloudy and cold. Saturday morning broke drizzly and dismal. A northeast wind tore off the tops of the drearily tossing billows. All was gray—enduring, hopeless gray. Along the coast the waves kept roaring on the sands, persistent and fateful; the Scaurnose was one mass of foaming white: and in the caves still haunted by the tide, the bellowing was like that of thunder.

Through the drizzle-shot wind and the fog blown in shreds from the sea, a large number of the most respectable of the male population of the burgh, clothed in Sunday gloom deepened by the crape on their hats, made their way to Miss Horn's, for, despite her rough manners, she was held in high repute. It was only such as had reason to dread the secret communication between closet and housetop that feared her tongue; if she spoke loud, she never spoke false, or backbit in the dark. What chiefly conduced however to the respect in which she was held, was that she was one of their own people, her father having died minister of the parish some twenty years before.

Comparatively little was known of her deceased cousin, who had been much of an invalid, and had mostly kept to the house, but all had understood that Miss Horn was greatly attached to her; and it was for the sake of the living mainly that the dead was thus honoured.

As the prayer drew to a close, the sounds of trampling and scuffling feet bore witness that Watty Witherspail and his assistants were carrying the coffin down the stair. Soon the company rose to follow it, and trooping out, arranged themselves behind the hearse, which, horrid with nodding plumes and gold and black panelling, drew away from the door to make room for them.

Just as they were about to move off, to the amazement of the company and the few onlookers who, notwithstanding the weather, stood around to represent the commonalty, Miss Horn herself, solitary, in a long black cloak and somewhat awful bonnet, issued, and made her way through the mourners until she stood immediately behind the hearse, by the side of Mr Cairns, the parish minister. The next moment, Watty Witherspail, who had his station at the further side of the hearse, arriving somehow at a knowledge of the apparition, came round by the horses' heads, and with a look of positive alarm at the glaring infringement of time-honoured customs, addressed her in half whispered tones expostulatory:

"Ye'll never be thinkin' o' gauin' yersel', mem!" he said.

"What for no, Watty, I wad like to ken," growled Miss Horn from the vaulted depths of her bonnet.

"The like was never hard tell o'!" returned Watty, with the dismay of an orthodox undertaker, righteously jealous of all innovation.

"It'll *be* to tell o' hencefurth," rejoined Miss Horn, who in her risen anger spoke aloud, caring nothing who heard her. "Daur *ye* preshume, Watty Witherspaill," she went on, "for no rizzon but that I ga'e you the job, an' unnertook to pay ye for't—an' that far abune its market value,—daur ye preshume, I say, to dictate to *me* what to du an' what no to du anent the maitter in han'? Think ye I hae been a mither to the puir yoong thing for sae mony a year to lat her gang awa' her lane at the last wi' the likes o' *you* for company!"

"Hoot, mem! there's the minister at yer elbuck."

"I tell ye, ye're but a wheen rouch men fowk! There's no a wuman amon' ye to haud things dacent, 'cep I gang mysel'. I'm no beggin' the minister's pardon aither. *I'll gang.* I *maun* see my puir Grizel till her last bed."

"I dread it may be too much for your feelings, Miss Horn," said the minister, who being an ambitious young man of lowly origin, and very shy of the ridiculous, did not in the least wish her company.

"You'll never be thinking of going yourself, ma'am!" he said.

"Why not, Watty, I'd like to know," growled Miss Horn from the vaulted depths of her bonnet.

"The like was never heard tell of!" returned Watty, with the dismay of an orthodox undertaker, righteously jealous of all innovation.

"It'll *be* to tell of henceforth," rejoined Miss Horn, who in her risen anger spoke aloud, caring nothing who heard her. "Dare *you* presume, Watty Witherspaill," she went on, "for no reason but that I gave you the job, and undertook to pay you for it—and that far above its market value,—dare you presume, I say, to dictate to *me* what to do and what not to do about the matter in hand? Do you think I've been a mother to the poor young thing for so many years to let her take her last journey alone with the likes of *you* for company!"

"Heavens, ma'am! there's the minister at your elbow."

"I tell you, you're but a set of rough men-folk! There's not a woman among you to keep things decent, except I go myself. I'm not begging the minister's pardon either. *I'll go.* I *must* see my poor Grizel to her last bed."

"I dread it may be too much for your feelings, Miss Horn," said the minister, who being an ambitious young man of lowly origin, and very shy of the ridiculous, did not in the least wish her company.

"Feelin's!" exclaimed Miss Horn, in a tone of indignant repudiation; "I'm gauin' to du what's richt. I s' *gang*, and gien ye dinna like my company, Mr Cairns, ye can gang hame, an' I s' gang withoot ye. Gien she sud happen to be luikin doon, she sanna see me wantin' at the last o' her. But I s' mak' no wark aboot it. I s' no putt mysel' ower forret."

"Feelings!" exclaimed Miss Horn, in a tone of indignant repudiation; "I'm going to do what's right. I shall *go*, and if you don't like my company, Mr Cairns, you can go home, and I'll go without you. If she should happen to be looking down, she shan't see me abandon her at the last. But I'll make no fuss about it. I won't put myself too far forward."

And ere the minister could utter another syllable, she had left her place to go to the rear. The same instant the procession began to move, corpse-marshalled, towards the grave; and stepping aside, she stood erect, sternly eyeing the irregular ranks of two and three and four as they passed her, intending to bring up the rear alone. But already there was one in that solitary position: with bowed head, Alexander Graham walked last and single. The moment he caught sight of Miss Horn, he perceived her design, and, lifting his hat, offered his arm. She took it almost eagerly, and together they followed in silence, through the gusty wind and monotonous drizzle.

The school-house was close to the churchyard. An instant hush fell upon the scholars when the hearse darkened the windows, lasting while the horrible thing slowly turned to enter the iron gates,—a deep hush, as if a wave of the eternal silence which rounds all our noises had broken across its barriers. The mad laird, who had been present all the morning, trembled from head to foot; yet rose and went to the door with a look of strange, subdued eagerness. When Miss Horn and Mr Graham had passed into the churchyard, he followed.

With the bending of uncovered heads, in a final gaze of leave-taking, over the coffin at rest in the bottom of the grave, all that belonged to the ceremony of burial was fulfilled; but the two facts that no one left the churchyard, although the wind blew and the rain fell, until the mound of sheltering earth was heaped high over the dead, and that the hands of many friends assisted with spade and shovel, did much to compensate for the lack of a service.

As soon as this labour was ended, Mr Graham again offered his arm to Miss Horn, who had stood in perfect calmness watching the whole with her eagle's eyes. But although she accepted his offer, instead of moving towards the gate, she kept her position in the attitude of a hostess who will follow her friends. They were the last to go from the churchyard. When they reached the schoolhouse she would have had Mr Graham leave her, but he insisted on seeing her home. Contrary to her habit she yielded, and they slowly followed the retiring company.

"Safe at last!" half-sighed Miss Horn, as they entered the town—her sole remark on the way.

Rounding a corner, they came upon Mrs Catanach standing at a neighbour's door, gazing out upon nothing, as was her wont at times, but talking to some one in the house behind her. Miss Horn turned her head aside as she passed. A look of low, malicious, half-triumphant cunning lightened across the puffy face of the *howdy*. She cocked one bushy eyebrow, setting one eye wide open, drew down the other eyebrow, nearly closing the eye under it, and stood looking after them until they were out of sight. Then turning her head over her shoulder, she burst into a laugh, softly husky with the general flabbiness of her corporeal conditions.

"What ails ye, Mistress Catanach?" cried a voice from within.	"What ails you, Mistress Catanach?" cried a voice from within.
"Sic a couple 's yon twasum wad mak!" she replied, again bursting into gelatinous laughter.	"Such a couple as that pair would make!" she replied, again bursting into gelatinous laughter.
"Wha, than? I canna lea' my milk-parritch to come an' luik."	"Who do you mean? I can't leave my milk-porridge to come and look."
"Ow! jist Meg Horn, the auld kail runt, an' Sanny Graham, the stickit minister. I wad like weel to be at the beddin' o' them. Eh! the twa heids o' them upon ae bowster!"	"Oh! just Meg Horn, the old kale runt, and Sanny Graham, the stickit minister[8]. Wouldn't I like to be at the bedding of them! Eh! the two heads of them on one pillow!"

And chuckling a low chuckle, Mrs Catanach moved for her own door.

As soon as the churchyard was clear of the funeral train, the mad laird peeped from behind a tall stone, gazed cautiously around him, and then with slow steps came and stood over the new-made grave, where the sexton was now laying the turf, "to mak a' snod for the Sawbath." (to make all trim for the Sabbath.)

"Whaur is she gane till?" he murmured to himself—He could generally speak better when merely uttering his thoughts without attempt at communication.—"I dinna ken whaur I cam frae, an' I dinna ken whaur she's gane till; but whan I gang mysel', maybe I'll ken baith.—I dinna ken, I dinna ken, I dinna ken whaur I cam frae."	"Where's she gone to?" he murmured to himself—He could generally speak better when merely uttering his thoughts without attempt at communication.—"I don't know where I came from, and I don't know where she's gone to; but when I go myself, maybe I'll know both.—I don't know, I don't know, I don't know where I came from."

Thus muttering, so lost in the thoughts that originated them that he spoke the words mechanically, he left the churchyard and returned to the school, where, under the superintendence of Malcolm, everything had been going on in the usual Saturday fashion—the work of the day which closed the week's labours, being to repeat a certain number of *questions* of the Shorter Catechism (which term, alas! included the answers), and next to buttress them with a number of suffering caryatids, as it were—texts of Scripture, I mean, first petrified and then dragged into the service. Before Mr Graham returned, every one

---

8 STICKIT MINISTER (idiomatic Scots): a failed candidate for Holy Orders

had done his part except Sheltie, who, excellent at asking questions for himself, had a very poor memory for the answers to those of other people, and was in consequence often a *keepie-in*. He did not generally heed it much, however, for the master was not angry with him on such occasions, and they gave him an opportunity of asking in his turn a multitude of questions of his own.

When he entered, he found Malcolm reading *The Tempest* and Sheltie sitting in the middle of the waste schoolroom, with his elbows on the desk before him, and his head and the Shorter Catechism between them; while in the farthest corner sat Mr Stewart, with his eyes fixed on the ground, murmuring his answerless questions to himself.

"Come up, Sheltie," said Mr Graham, anxious to let the boy go. "Which of the questions did you break down in today?"

"Please, sir, I couldn't rest in my grave till the resurrection," answered Sheltie, with but a dim sense of the humour involved in the reply.

"'What benefits do believers receive from Christ at death?'" said Mr Graham, putting the question with a smile.

"'The souls of believers are at their death made perfect in holiness, and do immediately pass into glory; and their bodies, being still united to Christ, do rest in their graves till the resurrection,'" replied Sheltie, now with perfect accuracy; whereupon the master, fearing the outbreak of a torrent of counter-questions, made haste to dismiss him.

"That'll do, Sheltie," he said. "Run home to your dinner."

Sheltie shot from the room like a shell from a mortar.

He had barely vanished when Mr Stewart rose and came slowly from his corner, his legs appearing to tremble under the weight of his hump, which moved fitfully up and down in his futile attempts to utter the word *resurrection*. As he advanced, he kept heaving one shoulder forward, as if he would fain bring his huge burden to the front, and hold it out in mute appeal to his instructor; but before reaching him he suddenly stopped, lay down on the floor on his back, and commenced rolling from side to side, with moans and complaints. Mr Graham interpreted the action into the question—How was such a body as his to rest in its grave till the resurrection—perched thus on its own back in the coffin? All the answer he could think of was to lay hold of his hand, lift him, and point upwards. The poor fellow shook his head, glanced over his shoulder at his hump, and murmured "Heavy, heavy!" seeming to imply that it would be hard for him to rise and ascend at the last day.

He had doubtless a dim notion that all his trouble had to do with his hump.

I dinna ken whaur I cam frae, an' I dinna ken whaur she's gane till.

CHAPTER XI

THE OLD CHURCH

The next day, the day of the Resurrection, rose glorious from its sepulchre of sea-fog and drizzle. It had poured all night long, but at sunrise the clouds had broken and scattered, and the air was the purer for the cleansing rain, while the earth shone with that peculiar lustre which follows the weeping which has endured its appointed night. The larks were at it again, singing as if their hearts would break for joy as they hovered in brooding exultation over the song of the future; for their nests beneath hoarded a wealth of larks for summers to come. Especially about the old church—half-buried in the ancient trees of Lossie House, the birds that day were jubilant; their throats seemed too narrow to let out the joyful air that filled all their hollow bones and quills: they sang as if they must sing, or choke with too much gladness. Beyond the short spire and its shining cock, rose the balls and stars and arrowy vanes of the House, glittering in gold and sunshine.

The inward hush of the Resurrection, broken only by the prophetic birds, the poets of the groaning and travailing creation, held time and space as in a trance; and the centre from which radiated both the hush and the carolling expectation seemed to Alexander Graham to be the churchyard in which he was now walking in the cool of the morning. It was more carefully kept than most Scottish churchyards, and yet was not too trim. Nature had a word in the affair—was allowed her part of mourning, in long grass and moss and the crumbling away of stone. The wholesomeness of decay, which both in nature and humanity is but the miry road back to life, was not unrecognized here; there was nothing of the hideous attempt to hide death in the garments of life. The master walked about gently, now stopping to read some well-known inscription and ponder for a moment over the words; and now wandering across the stoneless mounds, content to be forgotten by all but those who loved the departed. At length he seated himself on a slab by the side of the mound that rose but yesterday: it was sculptured with symbols of decay—needless surely where the originals lay about the mouth of every newly opened grave, and as surely ill-befitting the precincts of a church whose indwelling gospel is of life victorious over death!

"What are these stones," he said to himself, "but monuments to oblivion? They are not memorials of the dead, but memorials of the forgetfulness of the living. How vain it is to send a poor forsaken name, like the title page of a lost book, down the careless stream of time! Let me serve my generation, and let God remember me!"

The morning wore on; the sun rose higher and higher. He drew from his pocket the *Nosce Teipsum* of Sir John Davies, and was still reading, in quiet enjoyment of the fine logic of the lawyer-poet, when he heard the church key, in the trembling hand of Jonathan Auld, the sexton, jar feebly battling with the reluctant lock. Soon the people began to gather, mostly in groups and couples. At length came solitary Miss Horn, whom the neighbours, from respect to her sorrow, had left to walk alone. But Mr Graham went to meet her, and accompanied her into the church.

It was a cruciform building, as old as the vanished monastery, and the burial place of generations of noble blood; the dust of royalty even lay under its floor. A knight of stone reclined cross-legged in a niche with an arched Norman canopy in one of the walls, the rest of which was nearly encased in large tablets of white marble, for at his foot lay the ashes of barons and earls whose title was extinct, and whose lands had been inherited by the family of Lossie. Inside as well as outside of the church the ground had risen with the dust of generations, so that the walls were low; and heavy galleries having been erected in parts, the place was filled with shadowy recesses and haunted with glooms. From a window in the square pew where he sat, so small and low that he had to bend his head to look out of it, the schoolmaster could see a rivulet of sunshine, streaming through between two upright gravestones, and glorifying the long grass of a neglected mound that lay close to the wall under the wintry drip from the eaves: when he raised his head, the church looked very dark. The best way there to preach the Resurrection, he thought, would be to contrast the sepulchral gloom of the church, its dreary psalms and drearier sermons, with the sunlight on the graves, the lark-filled sky, and the wind blowing where it listed. But although the minister was a young man of the commonest order, educated to the church that he might eat bread, hence a mere willing slave to the beck of his lord and master, the patron, and but a parrot in the pulpit, the schoolmaster not only endeavoured to pour his feelings and desires into the mould of his prayers, but listened to the sermon with a countenance that revealed no distaste for the weak and unsavoury broth ladled out him to nourish his soul withal. When however the *service*—though whose purposes the affair could be supposed to *serve* except those of Mr Cairns himself, would have been a curious question—was over, he did breathe a sigh of relief; and when he stepped out into the sun and wind which had been shining and blowing all the time of the dreary ceremony, he wondered whether the larks might not have had the best of it in the God-praising that had been going on for two slow-paced hours. Yet, having been so long used to the sort of thing, he did not mind it half so much as his friend Malcolm, who found the Sunday observances an unspeakable weariness to both flesh and spirit.

On the present occasion, however, Malcolm did not find the said observances dreary, for he observed nothing but the vision which radiated from the dusk of the small gallery forming Lossie pew, directly opposite the Norman canopy and stone crusader. Unconventional, careless girl as Lady Florimel had hitherto shown herself to him, he saw her sit that morning like the proudest of her race, alone, and, to all appearance, unaware of a single other person's being in the church besides herself. She manifested no interest in what was going on, nor indeed felt any—how could she? never parted her lips to sing; sat during the prayer; and throughout the sermon seemed to Malcolm not once to move her eyes from the carved crusader. When all was over, she still sat motionless—sat until the last old woman had hobbled out. Then she rose, walked slowly from the gloom of the church, flashed into the glow of the churchyard, gleamed across it to a private door in the wall, which a servant held for her, and vanished. If a moment after, the notes of a merry song invaded the ears of those who yet lingered, who could dare suspect that proudly sedate damsel thus suddenly breaking the ice of her public behaviour?

For a mere school-girl she had certainly done the lady's part well. What she wore I do not exactly know; nor would it perhaps be well to describe what might seem grotesque to such prejudiced readers as have no judgment beyond the fashions of the day. But I will not let pass the opportunity of reminding them how sadly old-fashioned we of the present hour also look in the eyes of those equally infallible judges who have been in dread procession towards us ever since we began to be—our posterity—judges who perhaps will doubt with a smile whether we even knew what love was, or ever had a dream of the grandeur they are on the point of grasping. But at least bethink yourselves, dear posterity: we have not ceased because you have begun.

Out of the church the blind Duncan strode with long, confident strides. He had no staff to aid him, for he never carried one when in his best clothes; but he leaned proudly on Malcolm's arm, if one who walked so erect could be said to lean. He had adorned his bonnet the autumn before with a sprig of the large purple heather, but every bell had fallen from it, leaving only the naked spray, pitiful analogue of the whole withered exterior of which it formed part. His sporran, however, hid the stained front of his kilt, and his Sunday coat had been new within ten years—the gift of certain ladies of Portlossie, some of whom, to whose lowland eyes the kilt was obnoxious, would have added a pair of trowsers, had not Miss Horn stoutly opposed them, confident that Duncan would regard the present as an insult. And she was right; for rather than wear anything instead of the philibeg, Duncan would have plaited himself one with his own blind fingers out of an old sack. Indeed, although the *trews* were never at any time unknown in the Highlands, Duncan had always regarded them as effeminate, and especially in his lowland exile would have looked upon the wearing of them as a disgrace to his highland birth.

"Tat wass a fery coot sairmon today, Malcolm," he said, as they stepped from the churchyard upon the road.

"Tat wass a fery coot sermon today, Malcolm," he said, as they stepped from the churchyard upon the road.

Malcolm, knowing well whither conversation on the subject would lead, made no reply. His grandfather, finding him silent, iterated his remark, with the addition—

"Put how could it pe a paad one, you'll pe thinking, my poy, when he'd pe hafing such a text to keep him straight."

"But how could it be a baad one, you'll be thinking, my boy, when he'd be hafing such a text to keep him straight."

Malcolm continued silent, for a good many people were within hearing, whom he did not wish to see amused with the remarks certain to follow any he could make. But Mr Graham, who happened to be walking near the old man on the other side, out of pure politeness made a partial response.

"Yes, Mr MacPhail," he said, "it was a grand text."

"Yes, and it wass'll pe a cran' sairmon," persisted Duncan. "'Fenchence is mine—I will repay.' Ta Lord loves fenchence. It's a fine thing, fenchence. To make ta wicked know tat tey'll pe peing put men! Yes; ta Lord will slay ta wicked. Ta Lord will gif ta honest man fenchence upon his enemies. It wass a cran' sairmon!"

"Don't you think vengeance a very dreadful thing, Mr MacPhail?" said the schoolmaster.

"Yes, for ta von tat'll pe in ta wrong—I wish ta fenchence was mine!" he added with a loud sigh.

"But the Lord doesn't think any of *us* fit to be trusted with it, and so keeps it to himself, you see."

"Yes, and tat'll pe pecause it'll pe too coot to be gifing to another. And some people would be waik of heart, and be letting teir enemies co."

"I suspect it's for the opposite reason, Mr MacPhail:—we would go much too far, making no allowances, causing the innocent to suffer along with the guilty, neither giving fair play nor avoiding cruelty,—and indeed—"

"No fear!" interrupted Duncan eagerly,—"no fear, when ta wrong wass as larch as Morven!"

Malcolm continued silent, for a good many people were within hearing, whom he did not wish to see amused with the remarks certain to follow any he could make. But Mr Graham, who happened to be walking near the old man on the other side, out of pure politeness made a partial response.

"Yes, Mr MacPhail," he said, "it was a grand text."

"Yes, and it wass'll be a cran' sermon," persisted Duncan. "'Fenchence is mine—I will repay.' Ta Lord loves fenchence. It's a fine thing, fenchence. To make ta wicked know tat tey'll be being but men! Yes; ta Lord will slay ta wicked. Ta Lord will gif ta honest man fenchence upon his enemies. It wass a cran' sermon!"

"Don't you think vengeance a very dreadful thing, Mr MacPhail?"said the schoolmaster.

"Yes, for ta one tat'll be in ta wrong—I wish ta fenchence was mine!" he added with a loud sigh.

"But the Lord doesn't think any of *us* fit to be trusted with it, and so keeps it to himself, you see."

"Yes, and tat'll be because it'll be too coot to be gifing to another. And some people would be waik of heart, and be letting teir enemies co."

"I suspect it's for the opposite reason, Mr MacPhail:—we would go much too far, making no allowances, causing the innocent to suffer along with the guilty, neither giving fair play nor avoiding cruelty,—and indeed—"

"No fear!" interrupted Duncan eagerly—"no fear, when ta wrong was as large as Morven!"

In the sermon there had not been one word as to St Paul's design in quoting the text. It had been but a theatrical setting forth of the vengeance of God upon sin, illustrated with several common tales of the discovery of murder by strange means—a sermon after Duncan's own heart; and nothing but the way in which he now snuffed the wind with head thrown back and nostrils dilated, could have given an adequate idea of how much he enjoyed the recollection of it.

Mr Graham had for many years believed that he must have some personal wrongs to brood over,—wrongs, probably, to which were to be attributed his loneliness and exile; but of such Duncan had never spoken, uttering no maledictions except against the real or imagined foes of his family.[9]

The master placed so little value on any possible results of mere argument, and had indeed so little faith in any words except such as came hot from the heart, that he said no more, but, with an invitation to Malcolm to visit him in the evening, wished them good day, and turned in at his own door.

The two went slowly on towards the sea-town. The road was speckled with home-goers, single and in groups, holding a quiet Sunday pace to their dinners. Suddenly Duncan grasped Malcolm's arm with the energy of perturbation, almost of fright, and said in a loud whisper:

"Tere'll be something efil not far from her, Malcolm, my son! Look apout, look apout, and take care how you'll pe leading her."

Malcolm looked about, and replied, pressing Duncan's arm, and speaking in a low voice, far less audible than his whisper,

"There's naebody near, daddy—naebody but the howdie-wife."

"What howdie-wife do you mean, Malcolm?"

"Tere'll be something efil not far from her, Malcolm, my son! Look about, look about, and take care how you'll be leading her."

Malcolm looked about, and replied, pressing Duncan's arm, and speaking in a low voice, far less audible than his whisper,

"There's nobody near, daddy—nobody but the midwife."

"What midwife do you mean, Malcolm?"

---

9 What added to the likelihood of Mr Graham's conjecture was the fact, well enough known to him, though to few lowlanders besides, that revenge is not a characteristic of the Gael. Whatever instances of it may have appeared, and however strikingly they may have been worked up in fiction, such belong to the individual and not to the race. A remarkable proof of this occurs in the history of the family of Glenco itself. What remained of it after the massacre in 1689, rose in 1745, and joined the forces of Prince Charles Edward. Arriving in the neighbourhood of the residence of Lord Stair, whose grandfather had been one of the chief instigators of the massacre, the prince took special precautions lest the people of Glenco should wreak inherited vengeance on the earl. But they were so indignant at being supposed capable of visiting on the innocent the guilt of their ancestors, that it was with much difficulty they were prevented from forsaking the standard of the prince, and returning at once to their homes. Perhaps a yet stronger proof is the fact, fully asserted by one Gaelic scholar at least, that their literature contains nothing to foster feelings of revenge.

"Hoot! Mistress Catanach, ye ken. Dinna lat her hear ye."

"Heavens! Mistress Catanach, you know. Don't let her hear you."

"I had a feeshion, Malcolm—one moment, and no more; ta darkness closed arount it: I saw a ped, Malcolm, and—"

"I had a feeshion, Malcolm—one moment, and no more; ta darkness closed arount it: I saw a bed, Malcolm, and—"

"Wheesht, wheesht, daddy!" pleaded Malcolm importunately. "She hears ilka word ye're sayin'. She's awfu' gleg, and she's as poozhonous as an edder. Haud yer tongue, daddy; for guid-sake haud yer tongue."

"Shush, shush, daddy!" pleaded Malcolm importunately. "She hears every word you're saying. She's awfully sharp, and she's as poisonous as an adder. Hold your tongue, daddy; for goodness' sake hold your tongue."

The old man yielded, grasping Malcolm's arm, and quickening his pace, though his breath came hard, as through the gathering folds of asthma. Mrs. Catanach also quickened her pace, and came gliding along the grass by the side of the road, noiseless as the adder to which Malcolm had likened her, and going much faster than she seemed. Her great round body looked a persistent type of her calling, and her arms seemed to rest in front of her as upon a ledge. In one hand she carried a small bible, round which was folded her pocket handkerchief, and in the other a bunch of southernwood and rosemary. She wore a black silk gown, a white shawl, and a great straw bonnet with yellow ribbons in huge bows, and looked the very pattern of Sunday respectability; but her black eyebrows gloomed ominous, and an evil smile shadowed about the corners of her mouth as she passed without turning her head or taking the least notice of them. Duncan shuddered, and breathed yet harder, but seemed to recover as she increased the distance between them. They walked the rest of the way in silence, however; and even after they reached home, Duncan made no allusion to his late discomposure.

"What was't ye thocht ye saw, as we cam frae the kirk, daddy?" asked Malcolm when they were seated at their dinner of broiled mackerel and boiled potatoes.

"What was it you thought you saw, as we came from the church, daddy?" asked Malcolm when they were seated at their dinner of broiled mackerel and boiled potatoes.

"In other times she'll pe hafing such feeshions often, Malcolm, my son," he returned, avoiding an answer. "Like other pards of her race she would pe seeing—in the speerit, where old Tuncan *can* see. And she'll pe telling you, Malcolm—peware of tat voman; for ta voman was thinking pad thoughts; and tat will pe what make her shutter and shake, my son, as she'll pe coing py."

"In other times she'll be hafing such feeshions often, Malcolm, my son," he returned, avoiding an answer. "Like other bards of her race she would be seeing—in the speerit, where old Tuncan *can* see. And she'll be telling you, Malcolm—beware of tat woman; for ta woman was thinking bad thoughts; and that will be what make her shutter and shake, my son, as she'll be coing by."

CHAPTER XII

THE CHURCHYARD

On Sundays, Malcolm was always more or less annoyed by the obtrusive presence of his arms and legs, accompanied by a vague feeling that, at any moment, and no warning given, they might, with some insane and irrepressible flourish, break the Sabbath on their own account, and degrade him in the eyes of his fellow-townsmen, who seemed all silently watching how he bore the restraints of the holy day. It must be conceded, however, that the discomfort had quite as much to do with his Sunday clothes as with the Sabbath-day, and that it interfered but little with an altogether peculiar calm which appeared to him to belong in its own right to the Sunday, whether its light flowed in the sunny cataracts of June, or oozed through the spongy clouds of November. As he walked again to the Alton, or Old Town in the evening, the filmy floats of white in the lofty blue, the droop of the long dark grass by the side of the short brown corn, the shadows pointing like all lengthening shadows towards the quarter of hope, the yellow glory filling the air and paling the green below, the unseen larks hanging aloft—like air-pitcher-plants that overflowed in song—like electric jars emptying themselves of the sweet thunder of bliss in the flashing of wings and the trembling of melodious throats; these were indeed of the summer but the cup of rest had been poured out upon them; the Sabbath brooded like an embodied peace over the earth, and under its wings they grew sevenfold peaceful— with a peace that might be felt, like the hand of a mother pressed upon the half-sleeping child. The rusted iron cross on the eastern gable of the old church stood glowing lustreless in the westering sun; while the gilded vane, whose business was the wind, creaked radiantly this way and that, in the flaws from the region of the sunset: its shadow flickered soft on the new grave, where the grass of the wounded sod was drooping. Again seated on a neighbour stone, Malcolm found his friend.

"See," said the schoolmaster as the fisherman sat down beside him, "how the shadow from one grave stretches like an arm to embrace another! In this light the churchyard seems the very birthplace of shadows: see them flowing out of the tombs as from fountains, to overflow the world! Does the morning or the evening light suit such a place best, Malcolm?"

The pupil thought for a while.

"The evenin' licht, sir," he answered at length; "for ye see the sun's deein' like, an' deith's like a fa'in asleep, an' the grave's the bed, an' the sod's the bedclaes, an' there's a lang nicht to the fore."

"Are ye sure o' that, Malcolm?"

"It's the wye folk thinks an' says aboot it, sir."

"Or maybe doesna think, an' only says?"

"Maybe, sir; I dinna ken."

"The evening light, sir," he answered at length; "for you see the sun is dying, and death's like falling asleep, and the grave's the bed, and the sod's the bedclothes, and there's a long night to come."

"Are you sure of that, Malcolm?"

"It's the way folk think and talk about it, sir."

"Or maybe don't think and only talk?"

"Maybe, sir; I don't know."

"Come here, Malcolm," said Mr Graham, and took him by the arm, and led him towards the east end of the church, where a few tombstones were crowded against the wall, as if they would press close to a place they might not enter.

"Read that," he said, pointing to a flat stone, where every hollow letter was shown in high relief by the growth in it of a lovely moss. The rest of the stone was rich in gray and green and brown lichens, but only in the letters grew the bright moss; the inscription stood as it were in the hand of nature herself—*"He is not here; he is risen."*

While Malcolm gazed, trying to think what his master would have him think, the latter resumed.

"If he is risen—if the sun is up, Malcolm—then the morning and not the evening is the season for the place of tombs; the morning when the shadows are shortening and separating, not the evening when they are growing all into one. I used to love the churchyard best in the evening, when the past was more to me than the future; now I visit it almost every bright summer morning, and only occasionally at night."

"But, sir, isna deith a dreidfu' thing?" said Malcolm.

"That depends on whether a man regards it as his fate, or as the will of a perfect God. Its obscurity is its dread; but if God be light, then death itself must be full of splendour—a splendour probably too keen for our eyes to receive."

"But there's the deein' itsel': isna that fearsome? It's that I wad be fleyed at."

"I don't see why it should be. It's the want of a God that makes it dreadful, and *you* will be greatly to blame, Malcolm, if you haven't found your God by the time you have to die."

"But, sir, isn't death a dreadful thing?" said Malcolm.

"That depends on whether a man regards it as his fate, or as the will of a perfect God. Its obscurity is its dread; but if God be light, then death itself must be full of splendour—a splendour probably too keen for our eyes to receive."

"But there's the dying itself: isn't that fearsome? It's that I would be afraid of."

"I don't see why it should be. It's the want of a God that makes it dreadful, and *you* will be greatly to blame, Malcolm, if you haven't found your God by the time you have to die."

They were startled by a gruff voice near them. The speaker was hidden by a corner of the church.

"Ay, she's weel happit," it said. "But a grave never luiks richt wantin' a stane, an' her auld cousin wad hear o' nane bein' laid ower *her*. I said it micht be set up at her heid, whaur she wad never fin' the weicht o' 't; but na, na! nane o' 't for *her*! She's ane 'at maun tak her ain gait, say the ither thing wha likes."

It was Wattie Witherspail who spoke—a thin shaving of a man, with a deep, harsh, indeed startling voice.

"An' what ailed her at a stane?" returned the voice of Jonathan Auldbuird, the sexton.—"Nae doobt it wad be the expense?"

"Amna I tellin' ye what it was? Deil a bit o' the expense cam intil the calcalation! The auld maiden's nane sae close as fowk 'at disna ken her wad mak her oot. *I* ken her weel. She wadna hae a stane laid upon her as gien she wanted to haud her doon, puir thing! She said, says she, 'The yerd's eneuch upo' the tap o' her, wantin' that!'"

"It micht be some sair, she wad be thinkin' doobtless, for sic a waik worn cratur to lift whan the trump was blawn," said the sexton, with the feeble laugh of one who doubts the reception of his wit.

"Weel, I div whiles think," responded Wattie,—but it was impossible from his tone to tell whether or not he spoke in earnest,— "'at maybe my boxies *is* a wheen ower weel made for the use they're pitten till. They sudna be that ill to rive—gien a' be true 'at the minister says. Ye see, we dinna ken whan that day may come, an' there may na be time for the wat an' the worm to ca the boords apairt."

They were startled by a gruff voice near them. The speaker was hidden by a corner of the church.

"Ay, she's well covered," it said. "But a grave never looks right without a stone, and her old cousin wouldn't hear of one being laid over *her*. I said it might be set up at her head, where she would never feel the weight of it; but na, na! none of it for *her*! She's one that must take her own way, whatever others say."

It was Wattie Witherspail who spoke—a thin shaving of a man, with a deep, harsh, indeed startling voice.

"And why wouldn't she have a stone?" returned the voice of Jonathan Auldbuird, the sexton.—"No doubt it would be the expense?"

"Haven't I just told you what it was? Devil a bit of the expense came into the calculation! The old maiden's none so tight-fisted as strangers would have you think. *I* know her well. She wouldn't have a stone laid upon her as if she wanted to hold her down, poor thing! She said, says she, 'The earth's enough upon the top of her, without that!'"

"It might be hard, she would doubtless be thinking, for such a weak worn creature to lift when the trump was blown," said the sexton, with the feeble laugh of one who doubts the reception of his wit.

"Well, I do sometimes think," responded Wattie,—but it was impossible from his tone to tell whether or not he spoke in earnest,— "that maybe my boxes *are* a bit too well made for the use they're put to. They shouldn't be that hard to break—if all be true that the minister says. You see, we don't know when that day may come, and there might not be time for the wet and the worms to drive the boards apart."

"Hoots, man! it's no *your* lang nails nor yet yer heidit screws 'll haud doon the redeemt, gien the jeedgement war the morn's mornin'," said the sexton; "an' for the lave, they wad be glaid eneuch to bide whaur they are; but they'll a' be howkit oot,—fear na ye that."

"The Lord grant a blessed uprisin' to you an' me, Jonathan, at that day!" said Wattie, in the tone of one who felt himself uttering a more than ordinarily religious sentiment and on the word followed the sound of their retreating footsteps.

"How closely together may come the solemn and the grotesque! the ludicrous and the majestic!" said the schoolmaster. "Here, to us lingering in awe about the doors beyond which lie the gulfs of the unknown—to our very side come the wright and the grave-digger with their talk of the strength of coffins and the judgment of the living God!"

"I hae whiles thoucht mysel', sir," said Malcolm, "it was gey strange-like to hae a wuman o' the mak o' Mistress Catanach sittin' at the receipt o' bairns, like the gatekeeper o' the ither warl', wi' the hasp o' 't in her han': it doesna promise ower weel for them 'at she lats in. An' noo ye hae pitten't intil my heid that there's Wattie Witherspail an' Jonathan Auldbuird for the porters to open an' lat a' that's left o' 's oot again! Think o' sic like haein' sic a han' in sic solemn maitters!"

"Indeed some of us have strange porters," said Mr Graham, with a smile, "both to open to us and to close behind us! yet even in them lies the human nature, which, itself the embodiment of the unknown, wanders out through the gates of mystery, to wander back, it may be, in a manner not altogether unlike that by which it came."

"Heavens, man! it's not *your* long nails nor yet your headed screws that'll hold down the redeemed, though the judgement were tomorrow morning," said the sexton; "and for the rest, they would be glad enough to stay where they are; but they'll all be rooted out—never fear."

"The Lord grant a blessed uprising to you and me, Jonathan, at that day!" said Wattie, in the tone of one who felt himself uttering a more than ordinarily religious sentiment and on the word followed the sound of their retreating footsteps.

"How closely together may come the solemn and the grotesque! the ludicrous and the majestic!" said the schoolmaster. "Here, to us lingering in awe about the doors beyond which lie the gulfs of the unknown—to our very side come the wright and the grave-digger with their talk of the strength of coffins and the judgment of the living God!"

"I have sometimes thought myself, sir," said Malcolm, "it was the oddest thing to have a woman such as Mistress Catanach sitting at the receipt of babies, like the gatekeeper of the other world, with the hasp of it in her hand: it doesn't bode very well for those she lets in. An now you've put it in my head that there's Wattie Witherspail and Jonathan Auldbuird for the porters to open and let all that's left of us out again! Think of the likes of them being so involved in such solemn matters!"

"Indeed some of us have strange porters," said Mr Graham, with a smile, "both to open to us and to close behind us! yet even in them lies the human nature, which, itself the embodiment of the unknown, wanders out through the gates of mystery, to wander back, it may be, in a manner not altogether unlike that by which it came."

In contemplative moods, the schoolmaster spoke in a calm and loftily sustained style of book-English—quite another language from that he used when he sought to rouse the consciences of his pupils, and strangely contrasted with that in which Malcolm kept up his side of the dialogue.

"I houp, sir," said the latter, "it'll be nae sort o' a celestial Mistress Catanach 'at 'll be waiting for me o' the ither side; nor yet for my puir daddy, wha cud ill bide bein' wamled aboot upo' *her* knee."

Mr Graham laughed outright.

"If there be one to act the nurse," he answered, "I presume there will be one to take the mother's part too."

"But speakin' o' the grave, sir," pursued Malcolm, "I wiss ye cud drop a word 'at micht be o' some comfort to my daddy. It's plain to me, frae words he lats fa' noo an' than, that, instead o' lea'in' the warl' ahint him whan he dees, he thinks to lie smorin' an' smocherin' i' the mools, clammy an' weet, but a' there, an' trimlin' at the thocht o' the suddent awfu' roar an' din o' the brazen trumpet o' the archangel. I wiss ye wad luik in an' say something till him some nicht. It's nae guid mentionin' 't to the minister; he wad only gie a lauch an' gang awa'. An' gien ye cud jist slide in a word aboot forgien' his enemies, sir! I made licht o' the maitter to Mistress Courthope, 'cause she only maks him waur. She does weel wi' what the minister pits intill her, but she has little o' her ain to mix't up wi', an' sae has but sma' weicht wi' the likes o' my gran'father. Only ye winna lat him think ye called on purpose."

In contemplative moods, the schoolmaster spoke in a calm and loftily sustained style of book-English—quite another language from that he used when he sought to rouse the consciences of his pupils, and strangely contrasted with that in which Malcolm kept up his side of the dialogue.

"I hope, sir," said the latter, "it'll be no sort of a celestial Mistress Catanach that'll be waiting for me on the other side; nor yet for my poor daddy, who could ill endure being bounced about on *her* knee."

Mr Graham laughed outright.

"If there be one to act the nurse," he answered, "I presume there will be one to take the mother's part too."

"But speaking of the grave, sir," pursued Malcolm, "I wish you could drop a word that might be of some comfort to my daddy. It's plain to me, from words he lets fall now and then, that, instead of leaving the world behind him when he dies, he expects to lie snuffling and stifling in the mould, clammy and wet, but all there, and trembling at the thought of the sudden awful roar and din of the brazen trumpet of the archangel. I wish you would look in and say something to him some night. It's no good mentioning it to the minister; he would just laugh and turn away. And if you could just slide in a word about forgiving his enemies, sir! I made light of the matter to Mistress Courthope, for she only makes him worse. She does well with what the minister puts into her, but she has little of her own to mix it up with, and so has but small weight with the likes of my grandfather. Only you won't let him think you called on purpose."

They walked about the churchyard until the sun went down in what Mr Graham called the grave of his endless resurrection—the clouds on the one side bearing all the pomp of his funeral, the clouds on the other all the glory of his uprising; and when now the twilight trembled filmy on the borders of the dark, the master once more seated himself beside the new grave, and motioned to Malcolm to take his place beside him: there they talked and dreamed together of the life to come, with many wanderings and returns; and little as the boy knew of the ocean-depths of sorrowful experience in the bosom of his companion whence floated up the breaking bubbles of rainbow-hued thought, his words fell upon his heart—not to be provender for the birds of flitting fancy and airy speculation, but the seed—it might be decades ere it ripened—of a coming harvest of hope. At length the master rose and said, "Malcolm, I'm going in: I should like you to stay here half an hour alone, and then go straight home to bed."

For the master believed in solitude and silence. Say rather, he believed in God. What the youth might think, feel, or judge, he could not tell; but he believed that when the Human is still, the Divine speaks to it, because it is its own.

Malcolm consented willingly. The darkness had deepened, the graves all but vanished; an old setting moon appeared, boatlike over a great cloudy chasm, into which it slowly sank; blocks of cloud, with stars between, possessed the sky; all nature seemed thinking about death; a listless wind began to blow, and Malcolm began to feel as if he were awake too long, and *ought* to be asleep—as if he were out in a dream—a dead man that had risen too soon or lingered too late—so lonely, so forsaken! The wind, soft as it was, seemed to blow through his very soul. Yet something held him, and his half-hour was long over when he left the churchyard.

As he walked home, the words of a German poem, a version of which Mr Graham had often repeated to him, and once more that same night, kept ringing in his heart:

Uplifted is the stone,
And all mankind arisen!
We men remain thine own,
And vanished is our prison!
What bitterest grief can stay
Before thy golden cup,
When earth and life give way,
And with our Lord we sup.

To the marriage Death doth call.
The maidens are not slack;
The lamps are burning all—
Of oil there is no lack.
Afar I hear the walking
Of thy great marriage throng
And hark! the stars are talking
With human tone and tongue!

Courage! for life is hasting
To endless life away;
The inner fire, unwasting,
Transfigures our dull clay
See the stars melting, sinking,
In life-wine, golden-bright
We, of the splendour drinking,
Shall grow to stars of light.

Lost, lost are all our losses;
Love set for ever free;
The full life heaves and tosses
Like an eternal sea!
One endless living story!
One poem spread abroad!
And the sun of all our glory
Is the countenance of God.

CHAPTER XIII

THE MARQUIS OF LOSSIE

The next morning rose as lovely as if the mantle of the departing Resurrection-day had fallen upon it. Malcolm rose with it, hastened to his boat, and pulled out into the bay for an hour or two's fishing. Nearly opposite the great conglomerate rock at the western end of the dune, called the Bored Craig (*Perforated Crag*) because of a large hole that went right through it, he began to draw in his line. Glancing shoreward as he leaned over the gunwale, he spied at the foot of the rock, near the opening, a figure in white, seated, with bowed head. It was of course the mysterious lady, whom he had twice before seen thereabout at this unlikely if not untimely hour; but with yesterday fresh in his mind, how could he fail to see in her an angel of the resurrection waiting at the sepulchre to tell the glad news that the Lord was risen?

Many were the glances he cast shoreward as he re-baited his line, and, having thrown it again into the water, sat waiting until it should be time to fire the swivel. Still the lady sat on, in her whiteness a creature of the dawn, without even lifting her head. At length, having added a few more fishes to the little heap in the bottom of his boat, and finding his watch bear witness that the hour was at hand, he seated himself on his thwart, and rowed lustily to the shore, his bosom filled with the hope of yet another sight of the lovely face, and another hearing of the sweet English voice and speech. But the very first time he turned his head to look, he saw but the sloping foot of the rock sink bare into the shore. No white-robed angel sat at the gate of the resurrection; no moving thing was visible on the far-vacant sands. When he reached the top of the dune, there was no living creature beyond but a few sheep feeding on the thin grass. He fired the gun, rowed back to the Seaton, ate his breakfast, and set out to carry the best of his fish to the House.

The moment he turned the corner of her street, he saw Mrs Catanach standing on her threshold with her arms akimbo; although she was always tidy, and her house spotlessly trim, she yet seemed forever about the door, on the outlook at least, if not on the watch.

"What hae ye in yer bit basket the day, Ma'colm?" she said, with a peculiar smile, which was not sweet enough to restore vanished confidence.

"What have you in your basket today, Malcolm?" she said, with a peculiar smile, which was not sweet enough to restore vanished confidence.

"Naething guid for dogs," answered Malcolm, and was walking past.

But she made a step forward, and, with a laugh meant to indicate friendly amusement, said,

"Let's see what's intill't, ony gait.—The doggie's awa on 's traivels the day."

"'Deed, Mistress Catanach," persisted Malcolm, "I canna say I like to hae my ain fish flung i' my face, nor yet to see ill-faured tykes rin awa' wi' 't afore my verra een."

After the warning given him by Miss Horn, and the strange influence her presence had had on his grandfather, Malcolm preferred keeping up a negative quarrel with the woman.

"Dinna ca' ill names," she returned: "my dog wad tak it waur to be ca'd an ill-faured tyke, nor to hae fish flung in *his* face. Lat's see what's i' yer basket, I say."

As she spoke, she laid her hand on the basket, but Malcolm drew back, and turned away towards the gate.

"Lord safe us!" she cried, with a yelling laugh; "ye're no feared at an auld wife like me?"

"I dinna ken; maybe ay an' maybe no—I wadna say. But I dinna want to hae onything to du wi' ye, mem."

"Ma'colm MacPhail," said Mrs Catanach, lowering her voice to a hoarse whisper, while every trace of laughter vanished from her countenance, "ye hae had mair to du wi' me nor ye ken, an' aiblins ye'll hae mair yet nor ye can weel help. Sae caw canny, my man."

"Ye may hae the layin' o' me oot," said Malcolm, "but it sanna be wi' my wull; an' gien I hae ony life left i' me, I s' gie ye a fleg."

"Nothing good for dogs," answered Malcolm, and was walking past.

But she made a step forward, and, with a laugh meant to indicate friendly amusement, said,

"Let's see what's in it, anyway.—The dog's away on his travels today."

"Indeed, Mistress Catanach," persisted Malcolm, "I can't say I like to have my own fish flung in my face, nor yet to see ugly-looking mutts run away with it before my very eyes."

After the warning given him by Miss Horn, and the strange influence her presence had had on his grandfather, Malcolm preferred keeping up a negative quarrel with the woman.

"Don't call names," she returned: "my dog would take it worse to be called an ugly mutt than to have fish flung in *his* face. Let's see what's in your basket, I say."

As she spoke, she laid her hand on the basket, but Malcolm drew back, and turned away towards the gate.

"Lord save us!" she cried, with a yelling laugh; "you're not afraid of an old wife (woman) like me?"

"I don't know; maybe ay and maybe no—I wouldn't say. But I don't want to have anything to do with you, ma'am."

"Malcolm MacPhail," said Mrs Catanach, lowering her voice to a hoarse whisper, while every trace of laughter vanished from her countenance, "You've had more to do with me than you know, and maybe you'll have more yet than you can well avoid. So watch your step, my man."

"You may have the laying out of me," said Malcolm, "but not with my consent; and if I have any life left in me, I'll give you a fright."

"Ye may get a war yersel': I hae frichtit the deid afore noo. Sae gang yer wa's to Mistress Coorthoup, wi' a flech i' yer lug. I wuss ye luck—sic luck as I wad wuss ye!"

"You may get a worse yourself: I've frightened the dead before now. So be off with you to Mistress Courthope, with a flea in your ear. I wish you luck—such luck as I would wish you!"

Her last words sounded so like a curse, that to overcome a *cauld creep*,[10] Malcolm had to force a laugh.

The cook at the House bought all his fish, for they had had none for the last few days, because of the storm; and he was turning to go home by the river side, when he heard a tap on a window, and saw Mrs Courthope beckoning him to another door.

"His lordship desired me to send you to him, Malcolm, the next time you called," she said.

"Weel, mem, here I am," answered the youth.

"Well, ma'am, here I am," answered the youth.

"You'll find him in the flower-garden," she said. "He's up early today for a wonder."

"You'll find him in the flower-garden," she said. "He's up early today for a wonder."

He left his basket at the top of the stairs that led down the rock to the level of the burn, and walked up the valley of the stream.

The garden was a curious old-fashioned place, with high hedges, and close alleys of trees, where two might have wandered long without meeting, and it was some time before he found any hint of the presence of the marquis. At length, however, he heard voices, and following the sound, walked along one of the alleys till he came to a little arbour, where he discovered the marquis seated, and, to his surprise, the white-robed lady of the sands beside him. A great deer-hound at his master's feet was bristling his mane, and baring his eye-teeth with a growl, but the girl had a hold of his collar.

"Who are *you?*" asked the marquis rather gruffly, as if he had never seen him before.

"I beg yer lordship's pardon," said Malcolm, "but they telled me yer lordship wantit to see me, and sent me to the flooer-garden. Will I gang, or will I bide?"

"I beg your lordship's pardon," said Malcolm, "but they told me your lordship wanted to see me, and sent me to the flower-garden. Will I go, or will I stay?"

The marquis looked at him for a moment, frowningly, and made no reply. But the frown gradually relaxed before Malcolm's modest but unflinching gaze, and the shadow of a smile slowly usurped its place. He still kept silent, however.

The marquis looked at him for a moment, frowningly, and made no reply. But the frown gradually relaxed before Malcolm's modest but unflinching gaze, and the shadow of a smile slowly usurped its place. He still kept silent, however.

"Am I to gang or bide, my lord?" repeated Malcolm.

"Am I to go or stay, my lord?" repeated Malcolm.

"Can't you wait for an answer?'

"Can't you wait for an answer?"

---

10 CAULD CREEP: cold creep (i.e., a creeping of the flesh)

"As lang's yer lordship likes—Will I gang an' walk aboot, mem —my leddy, till his lordship's made up his min'? Wad that please him, duv ye think?" he said, in the tone of one who seeks advice.

But the girl only smiled, and the marquis said, "Go to the devil."

"I maun luik to yer lordship for the necessar' directions," rejoined Malcolm.

"Your tongue's long enough to inquire as you go," said the marquis.

A reply in the same strain rushed to Malcolm's lips, but he checked himself in time, and stood silent, with his bonnet in his hand, fronting the two. The marquis sat gazing as if he had nothing to say to him, but after a few moments the lady spoke—not to Malcolm, however.

"Is there any danger in boating here, papa?" she said.

"Not more, I daresay, than there ought to be," replied the marquis listlessly. "Why do you ask?"

"Because I should so like a row! I want to see how the shore looks to the mermaids."

"Well, I will take you some day, if we can find a proper boat."

"Is yours a proper boat?" she asked, turning to Malcolm with a sparkle of fun in her eyes.

"That depen's on my lord's definition o' *proper*."

"Definition!" repeated the marquis.

"Is 't ower lang a word, my lord?" asked Malcolm.

The marquis only smiled.

"I ken what ye mean. It's a strange word in a fisher lad's mou', ye think. But what for should na a fisher-lad hae a smatterin' o' loagic, my lord? For Greek

"As long as your lordship likes.—Will I go and walk about, ma'am—my lady, till his lordship's made up his mind? Would that please him, do you think?" he said, in the tone of one who seeks advice.

But the girl only smiled, and the marquis said, "Go to the devil."

"I must look to your lordship for the needful directions," rejoined Malcolm.

"Your tongue's long enough to inquire as you go," said the marquis.

A reply in the same strain rushed to Malcolm's lips, but he checked himself in time, and stood silent, with his bonnet in his hand, fronting the two. The marquis sat gazing as if he had nothing to say to him, but after a few moments the lady spoke—not to Malcolm, however.

"Is there any danger in boating here, papa?" she said.

"Not more, I daresay, than there ought to be," replied the marquis listlessly. "Why do you ask?"

"Because I should so like a row! I want to see how the shore looks to the mermaids."

"Well, I will take you some day, if we can find a proper boat."

"Is yours a proper boat?" she asked, turning to Malcolm with a sparkle of fun in her eyes.

"That depends on my lord's definition of *proper*."

"Definition!" repeated the marquis.

"Is it too long a word, my lord?" asked Malcolm.

The marquis only smiled.

"I know what you mean. It's a strange word in a fisher lad's mouth, you think. But why shouldn't a fisher-lad have a smattering of logic, my lord? For Greek or Latin or Laitin there's but sma' opportunity o' exerceese in oor pairts; but for loagic, a fisher-body may aye haud his han' in i' that. He can aye be tryin' 't upo' 's wife, or 's guid mother, or upo' 's boat, or upo' the fish whan they winna tak. Loagic wad save a heap o' cursin' an' ill words—amo' the fisher-fowk, I mean, my lord."

"Have you been to college?"

"Na, my lord—the mair's the pity! But I've been to the school sin' ever I can min'."

"Do they teach logic there?"

"A kin' o' 't. Mr Graham sets us to try oor han' whiles—jist to mak 's a bit gleg, ye ken."

"You don't mean you go to school still?"

"I dinna gang reg'lar; but I gang as aften as Mr Graham wants me to help him, an' I aye gether something."

"So it's schoolmaster you are as well as fisherman? Two strings to your bow!—Who pays you for teaching?"

"Ow! naebody. Wha wad pay me for that?"

"Why, the schoolmaster."

"Na, but that wad be an affront, my lord!"

"How can you afford the time for nothing?"

"The time comes to little, compairt wi' what Mr Graham gies me i' the lang forenichts—i' the winter time, ye ken, my lord, whan the sea's whiles ower contumahcious to be meddlet muckle wi'."

"But you have to support your grandfather."

"My gran'father wad be ill-pleased to hear ye say 't, my lord. He's terrible independent; an' what wi' his pipes, an' his lamps, an' his shop, he could keep's baith.

there's but small opportunity of exercise in our parts; but for logic, any fisher-body may always keep in training. He can always be trying it upon his wife, or his mother in law, or upon his boat, or upon the fish when they won't bite. Logic would save a heap of cursing and ill words—among the fisher-folk, I mean, my lord."

"Have you been to college?"

"Na, my lord—the more's the pity! But I've been to the school for as long as I can remember."

"Do they teach logic there?"

"After a fashion. Mr Graham sets us to try our hand sometimes—just to sharpen us, you know."

"You don't mean you go to school still?"

"Not as a regular pupil; but I go as often as Mr Graham wants me to help him, and I always get some benefit."

"So it's schoolmaster you are as well as fisherman? Two strings to your bow!—Who pays you for teaching?"

"Oh! nobody. Who would pay me for that?"

"Why, the schoolmaster."

"Na, but that wad be an affront, my lord!"

"How can you afford the time for nothing?"

"The time comes to little, compared with what Mr Graham gives me in the long forenights—in the winter time, you know, my lord, when the sea's sometimes too wild to be meddled with much."

"But you have to support your grandfather."

"My grandfather would be ill-pleased to hear you say it, my lord. He's terribly independent; and what with his pipes, and his lamps, and his shop, he could keep us

It's no muckle the likes o' us wants. He winna lat me gang far to the fishin', so that I hae the mair time to read an' gang to Mr Graham."

As the youth spoke, the marquis eyed him with apparently growing interest.

"But you haven't told me whether your boat is a proper one," said the lady.

"Proper eneuch, mem, for what's required o' her. She taks guid fish."

"But is it a proper boat for me to have a row in?"

"No wi' that goon on, mem, as I telled ye afore."

"The water won't get in, will it?"

"No more than 's easy gotten oot again."

"Do you ever put up a sail?"

"Whiles—a wee bit o' a lug sail."

"Nonsense, Flow!" said the marquis. "I'll see about it."

Then turning to Malcolm,—"You may go," he said. "When I want you I will send for you."

both. The likes of us live very simply. He won't let me go far to the fishing, so that I have the more time to read and go to Mr Graham."

As the youth spoke, the marquis eyed him with apparently growing interest.

"But you haven't told me whether your boat is a proper one," said the lady.

"Proper enough, ma'am, for what's required of her. She takes good fish."

"But is it a proper boat for me to have a row in?"

"Not with that gown on, ma'am, as I told you before."

"The water won't get in, will it?"

"No more than is easily got out again."

"Do you ever put up a sail?"

"Sometimes—a wee bit of a lug sail."

"Nonsense, Flow!" said the marquis. "I'll see about it."

Then turning to Malcolm,—"You may go," he said. "When I want you I will send for you."

Malcolm thought with himself that he had sent for him this time before he wanted him; but he made his bow, and departed—not without disappointment, for he had expected the marquis to say something about his grandfather going to the House with his pipes, a request he would fain have carried to the old man to gladden his heart withal.

Lord Lossie had been one of the boon companions of the Prince of Wales—considerably higher in type, it is true, yet low enough to accept usage for law, and measure his obligation by the custom of his peers: duty merely amounted to what was expected of him, and honour, the flitting shadow of the garment of truth, was his sole divinity. Still he had a heart, and it would speak,—so long at least, as the object affecting it was present. But, alas! it had no memory. Like the unjust judge, he might redress a wrong that cried to him, but out of sight and hearing it had for him no existence. To a man he would not have told a deliberate lie—except, indeed, a woman was in the case; but to women he had lied enough to sink the whole ship of fools. Nevertheless, had the accusing angel himself called him a liar, he would have instantly offered him his choice of weapons.

There was in him by nature, however, a certain generosity which all the vice he had shared in had not quenched. Overbearing, he was not yet too overbearing to appreciate a manly carriage, and had been pleased with what some would have considered the boorishness of Malcolm's behaviour—such not perceiving that it had the same source as the true aristocratic bearing—namely, a certain unselfish confidence which is the mother of dignity.

He had, of course, been a spendthrift—and so much the better, being otherwise what he was; for a cautious and frugal voluptuary is about the lowest style of man. Hence he had never been out of difficulties, and when, a year or so agone, he succeeded to his brother's marquisate, he was, notwithstanding his enlarged income, far too much involved to hope any immediate rescue from them. His new property, however, would afford him a refuge from troublesome creditors; there he might also avoid expenditure for a season, and perhaps rally the forces of a dissolute life; the place was not new to him, having, some twenty years before, spent nearly twelve months there, of which time the recollections were not altogether unpleasant: weighing all these things he had made up his mind, and here he was at Lossie House.

The marquis was about fifty years of age, more worn than his years would account for, yet younger than his years in expression, for his conscience had never bitten him very deep. He was middle-sized, broad-shouldered but rather thin, with fine features of the aquiline Greek type, light blue hazy eyes, and fair hair, slightly curling and streaked with gray. His manners were those of one polite for his own sake. To his remote inferiors he was kind—would even encourage them to liberties, but might in turn take greater with them than they might find agreeable. He was fond of animals—would sit for an hour stroking the head of Demon, his great Irish deerhound; but at other times would tease him to a wrath which touched the verge of dangerous. He was fond of practical jokes, and would not hesitate to indulge himself even in such as were incompatible with any genuine refinement: the sort had been in vogue in his merrier days, and Lord Lossie had ever been one of the most fertile in inventing, and loudest in enjoying them. For the rest, if he was easily enraged, he was readily appeased; could drink a great deal, but was no drunkard; and held as his creed that a God had probably made the world and set it going, but that he did not care a brass farthing, as he phrased it, how it went on, or what such an insignificant being as a man did or left undone in it. Perhaps he might amuse himself with it, he said, but he doubted it. As to men, he believed every man loved himself supremely, and therefore was in natural warfare with every other man. Concerning women he professed himself unable to give a definite utterance of any sort—and yet, he would add, he had had opportunities.

The mother of Florimel had died when she was a mere child, and from that time she had been at school until her father brought her away to share his fresh honours. She knew little, that little was not correct, and had it been, would have yet been of small value. At school she had been under many laws, and had felt their slavery: she was now in the third heaven of delight with her liberty. But the worst of foolish laws is, that when the insurgent spirit casts them off, it is but too ready to cast away with them the genial self-restraint which these fretting trammels have smothered beneath them.

Her father regarded her as a child, of whom it was enough to require that she should keep out of mischief. He said to himself now and then that he must find a governess for her; but as yet he had not begun to look for one. Meantime he neither exercised the needful authority over her, nor treated her as a companion. His was a shallow nature, never very pleasantly conscious of itself except in the whirl of excitement, and the glitter of crossing lights: with a lovely daughter by his side, he neither sought to search into her being, nor to aid its unfolding, but sat brooding over past pleasures, or fancying others yet in store for him—lost in the dull flow of life along the lazy reach to whose mire its once tumultuous torrent had now descended. But, indeed, what could such a man have done for the education of a young girl? How many of the qualities he understood and enjoyed in women could he desire to see developed in his daughter? There was yet enough of the father in him to expect those qualities in her to which in other women he had been an insidious foe; but had he not done what in him lay to destroy his right of claiming such from her?

So Lady Florimel was running wild, and enjoying it. As long as she made her appearance at meals, and looked happy, her father would give himself no trouble about her. How he himself managed to live in those first days without company—what he thought about or speculated upon, it were hard to say. All he could be said to do was to ride here and there over the estate with his steward, Mr Crathie, knowing little and caring less about farming, or crops, or cattle. He had by this time, however, invited a few friends to visit him, and expected their arrival before long.

"How do you like this dull life, Flory?" he said, as they walked up the garden to breakfast.

"Dull, papa!" she returned. "You never were at a girls' school, or you wouldn't call this dull. It is the merriest life in the world. To go where you like, and have miles of room! And such room! It's the loveliest place in the world, papa!"

He smiled a small, satisfied smile, and stooping stroked his Demon.

CHAPTER XIV

MEG PARTAN'S LAMP

Malcolm went down the riverside, not over pleased with the marquis; for, although unconscious of it as such, he had a strong feeling of personal dignity. As he threaded the tortuous ways of the Seaton towards his own door, he met sounds of mingled abuse and apology. Such were not infrequent in that quarter, for one of the women who lived there was a termagant, and the door of her cottage was generally open. She was known as Meg Partan. Her husband's real name was of as little consequence in life as it is in my history, for almost everybody in the fishing villages of that coast was and is known by his *to-name*, or nickname, a device for distinction rendered absolutely necessary by the paucity of surnames occasioned by the persistent intermarriage of the fisher folk. *Partan* is the Scotch for *crab*, but the immediate recipient of the name was one of the gentlest creatures in the place, and hence it had been surmised by some that, the grey mare being the better horse, the man was thus designated from the crabbedness of his wife; but the probability is he brought the agnomen with him from school, where many such apparently misfitting names are unaccountably generated.

In the present case, however, the apologies were not issuing as usual from the mouth of Davy Partan, but from that of the blind piper. Malcolm stood for a moment at the door to understand the matter of contention, and prepare him to interfere judiciously.

"Gien ye suppose, piper, 'at ye're peyed to drive fowk oot o' their beds at sic hoors as yon, it's time the toon cooncil was informed o' yer mistak," said Meg Partan, with emphasis on the last syllable.

"Ta coot peoples up in ta town are not half so hart upon her as you, Mistress Partan," insinuated poor Duncan, who, knowing himself in fault, was humble; "and it's tere tat she's paid," he added, with a bridling motion, "and not town here pelow."

"If you suppose, piper, that you're paid to drive folk out of their beds at such ungodly hours, it's time the town council was informed of your mistake," said Meg Partan, with emphasis on the last syllable.

"Ta coot peoples up in ta town are not half so hart upon her as you, Mistress Partan," insinuated poor Duncan, who, knowing himself in fault, was humble; "and it's tere tat she's paid," he added, with a bridling motion, "and not town here below."

"Dinna ye glorifee yersel' to suppose there's a fisher, lat alane a fisher's wife, in a' the haill Seaton 'at wad lippen till an auld haiveril like you to hae them up i' the mornin'! Haith! I was oot o' my bed hoors or I hard the skirlin' o' *your* pipes. Troth I ken weel hoo muckle ower ear' ye was! But what fowk taks in han', fowk sud put oot o' han' in a proper mainner, and no misguggle 't a'thegither like yon. An' for what they say i' the toon, there's Mistress Catanach—"

"Mistress Catanach is a paad 'oman," said Duncan.

"I wad advise *you*, piper, to haud a quaiet sough about *her*. *She's* no to be meddlet wi', Mistress Catanach, I can tell ye. Gien ye anger her, it'll be the waur for ye. The neist time ye hae a lyin' in,[11] she'll be raxin' ye a hairless pup, or, deed, maybe a stan' o' bagpipes, as the produck."

"Her nain sel' will not pe requiring her sairvices, Mistress Partan; she'll pe leafing tat to you, if you'll excuse me," said Duncan.

"Deed, ye're richt there! An auld speldin' like you! Ha! ha! ha!"

"Don't you be puffed-up, Duncan MacPhail! For as grand as you think yourself, there's not a fisher, let alone a fisher's wife, in the whole Seaton that would trust to an old fool like you to wake them in the morning! Faith! I was out of my bed hours before I heard the skirling of *your* pipes. I know full well how far you were before your time! But what folk take in hand, folk should manage properly, and not make such a hash of as that. And for what they say in the town, there's Mistress Catanach—"

"Mistress Catanach is a baad woman," said Duncan.

"I would advise *you*, piper, to hold your tongue about *her*. *She's* not to be meddled with, Mistress Catanach, I can tell you. If you anger her, it'll be the worse for you. The next time you have a lying-in,[11] she'll leave you a hairless pup, or maybe a stand of bagpipes, as the product."

"Her nain sel' (Her own self) will not be requiring her sairvices, Mistress Partan; she'll be leafing tat to you, if you'll excuse me," said Duncan.

"I believe you there! A dried up old haddock like you! Ha! ha! ha!"

Malcolm judged it time to interfere, and stepped into the cottage. Duncan was seated in the darkest corner of the room, with an apron over his knees, occupied with a tin lamp. He had taken out the wick and laid its flat tube on the hearth, had emptied the oil into a saucer, and was now rubbing the lamp vigorously: cleanliness rather than brightness must have been what he sought to produce.

Malcolm's instinct taught him to side so far with the dame concerning Mrs Catanach, and thereby turn the torrent away from his grandfather.

"Deed ye're richt there, Mistress Findlay" he said. "*She's* no to be meddlet wi'. She's no mowse."

"Indeed, you're right there, Mistress Findlay" he said. "*She's* not to be meddled with. She isn't safe."

Malcolm was a favourite with Meg, as with all the women of the place; hence she did not even start in resentment at

Malcolm was a favourite with Meg, as with all the women of the place; hence she did not even start in resentment at

---

11 LYIN' IN/LYING-IN (archaic): a woman's period of confinement before and after childbirth

his sudden appearance, but, turning to Duncan, exclaimed victoriously,—

"Hear till yer ain oye! He's a laad o' sense!"

"Ay, hear to him!" rejoined the old man with pride. "My Malcolm will always pe speaking tat which will pe worth ta hearing with ta ears. Poth of you and me will be knowing ta Mistress Catanach pretty well—eh, Malcolm, my son? We'll not be trusting her fery too much—will we, my son?"

"No a hair, daddy," returned Malcolm.

"She's a dooms clever wife, though; an' ane 'at ye may lippen till i' the w'y o' her ain callin'," said Meg Partan, whose temper had improved a little under the influence of the handsome youth's presence and cheery speech.

"She'll not pe toubting it," responded Duncan; "put, ach! ta voman 'll be hafing a crim feesage and a fearsome eye!"

Like all the blind, he spoke as if he saw perfectly.

"Weel, I hae hard fowk say 'at ye bude to hae the second sicht," said Mrs Findlay, laughing rudely; "but wow! it stan's ye in sma' service gien that be a' it comes till. She's a guid natur'd, sonsy luikin' wife as ye wad see; an' for her een, they're jist sic likes mine ain.—Haena ye near dune wi' that lamp yet?"

"The week of it 'll pe shust a lettle out of orter," answered the old man. "Ta pairns has been pulling it up with a peen from ta top, and not putting it in at ta hole for ta purpose. And she'll pe thinking you'll be cleaning off ta purnt part with a peen yourself, ma'am, and not with ta pair of scissors she tolt you of, Mistress Partan."

his sudden appearance, but, turning to Duncan, exclaimed victoriously,—

"Hear to your own grandson! He's a lad o' sense!"

"Ay, hear to him!" rejoined the old man with pride. "My Malcolm will always be speaking tat which will be worth ta hearing with ta ears. Both of you and me will be knowing ta Mistress Catanach pretty well—eh, Malcolm, my son? We'll not be trusting her fery too much—will we, my son?"

"Not a hair, daddy," returned Malcolm.

"She's clever as a fox, though; and one that you may trust to in the way of her own calling," said Meg Partan, whose temper had improved a little under the influence of the handsome youth's presence and cheery speech.

"She'll not be toubting it," responded Duncan; "but, ach! ta woman 'll be hafing a grim feesage and a fearsome eye!"

Like all the blind, he spoke as if he saw perfectly.

"Well, I have heard folk say that you must have the second sight," said Mrs Findlay, laughing rudely; "but wow! it stands you in small service if that be all it comes to. She's a good natured, cheerful looking wife as you would see; and for her eyes, they're just such another pair as mine.—Haven't you nearly done with that lamp yet?"

"The wick of it 'll be shust a little out of orter," answered the old man. "Ta chiltren has been pulling it up with a pin from ta top, and not putting it in at ta hole for ta purpose. And she'll be thinking you'll be cleaning off ta burnt part with a pin yourself, ma'am, and not with ta pair of scissors she tolt you of, Mistress Partan."

"Gae 'wa' wi' yer nonsense!" cried Meg. "Daur ye say I dinna ken hoo to trim an uilyie lamp wi' the best blin' piper that ever cam frae the bare-leggit Heelans?"

"A choke's a choke, ma'am," said Duncan, rising with dignity; "put for a laty to make a choke of a man's pare leks is not ta propriety!"

"Oot o' my hoose wi' ye!" screamed the she-Partan. "Wad ye threep upo' me onything I said was less nor proaper? 'At I sud say what wadna stan' the licht as weel's the bare houghs o' ony heelan' rascal 'at ever lap a lawlan' dyke!"

"Hoot toot, Mistress Findlay," interposed Malcolm, as his grandfather strode from the door; "ye maunna forget 'at he's auld an' blin'; an' a' heelan' fowk's some kittle about their legs."

"Deil shochle them!" exclaimed the Partaness; "what care I for 's legs!"

"Go away with your nonsense!" cried Meg. "Dare you say I don't know how to trim an oil lamp with the best blind piper that ever came from the bare-legged Highlands?"

"A choke's a choke, ma'am," said Duncan, rising with dignity; "but for a laty to make a choke of a man's bare leks is not ta propriety!"

"Out of my house with you!" screamed the she-Partan. "Would you tell me to my face that anything I said was less than proper? That I should say what wouldn't stand the light as well as the bare knees of any highland rascal that ever leaped a lowland dyke (wall)!"

"Come, come, Mistress Findlay," interposed Malcolm, as his grandfather strode from the door; "you mustn't forget that he's old and blind; and all highlanders are touchy about their legs."

"Devil shake their bones!" exclaimed the Partaness; "what care I for his legs!"

Duncan had brought the germ of this ministry of light from his native Highlands, where he had practised it in his own house, no one but himself being permitted to clean, or fill, or, indeed, trim the lamp. How first this came about, I do not believe the old man himself knew. But he must have had some feeling of a call to the work; for he had not been a month in Portlossie, before he had installed himself in several families as the genius of their lamps, and he gradually extended the relation until it comprehended almost all the houses in the village.

It was strange and touching to see the sightless man thus busy about light for others. A marvellous symbol of faith he was—not only believing in sight, but in the mysterious, and to him altogether unintelligible means by which others saw! In thus lending his aid to a faculty in which he had no share, he himself followed the trail of the garments of Light, stooping ever and anon to lift and bear her skirts. He haunted the steps of the unknown Power, and flitted about the walls of her temple as we mortals haunt the borders of the immortal land, knowing nothing of what lies behind the unseen veil, yet believing in an unrevealed grandeur. Or shall we say he stood like the forsaken merman, who, having no soul to be saved, yet lingered and listened outside the prayer-echoing church? Only old Duncan had got farther: though he saw not a glimmer of the glory, he yet asserted his part and lot in it, by the aiding of his fellows to that of which he lacked the very conception himself. He was a doorkeeper in the house, yea, by faith the blind man became even a priest in the temple of Light.

Even when his grandchild was the merest baby, he would never allow the gloaming to deepen into night without kindling for his behoof the brightest and cleanest of train-oil-lamps. The women who at first looked in to offer their services, would marvel at the trio of blind man, babe, and burning lamp, and some would expostulate with him on the needless waste. But neither would he listen to their words, nor accept their offered assistance in dressing or undressing the child. The sole manner in which he would consent to avail himself of their willingness to help him, was to leave the baby in charge of this or that neighbour while he went his rounds with the bagpipes: when he went lamp-cleaning he always took him along with him.

By this change of guardians Malcolm was a great gainer, for thus he came to be surreptitiously nursed by a baker's dozen of mothers, who had a fund of not very wicked amusement in the lamentations of the old man over his baby's refusal of nourishment, and his fears that he was pining away. But while they honestly declared that a healthier child had never been seen in Portlossie, they were compelled to conceal the too satisfactory reasons of the child's fastidiousness; for they were persuaded that the truth would only make Duncan terribly jealous, and set him on contriving how at once to play his pipes and carry his baby.

He had certain days for visiting certain houses, and cleaning the lamps in them. The housewives had at first granted him as a privilege the indulgence of his whim, and as such alone had Duncan regarded it; but by and by, when they found their lamps burn so much better from being properly attended to, they began to make him some small return; and at length it became the custom with every housewife who accepted his services, to pay him a halfpenny a week during the winter months for cleaning her lamp. He never asked for it; if payment was omitted, never even hinted at it; received what was given him thankfully; and was regarded with kindness, and, indeed, respect, by all. Even Mrs Partan, as he alone called her, was his true friend: no intensity of friendship could have kept her from scolding. I believe if we could thoroughly dissect the natures of scolding women, we should find them in general not at all so unfriendly as they are unpleasant.

A small trade in oil arose from his connection with the lamps, and was added to the list of his general dealings. The fisher-folk made their own oil, but sometimes it would run short, and then recourse was had to Duncan's little store, prepared by himself of the best; chiefly, now, from the livers of fish caught by his grandson. With so many sources of income, no one wondered at his getting on. Indeed no one would have been surprised to hear, long before Malcolm had begun to earn anything, that the old man had already laid by a trifle.

CHAPTER XV

THE SLOPE OF THE DUNE

Looking at Malcolm's life from the point of his own consciousness, and not from that of the so-called world, it was surely pleasant enough. Innocence, devotion to another, health, pleasant labour with an occasional shadow of danger to arouse the energies, leisure, love of reading, a lofty-minded friend, and, above all, a supreme presence, visible to his heart in the meeting of vaulted sky and outspread sea, and felt at moments in any waking wind that cooled his glowing cheek and breathed into him anew of the breath of life,—lapped in such conditions, bathed in such influences, the youth's heart was swelling like a rosebud ready to burst into blossom.

But he had never yet felt the immediate presence of woman in any of her closer relations. He had never known mother or sister; and, although his voice always assumed a different tone and his manner grew more gentle in the presence of a woman, old or young, he had found little individually attractive amongst the fisher-girls. There was not much in their circumstances to bring out the finer influences of womankind in them: they had rough usage, hard work at the curing and carrying of fish and the drying of nets, little education, and but poor religious instruction. At the same time any failure in what has come to be specially called *virtue*, was all but unknown amongst them; and the profound faith in women, and corresponding worship of everything essential to womanhood which essentially belonged to a nature touched to fine issues, had as yet met with no check. It had never come into Malcolm's thoughts that there were live women capable of impurity. Mrs. Catanach was the only woman he had ever looked upon with dislike—and that dislike had generated no more than the vaguest suspicion. Let a woman's faults be all that he had ever known in woman; he yet could look on her with reverence—and the very heart of reverence is love, whence it may be plainly seen that Malcolm's nature was at once prepared for much delight, and exposed to much suffering. It followed that all the women of his class loved and trusted him; and hence in part it came that, absolutely free of arrogance, he was yet confident in the presence of women. The tradesmen's daughters in the upper town took pains to show him how high above him they were, and women of better position spoke to him with a kind condescension that made him feel the gulf that separated them; but to one and all he spoke with the frankness of manly freedom.

But he had now arrived at that season when, in the order of things, a man is compelled to have at least a glimmer of the life which consists in sharing life with another. When once, through the thousand unknown paths of creation, the human being is so far divided from God that his individuality is secured, it has become yet more needful that the crust gathered around him in the process should be broken; and the love between man and woman arising from a difference deep in the heart of God, and essential to the very being of each—for by no words can I express my scorn of the evil fancy that the distinction between them is solely or even primarily physical—is one of his most powerful forces for blasting the wall of separation, and first step towards the universal harmony of twain making one. That love should be capable of ending in such vermiculate results as too often appear, is no more against the loveliness of the divine idea, than that the forms of man and woman, the spirit gone from them, should degenerate to such things as may not be looked upon. There is no plainer sign of the need of a God, than the possible fate of love. The celestial Cupido may soar aloft on seraph wings that assert his origin, or fall down on the belly of a snake and creep to hell.

But Malcolm was not of the stuff of which coxcombs are made, and had not begun to think even of the abyss that separated Lady Florimel and himself—an abyss like that between star and star, across which stretches no mediating air—a blank and blind space. He felt her presence only as that of a being to be worshipped, to be heard with rapture, and yet addressed without fear.

Though not greatly prejudiced in favour of books, Lady Florimel had burrowed a little in the old library at Lossie House, and had chanced on the Faerie Queene. She had often come upon the name of the author in books of extracts, and now, turning over its leaves, she found her own. Indeed, where else could her mother have found the name *Florimel?* Her curiosity was roused, and she resolved—no light undertaking—to read the poem through, and see who and what the lady, Florimel, was. Notwithstanding the difficulty she met with at first, she had persevered, and by this time it had become easy enough. The copy she had found was in small volumes, of which she now carried one about with her wherever she wandered; and making her first acquaintance with the sea and the poem together, she soon came to fancy that she could not fix her attention on the book without the sound of the waves for an accompaniment to the verse—although the gentler noise of an ever flowing stream would have better suited the nature of Spenser's rhythm; for indeed, he had composed the greater part of the poem with such a sound in his ears, and there are indications in the poem itself that he consciously took the river as his chosen analogue after which to model the flow of his verse.

It was a sultry afternoon, and Florimel lay on the seaward side of the dune, buried in her book. The sky was foggy with heat, and the sea lay dull, as if oppressed by the superincumbent air, and leaden in hue, as if its colour had been destroyed by the sun. The tide was rising slowly, with a muffled and sleepy murmur on the sand; for here were no pebbles to impart a hiss to the wave as it rushed up the bank, or to go softly hurtling down the slope with it as it sank. As she read, Malcolm was walking towards her along the top of the dune, but not until he came almost above where she lay, did she hear his step in the soft quenching sand.

She nodded kindly, and he descended approaching her.

"Did ye want me, my leddy?" he asked.

"No," she answered.

"I wasna sure whether ye noddit 'cause ye wantit me or no," said Malcolm, and turned to reascend the dune.

"Where are you going now?" she asked.

"Ow! nae gait in particlar. I jist cam oot to see hoo things war luikin."

"What things?"

"Ow! jist the lift, an' the sea, an' sic generals."

That Malcolm's delight in the presences of Nature—I say *presences*, as distinguished from forms and colours and all analyzed sources of her influences—should have already become a conscious thing to himself requires to account for it the fact that his master, Graham, was already under the influences of Wordsworth, whom he had hailed as a Crabbe that had burst his shell and spread the wings of an eagle: the virtue passed from him to his pupil.

"I won't detain you from such important business," said Lady Florimel, and dropped her eyes on her book.

"Gien ye want my company, my leddy, I can luik aboot me jist as weel here as ony ither gait," said Malcolm.

"Did you want me, my lady?" he asked.

"No," she answered.

"I wasn't sure if you nodded because you wanted me or not," said Malcolm, and turned to reascend the dune.

"Where are you going now?" she asked.

"Oh! nowhere in particular. I just came out to see how things were looking."

"What things?"

"Oh! just the sky and the sea, and the world in general."

That Malcolm's delight in the presences of Nature—I say *presences*, as distinguished from forms and colours and all analyzed sources of her influences—should have already become a conscious thing to himself requires to account for it the fact that his master, Graham, was already under the influences of Wordsworth, whom he had hailed as a Crabbe that had burst his shell and spread the wings of an eagle: the virtue passed from him to his pupil.

"I won't detain you from such important business," said Lady Florimel, and dropped her eyes on her book.

"If you want my company, my lady, I can look about me just as well here as anywhere else," said Malcolm.

And as he spoke, he gently stretched himself on the dune, about three yards aside and lower down. Florimel looked half amused and half annoyed, but she had brought it on herself, and would punish him only by dropping her eyes again on her book, and keeping silent. She had come to the Florimel of snow.

Malcolm lay and looked at her for a few moments pondering; then fancying he had found the cause of her offence, rose, and, passing to the other side of her, again lay down, but at a still more respectful distance.

"Why do you move?" she asked, without looking up.

"'Cause there's jist a possible air o' win' frae the nor'east."

"And you want me to shelter you from it?" said Lady Florimel.

"Na, na, my leddy," returned Malcolm, laughing; "for as bonny's ye are, ye wad be but sma' scoug."

"Why did you move, then?" persisted the girl, who understood what he said just about half.

"Weel, my leddy, ye see it's het, an' I'm aye amang the fish mair or less, an' I didna ken 'at I was to hae the honour o' sittin' doon aside ye; sae I thocht ye was maybe smellin' the fish. It's healthy eneuch, but some fowk disna like it; an' for a' that I ken, you gran' fowk's senses may be mair ready to scunner than oors. 'Deed, my leddy, we wadna need to be particlar, whiles, or it wad be the waur for 's."

"Why do you move?" she asked, without looking up.

"Because there's just a possible air of wind from the northeast."

"And you want me to shelter you from it?" said Lady Florimel.

"Na, na, my lady," returned Malcolm, laughing; "for as bonny as you are, you'd be but small shelter."

"Why did you move, then?" persisted the girl, who understood what he said just about half.

"Well, my lady, you see it's hot, and I'm always more or less among the fish, and I didn't know I'd be having the honour of sitting down beside you; so I thought you were maybe smelling the fish. It's healthy enough, but some folk don't like it; and for all that I know, you grand folk's senses may be more ready to take offence than ours. Indeed, my lady, we can't afford to be particular, at times, or it would be the worse for us."

Simple as it was, the explanation served to restore her equanimity, disturbed by what had seemed his presumption in lying down in her presence: she saw that she had mistaken the action. The fact was, that, concluding from her behaviour she had something to say to him, but was not yet at leisure for him, he had lain down, as a loving dog might, to await her time. It was devotion, not coolness. To remain standing before her would have seemed a demand on her attention; to lie down was to withdraw and wait. But Florimel, although pleased, was only the more inclined to torment—a peculiarity of disposition which she inherited from her father: she bowed her face once more over her book, and read through three whole stanzas, without however understanding a single phrase in them, before she spoke. Then looking up, and regarding for a moment the youth who lay watching her with the eyes of the servants in the psalm, she said,—

"Well? What are you waiting for?"

"I thocht ye wantit me, my leddy! I beg yer pardon," answered Malcolm, springing to his feet, and turning to go.

"Do you ever read?" she asked.

"Well? What are you waiting for?"

"I thought you wanted me, my lady! I beg your pardon," answered Malcolm, springing to his feet, and turning to go.

"Do you ever read?" she asked.

"Aften that," replied Malcolm, turning again, and standing stock still. "An' I like best to read jist as yer leddyship's readin' the noo, lyin' o' the san'-hill, wi' the haill sea afore me, an naething atween me an' the icebergs but the watter an' the stars an' a wheen islands. It's like readin' wi' fower een, that!"

"And what do you read on such occasions?" carelessly drawled his persecutor.

"Whiles ae thing an' whiles anither—whiles onything I can lay my han's upo'. I like traivels an' sic like weel eneuch; an' history, gien it be na ower dry like. I div *not* like sermons, an' there's mair o' them in Portlossie than onything ither. Mr Graham—that's the schoolmaister—has a gran' libbrary, but it's maist Laitin an' Greek, an' though I like the Laitin weel, it's no what I wad read i' the face o' the sea. When ye're in dreid o' wantin' a dictionar', that spiles a'."

"Can you read Latin then?"

"Ay: what for no, my leddy? I can read Virgil middlin'; an' Horace's *Ars Poetica*, the whilk Mr Graham says is no its richt name ava, but jist *Epistola ad Pisones*; for gien they bude to gie 't anither it sud ha' been *Ars Dramatica*. But leddies dinna care aboot sic things."

"You gentlemen give us no chance. You won't teach us."

"Noo, my leddy, dinna begin to mak' ghem o' me, like my lord. I cud ill bide it frae him, an' gien ye tak till 't as weel, I maun jist haud oot o' yer gait. I'm nae gentleman, an' hae ower muckle respeck for what becomes a gentleman to be pleased at bein' ca'd ane. But as for the Laitin, I'll be prood to instruck yer leddyship whan ye please."

"Ay, often," replied Malcolm, turning again, and standing stock still. "And I like best to read just as your ladyship's reading now, lying on the sand-hill, with the whole sea before me, and nothing between me and the icebergs but the water and the stars and a few islands. It's like reading with four eyes, that!"

"And what do you read on such occasions?" carelessly drawled his persecutor.

"Sometimes one thing and sometimes another—sometimes anything I can lay my hands upon. I like travels and suchlike well enough; and history, if it's not too dry. I *don't* like sermons, and there's more of them in Portlossie than anything else. Mr Graham—that's the schoolmaster—has a grand library, but it's mostly Latin and Greek, and though I'm fond of the Latin, it's not what I would read in the face of the sea. When you're in dread of needing a dictionary, that spoils all."

"Can you read Latin then?"

"Ay: why not, my lady? I can read Virgil fairly well; and Horace's *Ars Poetica*, which Mr Graham says is not its right name at all, but just *Epistola ad Pisones*; for if they have to give it another it should have been *Ars Dramatica*. But ladies don't care about such things."

"You gentlemen give us no chance. You won't teach us."

"Now, my lady, don't start making game of me, like my lord. I could scarce stand it from him, and if you take to it as well, I'll be forced to steer clear of you. I'm no gentleman, and have too much respect for what becomes a gentleman to be pleased at being called one. But as for the Latin, I'll be proud to instruct your ladyship when you please."

"I'm afraid I've no great wish to learn," said Florimel.

"I daur say no," said Malcolm quietly, and again addressed himself to go.

"Do you like novels?" asked the girl.

"I never saw a novelle. There's no ane amo' a' Mr Graham's buiks, an' I s' warran' there's full twa hunner o' *them*. I dinna believe there's a single novelle in a' Portlossie."

"Don't be too sure: there are a good many in our library."

"I hadna the presumption, my leddy, to coont the Hoose in Portlossie—Ye'll hae a sicht o' buiks up there, no?"

"Have you never been in the library?"

"I never set fut i' the hoose—'cep' i' the kitchie, an' ance or twise steppin' across the ha' frae the ae door to the tither. I wad fain see what kin' o' a place great fowk like you bides in, an' what kin' o' things, buiks an' a', ye hae aboot ye. It's no easy for the like o' huz 'at has but a but an' a ben, to unnerstan' hoo ye fill sic a muckle place as yon. I wad be aye i' the libbrary, I think. But," he went on, glancing involuntarily at the dainty little foot that peered from under her dress, "yer leddyship's sae licht-fittit, ye'll be ower the haill dwallin', like a wee bird in a muckle cage. Whan I want room, I like it wantin' wa's." Once more he was on the point of going, but once more a word detained him.

"Do you ever read poetry?"

"Ay, sometimes—whan it's auld."

"One would think you were talking about wine! Does age improve poetry as well?"

"I'm afraid I've no great wish to learn," said Florimel.

"I dare say not," said Malcolm quietly, and again addressed himself to go.

"Do you like novels?" asked the girl.

"I never saw a novelle. There's not one among all Mr Graham's books, and I'll wager he has a good two hundred of *them*. I don't believe there's a single novelle in all Portlossie."

"Don't be too sure: there are a good many in our library."

"I hadn't the presumption, my lady, to count the House in Portlossie—You'll doubtless have piles of books up there?"

"Have you never been in the library?"

"I never set foot in the house—except in the kitchen, and once or twice the hall, stepping across from one door to the other. I would fain see what kind of a place great folk like you live in, and what kind of things, books and all, you have about you. It's not easy for the likes of us that have but a but an' ben *(outer and inner room)* to understand how you fill such a great place as that. I'd never be out of the library, I think. But," he went on, glancing involuntarily at the dainty little foot that peered from under her dress, "Your ladyship's so light-footed, you'll be over the whole dwelling, like a wee bird in a big cage. When I want room, I like it without walls." Once more he was on the point of going, but once more a word detained him.

"Do you ever read poetry?"

"Ay, sometimes—when it's old."

"One would think you were talking about wine! Does age improve poetry as well?"

"I ken naething aboot wine, my leddy. Miss Horn gae me a glaiss the ither day, an' it tastit weel, but whether it was *merum* or *mixtum,* I couldna tell mair nor a haddick. Doobtless age does gar poetry smack a wee better; but I said *auld* only 'cause there's sae little new poetry that I care aboot comes my gait. Mr Graham's unco ta'en wi' Maister Wordsworth—no an ill name for a poet; do ye ken onything aboot *him,* my leddy?"

"I never heard of him."

"I wadna gie an auld Scots ballant for a barrowfu' o' his. There's gran' bits here an' there, nae doobt, but it 's ower mim mou'ed for me."

"What do you mean by that?"

"It's ower saft an' sliddery like i' yer mou', my leddy."

"What sort do you like then?"

"I like Milton weel. Ye get a fine mou'fu' o' *him.* I dinna like the verse 'at ye can murle oot atween yer lips an' yer teeth. I like the verse 'at ye maun open yer mou' weel to lat gang. Syne it 's worth yer while, whether ye unnerstan' 't or no."

"I don't see how you can say that."

"Jist hear, my leddy! Here's a bit I cam upo' last nicht:

"I know nothing about wine, my lady. Miss Horn gave me a glass the other day, and it tasted well, but whether it was *merum* or *mixtum,* I couldn't tell more than a haddock. Doubtless age does give poetry a little more flavour; but I said *old* only because I see so little new poetry that I care about. Mr Graham's fairly taken with Mister Wordsworth—not a bad name for a poet; do you know anything about *him,* my lady?"

"I never heard of him."

"I wouldn't give an old Scots ballad for a barrowful of his. There's grand bits here and there, no doubt, but it's too *mim mou'ed* for me."

"What do you mean by that?"

"It's too soft and slithery in your mouth, my lady."

"What sort do you like then?"

"I like Milton well. You get a fine mouthful of *him.* I don't like the verse that you can crumble out between your lips and your teeth. I like the verse that you have to open your mouth wide for. Then it's worth your while, whether you understand it or not."

"I don't see how you can say that."

"Just hear, my lady! Here's a bit I came upon last night:

...His volant touch,
Instinct through all proportions, low and high,
Fled and pursued transverse the resonant fugue.

Hear till 't! It's gran'—even though ye dinna ken what it means a bit."

"I do know what it means," said Florimel. "Let me see: *volant* means—what does *volant* mean?"

"It means *fleein',* I suppose."

"Well, he means some musician or other."

Hear to it! It's grand—even though you don't know what it means a bit."

"I do know what it means," said Florimel. "Let me see: *volant* means—what does *volant* mean?"

"It means *flying,* I suppose."

"Well, he means some musician or other."

"Of coorse: it maun be Jubal[12]—I ken a' the words but *fugue*; though I canna tell what business *instinct* an' *proportions* hae there."

"It's describing how the man's fingers, playing a fugue—on the organ, I suppose,—"

"A *fugue* 'll be some kin' o' a tune, than? That casts a heap o' licht on't, my leddy—I never saw an organ: what is 't like?"

"Something like a pianoforte."

"But I never saw ane o' them either. It's ill makin' things a'thegither oot o' yer ain heid."

"Well, it's played with the fingers—like this," said Florimel. "And the fugue is a kind of piece where one part pursues the other,—"

"An' syne," cried Malcolm eagerly, "that ane turns roon' an' rins efter the first;—that 'll be *'fled and pursued transverse.'* I hae't! I hae't! See, my leddy, what it is to hae sic schoolin', wi' music an' a'! The *proportions*—that's the relation o' the notes to ane anither; an' *fugue*—that comes frae *fugere to flee* — *'fled* and pursued transverse the resonant fugue'—the tane rinnin' efter the tither, roon' an' roon'. Ay, I hae't noo!—*Resonant*—that's *echoing* or *resounding*. But what's *instinct*, my leddy? It maun be an adjective, I'm thinkin'."

Although the modesty of Malcolm had led him to conclude the girl immeasurably his superior in learning because she could tell him what a fugue was, he soon found she could help him no further, for she understood scarcely anything about grammar, and her vocabulary was limited enough. Not a doubt interfered, however, with her acceptance of the imputed superiority; for it is as easy for some to assume as it is for others to yield.

"Of course: it must be Jubal[12]—I know all the words but *fugue*; though I can't tell what business *instinct* and *proportions* have there."

"It's describing how the man's fingers, playing a fugue—on the organ, I suppose,—"

"A *fugue* will be some kind of a tune, then? That casts a heap of light on it, my lady—I never saw an organ: what is it like?"

"Something like a pianoforte."

"But I never saw one of them either. It's not easy making things altogether out of your own head."

"Well, it's played with the fingers—like this," said Florimel. "And the fugue is a kind of piece where one part pursues the other,—"

"And then," cried Malcolm eagerly, "that one turns round and runs after the first—that'll be *'fled and pursued transverse.'* I have it! I have it! See, my lady, what it is to have such schooling, with music and all! The *proportions*—that's the relation of the notes to one another; and *fugue*—that comes from *fugere to flee*—*'fled* and pursued transverse the resonant fugue'—the one running after the other, round and round. Ay, I have it now!—*Resonant*—that's *echoing* or *resounding*. But what's *instinct*, my lady? It must be an adjective, I'm thinking."

Although the modesty of Malcolm had led him to conclude the girl immeasurably his superior in learning because she could tell him what a fugue was, he soon found she could help him no further, for she understood scarcely anything about grammar, and her vocabulary was limited enough. Not a doubt interfered, however, with her acceptance of the imputed superiority; for it is as easy for some to assume as it is for others to yield.

---

12 JUBAL: "the father of all such as handle the harp and organ." (Genesis 4:21)

"I hae't! It *is* an adjective," cried Malcolm, after a short pause of thought. "It's the *touch* that's *instinct*. But I fancy there sud be a comma efter *instinct*.—His fingers were sae used till 't that they could 'maist do the thing o' themsel's—Isna 't lucky, my leddy, that I thocht o' sayin' 't ower to *you!* I'll read the buik frae the beginnin',—it 's the neist to the last, I think,—jist to come upo' the twa lines i' their ain place, ohn their expeckin' me like, an' see hoo gran' they soon' whan a body unnerstan's them. Thank ye, my leddy."

"I suppose you read Milton to your grandfather?"

"Ay, sometimes—i' the lang forenights."

"What do you mean by the *forenights?*"

"I mean efter it's dark an' afore ye gang to yer bed.—He likes the battles o' the angels best. As sune 's it comes to ony fechtin', up he gets, an' gangs stridin' aboot the flure; an' whiles he maks a claucht at 's claymore; an' faith! ance he maist cawed aff my heid wi' 't, for he had made a mistak aboot whaur I was sittin'."

"What's a *claymore?*"

"A muckle heelan' braidswoord, my leddy. *Clay* frae *gladius* verra likly; an' *more* 's the Gaelic for *great: claymore*, great sword. Blin' as my gran'father is, ye wad sweer he had fochten in 's day, gien ye hard hoo he'll gar 't whurr an' whustle aboot 's heid as gien 't war a bit lath o' wud."

"But that's very dangerous," said Florimel, something aghast at the recital.

"Ow, ay!" assented Malcolm, indifferently,—"Gien ye wad luik in, my leddy, I wad lat ye see his claymore, an' his dirk, an' his skene dhu, an' a'."

"I have it! It *is* an adjective," cried Malcolm, after a short pause of thought. "It's the *touch* that's *instinct*. But I fancy there should be a comma after *instinct*.—His fingers were so used to it that they could all but do the thing of themselves—isn't it lucky, my lady, that I thought of saying it over to *you!* I'll read the book from the beginning—it's the second last one, I think—just to come upon the two lines in their own place, as if to surprise them, and see how they sound when a body understands them. Thank you, my lady."

"I suppose you read Milton to your grandfather?"

"Ay, sometimes—in the long forenights."

"What do you mean by the *forenights?*"

"I mean after it's dark and before you go to your bed.—He likes the battles of the angels best. As soon as it comes to any fighting, up he gets, and goes striding about the floor; and sometimes he makes a grab at his claymore; and faith! once he nearly lopped my head off with it, for he had misjudged where I was sitting."

"What's a *claymore?*"

"A big highland broadsword, my lady. *Clay* from *gladius* very likely; and *more's* the Gaelic for *great: claymore*, great sword. Blind as my grandfather is, you would swear he had fought in his day, if you heard how he'll make it whirr and whistle about his head as if it were a mere lath of wood."

"But that's very dangerous," said Florimel, something aghast at the recital.

"Oh, ay!" assented Malcolm, indifferently,— "If you would look in, my lady, I would let you see his claymore, and his dirk, and his skene dhu, and all."

"I don't think I could venture. He's too dreadful! I should be terrified at him."

"Dreidfu' my leddy? He's the quaietest, kin'liest auld man! that is, providit ye say naething *for* a Cawmill, or *agen* ony ither hielanman. Ye see he comes o' Glenco, an' the Cawmills are jist a hate till him—specially Cawmill o' Glenlyon, wha was the warst o' them a'. Ye sud hear him tell the story till 's pipes, my leddy! It's gran' to hear him! An' the poetry a' his ain!"

"I don't think I could venture. He's too dreadful! I should be terrified at him."

"Dreadful, my lady? He's the quietest, kindliest old man! that is, provided you say nothing *for* a Campbell, or *against* any other highlandman. You see he comes of Glencoe, and he loathes the Campbells—especially Campbell of Glenlyon, who was the worst of them all. You should hear him tell the story to his pipes, my lady! It's grand to hear him! And the poetry all his own!"

CHAPTER XVI

THE STORM

There came a blinding flash, and a roar through the leaden air, followed by heavy drops mixed with huge hailstones. At the flash, Florimel gave a cry and half rose to her feet, but at the thunder, fell as if stunned by the noise, on the sand. As if with a bound, Malcolm was by her side, but when she perceived his terror, she smiled, and laying hold of his hand, sprung to her feet.

"Come, come," she cried; and still holding his hand, hurried up the dune, and down the other side of it. Malcolm accompanied her step for step, strongly tempted, however, to snatch her up, and run for the bored craig: he could not think why she made for the road—high on an unscalable embankment, with the park wall on the other side. But she ran straight for a door in the embankment itself, dark between two buttresses, which, never having seen it open, he had not thought of. For a moment she stood panting before it, while with trembling hand she put a key in the lock; the next she pushed open the creaking door and entered. As she turned to take out the key, she saw Malcolm yards away in the middle of the road and in a cataract of rain, which seemed to have with difficulty suspended itself only until the lady should be under cover. He stood with his bonnet in his hand, watching for a farewell glance.

"Why don't you come in?" she said impatiently.

He was beside her in a moment.

"I didna ken ye wad lat me in," he said.

"I wouldn't have you drowned," she returned, shutting the door.

"Droont!" he repeated, "It wad tak a hantle to droon me. I stack to the boddom o' a whumled boat a haill nicht whan I was but fifeteen."

They stood in a tunnel which passed under the road, affording immediate communication between the park and the shore. The further end of it was dark with trees. The upper half of the door by which they had entered was a wooden grating, for the admission of light, and through it they were now gazing, though they could see little but the straight lines of almost perpendicular rain that scratched out the colours of the landscape. The sea was troubled, although no wind blew; it heaved as with an inward unrest. But suddenly there was a great broken sound somewhere in the air; and the next moment a storm came tearing over the face of the sea, covering it with blackness innumerably rent into spots of white. Presently it struck the shore, and a great rude blast came roaring through the grating, carrying with it a sheet of rain, and, catching Florimel's hair, sent it streaming wildly out behind her.

"Dinna ye think, my leddy," said Malcolm, "ye had better mak for the hoose? What wi' the win' an' the weet thegither, ye'll be gettin' yer deith o' cauld. I s' gang wi' ye sae far, gien ye'll alloo me, jist to haud it ohn blawn ye awa'."	"Don't you think, my lady," said Malcolm, "you had better make for the house? What with the wind and the wet together, you'll be getting your death of cold. I'll go with you so far, if you'll allow me, just to keep it from blowing you away."
The wind suddenly fell, and his last words echoed loud in the vaulted sky. For a moment it grew darker in the silence, and then a great flash carried the world away with it, and left nothing but blackness behind. A roar of thunder followed, and even while it yet bellowed, a white face flitted athwart the grating, and a voice of agony shrieked aloud:	The wind suddenly fell, and his last words echoed loud in the vaulted sky. For a moment it grew darker in the silence, and then a great flash carried the world away with it, and left nothing but blackness behind. A roar of thunder followed, and even while it yet bellowed, a white face flitted athwart the grating, and a voice of agony shrieked aloud:
"I dinna ken whaur it comes frae!"	"I don't know where it comes from!"

Florimel grasped Malcolm's arm: the face had passed close to hers—only the grating between, and the cry cut through the thunder like a knife.

Instinctively, almost unconsciously, he threw his arm around her, to shield her from her own terror.

"Dinna be fleyt, my leddy," he said. "It's naething but the mad laird. He's a quaiet cratur eneuch, only he disna ken whaur he comes frae—he disna ken whaur onything comes frae—an' he canna bide it. But he wadna hurt leevin' cratur, the laird."	"Don't be frightened, my lady," he said. "It's nothing but the mad laird. He's a quiet enough sort, only he doesn't know where he comes from—he doesn't know where anything comes from—and he can't stand it. But he wouldn't hurt a soul, the laird."
"What a dreadful face!" said the girl, shuddering.	"What a dreadful face!" said the girl, shuddering.
"It's no an ill-faured face," said Malcolm, "only the storm's frichtit him by ord'nar, an' it 's unco ghaistly the noo."	"It's not an ill-favoured one," said Malcolm, "only the storm's given him a dreadful fright, and it's very ghostly just now."
"Is there nothing to be done for him?" she said compassionately.	"Is there nothing to be done for him?" she said compassionately.

"No upo' this side the grave, I doobt, my leddy," answered Malcolm.

Here coming to herself the girl became aware of her support, and laid her hand on Malcolm's to remove his arm. He obeyed instantly, and she said nothing.

"There was some speech," he went on hurriedly, with a quaver in his voice, "o' pittin' him intill the asylum at Aberdeen, an' no lattin' him scoor the queentry this gait, they said; but it wad hae been sheer cruelty, for the cratur likes naething sae weel as rinnin' aboot, an' does no' mainner o' hurt. A verra bairn can guide him. An' he has jist as guid a richt to the leeberty God gies him as ony man alive, an' mair nor a hantle."

"Is nothing known about him?"

"A' thing's known aboot him, my leddy, 'at 's known aboot the lave o' 's. His father was the laird o' Gersefell—an' for that maitter he's laird himsel' noo. But they say he's taen sic a scunner at his mither, that he canna bide the verra word o' *mither*; he jist cries oot whan he hears 't."

"It seems clearing," said Florimel.

"I doobt it 's only haudin' up for a wee," returned Malcolm, after surveying as much of the sky as was visible through the bars; "but I do think ye had better run for the hoose, my leddy. I s' jist follow ye, a feow yairds ahin', till I see ye safe. Dinna ye be feared—I s' tak guid care: I wadna hae ye seen i' the company o' a fisher-lad like me."

"Not on this side of the grave, I expect, my lady," answered Malcolm.

Here coming to herself the girl became aware of her support, and laid her hand on Malcolm's to remove his arm. He obeyed instantly, and she said nothing.

"There was some talk," he went on hurriedly, with a quaver in his voice, "of putting him into the asylum at Aberdeen, and not letting him scour the country this way, they said; but it would have been sheer cruelty, for the laird likes nothing so well as running about, and does no manner of hurt. A very child can manage him. And he has just as good a right to the liberty God gives him as any man alive, and more than many."

"Is nothing known about him?"

"Everything's known about him, my lady, that's known about the rest of us. His father was the laird of Gersefell—and for that matter he's laird himself now. But they say he's taken such a horror at his mother, that he can't stand the very word of *mother*; he just cries out when he hears it."

"It seems clearing," said Florimel.

"I expect it's only holding up for a bit," returned Malcolm, after surveying as much of the sky as was visible through the bars; "but I do think you had better run for the house, my lady. I'll just follow you, a few yards behind, till I see you safe. Never fear—I'll be careful: I wouldn't have you seen in the company of a fisher-lad like me."

There was no doubting the perfect simplicity with which this was said, and the girl took no exception. They left the tunnel, and skirting the bottom of the little hill on which stood the temple of the winds, were presently in the midst of a young wood, through which a gravelled path led towards the House. But they had not gone far ere a blast of wind, more violent than any that had preceded it, smote the wood, and the trees, young larches and birches and sycamores, bent streaming before it. Lady Florimel turned to see where Malcolm was, and her hair went from her like a Maenad's, while her garments flew fluttering and straining, as if struggling to carry her off. She had never in her life before been out in a storm, and she found the battle joyously exciting. The roaring of the wind in the trees was grand; and what seemed their terrified struggles while they bowed and writhed and rose but to bow again, as in mad effort to unfix their earthbound roots and escape, took such sympathetic hold of her imagination, that she flung out her arms, and began to dance and whirl as if herself the genius of the storm. Malcolm, who had been some thirty paces behind, was with her in a moment.

"Isn't it splendid?" she cried.

"It blaws weel—verra near as weel 's my daddy," said Malcolm, enjoying it quite as much as the girl.

"How dare you make game of such a grand uproar?" said Florimel with superiority.

"Mak ghem o' a blast o' win' by comparin' 't to my gran'father!" exclaimed Malcolm. "Hoot, my leddy! It's a coamplement to the biggest blast 'at ever blew to be compairt till an auld man like *him*. I'm ower used to them to min' them muckle mysel', 'cep' to fecht wi' them. But whan I watch the seagoos dartin' like arrowheids throu' the win', I sometimes think it maun be gran' for the angels to caw aboot great flags o' wings in a mortal warstle wi' sic a hurricane as this."

"I don't understand you one bit," said Lady Florimel petulantly.

As she spoke, she went on, but, the blast having abated, Malcolm lingered, to place a proper distance between them.

"You needn't keep so far behind," said Florimel, looking back.

"As yer leddyship pleases," answered Malcolm, and was at once by her side. "I'll gang till ye tell me to stan'.—Eh, sae different 's ye look frae the ither mornin'!"

"What morning?"

"Whan ye was sittin' at the fut o' the bored craig."

"Isn't it splendid?" she cried.

"It blows well—very near as well as my daddy," said Malcolm, enjoying it quite as much as the girl.

"How dare you make game of such a grand uproar?" said Florimel with superiority.

"Make game of a blast of wind by comparing it to my grandfather!" exclaimed Malcolm. "Heavens, my lady! it's a compliment to the biggest blast that ever blew to be compared to an old man like *him*. I'm too used to them to mind them much myself, except to fight with them. But when I watch the seagulls darting like arrowheads through the wind, I sometimes think it must be grand for the angels to drive about great flags of wings in a mortal struggle with such a tempest."

"I don't understand you one bit," said Lady Florimel petulantly.

As she spoke, she went on, but, the blast having abated, Malcolm lingered, to place a proper distance between them.

"You needn't keep so far behind," said Florimel, looking back.

"As your ladyship pleases," answered Malcolm, and was at once by her side. "I'll go till you tell me to stand.—Eh, so different as you look from the other morning!"

"What morning?"

"When you were sitting at the foot of the bored craig."

"*Bored craig!* What's that?"

"The rock wi' a hole throu' 'it. Ye ken the rock weel eneuch, my leddy. Ye was sittin' at the fut o' 't, readin' yer buik, as white 's gien ye had been made o' snaw. It cam to me that the rock was the sepulchre, the hole the open door o' 't, an' yersel' ane o' the angels that had faulded his wings an' was waitin' for somebody to tell the guid news till, that he was up an awa'."

"And what do I look like today?" she asked.

"Ow! the day, ye luik like some cratur o' the storm; or the storm itsel' takin' a leevin' shape, an' the bonniest it could; or maybe, like Ahriel, gaein' afore the win', wi' the blast in 's feathers, rufflin' them a' gaits at ance."

"Who's Ahriel?"

"Ow, the fleein' cratur i' the Tempest! But in your bonny southern speech, I daursay ye wad ca' him—or her, I dinna ken whilk the cratur was—ye wad ca' 't Ayriel?"

"I don't know anything about him or her or it," said Lady Florimel.

"Ye'll hae a' aboot him up i' the libbrary there though," said Malcolm. "The Tempest's the only ane o' Shakspere's plays 'at I hae read, but it 's a gran' ane, as Maister Graham has empooered me to see."

"Oh, dear!" exclaimed Florimel, "I've lost my book!"

"I'll gang back an' luik for 't this meenute, my leddy," said Malcolm. "I ken ilka fit o' the road we've come, an' it 's no possible but I fa' in wi' 't.—Ye'll sune be hame noo, an' it'll hardly be on again afore ye win in," he added, looking up at the clouds.

"But how am I to get it? I want it very much."

"*Bored craig!* What's that?"

"The rock with a hole through it. You know the rock well enough, my lady. You were sitting at the foot of it, reading your book, as white as if you had been made of snow. It came to me that the rock was the sepulchre, the hole the open door of it, and you one of the angels that had folded his wings and was waiting for somebody to tell the good news to, that he was up and away."

"And what do I look like today?" she asked.

"Oh! today, you look like some creature of the storm; or the storm itself taking a living shape, and the bonniest it could; or maybe, like Ahriel, going before the wind, with the blast in his feathers, ruffling them every way at once."

"Who's Ahriel?"

"Oh, the flying creature in the Tempest! But in your bonny southern speech, I daresay you would call him—or her, I don't know which the creature was—you would call it Ayriel?"

"I don't know anything about him or her or it," said Lady Florimel.

"You'll have it all up in the library there though," said Malcolm. "The Tempest's the only one of Shakespeare's plays that I've read, but it's a grand one, as Mister Graham has shown me."

"Oh, dear!" exclaimed Florimel, "I've lost my book!"

"I'll go back and look for it this minute, my lady," said Malcolm. "I know every foot of the way we've come, and I can't help but fall in with it.—You'll soon be home now, and it'll hardly be on again before you're indoors," he added, looking up at the clouds.

"But how am I to get it? I want it very much."

"I'll jest fess 't up to the Hoose, an' say 'at I fan' 't whaur I will fin' 't. But I wiss ye wad len' me yer pocket nepkin to row 't in, for I'm feared for blaudin' 't afore I get it back to ye."

"I'll just bring it up to the House, and say that I found it wherever I do find it. But I wish you would lend me your pocket napkin to wrap it in, for I'm afraid of spoiling it before I get it back to you."

Florimel gave him her handkerchief, and Malcolm took his leave, saying.—"I'll be up i' the coorse o' a half-hoor at farthest."

Florimel gave him her handkerchief, and Malcolm took his leave, saying— "I'll be up in the course of half an hour at the farthest."

The humble devotion and absolute service of the youth, resembling that of a noble dog, however unlikely to move admiration in Lady Florimel's heart, could not fail to give her a quiet and welcome pleasure. He was an inferior who could be depended upon, and his worship was acceptable. Not a fear of his attentions becoming troublesome ever crossed her mind. The wider and more impassable the distinctions of rank, the more possible they make it for artificial minds to enter into simply human relations; the easier for the oneness of the race to assert itself, in the offering and acceptance of a devoted service. There is more of the genuine human in the relationship between some men and their servants, than between those men and their own sons.

With eyes intent, and keen as those of a gazehound, Malcolm retraced every step, up to the grated door. But no volume was to be seen. Turning from the door of the tunnel, for which he had no *Sesame*, he climbed to the foot of the wall that crossed it above, and with a bound, a clutch at the top, a pull and a scramble, was in the high road in a moment. From the road to the links was an easy drop, where, starting from the grated door, he retraced their path from the dune. Lady Florimel had dropped the book when she rose, and Malcolm found it lying on the sand, little the worse. He wrapped it in its owner's handkerchief, and set out for the gate at the mouth of the river.

As he came up to it, the keeper, an ill-conditioned snarling fellow, who, in the phrase of the Seaton folk, "rade on the riggin o' 's authority," (rode on the ridge of his authority) rushed out of the lodge, and just as Malcolm was entering, shoved the gate in his face.

"Ye comena in wi'oot the leave o' me," he cried, with a vengeful expression.

"You don't come in without my leave," he cried, with a vengeful expression.

"What's that for?" said Malcolm, who had already interposed his great boot, so that the spring-bolt could not reach its catch.

"What's that for?" said Malcolm, who had already interposed his great boot, so that the spring-bolt could not reach its catch.

"There s' nae lan'-loupin' rascals come in here," said Bykes, setting his shoulder to the gate.

"There's no vagabonds shall come in here," said Bykes, setting his shoulder to the gate.

That instant he went staggering back to the wall of the lodge, with the gate after him.

That instant he went staggering back to the wall of the lodge, with the gate after him.

"Stick to the wa' there," said Malcolm, as he strode in.

"Stick to the wall there," said Malcolm, as he strode in.

The keeper pursued him with frantic abuse, but he never turned his head. Arrived at the House, he committed the volume to the cook, with a brief account of where he had picked it up, begging her to inquire whether it belonged to the House. The cook sent a maid with it to Lady Florimel, and Malcolm waited until she returned—with thanks and a half-crown. He took the money, and returned by the upper gate through the town.

CHAPTER XVII

THE ACCUSATION

The next morning, soon after their early breakfast, the gate keeper stood in the door of Duncan MacPhail's cottage, with a verbal summons for Malcolm to appear before his lordship.

"An' I'm no to lowse sicht o' ye till ye hae put in yer appearance," he added; "sae gien ye dinna come peaceable, I maun gar ye."

"And I'm not to lose sight of you till you've put in your appearance," he added; "so if you don't come quietly, I must force you."

"Whaur's yer warrant?" asked Malcolm coolly.

"Where's your warrant?" asked Malcolm coolly.

"Ye wad hae the impidence to deman' my warrant, ye young sorner!" cried Bykes indignantly. "Come yer wa's, my man, or I s' gar ye smairt for 't."

"You would have the impudence to demand my warrant, you young beggar!" cried Bykes indignantly. "Come with me, my man, or I shall make you smart for it."

"Haud a quaiet sough, an' gang hame for yer warrant," said Malcolm. "It's lyin' there, doobtless, or ye wadna hae daured to shaw yer face on sic an eeran'."

"Hold your tongue, and go home for your warrant," said Malcolm. "It's lying there, doubtless, or you wouldn't have dared to show your face on such an errand."

Duncan, who was dozing in his chair, awoke at the sound of high words. His jealous affection perceived at once that Malcolm was being insulted. He sprang to his feet, stepped swiftly to the wall, caught down his broadsword, and rushed to the door, making the huge weapon quiver and whir about his head as if it had been a slip of tin plate.

"Where is ta rascal?" he shouted. "She'll cut him town! Show her ta lowlan' thief! She'll cut him town! Who'll be insulting her Malcolm?"

"Where is ta rascal?" he shouted. "She'll cut him town! Show her ta lowlan' thief! She'll cut him town! Who'll be insulting her Malcolm?"

But Bykes, at first sight of the weapon, had vanished in dismay.

But Bykes, at first sight of the weapon, had vanished in dismay.

"Hoot toot, daddy," said Malcolm, taking him by the arm; "there's naebody here. The puir cratur couldna bide the sough o' the claymore. He fled like the autumn wind over the stubble. There's Ossian for't."

"Ta Lord pe praised!" cried Duncan. "She'll be confounded her foes. But what would ta rascal pe wanting, my son?"

Leading him back to his chair, Malcolm told him as much as he knew of the matter.

"Ton't you co for *no* warrant," said Duncan. "If my lort marquis will pe senting for you as one chentleman sends for another, *then* you co."

Within an hour Bykes reappeared, accompanied by one of the gamekeepers— an Englishman. The moment he heard the door open, Duncan caught again at his broadsword.

"We want you, my young man," said the gamekeeper, standing on the threshold, with Bykes peeping over his shoulder, in an attitude indicating one foot already lifted to run.

"What for?"

"That's as may appear."

"Whaur's yer warrant?"

"There."

"Lay 't doon o' the table, an' gang back to the door, till I get a sklent at it," said Malcolm. "Ye're an honest man, Wull—but I wadna lippen a snuff-mull 'at had mair nor ae pinch intill 't wi' yon cooard cratur ahin' ye."

He was afraid of the possible consequences of his grandfather's indignation.

"Come, come, daddy," said Malcolm, taking him by the arm; "there's nobody here. The poor fellow couldn't stand the whirr of the claymore. He fled like the autumn wind over the stubble. There's Ossian for it."

"Ta Lord be praised!" cried Duncan. "She'll be confounded her foes. But what would ta rascal be wanting, my son?"

Leading him back to his chair, Malcolm told him as much as he knew of the matter.

"Ton't you co for *no* warrant," said Duncan. "If my lort marquis will be senting for you as one chentleman sends for another, *then* you co."

Within an hour Bykes reappeared, accompanied by one of the gamekeepers— an Englishman. The moment he heard the door open, Duncan caught again at his broadsword.

"We want you, my young man," said the gamekeeper, standing on the threshold, with Bykes peeping over his shoulder, in an attitude indicating one foot already lifted to run.

"What for?"

"That's as may appear."

"Where's your warrant?"

"There."

"Lay it down on the table, and go back to the door, till I get a glance at it," said Malcolm. "You're an honest man, Wull— but I wouldn't trust a snuff-mill that had more than a pinch in it with that coward behind you there."

He was afraid of the possible consequences of his grandfather's indignation.

The gamekeeper did at once as he was requested, evidently both amused with the bearing of the two men and admiring it. Having glanced at the paper, Malcolm put it in his pocket, and whispering a word to his grandfather, walked away with his captors.

As they went to the House, Bykes was full of threats of which he sought to enhance the awfulness by the indefiniteness; but Will told Malcolm as much as he knew of the matter—namely, that the head gamekeeper, having lost some dozen of his sitting pheasants, had enjoined a strict watch; and that Bykes having caught sight of Malcolm in the very act of getting over the wall, had gone and given information against him.

No one about the premises except Bykes would have been capable of harbouring suspicion of Malcolm; and the head gamekeeper had not the slightest; but, knowing that his lordship found little enough to amuse him, and anticipating some laughter from the confronting of two such opposite characters, he had gone to the marquis with Bykes' report,—and this was the result. His lordship was not a magistrate, and the so-called warrant was merely a somewhat sternly-worded expression of his desire that Malcolm should appear and answer to the charge.

The accused was led into a vaulted chamber opening from the hall—a genuine portion, to judge from its deep low-arched recesses, the emergence of truncated portions of two or three groins, and the thickness of its walls, of the old monastery. Close by the door ascended a right-angled modern staircase.

Lord Lossie entered, and took his seat in a great chair in one of the recesses.

"So, you young jackanapes!" he said, half angry, and half amused, "you decline to come, when I send for you, without a magistrate's warrant, forsooth! It looks bad to begin with, I must say!"

"Yer lordship wad never hae had me come at sic a summons as that cankert ted Johnny Bykes broucht me. Gien ye had but hard him! He spak as gien he had been sent to fess me to yer lordship by the scruff o' the neck, an' I didna believe yer lordship wad do sic a thing. Ony gait, I wasna gauin' to stan' that. Ye wad hae thocht him a cornel at the sma'est, an' me a wheen heerin' guts. But it *wad* hae garred ye lauch, my lord, to see hoo the body ran whan my blin' gran'father—he canna bide onybody interferin' wi' me—made at him wi' his braid swoord!"

"Your lordship would never have had me answer such a summons as that cankered toad Johnny Bykes brought me. If you had but heard him! He spoke as if he had been sent to bring me to your lordship by the scruff of the neck, and I didn't believe your lordship would do such a thing. Anyway, I wasn't going to stand that. You would have thought him a colonel at the least, and me a handful of herring guts. But you *would* have laughed, my lord, to see how he ran when my blind grandfather—he can't stand anybody interfering with me—made at him with his broadsword!"

"Ye leein' rascal!" cried Bykes; "—*me* feared at an auld spidder, 'at hasna breath eneuch to fill the bag o' 's pipes!"

"You lying rascal!" cried Bykes; "—*me* afraid of an old spider, that hasn't breath enough to fill the bag of his pipes!"

"Caw canny, Johnny Bykes. Gien ye say an ill word o' my gran'father, I s' gie your neck a thraw—an' that the meenute we're oot o' 's lordship's presence."

"Threits! my lord," said the gatekeeper, appealing.

"And well merited," returned his lordship. "—Well, then," he went on, again addressing Malcolm, "What have you to say for yourself in regard of stealing my brood pheasants?"

"Maister MacPherson," said Malcolm, with an inclination of his head towards the gamekeeper, "micht ha' fun' a fitter neuk to fling that dirt intill. 'Deed, my lord, it 's sae ridic'lous, it hardly angers me. A man 'at can hae a' the fish i' the haill ocean for the takin' o' them, to be sic a sneck-drawin' contemptible wratch as tak yer lordship's bonny hen-craturs frae their chuckies—no to mention the sin o't!—it 's past an honest man's denyin', my lord. An' Maister MacPherson kens better, for luik at him lauchin' in 's ain sleeve."

"Well, we've no proof of it," said the marquis; "but what do you say to the charge of trespass?"

"The policies hae aye been open to honest fowk, my lord."

"Then where was the necessity for getting in over the wall!"

"I beg yer pardon, my lord: ye hae nae proof agen me o' that aither."

"Daur ye tell *me*," cried Bykes, recovering himself, "at I didna see ye wi' my twa een, loup the dyke aneth the temple—ay, an something flutterin' unco like bird-wings i' yer han'?"

"Oot or in, Johnny Bykes?"

"Ow! oot."

"Beware, Johnny Bykes. Bad mouth my grandfather, and I'll twist your neck for you—and that the minute we're out of his lordship's presence."

"Threats! my lord," said the gatekeeper, appealing.

"And well merited," returned his lordship. "—Well, then," he went on, again addressing Malcolm, "What have you to say for yourself in regard of stealing my brood pheasants?"

"Mister MacPherson," said Malcolm, with an inclination of his head towards the gamekeeper, "might have found a fitter place to fling that dirt. Indeed, my lord, it's so ridiculous, it hardly angers me. A man that can have all the fish in the whole ocean for the taking of them, to be such a crafty, contemptible wretch as take your lordship's bonny hen-birds from their chicks—not to mention the sin of it!—it's past an honest man's denying, my lord. And Mister MacPherson knows better, for look at him laughing in his own sleeve."

"Well, we've no proof of it," said the marquis; "but what do you say to the charge of trespass?"

"The policies have always been open to honest folk, my lord."

"Then where was the necessity for getting in over the wall!"

"I beg your pardon, my lord: you have no proof against me of that either."

"Dare you tell *me*," cried Bykes, recovering himself, "that I didn't see you with these two eyes, jump the wall beneath the temple—ay, and something fluttering very like bird-wings in your hand?"

"Out or in, Johnny Bykes?"

"Oh! out."

"I *did* loup the dyke my lord; but it was *oot*, no *in*."

"How did you get in then?" asked the marquis.

"I gat in, my lord," began Malcolm, and ceased.

"How did you get in?" repeated the marquis.

"Ow! There's mony w'ys o' winnin' in, my lord. The last time I cam in but ane, it was 'maist ower the carcass o' Johnny there, wha wad fain hae hauden me oot, only he hadna my blin' daddy ahint him to ile 's jints."

"An' dinna ye ca' *that* brakin' in?" said Bykes.

"Na; there was naething to brak, 'cep it had been your banes, Johnny; an' that wad hae been a peety—they're sae guid for rinnin wi'."

"You had no right to enter against the will of my gatekeeper," said his lordship. "What is a gatekeeper for?"

"I had a richt, my lord, sae lang 's I was upo' my leddy's business."

"And what was my lady's business, pray?" questioned the marquis.

"I faun' a buik upo' the links, my lord, which was like to be hers, wi' the twa beasts 'at stans at yer lordship's door inside the brod o' 't. An' sae it turned oot to be whan I took it up to the Hoose. There's the half-croon she gae me."

Little did Malcolm think where the daintiest of pearly ears were listening, and the brightest of blue eyes looking down, half in merriment, a quarter in anxiety, and the remaining quarter in interest! On a landing half way up the stair, stood Lady Florimel, peeping over the balusters, afraid to fix her eyes upon him lest she should make him look up.

"I *did* jump the wall my lord; but it was *out*, not *in*."

"How did you get in then?" asked the marquis.

"I got in, my lord," began Malcolm, and ceased.

"How did you get in?" repeated the marquis.

"Oh! there's many ways of getting in, my lord. The last time I came in but one, it was almost over the carcass of Johnny there, who would fain have kept me out, only he hadn't my blind daddy behind him to oil his joints."

"And don't you call *that* breaking in?" said Bykes.

"Na; there was nothing to break, except it had been your bones, Johnny; and that would have been a pity—they're so good for running with."

"You had no right to enter against the will of my gatekeeper," said his lordship. "What is a gatekeeper for?"

"I had a right, my lord, so long as I was upon my lady's business."

"And what was my lady's business, pray?" questioned the marquis.

"I found a book on the links, my lord, which was like to be hers, with the two beasts that stand at your lordship's door inside the board. And so it turned out to be when I took it up to the House. There's the half-crown she gave me."

Little did Malcolm think where the daintiest of pearly ears were listening, and the brightest of blue eyes looking down, half in merriment, a quarter in anxiety, and the remaining quarter in interest! On a landing half way up the stair, stood Lady Florimel, peeping over the balusters, afraid to fix her eyes upon him lest she should make him look up.

"Yes, yes, I daresay!" acquiesced the marquis; "but," he persisted, "what I want to know is, how you got in that time. You seem to have some reluctance to answer the question."

"Weel, I hev, my lord."

"Then I must insist on your doing so."

"Weel, I jist winna, my lord. It was a' straucht foret an' fair; an' gien yer lordship war i' my place, ye wadna say mair yersel'."

"He's been after one of the girls about the place," whispered the marquis to the gamekeeper.

"Speir at him, my lord, gien 't please yer lordship, what it was he hed in 's han' whan he lap the park wa'," said Bykes.

"Gien 't be a' ane till 's lordship," said Malcolm, without looking at Bykes, "it wad be better no to speir, for it gangs sair agen me to refeese him."

"I should like to know," said the marquis.

"Ye maun trust me, my lord, that I was efter no ill. I gie ye my word for that, my lord."

"But how am I to know what your word is worth?" returned Lord Lossie, well pleased with the dignity of the youth's behaviour.

"To ken what a body's word 's worth ye maun trust him first, my lord. It's no muckle trust I want o' ye: it comes but to this—that I hae rizzons, guid to me, an' no ill to you gien ye kent them, for *not* answerin' yer lordship's questions. I'm no denyin' a word 'at Johnny Bykes says. I never hard the cratur ca'd a leear. He's but a cantankerous argle-barglous body— no fit to be a gatekeeper 'cep it was up upo' the Binn-side, whaur 'maist naebody gangs oot or in. He wad maybe be safter-hertit till a fellow-cratur syne."

"Yes, yes, I daresay!" acquiesced the marquis; "but," he persisted, "what I want to know is, how you got in that time. You seem to have some reluctance to answer the question."

"Well, I have, my lord."

"Then I must insist on your doing so."

"Well, I just won't, my lord. It was all straightforward and fair; and if your lordship were in my place, you wouldn't say more yourself."

"He's been after one of the girls about the place," whispered the marquis to the gamekeeper.

"Ask him, my lord, if it please your lordship, what it was he had in his hand when he jumped the park wall," said Bykes.

"If it's all the same to his lordship," said Malcolm, without looking at Bykes, "it would be better not to ask, for it gives me small pleasure to refuse him."

"I should like to know," said the marquis.

"You must trust me, my lord, that I meant no harm. I give you my word for that, my lord."

"But how am I to know what your word is worth?" returned Lord Lossie, well pleased with the dignity of the youth's behaviour.

"To know what a man's word is worth, you must trust him first, my lord. It's not much trust I want of you: it comes but to this—that I have reasons, good to me, and not bad to you if you knew them, for *not* answering your lordship's questions. I'm not denying a word that Johnny Bykes says. I never heard him called a liar. He's but a cantankerous quarrelsome body—not fit to be a gatekeeper except it was upon the Binn-side, where hardly a soul goes out or in. He would maybe be softer-hearted to a fellow-creature then."

"Would you have him let in all the tramps in the country?" said the marquis.

"De'il ane o' them, my Lord; but I wad hae him no trouble the likes o' me 'at fesses the fish to your lordship's brakwast: sic 's no like to be efter mischeef."

"There is some glimmer of sense in what you say," returned his lordship. "But you know it won't do to let anybody that pleases get over the park walls. Why didn't you go out at the gate?"

"The burn was atween me an' hit, an' it 's a lang road roon'."

"Well, I must lay some penalty upon you, to deter others," said the marquis.

"Verra well, my lord. Sae lang 's it 's fair, I s' bide it ohn grutten."

"It shan't be too hard. It's just this—to give John Bykes the thrashing he deserves, as soon as you're out of sight of the House."

"Na, na, my lord; I canna do that," said Malcolm.

"So you're afraid of him, after all!"

"Feared at Johnnie Bykes, my lord! Ha! ha!"

"You threatened him a minute ago, and now, when I give you leave to thrash him, you decline the honour!"

"The disgrace, my lord. He's an aulder man, an' no abune half the size. But fegs! gien he says anither word agen my gran'father, I *will* gie 's neck a bit thraw."

"Well, well, be off with you both," said the marquis rising.

"Would you have him let in all the tramps in the country?" said the marquis.

"Na, no tramps, my Lord; but I would have him not trouble the likes of me that bring the fish to your lordship's breakfast: we're not the sort to be after mischief."

"There is some glimmer of sense in what you say," returned his lordship. "But you know it won't do to let anybody that pleases get over the park walls. Why didn't you go out at the gate?"

"The burn (stream) was between me and it, and it's a long way round."

"Well, I must lay some penalty upon you, to deter others," said the marquis.

"Very well, my lord. So long as it's fair, I'll take it, and not cry over it."

"It shan't be too hard. It's just this—to give John Bykes the thrashing he deserves, as soon as you're out of sight of the House."

"Na, na, my lord; I can't do that," said Malcolm.

"So you're afraid of him, after all!"

"Afraid of Johnnie Bykes, my lord! Ha! ha!"

"You threatened him a minute ago, and now, when I give you leave to thrash him, you decline the honour!"

"The disgrace, my lord. He's an older man, and no more than half my size. But faith! if he says another word against my grandfather, I *will* give his neck a twist."

"Well, well, be off with you both," said the marquis rising.

No one heard the rustle of Lady Florimel's dress as she sped up the stair, thinking with herself how very odd it was to have a secret with a fisherman; for a secret it was, seeing the reticence of Malcolm had been a relief to her; when she shrunk from what seemed the imminent mention of her name in the affair before the servants. She had even felt a touch of mingled admiration and gratitude when she found what a faithful squire he was—capable of an absolute obstinacy indeed, where she was concerned. For her own sake as well as his she was glad that he had got off so well, for otherwise she would have felt bound to tell her father the whole story, and she was not at all so sure as Malcolm that he would have been satisfied with his *reasons,* and would not have been indignant with the fellow for presuming even to be silent concerning his daughter. Indeed Lady Florimel herself felt somewhat irritated with him, as having brought her into the awkward situation of sharing a secret with a youth of his position.

CHAPTER XVIII

THE QUARREL

For a few days the weather was dull and unsettled, with cold flaws, and an occasional sprinkle of rain. But after came a still gray morning, warm and hopeful, and ere noon the sun broke out, the mists vanished, and the day was glorious in blue and gold. Malcolm had been to Scaurnose, to see his friend Joseph Mair, and was descending the steep path down the side of the promontory, on his way home, when his keen eye caught sight of a form on the slope of the dune which could hardly be other than that of Lady Florimel. She did not lift her eyes until he came quite near, and then only to drop them again with no more recognition than if he had been any other of the fishermen. Already more than half inclined to pick a quarrel with him, she fancied that, presuming upon their very commonplace adventure and its resulting secret, he approached her with an assurance he had never manifested before, and her head was bent motionless over her book when he stood and addressed her.

"My leddy," he began, with his bonnet by his knee.

"Well?" she returned, without even lifting her eyes, for, with the inherited privilege of her rank, she could be insolent with coolness, and call it to mind without remorse.

"I houp the bit buikie wasna muckle the waur, my leddy," he said.

"'Tis of no consequence," she replied.

"Gien it war mine, I wadna think sae," he returned, eyeing her anxiously. "—Here's yer leddyship's pocket nepkin," he went on. "I hae keepit it ready rowed up, ever sin' my daddy washed it oot. It's no ill dune for a blin' man, as ye'll see, an' I ironed it mysel' as weel's I cud."

"My lady," he began, with his bonnet by his knee.

"Well?" she returned, without even lifting her eyes, for, with the inherited privilege of her rank, she could be insolent with coolness, and call it to mind without remorse.

"I hope your book wasn't much spoiled, my lady," he said.

"'Tis of no consequence," she replied.

"If it were mine, I wouldn't think so," he returned, eyeing her anxiously. "—Here's your ladyship's pocket napkin," he went on. "I've kept it ready wrapped up, ever since my daddy washed it. It's not a bad job for a blind man, as you'll see, and I ironed it myself as well as I could."

As he spoke he unfolded a piece of brown paper, disclosing a little parcel in a cover of immaculate post, which he humbly offered her.

Taking it slowly from his hand, she laid it on the ground beside her with a stiff *"Thank you,"* and a second dropping of her eyes that seemed meant to close the interview.

"I doobt my company's no welcome the day, my leddy," said Malcolm with trembling voice; "but there's ae thing I maun refar till. Whan I took hame yer leddyship's buik the ither day, ye sent me half a croon by the han' o' yer servan' lass. Afore her I wasna gaein' to disalloo onything ye pleased wi' regaird to me; an' I thocht wi' mysel' it was maybe necessar' for yer leddyship's dignity an' the luik o' things—"

"How dare you hint at any understanding between you and me?" exclaimed the girl in cold anger.

"Lord, mem! what hev I said to fess sic a fire-flaucht oot o' yer bonny een? I thocht ye only did it 'cause ye wadna like to luik shabby afore the lass—no giein' onything to the lad 'at brocht ye yer ain—an' lippened to me to unnerstan' 'at ye did it but for the luik o' the thing, as I say."

He had taken the coin from his pocket, and had been busy while he spoke rubbing it in a handful of sand, so that it was bright as new when he now offered it.

"You are quite mistaken," she rejoined, ungraciously. "You insult me by supposing I meant you to return it."

As he spoke he unfolded a piece of brown paper, disclosing a little parcel in a cover of immaculate post, which he humbly offered her.

Taking it slowly from his hand, she laid it on the ground beside her with a stiff *"Thank you,"* and a second dropping of her eyes that seemed meant to close the interview.

"I suspect my company's not welcome today, my lady," said Malcolm with trembling voice; "but there's one thing I must refer to. When I took home your ladyship's book the other day, you sent me half a crown by the hand of your servant lass. Before her I wasn't going to deny you anything you pleased with regard to me; and I thought with myself it was maybe necessary for your ladyship's dignity and the look of things—"

"How dare you hint at any understanding between you and me?" exclaimed the girl in cold anger.

"Lord, ma'am! what have I said to bring such a fire-flash out of your bonny eyes? I thought you only did it because you wouldn't like to look shabby before the lass—not giving anything to the lad that brought you your own—and trusted to me to understand that you only did it for the look of the thing, as I say."

He had taken the coin from his pocket, and had been busy while he spoke rubbing it in a handful of sand, so that it was bright as new when he now offered it.

"You are quite mistaken," she rejoined, ungraciously. "You insult me by supposing I meant you to return it."

"Div ye think I cud bide to be paid for a turn till a neebor, lat alane the liftin' o' a buik till a leddy?" said Malcolm with keen mortification. "That wad be to despise mysel' frae keel to truck. I like to be paid for my wark, an' I like to be paid weel: but no a plack by siclike sall stick to my loof. It *can* be no offence to gie ye back yer half-croon, my leddy."

And again he offered the coin.

"I don't in the least see why, on your own principles, you shouldn't take the money," said the girl, with more than the coldness of an uninterested umpire. "You worked for it, I'm sure—first accompanying me home in such a storm, and then finding the book and bringing it back all the way to the house!"

"'Deed, my leddy, sic a doctrine wad tak a' grace oot o' the earth! What wad this life be worth gien a' was to be peyed for? I wad cut my throat afore I wad bide in sic a warl'.—Tak yer half-croon, my leddy," he concluded, in a tone of entreaty.

But the energetic outburst was sufficing, in such her mood, only to the disgust of Lady Florimel.

"Do anything with the money you please; only go away, and don't plague me about it," she said freezingly.

"What can I du wi' what I wadna pass throu' my fingers?" said Malcolm with the patience of deep disappointment.

"Give it to some poor creature: you know some one who would be glad of it, I daresay."

"I ken mony ane, my leddy, wham it wad weel become yer ain bonny han' to gie 't till; but I'm no gaein' to tak' credit fer a leeberality that wad ill become me."

"Do you think I could bear to be paid for a turn to a neighbour, let alone the lifting of a book to a lady?" said Malcolm with keen mortification. "That would be to despise myself from keel to truck. I like to be paid for my work, and I like to be paid well: but not a brass farthing beyond that shall stick to my palm. It *can* be no offence to give you back your half-crown, my lady."

And again he offered the coin.

"I don't in the least see why, on your own principles, you shouldn't take the money," said the girl, with more than the coldness of an uninterested umpire. "You worked for it, I'm sure—first accompanying me home in such a storm, and then finding the book and bringing it back all the way to the house!"

"Indeed, my lady, such a doctrine would take all grace from the earth! What would this life be worth if all was to be paid for? I would cut my throat before I'd live in such a world. Take your half-crown, my lady," he concluded, in a tone of entreaty.

But the energetic outburst was sufficing, in such her mood, only to the disgust of Lady Florimel.

"Do anything with the money you please; only go away, and don't plague me about it," she said freezingly.

"What can I do with what I wouldn't pass through my fingers?" said Malcolm with the patience of deep disappointment.

"Give it to some poor creature: you know some one who would be glad of it, I daresay."

"I know many, my lady, whom it would well become your own bonny hand to give it to; but I'm not going to take credit for a liberality that would ill become me."

"You can tell how you earned it."

"And profess mysel' disgraced by takin' a reward frae a born leddy for what I wad hae dune for ony beggar wife i' the lan'. Na, na, my leddy."

"Your services are certainly flattering, when you put me on a level with any beggar in the country!"

"In regaird o' sic service, my leddy: ye ken weel eneuch what I mean. Obleege me by takin' back yer siller."

"How dare you ask me to take back what I once gave?"

"Ye cudna hae kent what ye was doin' whan ye gae 't, my leddy. Tak it back, an tak a hunnerweicht aff o' my hert."

He actually mentioned his heart!—was it to be borne by a girl in Lady Florimel's mood?

"I beg you will not annoy me," she said, muffling her anger in folds of distance, and again sought her book.

Malcolm looked at her for a moment, then turned his face towards the sea, and for another moment stood silent. Lady Florimel glanced up, but Malcolm was unaware of her movement. He lifted his hand, and looked at the half-crown gleaming on his palm; then, with a sudden poise of his body, and a sudden fierce action of his arm, he sent the coin, swift with his heart's repudiation, across the sands into the tide. Ere it struck the water he had turned, and, with long stride but low-bent head, walked away. A pang shot to Lady Florimel's heart.

"Malcolm!" she cried.

He turned instantly, came slowly back, and stood erect and silent before her.

"You can tell how you earned it."

"And profess myself disgraced by taking a reward from a born lady for what I would have done for any beggar wife in the land. Na, na, my lady."

"Your services are certainly flattering, when you put me on a level with any beggar in the country!"

"In regard of such service, my lady: you know well enough what I mean. Oblige me by taking back your money."

"How dare you ask me to take back what I once gave?"

"You couldn't have known what you were doing when you gave it, my lady. Take it back, and take a hundredweight from off my heart."

He actually mentioned his heart!—was it to be borne by a girl in Lady Florimel's mood?

"I beg you will not annoy me," she said, muffling her anger in folds of distance, and again sought her book.

Malcolm looked at her for a moment, then turned his face towards the sea, and for another moment stood silent. Lady Florimel glanced up, but Malcolm was unaware of her movement. He lifted his hand, and looked at the half-crown gleaming on his palm; then, with a sudden poise of his body, and a sudden fierce action of his arm, he sent the coin, swift with his heart's repudiation, across the sands into the tide. Ere it struck the water he had turned, and, with long stride but low-bent head, walked away. A pang shot to Lady Florimel's heart.

"Malcolm!" she cried.

He turned instantly, came slowly back, and stood erect and silent before her.

She must say something. Her eye fell on the little parcel beside her, and she spoke the first thought that came.

"Will you take this?" she said, and offered him the handkerchief.

In a dazed way he put out his hand and took it, staring at it as if he did not know what it was.

"It's some sair!" he said at length, with a motion of his hands as if to grasp his head between them. "Ye winna tak even the washin' o' a pocket nepkin frae me, an' ye wad gar me tak a haill half-croon frae yersel'! Mem, ye're a gran' leddy an' a bonny; an ye hae turns aboot ye, gien 'twar but the set o' yer heid, 'at micht gar an angel lat fa' what he was carryin', but afore I wad affront ane that wantit naething o' me but gude will, I wad—I wad—raither be the fisher-lad that I am."

A weak-kneed peroration, truly; but Malcolm was over-burdened at last. He laid the little parcel on the sand at her feet, almost reverentially, and again turned. But Lady Florimel spoke again.

"It is you who are affronting me now," she said gently. "When a lady gives her handkerchief to a gentleman, it is commonly received as a very great favour indeed."

"Gien I hae made a mistak, my leddy, I micht weel mak it, no bein' a gentleman, and no bein' used to the traitment o' ane. But I doobt gien a gentleman wad ha' surmised what ye was efter wi' yer nepkin', gien ye had offert him half a croon first."

"Oh, yes, he would—perfectly!" said Florimel with an air of offence.

"Then, my leddy, for the first time i' my life, I wish I had been born a gentleman."

She must say something. Her eye fell on the little parcel beside her, and she spoke the first thought that came.

"Will you take this?" she said, and offered him the handkerchief.

In a dazed way he put out his hand and took it, staring at it as if he did not know what it was.

"It's hard to bear!" he said at length, with a motion of his hands as if to grasp his head between them. "You won't take even the washing of a pocket napkin from me, and you would have me take a whole half-crown from yourself! Ma'am, you're a grand lady and a bonny; and you have turns about you, if it were but the set of your head, that might make an angel let fall what he was carrying, but before I would affront one that wanted nothing of me but good will, I would—I would—rather be the fisher-lad that I am."

A weak-kneed peroration, truly; but Malcolm was over-burdened at last. He laid the little parcel on the sand at her feet, almost reverentially, and again turned. But Lady Florimel spoke again.

"It is you who are affronting me now," she said gently. "When a lady gives her handkerchief to a gentleman, it is commonly received as a very great favour indeed."

"If I have made a mistake, my lady, I might well make it, not being a gentleman, and not being used to the treatment of one. But I doubt if a gentleman would have surmised what you meant with your napkin, if you had offered him half a crown first."

"Oh, yes, he would—perfectly!" said Florimel with an air of offence.

"Then, my lady, for the first time in my life, I wish I had been born a gentleman."

"Then I certainly wouldn't have given it you," said Florimel with perversity.

"What for no, my leddy? I dinna unnerstan' ye again. There maun be an unco differ atween 's!"

"Because a gentleman would have presumed on such a favour."

"I'm glaidder nor ever 'at I wasna born ane," said Malcolm, and, slowly stooping, he lifted the handkerchief; "an' I was aye glaid o' that, my leddy, 'cause gien I had been, I wad hae been luikin' doon upo' workin' men like mysel' as gien they warna freely o' the same flesh an' blude. But I beg yer leddyship's pardon for takin' ye up amiss. An' sae lang's I live, I'll regaird this as ane o' her fedders 'at the angel moutit as she sat by the bored craig. An' whan I'm deid, I'll hae 't laid upo' my face, an' syne, maybe, I may get a sicht o' ye as I pass. Guid day my leddy."

"Good day," she returned kindly. "I wish my father would let me have a row in your boat."

"It's at yer service whan ye please, my leddy," said Malcolm.

One who had caught a glimpse of the shining yet solemn eyes of the youth, as he walked home, would wonder no longer that he should talk as he did—so sedately, yet so poetically—so long-windedly, if you like, yet so sensibly—even wisely.

"Then I certainly wouldn't have given it you," said Florimel with perversity.

"Why not, my lady? I don't understand you again. There must be a world of difference between us!"

"Because a gentleman would have presumed on such a favour."

"I'm gladder than ever that I wasn't born one," said Malcolm, and, slowly stooping, he lifted the handkerchief; "and I was always glad of that, my lady, because if I had been, I would have been looking down upon working men like myself as if they were hardly of the same flesh and blood. But I beg your ladyship's pardon for taking you up amiss. And so long as I live, I'll regard this as one of her feathers that the angel moulted as she sat by the bored craig. And when I'm dead, I'll have it laid upon my face, and then, maybe, I may get a sight of you as I pass. Good day my lady."

"Good day," she returned kindly. "I wish my father would let me have a row in your boat."

"It's at your service when you please, my lady," said Malcolm.

One who had caught a glimpse of the shining yet solemn eyes of the youth, as he walked home, would wonder no longer that he should talk as he did—so sedately, yet so poetically—so long-windedly, if you like, yet so sensibly—even wisely.

Lady Florimel lay on the sand, and sought again to read the "Faerie Queene." But for the last day or two she had been getting tired of it, and now the forms that entered by her eyes dropped half their substance and all their sense in the porch, and thronged her brain with the mere phantoms of things, with words that came and went and were nothing. Abandoning the harvest of chaff, her eyes rose and looked out upon the sea. Never, even from tropical shore, was richer-hued ocean beheld. Gorgeous in purple and green, in shadowy blue and flashing gold, it seemed to Malcolm, as if at any moment the ever new-born Anadyomene might lift her shining head from the wandering floor, and float away in her pearly lustre to gladden the regions where the glaciers glide seawards in irresistible silence, there to give birth to the icebergs in tumult and thunderous uproar. But Lady Florimel felt merely the loneliness. One deserted boat lay on the long sand, like the bereft and useless half of a double shell. Without show of life the moveless cliffs lengthened far into a sea where neither white sail deepened the purple and gold, nor red one enriched it with a colour it could not itself produce. Neither hope nor aspiration awoke in her heart at the sight. Was she beginning to be tired of her companionless liberty? Had the long stanzas, bound by so many interwoven links of rhyme, ending in long Alexandrines, the long cantos, the lingering sweetness long drawn out through so many unended books, begun to weary her at last? Had even a quarrel with a fisher-lad been a little pastime to her? and did she now wish she had detained him a little longer? Could she take any interest in him beyond such as she took in Demon, her father's dog, or Brazenose, his favourite horse?

Whatever might be her thoughts or feelings at this moment, it remained a fact, that Florimel Colonsay, the daughter of a marquis, and Malcolm, the grandson of a blind piper, were woman and man—and the man the finer of the two this time.

As Malcolm passed on his way one of the three or four solitary rocks which rose from the sand, the skeleton remnants of larger masses worn down by wind, wave, and weather, he heard his own name uttered by an unpleasant voice, and followed by a more unpleasant laugh.

He knew both the voice and the laugh, and, turning, saw Mrs Catanach, seated, apparently busy with her knitting, in the shade of the rock.

"Weel?" he said curtly.	"Well?" he said curtly.
"Weel!—Set ye up!—Wha's yon ye was play actin' wi' oot yonner?"	"Well!—insolence!—Who's that you were play acting with out yonder?"
"Wha telled ye to speir, Mistress Catanach?"	"Who told you to ask, Mistress Catanach?"
"Ay, ay, laad! Ye'll be abune speykin' till an auld wife efter colloguin' wi' a yoong ane, an' sic a ane! Isna she bonny, Malkie? Isna hers a winsome shape an' a lauchin' ee? Didna she draw ye on, an' luik i' the hawk's-een o' ye, an' lay herself oot afore ye, an'—?"	"Ay, ay, lad! You'll be above speaking to an old wife after keeping company with a young one, and such a one! Isn't she bonny, Malkie? Isn't hers a winsome shape and a laughing eye? Didn't she draw you on, and look in your hawk's-eyes, and lay herself out before you, and—?"
"She did naething o' the sort, ye ill-tongued wuman!" said Malcolm in anger.	"She did nothing of the sort, you ill-tongued woman!" said Malcolm in anger.
"Ho! ho!" trumpeted Mrs Catanach. "Ill-tongued, am I? An' what neist?"	"Ho! ho!" trumpeted Mrs Catanach. "Ill-tongued, am I? And what next?"
"Ill-deedit," returned Malcolm, "—whan ye flang my bonny salmon troot till yer oogly deevil o' a dog."	"Ill-behaved," returned Malcolm, "—when you flung my bonny salmon trout to your ugly devil of a dog."

"Ho! ho! ho! Ill-deedit, am I? I s' no forget thae bonny names! Maybe yer lordship wad alloo me the leeberty o' speirin' anither question at ye, Ma'colm MacPhail."

"Ye may speir 'at ye like, sae lang 's ye canna gar me stan' to hearken. Guid day to ye, Mistress Catanach. Yer company was nane o' my seekin': I may lea' 't whan I like."

"Dinna ye be ower sure o' that," she called after him venomously.

But Malcolm turned his head no more.

As soon as he was out of sight, Mrs Catanach rose, ascended the dune, and propelled her rotundity along the yielding top of it. When she arrived within speaking distance of Lady Florimel, who lay lost in her dreary regard of sand and sea, she paused for a moment, as if contemplating her.

Suddenly, almost by Lady Florimel's side, as if he had risen from the sand, stood the form of the mad laird.

"I dinna ken whaur I come frae," he said.

Lady Florimel started, half rose, and seeing the dwarf so near, and on the other side of her a repulsive-looking woman staring at her, sprung to her feet and fled. The same instant the mad laird, catching sight of Mrs Catanach, gave a cry of misery, thrust his fingers in his ears, darted down the other side of the dune and sped along the shore. Mrs. Catanach shook with laughter.

"I hae skailled the bonny doos!" she said. Then she called aloud after the flying girl,—"My leddy! My bonny leddy!"

"Ho! ho! ho! Ill-behaved, am I? I won't forget those bonny names! Maybe your lordship would allow me the liberty of asking you another question, Malcolm MacPhail."

"You may ask what you like, so long as you can't make me stand here and listen. Good day to you, Mistress Catanach. Your company was none of my seeking: I may leave it when I like."

"Don't you be too sure of that," she called after him venomously.

But Malcolm turned his head no more.

As soon as he was out of sight, Mrs Catanach rose, ascended the dune, and propelled her rotundity along the yielding top of it. When she arrived within speaking distance of Lady Florimel, who lay lost in her dreary regard of sand and sea, she paused for a moment, as if contemplating her.

Suddenly, almost by Lady Florimel's side, as if he had risen from the sand, stood the form of the mad laird.

"I don't know where I come from," he said.

Lady Florimel started, half rose, and seeing the dwarf so near, and on the other side of her a repulsive-looking woman staring at her, sprung to her feet and fled. The same instant the mad laird, catching sight of Mrs Catanach, gave a cry of misery, thrust his fingers in his ears, darted down the other side of the dune and sped along the shore. Mrs. Catanach shook with laughter.

"I've scattered the bonny doves!" she said. Then she called aloud after the flying girl,— "My lady! My bonny lady!"

Florimel paid no heed, but ran straight for the door of the tunnel, and vanished. Thence leisurely climbing to the temple of the winds, she looked down from a height of safety upon the shore and the retreating figure of Mrs. Catanach. Seating herself by the pedestal of the trumpet-blowing Wind, she assayed her reading again, but was again startled—this time by a rough salute from Demon. Presently her father appeared, and Lady Florimel felt something like a pang of relief at being found there, and not on the farther side of the dune making it up with Malcolm.

Florimel paid no heed, but ran straight for the door of the tunnel, and vanished. Thence leisurely climbing to the temple of the winds, she looked down from a height of safety upon the shore and the retreating figure of Mrs. Catanach. Seating herself by the pedestal of the trumpet-blowing Wind, she assayed her reading again, but was again startled—this time by a rough salute from Demon. Presently her father appeared, and Lady Florimel felt something like a pang of relief at being found there, and not on the farther side of the dune making it up with Malcolm.

CHAPTER XIX

DUNCAN'S PIPES

A few days after the events last narrated, a footman in the marquis's livery entered the Seaton, snuffing with emphasized discomposure the air of the village, all-ignorant of the risk he ran in thus openly manifesting his feelings; for the women at least were good enough citizens to resent any indignity offered their town. As vengeance would have it, Meg Partan was the first of whom, with supercilious airs and "clippit" (clipped) tongue, he requested to know where a certain blind man, who played on an instrument called the bagpipes, lived.

"Spit i' yer loof an' caw for him," she answered—a reply of which he understood the tone and one disagreeable word.

With reddening cheek he informed her that he came on his lord's business.

"I dinna doobt it," she retorted; "ye luik siclike as rins ither fowk's eeran's."

"I should be obliged if you would inform me where the man lives," returned the lackey—with polite words in supercilious tones.

"What d' ye want wi' *him*, honest man?" grimly questioned the Partaness, the epithet referring to Duncan, and not the questioner.

"That I shall have the honour of informing himself," he replied.

"Weel, ye can hae the honour o' informin' yersel' whaur he bides," she rejoined, and turned away from her open door.

All were not so rude as she, however, for he found at length a little girl willing to show him the way.

"Spit i' yer loof an' caw for him,"[13] she answered—a reply of which he understood the tone and one disagreeable word.

With reddening cheek he informed her that he came on his lord's business.

"I don't doubt it," she retorted; "you look like the kind who run other folk's errands."

"I should be obliged if you would inform me where the man lives," returned the lackey—with polite words in supercilious tones.

"What do you want with *him*, honest man?" grimly questioned the Partaness, the epithet referring to Duncan, and not the questioner.

"That I shall have the honour of informing himself," he replied.

"Well, you can have the honour of informing yourself where he lives," she rejoined, and turned away from her open door.

All were not so rude as she, however, for he found at length a little girl willing to show him the way.

---

13 "Spit in your palm and search for him,"

The style in which his message was delivered was probably modified by the fact that he found Malcolm seated with his grandfather at their evening meal of water-brose and butter; for he had been present when Malcolm was brought before the marquis by Bykes, and had in some measure comprehended the nature of the youth: it was in politest phrase, and therefore entirely to Duncan's satisfaction in regard of the manner as well as matter of the message, that he requested Mr Duncan MacPhail's attendance on the marquis the following evening at six o'clock, to give his lordship and some distinguished visitors the pleasure of hearing him play on the bagpipes during dessert. To this summons the old man returned stately and courteous reply, couched in the best English he could command; which, although considerably distorted by Gaelic pronunciation and idioms, was yet sufficiently intelligible to the messenger, who carried home the substance for the satisfaction of his master, and what he could of the form for the amusement of his fellow servants.

Duncan, although he received it with perfect calmness, was yet overjoyed at the invitation. He had performed once or twice before the late marquis, and having ever since assumed the style of Piper to the Marquis of Lossie, now regarded the summons as confirmation in the office. The moment the sound of the messenger's departing footsteps died away, he caught up his pipes from the corner, where, like a pet cat, they lay on a bit of carpet, the only piece in the cottage, spread for them between his chair and the wall, and, though cautiously mindful of its age and proved infirmity, filled the bag full, and burst into such a triumphant onset of battle, that all the children of the Seaton were in a few minutes crowded about the door. He had not played above five minutes, however, when the love of finery natural to the Gael, the Gaul, the Galatian, triumphed over his love of music, and he stopped with an abrupt groan of the instrument to request Malcolm to get him new streamers. Whatever his notions of its nature might be, he could not come of the Celtic race without having in him somewhere a strong faculty for colour, and no doubt his fancy regarding it was of something as glorious as his knowledge of it must have been vague. At all events he not only knew the names of the colours in ordinary use, but could describe many of the clan tartans with perfect accuracy; and he now gave Malcolm complete instructions as to the hues of the ribbons he was to purchase. As soon as he had started on the important mission, the old man laid aside his instrument, and taking his broadsword from the wall, proceeded with the aid of brick-dust and lamp-oil, to furbish hilt and blade with the utmost care, searching out spot after spot of rust, to the smallest, with the delicate points of his great bony fingers. Satisfied at length of its brightness, he requested Malcolm, who had returned long before the operation was over, to bring him the sheath, which, for fear of its coming to pieces, so old and crumbling was the leather, he kept laid up in the drawer with his sporran and his Sunday coat. His next business, for he would not commit it to Malcolm, was to adorn the pipes with the new streamers. Asking the colour of each, and going by some principle of arrangement known only to himself he affixed them, one after the other, as he judged right, shaking and drawing out each to its full length with as much pride as if it had been a tone instead of a ribbon. This done, he resumed his playing, and continued it, notwithstanding the remonstrances of his grandson, until bedtime.

That night he slept but little, and as the day went on grew more and more excited. Scarcely had he swallowed his twelve o'clock dinner of *sowens* and oatcake, when he wanted to go and dress himself for his approaching visit. Malcolm persuaded him however to lie down a while and hear him play, and succeeded, strange as it may seem with such an instrument, in lulling him to sleep. But he had not slept more than five minutes when he sprung from the bed, wide awake, crying—

"My poy, Malcolm! my son! you haf let her sleep in; and ta creat peoples will be impatient for her music, and cursing her in teir hearts!"

Nothing would quiet him but the immediate commencement of the process of dressing, the result of which was, as I have said, even pathetic, from its intermixture of shabbiness and finery. The dangling brass-capped tails of his sporran in front, the silver-mounted dirk on one side, with its hilt of black oak carved into an eagle's head, and the steel basket of his broadsword gleaming at the other; his great shoulder-brooch of rudely chased brass; the pipes with their withered bag and gaudy streamers; the faded kilt, oiled and soiled; the stockings darned in twenty places by the hands of the termagant Meg Partan; the brogues patched and patched until it would have been hard to tell a spot of the original leather; the round blue bonnet grown gray with wind and weather: the belts that looked like old harness ready to yield at a pull; his skene dhu sticking out grim and black beside a knee like a lean knuckle:—all combined to form a picture ludicrous to a vulgar nature, but gently pitiful to the lover of his kind, he looked like a half-mouldered warrior, waked from beneath an ancient cairn, to walk about in a world other than he took it to be. Malcolm, in his commonplace Sunday suit, served as a foil to his picturesque grandfather; to whose oft reiterated desire that he would wear the highland dress, he had hitherto returned no other answer than a humorous representation of the different remarks with which the neighbours would encounter such a solecism.

The whole Seaton turned out to see them start. Men, women, and children lined the fronts and gables of the houses they must pass on their way; for everybody knew where they were going, and wished them good luck. As if he had been a great bard with a henchman of his own, Duncan strode along in front, and Malcolm followed, carrying the pipes, and regarding his grandfather with a mingled pride and compassion lovely to see. But as soon as they were beyond the village the old man took the young one's arm, not to guide him, for that was needless, but to stay his steps a little, for when dressed he would, as I have said, carry no staff; and thus they entered the nearest gate of the grounds. Bykes saw them and scoffed, but with discretion, and kept out of their way.

When they reached the house, they were taken to the servants' hall, where refreshments were offered them. The old man ate sparingly, saying he wanted all the room for his breath, but swallowed a glass of whisky with readiness; for, although he never spent a farthing on it, he had yet a highlander's respect for whisky, and seldom refused a glass when offered him. On this occasion, besides, anxious to do himself credit as a piper, he was well pleased to add a little fuel to the failing fires of old age; and the summons to the dining-room being in his view long delayed, he had, before he left the hall, taken a second glass.

They were led along endless passages, up a winding stone stair, across a lobby, and through room after room.

"It will pe some glamour, sure, Malcolm!" said Duncan in a whisper as they went.

"It will be some glamour, sure, Malcolm!" said Duncan in a whisper as they went.

Requested at length to seat themselves in an anteroom, the air of which was filled with the sounds and odours of the neighbouring feast, they waited again through what seemed to the impatient Duncan an hour of slow vacuity; but at last they were conducted into the dining-room. Following their guide, Malcolm led the old man to the place prepared for him at the upper part of the room, where the floor was raised a step or two.

Duncan would, I fancy, even unprotected by his blindness, have strode unabashed into the very halls of heaven. As he entered there was a hush, for his poverty-stricken age and dignity told for one brief moment: then the buzz and laughter recommenced, an occasional oath emphasizing itself in the confused noise of the talk, the gurgle of wine, the ring of glass, and the chink of china.

In Malcolm's vision, dazzled and bewildered at first, things soon began to arrange themselves. The walls of the room receded to their proper distance, and he saw that they were covered with pictures of ladies and gentlemen, gorgeously attired; the ceiling rose and settled into the dim show of a sky, amongst the clouds of which the shapes of very solid women and children disported themselves; while about the glittering table, lighted by silver candelabra with many branches, he distinguished the gaily dressed company, round which, like huge ill-painted butterflies, the liveried footmen hovered. His eyes soon found the lovely face of Lady Florimel, but after the first glance he dared hardly look again. Whether its radiance had any smallest source in the pleasure of appearing like a goddess in the eyes of her humble servant, I dare not say, but more lucent she could hardly have appeared had she been the princess in a fairy tale, about to marry her much-thwarted prince. She wore far too many jewels for one so young, for her father had given her all that belonged to her mother, as well as some family diamonds, and her inexperience knew no reason why she should not wear them. The diamonds flashed and sparkled and glowed on a white rather than fair neck, which, being very much *uncollared* dazzled Malcolm far more than the jewels. Such a form of enhanced loveliness, reflected for the first time in the pure mirror of a high-toned manhood, may well be to such a youth as that of an angel with whom he has henceforth to wrestle in deadly agony until the final dawn; for lofty condition and gorgeous circumstance, while combining to raise a woman to an ideal height, ill suffice to lift her beyond love, or shield the lowliest man from the arrows of her radiation; they leave her human still. She was talking and laughing with a young man of weak military aspect, whose eyes gazed unshrinking on her beauty.

The guests were not numerous: a certain bold-faced countess, the fire in whose eyes had begun to tarnish, and the natural lines of whose figure were vanishing in expansion; the soldier, her nephew, a wasted elegance; a long, lean man, who dawdled with what he ate, and drank as if his bones thirsted; an elderly, broad, red-faced, bull-necked baron of the Hanoverian type; and two neighbouring lairds and their wives, ordinary, and well pleased to be at the marquis's table.

Although the waiting were as many as the waited upon, Malcolm, who was keen-eyed, and had a passion for service—a thing unintelligible to the common mind,—soon spied an opportunity of making himself useful. Seeing one of the men, suddenly called away, set down a dish of fruit just as the countess was expecting it, he jumped up, almost involuntarily, and handed it to her. Once in the current of things, Malcolm would not readily make for the shore of inactivity: he finished the round of the table with the dish, while the men looked indignant, and the marquis eyed him queerly.

While he was thus engaged, however, Duncan, either that his poor stock of patience was now utterly exhausted, or that he fancied a signal given, compressed of a sudden his full-blown waiting bag, and blasted forth such a wild howl of the pibroch, that more than one of the ladies gave a cry and half started from their chairs. The marquis burst out laughing, but gave orders to stop him—a thing not to be effected in a moment, for Duncan was in full tornado, with the avenues of hearing, both corporeal and mental, blocked by his own darling utterance. Understanding at length, he ceased with the air and almost the carriage of a suddenly checked horse, looking half startled, half angry, his cheeks puffed, his nostrils expanded, his head thrown back, the port-vent still in his mouth, the blown bag under his arm, and his fingers on the chanter, on the fret to dash forward again with redoubled energy. But slowly the strained muscles relaxed, he let the tube fall from his lips, and the bag descended to his lap.

"A man forbid," he heard the ladies rise and leave the room, and not until the gentlemen sat down again to their wine, was there any demand for the exercise of his art.

Now whether what followed had been prearranged, and old Duncan invited for the express purpose of carrying it out, or whether it was conceived and executed on the spur of the moment, which seems less likely, I cannot tell, but the turn things now took would be hard to believe, were they dated in the present generation. Some of my elder readers, however, will, from their own knowledge of similar actions, grant likelihood enough to my record.

While the old man was piping, as bravely as his lingering mortification would permit, the marquis interrupted his music to make him drink a large glass of sherry; after which he requested him to play his loudest, that the gentlemen might hear what his pipes could do. At the same time he sent Malcolm with a message to the butler about some particular wine he wanted. Malcolm went more than willingly, but lost a good deal of time from not knowing his way through the house. When he returned he found things frightfully changed.

As soon as he was out of the room, and while the poor old man was blowing his hardest, in the fancy of rejoicing his hearers with the glorious music of the highland hills, one of the company—it was never known which, for each merrily accused the other— took a penknife, and going softly behind him, ran the sharp blade into the bag, and made a great slit, so that the wind at once rushed out, and the tune ceased without sob or wail. Not a laugh betrayed the cause of the catastrophe: in silent enjoyment the conspirators sat watching his movements. For one moment Duncan was so astounded that he could not think; the next he laid the instrument across his knees, and began feeling for the cause of the sudden collapse. Tears had gathered in the eyes that were of no use but to weep withal, and were slowly dropping.

"She wass afrait, my lort and chentle-mans," he said, with a quavering voice, "tat her pag will pe near her latter end; put she pelieved she would pe living peyond her nainsel, my chentlemans."

He ceased abruptly, for his fingers had found the wound, and were prosecuting an inquiry: they ran along the smooth edges of the cut, and detected treachery. He gave a cry like that of a wounded animal, flung his pipes from him, and sprang to his feet, but forgetting a step below him, staggered forward a few paces and fell heavily. That instant Malcolm entered the room. He hurried in consternation to his assistance. When he had helped him up and seated him again on the steps, the old man laid his head on his boy's bosom, threw his arms around his neck, and wept aloud.

"Malcolm, my son," he sobbed, "Tuncan is wronged in ta halls of ta strancher; tey 'll haf stapped his pest friend to ta heart, and och hone! och hone! she'll pe aall too plint to take fencheance. Malcolm, son of heroes, traw ta claymore of ta pard, and fall upon ta traitors. She'll pe singing you ta onset, for ta pibroch is no more."

"She wass afrait, my lort and chentle-mans," he said, with a quavering voice, "tat her bag will be near her latter end; but she believed she would be living beyond her nainsel, my chentlemans."

He ceased abruptly, for his fingers had found the wound, and were prosecuting an inquiry: they ran along the smooth edges of the cut, and detected treachery. He gave a cry like that of a wounded animal, flung his pipes from him, and sprang to his feet, but forgetting a step below him, staggered forward a few paces and fell heavily. That instant Malcolm entered the room. He hurried in consternation to his assistance. When he had helped him up and seated him again on the steps, the old man laid his head on his boy's bosom, threw his arms around his neck, and wept aloud.

"Malcolm, my son," he sobbed, "Tuncan is wronged in ta halls of ta strancher; tey 'll haf stabbed his best friend to ta heart, and alas! alas! she'll be aall too blind to take fencheance. Malcolm, son of heroes, draw ta claymore of ta bard, and fall upon ta traitors. She'll be singing you ta onset, for ta pibroch is no more."

His quavering voice rose that instant in a fierce though feeble chant, and his hand flew to the hilt of his weapon.

Malcolm, perceiving from the looks of the men that things were as his grandfather had divined, spoke indignantly:

"Ye oucht to tak shame to ca' yersel's gentlefowk, an' play a puir blin' man, wha was doin' his best to please ye, sic an ill-faured trick."

As he spoke they made various signs to him not to interfere, but Malcolm paid them no heed, and turned to his grandfather, eager to persuade him to go home. They had no intention of letting him off yet, however. Acquainted—probably through his gamekeeper, who laid himself out to amuse his master—with the piper's peculiar antipathies, Lord Lossie now took up the game.

"It was too bad of you, Campbell," he said, "to play the good old man such a dog's trick."

At the word *Campbell* the piper shook off his grandson, and sprang once more to his feet, his head thrown back, and every inch of his body trembling with rage.

"She might haf known," he screamed, half choking, "that a cursed tog of a Cawmill was in it!"

He stood for a moment, swaying in every direction, as if the spirit within him doubted whether to cast his old body on the earth in contempt of its helplessness, or to fling it headlong on his foes. For that one moment silence filled the room.

"You needn't attempt to deny it; it really *was* too bad of you, Glenlyon," said the marquis.

His quavering voice rose that instant in a fierce though feeble chant, and his hand flew to the hilt of his weapon.

Malcolm, perceiving from the looks of the men that things were as his grandfather had divined, spoke indignantly:

"You should be ashamed to call yourselves gentlefolk, and play a poor blind man, who was doing his best to please you, such a cruel trick."

As he spoke they made various signs to him not to interfere, but Malcolm paid them no heed, and turned to his grandfather, eager to persuade him to go home. They had no intention of letting him off yet, however. Acquainted—probably through his gamekeeper, who laid himself out to amuse his master—with the piper's peculiar antipathies, Lord Lossie now took up the game.

"It was too bad of you, Campbell," he said, "to play the good old man such a dog's trick."

At the word *Campbell* the piper shook off his grandson, and sprang once more to his feet, his head thrown back, and every inch of his body trembling with rage.

"She might haf known," he screamed, half choking, "that a cursed dog of a Cawmill was in it!"

He stood for a moment, swaying in every direction, as if the spirit within him doubted whether to cast his old body on the earth in contempt of its helplessness, or to fling it headlong on his foes. For that one moment silence filled the room.

"You needn't attempt to deny it; it really *was* too bad of you, Glenlyon," said the marquis.

A howl of fury burst from Duncan's labouring bosom. His broadsword flashed from its sheath, and brokenly panting out the words: "Clenlyon! Ta creat dufil! Haf I peen trinking with ta hellhount, Clenlyon?"—he would have run a Malay muck through the room with his huge weapon. But he was already struggling in the arms of his grandson, who succeeded at length in forcing from his bony grasp the hilt of the terrible claymore. But as Duncan yielded his weapon, Malcolm lost his hold on him. He darted away, caught his dirk—a blade of unusual length—from its sheath, and shot in the direction of the last word he had heard. Malcolm dropped the sword and sprung after him.

"Gif her ta fillain by ta troat," screamed the old man. "*She'll* stap his pag! She'll cut *his* chanter in two! She'll pe toing it! Who put ta creat cranson of Inverriggen should pe cutting ta troat of ta tog Clenlyon!"

A howl of fury burst from Duncan's labouring bosom. His broadsword flashed from its sheath, and brokenly panting out the words: "Clenlyon! Ta creat defil! Haf I been trinking with ta hellhount, Clenlyon?"—he would have run a Malay muck through the room with his huge weapon. But he was already struggling in the arms of his grandson, who succeeded at length in forcing from his bony grasp the hilt of the terrible claymore. But as Duncan yielded his weapon, Malcolm lost his hold on him. He darted away, caught his dirk—a blade of unusual length—from its sheath, and shot in the direction of the last word he had heard. Malcolm dropped the sword and sprung after him.

"Gif her ta fillain by ta troat," screamed the old man. "*She'll* stab his bag! She'll cut *his* chanter in two! She'll be toing it! Who but ta creat-crandson of Inverriggen should be cutting ta troat of ta dog Clenlyon!"

As he spoke, he was running wildly about the room, brandishing his weapon, knocking over chairs, and sweeping bottles and dishes from the table. The clatter was tremendous: and the smile had faded from the faces of the men who had provoked the disturbance. The military youth looked scared: the Hanoverian pig-cheeks were the colour of lead; the long lean man was laughing like a skeleton: one of the lairds had got on the sideboard, and the other was making for the door with the bell-rope in his hand; the marquis, though he retained his coolness, was yet looking a little anxious; the butler was peeping in at the door, with red nose and pale cheekbones, the handle in his hand, in instant readiness to pop out again; while Malcolm was after his grandfather, intent upon closing with him. The old man had just made a desperate stab at nothing half across the table, and was about to repeat it, when, spying danger to a fine dish, Malcolm reached forward to save it. But the dish flew in splinters, and the dirk passing through the thick of Malcolm's hand, pinned it to the table, where Duncan, fancying he had at length stabbed Glenlyon, left it quivering.

"Tere, Clenlyon," he said, and stood trembling in the ebb of passion, and murmuring to himself something in Gaelic.

Meantime Malcolm had drawn the dirk from the table, and released his hand. The blood was streaming from it, and the marquis took his own handkerchief to bind it up; but the lad indignantly refused the attention, and kept holding the wound tight with his left hand. The butler, seeing Duncan stand quite still, ventured, with scared countenance, to approach the scene of destruction.

"Dinna gang near him," cried Malcolm. "He has his skene dhu yet, an' in grips that's warst ava."

"Don't go near him," cried Malcolm. "He has his skene dhu yet, and in grips that's worst of all."

Scarcely were the words out of his mouth when the black knife was out of Duncan's stocking, and brandished aloft in his shaking fist.

Scarcely were the words out of his mouth when the black knife was out of Duncan's stocking, and brandished aloft in his shaking fist.

"Daddy!" cried Malcolm, "ye wadna kill twa Glenlyons in ae day—wad ye?"

"Daddy!" cried Malcolm, "you wouldn't kill two Glenlyons in one day—would you?"

"She would, my son Malcolm!—fifty of ta poars in one preath! Tey are ta children of wrath, and tey *haf* to pe testructiont."

"She would, my son Malcolm!—fifty of ta boars in one breath! Tey are ta children of wrath, and tey *haf* to pe destroyed."

"For an auld man ye hae killed enew for ae nicht," said Malcolm, and gently took the knife from his trembling hand. "Ye maun come hame the noo."

"For an old man you've killed enough for one night," said Malcolm, and gently took the knife from his trembling hand. "You must come home now."

"Is ta tog tead then?" asked Duncan eagerly.

"Is ta dog dead then?" asked Duncan eagerly.

"Ow, na; he's breathin' yet," answered Malcolm.

"Oh, na; he's breathing yet," answered Malcolm.

"She'll not can co till ta tog will pe tead. Ta tog may want more killing."

"She'll not can go till ta dog will be dead. Ta dog may want more killing."

"What a horrible savage!" said one of the lairds, a justice of the peace. "He ought to be shut up in a madhouse."

"What a horrible savage!" said one of the lairds, a justice of the peace. "He ought to be shut up in a madhouse."

"Gien ye set aboot shuttin' up, sir, or my lord—I kenna whilk —ye'll hae to begin nearer hame," said Malcolm, as he stooped to pick up the broadsword, and so complete his possession of the weapons. "An' ye'll please to haud in min', that nane here is an injured man but my gran'father himsel'."

"If you set about shutting up, sir, or my lord—I don't know which—you'll have to begin nearer home," said Malcolm, as he stooped to pick up the broadsword, and so complete his possession of the weapons. "And you'll please to remember, that none here is an injured man but my grandfather himself."

"Hey!" said the marquis; "what do you make of all my dishes?"

"Hey!" said the marquis; "what do you make of all my dishes?"

"'Deed, my lord, ye may comfort yersel' that they warna dishes wi barns i' them; for sic 's some scarce i' the Hoose o' Lossie."

"Indeed, my lord, you may comfort yourself that they weren't dishes with brains in them; for such are in short supply in the House of Lossie."

"You're a long-tongued rascal," said the marquis.

"A lang tongue may whiles be as canny as a lang spune, my lord; an' ye ken what that's for?"

The marquis burst into laughter.

"What do you make then of that horrible cut in your own hand?" asked the magistrate.

"I mak my ain business o' 't," answered Malcolm.

While this colloquy passed, Duncan had been feeling about for his pipes: having found them he clasped them to his bosom like a hurt child.

"Come home, come home," he said; "your own pard has refenched you."

Malcolm took him by the arm and led him away. He went without a word, still clasping his wounded bagpipes to his bosom.

"You'll hear from me in the morning, my lad," said the marquis in a kindly tone, as they were leaving the room.

"I hae no wuss to hear onything mair o' yer lordship. Ye hae done eneuch this nicht, my lord, to mak ye ashamed o' yersel' till yer dyin' day—gien ye hed ony pooer o' shame left in ye."

The military youth muttered something about insolence, and made a step towards him. Malcolm quitted his grandfather, and stepped again into his room.

"Come on," he said.

"No, no," interposed the marquis. "Don't you see the lad is hurt?"

"Lat him come on," said Malcolm; "I hae ae soon' han'. Here, my lord, tak the wapons, or the auld man 'll get a grip o' them again."

"You're a long-tongued rascal," said the marquis.

"A long tongue may sometimes be as canny as a long spoon, my lord; and you know what that's for?"

The marquis burst into laughter.

"What do you make then of that horrible cut in your own hand?" asked the magistrate.

"I make my own business of it," answered Malcolm.

While this colloquy passed, Duncan had been feeling about for his pipes: having found them he clasped them to his bosom like a hurt child.

"Come home, come home," he said; "your own bard has refenched you."

Malcolm took him by the arm and led him away. He went without a word, still clasping his wounded bagpipes to his bosom.

"You'll hear from me in the morning, my lad," said the marquis in a kindly tone, as they were leaving the room.

"I have no wish to hear anything more of your lordship. You have done enough this night, my lord, to make you ashamed of yourself till your dying day—if you had any power of shame left in you."

The military youth muttered something about insolence, and made a step towards him. Malcolm quitted his grandfather, and stepped again into his room.

"Come on," he said.

"No, no," interposed the marquis. "Don't you see the lad is hurt?"

"Let him come on," said Malcolm; "I have one good hand. Here, my lord, take the weapons, or the old man will get a grip of them again."

"I tell you *no*," shouted Lord Lossie. "Fred, get out—will you!"

"I tell you *no*," shouted Lord Lossie. "Fred, get out—will you!"

The young gentleman turned on his heel, and Malcolm led his grandfather from the house without further molestation. It was all he could do, however, to get him home. The old man's strength was utterly gone. His knees bent trembling under him, and the arm which rested on his grandson's shook as with an ague-fit. Malcolm was glad indeed when at length he had him safe in bed, by which time his hand had swollen to a great size, and the suffering grown severe.

Thoroughly exhausted by his late fierce emotions, Duncan soon fell into a troubled sleep, whereupon Malcolm went to Meg Partan, and begged her to watch beside him until he should return, informing her of the way his grandfather had been treated, and adding that he had gone into such a rage, that he feared he would be ill in consequence; and if he should be unable to do his morning's duty, it would almost break his heart.

"Eh!" said the Partaness, in a whisper, as they parted at Duncan's door, "a baad temper 's a frichtsome thing. I'm sure the times I hae telled him it wad be the ruin o' 'im!"

To Malcolm's gentle knock Miss Horn's door was opened by Jean.

"What d'ye wint at sic an oontimeous hoor," she said, "whan honest fowk's a' i' their nicht caips?"

"I want to see Miss Horn, gien ye please," he answered.

"I s' warran' she'll be in her bed an' snorin'," said Jean; "but I s' gang an' see."

Ere she went, however, Jean saw that the kitchen door was closed, for, whether she belonged to the class "honest folk" or not, Mrs Catanach was in Miss Horn's kitchen, and not in her nightcap.

Jean returned presently with an invitation for Malcolm to walk up to the parlour.

"I hae gotten a sma' mishanter, Miss Horn," he said, as he entered: "an' I thocht I cudna du better than come to you, 'cause ye can haud yer tongue, an' that's mair nor mony ane i' the port o' Portlossie can, mem."

"Eh!" said the Partaness, in a whisper, as they parted at Duncan's door, "A bad temper's an awful thing. I'm sure I've told him often it would be the ruin of him!"

To Malcolm's gentle knock Miss Horn's door was opened by Jean.

"What do you want at this untimely hour," she said, "when honest folk are all in their night caps?"

"I want to see Miss Horn, if you please," he answered.

"I'm sure she'll be in her bed and snoring," said Jean; "but I'll go and see."

Ere she went, however, Jean saw that the kitchen door was closed, for, whether she belonged to the class "honest folk" or not, Mrs Catanach was in Miss Horn's kitchen, and not in her nightcap.

Jean returned presently with an invitation for Malcolm to walk up to the parlour.

"I've had a slight accident, Miss Horn," he said, as he entered: "and I thought I couldn't do better than come to you, since you can hold your tongue, and that's more than many in the port of Portlossie can, ma'am."

The compliment, correct in fact as well as honest in intent, was not thrown away on Miss Horn, to whom it was the more pleasing that she could regard it as a just tribute. Malcolm told her all the story, rousing thereby a mighty indignation in her bosom, a great fire in her hawk-nose, and a succession of wild flashes in her hawk-eyes; but when he showed her his hand,

"Lord, Malcolm!" she cried; "it's a mercy I was made wantin' feelin's, or I cudna hae bed the sicht. My puir bairn!"

Then she rushed to the stair and shouted,

"Jean, ye limmer! Jean! Fess some het watter, an' some linen cloots."

"I hae nane o' naither," replied Jean from the bottom of the stair.

"Mak up the fire an' put on some watter direckly.—I s' fin' some clooties," she added, turning to Malcolm, "gien I sud rive the tail frae my best Sunday sark."

She returned with rags enough for a small hospital, and until the grumbling Jean brought the hot water, they sat and talked in the glimmering light of one long-beaked tallow candle.

"It's a terrible hoose, yon o' Lossie," said Miss Horn; "and there's been terrible things dune intill't. The auld markis was an ill man. I daurna say what he wadna hae dune, gien half the tales be true 'at they tell o' 'im; an' the last ane was little better. This ane winna be sae ill, but it's clear 'at he's tarred wi' the same stick."

"I dinna think he means onything muckle amiss," agreed Malcolm, whose wrath had by this time subsided a little, through the quieting influences of Miss

The compliment, correct in fact as well as honest in intent, was not thrown away on Miss Horn, to whom it was the more pleasing that she could regard it as a just tribute. Malcolm told her all the story, rousing thereby a mighty indignation in her bosom, a great fire in her hawk-nose, and a succession of wild flashes in her hawk-eyes; but when he showed her his hand,

"Lord, Malcolm!" she cried; "it's a mercy I was made without feelings, or I couldn't have borne the sight. My poor child!"

Then she rushed to the stair and shouted,

"Jean, you hussy! Jean! Fetch some hot water, and some linen rags."

"I have none of either," replied Jean from the bottom of the stair.

"Make up the fire an put on some water directly.—I'll find some rags," she added, turning to Malcolm, "if I should tear the tail from my best Sunday dress."

She returned with rags enough for a small hospital, and until the grumbling Jean brought the hot water, they sat and talked in the glimmering light of one long-beaked tallow candle.

"It's a terrible place, Lossie House," said Miss Horn; "and there's been terrible things done there. The old marquis was a bad sort. I daren't say what he wouldn't have done, if half the tales be true that they tell of him; and the last one was little better. This one isn't so bad, but it's clear that he's tarred with the same stick."

"I don't think he means much harm," agreed Malcolm, whose wrath had by this time subsided a little, through the quieting influences of Miss Horn's sympathy.

Horn's sympathy. "He's mair thouchtless, I do believe, than ill contrived—an' a' for's fun. He spak unco kin'-like to me, efterhin, but I cudna accep' it, ye see, efter the w'y he had saired my daddy. But wadna ye hae thoucht he was auld eneuch to ken better by this time?"

"He's more thoughtless, I do believe, than ill contrived—and all to amuse himself. He spoke very kindly to me, afterwards, but I couldn't accept it, you see, after the way he had served my daddy. But wouldn't you have thought he was old enough to know better by this time?"

"An auld fule 's the warst fule ava'," said Miss Horn. "But naething o' that kin', be 't as mad an' pranksome as ever sic ploy could be, is to be made mention o' aside the things at was mutit o' 's brither. I budena come ower them till a young laad like yersel'. They war never said straucht oot, min' ye, but jist mintit at, like, wi' a doon-draw o' the broos, an' a wee side shak o' the heid, as gien the body wad say, 'I cud tell ye gien I daur.' But I doobt mysel' gien onything was *kent*, though muckle was mair nor suspeckit. An' whaur there's reik, there maun be fire."

"An old fool's the worst fool of all," said Miss Horn. "But nothing of that kind, be it as mad and pranksome as ever such ploy could be, is to be compared with the things that were rumoured about his brother. I had better not repeat them to a young lad like yourself. They were never said straight out, mind you, but just hinted at, like, with a lowering of the brows, and a wee side shake of the head, as if the body would say, 'I could tell you if I dared.' But I doubt myself if anything was *known*, though much was more than suspected. And where there's smoke, there must be fire."

As she spoke she was doing her best, with many expressions of pity, for his hand. When she had bathed and bound it up, and laid it in a sling, he wished her goodnight.

Arrived at home he found, to his dismay, that things had not been going well. Indeed, while yet several houses off he had heard the voices of the Partan's wife and his grandfather in fierce dispute. The old man was beside himself with anxiety about Malcolm; and the woman, instead of soothing him, was opposing everything he said, and irritating him frightfully. The moment he entered, each opened a torrent of accusations against the other, and it was with difficulty that Malcolm prevailed on the woman to go home. The presence of his boy soon calmed the old man, however, and he fell into a troubled sleep— in which Malcolm, who sat by his bed all night, heard him, at intervals, now lamenting over the murdered of Glenco, now exulting in a stab that had reached the heart of Glenlyon, and now bewailing his ruined bagpipes. At length towards morning he grew quieter, and Malcolm fell asleep in his chair.

CHAPTER XX

ADVANCES

When he woke, Duncan still slept, and Malcolm having got ready some tea for his grandfather's, and a little brose for his own breakfast, sat down again by the bedside, and awaited the old man's waking.

The first sign of it that reached him was the feebly-uttered question,—

"Will ta tog be tead, Malcolm?"

"As sure 's ye stabbit him," answered Malcolm.

"Then she'll pe getting herself ready," said Duncan, making a motion to rise.

"What for, daddy?"

"For ta hanging, my son," answered Duncan coolly.

"Time eneuch for that, daddy, whan they sen' to tell ye," returned Malcolm, cautious of revealing the facts of the case.

"Ferry coot!" said Duncan, and fell asleep again.

In a little while he woke with a start.

"She'll be hafing an efil tream, my son Malcolm," "or it was 'll pe more than a tream. Cawmill of Clenlyon, Cod curse him! came to her pedside; and he'll say to her, 'MacDhonuill,' he said, for pein' a tead man he would pe knowing my name,—'MacDhonuill,' he said, 'what tid you'll pe meaning py turking my posterity?' And she answered and said to him, 'I pray it had peen yourself, you tamned Clenlyon.' And he said to me, 'It 'll pe no

"Will ta dog be dead, Malcolm?"

"As sure as you stabbed him," answered Malcolm.

"Then she'll be getting herself ready," said Duncan, making a motion to rise.

"What for, daddy?"

"For ta hanging, my son," answered Duncan coolly.

"Time enough for that, daddy, when they send to tell you," returned Malcolm, cautious of revealing the facts of the case.

"Ferry coot!" said Duncan, and fell asleep again.

In a little while he woke with a start.

"She'll be hafing an efil dream, my son Malcolm," he said; "or it was 'll be more than a dream. Cawmill of Clenlyon, God curse him! came to her bedside; and he'll say to her, 'MacDhonuill,' he said, for bein' a dead man he would be knowing my name,—'MacDhonuill,' he said, 'what did you'll be meaning by dirking my posterity?' And she answered and said to him, 'I pray it had been yourself, you tamned Clenlyon.' And he said to me, 'It'll be no coot wishing tat; it would be toing you no coot to turk me, for I'm a tead man.'—'And a tamned man,' says herself, and would haf taken him py ta troat, put she couldn't mofe. 'Well, I'm not so sure of tat,' says he, 'for I'fe pecked all teir partons.'—'And tid tey gif tem to you, you tog?' says herself.—'Well, I'm not sure,' says he; 'anyhow, I'm not tamned fery much yet.'—'She'll pe much sorry to hear it,' says herself. And she took care aalways to pe calling him some paad name, so tat he shouldn't say *she'll* be forgifing him, whatever ta rest of tem might be toing. 'Put what troubles me,' says he, 'it 'll not pe apout myself at aall.'—'Tat 'll pe a wonter,' says her nain sel': 'and what may it pe apout, you cut-troat?'—'It 'll pe apout yourself,' says he. 'Apout herself?'—'Yes; apout yourself,' says he. 'I'm sorry for you—for ta ting tat's to pe tone with him tat killed a man aal pecaase he pore my name, and he wasn't a son of mine at aall! Tere is no pot in hell teep enough to put him in!'—'Ten tey must make haste and tig one,' says herself; 'for she'll pe hangt in a tay or two.'—So she'll wake up, and beholt it was a tream!"

"An' no sic an ill dream efter a', daddy!" said Malcolm.

"Not an efil tream, my son, when it makes her aalmost wish that she hadn't peen quite killing ta tog! Last night she would haf made a puoy of his skin like any other tog's skin, and totay—no, my son, it wass a fery efil tream. And to be tolt tat ta creat tefil, Clenlyon herself, was not fery much tamned!—it wass a fery efil tream, my son."

"Weel, daddy—maybe ye 'll tak it for ill news, but ye killed naebody."

coot wishing tat; it would be doing you no coot to dirk me, for I'm a dead man.'—'And a tamned man,' says herself, and would haf taken him by ta troat, but she couldn't mofe. 'Well, I'm not so sure of tat,' says he, 'for I'fe begged all teir partons.'—'And tid they gif them to you, you dog?' says herself.—'Well, I'm not sure,' says he, 'anyhow, I'm not tamned fery much yet.'—'She'll be much sorry to hear it,' says herself. And she took care aalways to be calling him some baad name, so tat he shouldn't say *she'll* be forgifing him, whatever ta rest of tem might be doing. 'But what troubles me,' says he, 'it'll not be about myself at aall.'—'Tat'll be a wonder,' says her nain sel': 'and what may it be about, you cut-throat?'—'It'll be about yourself,' says he. 'About herself?'—'Yes, about yourself,' says he. 'I'm sorry for you—for ta thing that's to be done with him that killed a man aal because he bore my name, and he wasn't a son of mine at aall! Tere is no pot in hell deep enough to put him in!'—'Ten tey must make haste and dig one,' says herself; 'for she'll be hangt in a tay or two.'—So she'll wake up, and beholt it was a tream!"

"And not such a bad dream after all, daddy!" said Malcolm.

"Not an efil tream, my son, when it makes her aalmost wish that she hadn't been quite killing ta dog! Last night she would haf made a buoy of his skin like any other dog's skin, and today—no, my son, it wass a fery efil tream. And to be tolt tat ta creat defil, Clenlyon herself, was not fery much tamned!—it wass a fery efil tream, my son."

"Well, daddy—maybe you'll take it for bad news, but you killed nobody."

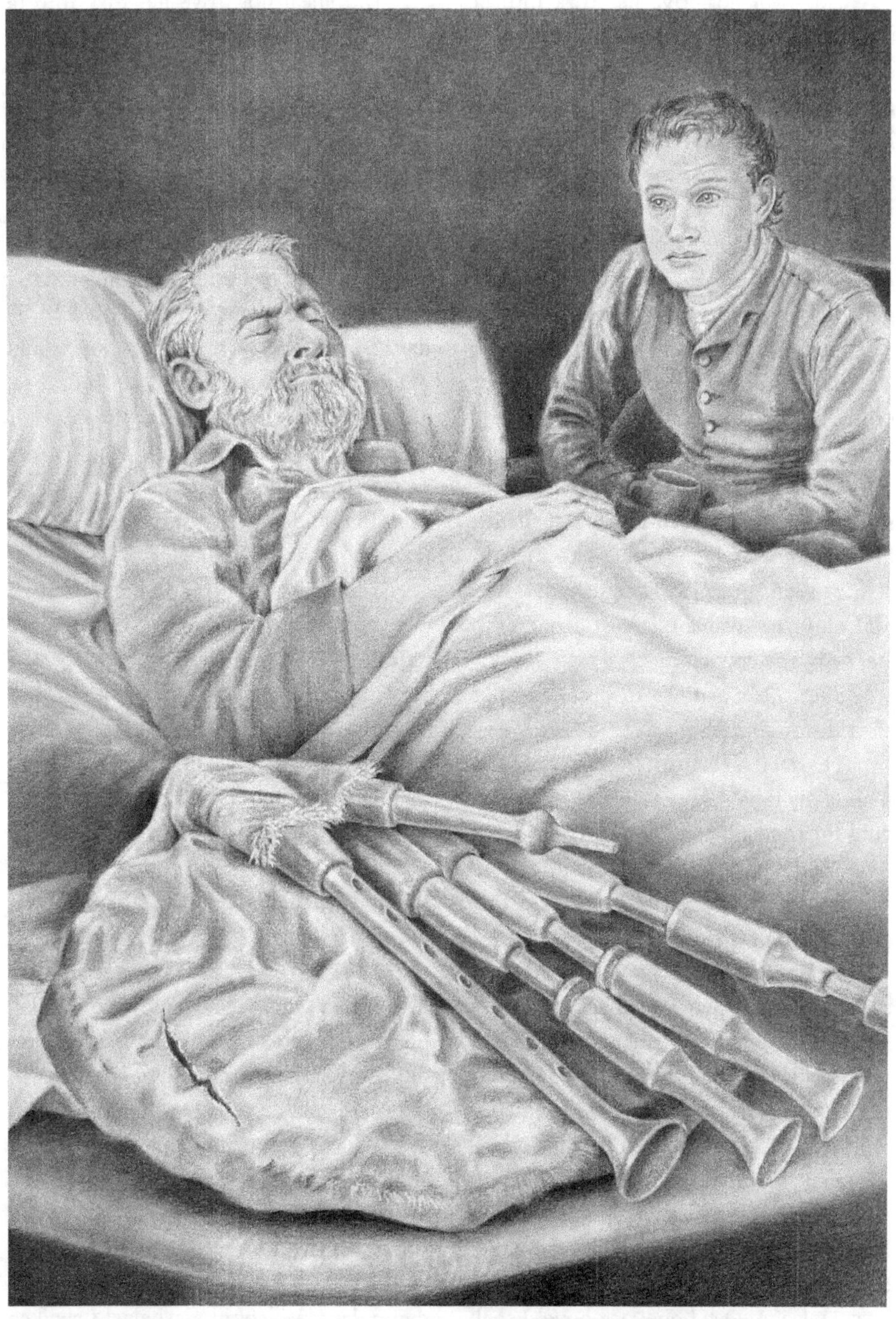

Malcolm...sat down by the bedside, and awaited the old man's waking.

"Tid she'll not trive her turk into ta tog?" cried Duncan fiercely. "Och hone! och hone!—Then she's ashamed of herself for efer, when she might have tone it. And it 'll hafe to be tone yet!"

He paused a few moments, and then resumed:

"And she'll not pe coing to be hangt?—Maype tat will pe petter, for you wouldn't hafe liket to see your olt cranfather to pe hangt, Malcolm, my son. Not tat she would hafe minted it herself in such a coot caause, Malcolm! Put she tidn't pe fery happy after she tid think she had tone it, for you see he wasn't ta fery man his ownself, and tat must pe counted. But she tid kill something: what was it, Malcolm?"

"Ye sent a gran' dish fleein'," answered Malcolm. "I s' warran' it cost a poun', to jeedge by the gowd upo' 't."

"She'll hear a noise of preaking; put she tid stap something soft."

"Ye stack yer durk intill my lord's mahogany table," said Malcolm. "It nott a guid rug to haul't oot."

"Then her arm has not lost aal its strength, Malcolm! I pray ta taple had peen ta rips of Clenlyon!"

"Ye maunna pray nae sic prayers, daddy. Min' upo' what Glenlyon said to ye last nicht. Gien I was you I wadna hae a pot howkit express for mysel'—doon yonner—i' yon place 'at ye dreamed aboot."

"Well, I'll forgife him a little, Malcolm—not ta one tat's tead, but ta one tat tidn't do it, you know.—Put how will she pe forgifing him for ripping her poor pag? Och hone! och hone! No more musics for her tying tays, Malcolm! Och hone! och hone! I shall co creeping to ta crafe with no loud noises to defy ta enemy. Her pipes is tumb for efer and efer. Och hone! och hone!"

"Did she'll not drive her dirk into ta dog?" cried Duncan fiercely. "Alas! alas!—Then she's ashamed of herself for efer, when she might have done it. And it'll haf to be done yet!"

He paused a few moments, and then resumed:

"And she'll not be going to be hangt?—Maybe tat will be better, for you wouldn't haf liket to see your olt cranfather to be hangt, Malcolm, my son. Not tat she would haf minted it herself in such a coot caause, Malcolm! But she tidn't be fery happy after she tid think she had done it, for you see he wasn't ta fery man his ownself, and tat must be counted. But she tid kill something: what was it, Malcolm?"

"You sent a grand dish flying," answered Malcolm. "I'll bet it cost a pound, to judge by the gold upon it."

"She'll hear a noise of breaking; but she tid stab something soft."

"You stuck your dirk into my lord's mahogany table," said Malcolm. "It needed a good pull to haul it out."

"Then her arm has not lost aal its strength, Malcolm! I pray ta table had been ta ribs of Clenlyon!"

"You mustn't pray such prayers, daddy. Remember what Glenlyon said to you last night. If I were you I wouldn't have a pit dug especially for me—down yonder—in that place you dreamed about."

"Well, I'll forgife him a little, Malcolm—not ta one tat's dead, but ta one tat tidn't do it, you know.—But how will she be forgifing him for ripping her poor bag? Alas! alas! No more musics for her dying days, Malcolm! Alas! alas! I shall co creeping to ta crafe with no loud noises to defy ta enemy. Her pipes is dumb for efer and efer. Alas! alas!"

The lengthening of his days had restored bitterness to his loss.

"I'll sune set the bag richt, daddy. Or, gien I canna du that, we'll get a new ane. Mony a pibroch 'll come skirlin' oot o' that chanter yet er' a' be dune."

They were interrupted by the unceremonious entrance of the same footman who had brought the invitation. He carried a magnificent set of ebony pipes, with silver mountings.

"A present from my lord, the marquis," he said bumptiously, almost rudely, and laid them on the table.

"Dinna lay them there; tak them frae that, or I'll fling them at yer poothered "wig," said Malcolm. "—It's a stan' o' pipes," he added, "an' that a gran' ane, daddy."

"Take tem away!" cried the old man, in a voice too feeble to support the load of indignation it bore. "She'll pe taking no presents from marquis or tuke tat would pe teceifing old Tuncan, and making him trink with ta cursed Clenlyon. Tell ta marquis he 'll pe sending her cray hairs with sorrow to ta crafe; for she 'll pe tishonoured for efer and henceforth."

The lengthening of his days had restored bitterness to his loss.

"I'll soon set the bag right, daddy. Or, if I can't do that, we'll get a new one. Many a pibroch will come skirling out of that chanter yet before all be done."

They were interrupted by the unceremonious entrance of the same footman who had brought the invitation. He carried a magnificent set of ebony pipes, with silver mountings.

"A present from my lord, the marquis," he said bumptiously, almost rudely, and laid them on the table.

"Don't lay them there; take them back, or I'll fling them at your powdered wig," said Malcolm. "—It's a stand of pipes," he added, "and a mighty grand one, daddy."

"Take tem away!" cried the old man, in a voice too feeble to support the load of indignation it bore. "She'll be taking no presents from marquis or duke tat would be deceifing old Tuncan, and making him trink with ta cursed Clenlyon. Tell ta marquis he'll be sending her gray hairs with sorrow to ta crafe; for she'll be dishonoured for efer and henceforth."

Probably pleased to be the bearer of a message fraught with so much amusement, the man departed in silence with the pipes.

The marquis, although the joke had threatened, and indeed so far taken a serious turn, had yet been thoroughly satisfied with its success. The rage of the old man had been to his eyes ludicrous in the extreme, and the anger of the young one so manly as to be even picturesque. He had even made a resolve, half-dreamy and of altogether improbable execution, to do something for the fisher fellow.

The pipes which he had sent as a solatium to Duncan, were a set that belonged to the house—ancient, and in the eyes of either connoisseur or antiquarian, exceedingly valuable; but the marquis was neither the one nor the other, and did not in the least mind parting with them. As little did he doubt a propitiation through their means, was utterly unprepared for a refusal of his gift, and was nearly as much perplexed as annoyed thereat.

For one thing, he could not understand such offence taken by one in Duncan's lowly position; for although he had plenty of highland blood in his own veins, he had never lived in the Highlands, and understood nothing of the habits or feelings of the Gael. What was noble in him, however, did feel somewhat rebuked, and he was even a little sorry at having raised a barrier between himself and the manly young fisherman, to whom he had taken a sort of liking from the first.

Of the ladies in the drawing-room, to whom he had recounted the vastly amusing joke with all the graphic delineation for which he had been admired at court, none, although they all laughed, had appeared to enjoy the bad recital thoroughly, except the bold-faced countess. Lady Florimel regarded the affair as undignified at the best, was sorry for the old man, who must be mad, she thought, and was pleased only with the praises of her squire of low degree. The wound in his hand the marquis either thought too trifling to mention, or serious enough to have clouded the clear sky of frolic under which he desired the whole transaction to be viewed.

They were seated at their late breakfast when the lackey passed the window on his return from his unsuccessful mission, and the marquis happened to see him, carrying the rejected pipes. He sent for him, and heard his report, then with a quick nod dismissed him—his way when angry, and sat silent.

"Wasn't it spirited—in such poor people too?" said Lady Florimel, the colour rising in her face, and her eyes sparkling.

"It was damned impudent," said the marquis.

"I think it was damned dignified," said Lady Florimel.

The marquis stared. The visitors, after a momentary silence, burst into a great laugh.

"I wanted to see," said Lady Florimel calmly, "whether *I* couldn't swear if I tried. I don't think it tastes nice. I shan't take to it, I think."

"You'd better not in my presence, my lady," said the marquis, his eyes sparkling with fun.

"I shall certainly not do it out of your presence, my lord," she returned. "—Now I think of it," she went on, "I know what I will do: every time you say a bad word in *my* presence, I shall say it after you. I shan't mind who's there—parson or magistrate. Now you'll see."

"You will get into the habit of it."

"Except you get out of the habit of it first, papa," said the girl, laughing merrily.

"You confounded little Amazon!" said her father.

"But what's to be done about those confounded pipes?" she resumed. "You can't allow such people to serve you so! Return your presents, indeed! Suppose I undertake the business?"

"By all means. What will you do?"

"Make them take them, of course. It would be quite horrible never to be quits with the old lunatic."

"As you please, puss."

"Then you put yourself in my hands, papa?"

"Yes; only you must mind what you're about, you know."

"That I will, and make them mind too," she answered, and the subject was dropped.

Lady Florimel counted upon her influence with Malcolm, and his again with his grandfather; but careful of her dignity, she would not make direct advances; she would wait an opportunity of speaking to him. But, although she visited the sand hill almost every morning, an opportunity was not afforded her. Meanwhile, the state of Duncan's bag and of Malcolm's hand forbidding, neither pipes were played nor gun was fired to arouse marquis or burgess. When a fortnight had thus passed, Lady Florimel grew anxious concerning the justification of her boast, and the more so that her father seemed to avoid all reference to it.

CHAPTER XXI

MEDIATION

At length it was clear to Lady Florimel that if her father had not forgotten her undertaking, but was, as she believed, expecting from her some able stroke of diplomacy, it was high time that something should be done to save her credit. Nor did she forget that the unpiped silence of the royal burgh was the memento of a practical joke of her father, so cruel that a piper would not accept the handsome propitiation offered on its account by a marquis.

On a lovely evening, therefore, the sunlight lying slant on waters that heaved and sunk in a flowing tide, now catching the gold on lifted crests, now losing it in purple hollows, Lady Florimel found herself for the first time, walking from the lower gate towards the Seaton. Rounding the west end of the village, she came to the sea front, where, encountering a group of children, she requested to be shown the blind piper's cottage. Ten of them started at once to lead the way, and she was presently knocking at the half-open door, through which she could not help seeing the two at their supper of dry oat cake and still drier skim-milk cheese, with a jug of cold water to wash it down. Neither, having just left the gentlemen at their wine, could she help feeling the contrast between the dinner just over at the House and the meal she now beheld.

At the sound of her knock, Malcolm, who was seated with his back to the door, rose to answer the appeal;—the moment he saw her, the blood rose from his heart to his cheek in similar response. He opened the door wide, and in low, something tremulous tones, invited her to enter; then caught up a chair, dusted it with his bonnet, and placed it for her by the window, where a red ray of the setting sun fell on a huge-flowered hydrangea. Her quick eye caught sight of his bound-up hand.

"How have you hurt your hand?" she asked kindly.

Malcolm made signs that prayed for silence, and pointed to his grandfather. But it was too late.

"Hurt your hand, Malcolm, my son," cried Duncan, with surprise and anxiety mingled. "How will you pe toing tat?"

"Hurt your hand, Malcolm, my son," cried Duncan, with surprise and anxiety mingled. "How will you be doing tat?"

"Here's a bonny yoong leddy come to see ye, daddy," said Malcolm, seeking to turn the question aside.

"She'll pe fery clad to see ta ponny young laty, and she's creatly obleeched for ta honour: put if ta ponny young laty will pe excusing her—what'll pe hurting your hand, Malcolm!"

"I'll tell ye efterhin, daddy. This is my Leddy Florimel, frae the Hoose."

"Hm!" said Duncan, the pain of his insult keenly renewed by the mere mention of the scene of it. "Put," he went on, continuing aloud the reflections of a moment of silence, "she'll pe a laty, and it's not to pe laid to her charch. Sit town, my laty. Ta poor place is your own."

But Lady Florimel was already seated, and busy in her mind as to how she could best enter on the object of her visit. The piper sat silent, revolving a painful suspicion with regard to Malcolm's hurt.

"So you won't forgive my father, Mr MacPhail?" said Lady Florimel.

"She would forgife any man put two men," he answered, "—Clenlyon, and ta man, whoefer he might pe, who would put upon her ta tiscrace of trinking in his company."

"But you're quite mistaken," said Lady Florimel, in a pleading tone. "I don't believe my father knows the gentleman you speak of."

"Chentleman!" echoed Duncan. "He is a tog!—No, he is no tog: togs is coot. He is a mongrel of a fox and a volf!"

"There was no Campbell at our table that evening," persisted Lady Florimel.

"Ten who tolt Tuncan MacPhail a lie!"

"Here's a bonny young lady come to see you, daddy," said Malcolm, seeking to turn the question aside.

"She'll be fery clad to see ta bonny young laty, and she's creatly obleeched for ta honour: put if ta bonny young laty will be excusing her—what'll be hurting your hand, Malcolm!"

"I'll tell you afterwards, daddy. This is my Lady Florimel, from the House."

"Hm!" said Duncan, the pain of his insult keenly renewed by the mere mention of the scene of it. "But," he went on, continuing aloud the reflections of a moment of silence, "she'll be a laty, and it's not to be laid to her charge. Sit town, my laty. Ta poor place is your own."

But Lady Florimel was already seated, and busy in her mind as to how she could best enter on the object of her visit. The piper sat silent, revolving a painful suspicion with regard to Malcolm's hurt.

"So you won't forgive my father, Mr MacPhail?" said Lady Florimel.

"She would forgife any man but two men," he answered, "—Clenlyon, and ta man, whoefer he might be, who would put upon her ta tiscrace of trinking in his company."

"But you're quite mistaken," said Lady Florimel, in a pleading tone. "I don't believe my father knows the gentleman you speak of."

"Chentleman!" echoed Duncan. "He is a dog!—No, he is no dog: dogs is coot. He is a mongrel of a fox and a volf!"

"There was no Campbell at our table that evening," persisted Lady Florimel.

"Then who tolt Tuncan MacPhail a lie!"

"It was nothing but a joke—indeed!" said the girl, beginning to feel humiliated.

"It wass a paad choke, and might have peen ta hanging of poor Tuncan," said the piper.

Now Lady Florimel had heard a rumour of some one having been hurt in the affair of the joke, and her quick wits instantly brought that and Malcolm's hand together.

"It might have been," she said, risking a miss for the advantage. "It *was* well that you hurt nobody but your own grandson."

"Oh, my leddy!" cried Malcolm with despairing remonstrance; "—an' me haudin' 't frae him a' this time! Ye sud ha' considert an auld man's feelin's! He's as blin' 's a mole, my leddy!"

"His feelings!" retorted the girl angrily. "He ought to know the mischief he does in his foolish rages."

Duncan had risen, and was now feeling his way across the room. Having reached his grandson, he laid hold of his head and pressed it to his bosom.

"Malcolm!" he said, in a broken and hollow voice, not to be recognized as his, "Malcolm, my eagle of the crag! my hart of the heather! was it yourself she stapped with her efil hand, my son? Tid she'll pe hurting her own poy!—She'll nefer wear turk more. Och hone! Och hone!"

He turned, and, with bowed head seeking his chair, seated himself and wept.

Lady Florimel's anger vanished. She was by his side in a moment, with her lovely young hand on the bony expanse of his, as it covered his face. On the other side, Malcolm laid his lips to his ear, and whispered with soothing expostulation,—

"It was nothing but a joke—indeed!" said the girl, beginning to feel humiliated.

"It wass a baad choke, and might have been ta hanging of poor Tuncan," said the piper.

Now Lady Florimel had heard a rumour of some one having been hurt in the affair of the joke, and her quick wits instantly brought that and Malcolm's hand together.

"It might have been," she said, risking a miss for the advantage. "It *was* well that you hurt nobody but your own grandson."

"Oh, my lady!" cried Malcolm with despairing remonstrance; "—and me keeping it from him all this time! You should have considered an old man's feelings! He's as blind as a mole, my lady!"

"His feelings!" retorted the girl angrily. "He ought to know the mischief he does in his foolish rages."

Duncan had risen, and was now feeling his way across the room. Having reached his grandson, he laid hold of his head and pressed it to his bosom.

"Malcolm!" he said, in a broken and hollow voice, not to be recognized as his, "Malcolm, my eagle of the crag! my hart of the heather! was it yourself she stabbed with her efil hand, my son? Did she'll be hurting her own boy!—She'll nefer wear dirk more. Alas! alas!"

He turned, and, with bowed head seeking his chair, seated himself and wept.

Lady Florimel's anger vanished. She was by his side in a moment, with her lovely young hand on the bony expanse of his, as it covered his face. On the other side, Malcolm laid his lips to his ear, and whispered with soothing expostulation,—

"It's maist as weel 's ever daddy. It's nane the waur. It was but a bit o' a scart. It's nae worth twise thinkin' o'."

"Ta turk went trough it, Malcolm! It went into ta table! She knows now! O Malcolm! Malcolm! would to Cod she had killed herself pefore she hurted her poy!"

He made Malcolm sit down beside him, and taking the wounded hand in both of his, sunk into a deep silence, utterly forgetful of the presence of Lady Florimel, who retired to her chair, kept silence also, and waited.

"It was not a coot choke," he murmured at length, "upon an honest man, and might pe calling herself a chentleman. A rache is not a choke. To put her in a rache was not coot. See to it. And it was a ferry paad choke, too, to make a pig hole in her poor pag! Och hone! och hone!—Put I'm clad Clenlyon was not there, for she was too plind to kill him."

"But you will surely forgive my father, when he wants to make it up! Those pipes have been in the family for hundreds of years," said Florimel.

"Her own pipes has peen in her own family for five or six chenerations at least," said Duncan. "—And she was wondering why her poy tidn't pe mending her pag! My poor poy! Och hone! Och hone!"

"We'll get a new bag, daddy," said Malcolm. "It's been lang past men'in' wi' auld age."

"And then you will be able to play together," urged Lady Florimel.

Duncan's resolution was visibly shaken by the suggestion. He pondered for a while. At last he opened his mouth solemnly, and said, with the air of one who had found a way out of a hitherto impassable jungle of difficulty:

"It's almost as well as ever, daddy. It's none the worse. It was but a scratch, and not worth a second thought."

"Ta dirk went through it, Malcolm! It went into ta table! She knows now! O Malcolm! Malcolm! would to God she had killed herself before she hurted her boy!"

He made Malcolm sit down beside him, and taking the wounded hand in both of his, sunk into a deep silence, utterly forgetful of the presence of Lady Florimel, who retired to her chair, kept silence also, and waited.

"It was not a coot choke," he murmured at length, "upon an honest man, and might be calling herself a chentleman. A rage is not a choke. To put her in a rage was not coot. See to it. And it was a ferry baad choke, too, to make a big hole in her poor bag! Alas! alas!—But I'm clad Clenlyon was not there, for she was too blind to kill him."

"But you will surely forgive my father, when he wants to make it up! Those pipes have been in the family for hundreds of years," said Florimel.

"Her own pipes has been in her own family for five or six chenerations at least," said Duncan. "—And she was wondering why her boy tidn't be mending her bag! My poor boy! Alas! alas!"

"We'll get a new bag, daddy," said Malcolm. "It's been long past mending with old age."

"And then you will be able to play together," urged Lady Florimel.

Duncan's resolution was visibly shaken by the suggestion. He pondered for a while. At last he opened his mouth solemnly, and said, with the air of one who had found a way out of a hitherto impassable jungle of difficulty:

"If her lord marquis will come to Tuncan's house, and say to Tuncan it was put a choke and he is sorry for it, then Tuncan will shake hands with ta marquis, and take ta pipes."

A smile of pleasure lighted up Malcolm's face at the proud proposal. Lady Florimel smiled also, but with amusement.

"Will my laty take Tuncan's message to my lord, ta marquis?" asked the old man.

Now Lady Florimel had inherited her father's joy in teasing; and the thought of carrying him such an overture was irresistibly delightful.

"I will take it," she said. "But what if he should be angry?"

"If her lord pe angry, Tuncan is angry too," answered the piper.

Malcolm followed Lady Florimel to the door.

"Put it as saft as ye can, my leddy," he whispered. "I canna bide to anger fowk mair than maun be."

"I shall give the message precisely as your grandfather gave it to me," said Florimel, and walked away.

"If her lord marquis will come to Tuncan's house, and say to Tuncan it was but a choke and he is sorry for it, then Tuncan will shake hands with ta marquis, and take ta pipes."

A smile of pleasure lighted up Malcolm's face at the proud proposal. Lady Florimel smiled also, but with amusement.

"Will my laty take Tuncan's message to my lord, ta marquis?" asked the old man.

Now Lady Florimel had inherited her father's joy in teasing; and the thought of carrying him such an overture was irresistibly delightful.

"I will take it," she said. "But what if he should be angry?"

"If her lord be angry, Tuncan is angry too," answered the piper.

Malcolm followed Lady Florimel to the door.

"Put it as softly as you can, my lady," he whispered. "I can't bear to anger folk more than I must."

"I shall give the message precisely as your grandfather gave it to me," said Florimel, and walked away.

While they sat at dinner the next evening, she told her father from the head of the table, all about her visit to the piper, and ended with the announcement of the condition—word for word—on which the old man would consent to a reconciliation.

Could such a proposal have come from an equal whom he had insulted, the marquis would hardly have waited for a challenge: to have done a wrong was nothing; to confess it would be disgrace. But here the offended party was of such ludicrously low condition, and the proposal therefore so ridiculous, that it struck the marquis merely as a yet more amusing prolongation of the joke. Hence his reception of it was with uproarious laughter, in which all his visitors joined.

"Damn the old windbag!" said the marquis.

"Damn the knife that made the mischief," said Lady Florimel.

When the merriment had somewhat subsided, Lord Meikleham, the youth of soldierly aspect, would have proposed whipping the highland beggar, he said, were it not for the probability the old clothes-horse would fall to pieces; whereupon Lady Florimel recommended him to try it on the young fisherman, who might possibly hold together; whereat the young lord looked both mortified and spiteful.

I believe some compunction, perhaps even admiration, mingled itself, in this case, with Lord Lossie's relish of an odd and amusing situation, and that he was inclined to compliance with the conditions of atonement, partly for the sake of mollifying the wounded spirit of the highlander. He turned to his daughter and said,—

"Did you fix an hour, Flory, for your poor father to make *amende honorable?*"

"No, papa; I did not go so far as that."

The marquis kept a few moments' grave silence.

"Your lordship is surely not meditating such a solecism?" said Mr Morrison, the justice-laird.

"Indeed I am," said the marquis.

"It would be too great a condescension," said Mr Cavins; "and your lordship will permit me to doubt the wisdom of it. These fishermen form a class by themselves; they are a rough set of men, and only too ready to despise authority. You will not only injure the prestige of your rank, my lord, but expose yourself to endless imposition."

"The spirit moves me, and we are commanded not to quench the spirit," rejoined the marquis with a merry laugh, little thinking that he was actually describing what was going on in him—that the spirit of good concerning which he jested, was indeed not only working in him, but gaining on him, in his resolution of that moment.

"Come, Flory," said the marquis, to whom it gave a distinct pleasure to fly in the face of advice, "we'll go at once, and have it over."

So they set out together for the Seaton, followed by the bagpipes, carried by the same servant as before, and were received by the overjoyed Malcolm, and ushered into his grandfather's presence.

Whatever may have been the projected attitude of the marquis, the moment he stood on the piper's floor, the *generosus*, that is the gentleman, in him, got the upper hand, and his behaviour to the old man was not polite merely, but respectful. At no period in the last twenty years had he been so nigh the kingdom of heaven as he was now when making his peace with the blind piper.

When Duncan heard his voice, he rose with dignity and made a stride or two towards the door, stretching forth his long arm to its full length, and spreading wide his great hand with the brown palm upwards:

"Her nainsel will pe proud to see my lord ta marquis under her roof," he said.

The visit itself had already sufficed to banish all resentment from his soul.

The marquis took the proffered hand kindly:

"I have come to apologise," he said.

"Not one vord more, my lort, I peg," interrupted Duncan. "My lort is come, out of his cootness, to pring her a creat kift; for he'll pe hearing of ta sad accident which pefell her poor pipes one efening lately. Tey was ferry old, my lort, and easily hurt."	"Not one vord more, my lort, I beg," interrupted Duncan. "My lort is come, out of his cootness, to bring her a creat kift; for he'll be hearing of ta sad accident which befell her poor pipes one efening lately. Tey was ferry old, my lort, and easily hurt."
"I am sorry—" said the marquis—but again Duncan interrupted him.	"I am sorry—" said the marquis—but again Duncan interrupted him.
"I am clad, my lort," he said, "for it prings me ta creat choy. If my lady and your lordship will honour her poor house py sitting town, she will haf ta pleasure of pe offering tem a little music."	"I am clad, my lort," he said, "for it brings me ta creat joy. If my lady and your lordship will honour her poor house by sitting town, she will haf ta pleasure of be offering them a little music."

His hospitality would give them of the best he had; but ere the entertainment was over, the marquis judged himself more than fairly punished by the pipes for all the wrong he had done the piper.

They sat down, and, at a sign from his lordship, the servant placed his charge in Duncan's hands, and retired. The piper received the instrument with a proud gesture of gratification, felt it all over, screwed at this and that for a moment, then filled the great bag gloriously full. The next instant a scream invaded the astonished air fit to rival the skirl produced by the towzie tyke of Kirk-Alloway[14]; another instant, and the piper was on his legs, as full of pleasure and pride as his bag of wind, strutting up and down the narrow chamber like a turkey-cock before his hens, and turning ever, after precisely so many strides, with a grand gesture and mighty sweep, as if he too had a glorious tail to mind, and was bound to keep it ceaselessly quivering to the tremor of the reed in the throat of his chanter.

Malcolm, erect behind their visitors, gazed with admiring eyes at every motion of his grandfather. To one who had from earliest infancy looked up to him with reverence, there was nothing ridiculous in the display, in the strut, in all that to other eyes too evidently revealed the vanity of the piper: Malcolm regarded it all only as making up the orthodox mode of playing the pipes. It was indeed well that he could not see the expression upon the faces of those behind whose chairs he stood, while for moments that must have seemed minutes, they succumbed to the wild uproar which issued from those splendid pipes. On an opposite hillside, with a valley between, it would have sounded poetic; in a charging regiment, none could have wished for more inspiriting battle-strains; even in a great hall, inspiring and guiding the merry reel, it might have been in place and welcome; but in a room of ten feet by twelve, with a wooden ceiling, acting like a drumhead, at the height of seven feet and a half!—It was little below torture to the marquis and Lady Florimel. Simultaneously they rose to make their escape.

---

14 TOWZIE TYKE OF KIRK-ALLOWAY: a reference to Burns' Tam O'Shanter, in which Satan appears as a piper in dog-like form. "A towzie tyke, black, grim, and large/To gie them music was his charge..."

"My lord an' my leddy maun be gauin', daddy," cried Malcolm.

Absorbed in the sound which his lungs created and his fingers modulated, the piper had forgotten all about his visitors; but the moment his grandson's voice reached him, the tumult ceased; he took the port-vent from his lips, and with sightless eyes turned full on Lord Lossie, said in a low earnest voice,—

"My lort, she'll pe ta craandest staand o' pipes she efer blew, and proud and thankful she'll pe to her lort marquis, and to ta Lort of lorts, for ta kift. Ta pipes shall co town from cheneration to cheneration to ta ent of time; yes, my lort, until ta loud cry of tem pe trownt in ta roar of ta trump of ta creat archanchel, when he'll pe setting one foot on ta laand and ta other foot upon ta sea, and Clenlyon shall pe cast into ta lake of fire."

"My lord and my lady must be going, daddy," cried Malcolm.

Absorbed in the sound which his lungs created and his fingers modulated, the piper had forgotten all about his visitors; but the moment his grandson's voice reached him, the tumult ceased; he took the port-vent from his lips, and with sightless eyes turned full on Lord Lossie, said in a low earnest voice,—

"My lort, she'll be ta graandest staand o' pipes she efer blew, and proud and thankful she'll be to her lort marquis, and to ta Lort of lorts, for ta kift. Ta pipes shall go down from cheneration to cheneration to ta ent of time; yes, my lort, until ta loud cry of them be drownt in ta roar of ta trump of ta creat archanchel, when he'll be setting one foot on ta laand and ta other foot upon ta sea, and Clenlyon shall be cast into ta lake of fire."

He ended with a low bow. They shook hands with him, thanked him for his music, wished him goodnight, and, with a kind nod to Malcolm, left the cottage.

Duncan resumed his playing the moment they were out of the house, and Malcolm, satisfied of his well-being for a couple of hours at least—he had been music-starved so long, went also out, in quest of a little solitude.

CHAPTER XXII

WHENCE AND WHITHER?

He wandered along the shore on the land side of the mound, with a favourite old book of Scottish ballads in his hand, every now and then stooping to gather a sea-anemone—a white flower something like a wild geranium, with a faint sweet smell, or a small, shortstalked harebell, or a red daisy, as large as a small primrose; for along the coast there, on cliff or in sand, on rock or in field, the daisies are remarkable for size, and often not merely tipped, but dyed throughout with a deep red.

He had gathered a bunch of the finest, and had thrown himself down on the side of the dune, whence, as he lay, only the high road, the park wall, the temple of the winds, and the blue sky were visible. The vast sea, for all the eye could tell, was nowhere—not a ripple of it was to be seen, but the ear was filled with the night gush and flow of it. A sweet wind was blowing, hardly blowing, rather gliding, like a slumbering river, from the west. The sun had vanished, leaving a ruin of gold and rose behind him, gradually fading into dull orange and lead and blue sky and stars. There was light enough to read by, but he never opened his book. He was thinking over something Mr Graham had said to him a few days before, namely, that all impatience of monotony, all weariness of best things even, are but signs of the eternity of our nature—the broken human fashions of the divine everlastingness.

"I dinna ken whaur it comes frae," said a voice above him.

He looked up. On the ridge of the mound, the whole of his dwarfed form relieved against the sky and looking large in the twilight, stood the mad laird, reaching out his forehead towards the west with his arms expanded as if to meet the ever coming wind.

"*Naebody* kens whaur the win' comes frae, or whaur it gangs till," said Malcolm. "Ye're no a hair waur aff nor ither fowk, there, laird."

"I don't know where it comes from," said a voice above him.

He looked up. On the ridge of the mound, the whole of his dwarfed form relieved against the sky and looking large in the twilight, stood the mad laird, reaching out his forehead towards the west with his arms expanded as if to meet the ever coming wind.

"*Nobody* knows where the wind comes from, or where it goes to," said Malcolm. "You're not a hair worse off than other folk, there, laird."

"Does't come frae a guid place, or frae an ill?" said the laird, doubtingly.

"Does it come from a good place, or from a bad?" said the laird, doubtingly.

"It's saft an' kin'ly i' the fin' o' 't," returned Malcolm suggestively, rising and joining the laird on the top of the dune, and like him spreading himself out to the western air.

"It has a soft and kindly feel to it," returned Malcolm suggestively, rising and joining the laird on the top of the dune, and like him spreading himself out to the western air.

The twilight had deepened, merging into such night as the summer in that region knows—a sweet pale memory of the past day. The sky was full of sparkles of pale gold in a fathomless blue; there was no moon; the darker sea lay quiet below, with only a murmur about its lip, and fitfully reflected the stars. The soft wind kept softly blowing. Behind them shone a light at the harbour's mouth, and a twinkling was here and there visible in the town above; but all was as still as if there were no life save in the wind and the sea and the stars. The whole feeling was as if something had been finished in heaven, and the outmost ripples of the following rest had overflowed and were now pulsing faintly and dreamily across the bosom of the labouring earth, with feeblest suggestion of the mighty peace beyond. Alas, words can do so little! even such a night is infinite.

"Ay," answered the laird; "but it maks me dowfart like, i' the inside."

"Ay," answered the laird; "but it saddens me like, in the inside."

"Some o' the best things does that," said Malcolm. "I think a kiss frae my mither wad gar me greet."

"Some of the best things do that," said Malcolm. "I think a kiss from my mother would make me weep."

He knew the laird's peculiarities well; but in the thought of his mother had forgotten the antipathy of his companion to the word. Stewart gave a moaning cry, put his fingers in his ears, and glided down the slope of the dune seawards.

Malcolm was greatly distressed. He had a regard for the laird far beyond pity, and could not bear the thought of having inadvertently caused him pain. But he dared not follow him, for that would be but to heighten the anguish of the tortured mind and the suffering of the sickly frame; for, when pursued, he would accomplish a short distance at an incredible speed, then drop suddenly and lie like one dead. Malcolm, therefore, threw off his heavy boots, and starting at full speed along the other side of the dune, made for the bored craig; his object being to outrun the laird without being seen by him, and so, doubling the rock, return with leisurely steps, and meet him. Sweetly the west wind whistled about his head as he ran. In a few moments he had rounded the rock, towards which the laird was still running, but now more slowly. The tide was high and came near its foot, leaving but a few yards of passage between, in which space they approached each other, Malcolm with sauntering step as if strolling homewards. Lifting his bonnet, a token of respect he never omitted when he met the mad laird, he stood aside in the narrow way. Mr Stewart stopped abruptly, took his fingers from his ears, and stared in perplexity.

"It's a richt bonny nicht, laird," said Malcolm.

"It's a right bonny night, laird," said Malcolm.

The poor fellow looked hurriedly behind him, then stared again, then made gestures backward, and next pointed at Malcolm with rapid pokes of his forefinger. Bewilderment had brought on the impediment in his speech, and all Malcolm could distinguish in the babbling efforts at utterance which followed, were the words,—"Twa (two) o' them! Twa o' them! Twa o' them!" often and hurriedly repeated.

"It's a fine, saft-sleekit win,' laird," said Malcolm, as if they were meeting for the first time that night. "I think it maun come frae the blue there, ayont the stars. There's a heap o' wonnerfu' things there, they tell me; an' whiles a strokin win' an' whiles a rosy smell, an' whiles a bricht licht, an' whiles, they say, an auld yearnin' sang, 'ill brak oot, an' wanner awa doon, an' gang flittin' an' fleein' amang the sair herts o' the men an' women fowk 'at canna get things putten richt."

"I think there *are* two fools of them!" said the marquis, referring to the words of the laird.

He was seated with Lady Florimel on the town side of the rock, hidden from them by one sharp corner. They had seen the mad laird coming, and had recognised Malcolm's voice.

"I dinna ken *whaur* I come frae," burst from the laird, the word *whaur* drawn out and emphasized almost to a howl; and as he spoke he moved on again, but gently now, towards the rocks of the Scaurnose. Anxious to get him thoroughly soothed before they parted, Malcolm accompanied him. They walked a little way side by side in silence, the laird every now and then heaving his head like a fretted horse towards the sky, as if he sought to shake the heavy burden from his back, straighten out his poor twisted spine, and stand erect like his companion.

"It's a fine, soft-smooth wind, laird," said Malcolm, as if they were meeting for the first time that night. "I think it must come from the blue there, beyond the stars. There's hundreds of wonderful things there, they tell me; and now a stroking wind and now a rosy smell, and now a bright light, and now, they say, an old yearning song, will break out, and wander away down, and go flitting and flying among the sore hearts of the men and women folk that can't win over their troubles."

"I think there *are* two fools of them!" said the marquis, referring to the words of the laird.

He was seated with Lady Florimel on the town side of the rock, hidden from them by one sharp corner. They had seen the mad laird coming, and had recognised Malcolm's voice.

"I don't know *where* I come from," burst from the laird, the word *where* drawn out and emphasized almost to a howl; and as he spoke he moved on again, but gently now, towards the rocks of the Scaurnose. Anxious to get him thoroughly soothed before they parted, Malcolm accompanied him. They walked a little way side by side in silence, the laird every now and then heaving his head like a fretted horse towards the sky, as if he sought to shake the heavy burden from his back, straighten out his poor twisted spine, and stand erect like his companion.

"Ay!" Malcolm began again, as if he had in the meantime been thinking over the question, and was now assured upon it, "—the win' *maun* come frae yont the stars; for dinna ye min', laird? Ye was at the kirk last Sunday—wasna ye?"

The laird nodded an affirmative, and Malcolm went on.

"An' didna ye hear the minister read frae the buik 'at hoo ilka guid an' ilka perfit gift was frae abune, an' cam frae the Father o' lichts?"

"Father o' lichts!" repeated the laird, and looked up at the stars. "I dinna ken whaur *I* cam frae. I hae nae father. I hae only a ... I hae only a wuman."

The moment he had said the word, he began to move his head from side to side like a scared animal seeking where to conceal itself.

"The Father o' lichts is your father an' mine—The Father o' a' o' 's," said Malcolm.

"O' a' guid fowk, I daursay," said the laird, with a deep and quivering sigh.

"Mr Graham says—o' a'body," returned Malcolm, "guid an' ill; —o' the guid to haud them guid an' mak them better—o' the ill to mak them guid."

"Eh! gien that war true!" said the laird.

"Ay!" Malcolm began again, as if he had in the meantime been thinking over the question, and was now assured upon it, "—the wind *must* come from beyond the stars; for don't you recall, laird? You were at church last Sunday—weren't you?"

The laird nodded an affirmative, and Malcolm went on.

"And didn't you hear the minister read from the book about how every good and every perfect gift was from above, and came from the Father of lights?"

"Father of lights!" repeated the laird, and looked up at the stars. "I don't know where *I* came from. I have no father. I have only a ... I have only a woman."

The moment he had said the word, he began to move his head from side to side like a scared animal seeking where to conceal itself.

"The Father of lights is your father and mine—the Father of all of us," said Malcolm.

"Of all good folk, I daresay," said the laird, with a deep and quivering sigh.

"Mr Graham says—of everyone," returned Malcolm, "good and bad—of the good to keep them good and make them better—of the bad to make them good."

"Eh! if that were true!" said the laird.

They walked on in silence for a minute. All at once the laird threw up his hands, and fell flat on his face on the sand, his poor hump rising skywards above his head. Malcolm thought he had been seized with one of the fits to which he was subject, and knelt down beside him, to see if he could do anything for him. Then he found he was praying: he heard him—he could but just hear him—murmuring over and over, all but inaudibly, "Father o' lichts! Father o' lichts! Father o' lichts!" It seemed as if no other word dared mingle itself with that cry. Maniac or not—the mood of the man was supremely sane, and altogether too sacred to disturb. Malcolm retreated a little way, sat down in the sand and watched beside him. It was a solemn time—the full tide lapping up on the long yellow sand from the wide sea darkening out to the dim horizon: the gentle wind blowing through the molten darkness; overhead, the great vault without arch or keystone, of dim liquid blue, and sown with worlds so far removed they could only shine; and, on the shore, the centre of all the cosmic order, a misshapen heap of man, a tumulus in which lay buried a live and lovely soul! The one pillar of its chapter house had given way, and the downrushing ruin had so crushed and distorted it, that thenceforth until some resurrection should arrive, disorder and misshape must appear to it the law of the universe, and loveliness but the passing dream of a brain glad to deceive its own misery, and so to fancy it had received from above what it had itself generated of its own poverty from below. To the mind's eye of Malcolm, the little hump on the sand was heaved to the stars, higher than ever Roman tomb or Egyptian pyramid, in silent appeal to the sweet heavens, a dumb prayer for pity, a visible groan for the resurrection of the body. For a few minutes he sat as still as the prostrate laird.

But bethinking himself that his grandfather would not go to bed until he went back, also that the laird was in no danger, as the tide was now receding, he resolved to go and get the old man to bed, and then return. For somehow he felt in his heart that he ought not to leave him alone. He could not enter into his strife to aid him, or come near him in any closer way than watching by his side until his morning dawned, or at least the waters of his flood assuaged, yet what he could he must: he would wake with him in his conflict.

He rose and ran for the bored craig, through which lay the straight line to his abandoned boots.

As he approached the rock, he heard the voices of Lord Lossie and Lady Florimel, who, although the one had not yet verified her being, the other had almost ruined his, were nevertheless enjoying the same thing, the sweetness of the night, together. Not hearing Malcolm's approach, they went on talking, and as he was passing swiftly through the bore, he heard these words from the marquis,—

"The world's an ill-baked cake, Flory, and all that a woman, at least, can do, is to cut as large a piece of it as possible, for immediate use."

The remark being a general one, Malcolm cannot be much blamed if he stood with one foot lifted to hear Florimel's reply.

"If it's an ill-baked one, papa," she returned, "I think it would be better to cut as small a piece of it as will serve for immediate use."

Malcolm was delighted with her answer, never thinking whether it came from her head or her heart, for the two were at one in himself.

As soon as he appeared on the other side of the rock, the marquis challenged him:

"Who goes there?" he said.	"Who goes there?" he said.
"Malcolm MacPhail, my lord."	"Malcolm MacPhail, my lord."
"You rascal!" said his lordship, good-humouredly; "you've been listening!"	"You rascal!" said his lordship, good-humouredly; "you've been listening!"
"No muckle, my lord. I heard but a word apiece. An' I maun say my leddy had the best o' the loagic."	"Not much, my lord. I heard but a word apiece. And I must say my lady had the best of the logic."

"My lady generally has, I suspect," laughed the marquis. "How long have you been in the rock there?"

"No ae meenute, my lord. I flang aff my butes to rin efter a freen', an' that's hoo ye didna hear me come up. I'm gaein' efter *them* noo, to gang hame i' them. Guid nicht, my lord. Guid nicht, my leddy."

He turned and pursued his way; but Florimel's face, glimmering through the night, went with him as he ran.

He told his grandfather how he had left the mad laird lying on his face, on the sands between the bored craig and the rocks of the promontory, and said he would like to go back to him.

"He'll be hafing a fit, poor man," said Duncan. "Yes, my son, you must co to him and to your pest for him. After such an honour as we'fe had this day, we mustn't pe forgetting our poor neighpours. Will you pe taking to him a trop of uisgebeatha?"

"He taks naething o' that kin'," said Malcolm.

"My lady generally has, I suspect," laughed the marquis. "How long have you been in the rock there?"

"Not one minute, my lord. I flung off my boots to run after a friend, and that's why you didn't hear me come up. I'm going after *them* now, to go home in them. Good night, my lord. Good night, my lady."

He turned and pursued his way; but Florimel's face, glimmering through the night, went with him as he ran.

He told his grandfather how he had left the mad laird lying on his face, on the sands between the bored craig and the rocks of the promontory, and said he would like to go back to him.

"He'll be hafing a fit, poor man," said Duncan. "Yes, my son, you must co to him and do your best for him. After such an honour as we'fe had this day, we mustn't be forgetting our poor neighbours. Will you be taking to him a trop of whisky?"

"He takes nothing of that kind," said Malcolm.

He could not tell him that the madman, as men called him, lay wrestling in prayer with the Father of lights. The old highlander was not irreverent, but the thing would have been unintelligible to him. He could readily have believed that the supposed lunatic might be favoured beyond ordinary mortals; that at that very moment, lost in his fit, he might be rapt in a vision of the future—a wave of time, far off as yet from the souls of other men, even now rolling over his; but that a soul should seek after vital content by contact with its maker, was an idea belonging to a region which, in the highlander's being, lay as yet an unwatered desert, an undiscovered land, whence even no faintest odour had been wafted across the still air of surprised contemplation.

About the time when Malcolm once more sped through the bored craig, the marquis and Lady Florimel were walking through the tunnel on their way home, chatting about a great ball they were going to give the tenants.

He found the laird where he had left him, and thought at first he must now surely be asleep; but once more bending over him, he could hear him still murmuring at intervals, "Father o' lichts! Father o' lichts!"

Not less compassionate, and more sympathetic than Eliphaz or Bildad or Zophar, Malcolm again took his place near him, and sat watching by him until the gray dawn began in the east. Then all at once the laird rose to his feet, and without a look on either side walked steadily away towards the promontory. Malcolm rose also, and gazed after him until he vanished amongst the rocks, no motion of his distorted frame witnessing other than calmness of spirit. So his watcher returned in peace through the cool morning air to the side of his slumbering grandfather.

No one in the Seaton of Portlossie ever dreamed of locking door or window at night.

CHAPTER XXIII

ARMAGEDDON

The home season of the herring fishery was to commence a few days after the occurrences last recorded. The boats had all returned from other stations, and the little harbour was one crowd of stumpy masts, each with its halliard, the sole cordage visible, rove through the top of it, for the hoisting of a lug sail, tanned to a rich red brown. From this underwood towered aloft the masts of a coasting schooner, discharging its load of coal at the little quay. Other boats lay drawn up on the beach in front of the Seaton, and beyond it on the other side of the burn. Men and women were busy with the brown nets, laying them out on the short grass of the shore, mending them with netting-needles like small shuttles, carrying huge burdens of them on their shoulders in the hot sunlight; others were mending, calking, or tarring their boats, and looking to their various fittings. All was preparation for the new venture in their own waters, and everything went merrily and hopefully. Wives who had not accompanied their husbands now had them home again, and their anxieties would henceforth endure but for a night—joy would come with the red sails in the morning, lovers were once more together, the one great dread broken into a hundred little questioning fears; mothers had their sons again, to watch with loving eyes as they swung their slow limbs at their labour, or in the evenings sauntered about, hands in pockets, pipe in mouth, and blue bonnet cast carelessly on the head: it was almost a single family, bound together by a network of intermarriages, so intricate as to render it impossible for any one who did not belong to the community to follow the threads or read the design of the social tracery.

And while the Seaton swarmed with "the goings on of life," the town of Portlossie lay above it still as a country hamlet, with more odours than people about: of people it was seldom indeed that three were to be spied at once in the wide street, while of odours you would always encounter a smell of leather from the saddler's shop, and a mingled message of bacon and cheese from the very general dealer's—in whose window hung what seemed three hams, and only he who looked twice would discover that the middle object was no ham, but a violin—while at every corner lurked a scent of gillyflowers and southernwood. Idly supreme, Portlossie the upper looked down in condescension, that is in half-concealed contempt, on the ant-heap below it.

The evening arrived on which the greater part of the boats was to put off for the first assay. Malcolm would have made one in the little fleet, for he belonged to his friend Joseph Mair's crew, had it not been found impossible to get the new boat ready before the following evening; whence, for this one more, he was still his own master, with one more chance of a pleasure for which he had been on the watch ever since Lady Florimel had spoken of having a row in his boat. True, it was not often she appeared on the shore in the evening; nevertheless he kept watching the dune with his keen eyes, for he had hinted to Mrs Courthope that perhaps her young lady would like to see the boats go out.

Although it was the fiftieth time his eyes had swept the links in vague hope, he could hardly believe their testimony when now at length he spied a form, which could only be hers, looking seaward from the slope, as still as a sphinx on Egyptian sands. He sauntered slowly towards her by the landward side of the dune, gathering on his way a handful of the reddest daisies he could find; then, ascending the sandhill, approached her along the top.

"Saw ye ever sic gowans in yer life, my leddy?" he said, holding out his posy.

"Is that what you call them?" she returned.

"Ow ay, my leddy—daisies ye ca' them. I dinna ken but yours is the bonnier name o' the twa—gien it be what Mr Graham tells me the auld poet Chaucer maks o' 't."

"What is that?"

"Ow, jist the een o' the day.—the *day's eyes*, ye ken. They're sma' een for sic a great face, but syne there's a lot o' them to mak up for that. They've begun to close a'ready, but the mair they close the bonnier they luik, wi' their bits o' screwed up mooies. But saw ye ever sic reid anes, or ony sic a size, my leddy?"

"I don't think I ever did. What is the reason they are so large and red?"

"I dinna ken. There canna be muckle nourishment in sic a thin soil, but there maun be something that agrees wi' *them*. It's the same a' roon' aboot here."

"Saw you ever such gowans in your life, my lady?" he said, holding out his posy.

"Is that what you call them?" she returned.

"Oh ay, my lady—daisies you call them. I'm not sure that yours isn't the bonnier name of the two—if it be what Mr Graham tells me the old poet Chaucer makes of it."

"What is that?"

"Oh, just the eyes of the day.—the *day's eyes*, you know. They're small eyes for such a great face, but then there's a lot of them to make up for that. They've begun to close already, but the more they close the bonnier they look, with those wee screwed up mouths of theirs. But saw you ever such red ones, or any such a size, my lady?"

"I don't think I ever did. What is the reason they are so large and red?"

"I don't know. There can't be much nourishment in such a thin soil, but there must be something that agrees with *them*. It's the same all round about here."

Lady Florimel sat looking at the daisies, and Malcolm stood a few yards off watching for the first of the red sails, which must soon show themselves, creeping out on the ebb tide. Nor had he waited long before a boat appeared, then another and another—six huge oars, ponderous to toil withal, urging each from the shelter of the harbour out into the wide weltering plain. The fishing boat of that time was not decked as now, and each, with every lift of its bows, revealed to their eyes a gaping hollow, ready, if a towering billow should break above it, to be filled with sudden death. One by one the whole fleet crept out, and ever as they gained the breeze, up went the red sails, and filled: aside leaned every boat from the wind, and went dancing away over the frolicking billows towards the sunset, its sails, deep-dyed in oak-bark, shining redder and redder in the growing redness of the sinking sun.

Nor did Portlossie alone send out her boats, like huge seabirds warring on the live treasures of the deep; from beyond the headlands east and west, out they glided on slow red wing,—from Scaurnose, from Sandend, from Clamrock, from the villages all along the coast,—spreading as they came, each to its work apart through all the laborious night, to rejoin its fellows only as home drew them back in the clear gray morning, laden and slow with the harvest of the stars. But the night lay between, into which they were sailing over waters of heaving green that for ever kept tossing up roses—a night whose curtain was a horizon built up of steady blue, but gorgeous with passing purple and crimson, and flashing with molten gold.

Malcolm was not one of those to whom the sea is but a pond for fish, and the sky a storehouse of wind and rain, sunshine and snow: he stood for a moment gazing, lost in pleasure. Then he turned to Lady Florimel: she had thrown her daisies on the sand, appeared to be deep in her book, and certainly caught nothing of the splendour before her beyond the red light on her page.

"Saw ye ever a bonnier sicht, my leddy?" said Malcolm.

She looked up, and saw, and gazed in silence. Her nature was full of poetic possibilities; and now a formless thought foreshadowed itself in a feeling she did not understand: why should such a sight as this make her feel sad? The vital connection between joy and effort had begun from afar to reveal itself with the question she now uttered.

"What is it all for?" she asked dreamily, her eyes gazing out on the calm ecstasy of colour, which seemed to have broken the bonds of law, and ushered in a new chaos, fit matrix of new heavens and new earth.

"To catch herrin'," answered Malcolm, ignorant of the mood that prompted the question, and hence mistaking its purport.

But a falling doubt had troubled the waters of her soul, and through the ripple she could descry it settling into form. She was silent for a moment.

"I want to know," she resumed, "why it looks as if some great thing were going on. Why is all this pomp and show? Something ought to be at hand. All I see is the catching of a few miserable fish! If it were the eve of a glorious battle now, I could understand it—if those were the little English boats rushing to attack the Spanish Armada, for instance. But they are only gone to catch fish. Or if they were setting out to discover the Isles of the West, the country beyond the sunset!—but this jars."

"I canna answer ye a' at ance, my leddy," said Malcolm; "I maun tak time to think aboot it. But I ken brawly what ye mean."

Even as he spoke he withdrew, and, descending the mound, walked away beyond the bored craig, regardless now of the far-lessening sails and the sinking sun. The motes of the twilight were multiplying fast as he returned along the shore side of the dune, but Lady Florimel had vanished from its crest. He ran to the top: thence, in the dim of the twilight, he saw her slow retreating form, phantom-like, almost at the grated door of the tunnel, which, like that of a tomb, appeared ready to draw her in, and yield her no more.

"My leddy, my leddy," he cried, "winna ye bide for 't?"

He went bounding after her like a deer. She heard him call, and stood holding the door half open.

"It's the battle o' Armageddon, my leddy," he cried, as he came within hearing distance.

But a falling doubt had troubled the waters of her soul, and through the ripple she could descry it settling into form. She was silent for a moment.

"I want to know," she resumed, "why it looks as if some great thing were going on. Why is all this pomp and show? Something ought to be at hand. All I see is the catching of a few miserable fish! If it were the eve of a glorious battle now, I could understand it—if those were the little English boats rushing to attack the Spanish Armada, for instance. But they are only gone to catch fish. Or if they were setting out to discover the Isles of the West, the country beyond the sunset!—but this jars."

"I can't answer you all at once, my lady," said Malcolm; "I must take time to think about it. But I know well what you mean."

Even as he spoke he withdrew, and, descending the mound, walked away beyond the bored craig, regardless now of the far-lessening sails and the sinking sun. The motes of the twilight were multiplying fast as he returned along the shore side of the dune, but Lady Florimel had vanished from its crest. He ran to the top: thence, in the dim of the twilight, he saw her slow retreating form, phantom-like, almost at the grated door of the tunnel, which, like that of a tomb, appeared ready to draw her in, and yield her no more.

"My lady, my lady," he cried, "won't you wait for it?"

He went bounding after her like a deer. She heard him call, and stood holding the door half open.

"It's the battle of Armageddon, my lady," he cried, as he came within hearing distance.

"The battle of what?" she exclaimed, bewildered. "I really can't understand your savage Scotch."

"Hoot, my leddy! the battle o' Armageddon 's no ane o' the Scots battles; it's the battle atween the richt and the wrang, 'at ye read aboot i' the buik o' the Revelations."

"What on earth are you talking about?" returned Lady Florimel in dismay, beginning to fear that her squire was losing his senses.

"It's jist what ye was sayin,' my leddy: sic a pomp as yon bude to hing abune a gran' battle some gait or ither."

"What *has* the catching of fish to do with a battle in the Revelations?" said the girl, moving a little within the door.

"Weel, my leddy, gien I took in han' to set it furth to ye, I wad hae to tell ye a' that Mr Graham has been learnin' me sin ever I can min.' He says 'at the whole economy o' natur is fashiont unco like that o' the kingdom o' haven: it's jist a gradation o' services, an' the highest en' o' ony animal is to contreebute to the life o' ane higher than itsel'; sae that it 's the gran' preevilege o' the fish we tak, to be aten by human bein's, an' uphaud what's abune them."

"That's a poor consolation to the fish," said Lady Florimel.

"Hoo ken ye that, my leddy? Ye can tell nearhan' as little aboot the hert o' a herrin'—sic as it has—as the herrin' can tell aboot yer ain, whilk, I'm thinkin', maun be o' the lairgest size."

"How should you know anything about my heart, pray?" she asked, with more amusement than offence.

"Jist by my ain," answered Malcolm.

"The battle of what?" she exclaimed, bewildered. "I really can't understand your savage Scotch."

"Heavens, my lady! the battle of Armageddon isn't one of the Scots battles; it's the battle between right and wrong, that you read about in the book of Revelation."

"What on earth are you talking about?" returned Lady Florimel in dismay, beginning to fear that her squire was losing his senses.

"It's just what you were saying, my lady: such a pomp as that must hang above a grand battle somewhere or other."

"What *has* the catching of fish to do with a battle in the Revelations?" said the girl, moving a little within the door.

"Well, my lady, if I set about explaining it to you, I would have to tell you all that Mr Graham has been teaching me for as far back as I can remember. He says that the whole economy of nature is fashioned very like that of the kingdom of heaven: it's just a gradation of services, and the highest end of any animal is to contribute to the life of one higher than itself; so that it's the grand privilege of the fish we take, to be eaten by human beings, and sustain what's above them."

"That's a poor consolation to the fish," said Lady Florimel.

"How do you know that, my lady? You can tell almost as little about the heart of a herring—such as it has—as the herring can tell about your own, which, I'm thinking, must be of the largest size."

"How should you know anything about my heart, pray?" she asked, with more amusement than offence.

"Just by my own," answered Malcolm.

Lady Florimel began to fear she must have allowed the fisher-lad more liberty than was proper, seeing he dared avow that he knew the heart of a lady of her position by his own. But indeed Malcolm was wrong, for in the scale of hearts, Lady Florimel's was far below his. She stepped quite within the door, and was on the point of shutting it, but something about the youth restrained her, exciting at least her curiosity; his eyes glowed with a deep, quiet light, and his face, even grand at the moment, had a greater influence upon her than she knew. Instead therefore of interposing the door between them, she only kept it poised, ready to fall-to the moment the sanity of the youth should become a hair's breadth more doubtful than she already considered it.

"It's a' pairt o' ae thing, my leddy," Malcolm resumed. "The herrin 's like the fowk 'at cairries the mate an' the pooder an' sic like for them 'at does the fechtin'. The hert o' the leevin' man's the place whaur the battle's foucht, an' it 's aye gaein' on an' on there atween God an' Sawtan; an' the fish they haud fowk up till 't."

"Do you mean that the herrings help you to fight for God?" said Lady Florimel with a superior smile.

"Aither for God or for the deevil, my leddy—that depen's upo' the fowk themsel's. I say it hauds them up to fecht, an' the thing maun be fouchten oot. Fowk to fecht maun live, an' the herrin' hauds the life i' them, an' sae the catchin' o' the herrin' comes in to be a pairt o' the battle."

"Wouldn't it be more sensible to say that the battle is between the fishermen and the sea, for the sake of their wives and children?" suggested Lady Florimel supremely.

Lady Florimel began to fear she must have allowed the fisher-lad more liberty than was proper, seeing he dared avow that he knew the heart of a lady of her position by his own. But indeed Malcolm was wrong, for in the scale of hearts, Lady Florimel's was far below his. She stepped quite within the door, and was on the point of shutting it, but something about the youth restrained her, exciting at least her curiosity; his eyes glowed with a deep, quiet light, and his face, even grand at the moment, had a greater influence upon her than she knew. Instead therefore of interposing the door between them, she only kept it poised, ready to fall-to the moment the sanity of the youth should become a hair's breadth more doubtful than she already considered it.

"It's all part of one thing, my lady," Malcolm resumed. "The herring are like the folk that carry the meat and the powder and such like for them that do the fighting. The heart of the living man's the place where the battle's fought, and it's always going on and on there between God and Satan; and the fish they give people strength to fight it."

"Do you mean that the herrings help you to fight for God?" said Lady Florimel with a superior smile.

"Either for God or for the devil, my lady—that depends upon the folk themselves. I say it strengthens them to fight, and the thing must be fought out. Folk to fight must live, and the herring keep the life in them, and so the catching of the herring comes in to be a part of the battle."

"Wouldn't it be more sensible to say that the battle is between the fishermen and the sea, for the sake of their wives and children?" suggested Lady Florimel supremely.

"Na, my leddy, it wadna be half sae sensible, for it wadna justifee the grandur that hings ower the fecht. The battle wi' the sea 's no sae muckle o' an affair. An', 'deed, gien it warna that the wives an' the verra weans hae themsel's to fecht i' the same battle o' guid an' ill, I dinna see the muckle differ there wad be atween them an' the fish, nor what for they sudna ate ane anither as the craturs i' the watter du. But gien 't be the battle I say, there can be no pomp o' sea or sky ower gran' for 't; an' it 's a' weel waured gien it but haud the gude anes merry an' strong, an' up to their wark. For that, weel may the sun shine a celestial rosy reid, an' weel may the boatie row, an' weel may the stars luik doon, blinkin' an' luikin' again—ilk ane duin' its bonny pairt to mak a man a richt-hertit guid-willed sodger!"

"And, pray, what may be your rank in this wonderful army?" asked Lady Florimel, with the air and tone of one humouring a lunatic.

"I'm naething but a raw recruit, my leddy; but gien I hed my chice, I wad be piper to my reg'ment."

"How do you mean?"

"I wad mak sangs. Dinna lauch at me, my leddy, for they're the best kin' o' wapon for the wark 'at I ken. But I'm no a makar, an' maun content mysel' wi' duin' my wark."

"Then why," said Lady Florimel, with the conscious right of social superiority to administer good counsel,—"why don't you work harder, and get a better house, and wear better clothes?"

Malcolm's mind was so full of far other and weightier things that the question bewildered him; but he grappled with the reference to his clothes.

"Na, my lady, it wouldn't be half so sensible, for it wouldn't justify the grandeur that hangs over the fight. The battle with the sea's not such a great matter. And, indeed, if it weren't that the wives and the very children had themselves to fight in the same battle of good and ill, I don't see the great difference there would be between them and the fish, nor why they shouldn't eat one another as the creatures in the water do. But if it be the battle I say, there can be no pomp of sea or sky too grand for it; and it's none of it wasted if it but keep the good ones merry and strong, and up to their work. For that, well may the sun shine a celestial rosy red, and well may the boat row, and well may the stars look down, blinking and looking again—each one doing its bonny part to make a man a right-hearted good-willed soldier!"

"And, pray, what may be your rank in this wonderful army?" asked Lady Florimel, with the air and tone of one humouring a lunatic.

"I'm nothing but a raw recruit, my lady; but if I had my choice, I would be piper to my regiment."

"How do you mean?"

"I would make songs. Don't laugh at me, my lady, for they're the best kind of weapon for the work that I know. But I'm not a poet, and must content myself with doing my work."

"Then why," said Lady Florimel, with the conscious right of social superiority to administer good counsel,—"why don't you work harder, and get a better house, and wear better clothes?"

Malcolm's mind was so full of far other and weightier things that the question bewildered him; but he grappled with the reference to his clothes.

"'Deed, my leddy," he returned, "ye may weel say that, seein' ye was never aboord a herrin' boat! but gien ye ance saw the inside o' ane fu' o' fish, whaur a body gangs slidderin' aboot, maybe up to the middle o' 's leg in wamlin' herrin,' an' the neist meenute, maybe, weet to the skin wi' the splash o' a muckle jaw, ye micht think the claes guid eneuch for the wark—though ill fit, I confess wi' shame, to come afore yer leddyship."

"I thought you only fished about close by the shore in a little boat; I didn't know you went with the rest of the fishermen: that's very dangerous work—isn't it?"

"No *ower* dangerous my leddy. There's some gangs doon ilka sizzon; but it 's a' i' the w'y o' yer wark."

"Then how is it you're not gone fishing tonight?"

"She's a new boat, an' there's anither day's wark on her afore we win oot.—Wadna ye like a row the nicht, my leddy?"

"No, certainly; it 's much too late."

"It'll be nane mirker nor 'tis; but I reckon ye're richt. I cam ower by jist to see whether ye wadna like to gang wi' the boats a bit; but yer leddyship set me aff thinkin' an' that pat it oot o' my heid."

"It's too late now anyhow. Come tomorrow evening, and I'll see if I can't go with you."

"I canna, my leddy—that's the fash o' 't! I maun gang wi' Blue Peter the morn's nicht. It was my last chance, I'm sorry to say."

"It's not of the slightest consequence," Lady Florimel returned; and, bidding him goodnight, she shut and locked the door.

"Indeed, my lady," he returned, "you may well say that, since you were never aboard a herring boat! but if you once saw the inside of one full of fish, where a body goes slithering about, maybe up to the middle of his leg in wriggling herring, and the next minute, maybe, wet to the skin with the splash of a great wave, you might think the clothes good enough for the work—though ill fit, I confess with shame, to come before your ladyship."

"I thought you only fished about close by the shore in a little boat; I didn't know you went with the rest of the fishermen: that's very dangerous work—isn't it?"

"Not *too* dangerous my lady. There's some of them go down every season; but it's all in the way of your work."

"Then how is it you're not gone fishing tonight?"

"She's a new boat, and there's another day's work on her before we can launch.—Wouldn't you like a row tonight, my lady?"

"No, certainly; it 's much too late."

"It won't grow any darker than this; but I reckon you're right. I came over just to see whether you wouldn't like to go with the boats a bit; but your ladyship set me off thinking and that put it out of my head."

"It's too late now anyhow. Come tomorrow evening, and I'll see if I can't go with you."

"I can't, my lady—that's the nuisance of it! I must go with Blue Peter tomorrow night. It was my last chance, I'm sorry to say."

"It's not of the slightest consequence," Lady Florimel returned; and, bidding him goodnight, she shut and locked the door.

The same instant she vanished, for the tunnel was now quite dark. Malcolm turned with a sigh, and took his way slowly homeward along the top of the dune. All was dim about him—dim in the heavens, where a thin veil of gray had gathered over the blue; dim on the ocean, where the stars swayed and swung, in faint flashes of dissolving radiance, cast loose like ribbons of seaweed: dim all along the shore, where the white of the breaking wavelet melted into the yellow sand; and dim in his own heart, where the manner and words of the lady had half hidden her starry reflex with a chilling mist.

The same instant she vanished, for the tunnel was now quite dark. Malcolm turned with a sigh, and took his way slowly homeward along the top of the dune. All was dim about him—dim in the heavens, where a thin veil of gray had gathered over the blue; dim on the ocean, where the stars swayed and swung, in faint flashes of dissolving radiance, cast loose like ribbons of seaweed: dim all along the shore, where the white of the breaking wavelet melted into the yellow sand; and dim in his own heart, where the manner and words of the lady had half hidden her starry reflex with a chilling mist.

CHAPTER XXIV

THE FEAST

To the entertainment which the marquis and Lady Florimel had resolved to give, all classes and conditions in the neighbourhood now began to receive invitations—shopkeepers, there called merchants, and all socially above them, individually, by notes, in the name of the marquis and Lady Florimel, but in the handwriting of Mrs Crathie and her daughters; and the rest generally, by the sound of bagpipes, and proclamation from the lips of Duncan MacPhail. To the satisfaction of Johnny Bykes the exclusion of improper persons was left in the hands of the gatekeepers.

The thing had originated with the factor. The old popularity of the lords of the land had vanished utterly during the life of the marquis's brother, and Mr Crathie, being wise in his generation, sought to initiate a revival of it by hinting the propriety of some general hospitality, a suggestion which the marquis was anything but loath to follow. For the present Lord Lossie, although as unready as most men to part with anything he cared for, could yet cast away magnificently, and had always greatly prized a reputation for liberality.

For the sake of the fishermen, the first Saturday after the commencement of the home-fishing was appointed. The few serious ones, mostly Methodists, objected on the ground of the proximity of the Sunday; but their attitude was, if possible, of still less consequence in the eyes of their neighbours that it was well known they would in no case have accepted such an invitation.

The day dawned propitious. As early as five o'clock Mr Crathie was abroad, booted and spurred—now directing the workmen who were setting up tents and tables; now conferring with house-steward, butler, or cook; now mounting his horse and galloping off to the home farm or the distillery, or into the town to the Lossie Arms, where certain guests from a distance were to be accommodated, and whose landlady had undertaken the superintendence of certain of the victualling departments; for canny Mr Crathie would not willingly have the meanest guest ask twice for anything he wanted—so invaluable did he consider a good word from the humblest quarter—and the best labours of the French cook, even had he reverenced instead of despising Scotch dishes, would have ill-sufficed for the satisfaction of appetites critically appreciative of hotch-potch, sheep's head, haggis, and black puddings.

The neighbouring nobility and landed gentlemen, the professional guests also, including the clergy, were to eat with the marquis in the great hall. On the grass near the house, tents were erected for the burgesses of the burgh, and the tenants of the marquis's farms. I would have said *on the lawn*, but there was no lawn proper about the place, the ground was so picturesquely broken—in parts with all but precipices—and so crowded with trees. Hence its aspect was specially unlike that of an English park and grounds. The whole was *Celtic*, as distinguished in character from *Saxon*. For the lake-like lawn, for the wide sweeps of airy room in which expand the mighty boughs of solitary trees, for the filmy gray-blue distances, and the far-off segments of horizon, here were the tree-crowded grass, the close windings of the long glen of the burn, heavily over-shadowed, and full of mystery and covert, but leading at last to the widest vantage of outlook—the wild heathery hill down which it drew its sharp furrow; while, in front of the house, beyond hidden river, and plane of treetops, and far-sunk shore with its dune and its bored crag and its tortuous caves, lay the great sea, a pouting under-lip, met by the thin, reposeful—shall I say sorrowful?—upper-lip of the sky.

A bridge of stately span, level with the sweep in front, honourable embodiment of the savings of a certain notable countess, one end resting on the same rock with the house, their foundations almost in contact, led across the burn to more and more trees, their roots swathed in the finest grass, through which ran broad carriage drives and nar-rower footways, hard and smooth with yellow gravel. Here amongst the trees were set long tables for the fishermen, mechanics, and farm-labourers. Here also was the place appointed for the piper.

As the hour drew near, the guests came trooping in at every entrance. By the sea-gate came the fisher-folk, many of the men in the blue jersey, the women mostly in short print gowns, of large patterns—the married with huge, wide-frilled caps, and the unmarried with their hair gathered in silken nets:—bonnets there were very few. Each group that entered had a joke or a jibe for Johnny Bykes, which he met in varying, but always surly fashion—in that of utter silence in the case of Duncan and Malcolm, at which the former was indignant, the latter merry. By the town gate came the people of Portlossie. By the new main entrance from the high road beyond the town, through lofty Greekish gates, came the lords and lairds, in yellow coaches, gigs, and post-chaises. By another gate, far up the glen, came most of the country-folk, some walking, some riding, some driving, all merry, and with the best intentions of enjoying themselves. As the common people approached the house, they were directed to their different tables by the sexton, for he knew everybody.

The marquis was early on the ground, going about amongst his guests, and showing a friendly offhand courtesy which prejudiced every one in his favour. Lady Florimel soon joined him, and a certain frank way she inherited from her father, joined to the great beauty her mother had given her, straightway won all hearts. She spoke to Duncan with cordiality; the moment he heard her voice, he pulled off his bonnet, put it under his arm, and responded with what I can find no better phrase to describe than a profuse dignity. Malcolm she favoured with a smile which swelled his heart with pride and devotion. The bold-faced countess next appeared; she took the marquis's other arm, and nodded to his guests condescendingly and often, but seemed, after every nod, to throw her head farther back than before. Then to haunt the goings of Lady Florimel came Lord Meikleham, receiving little encouragement, but eager after such crumbs as he could gather. Suddenly the great bell under the highest of the gilded vanes rang a loud peal, and the marquis having led his chief guests to the hall, as soon as he was seated, the tables began to be served simultaneously.

At that where Malcolm sat with Duncan, grace was grievously foiled by the latter, for, unaware of what was going on, he burst out, at the request of a waggish neighbour, with a tremendous blast, of which the company took advantage to commence operations at once, and presently the clatter of knives and forks and spoons was the sole sound to be heard in that division of the feast: across the valley, from the neighbourhood of the house, came now and then a faint peal of laughter, for there they knew how to be merry while they ate; but here, the human element was in abeyance, for people who work hard, seldom talk while they eat. From the end of an overhanging bough a squirrel looked at them for one brief moment, wondering perhaps that they should not prefer cracking a nut in private, and vanished—but the birds kept singing, and the scents of the flowers came floating up from the garden below, and the burn went on with its own noises and its own silences, drifting the froth of its last passion down towards the doors of the world.

In the hall, ancient jokes soon began to flutter their moulted wings, and musty compliments to offer themselves for the acceptance of the ladies, and meet with a reception varied by temperament and experience: what the bold-faced countess heard with a hybrid contortion, half sneer and half smile, would have made Lady Florimel stare out of big refusing eyes.

Those more immediately around the marquis were soon laughing over the story of the trick he had played the blind piper, and the apology he had had to make in consequence; and perhaps something better than mere curiosity had to do with the wish of several of the guests to see the old man and his grandson. The marquis said the piper himself would take care they should not miss him, but he would send for the young fellow, who was equally fitted to amuse them, being quite as much of a character in his way as the other.

He spoke to the man behind his chair, and in a few minutes Malcolm made his appearance, following the messenger.

"Malcolm," said the marquis kindly, "I want you to keep your eyes open, and see that no mischief is done about the place."

"I dinna think there's ane o' oor ain fowk wad dee ony mischeef, my lord," answered Malcolm; "but whan ye keep open yett, ye canna be sure wha wins in, specially wi' sic a gowk as Johnny Bykes at ane o' them. No 'at he wad wrang yer lordship a hair, my lord!"

"At all events you'll be on the alert," said the marquis.

"I wull that, my Lord. There's twa or three aboot a'ready 'at I dinna a'thegither like the leuks o'. They're no like country-fowk, an' they're no fisher-fowk. It's no far aff the time o' year whan the gipsies are i' the w'y o' payin' 's a veesit, an' they may ha' come in at the Binn yett, whaur there's nane but an auld wife to haud them oot."

"Well, well," said the marquis, who had no fear about the behaviour of his guests, and had only wanted a colour for his request of Malcolm's presence. "In the meantime," he added, "we are rather short-handed here. Just give the butler a little assistance—will you?"

"I don't think there's one of our own folk would do any mischief, my lord," answered Malcolm; "but when you keep open gate, you can't be sure who gets in, especially with such a fool as Johnny Bykes at one of them. Not that he would wrong your lordship a hair, my lord!"

"At all events you'll be on the alert," said the marquis.

"I will that, my Lord. There's two or three about already that I don't altogether like the looks of. They're not like country-folk, and they're not fisher-folk. It's about the time of year when the gipsies tend to visit us, and they may have come in at the Binn gate, where there's no one but an old wife to keep them out."

"Well, well," said the marquis, who had no fear about the behaviour of his guests, and had only wanted a colour for his request of Malcolm's presence. "In the meantime," he added, "we are rather short-handed here. Just give the butler a little assistance—will you?"

"Willin'ly, my lord," answered Malcolm, forgetting altogether, in the prospect of being useful and within sight of Lady Florimel, that he had but half finished his own dinner. The butler, who had already had an opportunity of admiring his aptitude, was glad enough to have his help; and after this day used to declare that in a single week he could make him a better servant than any of the men who waited at table. It was indeed remarkable how, with such a limited acquaintance with the many modes of an artificial life, he was yet, by quickness of sympathetic insight, capable not only of divining its requirements, but of distinguishing, amid the multitude of appliances around, those fitted to their individual satisfaction.

It was desirable, however, that the sitting in the hall should not be prolonged, and after a few glasses of wine, the marquis rose, and went to make the round of the other tables. Taking them in order, he came last to those of the rustics, mechanics, and fisher-folk. These had advanced considerably in their potations, and the fun was loud. His appearance was greeted with shouts, into which Duncan struck with a paean from his pipes; but in the midst of the tumult, one of the oldest of the fishermen stood up, and in a voice accustomed to battle with windy uproars, called for silence. He then addressed their host.

"Ye'll jist mak 's prood by drinkin' a tum'ler wi' 's, yer lordship," he said. "It's no ilka day we hae the honour o' yer lordship's company."

"You'll just make us proud by drinking a tumbler with us, your lordship," he said. "It's not every day we have the honour of your lordship's company."

"Or I of yours," returned the marquis with hearty courtesy. "I will do it with pleasure—or at least a glass: my head's not so well seasoned as some of yours."

"Or I of yours," returned the marquis with hearty courtesy. "I will do it with pleasure—or at least a glass: my head's not so well seasoned as some of yours."

"Gien your lordship's hed hed as mony blasts o' nicht win', an' as mony jaups o' cauld sea watter aboot its lugs as oors, it wad hae been fit to stan' as muckle o' the barley bree as the stievest o' the lot, I s' warran'."

"If your lordship's had had as many blasts of night wind, and as many dashes of cold sea water about its ears as ours, it would have been fit to stand as much of the barley bree as the stoutest of the lot, I'll wager."

"I hope so," returned Lord Lossie, who, having taken a seat at the end of the table, was now mixing a tumbler of toddy. As soon as he had filled his glass, he rose, and drank to the fishermen of Portlossie, their wives and their sweethearts, wishing them a mighty conquest of herring, and plenty of children to keep up the breed and the war on the fish. His speech was received with hearty cheers, during which he sauntered away to rejoin his friends.

Many toasts followed, one of which, "Damnation to the dogfish," gave opportunity to a wag, seated near the piper, to play upon the old man's well known foible by adding, "an' Cawmill o' Glenlyon;" whereupon Duncan, who had by this time taken more whisky than was good for him, rose, and made a rambling speech, in which he returned thanks for the imprecation, adding thereto the hope that never might one of the brood accursed go down with honour to the grave.

The fishermen listened with respectful silence, indulging only in nods, winks, and smiles for the interchange of amusement, until the utterance of the wish recorded, when, apparently carried away for a moment by his eloquence, they broke into loud applause. But, from the midst of it, a low gurgling laugh close by him reached Duncan's ear: excited though he was with strong drink and approbation, he shivered, sunk into his seat, and clutched at his pipes convulsively, as if they had been a weapon of defence.

"Malcolm! Malcolm, my son," he muttered feebly, "tere is a voman will pe laughing! She is a paad voman: she makes me cold!"

"Malcolm! Malcolm, my son," he muttered feebly, "tere is a voman will be laughing! She is a baad voman: she makes me cold!"

Finding from the no-response that Malcolm had left his side, he sat motionless, drawn into himself, and struggling to suppress the curdling shiver. Some of the women gathered about him, but he assured them it was nothing more than a passing sickness.

Malcolm's attention had, a few minutes before, been drawn to two men of somewhat peculiar appearance, who, applauding louder than any, only pretended to drink, and occasionally interchanged glances of intelligence. It was one of these peculiar looks that first attracted his notice. He soon discovered that they had a comrade on the other side of the table, who apparently, like themselves, had little or no acquaintance with any one near him. He did not like either their countenances or their behaviour, and resolved to watch them. In order therefore to be able to follow them when they moved, as he felt certain they would before long, without attracting their attention, he left the table and making a circuit took up his position behind a neighbouring tree. Hence it came that he was not, at the moment of his need, by his grandfather's side, whither he had returned as soon as dinner was over in the hall.

Meantime it became necessary to check the drinking by the counter attraction of the dance. Mr Crathie gave orders that a chair should be mounted on a table for Duncan; and the young hinds and fishermen were soon dancing zealously with the girls of their company to his strathspeys and reels. The other divisions of the marquis's guests made merry to the sound of a small brass band, a harp, and two violins.

When the rest forsook the toddy for the reel, the objects of Malcolm's suspicion remained at the table, not to drink, but to draw nearer to each other and confer. At length, when the dancers began to return in quest of liquor, they rose and went away loiteringly through the trees. As the twilight was now deepening, Malcolm found it difficult to keep them in sight, but for the same reason he was able the more quickly to glide after them from tree to tree. It was almost moonrise, he said to himself, and if they meditated mischief, now was their best time.

Presently he heard the sound of running feet, and in a moment more spied the unmistakeable form of the mad laird, darting through the thickening dusk of the trees, with gestures of wild horror. As he passed the spot where Malcolm stood, he cried out in a voice like a suppressed shriek,—

"It's my mither! It's my mither! I dinna ken whaur I come frae."

"It's my mother! It's my mother! I don't know where I come from."

His sudden appearance and outcry so startled Malcolm that for a moment he forgot his watch, and when he looked again the men had vanished. Not having any clue to their intent, and knowing only that on such a night the house was nearly defenceless, he turned at once and made for it. As he approached the front, coming over the bridge, he fancied he saw a figure disappear through the entrance, and quickened his pace. Just as he reached it, he heard a door bang, and supposing it to be that which shut off the second hall, whence rose the principal staircase, he followed this vaguest of hints, and bounded to the top of the stair. Entering the first passage he came to, he found it almost dark, with a half-open door at the end, through which shone a gleam from some window beyond: this light was plainly shut off for a moment, as if by some one passing the window. He hurried after— noiselessly, for the floor was thickly carpeted—and came to the foot of a winding stone stair. Afraid beyond all things of doing nothing, and driven by the formless conviction that if he stopped to deliberate he certainly should do nothing, he shot up the dark screw like an ascending bubble, passed the landing of the second floor without observing it, and arrived in the attic regions of the ancient pile, under low, irregular ceilings, here ascending in cones, there coming down in abrupt triangles, or sloping away to a hidden meeting with the floor in distant corners. His only light was the cold blue glimmer from here and there a storm-window or a sky-light. As the conviction of failure grew on him, the *ghostly* feeling of the place began to invade him. All was vague, forsaken, and hopeless, as a dreary dream, with the superadded miserable sense of lonely sleepwalking. I suspect that the feeling we call *ghostly* is but the sense of abandonment in the lack of companion life; but be this as it may, Malcolm was glad enough to catch sight of a gleam as from a candle, at the end of a long, low passage on which he had come after mazy wandering. Another similar passage crossed its end, somewhere in which must be the source of the light: he crept towards it, and laying himself flat on the floor, peeped round the corner. His very heart stopped to listen: seven or eight yards from him, with a small lantern in her hand, stood a short female figure, which, the light falling for a moment on her soft evil countenance, he recognised as Mrs Catanach. Beside her stood a tall graceful figure, draped in black from head to foot. Mrs Catanach was speaking in a low tone, and what Malcolm was able to catch was evidently the close of a conversation.

"I'll do my best, ye may be sure, my leddy," she said. "There's something no canny aboot the cratur, an' doobtless ye was an ill-used wuman, an' ye're i' the richt. But it 's a some fearsome ventur, an' may be luikit intill, ye ken. There I s' be yer scoug. Lippen to me, an' ye s' no repent it."

"I'll do my best, you may be sure, my lady," she said. "There's something not canny about the creature, and doubtless you were an ill-used woman, and you're in the right. But it's an unchancy venture, and may be looked into, you know. Should it come to that, I'll screen you. Trust to me, and you won't repent it."

As she ended speaking, she turned to the door, and drew from it a key, evidently after a foiled attempt to unlock it therewith; for from a bunch she carried she now made choice of another, and was already fumbling with it in the keyhole, when Malcolm bethought himself that, whatever her further intent, he ought not to allow her to succeed in opening the door. He therefore rose slowly to his feet, and stepping softly out into the passage, sent his round blue bonnet spinning with such a certain aim, that it flew right against her head. She gave a cry of terror, smothered by the sense of evil secrecy, and dropped her lantern. It went out. Malcolm pattered with his hands on the floor, and began to howl frightfully. Her companion had already fled, and Mrs Catanach picked up her lantern and followed. But her flight was soft-footed, and gave sign only in the sound of her garments, and a clank or two of her keys.

Gifted with a good sense of relative position, Malcolm was able to find his way back to the hall without much difficulty, and met no one on the way. When he stepped into the open air a round moon was visible through the trees, and their shadows were lying across the sward. The merriment had grown louder; for a good deal of whisky having been drunk by men of all classes, hilarity had ousted restraint, and the separation of classes having broken a little, there were many stragglers from the higher to the lower divisions, whence the area of the more boisterous fun had considerably widened. Most of the ladies and gentlemen were dancing in the chequer of the trees and moonlight, but, a little removed from the rest, Lady Florimel was seated under a tree, with Lord Meikleham by her side, probably her partner in the last dance. She was looking at the moon, which shone upon her from between two low branches, and there was a sparkle in her eyes and a luminousness upon her cheek which to Malcolm did not seem to come from the moon only. He passed on, with the first pang of jealousy in his heart, feeling now for the first time that the space between Lady Florimel and himself was indeed a gulf. But he cast the whole thing from him for the time with an inward scorn of his foolishness, and hurried on from group to group, to find the marquis.

Meeting with no trace of him, and thinking he might be in the flower-garden, which a few rays of the moon now reached, he descended thither. But he searched it through with no better success, and at the farthest end was on the point of turning to leave it and look elsewhere, when he heard a moan of stifled agony on the other side of a high wall which here bounded the garden. Climbing up an espalier, he soon reached the top, and looking down on the other side, to his horror and rage espied the mad laird on the ground, and the very men of whom he had been in pursuit, standing over him and brutally tormenting him, apparently in order to make him get up and go along with them. One was kicking him, another pulling his head this way and that by the hair, and the third punching and poking his hump, which last cruelty had probably drawn from him the cry Malcolm had heard.

Three might be too many for him: he descended swiftly, found some stones, and a stake from a bed of sweet-peas, then climbing up again, took such effectual aim at one of the villains that he fell without uttering a sound. Dropping at once from the wall, he rushed at the two with stick upheaved.

"Dinna be in sic a rage, man," cried the first, avoiding his blow; "we're aboot naething ayont the lawfu'. It's only the mad laird. We're takin' 'im to the asylum at Ebberdeen. By the order o' 's ain mither!"

"Don't be in such a rage, man," cried the first, avoiding his blow; "We're about nothing beyond the lawful. It's only the mad laird. We're taking him to the asylum at Aberdeen. By the order of his own mother!"

At the word a choking scream came from the prostrate victim. Malcolm uttered a huge imprecation, and struck at the fellow again, who now met him in a way that showed it was noise more than wounds he had dreaded. Instantly the other came up, and also fell upon him with vigour. But his stick was too much for them, and at length one of them, crying out—"It's the blin' piper's bastard—I'll mark him yet!" took to his heels, and was followed by his companion.

More eager after rescue than punishment, Malcolm turned to the help of the laird, whom he found in utmost need of his ministrations—gagged, and with his hands tied mercilessly tight behind his back. His knife quickly released him, but the poor fellow was scarcely less helpless than before. He clung to Malcolm, and moaned piteously, every moment glancing over his shoulder in terror of pursuit. His mouth hung open as if the gag were still tormenting him; now and then he would begin his usual lament and manage to say *"I dinna ken;"* but when he attempted the *whaur*, his jaw fell and hung as before. Malcolm sought to lead him away, but he held back, moaning dreadfully; then Malcolm would have him sit down where they were, but he caught his hand and pulled him away, stopping instantly, however, as if not knowing whither to turn from the fears on every side. At length the prostrate enemy began to move, when the laird, who had been unaware of his presence, gave a shriek, and took to his heels. Anxious not to lose sight of him, Malcolm left the wounded man to take care of himself; and followed him up the steep side of the little valley.

They had not gone many steps from the top of the ascent, however, before the fugitive threw himself on the ground exhausted, and it was all Malcolm could do to get him to the town, where, unable to go a pace further, he sank down on Mrs Catanach's doorstep. A light was burning in the cottage, but Malcolm would seek shelter for him anywhere rather than with her, and, in terror of her quick ears, caught him up in his arms like a child, and hurried away with him to Miss Horn's.

"Eh sirs!" exclaimed Miss Horn, when she opened the door—for Jean was among the merrymakers—"wha 's this 'at 's killt noo?"

"It's the laird—Mr Stewart," returned Malcolm. "He's no freely killt, but nigh han'."

"Na! weel I wat! Come in an' set him doon till we see," said Miss Horn, turning and leading the way up to her little parlour.

There Malcolm laid his burden on the sofa, and gave a brief account of the rescue.

"Lord preserve 's, Ma'colm!" cried Miss Horn, as soon as he had ended his tale, to which she had listened in silence, with fierce eyes and threatening nose; "isna 't a mercy I wasna made like some fowk, or I couldna ha' bidden to see the puir fallow misguidet that gait! It's a special mercy, Ma'colm MacPhail, to be made wantin' ony sic thing as feelin's."

"Eh sirs!" exclaimed Miss Horn, when she opened the door—for Jean was among the merrymakers—"who's this that's killed now?"

"It's the laird—Mr Stewart," returned Malcolm. "He's not quite killed, but nigh hand."

"Na! indeed! Come in and set him down till we see," said Miss Horn, turning and leading the way up to her little parlour.

There Malcolm laid his burden on the sofa, and gave a brief account of the rescue.

"Lord preserve us, Malcolm!" cried Miss Horn, as soon as he had ended his tale, to which she had listened in silence, with fierce eyes and threatening nose; "isn't it a mercy I wasn't made like some folk, or I couldn't have borne to see the poor fellow ill-treated that way! It's a special mercy, Malcolm MacPhail, to be made wanting any such things as feelings."

She was leaving the room as she spoke—to return instantly with brandy. The laird swallowed some with an effort, and began to revive.

"Eh, sirs!" exclaimed Miss Horn, regarding him now more narrowly—"but he's in an awfu' state o' dirt! I maun wash his face an' han's, an' pit him till 's bed. Could ye help aff wi' 's claes, Ma'colm? Though I haena ony feelin's, I'm jist some eerie-like at the puir body's back."

The last words were uttered in what she judged a safe aside.

As if she had been his mother, she washed his face and hands, and dried them tenderly, the laird submitting like a child. He spoke but one word—when she took him by the hand to lead him to the room where her cousin used to sleep: "Father o' lichts!" he said, and no more. Malcolm put him to bed, where he lay perfectly still, whether awake or asleep they could not tell.

He then set out to go back to Lossie House, promising to return after he had taken his grandfather home, and seen him also safe in bed.

She was leaving the room as she spoke—to return instantly with brandy. The laird swallowed some with an effort, and began to revive.

"Eh, sirs!" exclaimed Miss Horn, regarding him now more narrowly—"but he's in an awful state of dirt! I must wash his face and hands, and put him to bed. Could you help him off with his clothes, Malcolm? Though I haven't any feelings, I can't help a shudder at the poor body's back."

The last words were uttered in what she judged a safe aside.

As if she had been his mother, she washed his face and hands, and dried them tenderly, the laird submitting like a child. He spoke but one word—when she took him by the hand to lead him to the room where her cousin used to sleep: "Father o' lichts!" he said, and no more. Malcolm put him to bed, where he lay perfectly still, whether awake or asleep they could not tell.

He then set out to go back to Lossie House, promising to return after he had taken his grandfather home, and seen him also safe in bed.

CHAPTER XXV

THE NIGHT WATCH

When Malcolm returned, Jean had retired for the night, and again it was Miss Horn who admitted him, and led him to her parlour. It was a low-ceiled room, with lean spider-legged furniture and dingy curtains. Everything in it was suggestive of a comfort slowly vanishing. An odour of withered rose-leaves pervaded the air. A Japanese cabinet stood in one corner, and on the mantelpiece a pair of Chinese fans with painted figures whose faces were embossed in silk, between which ticked an old French clock, whose supporters were a shepherd and shepherdess in prettily painted china. Long faded as was everything in it, the room was yet very rich in the eyes of Malcolm, whose home was bare even in comparison with that of the poorest of the fisher-women, they had a passion for ornamenting their chimneypieces with china ornaments, and their dressers with the most gorgeous crockery that their money could buy—a certain metallic orange being the prevailing hue; while in Duncan's cottage, where woman had never initiated the taste, there was not even a china poodle to represent the finished development of luxury in the combination of the ugly and the useless.

Miss Horn had made a little fire in the old-fashioned grate, whose bars bellied out like a sail almost beyond the narrow chimney-shelf, and a tea-kettle was singing on the hob, while a decanter, a sugar basin, a nutmeg grater, and other needful things on a tray, suggested negus, beyond which Miss Horn never went in the matter of stimulants, asserting that, as she had no feelings, she never required anything stronger. She made Malcolm sit down at the opposite side of the fire, and mixing him a tumbler of her favourite drink, began to question him about the day, and how things had gone.

Miss Horn had the just repute of discretion, for, gladly hearing all the news, she had the rare virtue of not repeating things to the prejudice of others without some *good* reason for so doing; Malcolm therefore, seated thus alone with her in the dead of the night, and bound to her by the bond of a common well-doing, had no hesitation in unfolding to her all his adventures of the evening. She sat with her big hands in her lap, making no remark, not even an exclamation, while he went on with the tale of the garret; but her listening eyes grew—not larger—darker and fiercer as he spoke; the space between her nostrils and mouth widened visibly; the muscles knotted on the sides of her neck; and her nose curved more and more to the shape of a beak.

"There's some deevilry there!" she said at length after he had finished, breaking a silence of some moments, during which she had been staring into the fire. "Whaur twa ill women come thegither, there maun be the auld man himsel' atween them."

"I dinna doobt it," returned Malcolm. "An' ane o' them 's an ill wuman, sure eneuch; but I ken naething aboot the tither—only 'at she maun be a leddy, by the w'y the howdy wife spak till her."

"The waur token, when a leddy collogues wi' a wuman aneth her ain station, an' ane 'at has keppit mony a secret in her day, an' by her callin' has had mair opportunity—no to say farther—than ither fowk o' duin' ill things! An' gien *ye* dinna ken her, that's no rizzon 'at *I* sudna hae a groff guiss at her by the marks ye read aff o' her. I'll jist hae to tell ye a story sic as an auld wife like me seldom tells till a young man like yersel'."

"Yer ain bridle sall rule my tongue, mem," said Malcolm.

"I s' lippen to yer discretion," said Miss Horn, and straightway began.— "Some years ago—an' I s' warran' it 's weel ower twinty—that same wuman, Bawby Cat'nach,—wha was nae hameborn wuman, nor had been lang aboot the toon—comin' as she did frae naebody kent whaur, 'cep maybe it was the markis 'at than was, preshumed to mak up to me i' the w'y o' frien'ly acquantance—sic as a maiden leddy micht hae wi' a howdy—an' no 'at she forgot her proaper behaviour to ane like mysel'. But I cudna hae bidden the jaud, 'cep 'at I had rizzons for lattin' her jaw wag. She was cunnin', the auld vratch,—no that auld—maybe aboot forty,—but I was ower mony for her. She had the design

"There's some devilry there!" she said at length after he had finished, breaking a silence of some moments, during which she had been staring into the fire. "Where two bad women come together, there must be the old man himself between them."

"I don't doubt it," returned Malcolm. "And one of them's a bad woman, sure enough; but I know nothing about the other—only that she must be a lady, by the way the midwife spoke to her."

"The more suspicious, when a lady talks with a woman beneath her station, and one who's pocketed many a secret in her day, and by her calling has had more opportunity—to say no farther—than other folk of working evil! And if *you* don't know her, that's no reason that *I* shouldn't have a rough guess at her by the marks you read off her. I'll just have to tell you a story such as an old wife like me seldom tells to a young man like yourself."

"Your own bridle shall rule my tongue, ma'am," said Malcolm.

"I shall trust to your discretion," said Miss Horn, and straightway began.— "Some years ago—well over twenty, I make no doubt—that same woman, Bawby Catanach,—who was no home-born woman, nor had been long about the town—coming as she did from nobody knew where, except maybe it was the marquis that then was, presumed to make up to me in the way of friendly acquaintance—such as a maiden lady might have with a midwife—not forgetting either to behave properly to a woman like myself. But I couldn't have endured the jade, except that I had reasons for letting her jaw wag. She was cunning, the old wretch—not that old—maybe about forty—but I was too much for her. She was plotting to to win at something she thoucht I kent, an' sae, to enteece me to open my pock, she opent hers, an' tellt me story efter story about this neebour an' that—a' o' them things 'at ouchtna to ha' been true, an 'at she ouchtna to ha' loot pass her lips gien they war true, seein' she cam by the knowledge o' them so as she said she did. But she gat naething o' me—the fat-braint cat!—an' she hates me like the verra mischeef."

Miss Horn paused and took a sip of her negus.

"Ae day, I cam upon her sittin' by the ingleneuk i' my ain kitchen, haudin' a close an' a laich confab wi' Jean. I had Jean than, an' hoo I hae keepit the hizzy, I hardly ken. I think it maun be that, haein' nae feelin's o' my ain, I hae ower muckle regaird to ither fowk's, an' sae I never likit to pit her awa' wi'oot doonricht provocation. But dinna ye lippen to Jean, Malcolm—na, na! At that time, my cousin, Miss Grizel Cammell—my third cousin, she was—had come to bide wi' me—a bonny yoong thing as ye wad see, but in sair ill health; an' maybe she had her freits, an' maybe no, but she cudna bide to see the wuman Cat'nach aboot the place. An' in verra trowth, she was to mysel' like ane o' thae ill-faured birds, I dinna min' upo' the name o' them, 'at hings ower an airmy; for wharever there was onybody nae weel, or onybody deid, there was Bawby Cat'nach. I hae hard o' creepin' things 'at veesits fowk 'at 's no weel—an' Bawby was, an' is, ane sic like! Sae I was angert at seein' her colloguin' wi' Jean, an' I cried Jean to me to the door o' the kitchie. But wi' that up jumps Bawby, an' comin' efter her, says

win at something she thought I knew, and so, to entice me to open my bag, she opened hers, and told me story after story about this neighbour and that—all of them things that oughtn't to have been true, and that she oughtn't to have let pass her lips if they were true, seeing as she came by the knowledge of them in the way she said. But she got nothing out of me—the fat-brained cat!—and she hates me like the very mischief."

Miss Horn paused and took a sip of her negus.

"One day, I came upon her sitting by the fireside in my own kitchen, having a close and whispered talk with Jean. I had Jean then, and how I've kept the hussy, I hardly know. I think it must be that, having no feelings of my own, I have too much regard for other folk's, and so I never liked to dismiss her without downright provocation. But don't you trust to Jean, Malcolm—na, na! At that time, my cousin, Miss Grizel Campbell—my third cousin, she was—had come to stay with me—as bonny a young thing as you'd see, but in the poorest of health; and maybe she had her whims, and maybe not, but she couldn't stand the sight of that Catanach woman about the place. And it's true enough, she was to me like one of those ill-favoured birds, I forget the name of them, that hang over an army; for wherever there was someone taken ill, or a death in a family, there was Bawby Catanach. I've heard of creeping things that visit folk on their sickbeds—and Bawby was, and is, just another such! So I was angry at seeing her speaking with Jean, and I called Jean to me to the door of the kitchen. But with that up jumps Bawby, and coming after to me—says she, 'Eh, Miss Horn! there's terrible news: Leddy Lossie's deid;—she's been three ooks deid!'—'Weel,' says I, 'what's sae terrible aboot that?' For ye ken I never had ony feelin's, an' I cud see naething sae awfu' aboot a body deein' i' the ord'nar' w'y o natur like. 'We'll no miss her muckle doon here,' says I, 'for I never hard o' her bein' at the Hoose sin' ever I can min'.' 'But that's no a',' says she; 'only I wad be laith to speyk aboot it i' the transe. Lat me up the stair wi' ye, an' I'll tell ye mair.' Weel, pairtly 'at I was ta'en by surprise like, an' pairtly 'at I wasna sae auld as I am noo, an' pairtly that I was keerious to hear—ill 'at I likit her—what neist the wuman wad say, I did as I ouchtna, an' turned an' gaed up the stair, an' loot her follow me. Whan she cam' in, she pat tu the door ahint her, an' turnt to me, an' said—says she: 'An wha 's deid forbye, think ye?'—'I hae hard o' naebody,' I answered. 'Wha but the laird o' Gersefell!' says she. 'I'm sorry to hear that, honest man!' says I; for a'body likit Mr Stewart. 'An' what think ye o' 't?' says she, wi' a runklin o' her broos, an' a shak o' her heid, an' a settin o' her roon' nieves upo' the fat hips o' her. 'Think o' 't?' says I ; 'what sud I think o' 't, but that it 's the wull o' Providence?' Wi' that she leuch till she wabblet a' ower like cauld skink, an' says she—'Weel, that's jist what it is no, an' that lat me tell ye, Miss Horn!' I glowert at her, maist frichtit into believin' she was the witch fowk ca'd her. 'Wha's son 's the hump-backit cratur',' says she, "at comes in i' the gig whiles wi' the groom lad, think ye?'—'Wha's but the puir man's 'at 's deid?' says I. 'Deil a

her, says to me—says she, 'Eh, Miss Horn! there's terrible news: Lady Lossie's dead;—she's been three weeks dead!'—'Well,' says I, 'what's so terrible about that?' For you know I never had any feelings, and I could see nothing awful about a person dying in the ordinary, natural way. 'We won't miss her much down here,' says I, 'for I never heard of her being at the House since ever I can remember.' 'But that's not all,' says she; 'only I would be loath to speak about it in the hallway. Let's go upstairs, and I'll tell you more.' Well, partly that I was taken by surprise like, and partly that I wasn't so old as I am now, and partly that I was curious to hear—much as I disliked her—what she'd tell me next, I did what I shouldn't have, and turned and went up the stair, and let her follow me. When she came in, she shut the door behind her, and turned to me, and said, says she: 'And who's dead besides, think you?'—'I've heard of no one,' I answered. 'Who but the laird of Gersefell!' says she. 'I'm sorry to hear that, honest man!' says I; for everyone liked Mr Stewart. 'And what do you think of it?' says she, with a runkling of her brows, and a shake of her head, and a setting of her round fists upon her flabby hips. 'Think of it?' says I; 'what should I think of it, but that it's the will of Providence?' with that she laughed till she wobbled all over like cold skink, and says she—'Well, that's just what it is not, and that let me tell you, Miss Horn!' I glowered at her, almost frightened into believing her the witch folk called her. 'Who's son's the hump-backed creature,' says she, 'that comes in in the gig sometimes with the groom lad, think you?'—'Whose but the bit o' 't!' says she, 'an' I beg yer pardon for mentionin' o' *him*,' says she. An' syne she screwt up her mou', an' cam closs up till me—for I wadna sit doon mysel', an' less wad I bid her, an' was sorry eneuch by this time 'at I had broucht her up the stair—an' says she, layin' her han' upo' my airm wi' a clap, as gien her an' me was to be freen's upo' sic a gran' foondation o' dirt as that!—says she, makin' a laich toot-moot o' 't,—'He's Lord Lossie's!' says she, an' maks a face 'at micht hae turnt a cat sick—only by guid luck I had nae feelin's. 'An' nae suner's my leddy deid nor *her* man follows her!' says she. 'An' what do ye mak o' that?' says she. 'Ay, what do ye mak o' that?' says I till her again. 'Ow! what ken I?' says she, wi' anither ill leuk; an' wi' that she leuch an' turned awa, but turned back again or she wan to the door, an' says she—'Maybe ye didna ken 'at she was broucht to bed hersel' aboot a sax ooks ago?'—'Puir leddy!' said I, thinkin' mair o' her evil report nor o' the pains o' childbirth. 'Ay,' says she, wi' a deevilich kin' o' a lauch, like in spite o' hersel', 'for the bairn's deid, they tell me—as bonny a ladbairn as ye wad see, jist ooncoamon! An' whaur div ye think she had her doonlying? Jist at Lossie Hoose!' Wi' that she was oot at the door wi' a swag o' her tail, an' doon the stair to Jean again. I was jist at ane mair wi' anger at mysel' an' scunner at her, an' in twa min' s to gang efter her an' turn her oot o' the hoose, her an' Jean thegither. I could hear her snicherin' till hersel' as she gaed doon the stair. My verra stamack turned at the poozhonous ted.

poor man's that's dead?' says I. 'Devil a bit of it!' says she, 'and I beg your pardon for mentioning *him*,' says she. And then she screwed up her mouth, and came close up to me—for I wouldn't sit down myself, and less would I bid her, and I was sorry enough by this time that I had brought her upstairs—and says she, laying her hand upon my arm with a clap, as if she and I were to be friends upon such a grand foundation of dirt as that!—says she, making a low whisper of it—'He's Lord Lossie's!' says she, and makes a face that might have turned a cat sick—only by good luck I had no feelings. 'And no sooner's my lady dead than *her* man follows her!' says she. 'And what do you make of that?' says she. 'Ay, what do you make of that?' says I to her again. 'Oh, what do I know?' says she, with another evil look; and with that she laughed and turned away, but turned back again before she reached the door, and says she—'Maybe you didn't know that she was brought to bed herself about six weeks ago?' 'Poor lady!' said I, thinking more of her evil report than of the pains of childbirth. 'Ay,' says she, with a devilish kind of a laugh, in spite of herself, 'for the child's dead, they tell me—as bonny a wee boy as you would see, just uncommon! And where do you think she had her down-lying? Just at Lossie House!' With that she was out at the door with a swag of her tail and down the stair to Jean again. I was just mad with anger at myself and disgust at her, and in two minds to go after her, and turn her out of the house, her and Jean together. I could hear her snickering to herself as she went down the stair. My very stomach turned at the poisonous toad.

"I canna say what was true or what was fause i' the scandal o' her tale, nor what for she tuik the trouble to cairry 't to me, but it sune cam to be said 'at the yoong laird was but half-wittet as weel's humpit, an' 'at his mither cudna bide him. An' certain it was 'at the puir wee chap cud as little bide his mither. Gien she cam near him ohn luikit for, they said, he wad gie a great skriech, and rin as fast as his wee weyver legs cud wag aneth the wecht o' 's humpie—an' whiles her after him wi' onything she cud lay her han' upo', they said—but I kenna. Ony gait, the widow hersel' grew waur and waur i' the temper, an' I misdoobt me sair was gey hard upo' the puir wee objeck— fell cruel til 'm, they said—till at len'th, as a' body kens, he forhooit the hoose a'the-gither. An' puttin' this an' that thegither, for I hear a hantle said 'at I say na ower again, it seems to me 'at her first scunner at her puir misformt bairn, wha they say was humpit whan he was born an' maist cost her her life to get lowst o' him—her scunner at 'im 's been growin' an' growin' till it 's grown to doonricht hate."

"It's an awfu' thing 'at ye say, mem, an' I doobt it 's ower true. But hoo *can* a mither hate her ain bairn?" said Malcolm.

"'Deed it 's nae wonner ye sud speir, laddie! for it 's weel kent 'at maist mithers, gien there be a shargar or a nat'ral or a crookit ane amo' their bairns, mak mair o' that ane nor o' a' the lave putten the-gither—as gien they wad mak it up till 'im, for the fair play o' the warl. But ye see in this case, he's aiblins the child o' sin—for a leear *may* tell an ill trowth—an' beirs the marks o' 't, ye see; sae to her he's jist her sin rinnin' aboot the warl incarnat; an' that canna be pleasant to luik upo'."

"I can't say what was true or what was false in the scandal of her tale, nor why she took the trouble to carry it to me, but it soon came to be said that the young laird was but half-witted as well as humped, and that his mother couldn't stand him. And certain it was that the poor wee chap could as little stand his mother. If she came near him unlooked for, they said, he would give a great screech, and run as fast as his wee spider legs could wag beneath the weight of his hump—and her sometimes after him with anything she could lay her hand upon, they said—I don't know. Anyway, the widow herself grew worse and worse in her temper, and I more than suspect was very hard on the poor wee thing—fell cruel to him, they said—till at length, as everyone knows, he forsook the house altogether. And putting this and that together, for I hear a good deal said that I don't repeat, it seems to me that her first horror at her poor misformed child, who they say was humped from the first and almost cost her her life when she deliv-ered him—that horror's been growing and growing till it's grown to downright hate."

"It's an awful thing that you say, ma'am, and I suspect it's too true. But how *can* a mother hate her own child?" said Malcolm.

"Indeed it's no wonder you should ask, laddie! for it's well known that most mothers, if they have a runt or a slow-witted or a crooked child, make more of that one than of all the rest put together— as if they would make it up to him, for the fair play of the world. But you see in this case, he's perhaps the child of sin—for a liar *may* tell an ill truth—and bears the marks of it, you see; so to her he's just her sin running about the world incarnate; and that can't be pleasant to look upon."

"But excep' she war ashamed o' 't, she wadna tak it sae muckle to hert to be remin't o' 't."

"Mony ane's ashamed o' the consequences 'at's no ashamed o' the deed. Mony ane cud du the sin ower again, 'at canna bide the sicht or even the word o' 't. I hae seen a body 't wad steal a thing as sune's luik at it gang daft wi' rage at bein' ca'd a thief. An' maybe she wadna care gien 't warna for the oogliness o' 'im. Sae be he was a bonny sin, I'm thinkin' she wad bide him weel eneuch. But seein' he 's naither i' the image o' her 'at bore 'im nor him 'at got 'im, but beirs on 's back, for ever in her sicht, the sin 'at was the getting' o' 'im, he's a' hump to her, an' her hert's aye howkin a grave for 'im to lay 'im oot o' sicht intill: she bore 'im, an' she wad beery 'im. An' I'm thinkin' she beirs the markis—gien sae it be sae—deid an' gane as he is—a grutch yet, for passin' sic an offspring upo' her, an' syne no merryin' her efter an' a', an' the ro'd clear o' baith 'at stude atween them. It *was* said 'at the man 'at killt 'im in a twasum fecht, sae mony a year efter, was a freen' o' hers."

"But *wad* fowk du sic awfu' ill things, mem—her a married woman, an' him a merried man?"

"There's nae sayin', laddie, what a hantle o' men and some women wad du. I hae muckle to be thankfu' for 'at I was sic as no man ever luikit twice at. I wasna weel-faured eneuch; though I had bonny hair, an' my mither aye said 'at her Maggy hed guid sense; whatever else she micht or micht not hae. But gien I cud hae gotten a guid man, siclike's is

"But except she were ashamed of it, she wouldn't take it so much to heart to be reminded of it."

"Many are ashamed of the consequences that aren't ashamed of the deed. Many could commit the sin over again, that can't stand the sight or even the mention of it. I've seen a body that would steal a thing as soon as look at it go daft with rage at being called a thief. And maybe she wouldn't care if it weren't for his ugliness. Had he been a bonny sin, I'm thinking she would stand him well enough. But since he's neither in the image of her that bore him nor him that got him, but bears on his back, for ever in her sight, the sin that was the getting of him, he's all hump to her, and her heart's always digging his grave to lay him into out of sight: she bore him, and she would bury him. And I'm thinking she bears the marquis—if the thing be true—dead and gone as he is—a grudge yet, for passing such an offspring upon her, and then not marrying her after all, and the way clear of both that stood between them. It *was* said that the man that killed him in a duel, so many years after, was a friend of hers."

"But *would* folk do such awful things, ma'am—her a married woman, and him a married man?"

"There's no saying, laddie, what a great deal of men and some women would do. I have much to be thankful for that I was such as no man ever looked twice at. I wasn't pretty enough; though I had bonny hair, and my mother always said that her Maggy had good sense; whatever else she might or might not have. But if I could have gotten a good man, such as scarce, I cud hae lo'ed him weel eneuch. But that's naither here nor there, an' has naething to du wi' onybody ava. The pint I had to come till was this: the wuman ye saw haudin' a toot moot wi' that Cat'nach wife, was nane ither, I do believe, than Mistress Stewart, the puir laird's mither. An' I hae as little doobt that whan ye tuik 's pairt, ye broucht to noucht a plot o' the twasum against him. It bodes guid to naebody whan there's a conjunc o' twa sic wanderin' stars o' blackness as yon twa."

"His ain mither!" exclaimed Malcolm, brooding in horror over the frightful conjecture.

The door opened, and the mad laird came in. His eyes were staring wide, but their look and that of his troubled visage showed that he was awake only in some frightful dream. "Father o' lichts!" he murmured once and again, but making wild gestures, as if warding off blows. Miss Horn took him gently by the hand. The moment he felt her touch, his face grew calm, and he submitted at once to be led back to bed.

"Ye may tak yer aith upo' 't, Ma'colm," she said when she returned, "she means naething but ill by that puir cratur; but you and me—we'll ding her yet, gien't be *his* wull. She wants a grip o' 'm for some ill rizzon or ither—to lock him up in a madhoose, maybe, as the villains said, or 'deed, maybe, to mak awa' wi' him a'thegither."

"But what guid wad that du her?" said Malcolm.

"It's ill to say, but she wad hae him oot o' her sicht, ony gait."

"She can hae but little sicht o' him as 'tis," objected Malcolm.

isn't easily found, I could have loved him well enough. But that's neither here nor there, and has nothing to do with anybody at all. The point I had to come to was this: the woman you saw in cahoots with that Catanach wife, was none other, I do believe, than Mistress Stewart, the poor laird's mother. And I have as little doubt that when you took his part, you thwarted a plot the pair had hatched against him. It bodes good to nobody when there's a conjunction of two such wandering stars of blackness as them."

"His own mother!" exclaimed Malcolm, brooding in horror over the frightful conjecture.

The door opened, and the mad laird came in. His eyes were staring wide, but their look and that of his troubled visage showed that he was awake only in some frightful dream. "Father o' lichts!" he murmured once and again, but making wild gestures, as if warding off blows. Miss Horn took him gently by the hand. The moment he felt her touch, his face grew calm, and he submitted at once to be led back to bed.

"You may take your oath upon it, Malcolm," she said when she returned, "she means nothing but harm by that poor creature; but you and me—we'll foil her yet, if it be *his* will. She wants a grip of him for some ill reason or other—to lock him up in a madhouse, maybe, as the villains said, or indeed, maybe, to make away with him altogether."

"But what good would that do her?" said Malcolm.

"It's hard to say, but she would have him out of her sight, anyway."

"She can see him but little as it is," objected Malcolm.

"Ay! but she aye kens he's whaur she doesna ken, puttin' her to shame, a' aboot the country, wi' that hump o' his. Oot o' fowk's sicht wad be to her oot a' thegither."

A brief silence followed.

"Noo," said Malcolm, "we come to the question what the twa limmers could want wi' that door."

"Dear kens! It bude to be something wrang—that's a' 'at mortal can say; but ye may be sure o' that—I hae hard tell," she went on reflectingly—"o' some room or ither i' the hoose 'at there's a fearsome story aboot, an' 'at 's never opent on no accoont. I hae hard a' aboot it, but I canna min' upo' 't noo, for I paid little attention till 't at the time, an' it 's mony a year sin' syne. But it wad be some deevilich ploy o' their ain they wad be efter: it 's little the likes o' them wad heed sic auld warld tales."

"Wad ye hae me tell the markis?" asked Malcolm.

"Na, I wad no; an' yet ye maun du 't. Ye hae no business to ken o' onything wrang in a body's hoose, an' no tell them—forbye 'at he pat ye in chairge. But it 'll du naething for the laird; for what cares the markis for onything or onybody but himsel'?"

"He cares for 's dauchter," said Malcolm.

"Ow ay!—as sic fowk ca' carin'. There's no a bla'guard i' the haill queentry he wadna sell her till, sae be he was o' an auld eneuch faimily, and had rowth o' siller. Haith! noo a days the last 'ill come first, an' a fish cadger wi' siller 'ill be coontit a better bargain nor a lord wantin 't: only he maun hae a *heap* o' 't, to cower the stink o' the fish."

"Ay! but she always knows he's somewhere, putting her to shame, all about the country, with that hump of his. Out of folk's sight would be to her out altogether."

A brief silence followed.

"Now," said Malcolm, "we come to the question what the two jades could want with that door."

"Dear knows! It must be something wrong—that's all that mortal can say; but you may be sure of that—I have heard tell," she went on reflectingly—"of some room or other in the house that there's a fearsome story about, and that's never opened on any account. I've heard all about it, but I can't remember it now, for I paid little attention to it at the time, and it was many years ago. But it would be some devilish ploy of their own they'd be after: it's little the likes of them would heed such old world tales."

"Would you have me tell the marquis?" asked Malcolm.

"Na, I wouldn't; and yet you must do it. You have no business to know of anything wrong in a body's house, and not tell them—not to mention that he put you in charge. But it'll do nothing for the laird; for what cares the marquis for anything or anybody but himself?"

"He cares for his daughter," said Malcolm.

"Oh ay!—as such folk call caring. There's not a blackguard in the whole country he wouldn't sell her to, provided he was of an old enough family, and was rolling in money. Faith! nowadays the last will come first, and a fish cadger with money will be deemed a better bargain than a lord wanting it: only he must have a *heap* of it, to cover the stink of the fish."

"Dinna scorn the fish, mem," said Malcolm: "they're innocent craturs, an' dinna smell waur nor they can help; an' that's mair nor ye can say for ilka lord ye come athort."

"Ay, or cadger aither," rejoined Miss Horn. "They're aft eneuch jist sic like, the main differ lyin' in what they're defiled wi'; an' 'deed whiles there's no differ there, or maist ony gait, maybe, but i' the set o' the shoothers, an' the wag o' the tongue."

"An' what 'll we du wi' the laird?" said Malcolm.

"We maun first see what we *can* du wi' him. I wad try to keep him mysel', that is, gien he wad bide—but there's that jaud Jean! She's aye gabbin', an' claikin', an' cognostin' wi' the enemy, an' I canna lippen till her. I think it wad be better ye sud tak chairge o' 'm yersel', Malcolm. I wad willin'ly beir ony expense—for ye wadna be able to luik efter him an' du sae weel at the fishin', ye ken."

"Gien 't had been my ain line-fishin', I could aye ha' taen him i' the boat wi' me; but I dinna ken for the herrin'. Blue Peter wadna objeck, but it 's some rouch work, an' for a waikly body like the laird to be oot a' nicht some nichts, sic weather as we hae to encoonter whiles, micht be the deid o' 'm."

They came to no conclusion beyond this, that each would think it over, and Malcolm would call in the morning. Ere then, however, the laird had dismissed the question for them. When Miss Horn rose, after an all but sleepless night, she found that he had taken the affairs again into his own feeble hands, and vanished.

"Don't scorn the fish, ma'am," said Malcolm: "they're innocent creatures, and don't smell worse than they can help; and that's more than you can say for every lord you come across."

"Ay, or cadger either," rejoined Miss Horn. "They're just the same, often enough, the main difference lying in what they're defiled with; and indeed sometimes there's no odds even there, or almost anywhere, perhaps, but in the set of the shoulders, and the wag of the tongue."

"And what'll we do with the laird?" said Malcolm.

"We must first see what we *can* do with him. I would try to keep him myself, that is, if he would stay—but there's that jade Jean! She's always gabbing, and gossiping, and conspiring with the enemy, and I can't trust her. I think it would be better if you took charge of him yourself, Malcolm. I would willingly bear any expense—for you wouldn't be able to look after him and do so well at the fishing, you know."

"Had it been my own line-fishing, I could always have taken him in the boat with me; but I don't know about the herring. Blue Peter wouldn't object, but it's pretty rough work, and for a weak body like the laird to be out all night some nights, such weather as we have to face at times, might be the death of him."

They came to no conclusion beyond this, that each would think it over, and Malcolm would call in the morning. Ere then, however, the laird had dismissed the question for them. When Miss Horn rose, after an all but sleepless night, she found that he had taken the affairs again into his own feeble hands, and vanished.

CHAPTER XXVI

NOT AT CHURCH

It being well known that Joseph Mair's cottage was one of the laird's resorts, Malcolm, as soon as he learned his flight, set out to inquire whether they knew anything of him there.

Scaurnose was perched almost on the point of the promontory, where the land made its final slope, ending in a precipitous descent to the shore. Beneath lay rocks of all sizes and of fantastic forms, some fallen from the cape in tempests perhaps, some softly separated from it by the slow action of the winds and waves of centuries. A few of them formed, by their broken defence seawards, the unsafe natural harbour which was all the place enjoyed.

If ever there was a place of one colour it was this village: everything was brown; the grass near it was covered with brown nets; at the doors were brown heaps of oak-bark, which, after dyeing the nets, was used for fuel; the cottages were roofed with old brown thatch; and the one street and the many *closes* were dark brown with the peaty earth which, well mixed with scattered bark, scantily covered the surface of its huge foundation-rock. There was no pavement, and it was the less needed that the ways were rarely used by wheels of any description. The village was but a roost, like the dwellings of the sea birds which also haunted the rocks.

It was a gray morning with a gray sky and a gray sea; all was brown and gray, peaceful and rather sad. Brown-haired, gray-eyed Phemy Mair sat in the threshold, intently rubbing in her hands a small object like a moonstone. That she should be doing so on a Sunday would have shocked few in Scaurnose at that time, for the fisher folk then made but small pretensions to religion; and for his part Joseph Mair could not believe that the Almighty would be offended "at seein' a bairn sittin' douce wi' her playocks, (at seeing a child sitting quietly with her toys) though the day *was his*."

"Weel, Phemy, ye're busy!" said Malcolm.

"Ay," answered the child, without looking up. The manner was not courteous, but her voice was gentle and sweet.

"Well, Phemy, you're busy!" said Malcolm.

"Ay," answered the child, without looking up. The manner was not courteous, but her voice was gentle and sweet.

"What are ye doin' there?" he asked.

"Makin' a string o' beads, to weir at aunty's merriage."

"What are ye makin' them o'?" he went on.

"Haddicks' een."

"Are they a' haddicks'?"

"Na, there's some cods' amo' them; but they're maistly haddicks'. I pikes them out afore they're sautit, an' biles them; an' syne I polish them i' my han's till they're rale bonny."

"Can ye tell me onything about the mad laird, Phemy?" asked Malcolm, in his anxiety too abruptly.

"Ye can gang an' speir at my father: he's oot aboot," she answered, with a sort of marked coolness, which, added to the fact that she had never looked him in the face, made him more than suspect something behind.

"Div *ye* ken onything aboot him?" he therefore insisted.

"Maybe I div, an' maybe I divna," answered the child, with an expression of determined mystery.

"Ye'll tell me whaur ye *think* he is, Phemy?"

"Na, I winna."

"What for no?"

"Ow, jist for fear ye sud ken."

"But I'm a freen' till him."

"Ye may think ay, an' the laird may think no."

"Does he think *you* a freen', Phemy?" asked Malcolm, in the hope of coming at something by widening the sweep of the conversation.

"Ay, he *kens* I'm a freen'," she replied.

"An' do ye aye ken whaur he is?"

"What are you doing there?" he asked.

"Making a string of beads, to wear at aunty's marriage."

"What are you making them of?" he went on.

"Haddocks' eyes."

"Are they all haddocks'?"

"Na, there's some cods' among them; but they're mostly haddocks'. I pick them out before they're salted, and boil them; and then I polish them in my hands till they're real bonny."

"Can you tell me anything about the mad laird, Phemy?" asked Malcolm, in his anxiety too abruptly.

"You can go and ask my father: he's out and about," she answered, with a sort of marked coolness, which, added to the fact that she had never looked him in the face, made him more than suspect something behind.

"Do *you* know anything about him?" he therefore insisted.

"Maybe I do, and maybe I don't," answered the child, with an expression of determined mystery.

"You'll tell me where you *think* he is, Phemy?"

"Na, I won't."

"Why not?"

"Oh, just for fear you should know."

"But I'm a friend to him."

"You may think so, and the laird may think not."

"Does he think *you* a friend, Phemy?" asked Malcolm, in the hope of coming at something by widening the sweep of the conversation.

"Ay, he *knows* I'm a friend," she replied.

"And do you always know where he is?"

"Na, no aye. He gangs here an' he gangs there—jist as he likes. It's whan *naebody* kens whaur he is, that I ken, an' gang till him."

"Is he i' the hoose?"

"Na, he's no i' the hoose."

"Whaur is he than, Phemy?" said Malcolm coaxingly. "There's ill fowk aboot 'at's efter deein' him an ill turn."

"The mair need no to tell!" retorted Phemy.

"But I want to tak care o' 'im. Tell me whaur he is, like a guid lassie, Phemy."

"I'm no sure. I may say I dinna ken."

"Ye say ye ken whan ither fowk disna: noo naebody kens."

"Hoo ken ye that?"

"'Cause he's run awa."

"Wha frae? His mither?"

"Na, na; frae Miss Horn."

"I ken naething aboot *her*; but gien naebody kens, I ken whaur he is weel eneuch."

"Whaur than? Ye'll be duin' him a guid turn to tell me."

"Whaur I winna tell, an' whaur you nor nae ither body s' get him. An' ye needna speir, for it wadna be richt to tell; an' gien ye gang on speirin', you an' me winna be lang freen's."

As she spoke, the child looked straight up into his face with wide-opened blue eyes, as truthful as the heavens, and Malcolm dared not press her, for it would have been to press her to do wrong.

"Ye wad tell yer father, wadna ye?" he said kindly.

"My father wadna speir. My father's a guid man."

"Weel, Phemy, though ye winna trust *me*—supposin' I was to trust *you?*"

"Na, not always. He goes here and he goes there—just as he likes. It's when *nobody* knows where he is, that I know, and go to him."

"Is he in the house?"

"Na, he's not in the house."

"Where is he then, Phemy?" said Malcolm coaxingly. "There's bad folk about that are looking to do him a bad turn."

"The more need not to tell!" retorted Phemy.

"But I want to take care of him. Tell me where he is, like a good lassie, Phemy."

"I'm not sure. I may say I don't know."

"You say you know when other folk don't: now nobody knows."

"How do you know that?"

"Because he's run away."

"Who from? His mother?"

"Na, na; from Miss Horn."

"I know nothing about *her*; but if nobody knows, I know where he is well enough."

"Where then? You'll be doing him a good turn to tell me."

"Where I won't tell, and where you nor any other body shall get him. And you needn't ask, for it wouldn't be right to tell; and if you go on asking, you and me won't long be friends."

As she spoke, the child looked straight up into his face with wide-opened blue eyes, as truthful as the heavens, and Malcolm dared not press her, for it would have been to press her to do wrong.

"You would tell your father, wouldn't you?" he said kindly.

"My father wouldn't ask. My father's a good man."

"Well, Phemy, though you won't trust *me*—supposing I was to trust *you?*"

"Ye can du that gien ye like."

"An' ye winna tell?"

"I s' mak nae promises. It's no trustin', to gar me promise."

"Weel, I wull trust ye.—Tell the laird to haud weel oot o' sicht for a while."

"He'll du that," said Phemy.

"An' tell him gien onything befa' him, to sen' to Miss Horn, for Ma'colm MacPhail may be oot wi' the boats.—Ye winna forget that?"

"I'm no lickly to forget it," answered Phemy, apparently absorbed in boring a hole in a haddock's eye with a pin so bent as to act like a brace and bit.

"Ye'll no get yer string o' beads in time for the weddin', Phemy," remarked Malcolm, going on to talk from a desire to give the child a feeling of his friendliness.

"Ay will I—fine that," she rejoined.

"Whan is 't to be?"

"Ow, neist Setterday. Ye'll be comin' ower?"

"I haena gotten a call."

"Ye 'll be gettin ane."

"Div ye think they'll gie me ane?"

"As sune 's onybody.—Maybe by that time I'll be able to gie ye some news o' the laird."

"There's a guid lassie!"

"Na, na; I'm makin' nae promises," said Phemy.

"You can do that if you like."

"And you won't tell?"

"I'll make no promises. It's not trusting, to make me promise."

"Well, I will trust you.—Tell the laird to keep well out of sight for a while."

"He'll do that," said Phemy.

"And tell him if he's in any trouble, to send to Miss Horn, for Malcolm MacPhail may be out with the boats.—You won't forget that?"

"I'm not likely to forget it," answered Phemy, apparently absorbed in boring a hole in a haddock's eye with a pin so bent as to act like a brace and bit.

"You won't get your string of beads in time for the wedding, Phemy," remarked Malcolm, going on to talk from a desire to give the child a feeling of his friendliness.

"Ay I will—quite easily," she rejoined.

"When is it to be?"

"Oh, next Saturday. You'll be coming over?"

"I haven't had a *call*."

"You will, though."

"Do you think they'll ask me?"

"As soon as anyone.—Maybe by that time I'll be able to give you some news of the laird."

"There's a good lassie!"

"Na, na; I'm making no promises," said Phemy.

Malcolm left her and went to find her father, who, although it was Sunday, was already "oot aboot," as she had said. He found him strolling in meditation along the cliffs. They had a little talk together, but Joseph knew nothing of the laird.

Malcolm took Lossie House on his way back, for he had not yet seen the marquis, to whom he must report his adventures of the night before. The signs of past revelling were plentifully visible as he approached the house. The marquis was not yet up, but Mrs Courthope undertaking to send him word as soon as his lordship was to be seen, he threw himself on the grass and waited—his mind occupied with strange questions, started by the Sunday coming after such a Saturday—among the rest, how God could permit a creature to be born so distorted and helpless as the laird, and then permit him to be so abused in consequence of his helplessness. The problems of life were beginning to *bite*. Everywhere things appeared uneven. He was not one to complain of mere external inequalities: if he *was* inclined to envy Lord Meikleham, it was not because of his social position: he was even now philosopher enough to know that the life of a fisherman was preferable to that of such a marquis as Lord Lossie—that the desirableness of a life is to be measured by the amount of interest and not by the amount of ease in it, for the more ease the more unrest; neither was he inclined to complain of the gulf that yawned so wide between him and Lady Florimel; the difficulty lay deeper: such a gulf existing, by a social law only less inexorable than a natural one, why should he feel the rent invading his individual being? in a word, though Malcolm put it in no such definite shape: Why should a fisher lad find himself in danger of falling in love with the daughter of a marquis? Why should such a thing, seeing the very constitution of things rendered it an absurdity, be yet a possibility?

The church bell began, rang on, and ceased. The sound of the psalms came, softly mellowed, and sweetly harmonized, across the churchyard through the gray Sabbath air, and he found himself, for the first time, a stray sheep from the fold. The service must have been half through before a lackey, to whom Mrs Courthope had committed the matter when she went to church, brought him the message that the marquis would see him.

"Well, MacPhail, what do you want with me?" said his lordship as he entered.

"It's my duty to acquaint yer lordship wi' certain proceedin's 'at took place last night," answered Malcolm.

"Go on," said the marquis.

Thereupon Malcolm began at the beginning, and told of the men he had watched, and how, in the fancy of following them, he had found himself in the garret, and what he saw and did there.

"Did you recognize either of the women?" asked Lord Lossie.

"Ane o' them, my lord," answered Malcolm. "It was Mistress Catanach, the howdie."

"What sort of a woman is she?"

"Some fowk canna bide her, my lord. I ken no ill to lay till her chairge, but I winna lippen till her. My gran'father—an' he's blin', ye ken—jist trimles whan she comes near him."

The marquis smiled.

"It's my duty to acquaint your lordship with certain proceedings that took place last night," answered Malcolm.

"Go on," said the marquis.

Thereupon Malcolm began at the beginning, and told of the men he had watched, and how, in the fancy of following them, he had found himself in the garret, and what he saw and did there.

"Did you recognize either of the women?" asked Lord Lossie.

"One of them, my lord," answered Malcolm. "It was Mistress Catanach, the midwife."

"What sort of a woman is she?"

"Some folk can't stand her, my lord. I know no ill to lay to her charge, but I won't trust to her. My grandfather—and he's blind, you know—just trembles when she comes near him."

The marquis smiled.

"What do you suppose she was about?" he asked.

"I ken nae mair than the bonnet I flang in her face, my lord; but it could hardly be guid she was efter. At ony rate, seein' yer lordship pat me in a mainner in chairge, I bude to haud her oot o' a closed room—an' her gaein' creepin' aboot yer lordship's hoose like a worm."

"Quite right. Will you pull the bell there for me?"

He told the man to send Mrs Courthope; but he said she had not yet come home from church.

"Could you take me to the room, MacPhail?" asked his lordship.

"I'll try, my lord," answered Malcolm. As far as the proper quarter of the attics, he went straight as a pigeon; in that labyrinth he had to retrace his steps once or twice, but at length he stopped, and said confidently—"This is the door, my lord."

"Are you sure?"

"As sure's death, my lord."

The marquis tried the door and found it immovable. "You say she had the key?"

"No, my lord: I said she had keys, but whether she had *the* key, I doobt if she kent hersel'. It may ha' been ane o' the bundle yet to try."

"You're a sharp fellow," said the marquis. "I wish I had such a servant about me."

"I wad mak a some rouch ane, I doobt," returned Malcolm, laughing.

His lordship was of another mind, but pursued the subject no farther.

"I have a vague recollection," he said, "of some room in the house having an old story or legend connected with it. I must find out. I daresay Mrs Courthope knows. Meantime you hold your tongue. We may get some amusement out of this."

"What do you suppose she was about?" he asked.

"I know no more than the bonnet I flung in her face, my lord; but it could hardly be good she was after. At any rate, since your lordship put me in a manner in charge, I had to keep her out of a closed room—and her going creeping about your lordship's house like a worm."

"Quite right. Will you pull the bell there for me?"

He told the man to send Mrs Courthope; but he said she had not yet come home from church.

"Could you take me to the room, MacPhail?" asked his lordship.

"I'll try, my lord," answered Malcolm. As far as the proper quarter of the attics, he went straight as a pigeon; in that labyrinth he had to retrace his steps once or twice, but at length he stopped, and said confidently—"This is the door, my lord."

"Are you sure?"

"As sure's death, my lord."

The marquis tried the door and found it immovable. "You say she had the key?"

"No, my lord: I said she had keys, but whether she had *the* key, I doubt if she knew herself. It may have been one of the bundle yet to try."

"You're a sharp fellow," said the marquis. "I wish I had such a servant about me."

"I would make quite a rough one, I expect," returned Malcolm, laughing.

His lordship was of another mind, but pursued the subject no farther.

"I have a vague recollection," he said, "of some room in the house having an old story or legend connected with it. I must find out. I daresay Mrs Courthope knows. Meantime you hold your tongue. We may get some amusement out of this."

"I wull, my lord, like a deid man an' beeryt."

"You can—can you?"

"I can, my lord."

"You're a rare one!" said the marquis.

Malcolm thought he was making game of him as heretofore, and held his peace.

"You can go home now," said his lordship. "I will see to this affair."

"But jist be canny middlin' wi' Mistress Catanach, my lord: she's no mowse."

"What! you're not afraid of an old woman?"

"Deil a bit, my lord!—that is, I'm no feart at a dogfish or a rottan, but I wud tak tent an' grip them the richt gait, for they hae teeth. Some fowk think Mistress Catanach has mair teeth nor she shaws."

"Well, if she's too much for me, I'll send for you," said the marquis good-humouredly.

"Ye canna get me sae easy, my lord: we're efter the herrin' noo."

"Well, well, we'll see."

"But I wantit to tell ye anither thing my lord," said Malcolm, as he followed the marquis down the stairs.

"What is that?"

"I cam upo' anither plot—a mair serious ane, bein' against a man 'at can ill haud aff o' himsel', an' cud waur bide onything than yer lordship—the puir mad laird."

"Who's he?"

"Ilka body kens *him*, my lord! He's son to the leddy o' Kirkbyres."

"I remember *her*—an old flame of my brother's."

"I ken naething aboot that, my lord; but he's her son."

"What about him, then?"

"I will, my lord, like a man dead and buried."

"You can—can you?"

"I can, my lord."

"You're a rare one!" said the marquis.

Malcolm thought he was making game of him as heretofore, and held his peace.

"You can go home now," said his lordship. "I will see to this affair."

"But just be careful meddling with Mistress Catanach, my lord: she's not safe."

"What! you're not afraid of an old woman?"

"Devil a bit, my lord!—that is, I don't fear a dogfish or a rat, but I'd be careful how I held them, for they have teeth. Some folk think Mistress Catanach has more teeth than she shows."

"Well, if she's too much for me, I'll send for you," said the marquis good-humouredly.

"You can't get me so easy, my lord: we're after the herring now."

"Well, well, we'll see."

"But I wanted to tell you another thing my lord," said Malcolm, as he followed the marquis down the stairs.

"What is that?"

"I came upon another plot—a more serious one, being against a man that can ill defend himself, and is more vulnerable than your lordship—the poor mad laird."

"Who's he?"

"Everybody knows *him*, my lord! He's son to the lady of Kirkbyres."

"I remember *her*—an old flame of my brother's."

"I know nothing about that, my lord; but he's her son."

"What about him, then?"

They had now reached the hall, and, seeing the marquis impatient, Malcolm confined himself to the principal facts.

"I don't think you had any business to interfere, MacPhail," said his lordship, seriously. "His mother must know best."

"I'm no sae sure o' that, my lord! To say naething o' the ill guideship, which micht hae garred a minister sweer, it wud be a cruelty naething short o' deev'lich to lock up a puir hairmless cratur like that, as innocent as he 's ill-shapit."

"He's as God made him," said the marquis.

"He 's no as God *wull* mak him," returned Malcolm.

"What do you mean by that?" asked the marquis.

"It stan's to rizzon, my lord," answered Malcolm, "that what's ill-made maun be made ower again. There's a day comin' whan a' 'at's wrang 'll be set richt, ye ken."

"And the crooked made straight," suggested the marquis laughing.

"Doobtless, my lord. He'll be strauchtit oot bonny that day," said Malcolm with absolute seriousness.

"Bah! You don't think God cares about a misshapen lump of flesh like that!" exclaimed his lordship with contempt.

"As muckle's aboot yersel', or my leddy," said Malcolm. "Gien he didna, he wadna be nae God ava'."

The marquis laughed again: he heard the words with his ears, but his heart was deaf to the thought they clothed; hence he took Malcolm's earnestness for irreverence, and it amused him.

They had now reached the hall, and, seeing the marquis impatient, Malcolm confined himself to the principal facts.

"I don't think you had any business to interfere, MacPhail," said his lordship, seriously. "His mother must know best."

"I'm not so sure of that, my lord! To say nothing of the ill usage, which might have made a minister swear, it would be a cruelty nothing short of devilish to lock up a poor harmless creature like that, as innocent as he's ill-shaped."

"He's as God made him," said the marquis.

"He's not as God *will* make him," returned Malcolm.

"What do you mean by that?" asked the marquis.

"It stands to reason, my lord," answered Malcolm, "that what's ill-made, must be made over again. There's a day coming when all that's wrong will be set right, you know."

"And the crooked made straight," suggested the marquis laughing.

"Doubtless, my lord. He'll have a bonny straightening-out that day," said Malcolm with absolute seriousness.

"Bah! You don't think God cares about a misshapen lump of flesh like that!" exclaimed his lordship with contempt.

"As much as about yourself, or my lady," said Malcolm. "If he didn't, he would be no God at all."

The marquis laughed again: he heard the words with his ears, but his heart was deaf to the thought they clothed; hence he took Malcolm's earnestness for irreverence, and it amused him.

"You've not got to set things right, anyhow," he said. "You mind your own business."

"I'll try, my lord: it's the business o' ilka man, whaur he can, to lowse the weichty birns, an' lat the forfouchten gang free[15]. Guid day to ye, my lord."

So saying the young fisherman turned, and left the marquis laughing in the hall.

"You've not got to set things right, anyhow," he said. "You mind your own business."

"I'll try, my lord: it's the business of every man, where he can, to loose the heavy burdens, and let the oppressed go free[15]. Good day to you, my lord."

So saying the young fisherman turned, and left the marquis laughing in the hall.

---

15 Isaiah lviii

CHAPTER XXVII

LORD GERNON

When his housekeeper returned from church, Lord Lossie sent for her. "Sit down, Mrs Courthope," he said; "I want to ask you about a story I have a vague recollection of hearing when I spent a summer at this house some twenty years ago. It had to do with a room in the house that was never opened."

"There is such a story, my lord," answered the housekeeper. "The late marquis, I remember well, used to laugh at it, and threaten now and then to dare the prophecy; but old Eppie persuaded him not—or at least fancied she did."

"Who is old Eppie?"

"She's gone now, my lord. She was over a hundred then. She was born and brought up in the house, lived all her days in it, and died in it; so she knew more about the place than any one else."

"Is ever likely to know," said the marquis, superadding a close to her sentence. "And why wouldn't she have the room opened?" he asked.

"Because of the ancient prophecy, my lord."

"I can't recall a single point of the story."

"I wish old Eppie were alive to tell it," said Mrs Courthope.

"Don't *you* know it then?"

"Yes, pretty well; but my English tongue can't tell it properly. It doesn't sound right out of my mouth. I've heard it a good many times too, for I had often to take a visitor to her room to hear it, and the old woman liked nothing better than telling it. But I couldn't help remarking that it had grown a good bit even in my time. The story was like a tree: it got bigger every year."

"That's the way with a good many stories," said the marquis. "But tell me the prophecy at least."

"That is the only part I can give just as she gave it. It's in rhyme. I hardly understand it, but I'm sure of the words."

"Let us have them then, if you please."

Mrs Courthope reflected for a moment, and then repeated the following lines:

> "The lord quha wad sup on 3 thowmes o' cauld airn,
> The ayr quha wad kythe a bastard and carena,

The mayd quha wad tyne her man and her bairn,
Lift the sneck, and enter, and fearna."

"That's it, my lord," she said, in conclusion. "And there's one thing to be observed," she added, "—that that door is the only one in all the passage that has a sneck, as they call it."

"What is a sneck?" asked his lordship, who was not much of a scholar in his country's tongue.

"What we call a latch in England, my lord. I took pains to learn the Scotch correctly, and I've repeated it to your lordship, word for word."

"I don't doubt it," returned Lord Lossie, "but for the sense, I can make nothing of it.—And you think my brother believed the story?"

"He always laughed at it, my lord, but pretended at least to give in to old Eppie's entreaties."

"You mean that he was more near believing it than he liked to confess?"

"That's not what I mean, my lord."

"Why do you say *pretended* then?"

"Because when the news of his death came, some people about the place would have it that he must have opened the door some time or other."

"How did they make that out?"

"From the first line of the prophecy."

"Repeat it again."

"The lord quha wad sup on 3 thowmes o' cauld airn," said Mrs Courthope with emphasis, adding, "The *three* she always said was a figure 3."

"That implies it was written somewhere!"

"She said it was legible on the door in her day—as if burnt with a red-hot iron."

"And what does the line mean?"

"Eppie said it meant that the lord of the place who opened that door, would die by a sword-wound. Three inches of cold iron, it means, my lord."

The marquis grew thoughtful; his brother had died in a sword-duel. For a few moments he was silent.

"Tell me the whole story," he said at length.

Mrs Courthope again reflected, and began. I will tell the story, however, in my own words, reminding my reader that if he regards it as an unwelcome interruption, he can easily enough avoid this bend of the river of my narrative by taking a short cut across to the next chapter.

In an ancient time there was a lord of Lossie who practised unholy works. Although he had other estates, he lived almost entirely at the House of Lossie—that is, after his return from the East, where he had spent his youth and early manhood. But he paid no attention to his affairs: a steward managed everything for him, and Lord Gernon (for that was the outlandish name he brought from England, where he was born while his father was prisoner to Edward Longshanks) trusted him for a great while without making the least inquiry into his accounts, apparently contented with receiving money enough to carry on the various vile experiments which seemed his sole pleasure in life. There was no doubt in the minds of the people of the town—the old town that is, which was then much larger, and clustered about the gates of the House—that he had dealings with Satan, from whom he had gained authority over the powers of nature; that he was able to rouse and lay the winds, to bring down rain, to call forth the lightnings and set the thunders roaring over town and sea; nay, that he could even draw vessels ashore on the rocks, with the certainty that not one on board would be left alive to betray the pillage of the wreck: this and many other deeds of dire note were laid to his charge in secret. The town cowered at the foot of the House in terror of what its lord might bring down upon it—as a brood of chickens might cower if they had been hatched by a kite, and saw, instead of the matronly head and beak of the hen of their instinct, those of the bird of prey projected over them. Scarce one of them dared even look from the door when the thunder was rolling over their heads, the lightnings flashing about the roofs and turrets of the House, the wind raving in fits between as if it would rave its last, and the rain falling in sheets—not so much from fear of the elements, as for horror of the far more terrible things that might be spied careering in the storm. And indeed Lord Gernon himself was avoided in like fashion, although rarely had any one the evil chance of seeing him, so seldom did he go out of doors. There was but one in the whole community —and that was a young girl, the daughter of his steward—who declared she had no fear of him: she went so far as to uphold that Lord Gernon meant harm to nobody, and was in consequence regarded by the neighbours as unrighteously bold.

He worked in a certain lofty apartment on the ground floor—with cellars underneath, reserved, it was believed, for frightfullest conjurations and interviews; where, although no one was permitted to enter, they knew from the smoke that he had a furnace, and from the evil smells which wandered out, that he dealt with things altogether devilish in their natures and powers. They said he always washed there—in water medicated with distilments to prolong life and produce invulnerability; but of this they could of course know nothing. Strange to say, however, he always slept in the garret, as far removed from his laboratory as the limits of the house would permit; whence people said he dared not sleep in the neighbourhood of his deeds, but sought shelter for his unconscious hours in the spiritual shadow of the chapel, which was in the same wing as his chamber. His household saw nearly as little of him as his retainers: when his tread was heard, beating dull on the stone turnpike, or thundering along the upper corridors in the neighbourhood of his chamber or of the library—the only other part of the house he visited, man or maid would dart aside into the next way of escape—all believing that the nearer he came to finding himself the sole inhabitant of his house, the better he was pleased. Nor would he allow man or woman to enter his chamber any more than his laboratory. When they found sheets or garments outside his door, they removed them with fear and trembling, and put others in their place.

At length, by means of his enchantments, he discovered that the man whom he had trusted had been robbing him for many years: all the time he had been searching for the philosopher's stone, the gold already his had been tumbling into the bags of his steward. But what enraged him far more was, that the fellow had constantly pretended difficulty in providing the means necessary for the prosecution of his idolized studies: even if the feudal lord could have accepted the loss and forgiven the crime, here was a mockery which the man of science could not pardon. He summoned his steward to his presence, and accused him of his dishonesty. The man denied it energetically, but a few mysterious waftures of the hand of his lord, set him trembling, and after a few more, his lips, moving by a secret compulsion, and finding no power in their owner to check their utterance, confessed all the truth, whereupon his master ordered him to go and bring his accounts. He departed all but bereft of his senses, and staggered home as if in a dream. There he begged his daughter to go and plead for him with his lord, hoping she might be able to move him to mercy; for she was a lovely girl, and supposed by the neighbours, judging from what they considered her foolhardiness, to have received from him tokens of something at least less than aversion.

She obeyed, and from that hour disappeared. The people of the house averred afterwards that the next day, and for days following, they heard, at intervals, moans and cries from the wizard's chamber, or some where in its neighbourhood—certainly not from the laboratory; but as they had seen no one visit their master, they had paid them little attention, classing them with the other and hellish noises they were but too much accustomed to hear.

The steward's love for his daughter, though it could not embolden him to seek her in the tyrant's den, drove him, at length, to appeal to the justice of his country for what redress might yet be possible: he sought the court of the great Bruce, and laid his complaint before him. That righteous monarch immediately despatched a few of his trustiest men-at-arms, under the protection of a monk whom he believed a match for any wizard under the sun, to arrest Lord Gernon and release the girl. When they arrived at Lossie House, they found it silent as the grave. The domestics had vanished; but by following the minute directions of the steward, whom no persuasion could bring to set foot across the threshold, they succeeded in finding their way to the parts of the house indicated by him. Having forced the laboratory and found it forsaken, they ascended, in the gathering dusk of a winter afternoon, to the upper regions of the house. Before they reached the top of the stair that led to the wizard's chamber, they began to hear inexplicable sounds, which grew plainer, though not much louder, as they drew nearer to the door. They were mostly like the grunting of some small animal of the hog kind, with an occasional one like the yelling roar of a distant lion; but with these were now and then mingled cries of suffering, so fell and strange that their souls recoiled as if they would break loose from their bodies to get out of hearing of them. The monk himself started back when first they invaded his ear, and it was no wonder then that the men-at-arms should hesitate to approach the room; and as they stood irresolute, they saw a faint light go flickering across the upper part of the door, which naturally strengthened their disinclination to go nearer.

"If it weren't for the girl," said one of them in a scared whisper to his neighbour, "I would leave the wizard to the devil and his dam."

Scarcely had the words left his mouth, when the door opened, and out came a form—whether phantom or living woman none could tell. Pale, forlorn, lost, and purposeless, it came straight towards them, with wide unseeing eyes. They parted in terror from its path. It went on, looking to neither hand, and sank down the stair. The moment it was beyond their sight, they came to themselves and rushed after it; but although they searched the whole house, they could find no creature in it, except a cat of questionable appearance and behaviour, which they wisely let alone. Returning, they took up a position whence they could watch the door of the chamber day and night.

For three weeks they watched it, but neither cry nor other sound reached them. For three weeks more they watched it, and then an evil odour began to assail them, which grew and grew, until at length they were satisfied that the wizard was dead. They returned therefore to the king and made their report, whereupon Lord Gernon was decreed dead, and his heir was enfeoffed. But for many years he was said to be still alive; and indeed whether he had ever died in the ordinary sense of the word, was to old Eppie doubtful; for at various times there had arisen whispers of peculiar sounds, even strange cries, having been heard issue from that room—whispers which had revived in the house in Mrs Courthope's own time. No one had slept in that part of the roof within the memory of old Eppie: no one, she believed, had ever slept there since the events of her tale; certainly no one had in Mrs Courthope's time. It was said also, that, invariably, sooner or later after such cries were heard, some evil befell either the Lord of Lossie, or some one of his family.

"Show me the room, Mrs Courthope," said the marquis, rising, as soon as she had ended.

The housekeeper looked at him with some dismay.

"What!" said his lordship, "you an Englishwoman and superstitious!"

"I am cautious, my lord, though not a Scotchwoman," returned Mrs Courthope. "All I would presume to say is—Don't do it without first taking time to think over it."

"I will not. But I want to know which room it is."

Mrs Courthope led the way, and his lordship followed her to the very door, as he had expected, with which Malcolm had spied Mrs Catanach tampering. He examined it well, and on the upper part of it found what might be the remnants of a sunk inscription, so far obliterated as to convey no assurance of what it was. He professed himself satisfied, and they went down the stairs together again.

CHAPTER XXVIII

A FISHER WEDDING

When the next Saturday came, all the friends of the bride or bridegroom who had "gotten a call" to the wedding of Annie Mair and Charley Wilson, assembled respectively at the houses of their parents. Malcolm had received an invitation from both, and had accepted that of the bride.

Whisky and oatcake having been handed round, the bride, a short but comely young woman, set out with her father for the church, followed by her friends in couples. At the door of the church, which stood on the highest point in the parish, a centre of assault for all the winds that blew, they met the bridegroom and his party: the bride and he entered the church together, and the rest followed. After a brief and somewhat bare ceremony, they issued—the bride walking between her brother and the groomsman, each taking an arm of the bride, and the company following mainly in trios. Thus arranged they walked eastward along the highroad, to meet the bride's *first-foot.*

They had gone about halfway to Portlossie, when a gentleman appeared, sauntering carelessly towards them, with a cigar in his mouth. It was Lord Meikleham. Malcolm was not the only one who knew him: Lizzy Findlay, only daughter of the Partan, and the prettiest girl in the company, blushed crimson: she had danced with him at Lossie House, and he had said things to her, by way of polite attention, which he would never have said had she been of his own rank. He would have lounged past, with a careless glance, but the procession halted by one consent, and the bride, taking a bottle and glass which her brother carried, proceeded to pour out a bumper of whisky, while the groomsman addressed Lord Meikleham.

"Ye're the bride's first fut, sir," he said.

"What do you mean by that?" asked Lord Meikleham.

"Here's the bride, sir: she'll tell ye."

Lord Meikleham lifted his hat.

"Allow me to congratulate you," he said.

"You're the bride's first foot, sir," he said.

"What do you mean by that?" asked Lord Meikleham.

"Here's the bride, sir: she'll tell you."

Lord Meikleham lifted his hat.

"Allow me to congratulate you," he said.

"Ye're my first fut," returned the bride eagerly yet modestly, as she held out to him the glass of whisky.

"This is to console me for not being in the bridegroom's place, I presume; but notwithstanding my jealousy, I drink to the health of both," said the young nobleman, and tossed off the liquor.—"Would you mind explaining to me what you mean by this ceremony?" he added, to cover a slight choking caused by the strength of the dram.

"It's for luck, sir," answered Joseph Mair. "A first fut wha wadna bring ill luck upon a new merried couple, maun aye du as ye hae dune this meenute—tak a dram frae the bride."

"Is that the sole privilege connected with my good fortune?" said Lord Meikleham. "If I take the bride's dram, I must join the bride's regiment—My good fellow," he went on, approaching Malcolm, "you have more than your share of the best things of this world."

For Malcolm had two partners, and the one on the side next Lord Meikleham, who, as he spoke, offered her his arm, was Lizzy Findlay.

"No as shares gang, my lord," returned Malcolm, tightening his arm on Lizzie's hand. "Ye mauna gang wi' ane o' oor customs to gang *agane* anither. Fisher fowk 's ready eneuch to pairt wi' their whusky, but no wi' their lasses!—Na, haith!"

Lord Meikleham's face flushed, and Lizzy looked down, very evidently disappointed; but the bride's father, a wrinkled and brown little man, with a more gentle bearing than most of them, interfered.

"You're my first foot," returned the bride eagerly yet modestly, as she held out to him the glass of whisky.

"This is to console me for not being in the bridegroom's place, I presume; but notwithstanding my jealousy, I drink to the health of both," said the young nobleman, and tossed off the liquor.—"Would you mind explaining to me what you mean by this ceremony?" he added, to cover a slight choking caused by the strength of the dram.

"It's for luck, sir," answered Joseph Mair. "A first foot who wouldn't bring ill luck upon a new married couple, must always do as you have just done—take a dram from the bride."

"Is that the sole privilege connected with my good fortune?" said Lord Meikleham. "If I take the bride's dram, I must join the bride's regiment—My good fellow," he went on, approaching Malcolm, "you have more than your share of the best things of this world."

For Malcolm had two partners, and the one on the side next Lord Meikleham, who, as he spoke, offered her his arm, was Lizzy Findlay.

"Not as shares go, my lord," returned Malcolm, tightening his arm on Lizzie's hand. "You mustn't go with one of our customs to go *against* another. Fisher folk are ready enough to part with their whisky, but not with their lasses!—Na, faith!"

Lord Meikleham's face flushed, and Lizzy looked down, very evidently disappointed; but the bride's father, a wrinkled and brown little man, with a more gentle bearing than most of them, interfered.

"Ye see, my lord—gien it be sae I maun ca' ye, an' Ma'colm seems to ken—we're like by oorsel's for the present, an' we're but a rouch set o' fowk for such like 's yer lordship to haud word o' mou' wi'; but gien it wad please ye to come ower the gait ony time i' the evenin', an' tak yer share o' what's gauin', ye sud be welcome, an' we wad coont it a great honour frae sic 's yer lordship."

"I shall be most happy," answered Lord Meikleham; and taking off his hat he went his way.

"You see, my lord—if that's what I'm to call you, and Malcolm seems to know—we're by ourselves, like, for the present, and we're but a rough set of folk for such as your lordship to speak with; but if it would please you to step over the way any time in the evening, and take your share of what's going, you should be welcome, and we would count it a great honour from such as your lordship."

"I shall be most happy," answered Lord Meikleham; and taking off his hat he went his way.

The party returned to the home of the bride's parents. Her mother stood at the door with a white handkerchief in one hand, and a *quarter* of oatcake in the other. When the bride reached the threshold she stood, and her mother, first laying the handkerchief on her head, broke the oatcake into pieces upon it. These were distributed among the company, to be carried home and laid under their pillows.

The bridegroom's party betook themselves to his father's house, where, as well as at old Mair's, a substantial meal of tea, bread and butter, cake, and cheese, was provided. Then followed another walk, to allow of both houses being made tidy for the evening's amusements.

About seven, Lord Meikleham made his appearance, and had a hearty welcome. He had bought a showy brooch for the bride, which she accepted with the pleasure of a child. In their games, which had already commenced, he joined heartily, gaining high favour with both men and women. When the great clothesbasket full of *sweeties*, the result of a subscription among the young men, was carried round by two of them, he helped himself liberally with the rest; and at the inevitable game of forfeits met his awards with unflinching obedience; contriving ever through it all that Lizzy Findlay should feel herself his favourite. In the general hilarity, neither the heightened colour of her cheek, nor the vivid sparkle in her eyes attracted notice. Doubtless some of the girls observed the frequency of his attentions, but it woke nothing in their minds beyond a little envy of her passing good fortune.

Meikleham was handsome and a lord; Lizzy was pretty though a fisherman's daughter: a sort of Darwinian selection had apparently found place between them; but as the same entertainment was going on in two houses at once, and there was naturally a good deal of passing and repassing between them, no one took the least notice of several short absences from the company on the part of the pair.

Supper followed, at which his lordship sat next to Lizzy, and partook of dried skate and mustard, bread and cheese, and beer. Every man helped himself. Lord Meikleham and a few others were accommodated with knives and forks, but the most were independent of such artificial aids. Whisky came next, and Lord Meikleham being already, like many of the young men of his time, somewhat fond of strong drink, was not content with such sipping as Lizzy honoured his glass withal.

At length it was time, according to age-long custom, to undress the bride and bridegroom and put them to bed—the bride's stocking, last ceremony of all, being thrown amongst the company, as by its first contact prophetic of the person to be next married. Neither Lizzy nor Lord Meikleham, however, had any chance of being thus distinguished, for they were absent and unmissed.

As soon as all was over, Malcolm set out to return home. As he passed Joseph Mair's cottage, he found Phemy waiting for him at the door, still in the mild splendour of her pearl-like necklace.

"I tellt the laird what ye tellt me to tell him, Malcolm," she said.	"I told the laird what you told me to tell him, Malcolm," she said.
"An' what did he say, Phemy?" asked Malcolm.	"And what did he say, Phemy?" asked Malcolm.
"He said he kent ye was a freen'."	"He said he knew you were a friend."
"Was that a'?"	"Was that all?"
"Ay; that was a'."	"Ay; that was all."
"Weel, ye're a guid lassie."	"Well, you're a good lassie."
"Ow! middlin'," answered the little maiden.	"Oh! middling," answered the little maiden.

Malcolm took his way along the top of the cliffs, pausing now and then to look around him. The crescent moon had gone down, leaving a starlit night, in which the sea lay softly moaning at the foot of the broken crags. The sense of infinitude which comes to the soul when it is in harmony with the peace of nature, arose and spread itself abroad in Malcolm's being, and he felt with the Galilaeans of old, when they forsook their nets and followed him who called them, that catching fish was not the end of his being, although it was the work his hands had found to do. The stillness was all the sweeter for its contrast with the merriment he had left behind him, and a single breath of wind, like the waft from a passing wind, kissed his forehead tenderly, as if to seal the truth of his meditations.

CHAPTER XXIX

FLORIMEL AND DUNCAN

In the course of a fortnight, Lord Meikleham and his aunt, the bold-faced countess, had gone, and the marquis, probably finding it a little duller in consequence, began to pay visits in the neighbourhood. Now and then he would be absent for a week or two—at Bog o' Gight, or Huntly Lodge, or Frendraught, or Balvenie, and although Lady Florimel had not much of his society, she missed him at meals, and felt the place grown dreary from his being nowhere within its bounds.

On his return from one of his longer absences, he began to talk to her about a governess; but, though in a playful way, she rebelled utterly at the first mention of such an incubus. She had plenty of material for study, she said, in the library, and plenty of amusement in wandering about with the sullen Demon, who was her constant companion during his absences; and if he did force a governess upon her, she would certainly murder the woman, if only for the sake of bringing him into trouble. Her easygoing father was amused, laughed, and said nothing more on the subject at the time.

Lady Florimel did not confess that she had begun to feel her life monotonous, or mention that she had for some time been cultivating the acquaintance of a few of her poor neighbours, and finding their odd ways of life and thought and speech interesting. She had especially taken a liking to Duncan MacPhail, in which, strange to say, Demon, who had hitherto absolutely detested the appearance of any one not attired as a lady or gentleman, heartily shared. She found the old man so unlike anything she had ever heard or read of—so full of grand notions in such contrast with his poor conditions; so proud yet so overflowing with service—dusting a chair for her with his bonnet, yet drawing himself up like an offended hidalgo if she declined to sit in it—more than content to play the pipes while others dined, yet requiring a personal apology from the marquis himself for a practical joke! so full of kindness and yet of revenges—lamenting over Demon when he hurt his foot, yet cursing, as she overheard him once, in fancied solitude, with an absolute fervour of imprecation, a continuous blast of poetic hate which made her shiver; and the next moment sighing out a most wailful coronach on his old pipes. It was all so odd, so funny, so interesting! It nearly made her aware of human nature as an object of study. But lady Florimel had never studied anything yet, had never even perceived that anything wanted studying, that is, demanded to be understood. What appeared to her most odd, most inconsistent, and was indeed of all his peculiarities alone distasteful to her, was his delight in what she regarded only as the menial and dirty occupation of cleaning lamps and candlesticks; the poetic side of it, rendered tenfold poetic by his blindness, she never saw.

Then he had such tales to tell her—of mountain, stream, and lake; of love and revenge; of beings less and more than natural—brownie and Boneless, kelpie and fairy; such wild legends also, haunting the dim emergent peaks of mist-swathed Celtic history; such songs—come down, he said, from Ossian himself—that sometimes she would sit and listen to him for hours together.

It was no wonder then that she should win the heart of the simple old man speedily and utterly; for what can bard desire beyond a true listener—a mind into which his own may, in verse or tale or rhapsody, in pibroch or coronach, overflow? But when, one evening, in girlish merriment, she took up his pipes, blew the bag full, and began to let a highland air burst fitfully from the chanter, the jubilation of the old man broke all the bounds of reason. He jumped from his seat and capered about the room, calling her all the tenderest and most poetic names his English vocabulary would afford him; then abandoning the speech of the Sassenach, as if in despair of ever uttering himself through its narrow and rugged channels, overwhelmed her with a cataract of soft-flowing Gaelic, returning to English only as his excitement passed over into exhaustion—but in neither case aware of the transition.

Her visits were the greater comfort to Duncan, that Malcolm was now absent almost every night, and most days a good many hours asleep; had it been otherwise, Florimel, invisible for very width as was the gulf between them, could hardly have made them so frequent. Before the fishing-season was over, the piper had been twenty times on the verge of disclosing every secret in his life to the high-born maiden.

"It's a pity you haven't a wife to take care of you, Mr MacPhail," she said one evening. "You must be so lonely without a woman to look after you!"

A dark cloud came over Duncan's face, out of which his sightless eyes gleamed.

"She'll haf her poy, and she'll pe wanting no wife," he said sullenly. "Wifes is paad."

"Ah!" said Florimel, the teasing spirit of her father uppermost for the moment, "that accounts for your swearing so shockingly the other day?"

"Swearing was she? Tat will pe wrong. And who was she'll pe swearing at?"

"That's what I want you to tell me, Mr MacPhail."

"Tid you'll hear me, my laty?" he asked in a tone of reflection, as if trying to recall the circumstance.

"She'll haf her boy, and she'll be wanting no wife," he said sullenly. "Wifes is baad."

"Ah!" said Florimel, the teasing spirit of her father uppermost for the moment, "that accounts for your swearing so shockingly the other day?"

"Swearing was she? Tat will be wrong. And who was she'll be swearing at?"

"That's what I want you to tell me, Mr MacPhail."

"Tid you'll hear me, my laty?" he asked in a tone of reflection, as if trying to recall the circumstance.

"Indeed I did. You frightened me so that I didn't dare come in."

"Ten she'll pe punished enough. Put it wass no harm to curse ta wicket Cawmill."

"It was not Glenlyon—it wasn't a man at all; it was a woman you were in such a rage with."

"Was it ta rascal's wife, ten, my laty?" he asked, as if he were willing to be guided to the truth that he might satisfy her, but so much in the habit of swearing, that he could not well recollect the particular object at a given time.

"Is his wife as bad as himself then?"

"Wifes is aalways worser."

"But what is it makes you hate him so dreadfully? Is he a bad man?"

"A fery pad man, my tear laty! He is tead more than a hundert years."

"Then why do you hate him so?"

"Och hone! Ton't you'll never hear why?"

"He can't have done *you* any harm."

"Not done old Tuncan any harm! Tidn't you'll know what ta tog would pe toing to her aancestors of Glenco? Och hone! Och hone! Gif her ta tog's heart of him in her teeth, and she'll pe tearing it—tearing it—tearing it!" cried the piper in a growl of hate, and with the look of a maddened tiger, the skin of his face drawn so tight over the bones that they seemed to show their whiteness through it.

"You quite terrify me," said Florimel, really shocked. "If you talk like that, I must go away. Such words are not fit for a lady to hear."

The old man heard her rise: he fell on his knees, and held out his arms in entreaty.

"Indeed I did. You frightened me so that I didn't dare come in."

"Ten she'll be punished enough. But it wass no harm to curse ta wicket Cawmill."

"It was not Glenlyon—it wasn't a man at all; it was a woman you were in such a rage with."

"Was it ta rascal's wife, then, my laty?" he asked, as if he were willing to be guided to the truth that he might satisfy her, but so much in the habit of swearing, that he could not well recollect the particular object at a given time.

"Is his wife as bad as himself then?"

"Wifes is aalways worser."

"But what is it makes you hate him so dreadfully? Is he a bad man?"

"A fery bad man, my tear laty! He is dead more than a hundert years."

"Then why do you hate him so?"

"Alas! Ton't you'll never hear why?"

"He can't have done *you* any harm."

"Not done old Tuncan any harm! Tidn't you'll know what ta dog would be toing to her aancestors of Glenco? Alas! Alas! Gif her ta dog's heart of him in her teeth, and she'll be tearing it—tearing it—tearing it!" cried the piper in a growl of hate, and with the look of a maddened tiger, the skin of his face drawn so tight over the bones that they seemed to show their whiteness through it.

"You quite terrify me," said Florimel, really shocked. "If you talk like that, I must go away. Such words are not fit for a lady to hear."

The old man heard her rise: he fell on his knees, and held out his arms in entreaty.

"She's pegging your pardons, my laty. Sit town once more, anchel from hefen, and she'll not say it no more. Put she'll pe telling you ta story, and then you'll pe knowing tat what 'll not pe fit for laties to hear, as coot laties had to pear!"

"She's begging your pardons, my laty. Sit town once more, anchel from hefen, and she'll not say it no more. But she'll be telling you ta story, and then you'll be knowing tat what 'll not be fit for laties to hear, as coot laties had to bear!"

He caught up the Lossie pipes, threw them down again, searched in a frenzy till he found his own, blew up the bag with short thick pants, forced from them a low wail, which ended in a scream—then broke into a kind of chant, the words of which were something like what follows: he had sense enough to remember that for his listener they must be English. Doubtless he was translating as he went on. His chanter all the time kept up a low pitiful accompaniment, his voice only giving expression to the hate and execration of the song.

> Black rise the hills round the vale of Glenco;
> Hard rise its rocks up the sides of the sky;
> Cold fall the streams from the snow on their summits;
> Bitter are the winds that search for the wanderer;
> False are the vapours that trail o'er the corrie:
> Blacker than caverns that hollow the mountain,
> Harder than crystals in the rock's bosom,
> Colder than ice borne down in the torrents,
> More bitter than hail windswept o'er the correi,
> Falser than vapours that hide the dark precipice,
> Is the heart of the Campbell, the hell hound Glenlyon.
>
> Is it blood that is streaming down into the valley?
> Ha! 'tis the red-coated blood-hounds of Orange.
>
> To hunt the red deer, is this a fit season?
> Glenlyon, said Ian, the son of the chieftain:
> What seek ye with guns and with gillies so many?
>
> Friends, a warm fire, good cheer, and a drink,
> Said the liar of hell, with the death in his heart.
>
> Come home to my house—it is poor, but your own.
>
> Cheese of the goat, and flesh of black cattle,
> And dew of the mountain to make their hearts joyful,
> They gave them in plenty, they gave them with welcome;
> And they slept on the heather, and skins of the red deer.

Och hone for the chief! God's curse on the traitors!
Och hone for the chief—the father of his people!
He is struck through the brain, and not in the battle!

Och hone for his lady! the teeth of the badgers
Have torn the bright rings from her slender fingers!
They have stripped her and shamed her in sight of her clansmen!
They have sent out her ghost to cry after her husband.

Nine men did Glenlyon slay, nine of the true hearts!
His own host he slew, the laird of Inverriggen.

Fifty they slew—the rest fled to the mountains.
In the deep snow the women and children
Fell down and slept, nor awoke in the morning.

The bard of the glen, alone among strangers,
Allister, bard of the glen and the mountain,
Sings peace to the ghost of his father's father,
Slain by the curse of Glenco, Glenlyon.

Curse on Glenlyon! His wife's fair bosom
Dry up with weeping the fates of her children!
Curse on Glenlyon! Each drop of his heart's blood
Turn to red fire and hum through his arteries!
The pale murdered faces haunt him to madness!
The shrieks of the ghosts from the mists of Glenco
Ring in his ears through the caves of perdition!
Man, woman, and child, to the last-born Campbell,
Rush howling to hell, and fall cursing Glenlyon—
The liar who drank with his host and then slew him!

While he chanted, the whole being of the bard seemed to pour itself out in the feeble and quavering tones that issued from his withered throat. His voice grew in energy for a while as he proceeded, but at last gave way utterly under the fervour of imprecation, and ceased. Then, as if in an agony of foiled hate, he sent from chanter and drone a perfect screech of execration, with which the instrument dropped from his hands, and he fell back in his chair, speechless.

Lady Florimel started to her feet, and stood trembling for a moment, hesitating whether to run from the cottage and call for help, or do what she might for the old man herself. But the next moment he came to himself, saying, in a tone of assumed composure:

"You'll pe knowing now, my laty, why she'll pe hating ta very name of Clenlyon."

"But it was not *your* grandfather that Glenlyon killed, Mr MacPhail—was it?"

"And whose grandfather would it pe then, my laty?" returned Duncan, drawing himself up.

"The Glenco people weren't MacPhails. I've read the story of the massacre, and know all about that."

"He might haf been her mother's father, my laty."

"But you said *father's* father, in your song."

"She said *Allister's* father's father, my laty, she pelieves."

"I can't quite understand you, Mr MacPhail."

"Well, you see, my laty, her father was out in the forty-five, and fought ta red-coats at Culloden. Tat's his claymore on ta wall there—a coot plade—though she's not an Andrew Ferrara. She wass forched in Clenco, py a cousin of her own, Angus py name, and she's a fery coot plade: she'll can well whistle ta pibroch of Ian Loin apout ta ears of ta Sassenach. Her crand-father wass with his uncle in ta pattle of Killiecrankie after Tundee—a creat man, my laty, and he died there; and so tid her cranduncle, for a fillain of a Mackay, from Lord Reay's cursed country—where they aalways wass repels, my laty—chust as her uncle was pe cutting town ta wicket Chen-eral Mackay, turned him round, without gifing no warnings, and killed ta poor man at won plow."

"You'll be knowing now, my laty, why she'll be hating ta very name of Clenlyon."

"But it was not *your* grandfather that Glenlyon killed, Mr MacPhail—was it?"

"And whose grandfather would it be then, my laty?" returned Duncan, drawing himself up.

"The Glenco people weren't MacPhails. I've read the story of the massacre, and know all about that."

"He might haf been her mother's father, my laty."

"But you said *father's* father, in your song."

"She said *Allister's* father's father, my laty, she believes."

"I can't quite understand you, Mr MacPhail."

"Well, you see, my laty, her father was out in the forty-five, and fought ta red-coats at Culloden. Tat's his claymore on ta wall there—a coot blade—though she's not an Andrew Ferrara. She wass forged in Clenco, by a cousin of her own, Angus by name, and she's a fery coot blade: she'll can well whistle ta pibroch of Ian Loin about ta ears of ta Sassenach. Her crand-father wass with his uncle in ta battle of Killiecrankie after Dundee—a creat man, my laty, and he died there; and so tid her cranduncle, for a fillain of a Mackay, from Lord Reay's cursed country—where they aalways wass rebels, my laty—chust as her uncle was be cutting down ta wicket Chen-eral Mackay, turned him round, without gifing no warnings, and killed ta poor man at one blow."

"But what has it all to do with your name? I declare I don't know what to call you."

"Call her your own pard, old Tuncan MacPhail, my sweet laty, and haf ta patience with her, and she'll pe telling you aall apout eferyting, only you must gif her olt prains time to tumple temselfs apout. Her head grows fery stupid.—Yes, as she was saying, after ta ploody massacre at Culloden, her father had to hide himself away out of sight, and to forge himself—I mean to put upon himself a name tat tidn't mean himself at aal. And my poor mother, who pored me—pig old Tuncan—ta fery tay of ta pattle, would not be hearing won wort of him for tree months tat he was away; and when he would pe creep pack like a fox to see her one fine night when ta moon was not pe up, they'll make up an acreement to co away together for a time, and to call temselfs MacPhails. But py and py tey took their own nems again."

"And why haven't you your own name now? I'm sure it's a much prettier name."

"Pecause she'll pe taking the other, my tear laty."

"And why?"

"Pecause—pecause ... She will tell you another time. She'll pe tired to talk more apout ta cursed Cawmills this fery tay."

"Then Malcolm's name is not MacPhail either?"

"No, it is not, my lady."

"Is he your son's son, or your daughter's son?"

"Perhaps not, my laty."

"I want to know what his real name is. Is it the same as yours? It doesn't seem respectable not to have your own names."

"But what has it all to do with your name? I declare I don't know what to call you."

"Call her your own bard, old Tuncan MacPhail, my sweet laty, and haf ta patience with her, and she'll be telling you aall apout eferyting, only you must gif her olt brains time to tumble temselfs about. Her head grows fery stupid.—Yes, as she was saying, after ta bloody massacre at Culloden, her father had to hide himself away out of sight, and to forge himself—I mean to put upon himself a name tat tidn't mean himself at aal. And my poor mother, who bore me—big old Tuncan—ta fery day of ta battle, would not be hearing one word of him for tree months tat he was away; and when he would be creep back like a fox to see her one fine night when ta moon was not be up, they'll make up an acreement to co away together for a time, and to call temselfs MacPhails. But by and by tey took their own names again."

"And why haven't you your own name now? I'm sure it's a much prettier name."

"Because she'll be taking the other, my dear laty."

"And why?"

"Because—because ... She will tell you another time. She'll be tired to talk more apout ta cursed Cawmills this fery day."

"Then Malcolm's name is not MacPhail either?"

"No, it is not, my lady."

"Is he your son's son, or your daughter's son?"

"Perhaps not, my laty."

"I want to know what his real name is. Is it the same as yours? It doesn't seem respectable not to have your own names."

"Oh yes, my laty, fery respectable. Many coot men has to porrow nems of teir neighpours. We've all cot our fery own names, only in pad tays, my laty, we ton't aalways know which tey are exactly; but we aal know which we are each other, and we get on fery coot without the names. We lay tem py with our Sappath clothes for a few tays, and they come out ta fresher and ta sweeter for keeping ta Sappath so long, my laty. And now she'll pe playing you ta coronach of Clenco, which she was make herself for her own pipes."

"I want to know first what Malcolm's real name is," persisted Lady Florimel.

"Well, you see, my laty," returned Duncan, "some people has names and does not know them; and some people hasn't names, and will pe supposing they haf."

"You are talking riddles, Mr MacPhail, and I don't like riddles," said Lady Florimel, with an offence which was not altogether pretended.

"Yes surely—oh, yes! Call her Tuncan MacPhail, and neither more or less, my laty—not yet," he returned, most evasively.

"I see you won't trust me," said the girl, and rising quickly, she bade him good-night, and left the cottage.

"Oh yes, my laty, fery respectable. Many coot men has to borrow names of teir neighbours. We've all cot our fery own names, only in bad days, my laty, we ton't aalways know which tey are exactly; but we aal know which we are each other, and we get on fery coot without the names. We lay tem by with our Sabbath clothes for a few days, and they come out ta fresher and ta sweeter for keeping ta Sabbath so long, my laty. And now she'll pe playing you ta coronach of Clenco, which she was make herself for her own pipes."

"I want to know first what Malcolm's real name is," persisted Lady Florimel.

"Well, you see, my laty," returned Duncan, "some people has names and does not know them; and some people hasn't names, and will be supposing they haf."

"You are talking riddles, Mr MacPhail, and I don't like riddles," said Lady Florimel, with an offence which was not altogether pretended.

"Yes surely—oh, yes! Call her Tuncan MacPhail, and neither more or less, my laty—not yet," he returned, most evasively.

"I see you won't trust me," said the girl, and rising quickly, she bade him good-night, and left the cottage.

Duncan sat silent for a few minutes, as if in distress: then slowly his hand went out feeling for his pipes, wherewithal he consoled himself till bedtime.

Having plumed herself upon her influence with the old man, believing she could do anything with him she pleased, Lady Florimel was annoyed at failing to get from him any amplification of a hint in itself sufficient to cast a glow of romance about the youth who had already interested her so much. Duncan also was displeased, but with himself; for disappointing one he loved so much. With the passion for confidence which love generates, he had been for some time desirous of opening his mind to her upon the matter in question, and had indeed, on this very occasion, intended to lead up to a certain disclosure; but just at the last he clung to his secret, and could not let it go.

Compelled thereto against the natural impulse of the Celtic nature, which is open and confiding, therefore in the reaction cunning and suspicious, he had practised reticence so long, that he now recoiled from a breach of the habit which had become a second, false nature. He felt like one who, having caught a bird, holds it in his hand with the full intention of letting it go, but cannot make up his mind to do it just yet, knowing that, the moment he opens his hand, nothing can make that bird his again.

A whole week passed, during which Lady Florimel did not come near him, and the old man was miserable. At length one evening, for she chose her time when Malcolm must be in some vague spot between the shore and the horizon, she once more entered the piper's cottage. He knew her step the moment she turned the corner from the shore, and she had scarcely set her foot across the threshold before he broke out:

"Ach, my tear laty! and tid you'll think old Tuncan such a stoopit old man as not to 'll pe trusting ta light of her plind eyes? Put her laty must forgif her, for it is a long tale, not like anything you'll pe in ta way of peliefing; and aalso, it'll pe put ta tassel to another long tale which tears ta pag of her heart, and makes her feel a purning tevil in ta pocket of her posom. Put she'll tell you ta won half of it that pelongs to her poy Malcolm. He 's a pig poy now, put he wasn't aalways. No. He was once a fery little smaal chylt, in her old plind aarms. Put tey wasn't old ten. Why must young peoples crow old, my laty? Put she'll pe clad of it herself; for she'll can hate ta petter."

"Ach, my dear laty! and did you'll think old Tuncan such a stoopit old man as not to 'll be trusting ta light of her blind eyes? But her laty must forgif her, for it is a long tale, not like anything you'll be in ta way of beliefing; and aalso, it'll be but ta tassel to another long tale which tears ta bag of her heart, and makes her feel a burning devil in ta pocket of her bosom. But she'll tell you ta one half of it that belongs to her boy Malcolm. He's a big boy now, but he wasn't aalways. No. He was once a fery little smaal chylt, in her old blind aarms. But tey wasn't old then. Why must young peoples crow old, my laty? But she'll pe glad of it herself; for she'll can hate ta better."

Lady Florimel, incapable either of setting forth the advantages of growing old, or of enforcing the duty, which is the necessity, of forgiveness, answered with some commonplace; and as, to fortify his powers of narration, a sailor would cut himself a quid, and a gentleman fill his glass, or light a fresh cigar, Duncan slowly filled his bag. After a few strange notes as of a spirit wandering in pain, he began his story. But I will tell the tale for him, lest the printed oddities of his pronunciation should prove wearisome. I must mention first, however, that he did not commence until he had secured a promise from Lady Florimel that she would not communicate his revelations to Malcolm, having, he said, very good reasons for desiring to make them himself so soon as a fitting time should have arrived.

Avoiding all mention of his reasons either for assuming another name or for leaving his native glen, he told how, having wandered forth with no companion but his bagpipes, and nothing he could call his own beyond the garments and weapons which he wore, he traversed the shires of Inverness and Nairn and Moray, offering at every house on his road, to play the pipes, or clean the lamps and candlesticks, and receiving sufficient return, mostly in the shape of food and shelter, but partly in money, to bring him all the way from Glenco to Portlossie: somewhere near the latter was a cave in which his father, after his flight from Culloden, had lain in hiding for six months, in hunger and cold, and in constant peril of discovery and death, all in that region being rebels—for as such Duncan of course regarded the adherents of the houses of Orange and Hanover; and having occasion, for reasons, as I have said, unexplained, in his turn to seek, like a hunted stag, a place far from his beloved glen, wherein to hide his head, he had set out to find the cave, which the memory of his father would render far more of a home to him now than any other place left him on earth.

On his arrival at Portlossie, he put up at a small public house in the Seaton, from which he started the next morning to find the cave—a somewhat hopeless as well as perilous proceeding; but his father's description of its situation and character had generated such a vivid imagination of it in the mind of the old man, that he believed himself able to walk straight into the mouth of it; nor was the peril so great as must at first appear, to one who had been blind all his life. But he searched the whole of the east side of the promontory of Scaurnose, where it must lie, without finding such a cave as his father had depicted. Again and again he fancied he had come upon it, but was speedily convinced of his mistake. Even in one who had his eyesight, however, such a failure would not surprise those who understand how rapidly as well as constantly the whole faces of some cliffs are changing by the fall of portions—destroying the very existence of some caves, and utterly changing the mouths of others.

From a desire of secrecy, occasioned by the haunting dread of its approaching necessity, day and night being otherwise much alike to him, Duncan generally chose the night for his wanderings amongst the rocks, and probings of their hollows. One night, or rather morning, for he believed it was considerably past twelve o'clock, he sat weary in a large open cave, listening to the sound of the rising tide, and fell fast asleep, his bagpipes, without which he never went abroad, across his knees. He came to himself with a violent start, for the bag seemed to be moving, and its last faint sound of wail was issuing. Heavens! there was a baby lying upon it.—For a time he sat perfectly bewildered, but at length concluded that some wandering gipsy had made him a too ready gift of the child she did not prize. Some one must be near. He called aloud, but there was no answer. The child began to cry. He sought to soothe it, and its lamentation ceased. The moment that its welcome silence responded to his blandishments, the still small "Here I am" of the Eternal Love whispered its presence in the heart of the lonely man: something lay in his arms so helpless that to it, poor and blind and forsaken of man and woman as he was, he was yet a tower of strength. He clasped the child to his bosom, and rising forthwith set out, but with warier steps than heretofore, over the rocks for the Seaton.

Already he would have much preferred concealing him lest he should be claimed—a thing, in view of all the circumstances, not very likely—but for the child's sake, he must carry him to The Salmon, where he had free entrance at any hour—not even the public-house locking its doors at night.

Thither then he bore his prize, shielding him from the night air as well as he could, with the bag of his pipes. But he waked none of the inmates; lately fed, the infant slept for several hours, and then did his best both to rouse and astonish the neighbourhood.

Closely questioned, Duncan told the truth, but cunningly, in such manner that some disbelieved him altogether, while others, who had remarked his haunting of the rocks ever since his arrival, concluded that he had brought the child with him and had kept him hidden until now. The popular conviction at length settled to this, that the child was the piper's grandson—but base-born, whom therefore he was ashamed to acknowledge, although heartily willing to minister to and bring up as a foundling. The latter part of this conclusion, however, was not alluded to by Duncan in his narrative: it was enough to add that he took care to leave the former part of it undisturbed.

The very next day, he found himself attacked by a low fever; but as he had hitherto paid for everything he had at the inn, they never thought of turning him out when his money was exhausted; and as he had already by his discreet behaviour, and the pleasure his bagpipes afforded, made himself not a few friends amongst the simple-hearted people of the Seaton, some of the benevolent inhabitants of the upper town, Miss Horn in particular, were soon interested in his favour, who supplied him with everything he required until his recovery. As to the baby, he was gloriously provided for; he had at least a dozen foster-mothers at once—no woman in the Seaton who could enter a claim founded on the possession of the special faculty required, failing to enter that claim—with the result of an amount of jealousy almost incredible.

Meantime the town-drummer fell sick and died, and Miss Horn made a party in favour of Duncan. But for the baby, I doubt if he would have had a chance, for he was a stranger and interloper; the women, however, with the baby in their forefront, carried the day. Then his opponents retreated behind the instrument, and strove hard to get the drum recognised as an essential of the office. When Duncan recoiled from the drum with indignation, but without losing the support of his party, the opposition had the effrontery to propose a bell: that he rejected with a vehemence of scorn that had nearly ruined his cause; and, assuming straightway the position of chief party in the proposed contract, declared that no noise of his making should be other than the noise of bagpipes; that he would rather starve than beat drum or ring bell; if he served in the case, it must be after his own fashion—and so on. Hence it was no wonder, some of the bailies being not only small men and therefore conceited, but powerful whigs, who despised everything highland, and the bagpipes especially, if the affair did for awhile seem hopeless. But the more noble-minded of the authorities approved of the piper none the less for his independence, a generosity partly rooted, it must be confessed, in the amusement which the annoyance of their weaker brethren afforded them—whom at last they were happily successful in outvoting, so that the bagpipes superseded the drum for a season.

It may be asked whence it arose that Duncan should now be willing to quit his claim to any paternal property in Malcolm, confessing that he was none of his blood.

One source of the change was doubtless the desire of confidences between himself and Lady Florimel, another, the growing conviction, generated it may be by the admiration which is born of love, that the youth had gentle blood in his veins; and a third, that Duncan had now so thoroughly proved the heart of Malcolm as to have no fear of any change of fortune ever alienating his affections, or causing him to behave otherwise than as his dutiful grandson.

It is not surprising that such a tale should have a considerable influence on Lady Florimel's imagination: out of the scanty facts which formed but a second volume, she began at once to construct both a first and a third. She dreamed of the young fisherman that night, and reflecting in the morning on her intercourse with him, recalled sufficient indications in him of superiority to his circumstances, noted by her now, however, for the first time, to justify her dream: he might indeed well be the last scion of a noble family.

I do not intend the least hint that she began to fall in love with him. To balance his good looks, and the nobility, to keener eyes yet more evident than to hers, in both his moral and physical carriage, the equally undeniable clownishness of his dialect and tone had huge weight, while the peculiar straightforwardness of his behaviour and address not unfrequently savoured in her eyes of rudeness; besides which objectionable things, there was the persistent odour of fish about his garments—in itself sufficient to prevent such a catastrophe. The sole result of her meditations was the resolve to get some amusement out of him by means of a knowledge of his history superior to his own.

CHAPTER XXX

THE REVIVAL

Before the close of the herring-fishing, one of those movements of the spiritual waters, which in different forms, and under different names, manifest themselves at various intervals of space and of time, was in full vortex. It was supposed by the folk of Portlossie to have begun in the village of Scaurnose, but by the time it was recognized as existent, no one could tell whence it had come, any more than he could predict whither it was going. Of its spiritual origin it may be also predicated with confidence that its roots lay deeper than human insight could reach, and were far more interwoven than human analysis could disentangle.

One notable fact bearing on its nature was, that it arose amongst the people themselves, without the intervention or immediate operation of the clergy, who indeed to a man were set against it. Hence the flood was at first free from the results of one influence most prolific of the pseudo-spiritual, namely, the convulsive efforts of men with faith in a certain evil system of theology, to rouse a galvanic life by working on the higher feelings through the electric sympathies of large assemblages, and the excitement of late hours, prolonged prayers and exhortations, and sometimes even direct appeal to individuals in public presence. The end of these things is death, for the reaction is towards spiritual hardness and a more confirmed unbelief: when the excitement has died away, those at least in whom the spiritual faculty is for the time exhausted, presume that they have tasted and seen, and found that nothing is there. The whole thing is closely allied to the absurdity of those who would throw down or who would accept the challenge to test the reality of answer to prayer by applying the force of a multitudinous petition to the will of the supposed divinity—I say *supposed divinity,* because a being whose will could be thus moved like a water-wheel could not be in any sense divine. If there might be a religious person so foolish and irreverent as to agree to such a test—crucial indeed, but in a far other sense than that imagined—I would put it to him whether the very sense of experiment would not destroy in his mind all faculty of prayer, placing him in the position, no more of a son of God, but of one who, tempting the Lord his God, may read his rebuke where it stands recorded for the ages.

But where such a movement has originated amongst the people, the very facts adduced to argue its falsehood from its vulgarity, are to me so many indications on the other side;

for I could ill believe in a divine influence which did not take the person such as he was; did not, while giving him power from beyond him, leave his individuality uninjured, yea intensify it, subjecting the very means of its purification, the spread of the new leaven, to the laws of time and growth. To look at the thing from the other side, the genuineness of the man's reception of it will be manifest in the meeting of his present conditions with the new thing—in the show of results natural to one of his degree of development. To hear a rude man utter his experience in the forms of cultivation, would be at once to suspect the mere glitter of a reflex, and to doubt an illumination from within. I repeat, the genuine influence shows itself such in showing that it has laid hold of the very man, at the very stage of growth he had reached. The dancing of David before the ark, the glow of St. Stephen's face, and the wild gestures and rude songs of miners and fishers and negroes, may all be signs of the presence of the same spirit in temples various. Children will rush and shout and hollo for the same joy which sends others of the family to weep apart.

Of course the one infallible test as to whether any such movement is of man without God, or of God within the man, is the following life; only a large space for fluctuation must be allowed where a whole world of passions and habits has to be subjected to the will of God through the vice-gerency of a human will hardly or only just awakened, and as yet unconscious of itself.

The nearest Joseph Mair could come to the origin of the present movement was the influence of a certain Stornoway fisherman, whom they had brought back with them on their return from the coasts of Lewis—a man of Celtic fervour and faith, who had agreed to accompany them probably in the hope of serving a set of the bravest and hardest-working men in the world, who yet spent a large part of their ease in drinking up the earnings of fierce and perilous labour. There were a few amongst them, he found, already prepared to receive the word, and to each of these he spoke in private. They spoke to one another, then each to his friend outside the little circle. Next a few met to pray. These drew others in, and at length it was delivered from mouth to mouth that on the following Sunday, at a certain early hour in the morning, a meeting would be held in the Bailie's Barn, a cave large enough to receive all the grown population of Scaurnose.

The news of this gathering of course reached the Seaton, where some were inclined to go and see, others to go and hear; most of even the latter class, however, being at the same time more than inclined to mock at the idea of a popular religious assembly.

Not so Duncan MacPhail, who, notwithstanding the more than half Pagan character of his ideas, had too much reverence to mock at anything in the form of religion, to all the claims of which he was even eager to assent: when the duty of forgiveness was pressed upon him too hard, he would take his last refuge in excepting to the authority of the messenger. He regarded the announcement of the meeting with the greater respect that the man from Stornoway was a MacLeod, and so of his mother's clan.

It was now the end of August, when the sky is of a paler blue in the day time, and greener about the sunset. The air had in it a touch of cold, which, like as a faint acid affects a sweet drink, only rendered the warmth more pleasant. On the appointed morning, the tide was low, and the waves died gently upon the sand, seeming to have crept away from the shore to get nearer to the sunrise. Duncan was walking along the hard wet sand towards the promontory, with Mr Graham on one side of him and Malcolm on the other. There was no gun to fire this morning; it was Sunday, and all might repose undisturbed: the longer sleep in bed, possibly the shorter in church.

"I wish you had your sight but for a moment, Mr MacPhail," said the schoolmaster. "How this sunrise would make you leap for joy."

"Ay!" said Malcolm, "it wad gar daddy grip till 's pipes in twa hurries."

"And what should she'll pe wanting her pipes for?" asked Duncan.

"To praise God wi'," answered Malcolm.

"Ay; ay;" murmured Duncan thoughtfully. "Tey are tat."

"What are they?" asked Mr Graham gently.

"For to praise Cod," answered Duncan solemnly.

"I almost envy you," returned Mr Graham, "when I think how you will praise God one day. What a glorious waking you will have!"

"Ten it 'll pe your opinion, Mr Craham, tat she'll pe sleeping her sound sleep, and not pe lying wite awake in her coffin all ta time?"

"A good deal better than that, Mr MacPhail!" returned the schoolmaster cheerily. "It's my opinion that you are, as it were, asleep now, and that the moment you die, you will feel as if you had just woke up, and for the first time in your life. For one thing, you will see far better then than any of us do now."

But poor Duncan could not catch the idea; his mind was filled with a preventing fancy.

"Ay!" said Malcolm, "it would make daddy grab hold of his pipes in a trice."

"And what should she'll pe wanting her pipes for?" asked Duncan.

"To praise God with," answered Malcolm.

"Ay; ay;" murmured Duncan thoughtfully. "Tey are that."

"What are they?" asked Mr Graham gently.

"For to praise God," answered Duncan solemnly.

"I almost envy you," returned Mr Graham, "when I think how you will praise God one day. What a glorious waking you will have!"

"Ten it 'll be your opinion, Mr Craham, tat she'll be sleeping her sound sleep, and not be lying wite awake in her coffin all ta time?"

"A good deal better than that, Mr MacPhail!" returned the schoolmaster cheerily. "It's my opinion that you are, as it were, asleep now, and that the moment you die, you will feel as if you had just woke up, and for the first time in your life. For one thing, you will see far better then than any of us do now."

But poor Duncan could not catch the idea; his mind was filled with a preventing fancy.

"Yes; I know; at ta tay of chutchment," he said. "Put what 'll pe ta use of ketting her eyes open pefore she'll pe up? How should she pe seeing with all ta earth apove her—and ta cravestone too tat I know my poy Malcolm will pe laying on ta top of his old cranfather to keep him waarm, and let peoples pe know tat ta plind piper will be lying town pelow wite awake and fery uncomfortable?"

"Excuse me, Mr MacPhail, but that's all a mistake," said Mr Graham positively. "The body is but a sort of shell that we cast off when we die, as the corn casts off its husk when it begins to grow. The life of the seed comes up out of the earth in a new body, as St Paul says,"

"Ten," interrupted Duncan, "she'll pe crowing up out of her crave like a seed crowing up to pe a corn or a parley?"

The schoolmaster began to despair of ever conveying to the piper the idea that the living man is the seed sown, and that when the body of this seed dies, then the new body, with the man in it, springs alive out of the old one—that the death of the one is the birth of the other. Far more enlightened people than Duncan never imagine, and would find it hard to believe, that the sowing of the seed spoken of might mean something else than the burying of the body; not perceiving what yet surely is plain enough, that that would be the sowing of a seed already dead, and incapable of giving birth to anything whatever.

"No, no," he said, almost impatiently, "*you* will never be in the grave: it is only your body that will go there, with nothing *like* life about it except the smile the glad soul has left on it. The poor body when thus

"Yes; I know; at ta day of chutchment," he said. "But what 'll be ta use of ketting her eyes open before she'll be up? How should she be seeing with all ta earth above her—and ta cravestone too tat I know my boy Malcolm will be laying on ta top of his old cranfather to keep him waarm, and let peoples be know tat ta blind piper will be lying down below wite awake and fery uncomfortable?"

"Excuse me, Mr MacPhail, but that's all a mistake," said Mr Graham positively. "The body is but a sort of shell that we cast off when we die, as the corn casts off its husk when it begins to grow. The life of the seed comes up out of the earth in a new body, as St Paul says,"

"Ten," interrupted Duncan, "she'll be crowing up out of her crave like a seed crowing up to be a corn or a barley?"

The schoolmaster began to despair of ever conveying to the piper the idea that the living man is the seed sown, and that when the body of this seed dies, then the new body, with the man in it, springs alive out of the old one—that the death of the one is the birth of the other. Far more enlightened people than Duncan never imagine, and would find it hard to believe, that the sowing of the seed spoken of might mean something else than the burying of the body; not perceiving what yet surely is plain enough, that that would be the sowing of a seed already dead, and incapable of giving birth to anything whatever.

"No, no," he said, almost impatiently, "*you* will never be in the grave: it is only your body that will go there, with nothing *like* life about it except the smile the glad soul has left on it. The poor body when thus forsaken is so dead that it can't even stop smiling. Get Malcolm to read to you out of the book of the Revelation how there were multitudes even then standing before the throne. They had died in this world, yet there they were, well and happy."

"Oh, yes!" said Duncan, with no small touch of spitefulness in his tone, "—twang twanging at teir fine colden herps! She'll not be thinking much of ta herp for a music maker! And peoples tells her she'll not pe hafing her pipes tere! Och hone! Och hone!—She'll chust pe lying still and not pe ketting up, and when ta work is ofer, and eferypody cone away, she'll chust pe ketting up, and taking a look apout her, to see if she'll pe finding a stand o' pipes that some coot highlandman has peen left pehint him when he tied lately."

"You'll find it rather lonely—won't you?"

"Yes; no toubt, for they'll aal be cone up. Well, she'll haf her pipes; and she could not co where ta pipes was looked town upon by all ta creat people—and all ta smaal ones too."

forsaken is so dead that it can't even stop smiling. Get Malcolm to read to you out of the book of the Revelation how there were multitudes even then standing before the throne. They had died in this world, yet there they were, well and happy."

"Oh, yes!" said Duncan, with no small touch of spitefulness in his tone, "—twang twanging at teir fine colden harps! She'll not be thinking much of ta harp for a music maker! And peoples tells her she'll not be hafing her pipes tere! Alas! Alas!— She'll chust be lying still and not be ketting up, and when ta work is ofer, and efery- pody cone away, she'll chust be ketting up, and taking a look about her, to see if she'll be finding a stand o' pipes that some coot highlandman has been left behint him when he died lately."

"You'll find it rather lonely—won't you?"

"Yes; no toubt, for they'll aal be gone up. Well, she'll haf her pipes; and she could not go where ta pipes was looked town upon by all ta creat people—and all ta smaal ones too."

They had now reached the foot of the promontory, and turned northwards, each of his companions taking an arm of the piper to help him over the rocks that lay between them and the mouth of the cave, which soon yawned before them like a section of the mouth of a great fish. Its floor of smooth rock had been swept out clean, and sprinkled with dry sea sand. There were many hollows and projections along its sides rudely fit for serving as seats, to which had been added a number of forms extemporized of planks and thwarts. No one had yet arrived when they entered, and they went at once to the further end of the cave, that Duncan, who was a little hard of hearing, might be close to the speakers. There his companions turned and looked behind them: an exclamation, followed by a full glance at each other, broke from each.

The sun, just clearing the end of the opposite promontory, shone right into the mouth of the cave, from the midst of a tumult of gold, in which all the other colours of his approach had been swallowed up. The triumph strode splendent over sea and shore, sub- duing waves and rocks to a path for its mighty entrance into that dark cave on the human coast. With his back to the light stood Duncan in the bottom of the cave, his white hair gleaming argentine, as if his poor blind head were the very goal of the heavenly progress. He turned round.

"Will it pe a fire? She feels something warm on her head," he said, rolling his sightless orbs, upon which the splendour broke waveless, casting a grim shadow of him on the jagged rock behind.

"No," answered Mr Graham; "it is the sun you feel. He's just out of his grave."

The old man gave a grunt.

"I often think," said the schoolmaster to Malcolm, "that possibly the reason why we are told so little about the world we are going to, is, that no description of it would enter our minds any more than a description of that sunrise would carry a notion of its reality into the mind of your grandfather."

"She's obleeched to you, Mr Craham!" said the piper with offence. "You take her fery stupid. You're so proud of your eyes, you think a plind man cannot see at aall! Chm!"

"Will it be a fire? She feels something warm on her head," he said, rolling his sightless orbs, upon which the splendour broke waveless, casting a grim shadow of him on the jagged rock behind.

"No," answered Mr Graham; "it is the sun you feel. He's just out of his grave."

The old man gave a grunt.

"I often think," said the schoolmaster to Malcolm, "that possibly the reason why we are told so little about the world we are going to, is, that no description of it would enter our minds any more than a description of that sunrise would carry a notion of its reality into the mind of your grandfather."

"She's obleeched to you, Mr Craham!" said the piper with offence. "You take her fery stupid. You're so proud of your eyes, you think a blind man cannot see at aall! Chm!"

But the folk began to assemble. By twos and threes, now from the one side, now from the other, they came dropping in as if out of the rush of the blinding sunshine, till the seats were nearly filled, while a goodly company gathered about the mouth of the cave, there to await the arrival of those who had called the meeting. Presently MacLeod, a small thin man, with iron-gray hair, keen, shrewd features, large head, and brown complexion, appeared, and made his way to the further end of the cave, followed by three or four of the men of Scaurnose, amongst whom walked a pale-faced, consumptive lad, with bowed shoulders and eyes on the ground: he it was who, feebly clambering on a ledge of rock, proceeded to conduct the worship of the assembly. His parents were fisher-people of Scaurnose, who to make a minister of him had been half-starving the rest of their family; but he had broken down at length under the hardships of endless work and wretched food. From the close of the session in March, he had been teaching in Aberdeen until a few days before, when he came home, aware that he was dying, and full of a fervour betraying anxiety concerning himself rather than indicating the possession of good news for others. The sun had now so far changed his position, that, although he still shone into the cave, the preacher stood in the shadow, out of which gleamed his wasted countenance, pallid and sombre and solemn, as first he poured forth an abject prayer for mercy, conceived in the spirit of a slave supplicating the indulgence of a hard master, and couched in words and tones that bore not a trace of the filial; then read the chapter containing the curses of Mount Ebal, and gave the congregation one of Duncan's favourite psalms to sing; and at length began a sermon on what he called the divine justice. Not one word was there in it, however, concerning God's love of fair dealing, either as betwixt himself and man, or as betwixt man and his fellow; the preacher's whole notion of justice was the punishment of sin; and that punishment was hell, and hell only; so that the whole sermon was about hell from beginning to end—hell appalling, lurid, hopeless. And the eyes of all were fixed upon him with that glow from within which manifests the listening spirit. Some of the women were as pale as himself from sympathetic horror, doubtless also from a vague stirring of the conscience, which, without accusing them of crime, yet told them that all was not right between them and their God; while the working of the faces of some of the men betrayed a mind not at all at ease concerning their prospects. It was an eloquent and powerful utterance, and might doubtless claim its place in the economy of human education; but it was at best a pagan embodiment of truths such as a righteous pagan might have discovered, and breathed nothing of the spirit of Christianity, being as unjust towards God as it represented him to be towards men: the God of the preacher was utterly unlike the father of Jesus. Urging his hearers to flee from the wrath to come, he drew such a picture of an angry Deity as in nothing resembled the revelation in the Son.

"Fellow sinners," he said in conclusion, "haste ye and flee from the wrath to come. Now is God waiting to be gracious—but only so long as his Son holds back the indignation ready to burst forth and devour you. He sprinkles its flames with the scarlet wool and the hyssop of atonement; he stands between you and justice, and pleads with his incensed Father for his rebellious creatures. Well for you that he so stands and so pleads! Yet even *he* could not prevail for ever against such righteous anger; and it is but for a season he will thus entreat; the day will come when he will stand aside and let the fiery furnace break forth and slay you. Then, with howling and anguish, with weeping and wailing and gnashing of teeth, ye shall know that God is a God of justice, that his wrath is one with his omnipotence, and his hate everlasting as the fires of hell. But do as ye will, ye cannot thwart his decrees, for to whom he will he showeth mercy, and whom he will he hardeneth."

Scarcely had he ceased, when a loud cry, clear and keen, rang through every corner of the cave. Well might the preacher start and gaze around him! for the cry was articulate, sharply modelled into the three words—"Father o' lichts!" Some of the men gave a scared groan, and some of the women shrieked. None could tell whence the cry had come, and Malcolm alone could guess who must have uttered it.

"Yes," said the preacher, recovering himself, and replying to the voice, "he *is* the Father of lights, but only to them that are in Christ Jesus;—he is no father, but an avenging deity, to them over whom the robe of his imputed righteousness is not cast. Jesus Christ himself will not be gracious for ever. Kiss ye the Son, lest even *he* be angry, and ye perish from the way, when his wrath is kindled but a little."

You're so proud of your eyes, you think a plind man cannot see at aall!

"Father o' lichts!" rang the cry again, and louder than before.

To Malcolm it seemed close behind him, but he had the self-possession not to turn his head. The preacher took no farther notice. MacLeod stood up, and having, in a few simple remarks, attempted to smooth some of the asperities of the youth's address, announced another meeting in the evening, and dismissed the assembly with a prayer.

Malcolm went home with his grandfather. He was certain it was the laird's voice he had heard, but he would attempt no search after his refuge that day, for dread of leading to its discovery by others.

That evening most of the boats of the Seaton set out for the fishing ground as usual, but not many went from Scaurnose. Blue Peter would go no more of a Sunday, hence Malcolm was free for the night, and again with his grandfather walked along the sands in the evening towards the cave.

The sun was going down on the other side of the promontory before them, and the sky was gorgeous in rose and blue, in peach and violet, in purple and green, barred and fretted, heaped and broken, scattered and massed—every colour edged and tinged and harmonized with a glory as of gold, molten with heat, and glowing with fire. The thought that his grandfather could not see, and had never seen such splendour, made Malcolm sad, and very little was spoken between them as they went.

When they arrived, the service had already commenced, but room was made for them to pass, and a seat was found for Duncan where he could hear. Just as they entered, Malcolm spied, amongst those who preferred the open air at the mouth of the cavern, a face which he was all but certain was that of one of the three men from whom he had rescued the laird.

MacLeod was to address them. He took for his text the words of the Saviour, "Come unto me, all ye that labour and are heavy laden, and I will give you rest," and founded upon them a simple, gracious, and all but eloquent discourse, very different in tone and influence from that of the young student. It must be confessed that the Christ he presented was very far off, and wrapped in a hazy nimbus of abstraction; that the toil of his revelation was forgotten, the life he lived being only alluded to, and that not for the sake of showing what he was, and hence what God is, but to illustrate the conclusions of men concerning him; and yet there was that heart of reality in the whole thing which no moral vulgarity of theory, no injustice towards God, no tyranny of stupid logic over childlike intuitions, could so obscure as to render it inoperative. From the form of the Son of Man, thus beheld from afar, came a warmth like the warmth from the first approach of the far-off sun in spring, sufficing to rouse the earth from the sleep of winter—in which all the time the same sun has been its warmth and has kept it from sleeping unto death.

MacLeod was a thinker—aware of the movements of his own heart, and able to reflect on others the movements of their hearts; hence, although in the main he treated the weariness and oppression from which Jesus offered to set them free, as arising from a sense of guilt and the fear of coming misery, he could not help alluding to more ordinary troubles, and depicting other phases of the heart's restlessness with such truth and sympathy that many listened with a vague feeling of exposure to a supernatural insight. The sermon soon began to show its influence; for a sense of the need of help is so present to every simple mind, that, of all messages, the offer of help is of easiest reception; some of the women were sobbing, and the silent tears were flowing down the faces of others; while of the men many were looking grave and thoughtful, and kept their eyes fixed on the speaker. At length, towards the close, MacLeod judged it needful to give a word of warning.

"But, my friends," he said, and his voice grew low and solemn, "I dare not make an end without reminding you that, if you stop your ears against the gracious call, a day will come when not even the merits of the Son of God will avail you, but the wrath of the—"

"*Father o' Lichts!*" once more burst ringing out, like the sudden cry of a trumpet in the night.

MacLeod took no notice of it, but brought his sermon at once to a close, and specified the night of the following Saturday for next meeting. They sung a psalm, and after a slow, solemn, thoughtful prayer, the congregation dispersed.

But Malcolm, who, anxious because of the face he had seen as he entered, had been laying his plans, after begging his grandfather in a whisper to go home without him for a reason he would afterwards explain, withdrew into a recess whence he could watch the cave, without being readily discovered.

Scarcely had the last voices of the retreating congregation died away, when the same ill-favoured face peeped round the corner of the entrance, gave a quick glance about, and the man came in. Like a snuffing terrier, he went peering in the dimness into every hollow, and behind every projection, until he suddenly caught sight of Malcolm, probably by a glimmering of his eyes.

"Hillo, Humpy!" he cried in a tone of exultation, and sprang up the rough ascent of a step or two to where he sat.

Malcolm half rose, and met him with a well-delivered blow between the eyes. He fell, and lay for a moment stunned. Malcolm sat down again and watched him. When he came to himself, he crept out, muttering imprecations. He knew it was not Humpy who dealt that blow.

As soon as he was gone, Malcolm in his turn began searching. He thought he knew every hole and corner of the cave, and there was but one where the laird, who, for as near him as he heard his voice the first time, certainly had not formed one of the visible congregation, might have concealed himself: if that was his covert, there he must be still, for he had assuredly not issued from it.

Immediately behind where he had sat in the morning, was a projection of rock, with a narrow cleft between it and the wall of the cavern, visible only from the very back of the cave, where the roof came down low. But when he thought of it, he saw that even here he could not have been hidden in the full light of the morning from the eyes of some urchins who had seated themselves as far back as the roof would allow them, and they had never looked as if they saw anything more than other people. Still, if he was to search at all, here he must begin. The cleft had scarcely more width than sufficed to admit his body, and his hands told him at once that there was no laird there. Could there be any opening further? If there was, it could only be somewhere above. Was advance in that direction possible?

He felt about, and finding two or three footholds, began to climb in the dark, and had reached the height of six feet or so, when he came to a horizontal projection, which, for a moment only, barred his further progress. Having literally surmounted this, that is, got on the top of it, he found there a narrow vertical opening: was it but a shallow recess, or did it lead into the heart of the rock?

Carefully feeling his way both with hands and feet, he advanced a step or two, and came to a place where the passage widened a little, and then took a sharp turn and became so narrow that it was with difficulty he forced himself through. It was, however, but one close pinch, and he found himself, as his feet told him, at the top of a steep descent. He stood for a moment hesitating, for prudence demanded a light. The sound of the sea was behind him, but all in front was still as the darkness of the grave. Suddenly up from unknown depths of gloom, came the tones of a sweet childish voice, singing—*The Lord's my Shepherd*.

Malcolm waited until the psalm was finished, and then called out:

"Mr Stewart! I'm here—Malcolm MacPhail. I want to see ye. Tell him it's me, Phemy."

A brief pause followed; then Phemy's voice answered:

"Come awa' doon. He says ye s' be welcome."

"Canna ye shaw a licht than; for I dinna ken a fit o' the ro'd," said Malcolm.

"Come on down. He says you'll be welcome."

"Can't you show a light then; for I don't know a foot of the way," said Malcolm.

The next moment a light appeared at some little distance below, and presently began to ascend, borne by Phemy, towards the place where he stood. She took him by the hand without a word, and led him down a slope, apparently formed of material fallen from the roof, to the cave already described. The moment he entered it, he marked the water in its side, the smooth floor, the walls hollowed into a thousand fantastic cavities, and knew he had come upon the cave in which his great-grandfather had found refuge so many years before. Changes in its mouth had rendered entrance difficult, and it had slipped by degrees from the knowledge of men.

At the bottom of the slope, by the side of the well, sat the laird. Phemy set the little lantern she carried on its edge. The laird rose and shook hands with Malcolm and asked him to be seated.

"I'm sorry to say they're efter ye again, laird," said Malcolm after a little ordinary chat.

Mr Stewart was on his feet instantly.

"I maun awa'. Tak care o' Phemy," he said hurriedly.

"I'm sorry to say they're after you again, laird," said Malcolm after a little ordinary chat.

Mr Stewart was on his feet instantly.

"I must leave. Take care of Phemy," he said hurriedly.

"Na, na, sir," said Malcolm, laying his hand on his arm; "there's nae sic hurry. As lang's I'm here ye may sit still; an', as far's I ken, naebody's fun' the w'y in but mysel', an' that was yer ain wyte, laird. But ye hae garred mair fowk nor me luik, an' that's the pity o' 't."

"I tauld ye, sir, ye sudna cry oot," said Phemy.

"I couldna help it," said Stewart apologetically.

"Weel, ye sudna ha' gane near them again," persisted the little woman.

"Wha kent but they kent whaur I cam frae?" persisted the laird.

"Sit ye doon, sir, an' lat's hae a word aboot it," said Malcolm cheerily.

The laird cast a doubting look at Phemy.

"Ay, sit doon," said Phemy.

Mr Stewart yielded, but nervous starts and sudden twitches of the muscles betrayed his uneasiness: it looked as if his body would jump up and run without his mind's consent.

"Hae ye ony w'y o' winnin' oot o' this, forbye the mou' o' the cave there?" asked Malcolm.

"Nane 'at I ken o'," answered Phemy. "But there's heaps o' hidy-holes i' the inside o' 't."

"That's a' very weel; but gien they keppit the mou' an' took their time till 't, they bude to grip ye."

"There *may* be, though," resumed Phemy. "It gangs back a lang road. I hae never been in sicht o' the end o' 't. It comes doon verra laich in some places, and gangs up heich again in ithers, but nae sign o' an en' till 't."

"Is there ony soon o' watter intill 't?" asked Malcolm.

"Na, na, sir," said Malcolm, laying his hand on his arm; "there's no such hurry. As long as I'm here you may sit sill; and, as far as I know, nobody's found the way in but myself, and that was your own fault, laird. But you've made more folk than me look, and that's the pity of it."

"I told you, sir, you shouldn't cry out," said Phemy.

"I couldn't help it," said Stewart apologetically.

"Well, you shouldn't have gone near them again," persisted the little woman.

"Who could say but they knew where I came from?" persisted the laird.

"Have a seat, sir, and let's talk it over," said Malcolm cheerily.

The laird cast a doubting look at Phemy.

"Ay, sit down," said Phemy.

Mr Stewart yielded, but nervous starts and sudden twitches of the muscles betrayed his uneasiness: it looked as if his body would jump up and run without his mind's consent.

"Have you any way of getting out of this, besides the mouth of the cave there?" asked Malcolm.

"None that I know of," answered Phemy. "But there's heaps of hidey-holes in the inside of it."

"That's all very well; but if they stopped up the mouth and took their time to it, they'd be sure to have you."

"There *may* be, though," resumed Phemy. "It goes back a long way. I have never been in sight of the end of it. It comes down very low in some places, and goes up high again in others, but no sign of an end to it."

"Is there any sound of water in it?" asked Malcolm.

"Na, nane at ever I hard. But I'll tell ye what I *hae* hard: I hae hard the flails gaein' thud, thud, abune my heid."

"Hoot toot, Phemy!" said Malcolm; "we're a guid mile an' a half frae the nearest ferm toon, an' that I reckon, 'll be the Hoose ferm."

"I canna help that," persisted Phemy. "Gien 't wasna the flails, whiles ane, an' whiles twa, I dinna ken what it cud hae been. Hoo far it was I canna say, for it 's ill measurin' i' the dark, or wi' naething but a bowat i' yer han'; but gien ye ca'd it mair, I wadna won'er."

"It's a michty howkin!" said Malcolm; "but for a' that it wadna haud ye frae the grip o' thae scoonrels: wharever ye ran they cud rin efter ye."

"I think we cud sort them," said Phemy. "There's ae place, a guid bit farrer in, whaur the rufe comes doon to the flure, leavin' jist ae sma' hole to creep throu': it wad be fine to hae a gey muckle stane handy, jist to row athort it, an' gar't luik as gien 't was the en' o' a'thing. But the hole's sae sma' at the laird has ill getting' his puir back throu' 't."

"I couldna help won'erin' hoo he wan throu' at the tap there," said Malcolm.

At this the laird laughed almost merrily, and rising, took Malcolm by the hand and led him to the spot, where he made him feel a rough groove in the wall of the rocky strait: into this hollow he laid his hump, and so slid sideways through.

Malcolm squeezed himself through after him, saying,—

"Noo ye're oot, laird, hadna ye better come wi' me hame to Miss Horn's, whaur ye wad be as safe's gien ye war in h'aven itsel'?"

"Na, none that ever I heard. But I'll tell you what I *have* heard: I've heard the flails going thud, thud, above my head."

"Pooh, pooh, Phemy!" said Malcolm; "we're a good mile and a half from the nearest farm town, and that I reckon, will be the House farm."

"I can't help that," persisted Phemy. "If it wasn't the flails, now one, and now two, I don't know what it could have been. How far it was I can't say, for it's hard measuring in the dark, or with nothing but a lantern in your hand; but if you called it more, I wouldn't wonder."

"It's a mighty hollow!" said Malcolm; "but for all that it wouldn't save you from those scoundrels' clutches: wherever you ran they could run after you."

"I think we could sort them," said Phemy. "There's one place, a good bit further in, where the roof comes down to the floor, leaving just one small hole to creep through: it would be fine to have a huge stone handy, just to roll across it, and make it look as if it was the end of everything. But the hole's so small that the laird can scarce get his poor back through it."

"I couldn't help wondering how he won through at the top there," said Malcolm.

At this the laird laughed almost merrily, and rising, took Malcolm by the hand and led him to the spot, where he made him feel a rough groove in the wall of the rocky strait: into this hollow he laid his hump, and so slid sideways through.

Malcolm squeezed himself through after him, saying,—

"Now you're out, laird, hadn't you better come with me home to Miss Horn's, where you would be as safe as if you were in heaven itself?"

"Na, I canna gang to Miss Horn's," he replied.

"What for no, laird?"

Pulling Malcolm down towards him, the laird whispered in his ear,

"'Cause she's fleyt at my back."

"Na, I can't go to Miss Horn's," he replied.

"Why not, laird?"

Pulling Malcolm down towards him, the laird whispered in his ear,

"'Cause she's afraid of my back."

A moment or two passed ere Malcolm could think of a reply both true and fitting. When at length he spoke again there was no answer, and he knew that he was alone.

He left the cave and set out for the Seaton; but, unable to feel at peace about his friends, resolved, on the way, to return after seeing his grandfather, and spend the night in the outer cave.

CHAPTER XXXI

WANDERING STARS

He had not been gone many minutes, when the laird passed once more through the strait, and stood a moment waiting for Phemy; she had persuaded him to go home to her father's for the night.

But the next instant he darted back, with trembling hands, caught hold of Phemy, who was following him with the lantern, and stammered in her ear,—

"There's somebody there! I dinna ken whaur they come frae."

Phemy went to the front of the passage and listened, but could hear nothing, and returned.

"Bide ye whaur ye are, laird," she said; "I'll gang doon, an' gien I hear or see naething, I'll come back for ye."

"There's somebody there! I don't know where they come from."

Phemy went to the front of the passage and listened, but could hear nothing, and returned.

"Stay where you are, laird," she said; "I'll go down, and if I hear or see nothing, I'll come back for you."

With careful descent, placing her feet on the well-known points unerringly, she reached the bottom, and peeped into the outer cave. The place was quite dark. Through its jaws the sea glimmered faint in the low light that skirted the northern horizon; and the slow pulse of the tide upon the rocks, was the sole sound to be heard. No: another in the cave close beside her!—one small solitary noise, as of shingle yielding under the pressure of a standing foot! She held her breath and listened, her heart beating so loud that she feared it would deafen her to what would come next. A good many minutes, half an hour it seemed to her, passed, during which she heard nothing more; but as she peeped out for the twentieth time, a figure glided into the field of vision bounded by the cave's mouth. It was that of a dumpy woman. She entered the cave, tumbled over one of the forms, and gave a cry coupled with an imprecation.

"The deevil roast them 'at laid me sic a trap!" she said. "I hae broken the shins the auld markis laudit!"

"Hold your wicked tongue!" hissed a voice in return, almost in Phemy's very ear.

"The devil roast them that laid me such a trap!" she said. "I've broken the shins the old marquis lauded!"

"Hold your wicked tongue!" hissed a voice in return, almost in Phemy's very ear.

"Ow! ye're there, are ye, mem!" rejoined the other, in a voice that held internal communication with her wounded shins. "Coupit ye the crans like me?"

The question, Englished, was, "Did you fall heels over head like me?" but was capable of a metaphorical interpretation as well.

"Hold your tongue, I say, woman! Who knows but some of the saints may be at their prayers within hearing?"

"Na, na, mem, there's nae risk o' that; this is no ane o' yer creepy caves whaur otters an wullcats hae their habitations; it 's a muckle open-mou'd place, like them 'at prays intill 't—as toom an' clear-sidit as a tongueless bell. But what for ye wad hae 's come here to oor cracks, I canna faddom. A body wad think ye had an ill thoucht i' yer heid— eh, mem?"

The suggestion was followed by a low, almost sneering laugh. As she spoke, the sounds of her voice and step had been advancing, with cautious intermittent approach.

"I hae ye noo," she said, as she seated herself at length beside the other. "The gowk, Geordie Bray!" she went on, "—to tak it intill's oogly heid 'at the cratur wad be hurklin' here! It's no the place for ane 'at has to hide 's heid for verra shame o' slippin' aff the likes o' himsel' upo' sic a braw mither! Could he get nae ither door to win in at, haith!"

"Woman, you'll drive me mad!" said the other.

"Weel, hinney," returned the former, suddenly changing her tone, "I'm mair an' mair convenced 'at yon's the verra laad for yer purpose. For ae thing, ye see, naebody kens whaur he cam frae, as the laird,

"Oh! you're there, are you, ma'am!" rejoined the other, in a voice that held internal communication with her wounded shins. "Coupit ye the crans like me?"

The question, Englished, was, "Did you fall heels over head like me?" but was capable of a metaphorical interpretation as well.

"Hold your tongue, I say, woman! Who knows but some of the saints may be at their prayers within hearing?"

"Na, na, ma'am, there's no risk of that; this isn't one of your creepy caves where otters and wildcats set up house; it's a great open-mouthed place, like them that pray in it—as empty and clear-sided as a tongueless bell. But why you had us come here for our talk, I can't fathom. Anyone would think you had an ill thought in your head—eh, ma'am?"

The suggestion was followed by a low, almost sneering laugh. As she spoke, the sounds of her voice and step had been advancing, with cautious intermittent approach.

"I have you now," she said, as she seated herself at length beside the other. "The fool, Geordie Bray!" she went on, "—to take it into his ugly head that the fellow would be crouching here! It's not the place for one that has to hide his head for very shame at slipping off the likes of himself upon such a fine mother! Could he find no other door to come in at, faith!"

"Woman, you'll drive me mad!" said the other.

"Well, my dear," returned the former, suddenly changing her tone, "I'm more and more convinced that that's the very lad for your purpose. For one thing, you see, nobody knows where he came from, as the bonny laad, wad say, an' naebody can contradick a word—the auld man less than onybody, for I can tell him what he kens to be trowth. Only I winna muv till *I* ken whaur he comes frae."

"Wouldn't you prefer not knowing for certain? You could swear with the better grace."

"Deil a bit! It maitters na to me whilk side o' my teeth I chow wi'. But I winna sweir till I ken the trowth—'at I may haud off o' 't. He's the man, though, gien we can get a grip o' 'im! He luiks the richt thing, ye see, mem. He has a glisk o' the markis tu—divna ye think, mem?"

"Insolent wretch!"

"Caw canny, mem. A'thing maun be considered. It wad but gar the thing luik the mair likly. Fowk gangs the len'th o' sayin' 'at Humpy himsel' 's no the sin o' the auld laird, honest man."

"It's a wicked lie," burst with indignation from the other.

"There may be waur things nor a bit lee. Ony gait, ae thing's easy priven: ye lay verra dowie for a month or sax ooks ance upon a time at Lossie Hoose, an' that was a feow years, we needna speir hoo mony, efter ye was lichtened o' the tither. Whan they hear that at that time ye gae birth till a lad bairn, the whilk was stown awa', an' never hard tell o' till noo—'It may weel be,' fowk'll say: 'them 'at has drunk wad drink again!' It wad affoord rizzons, ye see, an' guid anes, for the bairn bein' putten oot a' sicht, and wad mak the haill story mair nor likly i' the jeedgment o' a' 'at hard it."

"You scandalous woman! That would be to confess to all the world that he was not the son of my late husband!"

laird, bonny lad, would say, and nobody can contradict a word—the old man less than anyone, for I can tell him what he knows to be truth. Only I won't move till *I* know where he comes from."

"Wouldn't you prefer not knowing for certain? You could swear with the better grace."

"Devil a bit! It doesn't matter to me which side of my teeth I chew with. But I won't swear till I know the truth—that I may avoid telling it. He's the man, though, if we can get our hands on him! He looks the right thing, you see, ma'am. He has a touch of the marquis too—don't you think, ma'am?"

"Insolent wretch!"

"Careful, ma'am. Everything must be considered. It would but make the thing look the more likely. Folk go as far as to say that Humpy himself isn't the son of the old laird, honest man."

"It's a wicked lie," burst with indignation from the other.

"There may be worse things than a wee lie. Anyway, one thing's easily proved: you lay very poorly for a month or six weeks once upon a time at Lossie House, and that was a few years, we needn't ask how many, after you were lightened of the other. When they hear that at that time you gave birth to a boy, who was stolen away, and never heard tell of till now—'It may well be,' folk'll say: 'them that have drunk would drink again!' It would afford reasons, you see, and good ones, for the child being put out of all sight, and would make the whole story more than likely in the judgement of all that heard it."

"You scandalous woman! That would be to confess to all the world that he was not the son of my late husband!"

"They say that o' him 'at *is*, an' hoo muckle the waur are ye? Lat them say 'at they like, sae lang 's we can shaw 'at he cam o' your body, an' was born i' wedlock. Ye hae yer lan's ance mair, for ye hae a sin 'at can guide them—and ye can guide him. He's a bonny lad—bonny eneuch to be yer leddyship's—*and* his lordship's: an' sae, as I was remarkin', i' the jeedgment a' ill thouchtit-fowk, the mair likly to be heir to auld Stewart o' Kirkbyres!"

She laughed huskily.

"But I maun hae a scart o' yer pen, mem, afore I wag tongue aboot it," she went on. "I ken brawly hoo to set it gauin'! I sanna be the first to ring the bell. Na, na; I s' set Miss Horn's Jean jawin', an' it 'll be a' ower the toon in a jiffy—at first in a kin o' a sough 'at naebody 'ill unnerstan': but it 'll grow looder an' plainer. At the lang last it 'll come to yer leddyship's hearin: an' syne ye hae me taen up an' questoned afore a justice o' the peace, that there may be no luik o' ony compack atween the twa o' 's. But, as I said afore, I'll no muv till I ken a' aboot the lad first, an' syne get a scart o' yer pen, mem."

"You must be the devil himself!" said the other, in a tone that was not of displeasure.

"I hae been tellt that afore, an' wi' less rizzon," was the reply—given also in a tone that was not of displeasure.

"But what if we should be found out?"

"Ye can lay 't a' upo' me."

"And what will you do with it?"

"Tak it wi' me," was the answer, accompanied by another husky laugh.

"Where to?"

"They say that of him that *is*, and how much the worse are you? Let them say what they like, so long as we can show that he came of your body, and was born in wedlock. You have your lands once more, for you have a son to manage them—and you can manage him. He's a bonny lad—bonny enough to be your ladyship's—*and* his lordship's: and so, as I was saying, in the judgement of all suspicious folk, the more likely to be heir to old Stewart of Kirkbyres!"

She laughed huskily.

"But I must have a scratch of your pen, before I spread the rumour," she went on. "I know well how to set it going! I shan't be the first to ring the bell. Na, na; I shall set Miss Horn's Jean jawing, and it'll be all over the town in a jiffey—at first in a kind of whisper that no one will understand: but it'll grow louder and plainer. At the long last it'll come to your ladyship's hearing: and then you have me taken up and questioned by a justice of the peace, that there may be no sign of conspiracy between the two of us. But, as I said before, I won't move till I know all about the lad first, and then get a scratch of your pen, ma'am."

"You must be the devil himself!" said the other, in a tone that was not of displeasure.

"I've been told that before, and with less reason," was the reply—given also in a tone that was not of displeasure.

"But what if we should be found out?"

"You can lay it all upon me."

"And what will you do with it?"

"Take it with me," was the answer, accompanied by another husky laugh.

"Where to?"

"Speir nae questons, an' ye'll be tellt nae lees. Ony gait, I s' lea' nae track ahin' me. An' for that same sake, I maun hae my pairt i' my han' the meenute the thing's been sworn till. Gien ye fail me, ye'll sune see me get mair licht upo' the subjec', an' confess till a great mistak. By the Michty, but I'll sweir the verra contrar the neist time I'm hed up! Ay, an' ilka body 'ill believe me. An' whaur'll ye be than, my leddy? For though *I* micht mistak, *ye* cudna! Faith! they'll hae ye ta'en up for perjury."

"You're a dangerous accomplice," said the lady.

"I'm a tule ye maun tak by the han'le, or ye'll rue the edge," returned the other quietly.

"As soon then as I get a hold of that misbegotten elf—"

"Mean ye the yoong laird, or the yoong markis, mem?"

"You forget, Mrs Catanach, that you are speaking to a lady!"

"Ye maun hae been unco like ane *ae* nicht, ony gait, mem. But I'm dune wi' my jokin'."

"As soon, I say, as I get my poor boy into proper hands, I shall be ready to take the next step."

"What for sud ye pit it aff till than? *He* canna du muckle ae w'y or ither."

"I will tell you. His uncle, Sir Joseph, prides himself on being an honest man, and if some busybody were to tell him that poor Stephen, as I am told people are saying, was no worse than harsh treatment had made him—for you know his father could not bear the sight of him till the day of his death—he would be the more determined to assert his guardianship, and keep things out of my hands. But if I once had the poor fellow in an asylum, or in my own keeping—you see—"

"Ask no questions, and you'll be told no lies. Anyway, I'll leave no track behind me. And for that same sake, I must have my part in my hand the minute the thing's been sworn to. If you fail me, you'll soon see me get more light upon the subject, and confess to a great mistake. By the Lord, but I'll swear the very opposite the next time I'm questioned! Ay, and everyone will believe me. And where will you be then, my lady? For though *I* might mistake, *you* couldn't! Faith! they'll have you arrested for perjury."

"You're a dangerous accomplice," said the lady.

"I'm a tool you must take by the handle, or you'll rue the edge," returned the other quietly.

"As soon then as I get a hold of that misbegotten elf—"

"Mean you the young laird, or the young marquis, ma'am?"

"You forget, Mrs Catanach, that you are speaking to a lady!"

"You must have been very like one *one* night, anyway, ma'am. But I'm done with my joking."

"As soon, I say, as I get my poor boy into proper hands, I shall be ready to take the next step."

"Why should you put it off till then? *He* can't do much one way or the other."

"I will tell you. His uncle, Sir Joseph, prides himself on being an honest man, and if some busybody were to tell him that poor Stephen, as I am told people are saying, was no worse than harsh treatment had made him—for you know his father could not bear the sight of him till the day of his death—he would be the more determined to assert his guardianship, and keep things out of my hands. But if I once had the poor fellow in an asylum, or in my own keeping—you see—"

"Weel, mem, gien I be potty, ye're panny!" exclaimed the midwife with her gelatinous laugh. "Losh, mem!" she burst out after a moment's pause, "gien you an' me was to fa' oot, there wad be a stramash! He! he! he!"

"Well ma'am, you're as bad as me!" exclaimed the midwife with her gelatinous laugh. "Lord, ma'am!" she burst out after a moment's pause, "if you and I were to fall out, there'd be a scuffle! He! he! he!"

They rose and left the cave together, talking as they went; and Phemy, trembling all over, rejoined the laird.

She could understand little of what she had heard, and yet, enabled by her affection, retained in her mind a good deal of it. After events brought more of it to her recollection, and what I have here given is an attempted restoration of the broken mosaic. She rightly judged it better to repeat nothing of what she had overheard to the laird, to whom it would only redouble terror; and when he questioned her in his own way concerning it, she had little difficulty, so entirely did he trust her, in satisfying him with a very small amount of information. When they reached her home, she told all she could to her father; whose opinion it was, that the best, indeed the only thing they could do, was to keep, if possible, a yet more vigilant guard over the laird and his liberty.

Soon after they were gone, Malcolm returned, and little thinking that there was no one left to guard, chose a sheltered spot in the cave, carried thither a quantity of dry sand, and lay down to sleep, covered with his tarpaulin coat. He found it something chilly, however, and did not rest so well but that he woke with the first break of day.

The morning, as it drew slowly on, was a strange contrast, in its gray and saffron, to the gorgeous sunset of the night before.

The sea crept up on the land as if it were weary, and did not care much to flow any more. Not a breath of wind was in motion, and yet the air even on the shore seemed full of the presence of decaying leaves and damp earth. He sat down in the mouth of the cave, and looked out on the still, half-waking world of ocean and sky before him—a leaden ocean, and a dull misty sky; and as he gazed, a sadness came stealing over him, and a sense of the endlessness of labour—labour ever returning on itself and making no progress. The mad laird was always lamenting his ignorance of his origin: Malcolm thought he knew whence he came—and yet what was the much good of life? Where was the end to it all? People so seldom got what they desired! To be sure his life was a happy one, or had been—but there was the poor laird! Why should he be happier than the laird? Why should the laird have a hump and he have none? If all the world were happy but one man, that one's misery would be as a cairn on which the countless multitudes of the blessed must heap the stones of endless questions and enduring perplexities.

It is one thing to know from whom we come, and another to know from Whom we come.

Then his thoughts turned to Lady Florimel. All the splendours of existence radiated from her, but to the glory he could never draw nearer; the celestial fires of the rainbow fountain of her life could never warm him; she cared about nothing he cared about; if they had a common humanity they could not share it; to her he was hardly human. If he were to unfold before her the deepest layers of his thought, she would look at them curiously, as she might watch the doings of an ant or a spider. Had he no right to look for more? He did not know, and sat brooding with bowed head.

Unseen from where he sat, the sun drew nearer the horizon, the light grew; the tide began to ripple up more diligently; a glimmer of dawn touched even the brown rock in the farthest end of the cave.

Where there was light there was work, and where there was work for any one, there was at least justification of his existence. That work must be done, if it should return and return in a never broken circle. Its theory could wait. For indeed the only hope of finding the theory of all theories, the divine idea, lay in the going on of things.

In the meantime, while God took care of the sparrows by himself, he allowed Malcolm a share in the protection of a human heart capable of the keenest suffering—that of the mad laird.

CHAPTER XXXII

THE SKIPPER'S CHAMBER

One day towards the close of the fishing season, the marquis called upon Duncan; and was received with a cordial unembarrassed welcome.

"I want you, Mr MacPhail," said his lordship, "to come and live in that little cottage, on the banks of the burn, which one of the under game-keepers, they tell me, used to occupy. I'll have it put in order for you, and you shall live rent free as my piper."

"I thank your lortship's crace," said Duncan, "and she would pe proud of ta honour, put it 'll pe too far away from ta shore for her poy's fishing."

"I have a design upon him too," returned the marquis. "They're building a little yacht for me—a pleasure boat, you understand—at Aberdeen, and I want Malcolm to be skipper. But he is such a useful fellow, and so thoroughly to be depended upon, that I should prefer his having a room in the house. I should like to know he was within call any moment I might want him."

Duncan did not clutch at the proposal. He was silent so long that the marquis spoke again.

"You do not quite seem to like the plan, Mr MacPhail," he said.

"If aal wass here as it used to wass in ta Highlants, my lort," said Duncan, "when every clansman wass son or prother or father to his chief tat would pe tifferent; put my poy must *not* co and eat with serfants

"I thank your lortship's grace," said Duncan, "and she would be proud of ta honour, but it'll be too far away from ta shore for her boy's fishing."

"I have a design upon him too," returned the marquis. "They're building a little yacht for me—a pleasure boat, you understand—at Aberdeen, and I want Malcolm to be skipper. But he is such a useful fellow, and so thoroughly to be depended upon, that I should prefer his having a room in the house. I should like to know he was within call any moment I might want him."

Duncan did not clutch at the proposal. He was silent so long that the marquis spoke again.

"You do not quite seem to like the plan, Mr MacPhail," he said.

"If all wass here as it used to be in ta Highlants, my lort," said Duncan, "when every clansman wass son or brother or father to his chief tat would be tifferent; but my boy must *not* co and eat with serfants who haf nothitng put teir waches to make tem love and opey your lortship. If her poy serfs another man, it must pe pecause he loves him, and looks upon him as his chief, who will shake haands with him and take ta father's care of him; and her poy must tie for him when ta time comes."

Even a feudal lord cannot be expected to have sympathized with such grand patriarchal ideas; they were much too like those of the kingdom of heaven; and feudalism itself had by this time crumbled away—not indeed into monthly, but into half-yearly wages. The marquis, notwithstanding, was touched by the old man's words, matter of fact as his reply must sound after them.

"I would make any arrangements you or he might wish," he said. "He should take his meals with Mrs Courthope, have a bedroom to himself and be required only to look after the yacht, and now and then do some bit of business I couldn't trust any one else with."

The highlander's pride was nearly satisfied.

"So," he said, "it'll pe his own henchman my lort will pe making of her poy?"

"Something like that. We'll see how it goes. If he doesn't like it, he can drop it. It's more that I want to have him about me than anything else. I want to do something for him when I have a chance. I like him."

"My lort will pe toing ta laad a creat honour," said Duncan. "Put," he added, with a sigh, "she'll pe lonely, her nainsel!"

"He can come and see you twenty times a day—and stop all night when you particularly want him. We'll see about some respectable woman to look after the house for you."

who haf nothing but teir wages to make tem love and obey your lortship. If her boy serfs another man, it must be because he loves him, and looks upon him as his chief, who will shake haands with him and take ta father's care of him; and her boy must tie for him when ta time comes."

Even a feudal lord cannot be expected to have sympathized with such grand patriarchal ideas; they were much too like those of the kingdom of heaven; and feudalism itself had by this time crumbled away—not indeed into monthly, but into half-yearly wages. The marquis, notwithstanding, was touched by the old man's words, matter of fact as his reply must sound after them.

"I would make any arrangements you or he might wish," he said. "He should take his meals with Mrs Courthope, have a bedroom to himself and be required only to look after the yacht, and now and then do some bit of business I couldn't trust any one else with."

The highlander's pride was nearly satisfied.

"So," he said, "it'll be his own henchman my lort will be making of her boy?"

"Something like that. We'll see how it goes. If he doesn't like it, he can drop it. It's more that I want to have him about me than anything else. I want to do something for him when I have a chance. I like him."

"My lort will be toing ta laad a creat honour," said Duncan. "But," he added, with a sigh, "she'll be lonely, her nainsel!"

"He can come and see you twenty times a day—and stop all night when you particularly want him. We'll see about some respectable woman to look after the house for you."

"She'll haf *no* womans to look after her," said Duncan fiercely.

"Oh, very well!—of course not, if you don't wish it," returned the marquis, laughing.

But Duncan did not even smile in return. He sat thoughtful and silent for a moment, then said:

"And what 'll pecome of her lamps and her shop?"

"You shall have all the lamps and candlesticks in the house to attend to and take charge of," said the marquis, who had heard of the old man's whim from Lady Florimel; "and for the shop, you won't want that when you're piper to the Marquis of Lossie."

He did not venture to allude to wages more definitely.

"Well, she'll pe talking to her poy apout it," said Duncan, and the marquis saw that he had better press the matter no further for the time.

"She'll haf *no* womans to look after her," said Duncan fiercely.

"Oh, very well!—of course not, if you don't wish it," returned the marquis, laughing.

But Duncan did not even smile in return. He sat thoughtful and silent for a moment, then said:

"And what 'll become of her lamps and her shop?"

"You shall have all the lamps and candlesticks in the house to attend to and take charge of," said the marquis, who had heard of the old man's whim from Lady Florimel; "and for the shop, you won't want that when you're piper to the Marquis of Lossie."

He did not venture to allude to wages more definitely.

"Well, she'll be talking to her boy apout it," said Duncan, and the marquis saw that he had better press the matter no further for the time.

To Malcolm the proposal was full of attraction. True, Lord Lossie had once and again spoken so as to offend him, but the confidence he had shown in him had gone far to atone for that. And to be near Lady Florimel!—to have to wait on her in the yacht and sometimes in the house!—to be allowed books from the library perhaps!—to have a nice room, and those lovely grounds all about him!—It *was* tempting!

The old man also, the more he reflected, liked the idea the more. The only thing he murmured at was, being parted from his grandson at night. In vain Malcolm reminded him that during the fishing season he had to spend most nights alone; Duncan answered that he had but to go to the door, and look out to sea, and there was nothing between him and his boy; but now he could not tell how many stone walls might be standing up to divide them. He was quite willing to make the trial, however, and see if he could bear it. So Malcolm went to speak to the marquis.

He did not *altogether* trust the marquis, but he had always taken a delight in doing anything for anybody—a delight rooted in a natural tendency to ministration, unusually strong, and specially developed by the instructions of Alexander Graham conjoined with the necessities of his blind grandfather; while there was an alluring something, it must be confessed, in the marquis's high position—which let no one set down to Malcolm's discredit: whether the subordination of class shall go to the development of reverence or of servility, depends mainly on the individual nature subordinated. Calvinism itself has produced as loving children as abject slaves, with a good many between partaking of the character of both kinds. Still, as he pondered over the matter on his way, he shrunk a good deal from placing himself at the beck and call of another; it threatened to interfere with that sense of personal freedom which is yet dearer perhaps to the poor than to the rich. But he argued with himself that he had found no infringement of it under Blue Peter; and that, if the marquis were really as friendly as he professed to be, it was not likely to turn out otherwise with him.

Lady Florimel anticipated pleasure in Malcolm's probable consent to her father's plan; but certainly he would not have been greatly uplifted by a knowledge of the sort of pleasure she expected. For some time the girl had been suffering from too much liberty. Perhaps there is no life more filled with a sense of oppression and lack of freedom than that of those under no external control, in whom Duty has not yet gathered sufficient strength to assume the reins of government and subject them to the highest law. Their condition is like that of a creature under an exhausted receiver—oppressed from within outwards for want of the counteracting external weight. It was amusement she hoped for from Malcolm's becoming in a sense one of the family at the House—to which she believed her knowledge of the extremely bare outlines of his history would largely contribute.

He was shown at once into the presence of his lordship, whom he found at breakfast with his daughter.

"Well, MacPhail," said the marquis, "have you made up your mind to be my skipper?"

"Willin'ly, my lord," answered Malcolm.

"Willingly, my lord," answered Malcolm.

"Do you know how to manage a sailboat?"

"Do you know how to manage a sailboat?"

"I wad need, my lord."

"I would need to, my lord."

"Shall you want any help?"

"Shall you want any help?"

"That depen's upo' saiveral things— her ain size, the wull o' the win', an' whether or no yer lordship or my leddy can tak the tiller."

"That depends upon several things— her own size, the will of the wind, and whether or not your lordship or my lady can take the tiller."

"We can't settle about that then till she comes. I hear she'll soon be on her way now. But I cannot have you dressed like a farmer!" said his lordship, looking sharply at the Sunday clothes which Malcolm had donned for the visit.

"We can't settle about that then till she comes. I hear she'll soon be on her way now. But I cannot have you dressed like a farmer!" said his lordship, looking sharply at the Sunday clothes which Malcolm had donned for the visit.

"What was I to du, my lord?" returned Malcolm apologetically. "The only ither claes I hae, are verra fishy, an' neither yersel' nor my leddy cud bide them i' the room aside ye."

"What was I to do, my lord?" returned Malcolm apologetically. "The only other clothes I have, are very fishy, and neither you nor my lady could stand them in the room beside you."

"Certainly not," responded the marquis, as in a leisurely manner he devoured his omelette: "I was thinking of your future position as skipper of my boat. What would you say to a kilt now?"

"Na, na, my lord," rejoined Malcolm; "a kilt's no seafarin' claes. A kilt wadna du ava', my lord."

"You cannot surely object to the dress of your own people," said the marquis.

"The kilt 's weel eneuch upon a hill-side," said Malcolm, "I dinna doobt; but faith! sea-farin', my lord, ye wad want the trews as weel."

"Well, go to the best tailor in the town, and order a naval suit—white ducks and a blue jacket—two suits you'll want."

"We s' gar ae shuit sair 's to begin wi', my lord. I'll jist gang to Jamie Sangster, wha maks a' my claes—no 'at their mony!—an' get *him* to mizzur me. He'll mak them weel eneuch for me. You're aye sure o' the worth o' yer siller frae *him*."

"I tell you to go to the best tailor in the town, and order two suits."

"Na, na, my lord; there's nae need. I canna affoord it forbye. We're no a' made o' siller like yer lordship."

"You booby! do you suppose I would tell you to order clothes I did not mean to pay for?"

Lady Florimel found her expectation of amusement not likely to be disappointed.

"Hoots, my lord!" returned Malcolm, "that wad never du. I *maun* pey for my ain claes. I wad be in a constant terror o blaudin' o' them gien I didna, an' that wad be eneuch to mak a body meeserable. It wad be a' the same, forbye, oot an' oot, as weirin' a leevry!"

"Certainly not," responded the marquis, as in a leisurely manner he devoured his omelette: "I was thinking of your future position as skipper of my boat. What would you say to a kilt now?"

"Na, na, my lord," rejoined Malcolm; "a kilt's not seafaring clothes. A kilt wouldn't do at all, my lord."

"You cannot surely object to the dress of your own people," said the marquis.

"The kilt's well enough upon a hill-side," said Malcolm, "I don't doubt; but faith! sea-faring, my lord, you would want the trews as well."

"Well, go to the best tailor in the town, and order a naval suit—white ducks and a blue jacket—two suits you'll want."

"We'll make do with one suit at first, my lord. I'll just go to Jamie Sangster, who makes all my clothes—not that they're many!—and get *him* to measure me. He'll make them well enough for me. You're always sure of getting your money's worth from *him*."

"I tell you to go to the best tailor in the town, and order two suits."

"Na, na, my lord; there's no need. Besides, I can't afford it. We're not all made of money like your lordship."

"You booby! do you suppose I would tell you to order clothes I did not mean to pay for?"

Lady Florimel found her expectation of amusement not likely to be disappointed.

"Heavens, my lord!" returned Malcolm, "that would never do. I *must* pay for my own clothes. I would be in constant terror of spoiling them if I didn't, and that would be enough to make me miserable. It would be all the same, anyway, out and out, as wearing a livery!"

"Well, well! please your pride, and be damned to you!" said the marquis.	"Well, well! please your pride, and be damned to you!" said the marquis.
"Yes, let him please his pride, and be damned to him!" assented Lady Florimel with perfect gravity.	"Yes, let him please his pride, and be damned to him!" assented Lady Florimel with perfect gravity.
Malcolm started and stared. Lady Florimel kept an absolute composure. The marquis burst into a loud laugh. Malcolm stood bewildered for a moment.	Malcolm started and stared. Lady Florimel kept an absolute composure. The marquis burst into a loud laugh. Malcolm stood bewildered for a moment.
"I'm thinkin' I'm gaein' daft!" he said at length, putting his hand to his head. "It's time I gaed. Guid mornin', my lord."	"I think I'm going daft!" he said at length, putting his hand to his head. "It's time I was going. Good morning, my lord."

He turned and left the room, followed by a fresh peal from his lordship, mingling with which his ear plainly detected the silvery veins of Lady Florimel's equally merry laughter.

When he came to himself and was able to reflect, he saw there must have been some joke involved: the behaviour of both indicated as much; and with this conclusion he heartened his dismay.

The next morning Duncan called on Mrs Partan, and begged her acceptance of his stock in trade, as, having been his lordship's piper for some time, he was now at length about to occupy his proper quarters within the policies. Mrs Findlay acquiesced, with an air better suited to the granting of slow leave to laboursome petition, than the accepting of such a generous gift; but she made some amends by graciously expressing a hope that Duncan would not forget his old friends now that he was going amongst lords and ladies, to which Duncan returned as courteous answer as if he had been addressing Lady Florimel herself.

Before the end of the week, his few household goods were borne in a cart through the sea-gate dragonised by Bykes, to whom Malcolm dropped a humorous "Weel Johnny!" ("Well Johnny!") as he passed, receiving a nondescript kind of grin in return. The rest of the forenoon was spent in getting the place in order, and in the afternoon, arrayed in his new garments, Malcolm reported himself at the House. Admitted to his lordship's presence, he had a question to ask and a request to prefer.

"Hae ye dune onything my lord," he said, "aboot Mistress Catanach?"	"Have you done anything my lord," he said, "about Mistress Catanach?"
"What do you mean?"	"What do you mean?"
"Anent yon cat-prowl aboot the hoose, my lord."	"About that cat-prowl about the house, my lord."
"No. You haven't discovered anything more—have you?"	"No. You haven't discovered anything more—have you?"
"Na, my lord; I haena had a chance. But ye may be sure she had nae guid design in 't."	"Na, my lord; I haven't had a chance. But you may be sure she had no good design in it."

"I don't suspect her of any."

"Weel, my lord, hae ye ony objection to lat me sleep up yonner?"

"None at all—only you'd better see what Mrs Courthope has to say to it. Perhaps you won't be so ready after you hear her story."

"But I hae yer lordship's leave to tak ony room I like?"

"Certainly. Go to Mrs Courthope, and tell her I wish you to choose your own quarters."

Having straightway delivered his lordship's message, Mrs Courthope, wondering a little thereat, proceeded to show him those portions of the house set apart for the servants. He followed her from floor to floor—last to the upper regions, and through all the confused rambling roofs of the old pile, now descending a sudden steep yawning stair, now ascending another where none could have been supposed to exist—oppressed all the time with a sense of the multitudinous and intricate, such as he had never before experienced, and such as perhaps only the works of man can produce, the intricacy and variety of those of nature being ever veiled in the grand simplicity which springs from primal unity of purpose.

I find no part of an ancient house so full of interest as the garret region. It has all the mystery of the dungeon cellars with a far more striking variety of form, and a bewildering curiosity of adaptation, the peculiarities of roof shapes and the consequent complexities of their relations and junctures being so much greater than those of foundation plans. Then the sense of lofty loneliness in the deeps of air, and at the same time of proximity to things aerial—doves and martins, vanes and gilded balls and lightning conductors, the waves of the sea of wind, breaking on the chimneys for rocks, and the crashing roll of the thunder—is in harmony with the highest spiritual instincts; while the clouds and the stars look, if not nearer, yet more germane, and the moon gazes down on the lonely dweller in uplifted places, as if she had secrets with such. The cellars are the metaphysics, the garrets the poetry of the house.

Mrs Courthope was more than kind, for she was greatly pleased at having Malcolm for an inmate. She led him from room to room, suggesting now and then a choice, and listening amusedly to his remarks of liking or disliking, and his marvel at strangeness or extent. At last he found himself following her along the passage in which was the mysterious door, but she never stayed her step, or seemed to intend showing one of the many rooms opening upon it.

"Sic a bee's byke o' rooms!" said Malcolm, making a halt. "Wha sleeps here?"

"Nobody has slept in one of these rooms for I dare not say how many years," replied Mrs Courthope, without stopping; and as she spoke she passed the fearful door.

"I wad like to see intil this room," said Malcolm.

"That door is never opened," answered Mrs Courthope, who had now reached the end of the passage, and turned, lingering as in act while she spoke to move on.

"And what for that?" asked Malcolm, continuing to stand before it.

"I would rather not answer you just here. Come along. This is not a part of the house where you would like to be, I am sure."

"Hoo ken ye that, mem? An' hoo can I say mysel' afore ye hae shawn me what the room 's like? It may be the verra place to tak my fancy. Jist open the door, mem, gien ye please, an lat's hae a keek intill 't."

"I daren't open it. It's never opened, I tell you. It's against the rules of the house. Come to my room, and I'll tell you the story about it."

"Weel, ye'll lat me see intil the neist—winna ye? There's nae law agane openin' hit—is there?" said Malcolm, approaching the door next to the one in dispute.

"Certainly not; but I'm pretty sure, once you've heard the story I have to tell, you won't choose to sleep in this part of the house."

"Lat's luik, ony gait."

So saying, Malcolm took upon himself to try the handle of the door. It was not locked: he peeped in, then entered. It was a small room, low-ceiled, with a deep

"Nobody has slept in one of these rooms for I dare not say how many years," replied Mrs Courthope, without stopping; and as she spoke she passed the fearful door.

"I'd like to see into this room," said Malcolm.

"That door is never opened," answered Mrs Courthope, who had now reached the end of the passage, and turned, lingering as in act while she spoke to move on.

"And why is that?" asked Malcolm, continuing to stand before it.

"I would rather not answer you just here. Come along. This is not a part of the house where you would like to be, I am sure."

"How do you know that, ma'am? And how can I say myself before you've shown me what the room is like? It may be the very place to take my fancy. Just open the door, ma'am, if you please, and let's have a peep into it."

"I daren't open it. It's never opened, I tell you. It's against the rules of the house. Come to my room, and I'll tell you the story about it."

"Well, you'll let me see into the next—won't you? There's no law against opening it—is there?" said Malcolm, approaching the door next to the one in dispute.

"Certainly not; but I'm pretty sure, once you've heard the story I have to tell, you won't choose to sleep in this part of the house."

"Let's look, anyway."

So saying, Malcolm took upon himself to try the handle of the door. It was not locked: he peeped in, then entered. It was a small room, low-ceiled, with a deep dormer window in the high pediment of a roof, and a turret recess on each side of the window. It seemed very light after the passage, and looked down upon the burn. It was comfortably furnished, and the curtains of its tent-bed were chequered in squares of blue and white.

"This is the verra place for me, mem," said Malcolm, reissuing;— "that is," he added, "gien ye dinna think it's ower gran' for the likes o' me 'at 's no been used to onything half sae guid."

"You're quite welcome to it," said Mrs Courthope, all but confident he would not care to occupy it after hearing the tale of Lord Gernon.

She had not moved from the end of the passage while Malcolm was in the room—somewhat hurriedly she now led the way to her own. It seemed half a mile off to the wondering Malcolm, as he followed her down winding stairs, along endless passages, and round innumerable corners. Arrived at last, she made him sit down, and gave him a glass of home-made wine to drink, while she told him the story much as she had already told it to the marquis, adding a hope to the effect that, if ever the marquis should express a wish to pry into the secret of the chamber, Malcolm would not encourage him in a fancy, the indulgence of which was certainly useless, and might be dangerous.

"*Me!*" exclaimed Malcolm with surprise. "—As gien he wad heed a word *I* said!"

"Very little sometimes will turn a man either in one direction or the other," said Mrs Courthope.

dormer window in the high pediment of a roof, and a turret recess on each side of the window. It seemed very light after the passage, and looked down upon the burn. It was comfortably furnished, and the curtains of its tent-bed were chequered in squares of blue and white.

"This is the very place for me, ma'am," said Malcolm, reissuing;—"that is," he added, "if you don't think it's too grand for the likes of me that hasn't been used to anything half so good."

"You're quite welcome to it," said Mrs Courthope, all but confident he would not care to occupy it after hearing the tale of Lord Gernon.

She had not moved from the end of the passage while Malcolm was in the room—somewhat hurriedly she now led the way to her own. It seemed half a mile off to the wondering Malcolm, as he followed her down winding stairs, along endless passages, and round innumerable corners. Arrived at last, she made him sit down, and gave him a glass of home-made wine to drink, while she told him the story much as she had already told it to the marquis, adding a hope to the effect that, if ever the marquis should express a wish to pry into the secret of the chamber, Malcolm would not encourage him in a fancy, the indulgence of which was certainly useless, and might be dangerous.

"*Me!*" exclaimed Malcolm with surprise. "—As if he would heed a word *I* said!"

"Very little sometimes will turn a man either in one direction or the other," said Mrs Courthope.

"But surely, mem, ye dinna believe in sic fule auld warld stories as that! It's weel eneuch for a tale, but to think o' a body turnin' ae fit oot o' 's gait for 't, blecks me."

"I don't say I believe it," returned Mrs Courthope, a little pettishly; "but there's no good in mere foolhardiness."

"Ye dinna surely think, mem, 'at God wad lat onything depen' upo' whether a man opent a door in 's ain hoose or no! It's agane a' rizzon!" persisted Malcolm.

"There might be reasons we couldn't understand," she replied. "To do what we are warned against from any quarter, without good reason, must be foolhardy at best."

"Weel, mem, I maun hae the room neist the auld warlock's, ony gait, for in that I'm gauin' to sleep, an' in nae ither in a' this muckle hoose."

Mrs Courthope rose, full of uneasiness, and walked up and down the room.

"I'm takin' upo' me naething ayont his lordship's ain word," urged Malcolm.

"If you're to go by the very word," rejoined Mrs Courthope, stopping and looking him full in the face, "you might insist on sleeping in Lord Gernon's chamber itself."

"Weel, an' sae I micht," returned Malcolm.

The hinted possibility of having to change bad for so much worse, appeared to quench further objection.

"I must get it ready myself then," she said resignedly, "for the maids won't even go up that stair. And as to going into any of those rooms!"

"But surely, ma'am, you don't believe in such foolish old world stories as that! It's well enough for a tale, but to think of anyone turning one foot out of his way for it, just baffles me."

"I don't say I believe it," returned Mrs Courthope, a little pettishly; "but there's no good in mere foolhardiness."

"You don't surely think, ma'am, that God would let anything depend upon whether a man opened a door in his own house or not! It's against all reason!" persisted Malcolm.

"There might be reasons we couldn't understand," she replied. "To do what we are warned against from any quarter, without good reason, must be foolhardy at best."

"Well, ma'am, I must have the room next the old warlock's, anyway, for in that I'm going to sleep, and in no other in all this great house."

Mrs Courthope rose, full of uneasiness, and walked up and down the room.

"I'm doing nothing beyond what his lordship gave me leave to do," urged Malcolm.

"If you're to go by the very word," rejoined Mrs Courthope, stopping and looking him full in the face, "you might insist on sleeping in Lord Gernon's chamber itself."

"Well, and so I might," returned Malcolm.

The hinted possibility of having to change bad for so much worse, appeared to quench further objection.

"I must get it ready myself then," she said resignedly, "for the maids won't even go up that stair. And as to going into any of those rooms!"

"'Deed no, mem! ye sanna du that," cried Malcolm. "Sayna a word to ane o' them. I s' wadger I'm as guid's the auld warlock himsel' at makin' a bed. Jist gie me the sheets an' the blankets, an' I'll du 't as trim 's ony lass i' the hoose."

"Indeed no, ma'am! you shan't do that," cried Malcolm. "Don't breathe a word to any of them. I'll wager I'm as good as the old warlock himself at making a bed. Just give me the sheets and the blankets, and I'll do it as trim as any lass in the house."

"But the bed will want airing," objected the housekeeper.

"But the bed will want airing," objected the housekeeper.

"By a' accoonts, that's the last thing it 's likly to want—lyin' neist door to *yon* chaumer. But I hae sleepit mony 's the time er' noo upo' the tap o' a boat-load o' herrin', an' gien that never did me ony ill, it 's no likly a guid bed 'll kill me gien it sud be a wee mochy."

"By all accounts, that's the last thing it's likely to want—lying next door to *that* room. But I've slept many a time before now on top of a boat-load of herring, and if that never hurt me, it's not likely I'll be killed by a good bed though it *should* be a little mothy."

Mrs Courthope yielded and gave him all that was needful, and before night Malcolm had made his new quarters quite comfortable. He did not retire to them, however, until he had seen his grandfather laid down to sleep in his lonely cottage.

About noon the next day the old man made his appearance in the kitchen. How he had found his way to it, neither he nor any one else could tell. There happened to be no one there when he entered, and the cook when she returned stood for a moment in the door, watching him as he felt flitting about with huge bony hands whose touch was yet light as the poise of a butterfly. Not knowing the old man, she fancied at first he was feeling after something in the shape of food, but presently his hands fell upon a brass candlestick. He clutched it, and commenced fingering it all over. Alas! it was clean, and with a look of disappointment he replaced it. Wondering yet more what his quest could be, she watched on. The next instant he had laid hold of a silver candlestick not yet passed through the hands of the scullery maid; and for a moment she fancied him a thief, for he had rejected the brass and now took the silver; but he went no farther with it than the fireplace, where he sat down on the end of the large fender, and, having spread his pocket handkerchief over his kilted knees, drew a similar rag from somewhere, and commenced cleaning it.

By this time one of the maids who knew him had joined the cook, and also stood watching him with amusement. But when she saw the old knife drawn from his stocking, and about to be applied to the nozzle, to free it from adhering wax, it seemed more than time to break the silence.

"Eh! that's a siller can'lestick, Maister MacPhail," she cried, "an' ye maunna tak a knife till 't, or ye'll scrat it a' dreidfu'."

"Eh! that's a silver candlestick, Mister MacPhail," she cried, "and you mustn't take a knife to it, or you'll scratch it all to bits."

An angry flush glowed in the withered cheeks of the piper, as, without the least start at the suddenness of her interference, he turned his face in the direction of the speaker.

"You take old Tuncan's finkers for persons of no etchucation, mem! As if tey couldn't know ta silfer from ta prass! If tey wass so stupid, her nose would pe telling tem so. Efen old Tuncan's knife 'll pe knowing petter than to scratch ta silfer—or ta prass either; old Tuncan's knife would pe scratching nothing petter tan ta skin of a Cawmill."

An angry flush glowed in the withered cheeks of the piper, as, without the least start at the suddenness of her interference, he turned his face in the direction of the speaker.

"You take old Tuncan's finkers for persons of no education, mem! As if tey couldn't know ta silfer from ta brass! If tey wass so stupid, her nose would be telling tem so. Efen old Tuncan's knife 'll be knowing better than to scratch ta silfer—or ta brass either; old Tuncan's knife would be scratching nothing better tan ta skin of a Cawmill."

Now the candlestick had no business in the kitchen, and if it were scratched, the butler would be indignant; but the girl was a Campbell, and Duncan's words so frightened her that she did not dare interfere. She soon saw, however, that the piper had not over-vaunted his skill: the skene left not a mark upon the metal; in a few minutes he had melted away the wax he could not otherwise reach, and had rubbed the candlestick perfectly bright, leaving behind him no trace except an unpleasant odour of train oil from the rag. From that hour he was cleaner of lamps and candlesticks, as well as blower of bagpipes, to the House of Lossie; and had everything provided necessary to the performance of his duties with comfort and success.

Before many weeks were over, he had proved the possession of such a talent for arrangement and general management, at least in everything connected with illumination, that the entire charge of the lighting of the house was left in his hands,—even to that of its stores of wax and tallow and oil; and great was the pleasure he derived, not only from the trust reposed in him, but from other more occult sources connected with the duties of his office.

THE LIBRARY

Malcolm's first night was rather troubled,—not primarily from the fact that but a thin partition separated him from the wizard's chamber, but from the deadness of the silence around him; for he had been all his life accustomed to the near noise of the sea, and its absence had upon him the rousing effect of an unaccustomed sound. He kept hearing the dead silence—was constantly dropping, as it were into its gulf; and it was no wonder that a succession of sleepless fits, strung together rather than divided by as many dozes little better than startled rousings, should at length have so shaken his mental frame as to lay it open to the assaults of nightly terrors, the position itself being sufficient to seduce his imagination, and carry it over to the interests of the enemy.

But Malcolm had early learned that a man's will must, like a true monarch, rule down every rebellious movement of its subjects, and he was far from yielding to such inroads as now assailed him: still it was long before he fell asleep, and then only to dream without quite losing consciousness of his peculiar surroundings. He seemed to know that he lay in his own bed, and yet to be somehow aware of the presence of a pale woman in a white garment, who sat on the side of the bed in the next room, still and silent, with her hands in her lap, and her eyes on the ground. He thought he had seen her before, and knew, notwithstanding her silence, that she was lamenting over a child she had lost. He knew also where her child was,—that it lay crying in a cave down by the sea-shore; but he could neither rise to go to her, nor open his mouth to call. The vision kept coming and coming, like the same tune played over and over on a barrel organ, and when he woke seemed to fill all the time he had slept.

About ten o'clock he was summoned to the marquis's presence, and found him at breakfast with Lady Florimel.

"Where did you sleep last night?" asked the marquis.

"Neist door to the auld warlock," answered Malcolm.

Lady Florimel looked up with a glance of bright interest: her father had just been telling her the story.

"Where did you sleep last night?" asked the marquis.

"Next door to the old warlock," answered Malcolm.

Lady Florimel looked up with a glance of bright interest: her father had just been telling her the story.

"You did!" said the marquis. "Then Mrs Courthope—did she tell you the legend about him?"

"Ay did she, my lord."

"Well, how did you sleep?"

"Middlin' only."

"How was that?"

"I dinna ken, 'cep it was 'at I was fule eneuch to fin' the place gey eerie like."

"Aha!" said the marquis. "You've had enough of it! You won't try it again!"

"What's that ye say, my lord?" rejoined Malcolm. "Wad ye hae a man turn 's back at the first fleg? Na, na, my lord; that wad never du!"

"Oh! then, you did have a fright?"

"Na, I canna say that aither. Naething waur cam near me nor a dream 'at plaguit me—an' it wasna sic an ill ane efter a'."

"What was it?"

"I thocht there was a bonny leddy sittin' o' the bed i' the neist room, in her nichtgoon like, an' she was greitin' sair in her hert, though she never loot a tear fa' doon. She was greitin' about a bairnie she had lost, an' I kent weel whaur the bairnie was—doon in a cave upo' the shore, I thoucht—an' I was jist yirnin' to gang till her an' tell her, an' stop the greitin' o' her hert, but I cudna muv han' nor fit, naither cud I open my mou' to cry till her. An' I gaed dreamin' on at the same thing ower an' ower, a' the time I was asleep. But there was naething sae frichtsome aboot that, my lord."

"No, indeed," said his lordship.

"Only it garred me greit tu, my lord, 'cause I cudna win at her to help her."

His lordship laughed, but oddly, and changed the subject.

"You did!" said the marquis. "Then Mrs Courthope—did she tell you the legend about him?"

"Ay, she did, my lord."

"Well, how did you sleep?"

"Just middling."

"How was that?"

"I don't know, unless it was that I was fool enough to feel it very eerie up there."

"Aha!" said the marquis. "You've had enough of it! You won't try it again!"

"What's that you say, my lord?" rejoined Malcolm. "Would you have a man turn his back at the first fright? Na, na, my lord; that would never do!"

"Oh! then, you did have a fright?"

"Na, I can't say that either. Nothing worse came near me than a dream that plagued me—and it wasn't such a bad one after all."

"What was it?"

"I thought there was a bonny lady sitting on the bed in the next room, in her nightgown, and she was weeping sore in her heart, though she never let fall a tear. She was weeping about a child she had lost, and I knew well where the child was—down in a cave upon the shore, I thought—and I was just yearning to go to her and tell her, and stop the crying of her heart, but I couldn't move hand nor foot, neither could I open my mouth to call to her. And I went dreaming on at the same thing over and over, all the time I was asleep. But there was nothing so frightsome about that, my lord."

"No, indeed," said his lordship.

"Only it made me weep too, my lord, because I couldn't get near her to help her."

His lordship laughed, but oddly, and changed the subject.

"There's no word of that boat yet," he said. "I must write again."

"May I show Malcolm the library, papa?" asked Lady Florimel.

"I *wad* fain see the buiks," adjected Malcolm.

"You don't know what a scholar he is, papa!"

"Little eneuch o' that!" said Malcolm.

"Oh yes! I do," said the marquis, answering his daughter. "But he must keep the skipper from my books and the scholar from my boat."

"Ye mean a scholar wha wad skip yer buiks, my lord! Haith! sic wad be a skipper wha wad ill scull yer boat!" said Malcolm, with a laugh at the poor attempt.

"Bravo!" said the marquis, who certainly was not over critical. "Can you write a good hand?"

"No ill, my lord."

"So much the better! I see you'll be worth your wages."

"That depen's on the wages," returned Malcolm.

"And that reminds me you've said nothing about them yet."

"Naither has yer lordship."

"Well, what are they to be?"

"Whatever ye think proper, my lord. Only dinna gar me gang to Maister Crathie for them."

The marquis had sent away the man who was waiting when Malcolm entered, and during this conversation Malcolm had of his own accord been doing his best to supply his place. The meal ended, Lady Florimel desired him to wait a moment in the hall.

"There's no word of that boat yet," he said. "I must write again."

"May I show Malcolm the library, papa?" asked Lady Florimel.

"I *would* fain see the books," adjected Malcolm.

"You don't know what a scholar he is, papa!"

"Little enough of that!" said Malcolm.

"Oh yes! I do," said the marquis, answering his daughter. "But he must keep the skipper from my books and the scholar from my boat."

"You mean a scholar who would skip your books, my lord! Faith! such would be a poor skipper to scull your boat!" said Malcolm, with a laugh at the poor attempt.

"Bravo!" said the marquis, who certainly was not over critical. "Can you write a good hand?"

"Not bad, my lord."

"So much the better! I see you'll be worth your wages."

"That depends on the wages," returned Malcolm.

"And that reminds me you've said nothing about them yet."

"Neither has your lordship."

"Well, what are they to be?"

"Whatever you think proper, my lord. Only don't make me go to Mister Crathie to get them."

The marquis had sent away the man who was waiting when Malcolm entered, and during this conversation Malcolm had of his own accord been doing his best to supply his place. The meal ended, Lady Florimel desired him to wait a moment in the hall.

"He's so amusing, papa!" she said. "I want to see him stare at the books. He thinks the schoolmaster's hundred volumes a grand library! He's such a goose! It's the greatest fun in the world watching him."

"No such goose!" said the marquis; but he recognized himself in his child, and laughed.

Florimel ran off merrily, as bent on a joke, and joined Malcolm.

"Now, I'm going to show you the library," she said.

"Thank ye, my leddy; that *will* be gran'!" replied Malcolm.

He followed her up two staircases, and through more than one long narrow passage: all the ducts of the house were long and narrow, causing him a sense of imprisonment—vanishing ever into freedom at the opening of some door into a great room. But never had he had a dream of such a room as that at which they now arrived. He started with a sort of marvelling dismay when she threw open the door of the library, and he beheld ten thousand volumes at a glance, all in solemn stillness. It was like a sepulchre of kings. But his astonishment took a strange form of expression, the thought in which was beyond the reach of his mistress.

"Eh, my leddy!" he cried, after staring for a while in breathless bewilderment, "it 's jist like a byke o' frozen bees! Eh! gien they war a' to come to life an' stick their stangs o' trowth intill a body, the waukin' up wad be awfu'!—It jist gars my heid gang roon'!" he added, after a pause.

"It is a fine thing," said the girl, "to have such a library."

"He's so amusing, papa!" she said. "I want to see him stare at the books. He thinks the schoolmaster's hundred volumes a grand library! He's such a goose! It's the greatest fun in the world watching him."

"No such goose!" said the marquis; but he recognized himself in his child, and laughed.

Florimel ran off merrily, as bent on a joke, and joined Malcolm.

"Now, I'm going to show you the library," she said.

"Thank you, my lady; that *will* be grand!" replied Malcolm.

He followed her up two staircases, and through more than one long narrow passage: all the ducts of the house were long and narrow, causing him a sense of imprisonment—vanishing ever into freedom at the opening of some door into a great room. But never had he had a dream of such a room as that at which they now arrived. He started with a sort of marvelling dismay when she threw open the door of the library, and he beheld ten thousand volumes at a glance, all in solemn stillness. It was like a sepulchre of kings. But his astonishment took a strange form of expression, the thought in which was beyond the reach of his mistress.

"Eh, my lady!" he cried, after staring for a while in breathless bewilderment, "it's just like a hive of frozen bees! Eh! if they were all to come to life and pierce you with their stings of truth, the waking up would be awful!—It just makes my head go round!" he added, after a pause.

"It is a fine thing," said the girl, "to have such a library."

"'Deed is 't, my leddy! It's ane o' the preevileeges o' rank," said Malcolm. "It taks a faimily that hauds on throu' centeries in a hoose whaur things gether, to mak sic an unaccoontable getherin' o' buiks as that. It's a gran' sicht—worth livin' to see."

"Suppose you were to be a rich man some day," said Florimel, in the condescending tone she generally adopted when addressing him, "it would be one of the first things you would set about—wouldn't it—to get such a library together?"

"Na, my leddy; I wad hae mair wut. A leebrary canna be made a' at ance, ony mair nor a hoose, or a nation, or a muckle tree: *they* maun a' tak time to grow, an' sae maun a leebrary. I wadna even ken what buiks to gang an' speir for. I daursay, gien I war to try, I cudna at a moment's notice tell ye the names o' mair nor a twa score o' buiks at the ootside. Fowk maun mak acquantance amo' buiks as they wad amo' leevin' fowk."

"But you could get somebody who knew more about them than yourself to buy for you."

"I wad as sune think o' gettin' somebody to ate my denner for me."

"No, that's not fair," said Florimel. "It would only be like getting somebody who knew more of cookery than yourself, to order your dinner for you."

"Ye're richt, my leddy; but still I wad as sune think o' the tane 's the tither. What wad come o' the like o' me, div ye think, broucht up upo' meal-brose, an' herrin', gien ye was to set me doon to sic a denner as my lord, yer father, wad ait ilka day, an' think naething o'? But gien some fowk hed the buyin' o' my buiks, I'm thinkin' the first thing I wad hae to du, wad be to fling the half o' them into the burn."

"Indeed it is, my lady! It's one of the privileges of rank," said Malcolm. "It takes centuries—many generations of a family in a house where things gather—to make such an endless gathering of books as that. It's a grand sight—worth living to see."

"Suppose you were to be a rich man some day," said Florimel, in the condescending tone she generally adopted when addressing him, "it would be one of the first things you would set about—wouldn't it—to get such a library together?"

"Na, my lady; I would have more sense. A library can't be made all at once, any more than a house, or a nation, or a great tree: they must all take time to grow, and so must a library. I wouldn't even know what books to go and ask for. I daresay, if I were to try, I couldn't at a moment's notice tell you the names of more than forty books at the outside. Folk must make acquaintance among books as they would among living folk."

"But you could get somebody who knew more about them than yourself to buy for you."

"I would as soon think of getting somebody to eat my dinner for me."

"No, that's not fair," said Florimel. "It would only be like getting somebody who knew more of cookery than yourself, to order your dinner for you."

"You're right, my lady; but still I would as soon think of the one as the other. What would become of the likes of me, do you think, brought up upon meal-brose, and herring, if you were to set me down to such a dinner as my lord, your father, would eat every day, and think nothing of it? But if some folk had the buying of my books, I'm thinking the first thing I would have to do, would be to fling the half of them into the burn."

"What good would that do?"

"Clear awa' the rubbitch. Ye see, my leddy, it 's no buiks, but what buiks. Eh! there maun be mony ane o' the richt sort here, though. I wonner gien Mr Graham ever saw them. He wad surely hae made mention o them i' my hearin'!"

"What would be the first thing you would do, then, Malcolm, if you happened to turn out a great man after all?" said Florimel, seating herself in a huge library chair, whence, having arranged her skirt, she looked up in the young fisherman's face.

"I doobt I wad hae to sit doon, an' turn ower the change a feow times afore I kent aither mysel' or what wad become me,"

"That's not answering my question," retorted Florimel.

"Weel, the second thing I wad du," said Malcolm, thoughtfully, and pausing a moment, "wad be to get Mr Graham to gang wi' me to Ebberdeen, an' cairry me throu' the classes there. Of coorse, I wadna try for prizes; that wadna be fair to them 'at cudna affoord a tutor at their lodgin's."

"But it's the *first* thing you would do that I want to know," persisted the girl.

"I tellt ye I wad sit doon an' think aboot it."

"I don't count that *doing* anything."

"'Deed, my leddy! thinkin 's the hardest wark I ken."

"Well, what is it you would think about first?" said Florimel—not to be diverted from her course.

"Ow, the third thing I wad du—"

"I want to know the first thing you would think about."

"What good would that do?"

"Clear away the rubbish. You see, my lady, it isn't just a question of books, but of *which* books. Eh! there must be many of the right sort here, though. I wonder if Mr Graham ever saw them—but then surely he would have mentioned them to me!"

"What would be the first thing you would do, then, Malcolm, if you happened to turn out a great man after all?" said Florimel, seating herself in a huge library chair, whence, having arranged her skirt, she looked up in the young fisherman's face.

"I expect I'd have to sit down, and turn over the change a few times before I knew either myself or what would become me," he said.

"That's not answering my question," retorted Florimel.

"Well, the second thing I would do," said Malcolm, thoughtfully, and pausing a moment, "would be to get Mr Graham to go with me to Aberdeen, and carry me through the classes there. Of course, I wouldn't compete for prizes; that wouldn't be fair to them that couldn't afford a tutor at their lodgings."

"But it's the *first* thing you would do that I want to know," persisted the girl.

"I told you I would sit down and think about it."

"I don't count that *doing* anything."

"Indeed, my lady! thinking's the hardest work I know."

"Well, what is it you would think about first?" said Florimel—not to be diverted from her course.

"Oh, the third thing I would do–"

"I want to know the first thing you would think about."

"I canna say yet what the third thing wad be. Fower year at the college wad gie me time to reflec upon a hantle o' things."

"I insist on knowing the first thing you would think about doing," cried Florimel, with mock imperiousness, but real tyranny.

"Weel, my leddy, gien ye wull hae 't—but hoo great a man wad ye be makin' o' me?"

"Oh!—let me see;—yes—yes—the heir to an earldom.—That's liberal enough—is it not?"

"That's as muckle as say I wad come to be a yerl some day, sae be I didna dee upo' the ro'd?"

"Yes—that's what it means."

"An' a yerl's neist door till a markis—isna he?"

"Yes—he's in the next lower rank."

"Lower?—Ay!—No that muckle, maybe?"

"No," said Lady Florimel consequentially; "the difference is not so great as to prevent their meeting on a level of courtesy."

"I dinna freely ken what that means; but gien 't be yer leddyship's wull to mak a yerl o' me, I'm no to raise ony objections."

He uttered it definitively, and stood silent.

"Well?" said the girl.

"What's yer wull, my leddy?" returned Malcolm, as if roused from a reverie.

"Where's your answer?"

"I said I wad be a yerl to please yer leddyship.—I wad be a flunky for the same rizzon, gien 't was to wait upo' yersel' an' nae ither."

"I ask you," said Florimel, more imperiously than ever, "what is the first thing you would do, if you found yourself no longer a fisherman, but the son of an earl?"

"I can't say yet what the third thing would be. Four years at the college would give me time to consider many things."

"I insist on knowing the first thing you would think about doing," cried Florimel, with mock imperiousness, but real tyranny.

"Well, my lady, if you will have it—but how great a man would you be making of me?"

"Oh!—let me see;—yes—yes—the heir to an earldom.—That's liberal enough—is it not?"

"That's as much as to say I'd become an earl some day, provided I lived so long?"

"Yes—that's what it means."

"And an earl's next door to a marquis—isn't he?"

"Yes—he's in the next lower rank."

"Lower?—Ay!—Not by much, maybe?"

"No," said Lady Florimel consequentially; "the difference is not so great as to prevent their meeting on a level of courtesy."

"I don't exactly know what that means; but if it be your ladyship's will to make an earl of me, I won't raise any objections."

He uttered it definitively, and stood silent.

"Well?" said the girl.

"What's your will, my lady?" returned Malcolm, as if roused from a reverie.

"Where's your answer?"

"I said I would be an earl to please your ladyship.—I would be a flunky for the same reason, if it was to wait upon yourself and no other."

"I ask you," said Florimel, more imperiously than ever, "what is the first thing you would do, if you found yourself no longer a fisherman, but the son of an earl?"

"But it maun be that I *was* a fisherman—to the en' o' a' creation, my leddy."

"You refuse to answer my question?"

"By no means, my leddy, gien ye wull hae an answer."

"I *will* have an answer."

"Gien ye wull hae 't than—But—"

"No *buts*, but an answer!"

"Weel—it's yer ain wyte, my leddy!—I wad jist gang doon upo' my k-nees, whaur I stude afore ye, and tell ye a heap o' things 'at maybe by that time ye wad ken weel eneuch a'ready."

"What would you tell me?"

"I wad tell ye 'at yer een war like the verra leme o' the levin itsel'; yer cheek like a white rose i' the licht frae a reid ane; yer hair jist the saft lattin' gang o' his han's whan the Maker cud du nae mair; yer mou' jist fashioned to drive fowk daft 'at daurna come nearer nor luik at it; an' for yer shape, it was like naething in natur' but itsel'.—Ye *wad* hae't my leddy!" he added apologetically—and well he might, for Lady Florimel's cheek had flushed, and her eye had been darting fire long before he got to the end of his Celtic outpouring. Whether she was really angry or not, she had no difficulty in making Malcolm believe she was. She rose from her chair—though not until he had ended—swept halfway to the door, then turned upon him with a flash.

"How *dare* you?" she said, her breed well obeying the call of the game.

"I'm verra sorry, my leddy," faltered Malcolm, trying to steady himself against a strange trembling that had laid hold upon him, "—but ye maun alloo it was a' yer ain wyte."

"Do you dare to say *I* encouraged you to talk such stuff to me?"

"But it must be that I *was* a fisherman—to the end of all creation, my lady."

"You refuse to answer my question?"

"By no means, my lady, if you will have an answer."

"I *will* have an answer."

"If you will have it then—But—"

"No *buts*, but an answer!"

"Well—it's your own fault, my lady!—I would just go down upon my knees, where I stood before you, and tell you a heap of things that maybe by that time you would know well enough already."

"What would you tell me?"

"I would tell you that your eyes were like the very lightning itself for brightness; your cheek like a white rose in the light from a red one; your hair just like the soft dropping of his hands when the Maker could do no more; your mouth just fashioned to drive folk daft that daren't come nearer than look at it; and for your shape, it was like nothing in nature but itself.—You *would* have it, my lady!" he added apologetically—and well he might, for Lady Florimel's cheek had flushed, and her eye had been darting fire long before he got to the end of his Celtic outpouring. Whether she was really angry or not, she had no difficulty in making Malcolm believe she was. She rose from her chair—though not until he had ended—swept halfway to the door, then turned upon him with a flash.

"How *dare* you?" she said, her breed well obeying the call of the game.

"I'm very sorry, my lady," faltered Malcolm, trying to steady himself against a strange trembling that had laid hold upon him, "—but you must allow it was all your own fault."

"Do you dare to say *I* encouraged you to talk such stuff to me?"

"Ye did gar me, my leddy."

Florimel turned and undulated from the room, leaving the poor fellow like a statue in the middle of it, with the books all turning their backs upon him.

"Noo," he said to himself, "she's aff to tell her father, and there'll be a bonny bane to pyke atween him an' me! But haith! I'll jist tell him the trowth o' 't, an' syne he can mak a kirk an' a mill o' 't, gien he likes."

"You did make me, my lady."

Florimel turned and undulated from the room, leaving the poor fellow like a statue in the middle of it, with the books all turning their backs upon him.

"Now," he said to himself, "she's off to tell her father, and there'll be a bonny bone to pick between him and me! But faith! I'll just tell him the truth of it, and then he can make a church and a mill of it, if he likes."

With this resolution he stood his ground, every moment expecting the wrathful father to make his appearance and at the least order him out of the house. But minute passed after minute, and no wrathful father came. He grew calmer by degrees, and at length began to peep at the titles of the books.

When the great bell rang for lunch, he was embalmed rather than buried in one of Milton's prose volumes—standing before the shelf on which he had found it—the very incarnation of study.

My reader may well judge that Malcolm could not have been very far gone in love, seeing he was thus able to read. I remark in return that it was not merely the distance between him and Lady Florimel that had hitherto preserved his being from absorption and his will from annihilation, but also the strength of his common sense, and the force of his individuality.

CHAPTER XXXIV

MILTON, AND THE BAY MARE

For some days Malcolm saw nothing more of Lady Florimel; but with his grandfather's new dwelling to see to, the carpenter's shop and the blacksmith's forge open to him, and an eye to detect whatever wanted setting right, the hours did not hang heavy on his hands. At length, whether it was that she thought she had punished him sufficiently for an offence for which she was herself only to blame, or that she had indeed never been offended at all and had only been keeping up her one-sided game, she began again to indulge the interest she could not help feeling in him, an interest heightened by the mystery which hung over his birth, and by the fact that she knew that concerning him of which he was himself ignorant. At the same time, as I have already said, she had no little need of an escape from the *ennui* which, now that the novelty of a country life had worn off, did more than occasionally threaten her. She began again to seek his company under the guise of his help, half requesting, half commanding his services; and Malcolm found himself admitted afresh to the heaven of her favour. Young as he was, he read himself a lesson suitable to the occasion.

One afternoon the marquis sent for him to the library, but when he reached it his master was not yet there. He took down the volume of Milton in which he had been reading before, and was soon absorbed in it again.

"Faith! it 's a big shame," he cried at length almost unconsciously, and closed the book with a slam.

"What is a big shame?" said the voice of the marquis close behind him.

Malcolm started, and almost dropped the volume.

"I beg yer lordship's pardon," he said; "I didna hear ye come in."

"What is the book you were reading?" asked the marquis.

"Faith! it 's a big shame," he cried at length almost unconsciously, and closed the book with a slam.

"What is a big shame?" said the voice of the marquis close behind him.

Malcolm started, and almost dropped the volume.

"I beg your lordship's pardon," he said; "I didn't hear you come in."

"What is the book you were reading?" asked the marquis.

"I was jist readin' a bit o' Milton's Eikonoklastes," answered Malcolm, "—a buik I hae hard tell o', but never saw wi' my ain een afore."

"And what's your quarrel with it?" asked his lordship.

"I canna mak oot what sud set a great man like Milton sae sair agane a puir cratur like Cherles."

"Read the history, and you'll see."

"Ow! I ken something aboot the politics o' the time, an' I'm no sayin' they war that wrang to tak the heid frae him, but what for sud Milton hate the man efter the king was deid?"

"Because he didn't think the king dead enough, I suppose."

"I see!—an' they war settin' him up for a saint. Still he had a richt to fair play.—Jist hearken, my lord."

So saying, Malcolm reopened the volume, and read the well-known passage, in the first chapter, in which Milton censures the king as guilty of utter irreverence, because of his adoption of the prayer of Pamela in the Arcadia.

"Noo, my lord," he said, half closing the book, "what wad ye expec' to come upo', efter sic a denunciation as that, but some awfu' haithenish thing? Weel, jist hearken again, for here's the verra prayer itsel' in a futnote."

His lordship had thrown himself into a chair, had crossed one leg over the other, and was now stroking its knee.

"Noo, my lord," said Malcolm again, as he concluded, "what think ye o' the jeedgment passed?"

"Really I have no opinion to give about it," answered the marquis. "I'm no theologian. I see no harm in the prayer."

"I was just reading a bit of Milton's Eikonoklastes," answered Malcolm, "—a book I know by name, but never saw with my own eyes before."

"And what's your quarrel with it?" asked his lordship.

"I can't make out what should set a great man like Milton so much against a poor soul like Charles."

"Read the history, and you'll see."

"Oh! I know something about the politics of the time, and I'm not saying they were that wrong to take his head from him, but why should Milton hate the man after the king was dead?"

"Because he didn't think the king dead enough, I suppose."

"I see!—and they were setting him up for a saint. Still he had a right to fair play.—Just listen, my lord."

So saying, Malcolm reopened the volume, and read the well-known passage, in the first chapter, in which Milton censures the king as guilty of utter irreverence, because of his adoption of the prayer of Pamela in the Arcadia.

"Now, my lord," he said, half closing the book, "what would you expect to come upon, after such a denunciation as that, but some awful heathenish thing? Well, just listen again, for here's the very prayer itself in a footnote."

His lordship had thrown himself into a chair, had crossed one leg over the other, and was now stroking its knee.

"Now, my lord," said Malcolm again, as he concluded, "what do you make of the judgement passed?"

"Really I have no opinion to give about it," answered the marquis. "I'm no theologian. I see no harm in the prayer."

"Hairm in 't, my lord! It's perfetly gran'! It's sic a prayer as cudna weel be aiqualt. It vexes me to the verra hert o' my sowl that a michty man like Milton—ane whase bein' was a crood o' hermonies—sud ca' that the prayer o' a haithen wuman till a haithen God. 'O all-seein' Licht, an' eternal Life o' a' things!'—Ca's he that a haithen God?—or her 'at prayed sic a prayer a haithen wuman?"

"Well, well," said the marquis, "I don't want it all over again. I see nothing to find fault with, myself, but I don't take much interest in that sort of thing."

"There's a wee bitty o' Laitin, here i' the note, 'at I canna freely mak oot," said Malcolm, approaching Lord Lossie with his finger on the passage, never doubting that the owner of such a library must be able to read Latin perfectly: Mr Graham would have put him right at once, and *his* books would have been lost in one of the window-corners of this huge place. But his lordship waved him back.

"I can't be your tutor," he said, not unkindly. "My Latin is far too rusty for use."

The fact was that his lordship had never got beyond Maturin Cordier's Colloquies.

"Besides," he went on, "I want you to do something for me."

Malcolm instantly replaced the book on its shelf, and approached his master, saying—

"Wull yer lordship lat me read whiles, i' this gran' place? I mean when I'm no wantit ither gaits, an' there's naebody here."

"To be sure," answered the marquis; "—only the scholar mustn't come with the skipper's hands."

"Harm in it, my lord! It's perfectly grand! It's such a prayer as could hardly be equalled. It vexes me to the very heart of my soul that a mighty man like Milton—one whose being was a crowd of harmonies—should call that the prayer of a heathen woman to a heathen God. 'O all-seeing Light, and eternal Life of all things!'—Calls he that a heathen God?—or she that prayed such a prayer a heathen woman?"

"Well, well," said the marquis, "I don't want it all over again. I see nothing to find fault with, myself, but I don't take much interest in that sort of thing."

"There's a wee bit of Latin, here in the note, that I can't quite make out," said Malcolm, approaching Lord Lossie with his finger on the passage, never doubting that the owner of such a library must be able to read Latin perfectly: Mr Graham would have put him right at once, and *his* books would have been lost in one of the window-corners of this huge place. But his lordship waved him back.

"I can't be your tutor," he said, not unkindly. "My Latin is far too rusty for use."

The fact was that his lordship had never got beyond Maturin Cordier's Colloquies.

"Besides," he went on, "I want you to do something for me."

Malcolm instantly replaced the book on its shelf, and approached his master, saying—

"Will your lordship let me read here sometimes, in this grand place? I mean when I'm not wanted elsewhere, and the room is empty?"

"To be sure," answered the marquis; "—only the scholar mustn't come with the skipper's hands."

"I s' tak guid care o' that, my lord. I wad as sune think o' han'lin' a book wi' wark-like han's as I wad o' branderin' a mackeral ohn cleaned it oot."

"I'll take good care of that, my lord. I would as soon think of handling a book with work-like hands as I would of grilling a mackerel I hadn't gutted."

"And when we have visitors, you'll be careful not to get in their way."

"And when we have visitors, you'll be careful not to get in their way."

"I wull that, my lord."

"I will that, my lord."

"And now," said his lordship rising, "I want you to take a letter to Mrs Stewart of Kirkbyres.—Can you ride?"

"And now," said his lordship rising, "I want you to take a letter to Mrs Stewart of Kirkbyres.—Can you ride?"

"I can ride the bare back weel eneuch for a fisher-loon," said Malcolm; "but I never was upon a saiddle i' my life."

"I can ride bare back well enough for a fisher-lad," said Malcolm; "but I never was upon a saddle in my life."

"The sooner you get used to one the better. Go and tell Stoat to saddle the bay mare. Wait in the yard: I will bring the letter out to you myself."

"The sooner you get used to one the better. Go and tell Stoat to saddle the bay mare. Wait in the yard: I will bring the letter out to you myself."

"Verra weel, my lord!" said Malcolm. He knew, from sundry remarks he had heard about the stables, that the mare in question was a ticklish one to ride, but would rather have his neck broken than object.

"Very well, my lord!" said Malcolm. He knew, from sundry remarks he had heard about the stables, that the mare in question was a ticklish one to ride, but would rather have his neck broken than object.

Hardly was she ready, when the marquis appeared, accompanied by Lady Florimel—both expecting to enjoy a laugh at Malcolm's expense. But when the mare was brought out, and he was going to mount her where she stood, something seemed to wake in the marquis's heart, or conscience, or wherever the pigmy Duty slept that occupied the all but sinecure of his moral economy: he looked at Malcolm for a moment, then at the ears of the mare hugging her neck, and last at the stones of the paved yard.

"Lead her on to the turf, Stoat," he said.

The groom obeyed, all followed, and Malcolm mounted. The same instant he lay on his back on the grass, amidst a general laugh, loud on the part of marquis and lady, and subdued on that of the servants. But the next he was on his feet, and, the groom still holding the mare, in the saddle again: a little anger is a fine spur for the side of even an honest intent. This time he sat for half a minute, and then found himself once more on the grass. It was but once more: his mother earth had claimed him again only to complete his strength. A third time he mounted—and sat. As soon as she perceived it would be hard work to unseat him, the mare was quiet.

"Bravo!" cried the marquis, giving him the letter.

"Will there be an answer, my lord?"

"Wait and see."

<table>
<tr>
<td>

"I s' gar you pey for't, gien we come upon a broon rig atween this an' Kirkbyres," said Malcolm, addressing the mare, and rode away.

</td>
<td>

"I shall make you pay for it, if we come upon a brown ridge between here and Kirkbyres," said Malcolm, addressing the mare, and rode away.

</td>
</tr>
</table>

Both the marquis and Lady Florimel, whose laughter had altogether ceased in the interest of watching the struggle, stood looking after him with a pleased expression, which, as he vanished up the glen, changed to a mutual glance and smile.

"He's got good blood in him, however he came by it," said the marquis. "The country is more indebted to its nobility than is generally understood."

Otherwise indebted at least than Lady Florimel could gather from her father's remark!

CHAPTER XXXV

KIRKBYRES

Malcolm felt considerably refreshed after his tussle with the mare and his victory over her, and much enjoyed his ride of ten miles. It was a cool autumn afternoon. A few of the fields were being reaped, one or two were crowded with stooks, while many crops of oats yet waved and rustled in various stages of vanishing green. On all sides kine were lowing; overhead rooks were cawing; the sun was nearing the west, and in the hollows a thin mist came steaming up. Malcolm had never in his life been so far from the coast before: his road led southwards into the heart of the country.

The father of the late proprietor of Kirkbyres had married the heiress of Gersefell, an estate which *marched* with his own, and was double its size, whence the lairdship was sometimes spoken of by the one name, sometimes by the other. The combined properties thus inherited by the late Mr Stewart were of sufficient extent to justify him, although a plain man, in becoming a suitor for the hand of the beautiful daughter of a needy baronet in the neighbourhood—with the already somewhat tarnished condition of whose reputation, having come into little contact with the world in which she moved, he was unacquainted. Quite unexpectedly she also, some years after their marriage, brought him a property of considerable extent, a fact which doubtless had its share in the birth and nourishment of her consuming desire to get the estates into her own management.

Towards the end of his journey, Malcolm came upon a bare moorland waste, on the long ascent of a low hill,—very desolate, with not a tree or house within sight for two miles. A ditch, half full of dark water, bordered each side of the road, which went straight as a rod through a black peat moss lying cheerless and dreary on all sides—hardly less so where the sun gleamed from the surface of some stagnant pool filling a hole whence peats had been dug, or where a patch of cotton-grass waved white and lonely in the midst of the waste expanse. At length, when he reached the top of the ridge, he saw the house of Kirkbyres below him; and, with a small modern lodge near by, a wooden gate showed the entrance to its grounds. Between the gate and the house he passed through a young plantation of larches and other firs for a quarter of a mile, and so came to an old wall with an iron gate in the middle of it, within which the old house, a gaunt meagre building—a bare house in fact, relieved only by four small turrets or bartizans, one at each corner—lifted its grey walls, pointed gables, and steep roof high into the pale blue air. He rode round the outer wall, seeking a back entrance, and arrived at a farm yard, where a boy took his horse. Finding the kitchen door open, he entered, and having delivered his letter to a servant girl, sat down to wait the possible answer.

In a few minutes she returned and requested him to follow her. This was more than he had calculated upon, but he obeyed at once. The girl led him along a dark passage, and up a winding stone-stair, much worn, to a room richly furnished, and older-fashioned, he thought, than any room he had yet seen in Lossie House.

On a settee, with her back to a window, sat Mrs Stewart, a lady tall and slender, with well-poised, easy carriage, and a motion that might have suggested the lithe grace of a leopard. She greeted him with a bend of the head and a smile, which, even in the twilight and her own shadow, showed a gleam of ivory, and spoke to him in a hard sweet voice, wherein an ear more experienced than Malcolm's might have detected an accustomed intent to please. Although he knew nothing of the so-called world, and hence could recognize neither the Parisian air of her dress nor the indications of familiarity with fashionable life prominent enough in her bearing, he yet could not fail to be at least aware of the contrast between her appearance and her surroundings. Yet less could the far stronger contrast escape him, between the picture in his own mind of the mother of the mad laird, and the woman before him; he could not by any effort cause the two to coalesce.

"You have had a long ride, Mr MacPhail," she said; "you must be tired."

"What wad tire me, mem?" returned Malcolm. "It's a fine caller evenin', an' I hed ane o' the marquis's best mears to carry me."

"You'll take a glass of wine, anyhow," said Mrs Stewart. "Will you oblige me by ringing the bell?"

"No, I thank ye, mem. The mear wad be better o' a mou'fu' o' meal an' watter, but I want naething mysel'."

A shadow passed over the lady's face. She rose and rang the bell, then sat in silence until it was answered.

"Bring the wine and cake," she said, then turned to Malcolm. "Your master speaks very kindly of you. He seems to trust you thoroughly."

"I'm verra glaid to hear 't, mem; but he has never had muckle cause to trust or distrust me yet."

"You have had a long ride, Mr MacPhail," she said; "you must be tired."

"What would tire me, ma'am?" returned Malcolm. "It's a fine fresh evening, and I had one of the marquis's best mares to carry me."

"You'll take a glass of wine, anyhow," said Mrs Stewart. "Will you oblige me by ringing the bell?"

"No, I thank you ma'am. The mare would be the better for a mouthful of meal and water, but I want nothing myself."

A shadow passed over the lady's face. She rose and rang the bell, then sat in silence until it was answered.

"Bring the wine and cake," she said, then turned to Malcolm. "Your master speaks very kindly of you. He seems to trust you thoroughly."

"I'm very glad to hear it, ma'am; but he has never had much cause to trust or distrust me yet."

"He seems even to think that *I* might place equal confidence in you."

"I dinna ken. I wadna hae ye lippen to me owre muckle," said Malcolm.

"You do not mean to contradict the good character your master gives you?" said the lady, with a smile and a look right into his eyes.

"I wadna hae ye lippen till me afore ye had my word," said Malcolm.

"I may use my own judgment about that," she replied, with another winning smile. "But oblige me by taking a glass of wine."

She rose and approached the decanters.

"'Deed no, mem! I'm no used till 't, an' it micht jummle *my* jeedgement," said Malcolm, who had placed himself on the defensive from the first, jealous of his own conduct as being the friend of the laird.

At his second refusal the cloud again crossed the lady's brow, but her smile did not vanish. Pressing her hospitality no more, she resumed her seat.

"My lord tells me," she said, folding a pair of lovely hands on her lap, "that you see my poor unhappy boy sometimes."

"No sae dooms unhappy, mem!" said Malcolm; but she went on without heeding the remark.

"And that you rescued him not long ago from the hands of ruffians."

Malcolm made no reply.

"Everybody knows," she continued, after a slight pause, "what an unhappy mother I am. It is many years since I lost the loveliest infant ever seen, while my poor Stephen was left to be the mockery of every urchin in the street!"

"He seems even to think that *I* might place equal confidence in you."

"I don't know. I wouldn't have you trust me too far," said Malcolm.

"You do not mean to contradict the good character your master gives you?" said the lady, with a smile and a look right into his eyes.

"I wouldn't have you trust to me before you had my word," said Malcolm.

"I may use my own judgment about that," she replied, with another winning smile. "But oblige me by taking a glass of wine."

She rose and approached the decanters.

"No indeed, ma'am! I'm not used to it, and it might jumble *my* judgement," said Malcolm, who had placed himself on the defensive from the first, jealous of his own conduct as being the friend of the laird.

At his second refusal the cloud again crossed the lady's brow, but her smile did not vanish. Pressing her hospitality no more, she resumed her seat.

"My lord tells me," she said, folding a pair of lovely hands on her lap, "that you see my poor unhappy boy sometimes."

"Not so very unhappy, ma'am!" said Malcolm; but she went on without heeding the remark.

"And that you rescued him not long ago from the hands of ruffians."

Malcolm made no reply.

"Everybody knows," she continued, after a slight pause, "what an unhappy mother I am. It is many years since I lost the loveliest infant ever seen, while my poor Stephen was left to be the mockery of every urchin in the street!"

She sighed deeply, and one of the fair hands took a hand kerchief from a work-table near.

"No in Portlossie, mem," said Malcolm. "There's verra feow o' them so hard-hertit or so ill-mainnert. They're used to seein' him at the schuil, whaur he shaws himsel' whiles; an' he's a great favourite wi' them, for he's ane o' the best craturs livin'."

"A poor, witless, unmanageable being! He's a dreadful grief to me," said the widowed mother, with a deep sigh.

"A bairn could manage him," said Malcolm in strong contradiction.

"Oh, if I could but convince him of my love! but he won't give me a chance. He has an unaccountable dread of me, which makes him as well as me wretched. It is a delusion which no argument can overcome, and seems indeed an essential part of his sad affliction. The more care and kindness he needs, the less will he accept at my hands. I long to devote my life to him, and he will not allow me. I should be but too happy to nurse him day and night. Ah, Mr MacPhail, you little know a mother's heart! Even if my beautiful boy had not been taken from me, Stephen would still have been my idol, idiot as he is—and will be as long as he lives. And—"

"He's nae idiot, mem," interposed Malcolm.

"And just imagine," she went on, "what a misery it must be to a widowed mother, poor companion as he would be at the best, to think of her boy roaming the country like a beggar! sleeping she doesn't know where! eating wretched food! and—"

She sighed deeply, and one of the fair hands took a hand kerchief from a work-table near.

"Not in Portlossie, ma'am," said Malcolm. "There's very few of them so hard-hearted or so ill-mannered. They're used to seeing him at the school, where he shows himself sometimes; and he's a great favourite with them, for he's one of the best creatures living."

"A poor, witless, unmanageable being! He's a dreadful grief to me," said the widowed mother, with a deep sigh.

"A child could manage him," said Malcolm in strong contradiction.

"Oh, if I could but convince him of my love! but he won't give me a chance. He has an unaccountable dread of me, which makes him as well as me wretched. It is a delusion which no argument can overcome, and seems indeed an essential part of his sad affliction. The more care and kindness he needs, the less will he accept at my hands. I long to devote my life to him, and he will not allow me. I should be but too happy to nurse him day and night. Ah, Mr MacPhail, you little know a mother's heart! Even if my beautiful boy had not been taken from me, Stephen would still have been my idol, idiot as he is—and will be as long as he lives. And—"

"He's no idiot, ma'am," interposed Malcolm.

"And just imagine," she went on, "what a misery it must be to a widowed mother, poor companion as he would be at the best, to think of her boy roaming the country like a beggar! sleeping she doesn't know where! eating wretched food! and—"

"Guid parritch an' milk, an' brose an' butter," said Malcolm parenthetically; "—whiles herrin' an' yallow haddies."

"Good porridge and milk, and brose and butter," said Malcolm parenthetically; "—sometimes herring and yellow haddocks."

"It's enough to break a mother's heart! If I could but persuade him to come home for a week so as to have a chance with him! But it's no use trying: ill-disposed people have made mischief between us, telling wicked lies, and terrifying the poor fellow almost to death. It is quite impossible except I get some one to help me—and there are so few who have any influence with him!"

"It's enough to break a mother's heart! If I could but persuade him to come home for a week so as to have a chance with him! But it's no use trying: ill-disposed people have made mischief between us, telling wicked lies, and terrifying the poor fellow almost to death. It is quite impossible except I get some one to help me—and there are so few who have any influence with him!"

Malcolm thought she must surely have had chances enough before he ran away from her; but he could not help feeling softened towards her.

Malcolm thought she must surely have had chances enough before he ran away from her; but he could not help feeling softened towards her.

"Supposin' I was to get ye speech o' 'im, mem?" he said.

"Supposing I were to arrange a meeting with him, ma'am?" he said.

"That would not be of the slightest use. He is so prejudiced against me, he would only shriek, and go into one of those horrible fits."

"That would not be of the slightest use. He is so prejudiced against me, he would only shriek, and go into one of those horrible fits."

"I dinna see what's to be dune than," said Malcolm.

"I don't see what's to be done then," said Malcolm.

"I must have him brought here—there is no other way."

"I must have him brought here—there is no other way."

"An' whaur wad be the guid o' that, mem? By yer ain shawin', he wad rin oot o' 's verra body to win awa' frae ye."

"And where would be the good of that, ma'am? By your own showing, he would run out of his very body to get away from you."

"I did not mean by force," returned Mrs Stewart. "Some one he has confidence in must come with him. Nothing else will give me a chance. He would trust you now; your presence would keep him from being terrified—at his own mother, alas! through you he would learn to trust me; and if a course of absolute indulgence did not bring him to live like other people—that of course is impossible —it might at least induce him to live at home, and cease to be a byword to the neighbourhood."

Her tone was so refined, and her voice so pleading; her sorrow was so gentle; and she looked, in the dimness, to Malcolm's imagination at least, so young and handsome, that the strong castle of his prejudices was swaying as if built on reeds; and had it not been that he was already the partizan of her son, and therefore in honour bound to give *him* the benefit of every doubt, he would certainly have been gained over to work her will. He *knew* absolutely nothing against her—not even that she was the person he had seen in Mrs Catanach's company in the garret of Lossie House. But he steeled himself to distrust her, and held his peace.

"It is clear," she resumed after a pause, "that the intervention of some friend of both is the only thing that can be of the smallest use. I know you are a friend of his—a true one, and I do not see why you should not be a friend of mine as well—Will you be my friend too?"

She rose as she said the words, and approaching him, bent on him out of the shadow the full strength of eyes whose light had not yet begun to pale before the dawn we call death, and held out a white hand glimmering in the dusk: she knew only too well the power of a still fine woman of any age over a youth of twenty.

Malcolm, knowing nothing about it, yet felt hers, and was on his guard. He rose also, but did not take her hand.

"I have had only too much reason," she added, "to distrust some who, unlike you, professed themselves eager to serve me; but I know neither Lord Lossie nor you will play me false."

She took his great rough hand between her two soft palms, and for one moment Malcolm was tempted—not to betray his friend, but to simulate a yielding sympathy, in order to come at the heart of her intent, and should it prove false, to foil it the more easily. But the honest nature of him shrunk from deception, even where the object of it was good: he was not at liberty to use falsehood for the discomfiture of the false even; a pretended friendship was of the vilest of despicable things, and the more holy the end, the less fit to be used for the compassing of it—least of all in the cause of a true friendship.

"I canna help ye, mem," he said; "I daurna. I hae sic a regaird for yer son 'at afore I wad du onything to hairm him, I wad hae my twa han's chappit frae the shackle bane."

"Surely, my dear Mr MacPhail," returned the lady in her most persuasive tones, and with her sweetest smile, "you cannot call it harming a poor idiot to restore him to the care of his own mother!"

"That's as it turnt oot," rejoined Malcolm. "But I'm sure o' ae thing, mem, an' that is, 'at he's no sae muckle o' an eediot as some fowk wad hae him."

Mrs Stewart's face fell, she turned from him, and going back to her seat hid her face in her handkerchief.

"I can't help you, ma'am," he said; "I daren't. I have such a regard for your son that before I would do anything to harm him, I would have my two hands chopped off at the wrist."

"Surely, my dear Mr MacPhail," returned the lady in her most persuasive tones, and with her sweetest smile, "you cannot call it harming a poor idiot to restore him to the care of his own mother!"

"That's yet to be seen," rejoined Malcolm. "But I'm sure of one thing, ma'am, and that is, that he's not so much of an idiot as some folk would have him."

Mrs Stewart's face fell, she turned from him, and going back to her seat hid her face in her handkerchief.

"I'm afraid," she said sadly, after a moment, "I must give up my last hope: you are not disposed to be friendly to me, Mr MacPhail; you too have been believing hard things of me."

"That's true; but no frae hearsay alane," returned Malcolm. "The luik o' the puir fallow whan he but hears the chance word *mither*, 's a sicht no to be forgotten. He grips his lugs atween 's twa han's, an' rins like a colley wi' a pan at 's tail. That couldna come o' naething."

Mrs Stewart hid her face on the cushioned arm of the settee, and sobbed. A moment after she sat erect again, but languid and red-eyed, saying, as if with sudden resolve:

"I will tell you all I know about it, and then you can judge for yourself. When he was a very small child, I took him for advice to the best physicians in London and Paris: all advised a certain operation which had to be performed for consecutive months, at intervals of a few days. Though painful it was simple, yet of such a nature that no one was so fit to attend to it as his mother. Alas! instead of doing him any good, it has done me the worst injury in the world: my child hates me!"

Again she hid her face on the settee.

The explanation was plausible enough, and the grief of the mother surely apparent! Malcolm could not but be touched.

"It's no 'at I'm no willin' to be your freen', mem; but I'm yer son's freen' a'ready, an' gien he war to hear onything 'at gart him mislippen till me, it wad gang to my hert."

"Then you can judge what I feel!" said the lady.

"I'm afraid," she said sadly, after a moment, "I must give up my last hope: you are not disposed to be friendly to me, Mr MacPhail; you too have been believing hard things of me."

"That's true; but not from hearsay alone," returned Malcolm. "The look of the poor fellow when he but hears the chance word *mother*, is a sight not to be forgotten. He grips his ears between his two hands, and runs like a colley with a pan at his tail. That couldn't come of nothing."

Mrs Stewart hid her face on the cushioned arm of the settee, and sobbed. A moment after she sat erect again, but languid and red-eyed, saying, as if with sudden resolve:

"I will tell you all I know about it, and then you can judge for yourself. When he was a very small child, I took him for advice to the best physicians in London and Paris: all advised a certain operation which had to be performed for consecutive months, at intervals of a few days. Though painful it was simple, yet of such a nature that no one was so fit to attend to it as his mother. Alas! instead of doing him any good, it has done me the worst injury in the world: my child hates me!"

Again she hid her face on the settee.

The explanation was plausible enough, and the grief of the mother surely apparent! Malcolm could not but be touched.

"It's not that I'm unwilling to be your friend, ma'am; but I'm your son's friend already, and if he were to hear anything that made him mistrust me, it would go to my heart."

"Then you can judge what I feel!" said the lady.

"Gien it wad hale your hert to hurt mine, I wad think aboot it, mem; but gien it hurtit a' three o' 's, and did guid to nane, it wad be a misfit a'thegither. I'll du naething till I'm doonricht sure it 's the pairt o' a freen'."

"That's just what makes you the only fit person to help me that I know. If I were to employ people in the affair, they might be rough with the poor fellow."

"Like eneuch, mem," assented Malcolm, while the words put him afresh on his guard.

"But I might be driven to it," she added.

Malcolm responded with an unuttered vow.

"It might become necessary to use force—whereas you could lead him with a word."

"Na; I'm naither sic witch nor sic traitor."

"Where would be the treachery when you knew it would be for his good?"

"That's jist what I dinna ken, mem," retorted Malcolm. "Luik ye here, mem," he continued, rousing himself to venture an appeal to the mother's heart; "—here's a man it has pleased God to mak no freely like ither fowk. His min' though cawpable a hantle mair nor a body wad think 'at didna ken him sae weel as I du, is certainly weyk—though maybe the weykness lies mair i' the tongue than i' the brain o' 'im efter a'—an' he's been sair frichtit wi' some guideship or ither; the upshot o 't a' bein', 'at he's unco timoursome, and ready to bursten himsel' rinnin' whan there's nane pursuin'. But he's the gentlest o' craturs—a doonricht gentleman, mem, gien ever there was ane—an' that kin'ly wi' a' cratur, baith man an' beast! A verra bairn cud guide him—ony gait but ane."

"If it would heal your heart to hurt mine, I would think about it, ma'am; but if it hurt all three of us, and did good to none, it would be a misfit altogether. I'll do nothing till I'm downright sure it's the part of a friend."

"That's just what makes you the only fit person to help me that I know. If I were to employ people in the affair, they might be rough with the poor fellow."

"Like enough, ma'am," assented Malcolm, while the words put him afresh on his guard.

"But I might be driven to it," she added.

Malcolm responded with an unuttered vow.

"It might become necessary to use force—whereas you could lead him with a word."

"Na; I'm neither such witch nor such traitor."

"Where would be the treachery when you knew it would be for his good?"

"That's just what I don't know, ma'am," retorted Malcolm. "See here, ma'am," he continued, rousing himself to venture an appeal to the mother's heart; "—here's a man it has pleased God to make differently from other folk. His mind, though a sight more capable than folk would think that didn't know him as I do, is certainly weak—though maybe the weakness lies more in his tongue than in his brain after all—and he's been frightened to death by some ill usage or other; the upshot of it all being, that he's very timorous, and ready to burst himself running when there's none pursuing. But he's the gentlest of souls—a downright gentleman, ma'am, if ever there was one—and that kindly with all creatures, both man and beast! A very child could lead him—any place but one."

"Anywhere but to his mother!" exclaimed Mrs Stewart, pressing her handkerchief to her eyes, and sobbed as she spoke. "There is a child he is very fond of, I am told," she added, recovering herself.

"He likes a' bairns," returned Malcolm, "an' they're maistly a' freen'ly wi' him. But there's but jist ae thing 'at maks life endurable till 'im. He suffers a hantle wi' that puir back o' his, an' wi' his breath tu whan he's frichtit, for his hert gangs loupin like a sawmon in a bag net. An' he suffers a hantle, forbye, in his puir feeble min tryin' to unnerstan' the guid things 'at fowk tells him, an' jaloosin' it 's his ain wyte 'at he disna unnerstan' them better; an' whiles he thinks himsel' the child o' sin and wrath, an' that Sawtan has some special propriety in him, as the carritchis says—"

"But," interrupted the lady hurriedly, "you were going to tell me the one comfort he has."

"It's his leeberty, mem—jist his leeberty; to gang whaur he lists like the win'; to turn his face whaur he wull i' the mornin', an' back again at nicht gien he likes; to wan'er—"

"Back *where?*" interrupted the mother, a little too eagerly.

"Whaur he likes, mem—I cudna say whaur wi' ony certainty. But aih! he likes to hear the sea moanin', an' watch the stars sheenin'!—There's a sicht o' oondevelopit releegion in him, as Maister Graham says; an' I div *not* believe 'at the Lord 'll see him wranged mair nor 's for 's guid. But it 's my belief, gien ye took the leeberty frae the puir cratur, ye wad kill him."

"Anywhere but to his mother!" exclaimed Mrs Stewart, pressing her handkerchief to her eyes, and sobbed as she spoke. "There is a child he is very fond of, I am told," she added, recovering herself.

"He likes all children," returned Malcolm, "and most of them are friendly with him. But there's just one thing that makes life worth living to him. He suffers a lot with his poor back, and with his breath too when he's frightened, for his heart goes leaping like a salmon in a bag net. And he suffers much, besides, in his poor feeble mind trying to understand the good things that folk tell him, and suspecting it's his own fault that he doesn't understand them better; and sometimes thinks himself the child of sin and wrath, and that Satan has some special property in him, as it says in the catechism—"

"But," interrupted the lady hurriedly, "you were going to tell me the one comfort he has."

"It's his liberty, ma'am—just his liberty; to go where he pleases like the wind; to turn his face where he will in the morning, and back again at night if he likes; to wander—"

"Back *where?*" interrupted the mother, a little too eagerly.

"Where he likes, ma'am—I couldn't say where with any certainty. But aih! he likes to hear the sea moaning, and watch the stars shining!—There's no end of undeveloped religion in him, as Mister Graham says; and I do *not* believe the Lord will see him wronged more than will help him in the end. But it's my belief, if you took away the poor man's liberty, you would kill him."

"Then you won't help me!" she cried despairingly. "They tell me you are an orphan yourself—and yet you will not take pity on a childless mother!—worse than childless, for I had the loveliest boy once—he would be about your age now, and I have never had any comfort in life since I lost him. Give me my son, and I will bless you—love you."

As she spoke she rose, and approaching him gently, laid a hand on his shoulder. Malcolm trembled, but stood his mental ground.

"'Deed, mem, I can an' wull promise ye naething!" he said. "Are ye to play a man fause 'cause he's less able to tak care o' himsel' than ither fowk? Gien I war sure 'at ye cud mak it up, an' 'at he would be happy wi' ye efterhin, it micht be anither thing; but excep' ye garred him, ye cudna get him to bide lang eneuch for ye to try—an' syne he wad dee afore ye hed convenced him. I doobt, mem, ye hae lost yer chance wi' him and maun du yer best to be content withoot him—I'll promise ye this muckle, gien ye like—I s' tell him what ye hae said upo' the subjec'."

"Much good that will be!" replied the lady, with ill-concealed scorn.

"Ye think he wadna unnerstan' 't; but he unnerstan's wonnerfu'."

"And you would come again, and tell me what he said?" she murmured, with the eager persuasiveness of reviving hope.

"Maybe ay, maybe no—I winna promise.—Hae ye ony answer to sen' back to my lord's letter, mem?"

"No; I cannot write; I cannot even think. You have made me so miserable!"

Malcolm lingered.

"Then you won't help me!" she cried despairingly. "They tell me you are an orphan yourself—and yet you will not take pity on a childless mother!—worse than childless, for I had the loveliest boy once—he would be about your age now, and I have never had any comfort in life since I lost him. Give me my son, and I will bless you—love you."

As she spoke she rose, and approaching him gently, laid a hand on his shoulder. Malcolm trembled, but stood his mental ground.

"Indeed, ma'am, I can and will promise you nothing!" he said. "Are you to play a man false because he's less able to take care of himself than other folk? If I were sure that you could make it up, and that he would be happy with you afterwards, it might be another thing; but except you forced him, you couldn't get him to stay long enough for you to try—and then he would die before you had convinced him. I suspect you've lost your chance with him ma'am, and must do your best to be content without him—I'll promise you this much, if you like—I'll tell him what you've said upon the subject."

"Much good that will be!" replied the lady, with ill-concealed scorn.

"You think he wouldn't understand it; but he understands things wonderfully."

"And you would come again, and tell me what he said?" she murmured, with the eager persuasiveness of reviving hope.

"Maybe ay, maybe no—I make no promise.—Have you any answer to send back to my lord's letter, ma'am?"

"No; I cannot write; I cannot even think. You have made me so miserable!"

Malcolm lingered.

"Go, go;" said the lady dejectedly. "Tell your master I am not well. I will write tomorrow. If you hear anything of my poor boy, do take pity upon me and come and tell me."

The stiffer partizan Malcolm appeared, the more desirable did it seem in Mrs Stewart's eyes to gain him over to her side. Leaving his probable active hostility out of the question, she saw plainly enough that, if he were called on to give testimony as to the laird's capacity, his witness would pull strongly against her plans; while, if the interests of such a youth were wrapped up in them, that fact in itself would prejudice most people in favour of them.

"Go, go;" said the lady dejectedly. "Tell your master I am not well. I will write tomorrow. If you hear anything of my poor boy, do take pity upon me and come and tell me."

The stiffer partizan Malcolm appeared, the more desirable did it seem in Mrs Stewart's eyes to gain him over to her side. Leaving his probable active hostility out of the question, she saw plainly enough that, if he were called on to give testimony as to the laird's capacity, his witness would pull strongly against her plans; while, if the interests of such a youth were wrapped up in them, that fact in itself would prejudice most people in favour of them.

CHAPTER XXXVI

THE BLOW

"Well, Malcolm," said his lordship, when the youth reported himself, "how's Mrs Stewart?"

"No ower weel pleased, my lord," answered Malcolm.

"What!—you haven't been refusing to—?"

"Deed hev I, my lord!"

"Tut! tut!—Have you brought me any message from her?"

He spoke rather angrily.

"Nane but that she wasna weel, an' wad write the morn."

The marquis thought for a few moments.

"If I make a personal matter of it, MacPhail—I mean—you won't refuse me if I ask a personal favour of you?"

"I maun ken what it is afore I say onything, my lord."

"You may trust me not to require anything you couldn't undertake."

"There micht be twa opinions, my lord."

"You young boor! What is the world coming to? By Jove!"

"As far 's I can gang wi' a clean conscience, I'll gang,—no ae step ayont," said Malcolm.

"Well, Malcolm," said his lordship, when the youth reported himself, "how's Mrs Stewart?"

"Not over pleased, my lord," answered Malcolm.

"What!—you haven't been refusing to—?"

"Indeed I have, my lord!"

"Tut! tut!—Have you brought me any message from her?"

He spoke rather angrily.

"None but that she wasn't well, and would write tomorrow."

The marquis thought for a few moments.

"If I make a personal matter of it, MacPhail—I mean—you won't refuse me if I ask a personal favour of you?"

"I must know what it is before I say anything, my lord."

"You may trust me not to require anything you couldn't undertake."

"There might be two opinions, my lord."

"You young boor! What is the world coming to? By Jove!"

"As far as I can go with a clean conscience, I'll go—not one step farther," said Malcolm.

"You mean to say your judgment is a safer guide than mine?"

"No, my lord; I micht weel follow yer lordship's jeedgment, but gien there be a conscience i' the affair, it's my ain conscience I'm bun' to follow, an' no yer lordship's, or ony ither man's. Suppose the thing 'at seemed richt to yer lordship, seemed wrang to me, what wad ye hae me du than?"

"Do as I told you, and lay the blame on me."

"Na, my lord, that winna haud: I bude to du what I thoucht richt, an' lay the blame upo' naebody, whatever cam o' 't."

"You young hypocrite! Why didn't you tell me you meant to set up for a saint before I took you into my service?"

"'Cause I had nae sic intention, my lord. Surely a body micht ken himsel' nae sant, an' yet like to haud his han's clean!"

"What did Mrs Stewart tell you she wanted of you?" asked the marquis almost fiercely, after a moment's silence.

"She wantit me to get the puir laird to gang back till her; but I sair misdoobt, for a' her fine words, it's a closed door, gien it bena a lid, she wad hae upon him; an' I wad suner be hangt nor hae a thoom i' that haggis."

"Why should you doubt what a lady tells you?"

"I wadna be ower ready, but I hae hard things, ye see, an' bude to be upo' my gaird."

"Well, I suppose, as you are a personal friend of the idiot—" His lordship had thought to sting him, and paused for a moment; but Malcolm's manner revealed nothing except waiting watchfulness.

"You mean to say your judgment is a safer guide than mine?"

"No, my lord; I might well follow your lordship's judgement, but if there be a conscience in the affair, it's my own conscience I'm bound to follow, and not your lordship's, or any other man's. Suppose the thing that seemed right to your lordship, seemed wrong to me, what would you have me do then?"

"Do as I told you, and lay the blame on me."

"Na, my lord, that won't wash: I'd have to do what I thought right, and lay the blame on nobody, whatever came of it."

"You young hypocrite! Why didn't you tell me you meant to set up for a saint before I took you into my service?"

"Because I had no such intention, my lord. Surely a man might know himself no saint, and yet like to keep his hands clean!"

"What did Mrs Stewart tell you she wanted of you?" asked the marquis almost fiercely, after a moment's silence.

"She wanted me to get the poor laird to go back to her; but I fear, for all her fine words, that it's a closed door, if not a lid, she would have upon him; and I would sooner be hanged than have a thumb in that haggis."

"Why should you doubt what a lady tells you?"

"I'd much rather not, but I have heard things, you see, and have to be on my guard."

"Well, I suppose, as you are a personal friend of the idiot—" His lordship had thought to sting him, and paused for a moment; but Malcolm's manner revealed nothing except waiting watchfulness.

"—I must employ some one else to get a hold of the fellow for her," he concluded.

"Ye winna du that, my lord," cried Malcolm, in a tone of entreaty; but his master chose to misunderstand him.

"Who's to prevent me, I should like to know?" he said.

Malcolm accepted the misinterpretation involved, and answered—but calmly:

"Me, my lord. *I* wull. At ony rate, I s' du my best."

"Upon my word!" exclaimed Lord Lossie, "you presume sufficiently on my good nature, young man!"

"Hear me ae moment, my lord," returned Malcolm. "I've been turnin' 't ower i' my min', an' I see, plain as the daylicht, that I'm bun', bein' yer lordship's servan' an' trustit by yer lordship, to say that to yersel' the whilk I was nowise bun' to say to Mistress Stewart. Sae, at the risk o' angerin' ye, I maun tell yer lordship, wi' a' respec', 'at gien *I* can help it, there sall no han', gentle or semple, be laid upo' the laird against his ain wull."

The marquis was getting tired of the contest. He was angry too, and none the less that he felt Malcolm was in the right.

"Go to the devil you booby!" he said—even more in impatience than in wrath.

"I'm thinkin' I needna budge," retorted Malcolm, angry also.

"What do you mean by that insolence?"

"I mean, my lord, that to gang will be to gang *frae* him. He canna be far frae yer lordship's lug this meenute."

All the marquis's gathered annoyance broke out at last in rage. He started from his chair, made three strides to Malcolm, and struck him in the face. Malcolm staggered back till he was brought up by the door.

"—I must employ some one else to get a hold of the fellow for her," he concluded.

"You won't do that, my lord," cried Malcolm, in a tone of entreaty; but his master chose to misunderstand him.

"Who's to prevent me, I should like to know?" he said.

Malcolm accepted the misinterpretation involved, and answered—but calmly:

"Me, my lord. *I* will. At any rate, I shall do my best."

"Upon my word!" exclaimed Lord Lossie, "you presume sufficiently on my good nature, young man!"

"Hear me one moment, my lord," returned Malcolm. "I've been turning it over in my mind, and I see, plain as the daylight, that I'm bound, being your lordship's servant and trusted by your lordship, to say that to you which I was nowise bound to say to Mistress Stewart. So, at the risk of angering you, I must tell your lordship, with all respect, that if *I* can help it, there shall no hand, gentle or common, be laid upon the laird against his own will."

The marquis was getting tired of the contest. He was angry too, and none the less that he felt Malcolm was in the right.

"Go to the devil you booby!" he said—even more in impatience than in wrath.

"I'm thinkin' I needn't budge," retorted Malcolm, angry also.

"What do you mean by that insolence?"

"I mean, my lord, that to go will be to go *from* him. He can't be very far from your lordship's ear this minute."

All the marquis's gathered annoyance broke out at last in rage. He started from his chair, made three strides to Malcolm, and struck him in the face. Malcolm staggered back till he was brought up by the door.

"Hoot, my lord!" he exclaimed, as he sought his blue cotton handkerchief, "ye sudna hae dune that: ye'll blaud the carpet!"

"You precious idiot!" cried his lordship, already repenting the deed; "why didn't you defend yourself?"

"The quarrel was my ain, an' I cud du as I likit, my lord."

"And why should you like to take a blow? Not to lift a hand, even to defend yourself!" said the marquis, vexed both with Malcolm and with himself.

"Because I saw I was i' the wrang, my lord. The quarrel was o' my ain makin': I hed no richt to lowse my temper an' be impident. Sae I didna daur defen' mysel'. An' I beg yer lordship's pardon. But dinna ye du me the wrang to imaigine, my lord, 'cause I took a flewet in guid pairt whan I kent mysel' i' the wrang, 'at that's hoo I wad cairry mysel' gien 'twas for the puir laird. Faith! I s' gar *ony* man ken a differ there!"

"Go along with you—and don't show yourself till you're fit to be seen. I hope it'll be a lesson to you."

"It wull, my lord," said Malcolm. "But," he added, "there was nae occasion to gie me sic a dirdum: a word wad hae pitten me mair i' the wrang."

"Heavens, my lord!" he exclaimed, as he sought his blue cotton handkerchief, "you shouldn't have done that: you'll spoil the carpet!"

"You precious idiot!" cried his lordship, already repenting the deed; "why didn't you defend yourself?"

"The quarrel was my own, and I could do as I liked, my lord."

"And why should you like to take a blow? Not to lift a hand, even to defend yourself!" said the marquis, vexed both with Malcolm and with himself.

"Because I saw I was in the wrong, my lord. The quarrel was of my own making: I had no right to lose my temper and be impudent. So I didn't dare defend myself. And I beg your lordship's pardon. But don't you do me the wrong to imagine, my lord, because I took a blow peaceably when I knew myself in the wrong, that I would carry myself the same if it was for the poor laird. Faith! I'll make *any* man know a difference there!"

"Go along with you—and don't show yourself till you're fit to be seen. I hope it'll be a lesson to you."

"It will, my lord," said Malcolm. "But," he added, "there was no occasion to give me such a buffet: a word would have put me more in the wrong."

So saying, he left the room, with his handkerchief to his face. The marquis was really sorry for the blow, chiefly because Malcolm, without a shadow of pusillanimity, had taken it so quietly. Malcolm would, however, have had very much more the worse of it had he defended himself, for his master had been a bruiser in his youth, and neither his left hand nor his right arm had yet forgot their cunning so far as to leave him less than a heavy overmatch for one unskilled, whatever his strength or agility.

For some time after he was gone, the marquis paced up and down the room, feeling strangely and unaccountably uncomfortable.

"The great lout!" he kept saying to himself; "why did he let me strike him?"

Malcolm went to his grandfather's cottage. In passing the window, he peeped in. The old man was sitting with his bagpipes on his knees, looking troubled. When he entered, he held out his arms to him.

"Tere 'll pe something cone wrong with you, Malcolm, my son!" he cried. "You'll pe hafing a hurt! She knows it. She has it within her, though she couldn't chust see it. Where is it?"

As he spoke he proceeded to feel his head and face. "God pless her sowl! you are plooding, Malcolm!" he cried the same moment.

"It's naething to greit aboot, daddy. It's hardly mair nor the flype o' a sawmon's tail."

"Put who 'll pe tone it?" asked Duncan angrily.

"Ow, the maister gae me a bit flewet!" answered Malcolm with indifference.

"Where is he?" cried the piper, rising in wrath. "Take her to him, Malcolm. She will stap him. She will pe killing him. She will trife her turk into his wicked pody."

"Na, na, daddy," said Malcolm; "we hae hed eneuch o' durks a'ready!"

"Tat you haf tone it yourself, ten, Malcolm? My prave poy!"

"No, daddy; I took my licks like a man, for I deserved them."

"Deserfed to pe peaten, Malcolm—to pe peaten like a tog? Ton't tell her tat! Ton't preak her heart, my poy."

"It wasna that muckle, daddy. I only telled him auld Horny was at 's lug."

"And she'll make no toubt it was true," cried Duncan, emerging sudden from his despondency.

"Ay, sae he was, only I had nae richt to say 't."

"Put you striked him pack, Malcolm? Ton't say you tidn't gif him pack his plow. Ton't tell it to her, Malcolm!"

"Tere'll be something gone wrong with you, Malcolm, my son!" he cried. "You'll pe hafing a hurt! She knows it. She has it within her, though she couldn't chust see it. Where is it?"

As he spoke he proceeded to feel his head and face. "God bless her sowl! you are blooding, Malcolm!" he cried the same moment.

"It's nothing to cry about, daddy. It's hardly more than the flip of a salmon's tail."

"But who 'll haf done it?" asked Duncan angrily.

"Oh, the master gave me a wee stroke!" answered Malcolm with indifference.

"Where is he?" cried the piper, rising in wrath. "Take her to him, Malcolm. She will stab him. She will be killing him. She will trife her dirk into his wicked body."

"Na, na, daddy," said Malcolm; "we have had enough of dirks already!"

"Tat you haf done it yourself, ten, Malcolm? My brave boy!"

"No, daddy; I took my licks like a man, for I deserved them."

"Deserfed to be beaten, Malcolm—to be beaten like a tog? Ton't tell her tat! Ton't break her heart, my boy."

"It wasn't that much, daddy. I only told him old Horny was at his ear."

"And she'll make no toubt it was true," cried Duncan, emerging sudden from his despondency.

"Ay, so he was, only I had no right to say it."

"But you striked him back, Malcolm? Ton't say you tidn't gif him back his blow. Ton't tell it to her, Malcolm!"

"Hoo cud I hit my maister, an' mysel' i' the wrang, daddy?"

"Then she'll must to it herself," said Duncan quietly, and, with the lips compressed of calm decision, turned towards the door, to get his dirk from the next room.

"Bide ye still, daddy," said Malcolm, laying hold of his arm, "an' sit ye doon till ye hear a' aboot it first."

Duncan yielded, for the sake of better instruction in the circumstances; over the whole of which Malcolm now went. But before he came to a close, he had skilfully introduced and enlarged upon the sorrows and sufferings and dangers of the laird, so as to lead the old man away from the quarrel, dwelling especially on the necessity of protecting Mr Stewart from the machinations of his mother. Duncan listened to all he said with marked sympathy.

"An' gien the markis daur to cross me in 't," said Malcolm at last, as he ended, "lat him leuk till himsel', for it 's no at a buffet or twa I wad stick, gien the puir laird was intill 't."

"How could I hit my master, and I in the wrong, daddy?"

"Then she'll must do it herself," said Duncan quietly, and, with the lips compressed of calm decision, turned towards the door, to get his dirk from the next room.

"Wait a moment, daddy," said Malcolm, laying hold of his arm, "and sit down till you hear all about it first.

Duncan yielded, for the sake of better instruction in the circumstances; over the whole of which Malcolm now went. But before he came to a close, he had skilfully introduced and enlarged upon the sorrows and sufferings and dangers of the laird, so as to lead the old man away from the quarrel, dwelling especially on the necessity of protecting Mr Stewart from the machinations of his mother. Duncan listened to all he said with marked sympathy.

"And if the marquis dares cross me in it," said Malcolm at last, as he ended, "let him look to himself, for it's not at a buffet or two I would stick, where the poor laird was concerned."

This assurance, indicative of a full courageous intent on the part of his grandson, for whose manliness he was jealous, greatly served to quiet Duncan; and he consented at last to postpone all quittance, in the hope of Malcolm's having the opportunity of a righteous quarrel for proving himself no coward. His wrath gradually died away, until at last he begged his boy to take his pipes, that he might give him a lesson. Malcolm made the attempt, but found it impossible to fill the bag with his swollen and cut lips, and had to beg his grandfather to play to him instead. He gladly consented, and played until bedtime; when, having tucked him up, Malcolm went quietly to his own room, avoiding supper and the eyes of Mrs Courthope together. He fell asleep in a moment, and spent a night of perfect oblivion, dreamless of wizard lord or witch lady.

CHAPTER XXXVII

THE CUTTER

Some days passed during which Malcolm contrived that no one should see him: he stole down to his grandfather's early in the morning, and returned to his own room at night. Duncan told the people about that he was not very well, but would be all better in a day or two. It was a time of jubilation to the bard, and he cheered his grandson's retirement with music, and with wild stories of highland lochs and moors, chanted or told. Malcolm's face was now much better, though the signs of the blow were still plain enough upon it, when a messenger came one afternoon to summon him to the marquis's presence.

"Where have you been sulking all this time?" was his master's greeting.

"I havena been sulkin', my lord," answered Malcolm. "Yer lordship tauld me to haud oot o' the gait till I was fit to be seen, an' no a sowl has set an ee upo' me till this verra moment 'at yer lordship has me in yer ain."

"Where have you been then?"

"I' my ain room at nicht, and doon at my gran'father's as lang's fowk was aboot—wi' a bit dauner up the burn i' the mirk."

"You couldn't encounter the shame of being seen with such a face—eh?"

"It micht ha' been thoucht a disgrace to the tane or the tither o' 's, my lord—maybe to baith."

"If you don't learn to curb that tongue of yours, it will bring you to worse."

"My lord, I confessed my faut, and I pat up wi' the blow. But if it hadna been that I was i' the wrang—weel, things micht hae differt."

"Where have you been sulking all this time?" was his master's greeting.

"I haven't been sulking, my lord," answered Malcolm. "Your lordship told me to keep out of the way till I was fit to be seen, and not a soul has set an eye upon me till this very moment that your lordship has me in your own."

"Where have you been then?"

"In my own room at night, and down at my grandfather's as long as folk were about—with a stroll up the burn in the dark."

"You couldn't encounter the shame of being seen with such a face—eh?"

"It might have been thought a disgrace to the one or the other of us, my lord—maybe to both."

"If you don't learn to curb that tongue of yours, it will bring you to worse."

"My lord, I confessed my fault, and I put up with the blow. But if it hadn't been that I was in the wrong—well, things might have differed."

"Hold your tongue, I tell you. You're an honest, good fellow, and I'm sorry I struck you. There!"

"I thank yer lordship."

"I sent for you because I've just heard from Aberdeen that the boat is on her way round. You must be ready to take charge of her the moment she arrives."

"I wull be that, my lord. It doesna shuit me at a' to be sae lang upo' the solid: like a cowt upon a toll ro'd."

"Hold your tongue, I tell you. You're an honest, good fellow, and I'm sorry I struck you. There!"

"I thank your lordship."

"I sent for you because I've just heard from Aberdeen that the boat is on her way round. You must be ready to take charge of her the moment she arrives."

"I will be that, my lord. It doesn't suit me at all to be so long on solid ground: like a colt upon a toll road."

The next morning he got a telescope, and taking with him his dinner of bread and cheese, and a book in his pocket, went up to the Temple of the Winds, to look out for the boat. Every few minutes he swept the offing, but morning and afternoon passed, and she did not appear. The day's monotony was broken only by a call from Demon. Malcolm looked landwards, and spied his mistress below amongst the trees, but she never looked in his direction.

He had just become aware of the first dusky breath of the twilight, when a tiny sloop appeared, rounding the Deid Heid, as they called the promontory which closed in the bay on the east. The sun was setting, red and large, on the other side of the Scaurnose, and filled her white sails with a rosy dye, as she came stealing round in a fair soft wind. The moon hung over her, thin, and pale, and ghostly, with hardly shine enough to show that it was indeed she, and not the forgotten scrap of a torn up cloud. As she passed the point and turned towards the harbour, the warm amethystine hue suddenly vanished from her sails, and she looked white and cold, as if the sight of the Death's Head had scared the blood out of her.

"It's hersel'!" cried Malcolm in delight. "Aboot the size a muckle herrin' boat, but nae mair like ane than Lady Florimel 's like Meg Partan! It'll be jist gran' to hae a cratur sae near leevin' to guide an' tak yer wull o'! I had nae idea she was gaein' to be onything like sae bonny. I'll no be fit to manage her in a squall though. I maun hae anither han'. An' I winna hae a laddie aither. It maun be a grown man, or I winna tak in han' to haud her abune the watter. I wull no. I s' hae Blue Peter himsel' gien I can get him. Eh! jist luik at her—wi' her bit gaff tappie set, and her jib an a', booin' an' booin', an' comin' on ye as gran' 's ony born leddy!"

"It's herself!" cried Malcolm in delight. "About the size of a big herring boat, but no more like one than Lady Florimel's like Meg Partan! It'll be just grand to have a creature so near living to order and guide! I had no idea she was going to be anything like so bonny. I won't be fit to manage her in a squall though. I must have another hand. And I won't have a laddie either. It must be a grown man, or I can't be sure to keep her afloat. I'll have Blue Peter himself if I can get him. Eh! just look at her—with her gaff top set, and her jib and all, bowing and bowing, and coming on you as grand as any born lady!"

He shut up his telescope, ran down the hill, unlocked the private door at its foot, and in three or four minutes was waiting her on the harbour-wall.

She was a little cutter—and a lovely show to eyes capable of the harmonies of shape and motion. She came walking in, as the Partan, whom Malcolm found on the pierhead, remarked, "like a leddy closin' her parasol as she cam." Malcolm jumped on board, and the two men who had brought her round, gave up their charge.

She was full-decked, with a dainty little cabin. Her planks were almost white—there was not a board in her off which one might not, as the Partan expanded the common phrase, "ait his parritch, an' never fin' a mote in 's mou'." Her cordage was all so clean, her standing rigging so taut, everything so ship-shape, that Malcolm was in raptures. If the burn had only been navigable so that he might have towed the graceful creature home and laid her up under the very walls of the House! It would have perfected the place in his eyes. He made her snug for the night, and went to report her arrival.

Great was Lady Florimel's jubilation. She would have set out on a "coasting voyage," as she called it, the very next day, but her father listened to Malcolm.

"Ye see, my lord," said Malcolm, "I maun ken a' aboot her afore I daur tak ye oot in her. An' I canna unnertak' to manage her my lane. Ye maun jist gie me anither man wi' me."

"Get one," said the marquis.

He shut up his telescope, ran down the hill, unlocked the private door at its foot, and in three or four minutes was waiting her on the harbour-wall.

She was a little cutter—and a lovely show to eyes capable of the harmonies of shape and motion. She came walking in, as the Partan, whom Malcolm found on the pierhead, remarked, "like a lady closing her parasol as she came." Malcolm jumped on board, and the two men who had brought her round, gave up their charge.

She was full-decked, with a dainty little cabin. Her planks were almost white—there was not a board in her off which one might not, as the Partan expanded the common phrase, "eat his porridge, and never taste a mote in his mouth." Her cordage was all so clean, her standing rigging so taut, everything so shipshape, that Malcolm was in raptures. If the burn had only been navigable so that he might have towed the graceful creature home and laid her up under the very walls of the House! It would have perfected the place in his eyes. He made her snug for the night, and went to report her arrival.

Great was Lady Florimel's jubilation. She would have set out on a "coasting voyage," as she called it, the very next day, but her father listened to Malcolm.

"You see, my lord," said Malcolm, "I must know all about her before I dare take you out in her. And I can't undertake to manage her single-handed. You'll have to give me another man to help me."

"Get one," said the marquis.

Early in the morning, therefore, Malcolm went to Scaurnose, and found Blue Peter amongst his nets. He could spare a day or two, and would join him. They returned together, got the cutter into the offing, and, with a westerly breeze, tried her every way. She answered her helm with readiness, rose as light as a bird, made a good board, and seemed every way a safe boat.

"She's the bonniest craft ever lainched!" said Malcolm, ending a description of her behaviour and qualities rather too circumstantial for his master to follow.

They were to make their first trip the next morning—eastward, if the wind should hold, landing at a certain ancient ruin on the coast, two or three miles from Portlossie.

Early in the morning, therefore, Malcolm went to Scaurnose, and found Blue Peter amongst his nets. He could spare a day or two, and would join him. They returned together, got the cutter into the offing, and, with a westerly breeze, tried her every way. She answered her helm with readiness, rose as light as a bird, made a good board, and seemed every way a safe boat.

"She's the bonniest craft ever launched!" said Malcolm, ending a description of her behaviour and qualities rather too circumstantial for his master to follow.

They were to make their first trip the next morning—eastward, if the wind should hold, landing at a certain ancient ruin on the coast, two or three miles from Portlossie.

CHAPTER XXXVIII

THE TWO DOGS

Lady Florimel's fancy was so full of the expected pleasure, that she woke soon after dawn. She rose and anxiously drew aside a curtain of her window. The day was one of God's odes written for men. Would that the days of our human autumn were as calmly grand, as gorgeously hopeful as the days that lead the aging year down to the grave of winter! If our white hairs were sunlit from behind like those radiance-bordered clouds; if our air were as pure as this when it must be as cold; if the falling at last of longest-cherished hopes did but, like that of the forest leaves, let in more of the sky, more of the infinite possibilities of the region of truth which is the matrix of fact; we should go marching down the hill of life like a battered but still bannered army on its way home. But alas! how often we rot, instead of march, towards the grave! "If he be not rotten before he die," said Hamlet's absolute grave digger.—If the year was dying around Lady Florimel, as she looked, like a deathless sun from a window of the skies, it was dying at least with dignity.

The sun was still revelling in the gift of himself. A thin blue mist went up to greet him, like the first of the smoke from the altars of the morning. The fields lay yellow below; the rich colours of decay hung heavy on the woods, and seemed to clothe them as with the trappings of a majestic sorrow; but the spider-webs sparkled with dew, and the gossamer films floated thick in the level sunbeams. It was a great time for the spiders, those visible Deaths of the insect race.

The sun, like a householder leaving his house for a time, was burning up a thousand outworn things before he went; hence the smoke of the dying hearth of summer was going up to the heavens; but there was a heart of hope left, for, when farthest away, the sun is never gone, and the snow is the earth's blanket against the frost. But, alas, it was not Lady Florimel who thought these things! Looking over her shoulder, and seeing both what she can and what she cannot see, I am having a think to myself.

"Which it is an offence to utter in the temple of Art!" cry the critics.

Not against Art, I think: but if it be an offence to the worshipper of Art, let him keep silence before his goddess; for me, I am a sweeper of the floors in the temple of Life, and his goddess is my mare, and shall go in the dust-cart; if I find a jewel as I sweep, I will fasten it on the curtains of the doors, nor heed if it should break the fall of a fold of the drapery.

Below Lady Florimel's oriel window, under the tall bridge, the burn lay dark in a deep pool, with a slow-revolving eddy, in which one leaf, attended by a streak of white froth, was performing solemn gyrations; away to the north the great sea was merry with waves and spotted with their broken crests; heaped against the horizon, it looked like a blue hill dotted all over with feeding sheep; but, today, she never thought *why* the waters were so busy—to what end they foamed and ran, flashing their laughter in the face of the sun: the mood of nature was in harmony with her own, and she felt no need to discover any higher import in its merriment. How could she, when she sought no higher import in her own—had not as yet once suspected that every human gladness—even to the most transient flicker of delight—is the reflex—from a potsherd it may be—but of an eternal sun of joy?—Stay, let me pick up the gem: every faintest glimmer, all that is not utter darkness, is from the shining face of the Father of Lights.—Not a breath stirred the ivy leaves about her window; but out there, on the wide blue, the breezes were frolicking; and in the harbour the new boat must be tugging to get free! She dressed in haste, called her stag-hound, and set out the nearest way, that is by the town-gate, for the harbour. She must make acquaintance with her new plaything.

Mrs Catanach in her nightcap looked from her upper window as she passed, like a great spider from the heart of its web, and nodded significantly after her, with a look and a smile such as might mean, that for all her good looks she might have the heartache some day. But she was to have the first herself, for that moment her ugly dog, now and always with the look of being fresh from an ash-pit, rushed from somewhere, and laid hold of Lady Florimel's dress, frightening her so, that she gave a cry. Instantly her own dog, which had been loitering behind, came tearing up, five lengths at a bound, and descended like an angel of vengeance upon the offensive animal, which would have fled, but found it too late. Opening his huge jaws, Demon took him across the flanks, much larger than his own, as if he had been a rabbit. His howls of agony brought Mrs Catanach out in her petticoats. She flew at the hound, which Lady Florimel was in vain attempting to drag from the cur, and seized him by the throat.

"Take care; he is dangerous!" cried the girl.

Finding she had no power upon him, Mrs Catanach forsook him, and, in despairing fury, rushed at his mistress. Demon saw it with one flaming eye, left the cur—which, howling hideously, dragged his hind quarters after him into the house—and sprang at the woman. Then indeed was Lady Florimel terrified, for she knew the savage nature of the animal when roused. Truly, with his eyes on fire as now, his long fangs bared, the bristles on his back erect, and his moustache sticking straight out, he might well be believed, much as civilization might have done for him, a wolf after all! His mistress threw herself between them, and flung her arms tight round his neck.

"Run, woman! Run for your life!" she shrieked. "I can't hold him long."

Mrs Catanach fled, cowed by terror. Her huge legs bore her huge body, a tragicomic spectacle, across the street to her open door. She had hardly vanished, flinging it to behind her, when Demon broke from his mistress, and going at the door as if launched from a catapult, burst it open and disappeared also.

Lady Florimel gave a shriek of horror, and darted after him.

The same moment the sound of Duncan's pipes as he issued from the town gate, at which he always commenced instead of ending his *reveillé* now, reached her, and bethinking herself of her inability to control the hound, she darted again from the cottage, and flew to meet him, crying aloud,—

"Mr MacPhail! Duncan! Duncan! stop your pipes and come here directly."

"And who may pe calling me?" asked Duncan, who had not thoroughly distinguished the voice through the near clamour of his instrument.

She laid her hand trembling with apprehension on his arm, and began pulling him along.

"It's me,—Lady Florimel," she said. "Come here directly. Demon has got into a house and is worrying a woman."

"Cod haf mercy!" cried Duncan. "Take her pipes, my laty, for fear anything paad should happen to tem."

She led him hurriedly to the door. But ere he had quite crossed the threshold he shivered and drew back.

"'Tis is an efil house," he said. "she'll not can co in." A great floundering racket was going on above, mingled with growls and shrieks, but there was no howling.

"Call the dog then. He will mind you, perhaps," she cried—knowing what a slow business an argument with Duncan was— and flew to the stair.

"Temon! Temon!" cried Duncan, with agitated voice. Whether the dog thought his friend was in trouble next, I cannot tell, but down he came that instant, with a single bound from the top of the stair, right over his mistress's head as she was running up, and leaping out to Duncan, laid a paw upon each of his shoulders, panting with out-lolled tongue. But the piper staggered back, pushing the dog from him. "It is plood!" he cried; "ta efil woman's plood!"

"Mr MacPhail! Duncan! Duncan! stop your pipes and come here directly."

"And who may be calling me?" asked Duncan, who had not thoroughly distinguished the voice through the near clamour of his instrument.

She laid her hand trembling with apprehension on his arm, and began pulling him along.

"It's me,—Lady Florimel," she said. "Come here directly. Demon has got into a house and is worrying a woman."

"God haf mercy!" cried Duncan. "Take her pipes, my laty, for fear anything baad should happen to tem."

She led him hurriedly to the door. But ere he had quite crossed the threshold he shivered and drew back.

"'Tis is an efil house," he said. "she'll not can go in." A great floundering racket was going on above, mingled with growls and shrieks, but there was no howling.

"Call the dog then. He will mind you, perhaps," she cried—knowing what a slow business an argument with Duncan was— and flew to the stair.

"Temon! Temon!" cried Duncan, with agitated voice. Whether the dog thought his friend was in trouble next, I cannot tell, but down he came that instant, with a single bound from the top of the stair, right over his mistress's head as she was running up, and leaping out to Duncan, laid a paw upon each of his shoulders, panting with out-lolled tongue. But the piper staggered back, pushing the dog from him. "It is blood!" he cried; "ta efil woman's blood!"

"Keep him out, Duncan dear," said Lady Florimel. "I will go and see. There! he'll be up again if you don't mind!"

Very reluctant, yet obedient, the bard laid hold of the growling animal by the collar; and Lady Florimel was just turning to finish her ascent of the stair and see what dread thing had come to pass, when, to her great joy, she heard Malcolm's voice, calling from the farther end of the street—

"Hey, daddy! What's happened 'at I dinna hear the pipes?"

She rushed out, the pipes dangling from her hand, so that the drone trailed on the ground behind her.

"Malcolm! Malcolm!" she cried; and he was by her side in scarcely more time than Demon would have taken.

Hurriedly and rather incoherently, she told him what had taken place. He sprang up the stair, and she followed.

In the front garret—with a dormer window looking down into the street—stood Mrs Catanach facing the door, with such a malignant rage in her countenance that it looked demoniacal. Her dog lay at her feet with his throat torn out.

As soon as she saw Malcolm, she broke into a fury of vulgar imprecation—most of it quite outside the pale of artistic record.

"Hoots! for shame, Mistress Catanach!" he cried, "Here's my leddy ahin' me, hearin' ilka word!"

"Deil stap her lugs wi' brunstane! What but a curse wad she hae frae me? I sweir by God I s' gar her pey for this, or my name's no—" She stopped suddenly.

"I thocht as muckle," said Malcolm with a keen look.

"Keep him out, Duncan dear," said Lady Florimel. "I will go and see. There! he'll be up again if you don't mind!"

Very reluctant, yet obedient, the bard laid hold of the growling animal by the collar; and Lady Florimel was just turning to finish her ascent of the stair and see what dread thing had come to pass, when, to her great joy, she heard Malcolm's voice, calling from the farther end of the street—

"Hey, daddy! What's happened that I didn't hear the pipes?"

She rushed out, the pipes dangling from her hand, so that the drone trailed on the ground behind her.

"Malcolm! Malcolm!" she cried; and he was by her side in scarcely more time than Demon would have taken.

Hurriedly and rather incoherently, she told him what had taken place. He sprang up the stair, and she followed.

In the front garret—with a dormer window looking down into the street—stood Mrs Catanach facing the door, with such a malignant rage in her countenance that it looked demoniacal. Her dog lay at her feet with his throat torn out.

As soon as she saw Malcolm, she broke into a fury of vulgar imprecation—most of it quite outside the pale of artistic record.

"Heavens! for shame, Mistress Catanach!" he cried, "Here's my lady behind me, hearing every word!"

"Devil stop her ears with brimstone! What but a curse would she have from me? I swear by God I'll make her pay for this, or my name's not—" She stopped suddenly.

"I thought as much," said Malcolm with a keen look.

"Ye'll think twise, ye deil's buckie, or ye think richt! Wha are *ye* to think? What sud my name be but Bawby Catanach? Ye're unco upsettin' sin' ye turned my leddy's flunky! Sorrow tak ye baith! My dawtit Beauty!—worriet by that hell tyke o' hers!"

"Gien ye gang on like that, the markis 'll hae ye drummed oot o' the toon or twa days be ower," said Malcolm.

"Wull he than?" she returned with a confident sneer, showing all the teeth she had left. "Ye'll be far ben wi' the markis, nae doobt! An' yon donnert auld deevil ye ca' yer gran'father 'ill be fain eneuch to be drummer, I'll sweir. Care 's my case!"

"My leddy, she's ower ill-tongued for you to hearken till," said Malcolm, turning to Florimel who stood in the door white and trembling. "Jist gang doon, an' tell my gran'father to sen' the dog up. There's surely some gait o' garrin' her haud her tongue!"

Mrs Catanach threw a terrified glance towards Lady Florimel.

"Indeed I shall do nothing of the kind!" replied Florimel. "For shame!"

"Hoots, my leddy!" returned Malcolm. "I only said it to try the effec' o' 't. It seems no that ill."

"Ye son o' a deevil's soo!" cried the woman; "I s' hae amen's o' ye for this, gien I sud ro'st my ain hert to get it."

"'Deed, but ye're duin that fine a'ready! That foul brute o' yours has gotten *his* arles tu. I wonner what he thinks o sawmon troot noo!—Eh, mem?"

"Have done, Malcolm," said Florimel. "I am ashamed of you. If the woman is not hurt, we have no business in her house."

"You'll think twice, you devil's imp,[16] before you think right! Who are *you* to think? What should my name be but Bawby Catanach? You're very upsetting since you turned my lady's flunky! Curse you both! My petted Beauty!—worried by that hell hound of hers!"

"Go on like that, and the marquis will have you drummed out of town before you're two days older," said Malcolm.

"Will he then?" she returned with a confident sneer, showing all the teeth she had left. "You'll be thick with the marquis, no doubt! And that doddered old devil you call your grandfather will be happy to play the drummer, I'll swear. Woe's me!"

"My lady, she's too ill-tongued to listen to," said Malcolm, turning to Florimel who stood in the door white and trembling. "Just go down, and tell my grandfather to send the dog up. There's surely some way of making her hold her tongue!"

Mrs Catanach threw a terrified glance towards Lady Florimel.

"Indeed I shall do nothing of the kind!" replied Florimel. "For shame!"

"Heavens, my lady!" returned Malcolm; "I only said it to try its effect. It seems to have worked pretty well."

"You son of a devil's sow!" cried the woman; "I'll have amends of you for this, if I should roast my own heart to get it."

"Faith, but you're doing that already! That foul brute of yours has had *his* wages too. I wonder what he thinks of salmon trout now!—Eh, ma'am?"

"Have done, Malcolm," said Florimel. "I am ashamed of you. If the woman is not hurt, we have no business in her house."

---

16 DEVIL'S IMP: The Scots *deil's buckie* (see left hand column) is a harsh phrase referring to a perverse, unmanageable person. I have translated it variously the three times it appears in MacDonald's text

"Hear till her!" cried Mrs Catanach contemptuously. *"The woman!"*

But Lady Florimel took no heed. She had already turned and was going down the stair. Malcolm followed in silence; nor did another word from Mrs Catanach overtake them.

Arrived in the street, Florimel restored his pipes to Duncan —who, letting the dog go, at once proceeded to fill the bag— and, instead of continuing her way to the harbour, turned back, accompanied by Malcolm, Demon, and Lady Stronach's Strathspey.

"What a horrible woman that is!" she said with a shudder.

"Ay is she; but I doobt she wad be waur gien she didna brak oot that gait whiles," rejoined Malcolm.

"How do you mean?"

"It frichts fowk at her, an' maybe sometimes pits 't oot o' her pooer to du waur. Gien ever she seek to mak it up wi' ye, my leddy, I wad hae little to say till her, gien I was you."

"What could I have to say to a low creature like that?"

"Ye wadna ken what she micht be up till, or hoo she micht set aboot it, my leddy. I wad hae ye mistrust her a'thegither. My daddy has a fine moral nose for vermin, an' he canna bide her, though he never had a glimp o' the fause face o' her, an' in trowth never spak till her."

"I will tell my father of her. A woman like that is not fit to live amongst civilized people."

"Ye're richt there, my leddy; but she wad only gang some ither gait amo' the same. Of coorse ye maun tell yer father, but she's no fit for him to tak ony notice o'."

"Hear to her!" cried Mrs Catanach contemptuously. *"The woman!"*

But Lady Florimel took no heed. She had already turned and was going down the stair. Malcolm followed in silence; nor did another word from Mrs Catanach overtake them.

Arrived in the street, Florimel restored his pipes to Duncan —who, letting the dog go, at once proceeded to fill the bag— and, instead of continuing her way to the harbour, turned back, accompanied by Malcolm, Demon, and Lady Stronach's Strathspey.

"What a horrible woman that is!" she said with a shudder.

"Ay, she is; but I expect she'd be worse if she didn't break out that way at times," rejoined Malcolm.

"How do you mean?"

"It makes folk afraid of her, and maybe sometimes puts it out of her power to do worse. If ever she seeks to make it up with you, my lady, I would have little to say to her, if I were you."

"What could I have to say to a low creature like that?"

"You wouldn't know what she might be up to, or how she might set about it, my lady. I would have you mistrust her altogether. My daddy has a fine moral nose for vermin, and he can't stand her, though he never had a glimpse of her false face, and in truth never spoke to her."

"I will tell my father of her. A woman like that is not fit to live amongst civilized people."

"You're right there, my lady; but she would only go somewhere else among the same. Of course you must tell your father, but she's not fit for him to take any notice of."

As they sat at breakfast, Florimel did tell her father. His first emotion, however—at least the first he showed—was vexation with herself.

"You must *not* be going out alone—and at such ridiculous hours," he said. "I shall be compelled to get you a governess."

"Really, papa," she returned, "I don't see the good of having a marquis for a father, if I can't go about as safe as one of the fisher-children. And I might just as well be at school, if I'm not to do as I like."

"What if the dog had turned on you!" he said.

"If he dared!" exclaimed the girl, and her eyes flashed.

Her father looked at her for a moment, said to himself—"There spoke a Colonsay!" and pursued the subject no further.

When they passed Mrs Catanach's cottage an hour after, on their way to the harbour, they saw the blinds drawn down, as if a dead man lay within: according to after report, she had the brute already laid out like a human being, and sat by the bedside awaiting a coffin which she had ordered of Watty Witherspail.

CHAPTER XXXIX

COLONSAY CASTLE

The day continued lovely, with a fine breeze. The whole sky and air and sea were alive—with moving clouds, with wind, with waves flashing in the sun. As they stepped on board amidst the little crowd gathered to see, Lady Florimel could hardly keep her delight within the bounds of so called propriety. It was all she could do to restrain herself from dancing on the little deck half-swept by the tiller. The boat of a schooner which lay at the quay towed them out of the harbour. Then the creature spread her wings like a bird—main-sail and gaff-topsail, staysail and jib—leaned away to leeward, and seemed actually to bound over the waves. Malcolm sat at the tiller, and Blue Peter watched the canvas.

Lady Florimel turned out to be a good sailor, and her enjoyment was so contagious as even to tighten certain strings about her father's heart which had long been too slack to vibrate with any simple gladness. Her questions were incessant—first about the sails and rigging, then about the steering; but when Malcolm proceeded to explain how the water reacted on the rudder, she declined to trouble herself with that.

"Let me steer first," she said, "and then tell me how things work."

"That is whiles the best plan," said Malcolm. "Jist lay yer han' upo' the tiller, my leddy, an' luik oot at yon pint they ca' the Deid Heid yonner. Ye see, whan I turn the tiller this gait, her heid fa's aff frae the pint; an' whan I turn't this ither gait, her heid turns till 't again: haud her heid jist aboot a twa yairds like aff o' 't."

Florimel was more delighted than ever when she felt her own hand ruling the cutter—so overjoyed indeed, that, instead of steering straight, she would keep playing tricks with the rudder—fretting the mouth of the sea palfrey, as it were. Every now and then Malcolm had to expostulate.

"Let me steer first," she said, "and then tell me how things work."

"That is sometimes the best plan," said Malcolm. "Just lay your hand upon the tiller, my lady, and look out at that point they call the Dead Head yonder. You see, when I turn the tiller this way, her head falls off from the point; and when I turn it this other way, her heard turns to it again: keep her head just about two yards or so off it."

Florimel was more delighted than ever when she felt her own hand ruling the cutter—so overjoyed indeed, that, instead of steering straight, she would keep playing tricks with the rudder—fretting the mouth of the sea palfrey, as it were. Every now and then Malcolm had to expostulate.

"Noo, my leddy, caw canny. Dinna steer sae wull. Haud her steddy.—My lord, wad ye jist say a word to my leddy, or I'll be forced to tak the tiller frae her."

But by and by she grew weary of the attention required, and, giving up the helm, began to seek the explanation of its influence, in a way that delighted Malcolm.

"Ye'll mak a guid skipper some day," he said: "ye spier the richt questions, an' that's 'maist as guid 's kennin' the richt answers."

At length she threw herself on the cushions Malcolm had brought for her, and, while her father smoked his cigar, gazed in silence at the shore. Here, instead of sands, low rocks, infinitively broken and jagged, filled all the tidal space—a region of ceaseless rush and shattered waters. High cliffs of gray and brown rock, orange and green with lichens here and there, and in summer crowned with golden furze, rose behind—untouched by the ordinary tide, but at high water lashed by the waves of a storm.

Beyond the headland which they were fast nearing, the cliffs and the sea met at half-tide.

The moment they rounded it—

"Luik there, my lord," cried Malcolm, "—there's Colonsay Castel, 'at yer lordship gets yer name, I'm thinkin', an', ony gait, ane o' yer teetles frae. It maun be mony a hunner year sin' ever Colonsay baid intill 't!"

Well might he say so! for they looked but saw nothing—only cliff beyond cliff rising from a white-fringed shore. Not a broken tower, not a ragged battlement invaded the horizon!

"There's nothing of the sort there!" said Lady Florimel.

"Easy now, my lady. Careful how you steer her. Hold her steady.—My lord, would you just say a word to my lady, or I'll be forced to take the tiller from her."

But by and by she grew weary of the attention required, and, giving up the helm, began to seek the explanation of its influence, in a way that delighted Malcolm.

"You'll make a good skipper some day," he said: "you ask the right questions, and that's almost as good as knowing the right answers."

At length she threw herself on the cushions Malcolm had brought for her, and, while her father smoked his cigar, gazed in silence at the shore. Here, instead of sands, low rocks, infinitively broken and jagged, filled all the tidal space—a region of ceaseless rush and shattered waters. High cliffs of gray and brown rock, orange and green with lichens here and there, and in summer crowned with golden furze, rose behind—untouched by the ordinary tide, but at high water lashed by the waves of a storm.

Beyond the headland which they were fast nearing, the cliffs and the sea met at half-tide.

The moment they rounded it—

"Look there, my lord," cried Malcolm, "—there's Colonsay Castle, that your lordship gets your name, I'm thinking, and, at any rate, one of your titles from. It must be a hundred years since ever a Colonsay lived in it!"

Well might he say so! for they looked but saw nothing—only cliff beyond cliff rising from a white-fringed shore. Not a broken tower, not a ragged battlement invaded the horizon!

"There's nothing of the sort there!" said Lady Florimel.

"Ye maunna luik for tooer or pinnacle, my leddy, for nane will ye see: their time's lang ower. But jist tak the sea-face o' the scaur i' yer ee, an' traivel alang 't oontil ye come till a bit 'at luiks like mason-wark. It scarce rises abune the scaur in ony but ae pairt, an' there it 's but a feow feet o' a wa'."

Following his direction, Lady Florimel soon found the ruin. The front of a projecting portion of the cliff was faced, from the very water's edge as it seemed, with mason-work; while on its side, the masonry rested here and there upon jutting masses of the rock, serving as corbels or brackets, the surface of the rock itself completing the wall-front. Above, grass-grown heaps and mounds, and one isolated bit of wall pierced with a little window, like an empty eyesocket with no skull behind it, was all that was visible from the sea of the structure which had once risen lordly on the crest of the cliff.

"It is poor for a ruin even!" said Lord Lossie.

"But jist consider hoo auld the place is, my lord!—as auld as the time o' the sea-rovin' Danes, they say. Maybe it 's aulder nor King Alfred! Ye maun regaird it only as a foondation; there's stanes eneuch lyin' aboot to shaw 'at there maun hae been a gran' supperstructur on 't ance. I some think it has been ance disconneckit frae the lan', an' jined on by a drawbrig. Mony a lump o' rock an' castel thegither has rowed doon the brae upon a' sides, an' the ruins may weel hae filled up the gully at last. It's a wonnerfu' auld place, my lord."

"What would you do with it if it were yours, Malcolm?" asked Lady Florimel.

"You mustn't look for tower or pinnacle, my lady, for there's none to be seen: their time's long over. But just take the sea-face of the cliff in your eye, and travel along it until you come to a bit that looks like mason-work. It scarce rises above the cliff in any but one part, and there it's but a few feet of a wall."

Following his direction, Lady Florimel soon found the ruin. The front of a projecting portion of the cliff was faced, from the very water's edge as it seemed, with mason-work; while on its side, the masonry rested here and there upon jutting masses of the rock, serving as corbels or brackets, the surface of the rock itself completing the wall-front. Above, grass-grown heaps and mounds, and one isolated bit of wall pierced with a little window, like an empty eyesocket with no skull behind it, was all that was visible from the sea of the structure which had once risen lordly on the crest of the cliff.

"It is poor for a ruin even!" said Lord Lossie.

"But just consider how old the place is, my lord!—as old as the time of the sea-roving Danes, they say. Maybe it's older than King Alfred! You must think of it only as a foundation; there are stones enough lying about to show that there must have been a grand superstructure on it once. I've a notion it's been disconnected from the land at one time, and joined on by a drawbridge. Many a lump of rock and castle together has rolled down the hill upon all sides, and the ruins may well have filled up the gully at last. It's a wonderful old place, my lord."

"What would you do with it if it were yours, Malcolm?" asked Lady Florimel.

"I wad spen' a my spare time patchin' 't up to gar 't stan' oot agane the wither. It's crum'let awa' a heap sin' I min'."

"What would be the good of that? A rickle of old stones!" said the marquis.

"It's a growth 'at there winna be mony mair like," returned Malcolm. "I wonner 'at yer lordship!"

He was now steering for the foot of the cliff. As they approached, the ruin expanded and separated, grew more massy, and yet more detailed. Still it was a mere root clinging to the soil.

"Suppose you were Lord Lossie, Malcolm, what would you do with it?" asked Florimel, seriously, but with fun in her eyes.

"I wad win at the boddom o' 't first."

"What do you mean by that?"

"Ye'll see whan ye win in till 't. There's a heap o' voutit places inside yon blin' face. Du ye see yon wee bit squaur winnock? That lats the licht in till ane o' them. There maybe vouts aneath vouts, for them 'at ye can win intill 's half fu' o' yird an' stanes. I wad hae a' that cleart oot, an syne begin frae the verra foondation, diggin', an' patchin', an' buttressin', till I got it a' as soun' as a whunstane; an' whan I cam to the tap o' the rock, there the castel sud tak to growin' again; an' grow it sud, till there it stude, as near what it was as the wit an' the han' o' man cud set it."

"That would ruin a tolerably rich man," said the marquis.

"Ony gait it 's no the w'y fowk ruins themsel's nooadays, my lord. They'll pu' doon an auld hoose ony day to save

"I would spend all my spare time patching it up to make it withstand the weather. It's crumbled away a lot since I remember."

"What would be the good of that? A rickle of old stones!" said the marquis.

"It's a growth that there won't be many more like," returned Malcolm. "I wonder at your lordship!"

He was now steering for the foot of the cliff. As they approached, the ruin expanded and separated, grew more massy, and yet more detailed. Still it was a mere root clinging to the soil.

"Suppose you were Lord Lossie, Malcolm, what would you do with it?" asked Florimel, seriously, but with fun in her eyes.

"I would get to the bottom of it first."

"What do you mean by that?"

"You'll see when once we're in it. There's a heap of vaulted places inside that blind face. Do you see that small square window? That lets the light into one of them. There may be vaults beneath vaults, for those you can enter are half full of earth and stones. I would have all that cleared out, and then begin from the very foundation, digging, and patching, and buttressing, till I got it all as sound as a whinstone; and when I came to the top of the rock, there the castle should take to growing again; and grow it should, till there it stood, as near to its former state as the wit and the hand of man could bring it."

"That would ruin a tolerably rich man," said the marquis.

"But not, at all events, the way folk ruin themselves nowadays, my lord. They'll pull down an old house any day to save themsel's blastin'-poother. There's that gran' place they ca' Huntly Castel!—a suckin' bairn to this for age, but wi' wa's, they tell me, wad stan' for thoosan's o' years: wad ye believe 't? there's a sowlless chiel' o' a factor there diggin' park-wa's an' a grainery oot o' 't, as gien 'twar a quarry o' blue stane! An' what 's ten times mair exterord'nar, there's the Duke o' Gordon jist lattin' the gype tak 's wull o' the hoose o' his grace's ain forbears! I wad maist as sune lat a man speyk ill o' my daddy!"

"But this is past all rebuilding," said his lordship. "It would be barely possible to preserve the remains as they are."

"It *wad* be ill to du, my lord, *ohn* set it up again. But jist think what a gran' place it wad be to bide in!"

The marquis burst out laughing.

"A grand place for gulls and kittiwakes and sea-crows!" he said. "But where is it, pray, that a fisherman like you gets such extravagant notions?—How do you come to think of such things?"

"Thoucht's free, my lord. Gien a thing be guid to think, what for sudna a fisher-lad think it? I hae read a heap aboot auld castles an' sic like i' the history o' Scotlan', an' there's mony an auld tale an' ballant aboot them.—Jist luik there, my leddy: ye see yon awfu' hole i' the wa,' wi' the verra inside o' the hill, like, rushin' oot at it?—I cud tell ye a fearfu' tale aboot that same."

"Do let us have it," said Florimel eagerly, setting herself to listen.

"Better wait till we land," said the marquis lazily.

"Ay, my lord; we're ower near the shore to begin a story.—Slack the mainsheet,

themselves blasting-powder. There's that grand place they call Huntly Castle!—a suckling babe to this for age, but with walls, they tell me, that would stand for thousands of years: would you believe it? there's a soulless factor fellow there digging park-walls and a grainery out of it, as if it were a quarry of blue stone! And what's ten times more a wonder, there's the Duke of Gordon just letting the fool do as he wills with the house of his grace's own forebears! I would almost as soon let a man speak ill of my daddy!"

"But this is past all rebuilding," said his lordship. "It would be barely possible to preserve the remains as they are."

"It *would* be hard to do, my lord, *without* setting it up again. But just think what a grand place it would be to live in!"

The marquis burst out laughing.

"A grand place for gulls and kittiwakes and sea-crows!" he said. "But where is it, pray, that a fisherman like you gets such extravagant notions?—How do you come to think of such things?"

"Thought's free, my lord. If a thing be good to think, why shouldn't a fisher-lad think it? I have read a heap about old castles and suchlike in the history of Scotland, and there's many an old tale and ballad about them.—Just look there, my lady: you see that awful hole in the wall, with the very inside of the hill, like, just rushing out at it?—I could tell you a fearful tale about that same."

"Do let us have it," said Florimel eagerly, setting herself to listen.

"Better wait till we land," said the marquis lazily.

"Ay, my lord; we're too near the shore to begin a story.—Slack the mainsheet,

Peter, an' stan' by the jib-doonhaul.—Dinna rise, my leddy; she'll be o' the grun' in anither meenute."

Almost immediately followed a slight grating noise, which grew loud, and before one could say her speed had slackened, the cutter rested on the pebbles, with the small waves of the just turned tide flowing against her quarter. Malcolm was overboard in a moment.

"How the deuce are we to land here?" said the marquis.

"Yes!" followed Florimel, half-risen on her elbow, "how the deuce *are* we to land here?"

"Hoot, my leddy!" said Malcolm, "sic words ill become yer bonny mou'."

The marquis laughed.

"I ask you how we are to get ashore?" said Florimel with grave dignity, though an imp was laughing in the shadows of her eyes.

"I'll sune lat ye see that, my leddy," answered Malcolm; and leaning over the low bulwark he had her in his arms almost before she could utter an objection. Carrying her ashore like a child— indeed, to steady herself, she had put an arm round his shoulders —he set her down on the shingle, and turning in the act, left her as if she had been a burden of nets, and waded back to the boat.

"And how, pray, am I to go?" asked the marquis. "Do you fancy you can carry me in that style?"

"Ow na, my lord! that wadna be dignifeed for a man. Jist loup upo' my back."

As he spoke he turned his broad shoulders, stooping.

The marquis accepted the invitation, and rode ashore like a schoolboy, laughing merrily.

Peter, and stand by the jib-downhaul.—Don't rise, my lady; she'll be grounded in another minute."

Almost immediately followed a slight grating noise, which grew loud, and before one could say her speed had slackened, the cutter rested on the pebbles, with the small waves of the just turned tide flowing against her quarter. Malcolm was overboard in a moment.

"How the deuce are we to land here?" said the marquis.

"Yes!" followed Florimel, half-risen on her elbow, "how the deuce *are* we to land here?"

"Heavens, my lady!" said Malcolm, "such words ill become your bonny mouth."

The marquis laughed.

"I ask you how we are to get ashore?" said Florimel with grave dignity, though an imp was laughing in the shadows of her eyes.

"I'll soon let you see that, my lady," answered Malcolm; and leaning over the low bulwark he had her in his arms almost before she could utter an objection. Carrying her ashore like a child— indeed, to steady herself, she had put an arm round his shoulders —he set her down on the shingle, and turning in the act, left her as if she had been a burden of nets, and waded back to the boat.

"And how, pray, am I to go?" asked the marquis. "Do you fancy you can carry me in that style?"

"Oh na, my lord! that wouldn't be dignified for a man. Just jump on my back."

As he spoke he turned his broad shoulders, stooping.

The marquis accepted the invitation, and rode ashore like a schoolboy, laughing merrily.

They were in a little valley, open only to the sea, one boundary of which was the small promontory whereon the castle stood. The side of it next them, of stone and live rock combined, rose perpendicular from the beach to a great height; whence, to gain the summit, they had to go a little way back, and ascend by a winding path till they reached the approach to the castle from the landward side.

"Noo, *wad* na this be a gran' place to bide at, my lord?" said Malcolm, as they reached the summit—the marquis breathless, Florimel fresh as a lark. "Jist see sic an outluik! The verra place for pirates like the auld Danes! Naething cud escape the sicht o' them here. Yon's the hills o' Sutherlan'. Ye see yon ane like a cairn? That's a great freen' to the fisher-fowk to tell them whaur they are. Yon's the laich co'st o' Caithness. An' yonner's the north pole, only ye canna see sae far. Jist think, my lord, hoo gran' wad be the blusterin' blap o' the win' aboot the turrets, as ye stude at yer window on a winter's day, luikin oot ower the gurly twist o' the watters, the air fu' o' flichterin snaw, the cloods a mile thick abune yer heid, an' no a leevin cratur but yer ain fowk nearer nor the fairm-toon ower the broo yonner!"

"I don't see anything very attractive in your description," said his lordship. "And where," he added, looking around him, "would be the garden?"

"What cud ye want wi' a gairden, an' the sea oot afore ye there? The sea's bonnier than ony gairden. A gairden's maist aye the same, or it changes sae slow, wi' the ae flooer gaein' in, an' the ither flooer comin' oot, 'at ye maist dinna nottice

They were in a little valley, open only to the sea, one boundary of which was the small promontory whereon the castle stood. The side of it next them, of stone and live rock combined, rose perpendicular from the beach to a great height; whence, to gain the summit, they had to go a little way back, and ascend by a winding path till they reached the approach to the castle from the landward side.

"Now, *wouldn't* this be a grand place to live, my lord?" said Malcolm, as they reached the summit—the marquis breathless, Florimel fresh as a lark. "How's that for an outlook! The very place for pirates like the old Danes! Nothing could escape the sight of them here. Those are the hills of Sutherland. You see that one like a cairn? That's a great friend to the fisher-folk to tell them where they are. That's the low coast of Caithness. And yonder's the north pole, only you can't see so far. Just imagine, my lord, the grandeur of the blustering wind about the turrets, as you stood at your window on a winter's day, looking out over the stormy twist of the waters, the air full of the fluttering snow, the clouds a mile thick above your head, and not a living creature but your own folk nearer than the farm-town over the brow yonder!"

"I don't see anything very attractive in your description," said his lordship. "And where," he added, looking around him, "would be the garden?"

"What could you want with a garden, when you've the sea there before you? The sea's bonnier than any garden. A garden's nearly always the same, or the change is so slow, with one flower going in, and the other flower coming out, that you hardly the odds. But the sea's never twa days the same. Even lauchin' she never lauchs twise wi' the same face, an' whan she sulks, she has a hunner w'ys o' sulkin'."

"And how would you get a carriage up here?" said the marquis.

"Fine that, my lord. There's a ro'd up as far's yon neuk. An' for this broo, I wad clear awa the lowse stanes, an' lat the nait'ral gerse grow sweet an' fine, an' turn a lot o' bonny heelan' sheep on till't. I wad keep yon ae bit o' whuns, for though they're rouch i' the leaf, they blaw sae gowden. Syne I wad gether a' the bits o' drains frae a' sides, till I had a bonny stream o' watter aff o' the sweet corn lan', rowin' doon here whaur we stan', an' ower to the castel itsel', an' throu' coort an' kitchie, gurglin' an' rinnin', an' syne oot again an' doon the face o' the scaur, splashin' an' loupin' like mad. I wad lea' a' the lave to Natur' hersel'. It _wad_ be a gran' place, my lord! An' whan ye was tired o' 't, ye cud jist rin awa' to Lossie Hoose, an' hide ye i' the how there for a cheenge. I wad like fine to hae the sortin' o' 't for yer lordship."

"I daresay!" said the marquis.

"Let's find a nice place for our luncheon, papa, and then we can sit down and hear Malcolm's story," said Florimel.

"Dinna ye think, my lord, it wad be better to get the baskets up first?" interposed Malcolm.

"Yes, I think so. Wilson can help you."

"Na, my lord; he canna lea' the cutter. The tide's risin, an' she's ower near the rocks."

"Well, well; we shan't want lunch for an hour yet, so you can take your time."

notice the difference. But the sea's never two days the same. Even laughing she never laughs twice with the same face, and when she sulks, she has a hundred ways of sulking."

"And how would you get a carriage up here?" said the marquis.

"Nothing easier, my lord. There's a road up as far as that corner. And for this brow, I would clear away the loose stones, and let the natural grass grow sweet and fine, and turn a lot of bonny highland sheep onto it. I would keep that one patch of whins, for though they're rough in the leaf, they bloom so golden. Then I would gather all the bits of drains from all sides, till I had a bonny stream of water from the sweet corn land, rolling down here where we stand, and over to the castle itself, and through court and kitchen, gurgling and running, and then out again and down the face of the cliff, splashing and jumping like mad. I would leave all the rest to Nature herself. It _would_ be a grand place, my lord! And when you tired of it, you could just run away to _Lossie House_, and hide there in the valley for a change. I would love to manage it all for your lordship."

"I daresay!" said the marquis.

"Let's find a nice place for our luncheon, papa, and then we can sit down and hear Malcolm's story," said Florimel.

"Don't you think, my lord, it would be better to get the baskets up first?" interposed Malcolm.

"Yes, I think so. Wilson can help you."

"Na, my lord; he can't leave the cutter. The tide's rising, and she's too near the rocks."

"Well, well; we shan't want lunch for an hour yet, so you can take your time."

"But ye maun tak tent, my lord, hoo ye gang amo' the ruins. There's awkward kin' o' holes aboot thae vouts, an' jist whaur ye think there's nane. I dinna a'thegither like yer gaein' wantin' me."

"Nonsense! Go along," said the marquis.

"But I'm no jokin'," persisted Malcolm.

"Yes, yes; we'll be careful," returned his master impatiently, and Malcolm ran down the hill, but not altogether satisfied with the assurance.

"But you must watch your step, my lord, among the ruins. There are awkward kinds of holes about those vaults, and just where you would think you were safest. I don't altogether like your going without me."

"Nonsense! Go along," said the marquis.

"But I'm not joking," persisted Malcolm.

"Yes, yes; we'll be careful," returned his master impatiently, and Malcolm ran down the hill, but not altogether satisfied with the assurance.

CHAPTER XL

THE DEIL'S WINNOCK[10]

Florimel was disappointed, for she longed to hear Malcolm's tale. But amid such surroundings it was not so very difficult to wait. They set out to have a peep at the ruins, and choose a place for luncheon.

From the point where they stood, looking seawards, the ground sunk to the narrow isthmus supposed by Malcolm to fill a cleft formerly crossed by a drawbridge, and, beyond it, rose again to the grassy mounds in which lay so many of the old bones of the ruined carcass.

Passing along the isthmus, where on one side was a steep descent to the shore of the little bay, and on the other the live rock hewn away to wall, shining and sparkling with crystals of a clear irony brown, they next clambered up a rude ascent of solid rock, and so reached what had been the centre of the seaward portion of the castle. Here they came suddenly upon a small hole at their feet, going right down. Florimel knelt, and peeping in, saw the remains of a small spiral stair. The opening seemed large enough to let her through, and, gathering her garments tight about her, she was halfway buried in the earth before her father, whose attention had been drawn elsewhere, saw what she was about. He thought she had fallen in, but her merry laugh reassured him, and ere he could reach her, she had screwed herself out of sight. He followed her in some anxiety, but, after a short descent, rejoined her in a small vaulted chamber, where she stood looking from the little square window Malcolm had pointed out to them as they neared the shore. The bare walls around them were of brown stone, wet with the drip of rains, and full of holes where the mortar had yielded and stones had fallen out. Indeed the mortar had all but vanished; the walls stood and the vaults hung chiefly by their own weight. By breaches in the walls, where once might have been doors, Florimel passed from one chamber to another and another, each dark, brown, vaulted, damp, and weather-eaten, while her father stood at the little window she had left, listlessly watching the two men on the beach far below landing the lunch, and the rippled sea, and the cutter rising and falling with every wave of the flowing tide.

At length Florimel found herself on the upper end of a steep sloping ridge of hard, smooth earth, lying along the side of one chamber, and leading across to yet another

---

17 The Devil's Window

beyond, which, unlike the rest, was full of light. The passion of exploration being by this time thoroughly roused in her, she descended the slope, half sliding, half creeping. When she thus reached the hole into the bright chamber, she almost sickened with horror, for the slope went off steeper, till it rushed, as it were, out of a huge gap in the wall of the castle, laying bare the void of space, and the gleam of the sea at a frightful depth below: if she had gone one foot further, she could not have saved herself from sliding out of the gap. It was the very breach Malcolm had pointed out to them from below, and concerning which he had promised them the terrible tale. She gave a shriek of terror, and laid hold of the broken wall. To heighten her dismay to the limit of mortal endurance, she found at the very first effort, partly, no doubt, from the paralysis of fear, that it was impossible to reascend; and there she lay on the verge of the steeper slope, her head and shoulders in the inner of the two chambers, and the rest of her body in the outer, with the hideous vacancy staring at her. In a few moments it had fascinated her so that she dared not close her eyes lest it should leap upon her. The wonder was that she did not lose her consciousness, and fall at once to the bottom of the cliff.

Her cry brought her father in terror to the top of the slope.

"Are you hurt, child?" he cried, not seeing the danger she was in.

"It's so steep, I can't get up again," she said faintly.

"I'll soon get you up," he returned cheerily, and began to descend.

"Oh, papa!" she cried, "don't come a step nearer. If you should slip, we should go to the bottom of the rock together. Indeed, indeed, there is great danger! Do run for Malcolm."

Thoroughly alarmed, yet mastering the signs of his fear, he enjoined her to keep perfectly still while he was gone, and hurried to the little window. Thence he shouted to the men below, but in vain, for the wind prevented his voice from reaching them. He rushed from the vaults, and began to descend at the first practicable spot he could find, shouting as he went.

The sound of his voice cheered Florimel a little, as she lay forsaken in her misery. Her whole effort now was to keep herself from fainting, and for this end, to abstract her mind from the terrors of her situation: in this she was aided by a new shock, which, had her position been a less critical one, would itself have caused her a deadly dismay. A curious little sound came to her, apparently from somewhere in the dusky chamber in which her head lay. She fancied it made by some little animal, and thought of the wild cats and otters of which Malcolm had spoken as haunting the caves; but, while the new fear mitigated the former, the greater fear subdued the less. It came a little louder, then again a little louder, growing like a hurried whisper, but without seeming to approach her. Louder still it grew, and yet was but an inarticulate whispering. Then it began to divide into some resemblance of articulate sounds. Presently, to her utter astonishment, she heard herself called by name.

"Lady Florimel! Lady Florimel!" said the sound plainly enough.

"Who's there?" she faltered, with her heart in her throat, hardly knowing whether she spoke or not.

"There's nobody here," answered the voice. "I'm in my own bedroom at home, where your dog killed mine."

It was the voice of Mrs Catanach, but both words and tone were almost English.

Anger, and the sense of a human presence, although an evil one, restored Lady Florimel's speech.

"How dare you talk such nonsense?" she said.

"Don't anger me again," returned the voice. "I tell you the truth. I'm sorry I spoke to your ladyship as I did this morning. It was the sight of my poor dog that drove me mad."

"*I* couldn't help it. I tried to keep mine off him, as you know."

"I do know it, my lady, and that's why I beg your pardon."

"Then there's nothing more to be said."

"Yes, there is, my lady: I want to make you some amends. I know more than most people, and I know a secret that some would give their ears for. Will you trust me?"

"I will hear what you've got to say."

"Well, I don't care whether you believe me or not: I shall tell you nothing but the truth. What do you think of Malcolm MacPhail, my lady?"

"What do you mean by asking me such a question?"

"Only to tell you that by birth he is a gentleman, and comes of an old family."

"But why do you tell *me*?" said Florimel. "What have *I* to do with it?"

"Nothing, my lady—or himself either. *I* hold the handle of the business. But you needn't think it's from any favour for *him*! I don't care what comes of him. There's no love lost between him and me. You heard yourself this very day, how he abused both me and my poor dog who is now lying dead on the bed beside me!"

"You don't expect me to believe such nonsense as that!" said Lady Florimel.

There was no reply. The voice had departed; and the terrors of her position returned with gathered force in the desolation of redoubled silence that closes around an unanswered question. A trembling seized her, and she could hardly persuade herself that she was not slipping by slow inches down the incline.

Minutes that seemed hours passed. At length she heard feet and voices, and presently her father called her name, but she was too agitated to reply except with a moan. A voice she was yet more glad to hear followed—the voice of Malcolm, ringing confident and clear.

"Haud awa', my lord," it said, "an' lat *me* come at her."

"You're not going down so!" said the marquis angrily. "You'll slip to a certainty, and send her to the bottom."

"My lord," returned Malcolm, "I ken what I'm aboot, an' ye dinna. I beg 'at ye'll haud ootby, an' no upset the lassie, for something maun depen' upon hersel'. Jist gang awa' back into that ither vout, my lord. I insist upo' 't."

"Stand clear, my lord," it said, "and let *me* come at her."

"You're not going down so!" said the marquis angrily. "You'll slip to a certainty, and send her to the bottom."

"My lord," returned Malcolm, "I know what I'm about, and you don't. I beg that you'll remain outside, and not upset the lassie, for something must depend on herself. Just go back there into that other vault, my lord. I insist upon it."

His lordship obeyed, and Malcolm, who had been pulling off his boots as he spoke, now addressed Mair.

"Here, Peter!" he said, "haud on to the tail o' that rope like grim deith.—Na, I dinna want it roon' me; it's to gang roon' her. But dinna ye haul, for it micht hurt her, an' she'll lippen to me and come up o' hersel."

"Dinna be feart, my bonny leddy: there's nae danger—no ae grain. I'm comin'."

With the rope in his hand, he walked down the incline, and kneeling by Florimel, close to the broken wall, proceeded to pass the rope under and round her waist, talking to her, as he did so, in the tone of one encouraging a child.

"Noo, my leddy! Noo, my bonny leddy! Ae meenute, an' ye're as safe's gien ye lay i' yer minnie's lap!"

"I daren't get up, Malcolm! I daren't turn my back to it! I shall drop right down into it if I do!" she faltered, beginning to sob.

"Nae fear o' that! There! ye canna fa' noo, for Blue Peter has the other en', and Peter's as strong 's twa pownies. I'm gaein to tak aff yer shune neist."

So saying, he lowered himself a little through the breach, holding on by the broken wall with one hand, while he gently removed her sandal shoes with the other. Drawing himself up again, he rose to his feet, and taking her hand, said,—

"Noo, my leddy, tak a gude grip o' my han', an' as I lift ye, gie a scram'le wi' yer twa bit feet, an' as sune's ye fin' them aneth ye, jist gang up as gien ye war clim'in' a gey stey brae. Ye cudna fa' gien ye tried yer warst."

His lordship obeyed, and Malcolm, who had been pulling off his boots as he spoke, now addressed Mair.

"Here, Peter!" he said, "hold on to the end of that rope like grim death.—Na, I don't want it round me; it's to go round her. But don't you haul on it, for it might hurt her, and she'll trust to me and come up of herself."

"Don't be afraid, my bonny lady: there's no danger—not one grain. I'm coming."

With the rope in his hand, he walked down the incline, and kneeling by Florimel, close to the broken wall, proceeded to pass the rope under and round her waist, talking to her, as he did so, in the tone of one encouraging a child.

"Now, my lady! Now, my bonny lady! One minute, and you're as safe as if you lay in your mother's lap!"

"I daren't get up, Malcolm! I daren't turn my back to it! I shall drop right down into it if I do!" she faltered, beginning to sob.

"No fear of that! There! you can't fall now, for Blue Peter has the other end, and Peter's as strong as two ponies. I'm going to take off your shoes next."

So saying, he lowered himself a little through the breach, holding on by the broken wall with one hand, while he gently removed her sandal shoes with the other. Drawing himself up again, he rose to his feet, and taking her hand, said,—

"Now, my lady, take a good grip of my hand, and as I lift you, give a scramble with your two feet, and as soon as you feel them beneath you, just go up as if you were climbing a good steep hill. You couldn't fall if you tried your worst."

At the grasp of his strong hand the girl felt a great gush of confidence rise in her heart; she did exactly as he told her, scrambled to her feet, and walked up the slippery way without one slide, holding fast by Malcolm's hand, while Joseph kept just feeling her waist with the loop of the rope as he drew it in. When she reached the top, she fell, almost fainting, into her father's arms; but was recalled to herself by an exclamation from Blue Peter: just as Malcolm relinquished her hand, his foot slipped. But he slid down the side of the mound only some six or seven feet to the bottom of the chamber, whence his voice came cheerily, saying he would be with them in a moment. When, however, ascending by another way, he rejoined them, they were shocked to see blood pouring from his foot: he had lighted amongst broken glass, and had felt a sting, but only now was aware that the cut was a serious one. He made little of it, however, bound it up, and, as the marquis would not now hear of bringing the luncheon to the top, having, he said, had more than enough of the place, limped painfully after them down to the shore.

Knowing whither they were bound, and even better acquainted with the place than Malcolm himself, Mrs Catanach, the moment she had drawn down her blinds in mourning for her dog, had put her breakfast in her pocket, and set out from her back door, contriving mischief on her way. Arrived at the castle, she waited a long time before they made their appearance, but was rewarded for her patience, as she said to herself, by the luck which had so wonderfully seconded her cunning. From a broken loophole in the foundation of a round tower, she now watched them go down the hill. The moment they were out of sight, she crept like a fox from his earth, and having actually crawled beyond danger of discovery, hurried away inland, to reach Portlossie by footpaths and byways, and there show herself on her own doorstep.

The woman's consuming ambition was to possess power over others—power to hurt them if she chose—power to pull hidden strings fastened to their hearts or consciences or history or foibles or crimes, and so reduce them, in her knowledge, if not in theirs, to the condition of being, more or less, her slaves. Hence she pounced upon a secret as one would on a diamond in the dust, any fact even was precious, for it might be allied to some secret—might, in combination with other facts, become potent. How far this vice may have had its origin in the fact that she had secrets of her own, might be an interesting question.

As to the mysterious communication she had made to her, Lady Florimel was not able to turn her mind to it—nor indeed for some time was she able to think of anything.

She fell, almost fainting, into her father's arms.

CHAPTER XLI

THE CLOUDED SAPPHIRES

Before they reached the bottom of the hill, however, Florimel had recovered her spirits a little, and had even attempted a laugh at the ridiculousness of her late situation; but she continued very pale. They sat down beside the baskets—on some great stones, fallen from the building above. Because of his foot, they would not allow Malcolm to serve them, but told Mair and him to have their dinner near, and called the former when they wanted anything.

Lady Florimel revived still more after she had had a morsel of partridge and a glass of wine, but every now and then she shuddered: evidently she was haunted by the terror of her late position, and, with the gladness of a discoverer, the marquis bethought himself of Malcolm's promised tale, as a means of turning her thoughts aside from it. As soon, therefore, as they had finished their meal he called Malcolm, and told him they wanted his story.

"It's some fearsome," said Malcolm, looking anxiously at the pale face of Lady Florimel.

"Nonsense!" returned the marquis; for he thought, and perhaps rightly, that if such it would only serve his purpose the better.

"I wad raither tell 't i' the gloamin' roon' a winter fire," said Malcolm, with another anxious look at Lady Florimel.

"Do go on," she said. "I want so much to hear it!"

"Go on," said the marquis; and Malcolm, seating himself near them, began.

I need not again tell my reader that he may take a short cut if he pleases.

"It's quite fearsome," said Malcolm, looking anxiously at the pale face of Lady Florimel.

"Nonsense!" returned the marquis; for he thought, and perhaps rightly, that if such it would only serve his purpose the better.

"I would rather tell it in the gloaming round a winter fire," said Malcolm, with another anxious look at Lady Florimel.

"Do go on," she said. "I want so much to hear it!"

"Go on," said the marquis; and Malcolm, seating himself near them, began.

I need not again tell my reader that he may take a short cut if he pleases.

"There was ance a great nobleman—like yersel', my lord, only no sae douce—an' he had a great followin', and was thoucht muckle o' in a' the country, frae John o' Groat's to the Mull o' Gallowa'. But he was terrible prood, an' thoucht naebody was to compare wi' him, nor onything 'at onybody had, to compare wi' onything 'at he had. His horse war aye swifter, an' his kye aye better milkers nor ither fowk's; there war nae deer sae big nor had sic muckle horns as the reid deer on his heelan' hills; nae gillies sae strang's his gillies; and nae castles sae weel biggit or sae auld as his! It may ha' been a' verra true for onything I ken, or onything the story says to the contrar'; but it wasna heumble or Christian-like o' him to be aye at it, ower an' ower, aye gloryin'—as gien he had a'thing sae by ord'nar' 'cause he was by ord'nar' himsel', an' they a' cam till him by the verra natur' o' things. There was but ae thing in which he was na fawvoured, and that was, that he had nae son to tak up what he left. But it maittered the less, that the teetle as weel's the lan's, wad, as the tale tells, gang a' the same till a lass bairn—an' a lass bairn he had."

"That is the case in the Lossie family," said the marquis.

"That's hoo I hae hard the tale, my lord; but I wad be sorry sud a' it conteens meet wi' like corroboration.—As I say, a dochter there was, an' gien a' was surpassin', she was surpassin' a'. The faimily piper, or sennachy, as they ca'd him—I wadna wonner, my lord, gien thae gran' pipes yer boonty gae my gran'father, had been his!—he said in ane o' his sangs, 'at the sun blinkit whanever she shawed hersel' at the hoose door. I s' warran' ae thing—'at a' the lads

"There was once a great nobleman—like yourself, my lord, only less of a sensible body—and he had a great following, and was much admired in all the country, from John o' Groat's to the Mull of Galloway. But he was terribly proud, and thought nobody was to compare with him, nor anything that anyone had, to compare with anything he had. His horses were always faster, and his cows always better milkers than other folk's; there were no deer so big, nor had such horns as the red deer on his highland hills; no gillies so strong as his gillies; and no castles so well built or so old as his! It may have been all very true for anything I know, or anything the story says to the contrary; but it wasn't humble or Christian-like of him to make it his constant theme, always glorying—as if he had everything of the best because he was the best himself, and they all came to him by the very nature of things. There was but one thing in which he wasn't favoured, and that was, that he had no son to whom to leave it all. But it mattered the less, that the title as well as the lands, would, as the tale tells, go to a daughter all the same—and a daughter he had."

"That is the case in the Lossie family," said the marquis.

"That's how I have heard the tale, my lord; but I would be sorry should all it contains meet with like corroboration.—As I say, a daughter there was, and if all was surpassing, she was surpassing all. The family piper, or sennachy, as they called him—I shouldn't wonder, my lord, if those grand pipes your bounty gave my grandfather, had been his!—he said in one of his songs, that the sun blinked whenever she showed herself at the house door. I'm blinkit whan she luikit at them, gien sae be she cud ever be said to condescen' sae far as to *luik* at ony; for gien ever she set ee upo' ane, she never loot it rist: her ee aye jist slippit ower a face as gien the face micht or micht not be there—she didna ken or care. A'body said she had sic a hauchty leuk as was never seen on human face afore; an' for freen'ly luik, she had nane for leevin' cratur, 'cep' it was her ain father, or her ain horse 'at she rade upo'. Her mither was deid.

"Her father wad fain hae seen her merriet afore he dee'd, but the pride he had gien her was like to be the en' o' a', for she coontit it naething less than a disgrace to pairt wi' maiden leeberty. 'There's no man,' she wad say, whan her father wad be pressin' upo' the subjec',—'there's no mortal man, but yersel', worth the turn o' my ee.' An' the father, puir man, was ower weel pleased wi' the flattery to be sae angry wi' her as he wad fain hae luikit. Sae time gaed on, till frae a bonny lassie she had grown a gran' leddy, an' cud win up the hill nae forder, but bude to gang doon o' the ither side; an' her father was jist near-han' daft wi' anxiety to see her wad. But no! never ane wad she hearken till.

"At last there cam to the hoose—that's Colonsay Castel, up there—ae day, a yoong man frae Norrawa', the son o' a great nobleman o' that country; an' wi' him she was some ta'en. He was a fine man to leuk at, an' he pat them a' to shame at onything that nott stren'th or skeel. But he was as heumble as he was fit, an' never teuk ony credit till himsel' for onything 'at he did or was; an' this she was ill pleased wi', though she cudna help likin' him, an' made nae banes o' lattin' him see 'at he wasna a'the-gither a scunner till her.

sure of one thing—that the lads blinked when she looked at them, if she could ever be said to have deigned to *look* at any; for if ever she set eye upon one, she never let it rest: it always just slipped over a face as if the face might or might not be there—she didn't know or care. Everyone said she had such a haughty look as never mortal had before; and for friendly look, she had none for living creature, except it was her own father, or her own horse that she rode upon. Her mother was dead.

"Her father would fain have seen her married before he died, but the pride he had given her was like to disappoint him, for she counted it nothing less than a disgrace to part with maiden liberty. 'There's no man,' she would say, when her father would be pressing upon the subject,—there's no mortal man, but yourself, worth the turn of my eye. And the father, poor man, was too well pleased with the flattery to be so angry with her has he would fain have looked. So time went on, till from a bonny lassie she had grown a grand lady, and could climb the hill no farther, but must needs go down the other side; and her father was just near-hand daft with anxiety to have her wed. But no! she would listen to no one.

"At last there came to the house—that's Colonsay Castle, up there—one day, a young man from Norway, the son of a great nobleman of that country; and with him she was quite taken. He was a fine man to look at, and he put them all to shame at anything that needed strength or skill. But he was as humble as he was fit, and never took any credit to himself for anything that he did or was; and this scarce pleased the lady, though she couldn't help liking him, and made no attempt to disguise that he wasn't altogether a horror to her.

"Weel, ae mornin', verra ear', she gaed oot intill her gairden, an luikit ower the hedge; an' what sud she see but this same yoong nobleman tak the bairn frae a puir traivellin' body, help her ower a dyke, and gie her her bairn again! He was at her ain side in anither meenute, but he was jist that meenute ahint his tryst, an' she was in a cauld rage at him. He tried to turn her hert, sayin'—wad she hae had him no help the puir thing ower the dyke, her bairnie bein' but a fortnicht auld, an' hersel' unco weaklike? but my leddy made a mou' as gien she was scunnert to hear sic things made mention o'. An' was *she* to stan' luikin' ower the hedge, an' him convoyin' a beggar wife an' her brat! An' syne to come to *her* ohn ever washen his han's! 'Hoot, my leddy,' says he, 'the puir thing was a human cratur!'—'Gien she had been a God's angel,' says she, 'ye had no richt to keep me waitin'.'—'Gien she had been an angel,' says he, 'there wad hae been little occasion, but the wuman stude in want o' help!'—'Gien 't had been to save her life, ye sudna hae keepit me waitin',' says she. The lad was scaret at that, as weel he micht, an' takin' aff 's bannet, he lowtit laich, an' left her. But this didna shuit my leddy; she wasna to be left afore she said *gang!* sae she cried him back, an' he cam, bannet in han'; an' she leuch, an' made as gien she had been but tryin' the smeddum o' 'im, an' thoucht him a true k-nicht. The puir fallow pluckit up at this, an' doon he fell upo 's knees, an' oot wi' a' 'at was in 's hert,—hoo 'at he lo'ed her mair nor tongue cud tell, an' gien she wad hae him, he wad be her slave for ever."

"Well, one morning, very early, she went out into her garden, and looked over the hedge; and what should she see but this same young nobleman take the child from a poor travelling body, help her over a wall, and give her her child again! He was at her side in another minute, but he was just that minute behind his tryst, and she was in a cold rage at him. He tried to turn her heart, saying—would she have had him not help the poor thing over the wall, her wee child being but a fortnight old, and her own strength all but gone? but my lady made a mouth as if she was shocked at the mere mention of such things. And was *she* to stand looking over the hedge, and him escorting a beggar wife and her brat! And then to come to *her* without ever washing his hands! 'Heavens, my lady,' says he, 'the poor thing was a human creature!'—'If she had been a God's angel,' says she, 'you had no right to keep me waiting.'—'If she had been an angel,' says he, 'there would have been little occasion, but the woman stood in want of help!'—'If it had been to save her life, you shouldn't have kept me waiting,' says she. The lad was scared at that, as well he might be, and taking off his bonnet, he bowed low, and left her. But this didn't suit my lady; she wasn't to be left before she said *go!* so she called him back, and he came, bonnet in hand; and she laughed, and made as if she had been but testing his spirit, and thought him a true knight. The poor fellow plucked up at this, and down he fell upon his knees, and out with all that was in his heart—how he loved her more than tongue could tell, and if she would have him, he would be her slave forever."

"'Ye s' be that,' says she, an' leuch him to scorn. 'Gang efter yer beggar wife,' she says; 'I'm sick o' ye.'

"He rase, an' teuk up 's bannet, an' loupit the hedge, an' gae a blast upo' 's horn, an' gethered his men, an' steppit aboord his boat, ower by Puffie Heid yonner, an' awa to Norrowa' ower the faem, 'an was never hard tell o' in Scotlan' again. An' the leddy was hauchtier, and cairried her heid heicher nor ever—maybe to hide a scaum she had taen, for a' her pride.

"Sae things gaed on as afore, till at len'th the tide o' *her* time was weel past the turn, an' a streak o' the snaw in her coal-black hair. For, as the auld sang says, Her hair was like the craw, An' her ble was like the snaw, An' her bow-bendit lip Was like the rose-hip, An' her ee was like the licht'nin', Glorious an' fricht'nin'. But a' that wad sune be ower!

"Aboot this time, ae day i' the gloamin', there cam on sic an awfu' storm, 'at the fowk o' the castel war frichtit 'maist oot o' their wits. The licht'nin' cam oot o' the yerd, an' no frae the lift at a'; the win' roared as gien 't had been an incarnat rage; the thunner rattlet an' crackit, as gien the mune an' a' the stars had been made kettledrums o' for the occasion; but never a drap o' rain or a stane o' hail fell; naething brak oot but blue licht an' roarin' win'. But the strangest thing was, that the sea lay a' the time as ooncorcerned as a sleepin' bairn; the win' got nae mair grip o' 't nor gien a' the angels had been poorin' ile oot o' widows' cruses upo' 't; the verra tide came up quaieter nor ord'nar; and the fowk war sair perplext as weel's frichtit.

"'That you shall be,' says she, and laughed him to scorn. 'Go after your beggar wife,' she says; 'I'm sick of you.'

"He rose, and took up his bonnet, and leaped the hedge, and gave a blast on his horn, and gathered his men, and stepped aboard his boat, over by Puffie Head yonder, and away to Norway over the foam, and was never heard tell of in Scotland again. And the lady was haughtier, and carried her head higher than ever—maybe to hide a scorch she had taken, for all her pride.

"So things went on as before, till at length the tide of *her* time was well past the turn, and a streak of the snow in her coal-black hair. For, as the old song says, Her hair was like the crow, And her skin was like the snow, And her bow-bended lip Was like the rose-hip, And her eye was like the lightning, Glorious and frightening. But all that would soon be over!

"About this time, one day in the gloaming, there came on such an awful storm, that the folk of the castle were frightened almost out of their wits. The lightning came out of the earth, and not from the sky at all; the wind roared as if it had been an incarnate rage; the thunder rattled and cracked, as if the moon and all the stars had been changed to kettledrums for the occasion; but never a raindrop nor a hailstone fell; nothing broke out but the blue light and roaring wind. But the strangest thing was, that the sea lay all the time as unconcerned as a sleeping child; the wind ruffled it no more than if all the angels had been pouring oil out of widows' lamps upon it; the very lapping of the tide was quieted; and the folk were sore perplexed as well as frightened.

"Jist as the clock o' the castel chappit the deid o' the nicht, the clamour o' v'ices was hard throu' the thunner an' the win', an' the warder—luikin' doon frae the heich bartizan o' the muckle tooer, saw i' the fire-flauchts, a company o' riders appro'chin' the castel, a' upo' gran' horses, he said, that sprang this gait an' that, an shot fire frae their een. At the drawbrig they blew a horn 'at rowtit like a' the bulls o' Bashan, an' whan the warder challencht them, claimt hoose-room for the nicht. Naebody had ever hard o' the place they cam frae; it was sae far awa 'at as sune 's a body hard the name o' 't, he forgot it again; but their beasts war as fresh an' as fu' o' smeddum as I tell ye, an' no a hair o' ane o' them turnt. There was jist a de'il's dizzen o' them an whaurever ye began to count them, the thirteent had aye a reid baird.

"Whan the news was taen to the markis—the yerl, I sud say— he gae orders to lat them in at ance; for whatever fau'ts he had, naither fear nor hainin' was amang them. Sae in they cam, clatterin' ower the drawbrig, 'at gaed up an' down aneth them as gien it wad hae cast them.

"Richt fremt fowk they luikit when they cam intill the coortyaird—a' spanglet wi' bonny bricht stanes o' a' colours. They war like nae fowk 'at ever the yerl had seen, an' he had been to Jeroozlem in 's day, an' had fouchten wi' the Saracenes. But they war coorteous men an' weel-bred—an' maistly weel-faured tu—ilk ane luikin' a lord's son at the least. They had na a single servin'-man wi' them, an' wad alloo nane o' the fowk aboot the place to lay han' upo' their beasts; an' ilk ane as he said *na*, wad gie the stallion aneth him a daig wi' 's spurs, or a kick i' the ribs, gien he was

"Just as the castle clock chimed the dead of the night, the clamour of voices was heard through the thunder and the wind, and the warder—looking down from the high bartizan of the great tower, saw in the fire-flashes, a company of riders approaching the castle, all upon grand horses, he said, that sprang this way and that, and shot fire from their eyes. At the drawbridge they blew a horn that roared like the bulls of Bashan, and when the warder challenged them, claimed house-room for the night. Nobody had ever heard of the place they came from; it was so far away that as soon as anyone heard the name of it, he forgot it again; but their beasts were as fresh and as feisty as I tell you, and not a hair of one of them turned. There was just a devil's dozen of them and wherever you began to count them, the thirteenth had always a red beard.

"When the news was taken to the marquis—the earl, I should say—he gave orders to let them in at once; for whatever faults he had, he was neither coward nor niggard. So in they came, clattering over the drawbridge, that went up and down beneath them as if it would have unhorsed them all.

"Strange enough folk they looked when they came into the courtyard—all spangled with bonny bright stones of all colours. They were like no folk that ever the earl had seen, and he had been to Jerusalem in his day, and had fought with the Saracens. But they were courteous men and well-bred— and mostly well-favoured too—each one looking like a lord's son at least. They hadn't a single servant with them, and would allow none of the folk about the place to handle their beasts; and each one as he refused, would give the stallion he rode a dig with his spurs, or a kick in the ribs, if he wasn't aff o' 's back, wi' the steel tae o' his bute; an' the brute wad lay his lugs i' the how o' 's neck, an' turn his heid asklent, wi' ae white ee gleyin' oot o' 't, an' lift a hin' leg wi' the glintin' shue turnt back, an' luik like Sawtan himsel' whan he daurna.

"Weel, my lord an' my leddy war sittin' i' the muckle ha', for they cudna gang to their beds in sic a byous storm, whan him 'at was the chief o' them was ushered in by the seneschal, that's the steward, like, booin' afore him, an' ca'in' him the Prence, an' nae mair, for he cudna min' the name o' 's place lang eneuch to say 't ower again.

"An' sae a prence he was! an', forbye that, jist a man by himsel' to luik at!—i' the prime o' life, maybe, but no freely i' the first o' 't, for he had the luik as gien he had had a hard time o' 't, an' had a white streak an' a craw's fit here and there—the liklier to please my leddy, wha lookit doon upo' a'body yoonger nor hersel'. He hae a commandin', maybe some owerbeirin' luik—ane at a man micht hae birstled up at, but a leddy like my leddy wad welcome as worth bringin' doon. He was dressed as never man had appeart in Scotlan' afore— glorious withoot—no like the leddy i' the Psalms—for yer ee cud licht nowhaur but there was the glitter o' a stane, sae 'at he flashed a' ower, ilka motion he made. He cairret a short swoord at his side—no muckle langer nor my daddy's dirk, as gien he never foucht but at closs quarters—the whilk had three sapphires—blue stanes, they tell me—an muckle anes, lowin' i' the sheath o' 't, an' a muckler ane still i' the heft; only they war some drumly, the leddy thoucht, bein' a jeedge o' hingars-at-lugs an' sic vainities.

mounted, with the steel toe of his boot; and the brute would lay his ears in the curve of his neck, and turn his head askance, with one white eye looking out of it, and lift a hind leg with the glinting shoe turned back, and look like Satan himself at bay.

"Well, my lord and my lady were sitting in the great hall, for they couldn't go to their beds in such a violent storm, when him that was the chief of them was ushered in by the seneschal—the steward, that is— bowing down before him, and calling him the Prince, and no more, for he couldn't remember the name of his country long enough to say it over again.

"And so a prince he was! and, besides that, just a man in ten thousand to look at!—in the prime of life, maybe, but not quite in its springtime, for he had the look of one who had known hardship, and had a white streak and a crow's foot here and there—the likelier to please my lady, who looked down upon everyone younger than herself. He had a commanding, per- haps quite an overbearing look—one that a man might have bristled up at, but a lady like my lady would welcome as worth bringing down. He was dressed as never man had appeared in Scotland before— glorious without—not like the lady in the Psalms—for your eye could light nowhere but there was the glitter of a stone, so that he flashed all over, every motion he made. He carried a short sword at his side—not much longer than my daddy's dirk, as if he never fought but at close quarters—which had three sapphires—blue stones, they tell me—and large ones, flaming in its sheath, and a larger one still in the heft; only they were something clouded, the lady thought, being a judge of earrings and such vanities.

"That may be 's it may, but in cam the prence, wi' a laich boo, an' a gran upstrauchtin' again; an' though, as I say, he was flashin' a' ower, his mainner was quaiet as the munelicht,—jist grace itsel'. He profest himsel unco' indebtit for the shelter accordit him; an' his een aye soucht the leddy's, an' his admiration o' her was plain in ilka luik an' gestur', an' though his words were feow, they a' meant mair nor they said. Afore his supper cam in, her hert was at his wull.

"They say that whan a wuman's late o' fa'in' in love—ye'll ken my lord—I ken naething aboot it—it 's the mair likly to be an oonrizzonin' an ooncontrollable fancy; in sic maitters it seems wisdom comesna wi' gray hairs: within ae hoor the leddy was enamoured o' the stranger in a fearfu' w'y. She poored oot his wine till him wi' her ain han'; an' the moment he put the glaiss till 's lips, the win' fell an' the lichtnin' devallt. She set hersel' to put questions till him, sic as she thoucht he wad like to answer—a' aboot himsel' an' what he had come throu'; an' sic stories as he tellt! She atten't till him as she had never dune to guest afore, an' her father saw 'at she was sair taen wi' the man. But he wasna a'thegither sae weel pleased, for there was something aboot him—he cudna say what—'at garred him grue. He wasna a man to hae fancies, or stan' upo' freits, but he cudna help the creep that gaed doon his backbane ilka time his ee encoontert that o' the prence— it was aye sic a strange luik the prence cuist upon him—a luik as gien him an' the yerl had been a'ready ower weel acquant, though the yerl cudna min' 'at ever he had set ee upo' him. A' the time, hooever, he

"That may be as it may, but in came the prince, with a low bow, and a grand upstraightening again; and though, as I say, he was flashing all over, his manner was quiet as the moonlight,—just grace itself. He professed himself much indebted for the shelter accorded him; and his eyes ever sought the lady's, and his admiration of her was plain in every look and gesture, and though his words were few, they all meant more than they said. Before his supper came in, her heart was his to command.

"They say that when a woman is late in falling in love—you'll know my lord—I know nothing about it—it's the more likely to be an irrational and uncontrollable fancy; in such matters it seems wisdom may not come with gray hairs: within a single hour the lady was enamoured of the stranger in a fearful way. She poured out his wine to him with her own hand; and the moment he put the glass to his lips, the wind fell and the lightning ceased. She set herself to put questions to him, such as she thought he would like to answer—all about himself and what he had come through; and such stories as he told! She hung on his words as she had never done with guest before, and her father saw that she was fairly taken with him. But he wasn't altogether so well pleased, for there was something about him—he couldn't say what—that made him shudder. He wasn't a fanciful or superstitious man, but he couldn't help the creep that went down his backbone every time his eye encountered the prince—it was always such a strange look the prince cast upon him—a look as if he and the earl had already been too well known to each other, though the earl couldn't remember ever having had a kin' o' suspicion 'at they bude to be auld acquantances, an' sair he soucht to mak him oot, but the prence wad never lat a body get a glimp o' his een 'cep' the body he was speykin' till—that is gien he cud help it, for the yerl did get twa or three glimps o' them as he spak till 's dauchter; an' he declaret efterhin to the king's commissioner, that a pale blue kin' o' a licht cam frae them, the whilk the body he was conversin' wi', an' luikin' straucht at, never saw.

"Weel, the short and the lang o' 't that nicht was, that they gaed a' to their beds.

"I' the mornin', whan the markis—the yerl, I sud say—an' his dochter cam doon the stair, the haill menyie was awa. Never a horse or horse was i' the stable, but the yerl's ain beasts—no ae hair left ahin' to shaw that they had been there! an' i' the chaumers allotted to their riders, never a pair o' sheets had been sleepit in.

"The yerl an my leddy sat doon to brak their fast—no freely i' the same humour, the twa o' them, as ye may weel believe. Whan they war aboot half throu', wha sud come stridin' in, some dour an' ill-pleased like, but the prence himsel'! Baith yerl an' leddy startit up: 'at *they* sud hae sitten doon till a meal ohn even adverteest their veesitor that sic was their purpose! They made muckle adu wi' apologies an' explanations, but the prence aye booed an' booed, an' said sae little, that they thocht him mortal angert, the whilk was a great vex to my leddy, ye may be sure. He had a wither-like luik, an' the verra diamonds in 's claes war douf like. A'thegither he had a brunt-oot kin' o' aissy leuk.

seen him before. All the time, however, he had a kind of suspicion that they must be old acquaintances, and he tried his best to make him out, but the prince would never let a body get a glimpse of his eyes except the one he was speaking to—that is if he could help it, for the earl did steal a few looks at them as he spoke to his daughter; and he declared afterwards to the king's commissioner, that they gave out a pale blue kind of light, which the one he was speaking to, and looking straight at, never saw.

"Well, the short and the long of it that night was, that they all retired to their beds.

"In the morning, when the marquis—the earl, I should say—and his daughter came downstairs, the whole company was gone. Never a horse was in the stable, but just the earl's own beasts—not one hair left behind to show that they had been there! and in the rooms allotted to their riders, never a pair of sheets had been slept in.

"The earl and my lady sat down to break their fast—hardly in the same humour, the two of them, as you may well believe. When they were about half finished, who should come striding in, not a little dour and ill-pleased, but the prince himself! Both earl and lady started up: that *they* should have sat down to a meal without informing their guest of their purpose! They made much ado with apologies and explanations, but the prince just bowed and bowed, and said so little, that they thought him in a mortal rage, which was a great vex to my lady, you may be sure. He had a withered-like look, and the very diamonds in his clothes were dulled. Altogether he had a burnt-out, ashy kind of look.

"At len'th the butler cam in, an' the prence signed till him, an' he gaed near, an' the prence drew him doon, an' tootmootit in 's lug—an' his breath, the auld man said, was like the grave: he hadna had 's mornin', he said, an' tell't him to put the whusky upo' the table. The butler did as he was tauld, an' set doon the decanter, an' a glaiss aside it; but the prence bannt him jist fearfu', an' ordert him to tak awa that playock, and fess a tum'ler.

"I'm thinkin', my lord, that maun be a modern touch," remarked Malcolm here, interrupting himself: "there wasna glaiss i' thae times—was there?"

"What do I know!" said the marquis. "Go on with your story."

"But there's mair intill 't than that," persisted Malcolm. "I doobt gien there was ony whusky i' thae times aither; for I hard a gentleman say the ither day 'at hoo he had tastit the first whusky 'at was ever distillt in Scotlan', an' horrible stuff it was, he said, though it was 'maist as auld as the forty-five."

"Confound your long wind! Go on," said the marquis peremptorily.

"We s' ca' 't whusky, than, ony gait," said Malcolm, and resumed.

"The butler did again as he was bidden, an' fiess a tum'ler, or mair likely a siller cup, an' the prence took the decanter, or what it micht be, an' filled it to the verra brim. The butler's een 'maist startit frae 's heid, but naebody said naething. He liftit it, greedy like, an' drank aff the whusky as gien 't had been watter. 'That's middlin',' he said, as he set it o' the table again. They luikit to see him fa' doon deid, but in place o' that he begoud

"At length the butler came in, and the prince signed to him, and he came near, and the prince drew him down, and whispered in his ear—and his breath, the old man said, was like the grave: he hadn't had his morning, he said, and told him to put the whisky upon the table. The butler did as he was told, and set down the decanter, and a glass beside it; but the prince cursed him dreadfully, and ordered him to take away that child's toy, and fetch a tumbler.

"I'm thinking, my lord, that must be a modern touch," remarked Malcolm here, interrupting himself: "there wasn't glass in those times—was there?"

"What do I know!" said the marquis. "Go on with your story."

"But there's more in it than that," persisted Malcolm. "I doubt if there was any whisky in those times either; for I heard a gentleman say the other day that he had tasted the first whisky that was ever distilled in Scotland, and horrible stuff it was, he said, though it was almost as old as the forty-five."

"Confound your long wind! Go on," said the marquis peremptorily.

"We'll call it whisky then, anyway," said Malcolm, and resumed.

"The butler did again as he was bidden, and fetched a tumbler, or more likely a silver cup, and the prince took the decanter, or what it might be, and filled it to the very brim. The butler's eyes nearly started from his head, but nobody spoke a word. He lifted it, greedily, and drank off the whisky as if it had been water. 'That's middling,' he said, as he set it on the table again. They looked to see him fall down dead, but instead of that he began to gether himsel' a bit, an' says he, 'We brew the same drink i' my country, but a wee mair pooerfu'.' Syne he askit for a slice o' boar-ham an' a raw aipple'; an' that was a' he ate. But he took anither waucht o' the whusky, an' his een grew brichter, an' the stanes aboot him began to flash again; an' my leddy admired him the mair, that what wad hae felled ony ither man ony waukened him up a bit. An' syne he telled them hoo, laith to be fashous, he had gi'en orders till 's menyie to be aff afore the mornin' brak, an' wait at the neist cheenge-hoose till he jined them. 'Whaur,' said the leddy, 'I trust ye'll lat them wait, or else sen' for them.' But the yerl sat an' said never a word. The prence gae him ae glower, an' declared that his leddy's word was law to him; he wad bide till she wulled him to gang. At this her een shot fire 'maist like his ain, an' she smilit as she had never smilit afore; an' the yerl cudna bide the sicht o' 't, but daurna interfere: he rase an' left the room an' them thegither.

"What passed atwixt the twa, there was nane to tell: but or an hoor was by, they cam oot upo' the gairden terrace thegither, han' in han', luikin' baith o' them as gran' an' as weel pleased as gien they had been king and queen. The lang an' the short o' 't was, that the same day at nicht the twa was married. Naither o' them wad hear o' a priest. Say what the auld yerl cud, they wad *not* hear o' sic a thing, an' the leddy was 'maist mair set agane 't nor the prence. She wad be married accordin' to Scots law, she said, an' wad hae nae ither ceremony, say 'at he likit!

to gather himself a bit, and says he, 'We brew the same drink in my country, but a shade more powerful.' Then he asked for a slice of boar-ham and a raw apple; and that was all he ate. But he took another large draught of the whisky, and his eyes grew brighter, and the stones about him began to flash again; and my lady admired him the more, that what would have felled any other man only wakened him up a bit. And then he told them how, loath to give trouble, he had given orders to his men to be off before the morning broke, and wait at the next change-house till he joined them. 'Where,' said the lady, 'I trust you'll let them wait, or else send for them.' But the earl sat and said never a word. The prince glowered at him once, and declared that his lady's word was law to him; he would stay till she wished him to go. At this her eyes shot fire almost like his own, and she smiled as she had never smiled before; and the earl couldn't stand the sight of it, but dared not interfere: he rose and left the room and them together.

"What the pair said in private, there was none to tell; but before an hour had passed, they came out upon the garden terrace together, hand in hand, looking both of them as grand and as well pleased as if they had been king and queen. The long and the short of it was, that the same day at night the two were married. Neither of them would hear of a priest. Say what the old earl could, they would *not* hear of it, and the lady was almost more insistent than the prince. She would be married according to Scots law, she said, and would have no other ceremony, say what he liked!

"A gran' feast was gotten ready, an' jist the meenute afore it was cairriet to the ha', the great bell o' the castel yowlt oot, an' a' the fowk o' the hoose was gaithered i' the coortyaird, an' oot cam the twa afore them, han' in han', declarin' themsel's merried fowk, the whilk, accordin' to Scots law, was but ower guid a merriage. Syne they sat doon to their denner, an' there they sat—no drinkin' muckle, they say, but merrily enjoyin' themsel's, the leddy singin' a sang noo an' again, an' the prence sayin' he ance cud sing, but had forgotten the gait o' 't: but never a prayer said, nor a blessin' askit—oontil the clock chappit twal, whaurupon the prence and the prencess rase to gang to their bed—in a room whaur the king himsel' aye sleepit whan he cam to see them. But there wasna ane o' the men or the maids 'at wad hae daured be their lanes wi' that man, prence as he ca'd himsel'.

"A meenute, or barely twa, was ower, whan a cry cam frae the king's room—a fearfu' cry—a lang lang skreigh. The men an' the maids luikit at ane anither wi' awsome luiks; an' 'He's killin' her!' they a'gaspit at ance.

"Noo she was never a favourite wi' ony ane o' her ain fowk, but still they couldna hear sic a cry frae her ohn run to the yerl.

"They fand him pacin' up and doon the ha', an' luikin' like a deid man in a rage o' fear. But when they telled him, he only leuch at them, an' ca'd them ill names, an' said he had na hard a cheep. Sae they tuik naething by that, an' gaed back trimlin'.

"A grand feast was prepared, and just the minute before it was carried to the hall, the great bell of the castle rang out, and all the folk of the house were gathered in the courtyard, and out came the two before them, hand in hand, declaring themselves married folk, which, according to Scots law, was but too good a marriage. Then they sat down to their dinner, and there they sat—not drinking much, they say, but all making merry, the lady singing a song now and then, and the prince saying he once could sing, but had forgotten how: but never a prayer said, nor a blessing asked—until the clock struck twelve, whereupon the prince and the princess rose to go to their bed—in a room where the king himself always slept when he came to see them. But not one of the men or the maids would have dared be alone with that man, prince though he called himself.

"A minute, or barely two, were over, when a cry came from the king's room—a fearful cry—a long long shriek. The men and the maids looked at one another with awesome looks; and 'He's killing her!' they all gasped at once.

"Now she was never a favourite with any one of her own folk, but still they couldn't hear such a cry from her and not run to the earl.

"They found him pacing up and down the hall, and looking like a dead man in a rage of fear. But when they told him, he only laughed at them, and called them ill names, and said he hadn't heard a cheep. So they were nothing solaced, and they went back trembling.

"Twa o' them, a man an' a maid to haud hert in ane anither, gaed up to the door o' the transe 'at led to the king's room; but for a while they hard naething. Syne cam the soon' o' moanin' an' greitin' an' prayin'.

"The neist meenute they war back again amo' the lave, luikin' like twa corps. They had opent the door o' the transe to hearken closer, an' what sud they see there but the fiery een an' the white teeth o' the prence's horse, lyin' athort the door o' the king's room, wi' 's heid atween 's fore feet, an keepin' watch like a tyke!

"Er' lang they bethoucht themsels, an twa o' them set oot an aff thegither for the priory—that's whaur yer ain hoose o' Lossie noo stan's, my lord, to fess a priest. It wad be a guid twa hoor or they wan back, an' a' that time, ilka noo an' than, the moaning an' the beggin' an' the cryin' wad come again. An' the warder upo' the heich tooer declared 'at ever sin' midnicht the prence's menyie, the haill twal o' them, was careerin' aboot the castel, roon' an roon', wi' the een o' their beasts lowin', and their heids oot, an' their manes up, an their tails fleein' ahint them. He aye lost sicht o' them whan they wan to the edge o' the scaur, but roon' they aye cam again upo' the ither side, as gien there had been a ro'd whaur there wasna even a ledge.

"The moment the priest's horse set fut upo' the drawbrig, the puir leddy gae anither ougsome cry, a hantle waur nor the first, an' up gat a suddent roar an' a blast o' win' that maist cairried the castel there aff o' the cliff intill the watter, an' syne cam a flash o' blue licht an' a rum'lin'. Efter that, a' was quaiet: it was a' ower afore the priest

"Two of them, a man and a maid to put heart in each other, went up to the door of the passage that led to the king's room; but for a while they heard nothing. Then came the sound of moaning and crying and praying.

"The next minute they were back again among the rest, looking like two corpses. They had opened the door of the passage to listen closer, and what should they see there but the fiery eyes and the white teeth of the prince's horse, lying across the door of the king's room, with his head between his fore feet, keeping watch like a dog!

"Ere long they bethought themselves, and two of them set out together for the priory—that's where your own house of Lossie now stands, my lord, to fetch a priest. It would be a good two hours before they returned, and all that time, every now and then, the moaning and the begging and the crying would come again. And the warder upon the high tower declared that ever since midnight the prince's escort, all twelve of them, were careering about the castle, round and round, with the eyes of their beasts flaming, and their heads out, and their manes up, and their tails flying behind them. He lost sight of them every time they reached the edge of the cliff, but round they came each time again upon the other side, as if there had been a road where there wasn't even a ledge.

"The moment the priest's horse set foot upon the drawbridge, the poor lady gave another horrible cry, a good deal worse than the first, and up got a sudden roar and blast of wind that almost carried the castle there off the cliff and into the water, and then came a flash of blue light and a rumbling. After that, all was quiet: it wan athort the coortyaird an' up the stair. For he crossed himsel' an' gaed straucht for the bridal chaumer. By this time the yerl had come up, an' followed cooerin' ahin' the priest.

"Never a horse was i' the transe; an' the priest, first layin' the cross 'at hang frae 's belt agane the door o' the chaumer, flang 't open wi'oot ony ceremony, for ye 'll alloo there was room for nane.

"An' what think ye was the first thing the yerl saw?—A great hole i' the wa' o' the room, an' the starry pleuch luikin' in at it, an' the sea lyin' far doon afore him— as quaiet as the bride upo' the bed—but a hantle bonnier to luik at; for ilka steek that had been on her was brunt aff, an' the bonny body o' her lyin' a' runklet, an' as black 's a coal frae heid to fut; an' the reek 'at rase frae 't was heedeous. I needna say the bridegroom wasna there. Some fowk thoucht it a guid sign that he hadna cairried the body wi' him; but maybe he was ower suddent scared by the fut o' the priest's horse upo' the drawbrig, an' dauredna bide his oncome. Sae the fower-fut stane-wa' had to flee afore him, for a throu-gang to the Prence o' the Pooer o'the Air. An' yon's the verra hole to this day, 'at ye was sae near ower weel acquaint wi' yersel', my leddy. For the yerl left the castel, and never a Colonsay has made his abode there sin' syne. But some say 'at the rizzon the castel cam to be desertit a'thegither was, that as aften as they biggit up the hole, it fell oot again as sure 's the day o' the year cam roon' whan it first happened. They say, that at twal o'clock that same nicht, the door o' that room aye gaed tu, an' that naebody daur touch 't, for the

was all over before the priest's short step could measure the courtyard and climb the stair. For he crossed himself and made straight for the bridal chamber. By this time the earl had come up, and followed cowering behind the priest.

"Never a horse was in the passage; and the priest, first laying the cross that hung from his belt against the door of the chamber, flung it open without any ceremony, for you'll allow there was room for none.

"And what do you think was the first thing the earl saw?—A great hole in the wall of the room, and the starry plough looking in at it, and the sea lying far down before him—as quiet as the bride upon the bed— but much bonnier to look at; for every stitch that had been on her was burnt off, and the bonny body of her lying all wrinkled, and as black as a coal from head to foot; and the smoke that rose from it was hideous. I needn't say the bridegroom wasn't there. Some folk thought it a good sign that he hadn't carried the body with him; but maybe he had had too sudden a scare when he heard the tramp of the priest's horse on the drawbridge, and didn't dare abide his coming. So the four-foot stone-wall had to flee before him, for a portal to the Prince of the Power of the Air. And that's the very hole to this day, that you had such a close brush with yourself, my lady. For the earl left the castle, and never a Colonsay since has set up home there. But some say that the reason the castle came to be deserted altogether was, that as often as they built up the hole, it fell out again as sure as the day of the year came round when it first happened. They say, that at twelve o'clock that same night, the door of that room always shut, and that nobody dared touch it, for the heat o' the han'le o' 't; an' syne cam the skreighin' an' the moanin', an' the fearsome skelloch at the last, an' a rum'le like thun'er, an' i' the mornin' there was the wa' oot! The hole's bigger noo, for a' the decay o' the castel has taen to slidin' oot at it, an' doobtless it'll spread an' spread till the haill structur vainishes; at least sae they say, my lord; but I wad hae a try at the haudin' o' 't thegither for a' that. I dinna see 'at the deil sud hae 't a' his ain gait, as gien we war a' fleyt at him. Fowk hae threepit upo' me that there i' the gloamin' they hae seen an' awsome face luikin' in upo' them throu' that slap i' the wa'; but I never believed it was onything but their ain fancy, though for a' 'at I ken, it may ha' been something no canny. Still, I say, wha's feart? The Ill Man has no pooer 'cep ower his ain kin. We're tellt to resist him an' he'll flee frae 's."

"A good story, and well told," said the marquis kindly. "Don't you think so, Florimel?"

"Yes, papa," Lady Florimel answered; "only he kept us waiting too long for the end of it."

"Some fowk, my leddy," said Malcolm, "wad aye be at the hin'er en' o' a'thing. But for mysel', the mair pleased I was to be gaein' ony gait, the mair I wad spin oot the ro'd til 't."

"How much of the story may be your own invention now?" said the marquis.

"Ow, nae that muckle, my lord; jist a feow extras an' partic'lars 'at micht weel hae been, wi' an adjective, or an adverb, or sic like, here an' there. I made ae mistak' though; gien 't was yon hole yonner, they bude till hae gane doon an' no up the stair to their chaumer."

searing heat of its handle; and then came the shrieking and the moaning, and the fearsome scream at the last, and a rumble like thunder, and in the morning the wall was gone! The hole's bigger now, for all the decay of the castle has taken to sliding out at it, and doubtless it'll spread and spread, till the whole structure vanishes; at least so they say, my lord; but I would try my hand at holding it together for all that. I don't see that the devil should have it all his own way, as if we were all afraid of him. Folk have assured me that there in the gloaming they have seen an awesome face looking in upon them through that gap in the wall; but I never believed it was anything but their own fancy, though for all that I know, it may have been something not canny. Still, I say, who's afraid? The Evil One has no power except over his own kin. We're told to resist him and he'll flee from us."

"A good story, and well told," said the marquis kindly. "Don't you think so, Florimel?"

"Yes, papa," Lady Florimel answered; "only he kept us waiting too long for the end of it."

"Some folk, my lady," said Malcolm, "would always be rushing on to the end of things. But for myself, the more pleased I was to be going anywhere, the more I would lengthen the journey."

"How much of the story may be your own invention now?" said the marquis.

"Oh, not that much, my lord; just a few extras and particulars that might well have been, with an adjective, or an adverb, or suchlike, here and there. I made one mistake though; if it was that hole yonder, they must have gone down and not up the stair to their chamber."

His lordship laughed, and, again commending the tale, rose: it was time to re-embark—an operation less arduous than before, for in the present state of the tide it was easy to bring the cutter so close to a low rock that even Lady Florimel could step on board.

As they had now to beat to windward, Malcolm kept the tiller in his own hand. But indeed, Lady Florimel did not want to steer; she was so much occupied with her thoughts that her hands must remain idle.

Partly to turn them away from the more terrible portion of her adventure, she began to reflect upon her interview with Mrs Catanach—if *interview* it could be called, where she had seen no one. At first she was sorry that she had not told her father of it, and had the ruin searched; but when she thought of the communication the woman had made to her, she came to the conclusion that it was, for various reasons—not to mention the probability that he would have set it all down to the workings of an unavoidably excited nervous condition—better that she should mention it to no one but Duncan MacPhail.

When they arrived at the harbour quay, they found the carriage waiting, but neither the marquis nor Lady Florimel thought of Malcolm's foot, and he was left to limp painfully home. As he passed Mrs Catanach's cottage, he looked up: there were the blinds still drawn down; the door was shut, and the place was silent as the grave. By the time he reached Lossie House, his foot was very much swollen. When Mrs Courthope saw it, she sent him to bed at once, and applied a poultice.

CHAPTER XLII

DUNCAN'S DISCLOSURE

The night long Malcolm kept dreaming of his fall; and his dreams were worse than the reality, inasmuch as they invariably sent him sliding out of the breach, to receive the cut on the rocks below. Very oddly this catastrophe was always occasioned by the grasp of a hand on his ankle. Invariably also, just as he slipped, the face of the Prince appeared in the breach, but it was at the same time the face of Mrs Catanach.

The next morning, Mrs Courthope found him feverish, and insisted on his remaining in bed—no small trial to one who had never been an hour ill in his life; but he was suffering so much that he made little resistance.

In the enforced quiescence, and under the excitements of pain and fever, Malcolm first became aware how much the idea of Lady Florimel had at length possessed him. But even in his own thought he never once came upon the phrase, *in love,* as representing his condition in regard of her: he only knew that he worshipped her, and would be overjoyed to die for her. The youth had about as little vanity as could well consist with individual coherence; if he was vain at all, it was neither of his intellectual nor personal endowments, but of the few tunes he could play on his grandfather's pipes. He could run and swim, rare accomplishments amongst the fishermen, and was said to be the best dancer of them all; but he never thought of such comparison himself. The rescue of Lady Florimel made him very happy: he had been of service to her; but so far was he from cherishing a shadow of presumption, that as he lay there he felt it would be utter content to live serving her for ever, even when he was old and wrinkled and gray like his grandfather: he never dreamed of her growing old and wrinkled and gray.

A single sudden thought sufficed to scatter—not the devotion, but its peace. Of course she would marry some day, and what then? He looked the inevitable in the face; but as he looked, that face grew an ugly one. He broke into a laugh: his soul had settled like a brooding cloud over the gulf that lay between a fisher-lad and the daughter of a peer! But although he was no coxcomb, neither had fed himself on romances, as Lady Florimel had been doing of late, and although the laugh was quite honestly laughed at himself, it was nevertheless a bitter one. For again came the question: Why should an absurdity be a possibility? It was absurd, and yet possible: there was the point. In mathematics it was not so: there, of two opposites to prove one an absurdity, was to prove the other a fact.

Neither in metaphysics was it so: there also an impossibility and an absurdity were one and the same thing. But here, in a region of infinitely more import to the human life than an eternity of mathematical truth, there was at least one absurdity which was yet inevitable—an absurdity—yet with a villainous attendance of direst heat, marrow-freezing cold, faintings, and ravings, and demoniacal laughter.

Had it been a purely logical question he was dealing with, he might not have been quite puzzled; but to apply logic here, as he was attempting to do, was like—not like attacking a fortification with a penknife, for a penknife might win its way through the granite ribs of Cronstadt—it was like attacking an eclipse with a broomstick: there was a solution to the difficulty; but as the difficulty itself was deeper than he knew, so the answer to it lay higher than he could reach—was in fact at once grander and finer than he was yet capable of understanding.

His disjointed meditations were interrupted quite by the entrance of the man to whom alone of all men he could at the time have given a hearty welcome. The schoolmaster seated himself by his bedside, and they had a long talk. I had set down this talk, but came to the conclusion I had better not print it: ranging both high and wide, and touching on points of vital importance, it was yet so odd, that it would have been to too many of my readers but a Chimera tumbling in a vacuum—as they will readily allow when I tell them that it started from the question—which had arisen in Malcolm's mind so long ago, but which he had not hitherto propounded to his friend—as to the consequences of a man's marrying a mermaid; and that Malcolm, reversing its relations, proposed next, the consequences of a man's being in love with a ghost or an angel.

"I'm dreidfu' tired o' lyin' here i' my bed," said Malcolm at length when, neither desiring to carry the conversation further, a pause had intervened. "I dinna ken what I want. Whiles I think it's the sun, whiles the win', and whiles the watter. But I canna rist. Haena ye a bit ballant ye could say till me Mr Graham? There's naething wad quaiet me like a ballant."

The schoolmaster thought for a few minutes, and then said, "I'll give you one of my own, if you like, Malcolm. I made it some twenty or thirty years ago."

"That *wad* be a trate, sir," returned Malcolm; and the master, with perfect rhythm, and a modulation amounting almost to melody, repeated the following verses:

"I'm dreadfully tired of lying here in bed," said Malcolm at length when, neither desiring to carry the conversation further, a pause had intervened. "I don't know what I want. Sometimes I think it's the sun, sometimes the wind, and sometimes the water. But I can't rest. Haven't you some wee ballad you could say to me Mr Graham? There's nothing would quiet me like a ballad."

The schoolmaster thought for a few minutes, and then said, "I'll give you one of my own, if you like, Malcolm. I made it some twenty or thirty years ago."

"That *would* be a treat, sir," returned Malcolm; and the master, with perfect rhythm, and a modulation amounting almost to melody, repeated the following verses:

The water ran doon frae the heich hope-heid,
   Wi' a Rin, burnie, rin;
It wimpled, an' waggled, an' sang a screed
   O' nonsense, an' wadna blin,
   Wi' its Rin, burnie, rin.

Frae the hert o' the warl', wi' a swirl an' a sway,
   An' a Rin, burnie, rin,
That water lap clear frae the dark till the day,
   An' singin' awa' did spin,
   Wi' its Rin, burnie, rin

Ae wee bit mile frae the heich hope-heid,
   Wi' a Rin, burnie, rin,
'Mang her yows an' her lambs the herd lassie stude
   An' she loot a tear fa' in,
   Wi' a Rin, burnie, rin.

Frae the hert o' the maiden that tear-drap rase,
   Wi' a Rin, burnie rin;
Wearily clim'in' up narrow ways,
   There was but a drap to fa' in,
   Sae slow did that burnie rin.

Twa wee bit miles frae the heich hope-heid,
   Wi' a Rin, burnie, rin,
Doon creepit a cowerin' streakie o' reid,
   An' meltit awa' within,
   Wi' a Rin, burnie, rin.

Frae the hert o' a youth cam the tricklin' reid,
   Wi' a Rin, burnie, rin;
It ran an' ran till it left him deid,
   An' syne it dried up i' the win',
   An' that burnie nae mair did rin.

Whan the wimplin' burn that frae three herts gaed
   Wi' a Rin, burnie, rin,
Cam to the lip o' the sea sae braid,
   It curled an' grued wi' pain o' sin—
   But it took that burnie in.

English

The water ran down from the high hope-head,   (head of the valley)
With a Run, river, run;
And it sang as it flowed o'er its stony bed
Such nonsense as never was sung,
With its Run, river run.

From the heart of the world, with a swirl and a sway,
And a Run, river, run,
That water leaped clear from the dark to the day,
Its revel anew begun,
With its Run, river, run.

Just one short mile from the high hope-head,
With a Run, river, run,
And a single tear which a shepherdess shed
Mixed with the rippling water dun,
With a Run, river, run.

From the heart of the maiden that tear-drop rose,
With a Run, river, run;
Wearily climbing like one who goes
Toiling uphill in the burning sun,
So slow did that river run.

Just two short miles from the high hope-head,
With a Run, river, run,
Down crept a cowering streak of red,
And became with the water one,
With a Run, river, run.

From the heart of a youth came the trickling red,
With a run, river, run;
It ran and ran till it left him dead,
And then its thread was outspun,
And that river no more did run.

When the river was forth from those three hearts sent
With a Win, river, win,
And at last with its parent-sea was blent,
The sea-waves curled with the pain of sin—
But they took that river in.

"It's a bonny, bonny sang," said Malcolm; "but I canna say I *a*'thegither like it."

"Why not?" asked Mr Graham, with an inquiring smile.

"Because the ocean sudna mak a mou' at the puir earth-burnie that cudna help what ran intill 't."

"It took it in though, and made it clean, for all the pain *it* couldn't help either."

"Weel, gien ye luik at it that gait!" said Malcolm.

In the evening his grandfather came to see him, and sat down by his bedside, full of a tender anxiety which he was soon able to alleviate.

"Wownded in ta hand and in ta foot!" said the seer: "what can it mean? It must mean something, Malcolm, my son."

"Weel, daddy, we maun jist bide till we see," said Malcolm cheerfully.

A little talk followed, in the course of which it came into Malcolm's head to tell his grandfather the dream he had had so much of the first night he had slept in that room—but more for the sake of something to talk about that would interest one who believed in all kinds of prefigurations, than for any other reason.

Duncan sat moodily silent for some time, and then, with a great heave of his broad chest, lifted up his head, like one who had formed a resolution, and said:

"The hour has come. She has long peen afrait to meet it, put it has come, and Allister will meet it.—she'll not pe your cran'father, my son."

He spoke the words with perfect composure, but as soon as they were uttered, burst into a wail, and sobbed like a child.

"Ye'll be my ain father than?" said Malcolm.

"It's a bonny, bonny song," said Malcolm; "but I can't say that I *al*together like it."

"Why not?" asked Mr Graham, with an inquiring smile.

"Because the ocean shouldn't scorn the poor earth-river that couldn't help what ran into it."

"It took it in though, and made it clean, for all the pain *it* couldn't help either."

"Well, if you look at it that way!" said Malcolm.

In the evening his grandfather came to see him, and sat down by his bedside, full of a tender anxiety which he was soon able to alleviate.

"Wounded in ta hand and in ta foot!" said the seer: "what can it mean? It must mean something, Malcolm, my son."

"Well, daddy, we'll have to wait and see," said Malcolm cheerfully.

A little talk followed, in the course of which it came into Malcolm's head to tell his grandfather the dream he had had so much of the first night he had slept in that room—but more for the sake of something to talk about that would interest one who believed in all kinds of prefigurations, than for any other reason.

Duncan sat moodily silent for some time, and then, with a great heave of his broad chest, lifted up his head, like one who had formed a resolution, and said:

"The hour has come. She has long been afrait to meet it, but it has come, and Allister will meet it.—she'll not pe your cran'father, my son."

He spoke the words with perfect composure, but as soon as they were uttered, burst into a wail, and sobbed like a child.

"You'll be my own father then?" said Malcolm.

"No, no, my son. She'll not pe anything that's your own at aal!"

And the tears flowed down his channelled cheeks.

For one moment Malcolm was silent, utterly bewildered. But he must comfort the old man first, and think about what he had said afterwards.

"Ye're my ain daddy, whatever ye are!" he said. "Tell me a' aboot it, daddy."

"She'll tell you all she'll pe knowing, my son, and she nefer told a lie efen to a Cawmill."

He began his story in haste, as if anxious to have it over, but had to pause often from fresh outbursts of grief. It contained nothing more of the essential than I have already recorded, and Malcolm was perplexed to think why what he had known all the time should affect him so much in the telling. But when he ended with the bitter cry—"And now you'll pe loving her no more, my poy: my chilt, my Malcolm!" he understood it.

"Daddy! daddy!" he cried, throwing his arms round his neck and kissing him, "I lo'e ye better nor ever. An' weel I may!"

"But how can you, when you've cot none of ta plood in you, my son?" persisted Duncan.

"I hae as muckle as ever I had, daddy."

"Yes, put you'll tidn't know."

"But ye did, daddy."

"Yes, and inteet she cannot tell why she'll pe loving you so much herself aal ta time!"

"Weel, daddy, gien ye cud lo'e me sae weel, kennin' me nae bluid's bluid o' yer ain—I canna help it: I *maun* lo'e ye mair nor ever, noo' at I ken 't tu.—Daddy, daddy, I had *nae* claim upo' ye, an' ye hae been father an' gran'father an' a' to me!"

"No, no, my son. She'll not be anything that's your own at aal!"

And the tears flowed down his channelled cheeks.

For one moment Malcolm was silent, utterly bewildered. But he must comfort the old man first, and think about what he had said afterwards.

"You're my own daddy, whatever you are!" he said. "Tell me all about it, daddy."

"She'll tell you all she'll be knowing, my son, and she nefer told a lie efen to a Cawmill."

He began his story in haste, as if anxious to have it over, but had to pause often from fresh outbursts of grief. It contained nothing more of the essential than I have already recorded, and Malcolm was perplexed to think why what he had known all the time should affect him so much in the telling. But when he ended with the bitter cry—"And now you'll be loving her no more, my boy: my chilt, my Malcolm!" he understood it.

"Daddy! daddy!" he cried, throwing his arms round his neck and kissing him, "I love you better than ever. And well I may!"

"But how can you, when you've got none of ta blood in you, my son?" persisted Duncan.

"I have as much as ever I had, daddy."

"Yes, but you'll tidn't know."

"But you did, daddy."

"Yes, and inteet she cannot tell why she'll be loving you so much herself aal ta time!"

"Well, daddy, if you could love me so well, knowing me none of your own blood—I can't help it: I *must* love you more than ever, now that I know it too.—Daddy, daddy, I had *no* claim upon you, and you have been father and grandfather and all to me!"

"What could she do, Malcolm, my poy? Ta chilt had no one, and she had no one, and so it wass. You must pe her own poy after all! And she'll not pe wondering put.—It might pe.—Yes, inteed not!"

His voice sank to the murmurs of a half-uttered soliloquy, and as he murmured he stroked Malcolm's cheek.

"What are ye efter noo daddy?" asked Malcolm.

The only sign that Duncan heard the question was the complete silence that followed. When Malcolm repeated it, he said something in Gaelic, but finished the sentence thus, apparently unaware of the change of language:

"—only how else should she pe lovin you so much, Malcolm, my son?"

"I ken what Maister Graham would say, daddy," rejoined Malcolm, at a half-guess.

"What would he say, my son? He's a coot man, your Maister Graham.—It could not pe without ta sem fathers, and ta sem chief."

"He wad say it was 'cause we war a' o' ae bluid—'cause we had a' ae father."

"Oh yes, no toubt! We aal come from ta same first paarents; put tat will be a fery long way off, pefore ta clans cot tokether. It'll not pe holding fery well now, my son. Tat waas pefore ta Cawmills."

"That's no what Maister Graham would mean, daddy," said Malcolm. "He would mean that God was the father o' 's a', and sae we cudna help lo'in' ane anither."

"No; tat cannot pe right, Malcolm; for then we should haf to love eferybody. Now she loves you, my son, and she hates Cawmill of Clenlyon. She loves Mistress Partan

"What could she do, Malcolm, my boy? Ta child had no one, and she had no one, and so it wass. You must be her own boy after all! And she'll not be wondering but.—It might be.—Yes, inteed not!"

His voice sank to the murmurs of a half-uttered soliloquy, and as he murmured he stroked Malcolm's cheek.

"What are you after now daddy?" asked Malcolm.

The only sign that Duncan heard the question was the complete silence that followed. When Malcolm repeated it, he said something in Gaelic, but finished the sentence thus, apparently unaware of the change of language:

"—only how else should she be lovin you so much, Malcolm, my son?"

"I know what Mister Graham would say, daddy," rejoined Malcolm, at a half-guess.

"What would he say, my son? He's a good man, your Maister Graham.—It could not be without ta same fathers, and ta same chief."

"He would say it was because we were all of one blood—because we all had one father."

"Oh yes, no toubt! We aal come from ta same first paarents; put tat will be a fery long way off, before ta clans got tokether. It'll not pe holding fery well now, my son. Tat waas before ta Cawmills."

"That's not what Mister Graham would mean, daddy," said Malcolm. "He would mean that God was the father of us all, and so we couldn't help loving one another."

"No; tat cannot be right, Malcolm; for then we should haf to love eferybody. Now she loves you, my son, and she hates Cawmill of Clenlyon. She loves Mistress Partan when she'll not pe too rude to her, and she hates tat Mistress Catanach. She's a paad woman, 'tat, she'll pe certain sure, though she'll nefer saw her to speak to her. She'll haf claaws to her poosoms."

"Weel, daddy, there was naething ither to gar ye lo'e me. I was jist a helpless human bein', an' sae for that, an' nae ither rizzon, ye tuik a' that fash wi' me! An' for mysel', I'm deid sure I cudna lo'e ye better gien ye war twise my gran'father."

"He's her own poy!" cried the piper, much comforted; and his hand sought his head, and lighted gently upon it. "Put, maype," he went on, "she might not haf loved you so much if she hadn't peen tinking sometimes—"

He checked himself. Malcolm's questions brought no conclusion to the sentence, and a long silence followed.

"Supposin' I was to turn oot a Cawmill?" said Malcolm, at length.

The hand that was fondling his curls withdrew as if a serpent had bit it, and Duncan rose from his chair.

"Wass it her own son to pe speaking such an efil thing?" he said, in a tone of injured and sad expostulation.

"For onything ye ken, daddy—ye canna tell but it *mith* be."

"Ton't preathe it, my son!" cried Duncan in a voice of agony, as if he saw unfolding a fearful game the arch-enemy had been playing for his soul. "Put it cannot pe," he resumed instantly, "for ten how should she pe loving you, my son?"

"'Cause ye was in for that afore ye kent wha the puir beastie was."

when she'll not be too rude to her, and she hates tat Mistress Catanach. She's a baad woman, that, she'll pe certain sure, though she'll nefer saw her to speak to her. She'll haf claaws to her boosoms."

"Well, daddy, there was nothing else to make you love me. I was just a helpless human being, and so for that, and no other reason, you took all that trouble with me! And for myself, I'm dead sure I couldn't love you better if you were quite my grandfather."

"He's her own boy!" cried the piper, much comforted; and his hand sought his head, and lighted gently upon it. "But, maybe," he went on, "she might not haf loved you so much if she hadn't peen thinking sometimes—"

He checked himself. Malcolm's questions brought no conclusion to the sentence, and a long silence followed.

"Supposing I was to turn out a Campbell?" said Malcolm, at length.

The hand that was fondling his curls withdrew as if a serpent had bit it, and Duncan rose from his chair.

"Wass it her own son to be speaking such an efil thing?" he said, in a tone of injured and sad expostulation.

"For anything you know, daddy—you can't tell but it *might* be."

"Ton't breathe it, my son!" cried Duncan in a voice of agony, as if he saw unfolding a fearful game the arch-enemy had been playing for his soul. "But it cannot be," he resumed instantly, "for ten how should she be loving you, my son?"

"Because you already loved it before you knew who the poor thing was."

"Ta tarling chilt! she could *not* haf loved him if he had peen a Cawmill. Her soul would haf chumped pack from him as from ta snake in ta tree. Ta hate in her heart to ta plood of ta Cawmill, would have killed ta chilt of ta Cawmill plood. No, Malcolm! no, my son!"

"Ye wadna hae me believe, daddy, that gien ye had kent by mark o' hiv an' horn, that the cratur they laid i' yer lap was a Cawmill—ye wad hae risen up, an' lootin it lie whaur it fell?"

"No, Malcolm; I would haf put my foot upon it, as I would on ta young fiper in ta heather."

"Gien I *was* to turn oot ane o' that ill race, ye wad hate me, than, daddy—efter a'! Ochone, daddy! Ye wad be weel pleased to think hoo ye stack yer durk throu' the ill han' o' me, an' wadna rist till ye had it throu' the waur hert.—I doobt I had better up an' awa', daddy, for wha' kens what ye mayna du to me?"

Malcolm made a movement to rise, and Duncan's quick ears understood it. He sat down again by his bedside and threw his arms over him.

"Lie town, lie town, my poy. If you ket up, tat will pe you are a Cawmill. No, no, my son! You are ferry cruel to your own old daddy. She would pe too much sorry for her poy to hate him. It will pe so treadful to pe a Cawmill! No, no, my poy! She would take you to her poosom, and tat would trive ta Cawmill out of you. Put ton't speak of it any more, my son, for it cannot pe.—She must co now, for her pipes will pe waiting for her."

"Ta tarling chilt! she could *not* haf loved him if he had been a Cawmill. Her soul would haf chumped pack from him as from ta snake in ta tree. Ta hate in her heart to ta blood of ta Cawmill, would have killed ta chilt of ta Cawmill blood. No, Malcolm! no, my son!"

"You wouldn't have me believe, daddy, that if you had known by mark of hoof and horn, that the wee thing they laid in your lap was a Campbell—you would have risen up, and let it lie where it fell?"

"No, Malcolm; I would haf put my foot upon it, as I would on ta young viper in ta heather."

"If I *did* turn out a Campbell, you would hate me, then, daddy—after all! Alas, daddy! You would rejoice to think how you stuck your dirk through my cursed hand, and wouldn't rest till you had it through my twice-cursed heart.—I think I had better march, daddy, for who knows what you mightn't do to me?"

Malcolm made a movement to rise, and Duncan's quick ears understood it. He sat down again by his bedside and threw his arms over him.

"Lie town, lie town, my boy. If you get up, tat will be you are a Cawmill. No, no, my son! You are ferry cruel to your own old daddy. She would be too much sorry for her boy to hate him. It will be so treadful to be a Cawmill! No, no, my boy! She would take you to her boosom, and tat would trive ta Cawmill out of you. But ton't speak of it any more, my son, for it cannot be.—She must go now, for her pipes will be waiting for her."

Malcolm feared he had ventured too far, for never before had his grandfather left him except for work. But the possibility he had started might do something to soften the dire endurance of his hatred.

His thoughts turned to the new darkness let in upon his history and prospects. All at once the cry of the mad laird rang in his mind's ear: "I dinna ken whaur I cam frae!"

Duncan's revelation brought with it nothing to be done—hardly anything to be *thought*—merely room for most shadowy, most unfounded conjecture—nay, not conjecture—nothing but the vaguest of castle-building! In merry mood, he would henceforth be the son of some mighty man, with a boundless future of sunshine opening before him; in sad mood, the son of some strolling gipsy or worse—his very origin better forgotten—a disgrace to the existence for his share in which he had hitherto been peacefully thankful.

Like a lurking phantom-shroud, the sad mood leaped from the field of his speculation, and wrapped him in its folds: sure enough he was but a beggar's brat—How henceforth was he to look Lady Florimel in the face? Humble as he had believed his origin, he had hitherto been proud of it: with such a high-minded sire as he deemed his own, how could he be other? But now! Nevermore could he look one of his old companions in the face! They were all honourable men; he a base-born foundling!

He would tell Mr Graham of course; but what could Mr Graham say to it? The fact remained. He must leave Portlossie.

His mind went on brooding, speculating, devising. The evening sunk into the night, but he never knew he was in the dark until the housekeeper brought him a light. After a cup of tea, his thoughts found pleasanter paths. One thing was certain: he must lay himself out, as he had never done before, to make Duncan MacPhail happy. With this one thing clear to both heart and mind, he fell fast asleep.

CHAPTER XLIII

THE WIZARD'S CHAMBER

He woke in the dark, with that strange feeling of bewilderment which accompanies the consciousness of having *been* waked: is it that the brain wakes before the mind, and like a servant unexpectedly summoned, does not know what to do with its master from home? or is it that the master wakes first, and the servant is too sleepy to answer his call? Quickly coming to himself, however, he sought the cause of the perturbation now slowly ebbing. But the dark into which he stared could tell nothing; therefore he abandoned his eyes, took his station in his ears, and thence sent out his messengers. But neither, for some moments, could the scouts of hearing come upon any sign.

At length, something seemed doubtfully to touch the sense—the faintest suspicion of a noise in the next room—the wizard's chamber: it was enough to set Malcolm on the floor.

Forgetting his wounded foot and lighting upon it, the agony it caused him dropped him at once on his hands and knees, and in this posture he crept into the passage. As soon as his head was outside his own door, he saw a faint gleam of light coming from beneath that of the next room. Advancing noiselessly, and softly feeling for the latch, his hand encountered a bunch of keys depending from the lock, but happily did not set them jingling. As softly, he lifted the latch, when, almost of itself, the door opened a couple of inches, and, with bated breath, he saw the back of a figure he could not mistake—that of Mrs Catanach. She was stooping by the side of a tent-bed much like his own, fumbling with the bottom hem of one of the check-curtains, which she was holding towards the light of a lantern on a chair. Suddenly she turned her face to the door, as if apprehending a presence; as suddenly, he closed it, and turned the key in the lock. To do so he had to use considerable force, and concluded its grating sound had been what waked him.

Having thus secured the prowler, he crept back to his room, considering what he should do next. The speedy result of his cogitations was, that he indued his nether garments, though with difficulty from the size of his foot, thrust his head and arms through a jersey, and set out on hands and knees for an awkward crawl to Lord Lossie's bedroom.

It was a painful journey, especially down the two spiral stone stairs, which led to the first floor where he lay. As he went, Malcolm resolved, in order to avoid rousing needless observers, to enter the room, if possible, before waking the marquis.

The door opened noiselessly. A night-light, afloat in a crystal cup, revealed the bed, and his master asleep, with one arm lying on the crimson quilt. He crept in, closed the door behind him, advanced halfway to the bed, and in a low voice called the marquis.

Lord Lossie started up on his elbow, and without a moment's consideration seized one of a brace of pistols which lay on a table by his side, and fired. The ball went with a sharp thud into the thick mahogany door.

"My lord! my lord!" cried Malcolm, "it's only me!"

"And who the devil are you?" returned the marquis, snatching up the second pistol.

"Malcolm, yer ain henchman, my lord."

"Damn you! what are you about then? Get up. What are you after there—crawling like a thief?"

As he spoke he leaped from the bed, and seized Malcolm by the back of the neck.

"It's a mercy I wasna mair like an honest man," said Malcolm, "or that bullet wad hae been throu' the hams o' me. Yer lordship's a wheen ower rash."

"Rash! you rascal!" cried Lord Lossie; "when a fellow comes into my room on his hands and knees in the middle of the night! Get up, and tell me what you are after, or, by Jove! I'll break every bone in your body."

A kick from his bare foot in Malcolm's ribs fitly closed the sentence.

"Ye *are* ower rash, my lord!" persisted Malcolm. "I canna get up. I hae a fit the size o' a sma' buoy!"

"Speak, then, you rascal!" said his lordship, loosening his hold, and retreating a few steps, with the pistol cocked in his hand.

"My lord! my lord!" cried Malcolm, "it's only me!"

"And who the devil are you?" returned the marquis, snatching up the second pistol.

"Malcolm, your own henchman, my lord."

"Damn you! what are you about then? Get up. What are you after there—crawling like a thief?"

As he spoke he leaped from the bed, and seized Malcolm by the back of the neck.

"It's a mercy I wasn't more like an honest man," said Malcolm, "or that bullet would have been through my legs. Your lordship's a touch too rash."

"Rash! you rascal!" cried Lord Lossie; "when a fellow comes into my room on his hands and knees in the middle of the night! Get up, and tell me what you are after, or, by Jove! I'll break every bone in your body."

A kick from his bare foot in Malcolm's ribs fitly closed the sentence.

"You *are* too rash, my lord!" persisted Malcolm. "I can't get up. I have a foot the size of a small buoy!"

"Speak, then, you rascal!" said his lordship, loosening his hold, and retreating a few steps, with the pistol cocked in his hand.

"Dinna ye think it wad be better to lock the door, for fear the shot sud bring ony o' the fowk?" suggested Malcolm, as he rose to his knees and leaned his hands on a chair.

"You're bent on murdering me—are you then?" said the marquis, beginning to come to himself and see the ludicrousness of the situation.

"Gien I had been that, my lord, I wadna hae waukent ye up first."

"Well, what the devil is it all about?—You needn't think any of the men will come. They're a pack of the greatest cowards ever breathed."

"Weel, my lord, I hae gruppit her at last, an' I bude to come an tell ye."

"Leave your beastly gibberish. You can speak what at least resembles English when you like."

"Weel, my lord, I hae her unner lock an' keye."

"Who, in the name of Satan?"

"Mistress Catanach, my lord!"

"Damn her eyes! What's she to me that I should be waked out of a good sleep for *her?*"

"That's what I wad fain yer lordship kent: *I* dinna."

"None of your riddles! Explain yourself;—and make haste; I want to go to bed again."

"'Deed, yer lordship maun jist pit on yer claes, an' come wi' me."

"Where to?"

"To the warlock's chaumer, my lord—whaur that ill wuman remains 'in durance vile,' as Spenser wad say—but no sae vile's hersel', I doobt."

Thus arrived at length, with a clear road before him, at the opening of his case, Malcolm told in few words what

"Don't you think it would be better to lock the door, for fear the shot should bring any of the folk?" suggested Malcolm, as he rose to his knees and leaned his hands on a chair.

"You're bent on murdering me—are you then?" said the marquis, beginning to come to himself and see the ludicrousness of the situation.

"If I had been, my lord, I wouldn't have wakened you up first."

"Well, what the devil is it all about?—You needn't think any of the men will come. They're a pack of the greatest cowards ever breathed."

"Weel, my lord, I hae gruppit her at last, an' I bude to come an tell ye."

"Leave your beastly gibberish. You can speak what at least resembles English when you like."

"Well, my lord, I have her under lock and key."

"Who, in the name of Satan?"

"Mistress Catanach, my lord!"

"Damn her eyes! What's she to me that I should be waked out of a good sleep for *her?*"

"That's what I wish your lordship knew: *I* don't."

"None of your riddles! Explain yourself;—and make haste; I want to go to bed again."

"Your lordship will have to put on your clothes rather, and come with me."

"Where to?"

"To the warlock's chamber, my lord—where that evil woman remains 'in durance vile,' as Spenser would say—but not so vile as herself, I think."

Thus arrived at length, with a clear road before him, at the opening of his case, Malcolm told in few words what had fallen out. As he went on, the marquis grew interested, and by the time he had finished, had got himself into dressing-gown and slippers.

"Wadna ye tak yer pistol?" suggested Malcolm slyly.

"What! to meet a woman?" said his lordship.

"Ow na! but wha kens there michtna be anither murderer aboot? There micht be twa in ae nicht."

had fallen out. As he went on, the marquis grew interested, and by the time he had finished, had got himself into dressing-gown and slippers.

"Won't you be taking your pistol?" suggested Malcolm slyly.

"What! to meet a woman?" said his lordship.

"Oh na! but who knows if there mightn't be another murderer about? There might be two in one night."

Impertinent as was Malcolm's humour, his master did not take it amiss: he lighted a candle, told him to lead the way, and took his revenge by making joke after joke upon him as he crawled along. With the upper regions of his house the marquis was as little acquainted, as with those of his nature, and required a guide.

Arrived at length at the wizard's chamber, they listened at the door for a moment, but heard nothing; neither was there any light visible at its lines of junction. Malcolm turned the key, and the marquis stood close behind, ready to enter. But the moment the door was unlocked, it was pulled open violently, and Mrs Catanach, looking too high to see Malcolm who was on his knees, aimed a good blow at the face she did see, in the hope, no doubt, of thus making her escape. But it fell short, being countered by Malcolm's head in the softest part of her person, with the result of a clear entrance. The marquis burst out laughing, and stepped into the room with a rough joke. Malcolm remained in the doorway.

"My lord," said Mrs Catanach, gathering herself together, and rising little the worse, save in temper, for the treatment he had commented upon, "I have a word for your lordship's own ear."

"Your right to be there does stand in need of explanation," said the marquis.

She walked up to him with confidence.

"You shall have an explanation, my lord," she said, "such as shall be my full quittance for intrusion even at this untimely hour of the night."

"Say on then," returned his lordship.

"Send that boy away then, my lord."

"I prefer having him stay," said the marquis.

"Not a word shall cross my lips till he's gone," persisted Mrs Catanach. "I know him too well! Awa' wi' ye, ye deil's buckie!" she continued, turning to Malcolm; "I ken mair aboot ye nor ye ken aboot yersel', an' deil hae't I ken o' guid to you or yours! But I s' gar ye lauch o' the wrang side o' *your* mou' yet, my man."

"Not a word shall cross my lips till he's gone," persisted Mrs Catanach. "I know him too well! Away with you, you devil's whelp!" she continued, turning to Malcolm; "I know more about you than you know about yourself, and devil a bit of it is good news to you or yours! But I'll make you laugh on the wrong side of *your* mouth yet, my man."

Malcolm, who had seated himself on the threshold, only laughed and looked reference to his master.

"Your lordship was never in the way of being frightened at a woman," said Mrs Catanach, with an ugly expression of insinuation.

The marquis shrugged his shoulders.

"That depends," he said. Then turning to Malcolm, "Go along," he added; "only keep within call. I may want you."

"Nane o' yer hearkenin' at the keye-hole, though, or I s' lug-mark ye, ye—!" said Mrs Catanach, finishing the sentence none the more mildly that she did it only in her heart.

"I wadna hae ye believe *a'* 'at she says, my lord," said Malcolm, with a significant smile, as he turned to creep away.

He closed the door behind him, and lest Mrs Catanach should repossess herself of the key, drew it from the lock, and, removing a few yards, sat down in the passage by his own door. A good many minutes passed, during which he heard not a sound.

At length the door opened, and his lordship came out. Malcolm looked up, and saw the light of the candle the marquis carried, reflected from a face like that of a corpse. Different as they were, Malcolm could not help thinking of the only dead face he had ever seen. It terrified him for the moment in which it passed without looking at him.

"My lord!" said Malcolm gently.

His master made no reply.

"My lord!" cried Malcolm, hurriedly pursuing him with his voice, "am I to lea' the keyes wi' yon hurdon, and lat her open what doors she likes?"

Malcolm, who had seated himself on the threshold, only laughed and looked reference to his master.

"Your lordship was never in the way of being frightened at a woman," said Mrs Catanach, with an ugly expression of insinuation.

The marquis shrugged his shoulders.

"That depends," he said. Then turning to Malcolm, "Go along," he added; "only keep within call. I may want you."

"None of your listening at the key-hole, or I'll clip your ear for you, you—!" said Mrs Catanach, finishing the sentence none the more mildly that she did it only in her heart.

"I wouldn't have you believe *all* that she says, my lord," said Malcolm, with a significant smile, as he turned to creep away.

He closed the door behind him, and lest Mrs Catanach should repossess herself of the key, drew it from the lock, and, removing a few yards, sat down in the passage by his own door. A good many minutes passed, during which he heard not a sound.

At length the door opened, and his lordship came out. Malcolm looked up, and saw the light of the candle the marquis carried, reflected from a face like that of a corpse. Different as they were, Malcolm could not help thinking of the only dead face he had ever seen. It terrified him for the moment in which it passed without looking at him.

"My lord!" said Malcolm gently.

His master made no reply.

"My lord!" cried Malcolm, hurriedly pursuing him with his voice, "am I to leave the keys with that harridan, and let her open what doors she likes?"

"Go to bed," said the marquis angrily, "and leave the woman alone;" with which words he turned into the adjoining passage, and disappeared.

"Go to bed," said the marquis angrily, "and leave the woman alone;" with which words he turned into the adjoining passage, and disappeared.

Mrs Catanach had not come out of the wizard's chamber, and for a moment Malcolm felt strongly tempted to lock her in once more. But he reflected that he had no right to do so after what his lordship had said—else, he declared to himself, he would have given her at least as good a fright as she seemed to have given his master, to whom he had no doubt she had been telling some horrible lies. He withdrew, therefore, into his room—to lie pondering again for a wakeful while.

This horrible woman claimed then to know more concerning him than his so-called grandfather, and, from her profession, it was likely enough; but information from her was hopeless—at least until her own evil time came; and then, how was any one to believe what she might choose to say? So long, however, as she did not claim him for her own, she could, he thought, do him no hurt he would be afraid to meet.

But what could she be about in that room still? She might have gone, though, without the fall of her soft fat foot once betraying her!

Again he got out of bed, and crept to the wizard's door, and listened. But all was still. He tried to open it, but could not: Mrs Catanach was doubtless spending the night there, and perhaps at that moment lay, evil conscience and all, fast asleep in the tent-bed. He withdrew once more, wondering whether she was aware that he occupied the next room; and, having, for the first time, taken care to fasten his own door, got into bed, finally this time, and fell asleep.

CHAPTER XLIV

THE HERMIT

Malcolm had flattered himself that he would at least be able to visit his grandfather the next day; but, instead of that, he did not even make an attempt to rise—head as well as foot aching so much, that he felt unfit for the least exertion—a phase of being he had never hitherto known. Mrs Courthope insisted on advice, and the result was that a whole week passed before he was allowed to leave his room.

In the meantime, a whisper awoke and passed from mouth to mouth in all directions through the little burgh—whence arising only one could tell, for even her mouthpiece, Miss Horn's Jean, was such a mere tool in the midwife's hands, that she never doubted but Mrs Catanach was, as she said, only telling the tale as it was told to her. Mrs Catanach, moreover, absolutely certain that no threats would render Jean capable of holding her tongue, had so impressed upon her the terrible consequences of repeating what she had told her, that, the moment the echo of her own utterances began to return to her own ears, she began to profess an utter disbelief in the whole matter—the precise result Mrs Catanach had foreseen and intended: now she lay unsuspected behind Jean, as behind a wall whose door was built up; for she had so graduated her threats, gathering the fullest and vaguest terrors of her supernatural powers about her name, that while Jean dared, with many misgivings, to tamper with the secret itself she dared not once mention Mrs Catanach in connection with it. For Mrs Catanach herself, she never alluded to the subject, and indeed when it was mentioned in her hearing pretended to avoid it; but at the same time she took good care that her silence should be not only eloquent, but discreetly so, that is, implying neither more nor less than she wished to be believed.

The whisper, in its first germinal sprout, was merely that Malcolm was not a MacPhail; and even in its second stage it only amounted to this, that neither was he the grandson of old Duncan.

In the third stage of its development, it became the assertion that Malcolm was the son of somebody of consequence; and in the fourth, that a certain person, not yet named, lay under shrewd suspicion.

The fifth and final form it took was, that Malcolm was the son of Mrs Stewart of Gersefell, who had been led to believe that he died within a few days of his birth, whereas he had in fact been carried off and committed to the care of Duncan MacPhail, who drew a secret annual stipend of no small amount in consequence—whence indeed his well-known riches!

Concerning this final form of the whisper, a few of the women of the burgh believed or thought or fancied they remembered both the birth and reported death of the child in question—also certain rumours afloat at the time, which cast an air of probability over the new reading of his fate. In circles more remote from authentic sources, the general reports met with remarkable embellishments, but the framework of the rumour—what I may call the bones of it—remained undisputed.

From Mrs Catanach's behaviour, every one believed that she knew all about the affair, but no one had a suspicion that she was the hidden fountain and prime mover of the report—so far to the contrary was it that people generally anticipated a frightful result for her when the truth came to be known, for that Mrs Stewart would follow her with all the vengeance of a bereaved tigress. Some indeed there were who fancied that the mother, if not in full complicity with the midwife, had at least given her consent to the *arrangement*; but these were not a little shaken in their opinion when at length Mrs Stewart herself began to figure more immediately in the affair, and it was witnessed that she had herself begun to search into the report. Certain it was that she had dashed into the town in a carriage and pair—the horses covered with foam—and had hurried, quite *raised-like*, (agitated) from house to house, prosecuting inquiries. It was said that, finding at length, after much labour that she could arrive at no certainty even as to the first promulgator of the assertion, she had a terrible fit of crying, and professed herself unable, much as she would have wished it, to believe a word of the report: it was far too good news to be true; no such luck ever fell to *her* share—and so on. That she did not go near Duncan MacPhail was accounted for by the reflection, that, on the supposition itself, he was of the opposite party, and the truth was not to be looked for from him.

At length it came to be known that, strongly urged, and battling with a repugnance all but invincible, she had gone to see Mrs Catanach, and had issued absolutely radiant with joy, declaring that she was now absolutely satisfied, and, as soon as she had communicated with the young man himself, would, without compromising any one, take what legal steps might be necessary to his recognition as her son.

Although, however, these things had been going on all the week that Malcolm was confined to his room, they had not reached this last point until after he was out again, and mean time not a whisper of them had come to his or Duncan's ears. Had they been still in the Seaton, one or other of the travelling ripples of talk must have found them; but Duncan had come and gone between his cottage and Malcolm's bedside, without a single downy feather from the still widening flap of the wings of Fame ever dropping on him; and the only persons who visited Malcolm besides were the Doctor—too discreet in his office to mix himself up with gossip; Mr Graham, to whom nobody, except it had been Miss Horn, whom he had not seen for a fortnight, would have dreamed of mentioning such a subject; and Mrs Courthope—not only discreet like the doctor, but shy of such discourse as any reference to the rumour must usher in its train.

At length he was sufficiently recovered to walk to his grandfather's cottage; but only now for the first time had he a notion of how far bodily condition can reach in the oppression and overclouding of the spiritual atmosphere.

"Gien I be like this," he said to himself, "what maun the weather be like aneth yon hump o' the laird's!"

"If I be like this," he said to himself, "what must the weather be like beneath that hump of the laird's!"

Now also for the first time he understood what Mr Graham had meant when he told him that he only was a strong man who was strong in weakness; he only a brave man who, inhabiting trembling, yet faced his foe; he only a true man who, tempted by *good*, yet abstained.

Duncan received him with delight, made him sit in his own old chair, got him a cup of tea, and waited upon him with the tenderness of a woman. While he drank his tea, Malcolm recounted his last adventure in connection with the wizard's chamber.

"Tat will be ta ped she'll saw in her feeshon," said Duncan, whose very eyes seemed to listen to the tale.

"Tat will be ta bed she'll saw in her vision," said Duncan, whose very eyes seemed to listen to the tale.

When Malcolm came to Mrs Catanach's assertion that she knew more of him than he did himself—

When Malcolm came to Mrs Catanach's assertion that she knew more of him than he did himself—

"Then she peliefs ta voman does, my poy. We are aall poth of us in ta efil voman's power," said Duncan sadly.

"Then she beliefs ta woman does, my boy. We are aall both of us in ta efil woman's power," said Duncan sadly.

"Never a hair, daddy!" cried Malcolm. "A' pooer 's i' the han's o' ane, that's no *her* maister. Ken she what she likes, she canna pairt you an' me, daddy."

"Never a hair, daddy!" cried Malcolm. "All power's in the hands of one, that's not *her* master. Whatever she knows, she can't part you and me, daddy."

"God forpid!" responded Duncan. "But we must pe on our kard."

"God forbid!" responded Duncan. "But we must be on our kard."

Close by the cottage stood an ivy-grown bridge, of old leading the king's highway across the burn to the Auld Toon, but now leading only to the flower-garden. Eager for the open air of which he had been so long deprived, and hoping he might meet the marquis or Lady Florimel, Malcolm would have had his grandfather to accompany him thither; but Duncan declined, for he had not yet attended to the lamps; and Malcolm therefore went alone.

He was slowly wandering, where never wind blew, betwixt rows of stately hollyhocks, on which his eyes fed, while his ears were filled with the sweet noises of a little fountain, issuing from the upturned beak of a marble swan, which a marble urchin sought in vain to check by squeezing the long throat of the bird, when the sounds of its many-toned fall in the granite basin seemed suddenly centupled on every side, and Malcolm found himself caught in a tremendous shower. Prudent enough to avoid getting wet in the present state of his health, he made for an arbour he saw near by, on the steep side of the valley—one he had never before happened to notice.

Now it chanced that Lord Lossie himself was in the garden, and, caught also by the rain while feeding some pet goldfishes in a pond, betook himself to the same summer-house, following Malcolm.

Entering the arbour, Malcolm was about to seat himself until the shower should be over, when, perceiving a mossy arched entrance to a gloomy recess in the rock behind, he went to peep into it, curious to see what sort of a place it was.

Now the foolish whim of a past generation had, in the farthest corner of the recess, and sideways from the door, seated the figure of a hermit, whose jointed limbs were so furnished with springs and so connected with the stone that floored the entrance, that as soon as a foot pressed the threshold, he rose, advanced a step, and held out his hand.

The moment, therefore, Malcolm stepped in, up rose a pale, hollow-cheeked, emaciated man, with eyes that stared glassily, made a long skeleton-like stride towards him, and held out a huge bony hand, rather, as it seemed, with the intent of clutching, than of greeting, him. An unaccountable horror seized him; with a gasp which had nearly become a cry, he staggered backwards out of the cave. It seemed to add to his horror that the man did not follow—remained lurking in the obscurity behind. In the arbour Malcolm turned—turned to flee!—though why, or from what, he had scarce an idea.

But when he turned he encountered the marquis, who was just entering the arbour.

"Well, MacPhail," he said kindly, "I'm glad—"

But his glance became fixed in a stare; he changed colour, and did not finish his sentence.

"I beg yer lordship's pardon," said Malcolm, wondering through all his perturbation at the look he had brought on his master's face; "I didna ken ye was at han'."

"What the devil makes you look like that?" said the marquis, plainly with an effort to recover himself.

Malcolm gave a hurried glance over his shoulder.

"Ah! I see!" said his lordship, with a mechanical kind of smile, very unlike his usual one; "—you've never been in there before?"

"No, my lord."

"And you got a fright?"

"Well, MacPhail," he said kindly, "I'm glad—"

But his glance became fixed in a stare; he changed colour, and did not finish his sentence.

"I beg your lordship's pardon," said Malcolm, wondering through all his perturbation at the look he had brought on his master's face; "I didn't know you were here."

"What the devil makes you look like that?" said the marquis, plainly with an effort to recover himself.

Malcolm gave a hurried glance over his shoulder.

"Ah! I see!" said his lordship, with a mechanical kind of smile, very unlike his usual one; "—you've never been in there before?"

"No, my lord."

"And you got a fright?"

"Ken ye wha's that, in there, my lord?"

"You booby! It's nothing but a dummy—with springs, and—and —all damned tomfoolery!"

While he spoke his mouth twitched oddly, but instead of his bursting into the laugh of enjoyment natural to him at the discomfiture of another, his mouth kept on twitching and his eyes staring.

"Ye maun hae seen him yersel' ower my shouther, my lord," hinted Malcolm.

"I saw your face, and that was enough to—" But the marquis did not finish the sentence.

"Weel, 'cep it was the oonnaiteral luik o' the thing—no human, an' yet sae dooms like it—I can not account for the grue or the trimmle 'at cam ower me, my lord, I never fan' onything like it i' my life afore. An' even noo 'at I unnerstan' what it is, I kenna what wad gar me luik the boody i' the face again."

"Go in at once," said the marquis fiercely.

Malcolm looked him full in the eyes.

"Ye mean what ye say, my lord?"

"Yes, by God!" said the marquis, with an expression I can describe only as of almost savage solemnity.

Malcolm stood silent for one moment.

"Do you think I'll have a man about me that has no more courage than—than—a woman!" said his master, concluding with an effort.

"I was jist turnin' ower an auld question, my lord—whether it be lawfu' to obey a tyrant. But it's na worth stan'in' oot upo'. I s' gang."

"Do you know who that is, in there, my lord?"

"You booby! It's nothing but a dummy—with springs, and—and —all damned tomfoolery!"

While he spoke his mouth twitched oddly, but instead of his bursting into the laugh of enjoyment natural to him at the discomfiture of another, his mouth kept on twitching and his eyes staring.

"You must have seen him yourself over my shoulder, my lord," hinted Malcolm.

"I saw your face, and that was enough to—" But the marquis did not finish the sentence.

"Well, except it was the unnatural look of the thing—not human, and yet so very like it—I can't account for the horror or the trembling that came over me, my lord, I never felt anything like it in my life before. And even now that I understand what it is, I don't know what would bring me to look the bogie in the face again."

"Go in at once," said the marquis fiercely.

Malcolm looked him full in the eyes.

"You mean what you say, my lord?"

"Yes, by God!" said the marquis, with an expression I can describe only as of almost savage solemnity.

Malcolm stood silent for one moment.

"Do you think I'll have a man about me that has no more courage than—than—a woman!" said his master, concluding with an effort.

"I was just turning over an old question, my lord—whether it be lawful to obey a tyrant. But it's not worth making a stand upon. I'll go."

He turned to the arch, placed a hand on each side of it, and leaning forward with outstretched neck, peeped cautiously in, as if it were the den of a wild beast. The moment he saw the figure—seated on a stool—he was seized with the same unaccountable agitation, and drew back shivering.	He turned to the arch, placed a hand on each side of it, and leaning forward with outstretched neck, peeped cautiously in, as if it were the den of a wild beast. The moment he saw the figure—seated on a stool—he was seized with the same unaccountable agitation, and drew back shivering.
"Go in," shouted the marquis.	"Go in," shouted the marquis.

Most Britons would count obedience to such a command slavish; but Malcolm's idea of liberty differed so far from that of most Britons, that he felt, if now he refused to obey the marquis, he might be a slave for ever; for he had already learned to recognize and abhor that slavery which is not the less the root of all other slaveries that it remains occult in proportion to its potency—self slavery: he must and would conquer this whim, antipathy, or whatever the loathing might be: it was a grand chance given him of proving his will supreme—that is himself a free man! He drew himself up, with a full breath, and stepped within the arch. Up rose the horror again, jerked itself towards him with a clank, and held out its hand. Malcolm seized it with such a gripe that its fingers came off in his grasp.

"Will that du, my lord?" he said calmly, turning a face rigid with hidden conflict, and gleaming white, from the framework of the arch, upon his master, whose eyes seemed to devour him.	"Will that do, my lord?" he said calmly, turning a face rigid with hidden conflict, and gleaming white, from the framework of the arch, upon his master, whose eyes seemed to devour him.
"Come out," said the marquis, in a voice that seemed to belong to some one else.	"Come out," said the marquis, in a voice that seemed to belong to some one else.
"I hae blaudit yer playock, my lord," said Malcolm ruefully, as he stepped from the cave and held out the fingers.	"I've broken that toy of yours, my lord," said Malcolm ruefully, as he stepped from the cave and held out the fingers.
Lord Lossie turned and left the arbour.	Lord Lossie turned and left the arbour.

Had Malcolm followed his inclination, he would have fled from it, but he mastered himself still, and walked quietly out. The marquis was pacing, with downbent head and hasty strides, up the garden: Malcolm turned the other way.

The shower was over, and the sun was drawing out millions of mimic suns from the drops that hung, for a moment ere they fell, from flower and bush and great tree. But Malcolm saw nothing. Perplexed with himself and more perplexed yet with the behaviour of his master, he went back to his grandfather's cottage, and, as soon as he came in, recounted to him the whole occurrence.

"He had a feeshon," said the bard, with wide eyes. "He comes of a race that sees."

"What cud the veesion hae been, daddy?"

"Tat she knows not, for ta feeshon tid not come to her," said the piper solemnly.

"He had a feeshon," said the bard, with wide eyes. "He comes of a race that sees."

"What could the vision have been, daddy?"

"Tat she knows not, for ta feeshon tid not come to her," said the piper solemnly.

Had the marquis had his vision in London, he would have gone straight to his *study*, as he called it, not without a sense of the absurdity involved, opened a certain cabinet, and drawn out a certain hidden drawer; being at Lossie, he walked up the glen of the burn to the bare hill, overlooking the House, the royal burgh, the great sea, and his own lands lying far and wide around him. But all the time he saw nothing of these—he saw but the low white forehead of his vision, a mouth of sweetness, and hazel eyes that looked into his very soul.

Malcolm walked back to the House, clomb the narrow duct of an ancient stone stair that went screwing like a great auger through the pile from top to bottom, sought the wide lonely garret, flung himself upon his bed, and from his pillow gazed through the little dormer window on the pale blue skies flecked with cold white clouds, while in his mind's eye he saw the foliage beneath burning in the flames of slow decay, diverse as if each of the seven in the prismatic chord had chosen and seared its own: the first nor'easter that drove the flocks of Neptune on the sands, would sweep its ashes away. Life, he said to himself, was but a poor gray kind of thing after all. The peacock summer had folded its gorgeous train, and the soul within him had lost its purple and green, its gold and blue. He never thought of asking how much of the sadness was owing to bodily conditions with which he was little acquainted, and to compelled idleness in one accustomed to an active life. But if he had, the sorrowful probabilities of life would have seemed just the same. And indeed he might have argued that, to be subject to any evil from a cause inadequate, only involves an absurdity that embitters the pain by its mockery. He had yet to learn what faith can do, in the revelation of the Moodless, for the subjugation of mood to will.

As he lay thus weighed upon rather than pondering, his eye fell on the bunch of keys which he had taken from the door of the wizard's chamber, and he wondered that Mrs Courthope had not seen and taken them—apparently had not missed them. And the chamber doomed to perpetual desertion lying all the time open to any stray foot! Once more at least, he must go and turn the key in the lock.

As he went the desire awoke to look again into the chamber, for that night he had had neither light nor time enough to gain other than the vaguest impression of it.

But for no lifting of the latch would the door open.—How could the woman—witch she must be—have locked it? He proceeded to unlock it. He tried one key, then another. He went over the whole bunch. Mystery upon mystery!—not one of them would turn. Bethinking himself, he began to try them the other way, and soon found one to throw the bolt *on*. He turned it in the contrary direction, and it threw the bolt off: still the door remained immovable! It must then—awful thought!—be fast on the inside! Was the woman's body lying there behind those check curtains? Would it lie there until it vanished, like that of the wizard,—vanished utterly—bones and all, to a little dust, which one day a housemaid might sweep up in a pan?

On the other hand, if she had got shut in, would she not have made noise enough to be heard?—he had been day and night in the next room! But it was not a spring-lock, and how could that have happened? Or would she not have been missed, and inquiry made after her? Only such an inquiry might well have never turned in the direction of Lossie House, and he might never have heard of it, if it had.

Anyhow he must do something; and the first rational movement would clearly be to find out quietly for himself whether the woman was actually missing or not.

Tired as he was he set out at once for the burgh, and the first person he saw was Mrs Catanach standing on her doorstep and shading her eyes with her hand, as she looked away out to the horizon over the roofs of the Seaton. He went no farther.

In the evening he found an opportunity of telling his master how the room was strangely closed; but his lordship pooh-poohed, and said something must have gone wrong with the clumsy old lock.

With vague foresight, Malcolm took its key from the bunch, and, watching his opportunity, unseen hung the rest on their proper nail in the housekeeper's room. Then, having made sure that the door of the wizard's chamber was locked, he laid the key away in his own chest.

CHAPTER XLV

MR CAIRNS AND THE MARQUIS

The religious movement amongst the fisher-folk was still going on. Their meeting was now held often during the week, and at the same hour on the Sunday as other people met at church. Nor was it any wonder that, having participated in the fervour which pervaded their gatherings in the cave, they should have come to feel the so-called divine service in the churches of their respective parishes a dull, cold, lifeless, and therefore unhelpful ordinance, and at length regarding it as composed of beggarly elements, breathing of bondage, to fill the Baillies' Barn three times every Sunday—a reverential and eager congregation.

Now, had they confined their prayers and exhortations to those which, from an ecclesiastical point of view, constitute the unholy days of the week, Mr Cairns would have neither condescended nor presumed to take any notice of them; but when the bird's-eye view from his pulpit began to show patches of bare board where human forms had wont to appear; and when these plague-spots had not only lasted through successive Sundays, but had begun to spread more rapidly, he began to think it time to put a stop to such fanatical aberrations—the result of pride and spiritual presumption—hostile towards God, and rebellious towards their lawful rulers and instructors.

For what an absurdity it was that the spirit of truth should have anything to communicate to illiterate and vulgar persons except through the mouths of those to whom had been committed the dispensation of the means of grace! Whatever wind might blow, except from their bellows, was, to Mr Cairns at least, not even of doubtful origin. Indeed the priests of every religion, taken in class, have been the slowest to recognize the wind of the spirit, and the quickest to tell whence the blowing came and whither it went—even should it have blown first on their side of the hedge. And how could it be otherwise? How should they recognize as a revival the motions of life unfelt in their own hearts, where it was most required? What could they know of doubts and fears, terrors and humiliations, agonies of prayer, ecstasies of relief, and thanksgiving, who regarded their high calling as a profession, with social claims and ecclesiastical rights; and even as such had so little respect for it that they talked of it themselves as *the cloth*? How could such a man as Mr Cairns, looking down from the height of his great soberness and the dignity of possessing the oracles and the ordinances, do other than contemn the enthusiasms and excitements of ignorant repentance? How could such as he recognize in the babble of babes the slightest indication of the revealing of truths hid from the wise and prudent; especially since their rejoicing also was that of babes, hence carnal, and accompanied by all the weaknesses and some of the vices which it had required the utmost energy of the prince of apostles to purge from one at least of the early churches?

He might, however, have sought some foundation for a true judgment, in a personal knowledge of their doctrine and collective behaviour; but, instead of going to hear what the babblers had to say, and thus satisfying himself whether the leaders of the movement spoke the words of truth and soberness, or of discord and denial—whether their teaching and their prayers were on the side of order and law, or tending to sedition—he turned a ready ear to all the reports afloat concerning them, and, misjudging them utterly, made up his mind to use all *lawful* means for putting an end to their devotions and exhortations. One fact he either had not heard or made no account of—that the public-houses in the villages whence these assemblies were chiefly gathered, had already come to be all but deserted.

Alone, then, and unsupported by one of his brethren of the Presbytery, even of those who suffered like himself, he repaired to Lossie House, and laid before the marquis the whole matter from his point of view—that the tabernacles of the Lord were deserted for dens and caves of the earth; that fellows so void of learning as not to be able to put a sentence together, or talk decent English, (a censure at which Lord Lossie smiled, for his ears were accustomed to a different quality of English from that which now invaded them) took upon themselves to expound the Scriptures; that they taught antinomianism, (for which assertion, it must be confessed, there was some *apparent* ground) and were at the same time suspected of Arminianism and Anabaptism: that, in a word, they were a terrible disgrace to the godly and hitherto sober-minded parishes in which the sect, if it might be dignified with even such a name, had sprung up.

The marquis listened with much indifference, and some impatience: what did he or any other gentleman care about such things? Besides, he had a friendly feeling towards the fisher folk, and a decided disinclination to meddle with their liberty, either of action or utterance.[18]

"But what have I to do with it, Mr Cairns?" he said, when the stream of the parson's utterance had at length ceased to flow. "I am not a theologian; and if I were, I do not see how that even would give me a right to interfere."

---

[18] Ill, from all artistic points of view, as such a note comes in, I must, for reasons paramount to artistic considerations, remind my readers, that not only is the date of my story half a century or so back, but, dealing with principles, has hardly anything to do with actual events, and nothing at all with persons. The *local* skeleton of the story alone is taken from the real, and I had not a model, not to say an original, for one of the characters in it—except indeed Mrs Catanach's dog.

"In such times of insubordination as these, my lord," said Mr Cairns, "when every cadger thinks himself as good as an earl, it is more than desirable that not a single foothold should be lost. There *must* be a general election soon, my lord. Besides, these men abuse your lordship's late hospitality, declaring it has had the worst possible influence on the morals of the people."

A shadow of truth rendered this assertion the worse misrepresentation: no blame to the marquis had even been hinted at; the speakers had only animadverted on the fishermen who had got drunk on the occasion.

"Still," said the marquis, smiling, for the reported libel did not wound him very deeply, "what ground of right have I to interfere?"

"The shore is your property, my lord—every rock and every buckie (*spiral shell*) upon it; the caves are your own—every stone and pebble of them: you can prohibit all such assemblies."

"And what good would that do? They would only curse me, and go somewhere else."

"Where could they go, where the same law wouldn't hold, my lord? The coast is yours for miles and miles on both sides."

"I don't know that it should be."

"Why not, my lord? It has belonged to your family from time immemorial, and will belong to it, I trust, while the moon endureth."

"They used to say," said the marquis thoughtfully, as if he were recalling something he had heard long ago, "that the earth was the Lord's."

"This part of it is Lord Lossie's," said Mr Cairns, combining the jocular with the complimentary in one irreverence; but, as if to atone for the freedom he had taken—" The Deity has committed it to the great ones of the earth to rule for him," he added, with a devout obeisance to the delegate.

Lord Lossie laughed inwardly.

"You can even turn them out of their houses, if you please, my lord," he superadded.

"God forbid!" said the marquis.

"A threat—the merest hint of such a measure is all that would be necessary."

"But are you certain of the truth of these accusations?"

"My lord!"

"Of course you believe them, or you would not repeat them, but it does not follow that they are fact."

"They are matter of common report, my lord. What I have stated is in every one's mouth."

"But you have not yourself heard any of their sermons, or what do they call them?"

"No, my lord," said Mr Cairns, holding up his white hands in repudiation of the idea; "it would scarcely accord with my position to act the spy."

"So, to keep yourself immaculate, you take all against them for granted! I have no such scruples, however. I will go and see, or rather hear, what they are about: after that I shall be in a position to judge."

"Your lordship's presence will put them on their guard."

"If the mere sight of me is a check," returned the marquis, "extreme measures will hardly be necessary."

He spoke definitively, and made a slight movement, which his visitor accepted as his dismissal. He laughed aloud when the door closed, for the spirit of what the Germans call *Schadenfreude* was never far from his elbow, and he rejoiced in the parson's discomfiture. It was in virtue of his simplicity, precluding discomfiture, that Malcolm could hold his own with him so well. For him he now sent.

"Well, MacPhail," he said kindly, as the youth entered, "how is that foot of yours getting on?"

"Brawly, my lord; there's naething muckle the maitter wi' hit or me aither, noo 'at we're up. But I was jist nearhan' deid o' ower muckle bed."

"Hadn't you better come down out of that cockloft?" said the marquis, dropping his eyes.

"Na, my lord; I dinna care aboot pairtin' wi' my neebour yet."

"What neighbour?"

"Ow, the auld warlock, or whatever it may be 'at hauds a reemish there."

"What! is *he* troublesome next?"

"Ow, na! I'm no thinkin' 't; but 'deed I dinna ken, my lord!" said Malcolm.

"What do you mean, then?"

"Gien yer lordship wad aloo me to force yon door, I wad be better able to tell ye."

"Then the old man is *not* quiet?"

"There's something no quaiet."

"Nonsense! It's all your imagination—depend on it."

"I dinna think it."

"What *do* you think, then? You're not afraid of ghosts, surely?"

"No muckle. I hae naething mair upo' my conscience nor I can bide i' the deidest o' the nicht."

"Well, MacPhail," he said kindly, as the youth entered, "how is that foot of yours getting on?"

"Very well, my lord; there's nothing much the matter with it or me either, now that we're up. But keeping to my bed so much has near-hand killed me."

"Hadn't you better come down out of that cockloft?" said the marquis, dropping his eyes.

"Na, my lord; I don't care to part with my neighbour yet."

"What neighbour?"

"Oh, the old warlock, or whatever it may be that keeps up a romage there."

"What! is *he* troublesome next?"

"Oh, na! I think not; but indeed I don't know, my lord!" said Malcolm.

"What do you mean, then?"

"If your lordship would allow me to force that door, I would be better able to tell you."

"Then the old man is *not* quiet?"

"There's something there that isn't."

"Nonsense! It's all your imagination—depend on it."

"I think not."

"What *do* you think, then? You're not afraid of ghosts, surely?"

"Not much. I have nothing more upon my conscience than I can stand in the deadest of the night."

"Then you think ghosts come of a bad conscience? A kind of moral *delirium tremens*—eh?"

"I dinna ken, my lord; but that's the only kin' o' ghaist I wad be fleyed at—at least 'at I wad rin frae. I wad a heap raither hae a ghaist i' my hoose nor ane far'er benn. An ill man, or wuman, like Mistress Catanach, for enstance, 'at's a' boady, 'cep' what o' her 's deevil,"

"Nonsense!" said the marquis, angrily; but Malcolm went on:

"—maun be jist fu' o' ghaists! An' for onything I ken, that 'll be what maks ghaists o' themsel's efter they're deid, settin' them *walkin'*, as they ca' 't. It's full waur nor bein' possessed wi' deevils, an' maun be a hantle mair ooncoamfortable.—But I wad hae yon door opent, my lord."

"Nonsense!" exclaimed the marquis once more, and shrugged his shoulders. "You must leave that room. If I hear anything more about noises, or that sort of rubbish, I shall insist upon it.—I sent for you now, however, to ask you about these clandestine meetings of the fisher-folk."

"Clandestine, my lord? There's no *clam* aboot them, but the clams upo' the rocks."

The marquis was not etymologist enough to understand Malcolm's poor pun, and doubtless thought it worse than it was.

"I don't want any fooling," he said. "Of course you know these people?"

"Ilka man, wuman, an' bairn o' them," answered Malcolm.

"And what sort are they?"

"Siclike as ye micht expec'."

"That's not a very luminous answer."

"Then you think ghosts come of a bad conscience? A kind of moral *delirium tremens*—eh?"

"I don't know, my lord; but that's the only kind of ghost that would frighten me—at least that I would run from. I would far rather have a ghost in my house than one inside of me. An evil man or woman, like Mistress Catanach, for instance, that's all body, except for the part of her that's devil,"

"Nonsense!" said the marquis, angrily; but Malcolm went on:

"—must be just full of ghosts! And for anything I know, that'll be what makes ghosts of themselves after they're dead, setting them *walking*, as they call it. It's rather worse than being possessed by devils, and must be much more uncomfortable. But I would have that door opened, my lord."

"Nonsense!" exclaimed the marquis once more, and shrugged his shoulders. "You must leave that room. If I hear anything more about noises, or that sort of rubbish, I shall insist upon it.—I sent for you now, however, to ask you about these clandestine meetings of the fisher-folk."

"Clandestine, my lord? There's no *clam* about them, but the clams upon the rocks."

The marquis was not etymologist enough to understand Malcolm's poor pun, and doubtless thought it worse than it was.

"I don't want any fooling," he said. "Of course you know these people?"

"Every man, woman, and child of them," answered Malcolm.

"And what sort are they?"

"Such as you might expect."

"That's not a very luminous answer."

"Weel, they're nae waur nor ither fowk, to begin wi'; an' gien this hauds, they'll be better nor mony."

"What sort are their leaders?"

"Guid, respectable fowk, my lord."

"Then there's not much harm in *them?*"

"There's nane but what they wad fain be rid o'. I canna say as muckle for a' 'at hings on to them. There's o' them, nae doobt, wha wad fain win to h'aven ohn left their sins ahin' them; but they get nae encouragement frae Maister MacLeod. Blue Peter, 'at gangs oot wi' 's i' yer lordship's boat—he's ane o' their best men—though he never gangs ayont prayin', I'm tauld."

"Which is far enough, surely," said his lordship, who, belonging to the Episcopal church, had a different idea concerning the relative dignities of preaching and praying.

"Ay, for a body's sel', surely; but maybe no aye eneuch for ither fowk," answered Malcolm, always ready after his clumsy fashion.

"Have you been to any of these meetings?"

"I was at the first twa, my lord."

"Why not more?"

"I didna care muckle aboot them, an' I hae aye plenty to du. Besides, I can get mair oot o' Maister Graham wi' twa words o' a question nor the haill crew o' them could tell me atween this an' eternity."

"Well, I am going to trust you," said the marquis slowly, with an air of question rather than of statement.

"Ye may du that, my lord."

"You mean I may with safety?"

"I div mean that same, my lord."

"Well, they're no worse than other folk, to begin with; and if this lasts, they'll be better than many."

"What sort are their leaders?"

"Good, respectable folk, my lord."

"Then there's not much harm in *them?*"

"There's none but what they would fain be rid of. I can't say as much for all their hangers-on. There's some of them, doubtless, who would fain get to heaven without leaving their sins behind; but they get no encouragement from Mister MacLeod. Blue Peter, who goes out with us in your lordship's boat—he's one of their best men—though he never goes beyond praying, I'm told."

"Which is far enough, surely," said his lordship, who, belonging to the Episcopal church, had a different idea concerning the relative dignities of preaching and praying.

"Ay, for a man himself, surely; but maybe not always enough for other folk," answered Malcolm, always ready after his clumsy fashion.

"Have you been to any of these meetings?"

"I was at the first two, my lord."

"Why not more?"

"I didn't care much about them, and I was always kept busy. Besides, I can get more out of Mister Graham with two words of a question than the whole crew of them could tell me between this and eternity."

"Well, I am going to trust you," said the marquis slowly, with an air of question rather than of statement.

"You may do that, my lord."

"You mean I may with safety?"

"That's just what I do mean, my lord."

"You can hold your tongue then?"

"I can, an' I wull my lord," said Malcolm; but added in haste, "—'cept it interfere wi' ony foregane agreement or nat'ral obligation."

It must be borne in mind that Malcolm was in the habit of discussing all sorts of questions with Mr Graham: some of the formulae wrought out between them he had made himself thoroughly master of.

"By Jupiter!" exclaimed the marquis, with a pause of amusement. "Well," he went on, "I suppose I must take you on your own terms.—They've been asking me to put a stop to these conventicles."

"Wha has, my lord?"

"That's my business."

"Lat it be nae ither body's, my lord."

"That's my intention. I told him I would go and judge for myself."

"Jist like yer lordship!"

"What do you mean by that?"

"I was aye sure ye was for fair play, my lord."

"It's little enough I've ever had," said the marquis.

"Sae lang's we gie plenty, my lord, it maitters less hoo muckle we get. A'body likes to get it."

"That doctrine won't carry you far, my lad."

"Far eneuch, gien 't cairry me throu', my lord."

"How absolute the knave is!" said his lordship good humouredly. "—Well, but," he resumed, "—about these fishermen: I'm only afraid Mr Cairns was right."

"What said he, my lord?"

"That, when they saw me there, they would fit their words to my ears."

"You can hold your tongue then?"

"I can, and I will my lord," said Malcolm; but added in haste, "—except it interfere with any prior trust or natural obligation."

It must be borne in mind that Malcolm was in the habit of discussing all sorts of questions with Mr Graham: some of the formulae wrought out between them he had made himself thoroughly master of.

"By Jupiter!" exclaimed the marquis, with a pause of amusement. "Well," he went on, "I suppose I must take you on your own terms.—They've been asking me to put a stop to these conventicles."

"Who has, my lord?"

"That's my business."

"Let it be no one else's, my lord."

"That's my intention. I told him I would go and judge for myself."

"Just like your lordship!"

"What do you mean by that?"

"I was always sure you were for fair play, my lord."

"It's little enough I've ever had," said the marquis.

"As long as we give plenty, my lord, it matters less how much we get. Everyone likes to get it."

"That doctrine won't carry you far, my lad."

"Far enough, if it carries me through, my lord."

"How absolute the knave is!" said his lordship good humouredly. "—Well, but," he resumed, "—about these fishermen: I'm only afraid Mr Cairns was right."

"What said he, my lord?"

"That, when they saw me there, they would fit their words to my ears."

"I ken them better nor ony black-coat atween Cromarty an' Peterheid; an' I can tell yer lordship there winna be ae word o' differ for your bein' there."

"If only I could be there and not there both at once! There's no other sure mode of testing your assertion. What a pity the only thorough way should be an impossible one!"

"To a' practical purpose, it 's easy eneuch, my lord. Jist gang ohn be seen the first nicht, an' the neist gang in a co'ch an' fower. Syne compaur."

"Quite satisfactory, no doubt, if I could bring myself to do it; but, though I said I would, I don't like to interfere so far even as to go at all."

"At ony public meetin', my lord, ye hae as guid a richt to be present, as the puirest body i' the lan'. An' forbye that, as lord o' the place, ye hae a richt to ken what's gaein' on: I dinna ken hoo far the richt o' interferin' gangs; that's anither thing a'thegither."

"I see you're a thorough-going rebel yourself."

"Naething o' the kind, my lord. I'm only sae far o' yer lordship's min' 'at I like fair play—gien a body could only be aye richt sure what was fair play!"

"Yes, there's the very point!—certainly, at least, when the question comes to be of eavesdropping—not to mention that I could never condescend to play the spy."

"What a body has a richt to hear, he may hear as he likes—either shawin' himsel' or hidin' himsel'. An' it 's the *only* plan 'at 's fair to them, my lord. It's no 's gien yer lordship was lyin' in wait to du them a mischeef: ye want raither to du them a kin'ness, an' tak their pairt."

"I know them better than any black-coat between Cromarty and Peterhead; and I can tell your lordship there won't be one word of difference for your being there."

"If only I could be there and not there both at once! There's no other sure mode of testing your assertion. What a pity the only thorough way should be an impossible one!"

"To all practical purpose, it's easy enough, my lord. Just go unseen the first night, and the next go in a coach and four. Then compare."

"Quite satisfactory, no doubt, if I could bring myself to do it; but, though I said I would, I don't like to interfere so far even as to go at all."

"At any public meeting, my lord, you have as good a right to be present, as the poorest body in the land. And besides, as lord of the place, you have a right to know what's going on: I don't know how far the right of interfering goes; that's another thing altogether."

"I see you're a thorough-going rebel yourself."

"Nothing of the kind, my lord. I'm only so far of your lordship's mind that I like fair play—if one could only be always certain what was fair play!"

"Yes, there's the very point!—certainly, at least, when the question comes to be of eavesdropping—not to mention that I could never condescend to play the spy."

"What a man has a right to hear, he may hear as he likes—either showing himself or hiding himself. And it's the *only* plan that's fair to them, my lord. It's not as if your lordship was lying in wait to do them a mischief: you want rather to do them a kindness, and take their part."

"I don't know that, Malcolm. It depends."

"It's plain yer lordship's prejudeezed i' their fawvour. Ony gait I'm sartin it 's fair play ye want; an' I canna for the life o' me see a hair o' wrang i' yer lordship's gaein' *in a cogue*, as auld Tammy Dyster ca's 't; for, at the warst, ye cud only interdick them, an' that ye cud du a' the same, whether ye gaed or no. An', gien ye be sae wulled, I can tak you an' my leddy whaur ye'll hear ilka word 'at 's uttered, an' no a body get a glimp o' ye, mair nor gien ye was sittin' at yer ain fireside as ye are the noo."

"That does make a difference!" said the marquis, a great part of whose unwillingness arose from the dread of discovery. "It would be very amusing."

"I'll no promise ye that," returned Malcolm. "I dinna ken aboot that.—There's jist ae objection hooever: ye wad hae to gang a guid hoor afore they begoud to gaither.—An' there's aye laadies aboot the place sin' they turned it intill a kirk!" he added thoughtfully. "But," he resumed, "we cud manage them."

"How?"

"I wad get my gran'father to strik' up wi' a spring upo' the pipes, o' the other side o' the bored craig—or lat aff a shot of the sweevil: they wad a' rin to see, an' i' the meantime we cud lan' ye frae the cutter. We wad hae ye in an' oot o' sicht in a moment—Blue Peter an' me—as quaiet as gien ye war ghaists, an' the hoor midnicht."

The marquis was persuaded, but objected to the cutter. They would walk there, he said. So it was arranged that Malcolm should take him and Lady Florimel to the Baillies' Barn the very next time the fishermen had a meeting.

"I don't know that, Malcolm. It depends."

"It's plain your lordship's prejudiced in their favour. Anyway I'm certain it's fair play you want; and I can't for the life of me see the least wrong in your lordship going *in a cogue*, as old Tammy Dyster calls it; for, at the worst, you could only put a stop to them, and that you could do regardless, whether you went or not. And, if you want, I can take you and my lady where you'll hear every word that's uttered, and no one get a glimpse of you, more than if you were sitting at your own fireside as you are just now."

"That does make a difference!" said the marquis, a great part of whose unwillingness arose from the dread of discovery. "It would be very amusing."

"I won't promise you that," returned Malcolm. "I don't know about that.—There's just one objection however: you would have to go a good hour before they began to gather.—And there are always laddies about the place since they turned it into a church!" he added thoughtfully. "But," he resumed, "we could manage them."

"How?"

"I would get my grandfather to strike up with a spring upon the pipes, on the other side of the bored craig—or let off a shot of the swivel: they would all run to see, and in the meantime we could land you from the cutter. We would have you in and out of sight in a moment—Blue Peter and me—as quiet as if you were ghosts, and the hour midnight."

The marquis was persuaded, but objected to the cutter. They would walk there, he said. So it was arranged that Malcolm should take him and Lady Florimel to the Baillies' Barn the very next time the fishermen had a meeting.

CHAPTER XLVI

THE BAILLIES' BARN

ady Florimel was delighted at the prospect of such an adventure. The evening
arrived. An hour before the time appointed for the meeting, the three issued from
the tunnel, and passed along the landward side of the dune, towards the promontory. There sat the piper on the swivel, ready to sound a pibroch the moment they should
have reached the shelter of the bored craig—his signal being Malcolm's whistle. The plan
answered perfectly. In a few minutes, all the children within hearing were gathered about
Duncan—a rarer sight to them than heretofore—and the way was clear to enter unseen.

It was already dusk, and the cave was quite dark, but Malcolm lighted a candle, and,
with a little difficulty, got them up into the wider part of the cleft, where he had arranged
comfortable seats with plaids and cushions. As soon as they were placed, he extinguished
the light.

"I wish you would tell us another story, Malcolm," said Lady Florimel.

"Do," said the marquis "the place is not consecrated yet."

"Did ye ever hear the tale o' the auld warlock, my leddy?" asked Malcolm. "Only my lord kens 't!" he added.

"*I* don't," said Lady Florimel.

"It's great nonsense," said the marquis.

"Do let us have it, papa."

"Very well. I don't mind hearing it again." He wanted to see how Malcolm would embellish it.

"It seems to me," said Malcolm, "that this ane aboot Lossie Hoose an' yon ane aboot Colonsay Castel, are verra likly but twa stalks frae the same rute. Ony gate, this ane aboot the warlock maun be the auldest o' the twa. Ye s' hae 't sic 's I hae 't mysel'. Mistress Coorthoup taul' 't to me."

"I wish you would tell us another story, Malcolm," said Lady Florimel.

"Do," said the marquis "the place is not consecrated yet."

"Did you ever hear the tale of the old warlock, my lady?" asked Malcolm. "Only my lord knows it!" he added.

"*I* don't," said Lady Florimel.

"It's great nonsense," said the marquis.

"Do let us have it, papa."

"Very well. I don't mind hearing it again." He wanted to see how Malcolm would embellish it.

"It seems to me," said Malcolm, "that this one about Lossie House and that one about Colonsay Castle, are very likely but two stalks from the rame root. Anyway, this one about the warlock must be the older of the two. You shall have it just as I've heard it myself. Mistress Courthope told it to me."

It was after his own more picturesque fashion, however, that he recounted the tale of Lord Gernon.

As the last words left his lips, Lady Florimel gave a startled cry, seized him by the arm, and crept close to him. The marquis jumped to his feet, knocked his head against the rock, uttered an oath, and sat down again.

"What ails ye, my leddy!" said Malcolm. "There's naething here to hurt ye."

"I saw a face," she said, "a white face!"

"Whaur?"

"Beyond you a little way—near the ground," she answered, in a tremulous whisper.

"It's as dark's pick!" said Malcolm, as if thinking it to himself.—He knew well enough that it must be the laird or Phemy, but he was anxious the marquis should not learn the secret of the laird's refuge.

"I saw a face anyhow," said Florimel. "It gleamed white for one moment, and then vanished."

"I wonner ye didna cry oot waur, my leddy," said Malcolm, peering into the darkness.

"I was too frightened. It looked so ghastly!—not more than a foot from the ground."

"Cud it hae been a flash, like, frae yer ain een?"

"No I am sure it was a face."

"How much is there of this cursed hole?" asked the marquis; rubbing the top of his head.

"A heap," answered Malcolm. "The grun' gangs down like a brae ahin' 's, intil a—"

"You don't mean right behind us?" cried the marquis.

It was after his own more picturesque fashion, however, that he recounted the tale of Lord Gernon.

As the last words left his lips, Lady Florimel gave a startled cry, seized him by the arm, and crept close to him. The marquis jumped to his feet, knocked his head against the rock, uttered an oath, and sat down again.

"What's the matter, my lady!" said Malcolm. "There's nothing here to hurt you."

"I saw a face," she said, "a white face!"

"Where?"

"Beyond you a little way—near the ground," she answered, in a tremulous whisper.

"It's as dark as pitch!" said Malcolm, as if thinking it to himself.—He knew well enough that it must be the laird or Phemy, but he was anxious the marquis should not learn the secret of the laird's refuge.

"I saw a face anyhow," said Florimel. "It gleamed white for one moment, and then vanished."

"I wonder you didn't cry out the more, my lady," said Malcolm, peering into the darkness.

"I was too frightened. It looked so ghastly!—not more than a foot from the ground."

"Could it have been a flash, like, from your own eyes?"

"No I am sure it was a face."

"How much is there of this cursed hole?" asked the marquis; rubbing the top of his head.

"A lot," answered Malcolm. "The ground goes down like a hill behind us, into a—"

"You don't mean right behind us?" cried the marquis.

"Nae jist doss, my lord. We're sittin' i' the mou' o' 't, like, wi' the thrapple o' 't ahin' 's, an' a muckle stamach ayont that."

"I hope there's no danger," said the marquis.

"Nane 'at I ken o'."

"No water at the bottom ?"

"Nane, my lord—that is, naething but a bonny spring i' the rock side."

"Come away, papa!" cried Florimel. "I don't like it. I've had enough of this kind of thing."

"Nonsense!" said the marquis, still rubbing his head.

"Ye wad spile a', my leddy! It's ower late, forbye," said Malcolm; "I hear a fut."

He rose and peeped out, but drew back instantly, saying in a whisper:

"It's Mistress Catanach wi' a lantren! Haud yer tongue, my bonny leddy; ye ken weel she's no mowse. Dinna try to leuk, my lord; she micht get a glimp o' ye—she's terrible gleg. I hae been hearin' mair yet aboot her. Yer lordship 's ill to convence, but depen' upo' 't, whaurever that woman is, there there's mischeef! Whaur she taks a scunner at a body, she hates like the verra deevil. She winna aye lat them ken 't, but taks time to du her ill turns. An' it 's no that only, but gien she gets a haud o' onything agane anybody, she'll save 't up upo' the chance o' their giein' her some offence afore they dee. She never lowses haud o' the tail o' a thing, an' at her ain proaper time, she's in her natur' bun' to mak the warst use o' 't."

Malcolm was anxious both to keep them still, and to turn aside any further inquiry as to the face Florimel had seen. Again he peeped out.

"Not quite plumb, my lord. We're sitting in the mouth of it, with its throat behind us, and a great stomach beyond that."

"I hope there's no danger," said the marquis.

"None that I know of."

"No water at the bottom?"

"None, my lord—that is, nothing but a bonny spring in the rock side."

"Come away, papa!" cried Florimel. "I don't like it. I've had enough of this kind of thing."

"Nonsense!" said the marquis, still rubbing his head.

"You would ruin all, my lady! It's too late, anyway," said Malcolm; "I hear a foot."

He rose and peeped out, but drew back instantly, saying in a whisper:

"It's Mistress Catanach with a lantern! Keep quiet, my bonny lady; you know well she isn't safe. Don't try to look, my lord; she might see you—she's terribly sharp. I've been hearing more of her yet. Your lordship's hard to convince, but depend upon it, wherever that woman is, there there's mischief! Where she takes offence at someone, she hates like the very devil. She won't always let them know it, but takes time to do her bad turns. And it's not only that, but if she once gets hold of anything against a person, she'll save it up upon the mere chance of their offending her in future. She never loses hold of the tail of a thing, and at her own proper time, she's in her nature bound to make the worst use of it."

Malcolm was anxious both to keep them still, and to turn aside any further inquiry as to the face Florimel had seen. Again he peeped out.

"What *is* she efter noo? she's comin' this gait," he went on, in a succession of whispers, turning his head back over his shoulder when he spoke. "Gien she thoucht ther was a hole i' the perris she didna ken a' the oots an' ins o', it wad haud her ohn sleepit.—Weesht! weesht! here she comes!" he concluded, after a listening pause, in the silence of which he could hear her step approaching.

He stretched out his neck over the ledge, and saw her coming straight for the back of the cave, looking right before her with slow-moving, keen, wicked eyes. It was impossible to say what made them look wicked: neither in form, colour, motion, nor light, were they ugly—yet in everyone of these they looked wicked, as her lantern, which, being of horn, she had opened for more light, now and then, as it swung in her hand, shone upon her pale, pulpy, evil countenance.

"Gien she tries to come up, I'll hae to caw her doon," he said to himself, "an' I dinna like it, for she's a wuman efter a', though a deevilich kin' o' a ane; but there's my leddy! I hae broucht her intill 't, an' I maun see her safe oot o' 't!"

But if Mrs. Catanach was bent on an exploration, she was for the time prevented from prosecuting it by the approach of the first of the worshippers, whose voices they now plainly heard. She retreated towards the middle of the cave, and sat down in a dark corner, closing her lantern and hiding it with the skirt of her long cloak. Presently a good many entered at once, some carrying lanterns, and most of them tallow candles, which they quickly lighted and disposed about the walls. The rest of the congregation, with its leaders, came trooping in so fast, that in ten minutes or so the service began.

"What *is* she after now? She's coming this way," he went on, in a succession of whispers, turning his head back over his shoulder when he spoke. "If she thought there was a hole in the parish she didn't know all the outs and ins of, it would give her sleepless nights.—Shush! shush! Here she comes!" he concluded, after a listening pause, in the silence of which he could hear her step approaching.

He stretched out his neck over the ledge, and saw her coming straight for the back of the cave, looking right before her with slow-moving, keen, wicked eyes. It was impossible to say what made them look wicked: neither in form, colour, motion, nor light, were they ugly—yet in everyone of these they looked wicked, as her lantern, which, being of horn, she had opened for more light, now and then, as it swung in her hand, shone upon her pale, pulpy, evil countenance.

"If she tries to come up, I'll have to push her down," he said to himself, "and I don't like it, for she's a woman after all, though a devilish sort of one; but there's my lady! I've brought her into it, and I must see her safe out of it!"

But if Mrs. Catanach was bent on an exploration, she was for the time prevented from prosecuting it by the approach of the first of the worshippers, whose voices they now plainly heard. She retreated towards the middle of the cave, and sat down in a dark corner, closing her lantern and hiding it with the skirt of her long cloak. Presently a good many entered at once, some carrying lanterns, and most of them tallow candles, which they quickly lighted and disposed about the walls. The rest of the congregation, with its leaders, came trooping in so fast, that in ten minutes or so the service began.

As soon as the singing commenced, Malcolm whispered to Lady Florimel, "Was 't a man's face or a lassie's ye saw, my leddy?"

"A man's face—the same we saw in the storm," she answered, and Malcolm felt her shudder as she spoke.

"It's naething but the mad laird," he said. "He's better nor hairmless. Dinna say a word to yer father my leddy. I dinna like to say that, but I'll tell ye a' what for efterhin'."

But Florimel, knowing that her father had a horror of lunatics, was willing enough to be silent.

As soon as the singing commenced, Malcolm whispered to Lady Florimel, "Was it a man's face or a girl's you saw, my lady?"

"A man's face—the same we saw in the storm," she answered, and Malcolm felt her shudder as she spoke.

"It's nothing but the mad laird," he said. "He's better than harmless. Don't say a word to your father my lady. I don't like to say that, but I'll explain it all to you after."

But Florimel, knowing that her father had a horror of lunatics, was willing enough to be silent.

No sooner was her terror thus assuaged, than the oddities of the singing laid hold upon her, stirring up a most tyrannous impulse to laughter. The prayer that followed made it worse. In itself the prayer was perfectly reverent, and yet, for dread of irreverence, I must not attempt a representation of the forms of its embodiment, or the manner of its utterance.

So uncontrollable did her inclination to merriment become, that she found at last the only way to keep from bursting into loud laughter was to slacken the curb, and go off at a canter—I mean, to laugh freely but gently. This so infected her father, that he straightway accompanied her, but with more noise. Malcolm sat in misery, from the fear not so much of discovery, though that would be awkward enough, as of the loss to the laird of his best refuge. But when he reflected, he doubted much whether it was even now a safe one; and, anyhow, knew it would be as vain to remonstrate as to try to stop the noise of a brook by casting pebbles into it.

When it came to the sermon, however, things went better; for MacLeod was the preacher,—an eloquent man after his kind, in virtue of the genuine earnestness of which he was full. If his anxiety for others appeared to be rather to save them from the consequences of their sins, his main desire for himself certainly was to be delivered from evil; the growth of his spiritual nature, while it rendered him more and more dissatisfied with himself, had long left behind all fear save of doing wrong. His sermon this evening was founded on the text: "The natural man receiveth not the things of the Spirit of God." He spoke fervently and persuasively; nor, although his tone and accent were odd, and his Celtic modes and phrases to those Saxon ears outlandish, did these peculiarities in the least injure the influence of the man. Even from Florimel was the demon of laughter driven; and the marquis, although not a single notion of what the man intended passed through the doors of his understanding, sat quiet, and disapproved of nothing. Possibly, had he been alone as he listened, he too, like one of old, might have heard, in the dark cave, the still small voice of a presence urging him forth to the light; but, as it was, the whole utterance passed without a single word or phrase or sentence having roused a thought, or suggested a doubt, or moved a question, or hinted an objection or a need of explanation. That the people present should interest themselves in such things, only set before him the folly of mankind. The text and the preacher both kept telling him that such as he could by no possibility have the slightest notion what *such things* were; but not the less did he, as if he knew all about them, wonder how the deluded fisher-folk could sit and listen. The more tired he grew, the more angry he got with the parson who had sent him there with his foolery: and the more convinced that the men who prayed and preached were as honest as they were silly; and that the thing to die of itself had only to be let alone. He heard the Amen of the benediction with a sigh of relief, and rose at once—cautiously this time.

"Ye maunna gang yet, my lord," said Malcolm. "They maun be a' oot first."

"I don't care who sees me," protested the weary man.

"But yer lordship wadna like to be descriet scram'lin' doon efter the back like the bear in Robinson Crusoe!"

The marquis grumbled, and yielded impatiently.

At length Malcolm, concluding from the silence that the meeting had thoroughly *skailed*, peeped cautiously out to make sure. But after a moment, he drew back, saying in a regretful whisper,

"I'm sorry ye canna gang yet, my lord. There's some half a dizzen o' ill-luikin' chields, cairds, I'm thinkin', or maybe waur, congregat doon there, an' it 's my opinion they're efter nae guid, my lord."

"How do you know that?"

"Ony body wad ken that, 'at got a glimp o' them."

"Let me look."

"Na, my lord; ye dinna understan' the lie o' the stanes eneuch to haud oot o' sicht."

"How long do you mean to keep us here?" asked the marquis impatiently.

"You mustn't go yet, my lord," said Malcolm. "The cave must be emptied first."

"I don't care who sees me," protested the weary man.

"But your lordship wouldn't like to be seen scrambling down backwards like the bear in Robinson Crusoe!"

The marquis grumbled, and yielded impatiently.

At length Malcolm, concluding from the silence that the meeting had thoroughly broken up, peeped cautiously out to make sure. But after a moment, he drew back, saying in a regretful whisper,

"I'm sorry you can't go yet, my lord. There's some half a dozen ill-looking men, gipsies, I'm thinking, or maybe worse, assembled down there, and it's my opinion they're after no good, my lord."

"How do you know that?"

"Anyone would know that, that caught a glimpse of them."

"Let me look."

"Na, my lord; you don't understand the lie of the stones enough to keep out of sight."

"How long do you mean to keep us here?" asked the marquis impatiently.

"Till it 's safe to gang, my lord. For onything I ken, they may be efter comin' up here. They may be used to the place—though I dinna think it."

"In that case we must go down at once. We must *not* let them find us here."

"They wad tak 's ane by ane as we gaed doon, my lord, an' we wadna hae a chance. Think o' my leddy there!"

Florimel heard all, but with the courage of her race.

"This is a fine position you have brought us into, MacPhail!" said his master, now thoroughly uneasy for his daughter's sake.

"Nae waur nor I'll tak ye oot o', gien ye lippen to me, my lord, an' no speyk a word."

"If you tell them who papa is," said Florimel, "they won't do us any harm, surely!"

"I'm nane sae sure o' that. They micht want to ripe 's pooches, an' my lord wad ill stan' that, I'm thinkin'! Na, na. Jist stan' ye back, my lord an' my leddy, an' dinna speyk a word. I s' sattle them. They're sic villains, there nae terms to be hauden wi' them."

His lordship was far from satisfied; but a light shining up into the crevice at the moment, gave powerful support to Malcolm's authority: he took Florimel's hand and drew her a little farther from the mouth of the cave.

"Don't you wish we had Demon with us?" whispered the girl.

"I was thinking how I never went without a dagger in Venice," said the marquis, "and never once had occasion to use it. Now I haven't even a penknife about me! It looks very awkward."

"Please don't talk like that," said Florimel. "Can't you trust Malcolm, papa?"

"Till it's safe to go, my lord. For anything I know, they may be planning to come up here. They may be used to the place—though I doubt it."

"In that case we must go down at once. We must *not* let them find us here."

"They would take us one by one as we went down, my lord, and we wouldn't have a chance. Think of my lady there!"

Florimel heard all, but with the courage of her race.

"This is a fine position you have brought us into, MacPhail!" said his master, now thoroughly uneasy for his daughter's sake.

"No worse than I'll take you out of, if you'll trust me, my lord, and not speak a word."

"If you tell them who papa is," said Florimel, "they won't do us any harm, surely!"

"I'm not so sure of that. They might want to go through his pockets, and my lord would hardly stand that, I'm thinking! Na, na. Just stand back, my lord and my lady, and don't speak a word. I'll settle them. They're such villains, there's no terms to be made with them."

His lordship was far from satisfied; but a light shining up into the crevice at the moment, gave powerful support to Malcolm's authority: he took Florimel's hand and drew her a little farther from the mouth of the cave.

"Don't you wish we had Demon with us?" whispered the girl.

"I was thinking how I never went without a dagger in Venice," said the marquis, "and never once had occasion to use it. Now I haven't even a penknife about me! It looks very awkward."

"Please don't talk like that," said Florimel. "Can't you trust Malcolm, papa?"

"Oh, yes; perfectly!" he answered; but the tone was hardly up to the words.

They could see the dim figure of Malcolm, outlined in fits of the approaching light, all but filling the narrow entrance, as he bent forward to listen. Presently he laid himself down, leaning on his left elbow, with his right shoulder only a little above the level of the passage. The light came nearer, and they heard the sound of scrambling on the rock, but no voice; then for one moment the light shone clear upon the roof of the cleft; the next, came the sound of a dull blow, the light vanished, and the noise of a heavy fall came from beneath.

"Ane o' them, my lord," said Malcolm, in a sharp whisper, over his shoulder.

A confusion of voices arose.

"You booby!" said one. "You climb like a calf. I'll go next."

Evidently they thought he had slipped and fallen, and he was unable to set them right. Malcolm heard them drag him out of the way.

The second ascended more rapidly, and met his fate the sooner. As he delivered the blow, Malcolm recognized one of the laird's assailants, and was now perfectly at his ease.

"Twa o' them, my lord," he said. "Gien we had ane mair doon, we cud manage the lave."

The second, however, had not lost his speech, and amidst the confused talk that followed, Malcolm heard the words: "Rin doon to the coble for the gun," and, immediately after, the sound of feet hurrying from the cave. He rose quietly, leaped into the midst of them, came down upon one, and struck out right and left. Two ran, and three lay where they were.

"Oh, yes; perfectly!" he answered; but the tone was hardly up to the words.

They could see the dim figure of Malcolm, outlined in fits of the approaching light, all but filling the narrow entrance, as he bent forward to listen. Presently he laid himself down, leaning on his left elbow, with his right shoulder only a little above the level of the passage. The light came nearer, and they heard the sound of scrambling on the rock, but no voice; then for one moment the light shone clear upon the roof of the cleft; the next, came the sound of a dull blow, the light vanished, and the noise of a heavy fall came from beneath.

"One of them, my lord," said Malcolm, in a sharp whisper, over his shoulder.

A confusion of voices arose.

"You booby!" said one. "You climb like a calf. I'll go next."

Evidently they thought he had slipped and fallen, and he was unable to set them right. Malcolm heard them drag him out of the way.

The second ascended more rapidly, and met his fate the sooner. As he delivered the blow, Malcolm recognized one of the laird's assailants, and was now perfectly at his ease.

"Two of them, my lord," he said. "If we had one more down, we could manage the rest."

The second, however, had not lost his speech, and amidst the confused talk that followed, Malcolm heard the words: "Run down to the coble for the gun," and, immediately after, the sound of feet hurrying from the cave. He rose quietly, leaped into the midst of them, came down upon one, and struck out right and left. Two ran, and three lay where they were.

"Gien ane o' ye muv han' or fit, I'll brain him wi' 's ain stick," he cried, as he wrenched a cudgel from the grasp of one of them. Then catching up a lantern, and hurrying behind the projecting rock— "Haste ye, an' come," he shouted. "The w'y 's clear, but only for a meenute."

Florimel appeared, and Malcolm got her down.

"Mind that fellow," cried the marquis from above.

Malcolm turned quickly, and saw the gleam of a knife in the grasp of his old enemy, who had risen, and crept behind him to the recess. He flung the lantern in his face, following it with a blow in which were concentrated all the weight and energy of his frame. The man went down again heavily, and Malcolm instantly trampled all their lanterns to pieces.

"Noo," he said to himself, "they winna ken but it's the laird an' Phemy wi' me!"

Then turning, and taking Florimel by the arm, he hurried her out of the cave, followed by the marquis.

They emerged in the liquid darkness of a starry night. Lady Florimel clung to both her father and Malcolm. It was a rough way for some little distance, but at length they reached the hard wet sand, and the marquis would have stopped to take breath; but Malcolm was uneasy, and hurried them on.

"What are you frightened at now?" asked his lordship.

"Naething," answered Malcolm, adding to himself however, "I'm fleyt *at* naethin'—I'm fleyt *for* the laird."

As they approached the tunnel, he fell behind.

"If one of you move hand or foot, I'll brain him with his own stick," he cried, as he wrenched a cudgel from the grasp of one of them. Then catching up a lantern, and hurrying behind the projecting rock— "Quickly now," he shouted. "The way's clear, but only for a minute."

Florimel appeared, and Malcolm got her down.

"Mind that fellow," cried the marquis from above.

Malcolm turned quickly, and saw the gleam of a knife in the grasp of his old enemy, who had risen, and crept behind him to the recess. He flung the lantern in his face, following it with a blow in which were concentrated all the weight and energy of his frame. The man went down again heavily, and Malcolm instantly trampled all their lanterns to pieces.

"Now," he said to himself, "they won't know but it's the laird and Phemy with me!"

Then turning, and taking Florimel by the arm, he hurried her out of the cave, followed by the marquis.

They emerged in the liquid darkness of a starry night. Lady Florimel clung to both her father and Malcolm. It was a rough way for some little distance, but at length they reached the hard wet sand, and the marquis would have stopped to take breath; but Malcolm was uneasy, and hurried them on.

"What are you frightened at now?" asked his lordship.

"Nothing," answered Malcolm, adding to himself however, "I'm frightened *at* nothing—I'm frightened *for* the laird."

As they approached the tunnel, he fell behind.

"Why don't you come on?" said his lordship.

"I'm gaein' back noo 'at ye're safe," said Malcolm.

"Going back! What for?" asked the marquis.

"I maun see what thae villains are up till," answered Malcolm.

"Not alone, surely!" exclaimed the marquis. "At least get some of your people to go with you."

"There's nae time, my lord. Dinna be fleyt for me: I s' tak care o' mysel'."

He was already yards away, running at full speed. The marquis shouted after him, but Malcolm would not hear.

"Why don't you come on?" said his lordship.

"I'm going back now that you're safe," said Malcolm.

"Going back! What for?" asked the marquis.

"I must see what those villains are up to," answered Malcolm.

"Not alone, surely!" exclaimed the marquis. "At least get some of your people to go with you."

"There's no time, my lord. Don't worry about me: I'll take care of myself."

He was already yards away, running at full speed. The marquis shouted after him, but Malcolm would not hear.

When he reached the Baillies' Barn once more, all was still. He groped his way in and found his own lantern where they had been sitting, and having lighted it, descended and followed the windings of the cavern a long way, but saw nothing of the laird or Phemy. Coming at length to a spot where he heard the rushing of a stream, he found he could go no farther: the roof of the cave had fallen, and blocked up the way with huge masses of stone and earth. He had come a good distance certainly, but by no means so far as Phemy's imagination had represented the reach of the cavern. He might however have missed a turn, he thought.

The sound he heard was that of the Lossie Burn, flowing along in the starlight through the grounds of the House. Of this he satisfied himself afterwards; and then it seemed to him not unlikely that in ancient times the river had found its way to the sea along the cave, for throughout its length the action of water was plainly visible. But perhaps the sea itself had used to go roaring along the great duct: Malcolm was no geologist, and could not tell.

CHAPTER XLVII

MRS STEWART'S CLAIM

The weather became unsettled with the approach of winter, and the marquis had a boat-house built at the west end of the Seaton: there the little cutter was laid up, well wrapt in tarpaulins, like a butterfly returned to the golden coffin of her internatal chrysalis. A great part of his resulting leisure, Malcolm spent with Mr Graham, to whom he had, as a matter of course, unfolded the trouble caused him by Duncan's communication.

The more thoughtful a man is, and the more conscious of what is going on within himself, the more interest will he take in what he can know of his progenitors, to the remotest generations; and a regard to ancestral honours, however contemptible the forms which the appropriation of them often assumes, is a plant rooted in the deepest soil of humanity. The high-souled labourer will yield to none in his respect for the dignity of his origin, and Malcolm had been as proud of the humble descent he supposed his own, as Lord Lossie was of his mighty ancestry. Malcolm had indeed a loftier sense of resulting dignity than his master.

He reverenced Duncan both for his uprightness and for a certain grandeur of spirit, which, however ridiculous to the common eye, would have been glorious in the eyes of the chivalry of old; he looked up to him with admiration because of his gifts in poetry and music; and loved him endlessly for his unfailing goodness and tenderness to himself. Even the hatred of the grand old man had an element of unselfishness in its retroaction, of power in its persistency, and of greatness in its absolute contempt of compromise. At the same time he was the only human being to whom Malcolm's heart had gone forth as to his own; and now, with the knowledge of yet deeper cause for loving him, he had to part with the sense of a filial relation to him! And this involved more; for so thoroughly had the old man come to regard the boy as his offspring, that he had nourished in him his own pride of family; and it added a sting of mortification to Malcolm's sorrow, that the greatness of the legendary descent in which he had believed, and the honourableness of the mournful history with which his thoughts of himself had been so closely associated, were swept from him utterly. Nor was this all even yet: in losing these he had had, as it were, to let go his hold, not of his clan merely, but of his race: every link of kin that bound him to humanity had melted away from his grasp. Suddenly he would become aware that his heart was sinking within him, and questioning it why, would learn anew that he was alone in the world, a being without parents, without sister or brother, with none to whom he might look in the lovely confidence of a right bequeathed by some common mother, near or afar. He had waked into being, but all around him was dark, for there was no window, that is, no kindred eye, by which the light of the world whence he had come, entering might console him.

But a gulf of blackness was about to open at his feet, against which the darkness he now lamented would show purple and gray.

One afternoon, as he passed through the Seaton from the harbour, to have a look at the cutter, he heard the Partaness calling after him.

"Weel, ye're a sicht for sair een—noo 'at ye're like to turn oot something worth luikin' at!" she cried, as he approached with his usual friendly smile.

"What du ye mean by that, Mistress Findlay?" asked Malcolm, carelessly adding: "Is yer man in?"

"Ay!" she went on, without heeding either question; "ye'll be gran' set up noo! Ye'll no be hain' a 'fine day' to fling at yer auld freen's, the puir fisher-fowk, or lang! Weel! it 's the w'y o' the warl! Hech, sirs!"

"What on earth 's set ye aff like that Mrs Findlay?" said Malcolm. "It's nae sic a feerious gran' thing to be my lord's skipper—or henchman, as my daddy wad hae 't—surely! It's a heap gran'er like to be a free fisherman, wi' a boat o' yer ain, like the Partan."

"Hoots! Nane o' yer clavers! Ye ken weel eneuch what I mean—as weel 's ilka ither creatit sowl o' Portlossie. An' gien ye dinna chowse to lat on aboot it till an auld freen' cause she's naething but a fisher-wife, it 's dune ye mair skaith a'ready nor I thocht it wad to the lang last, Ma'colm— for it 's yer ain name I s' ca' ye yet, gien ye war ten times a laird!—didna I gie ye the breist whan ye cud du naething i' the wardle but sowk?—An' weel ye sowkit, puir innocent—'at ye *was!*"

"Well, you're a sight for sore eyes— now that you're like to turn out something worth looking at!" she cried, as he approached with his usual friendly smile.

"What do you mean by that, Mistress Findlay?" asked Malcolm, carelessly adding: "Is your man in?"

"Ay!" she went on, without heeding either question; "you'll be a great man now! Soon you won't have even a 'fine day' to fling at your old friends, the poor fisher-folk! Well! it's the way of the world! Eh, sirs!"

"What on earth's set you off that way, Mrs Findlay?" said Malcolm. "It's not so mighty grand to be my lord's skipper— or henchman, as my daddy would have it—surely! It's a heap grander to be a free fisherman, with a boat of your own, like the Partan."

"Heavens! None of your nonsense! You know well enough what I mean—as well as every other living soul in Portlossie. And if you don't choose to let on about it to an old friend because she's nothing but a fisher-wife, it's done you more harm already than I thought it ever would, Malcolm—for I'll call you by your own name yet, if you were ten times a laird!—didn't I give you the breast when you could do nothing in the wide world but suck?—And well you sucked, poor innocent—that you *were!*"

"As sure's we're baith alive," asseverated Malcolm, "I ken nae mair nor a sawtit herrin' what ye're drivin' at."

"Tell me 'at ye dinna ken what a' the queentry kens—an' hit aboot yer ain sel'!" screamed the Partaness.

"I tell ye I ken naething; an' gien ye dinna tell me what ye're efter direckly, I s' haud awa' to Mistress Allison—she'll tell me."

This was a threat sufficiently prevailing.

"It's no in natur'!" she cried. "Here's Mistress Stewart o' the Gersefell been cawin' like mad aboot the place, in her cairriage an' hoo mony horse I dinna ken, declarin', ay, sweirin', they tell me, 'at ane cowmonly ca'd Ma'colm MacPhail is neither mair nor less nor the son born o' her ain boady in honest wadlock!—an' tell me *ye* ken naething aboot it! What are ye stan'in' like that for—as gray-mou'd 's a deein' skate?"

For the first time in his life, Malcolm, young and strong as he was, felt sick. Sea and sky grew dim before him, and the earth seemed to reel under him. "I dinna believe 't," he faltered—and turned away.

"Ye dinna believe what I tell ye!" screeched the wrathful Partaness. "Ye daur to say the word!"

But Malcolm did not care to reply. He wandered away, half unconscious of where he was, his head hanging, and his eyes creeping over the ground. The words of the woman kept ringing in his ears; but ever and anon, behind them as it were in the depth of his soul, he heard the voice of the mad laird, with its one lamentation: "I dinna ken whaur I cam' frae." Finding himself at length at Mr Graham's door, he wondered how he had got there.

"As sure as we both live," asseverated Malcolm, "I know no more than a salted herring what you're driving at."

"Tell me that you don't know what all the country knows—and that about your own self!" screamed the Partaness.

"I tell you I know nothing; and if you don't tell me the meaning of all this at once, I'll go straight to Mistress Allison— she'll tell me."

This was a threat sufficiently prevailing.

"It's not in nature!" she cried. "Here's Mistress Stewart of Gersefell been driving like mad about the place, in her carriage and I don't know how many horse, declaring, ay, swearing, they tell me, that one commonly called Malcolm MacPhail is neither more nor less than the son born of her own body in honest wedlock!—and tell me *you* know nothing about it! What are you standing like that for—as gray-mouthed as a dying skate?"

For the first time in his life, Malcolm, young and strong as he was, felt sick. Sea and sky grew dim before him, and the earth seemed to reel under him. "I don't believe it," he faltered—and turned away.

"You don't believe what I tell you!" screeched the wrathful Partaness. "You dare to say the word!"

But Malcolm did not care to reply. He wandered away, half unconscious of where he was, his head hanging, and his eyes creeping over the ground. The words of the woman kept ringing in his ears; but ever and anon, behind them as it were in the depth of his soul, he heard the voice of the mad laird, with its one lamentation: "I don't know where I came from." Finding himself at length at Mr Graham's door, he wondered how he had got there.

It was Saturday afternoon, and the master was in the churchyard. Startled by Malcolm's look, he gazed at him in grave silent enquiry.

"Hae ye h'ard the ill news, sir?" said the youth.

"No; I'm sorry to hear there is any."

"They tell me Mistress Stewart's rinnin' aboot the toon claimin' me!"

"Claiming you!—How do you mean?"

"For her ain!"

"Not for her son?"

"Ay, sir—that's what they say. But ye haena h'ard o' 't?"

"Not a word."

"Then I believe it 's a' havers!" cried Malcolm energetically. "It was sair eneuch upo' me a'ready to ken less o' whaur I cam frae than the puir laird himsel'; but to come frae whaur he cam frae, was a thocht ower sair!"

"You don't surely despise the poor fellow so much as to scorn to have the same parents with him!" said Mr Graham.

"The verra contrar', sir. But a wuman wha wad sae misguide the son o' her ain body, an' for naething but that, as she had broucht him furth, sic he was!—it 's no to be lichtly believed nor lichtly endured. I s' awa' to Miss Horn an' see whether *she* 's h'ard ony sic leeing clashes."

But as Malcolm uttered her name, his heart sank within him, for their talk the night he had sought her hospitality for the laird, came back to his memory, burning like an acrid poison.

"You can't do better," said Mr Graham. "The report itself may be false—or true, and the lady mistaken."

"She'll hae to pruv 't weel afore I say *haud*," rejoined Malcolm.

It was Saturday afternoon, and the master was in the churchyard. Startled by Malcolm's look, he gazed at him in grave silent enquiry.

"Have you heard the bad news, sir?" said the youth.

"No; I'm sorry to hear there is any."

"They tell me Mistress Stewart's running about the town claiming me!"

"Claiming you!—How do you mean?"

"For her own!"

"Not for her son?"

"Ay, sir—that's what they say. But you haven't heard of it?"

"Not a word."

"Then I believe it's all rubbish!" cried Malcolm energetically. "It was hard enough upon me already to know less of where I came from than the poor laird himself; but to come from where he came from was a thought too hard!"

"You don't surely despise the poor fellow so much as to scorn to have the same parents with him!" said Mr Graham.

"Just the reverse, sir. But a woman who would so ill treat the son of her own body, and for nothing but that, as she had brought him forth, such he was!—it's not to be lightly believed or lightly borne. I'll go to Miss Horn and see whether *she*'s heard any such false gossip."

But as Malcolm uttered her name, his heart sank within him, for their talk the night he had sought her hospitality for the laird, came back to his memory, burning like an acrid poison.

"You can't do better," said Mr Graham. "The report itself may be false—or true, and the lady mistaken."

"She'll have to prove it well before I say *hold*," rejoined Malcolm.

"And suppose she does?"

"In that case," said Malcolm, with a composure almost ghastly, "a man maun tak what mither it pleases God to gie him. But faith! she winna du wi' me as wi' the puir laird. Gien she taks me up, she'll repent 'at she didna lat me lie. She'll be as little pleased wi' the tane o' her sons as the tither—I can tell her, ohn propheseed!"

"But think what you might do between mother and son," suggested the master, willing to reconcile him to the possible worst.

"It's ower late for that," he answered. "The puir man's thairms are a' hingin' lowse, an' there's no grip eneuch i' the pegs to set them up again. He wad but think I had gane ower to the enemy, an' haud oot o' *my* gait as eident as he hauds oot o' hers. Na, it wad du naething for him. Gien 't warna for what I see in *him*, I wad hae a gran' rebutter to her claim; for hoo cud ony wuman's ain son hae sic a scunner at her as I hae i' my hert an' brain an' verra stamach? Gien she war my ain mither, there bude to be some nait'ral drawin's atween 's, a body wad think. But it winna haud, for there's the laird! The verra name o' mither gars him steik his lugs an' rin."

"Still, if she be your mother, it's for better for worse as much as if she had been your own choice."

"I kenna weel hoo it cud be for waur," said Malcolm, who did not yet, even from his recollection of the things Miss Horn had said, comprehend what worst threatened him.

"It does seem strange," said the master thoughtfully, after a pause, "that some women should be allowed to be mothers that through them sons and daughters of

"And suppose she does?"

"In that case," said Malcolm, with a composure almost ghastly, "a man must take what mother it pleases God to give him. But faith! she won't do with me as with the poor laird. If she takes me up, she'll be sorry she didn't let me lie. She'll be as little pleased with the one of her sons as the other—I can tell her that, without prophecy!"

"But think what you might do between mother and son," suggested the master, willing to reconcile him to the possible worst.

"It's too late for that," he answered. "The poor man's like a fiddle with the strings hanging loose, and the pegs haven't grip enough to set them up again. He would only think I'd gone over to the enemy, and avoid *me* as much as he does her. Na, it would do nothing for him. If it weren't for what I see in *him*, I'd have a grand rebuttal to her claim; for how could any woman's own son be so disgusted by her as I am in my heart and brain and very stomach? If she were my own mother, there'd have to be some natural attraction between us, surely. But then there's the laird! The very name of mother makes him stop his ears and run."

"Still, if she be your mother, it's for better for worse as much as if she had been your own choice."

"I hardly know how it could be for worse," said Malcolm, who did not yet, even from his recollection of the things Miss Horn had said, comprehend what worst threatened him.

"It does seem strange," said the master thoughtfully, after a pause, "that some women should be allowed to be mothers that through them sons and daughters of

God should come into the world—thief-babies, say! human parasites, with no choice but feed on the social body!"

"I wonner what God thinks aboot it a'! It gars a body spier whether he cares or no," said Malcolm gloomily.

"It does," responded Mr Graham solemnly.

"Div *ye* alloo that, sir?" returned Malcolm aghast. "That soon's as gien a'thing war rushin' thegither back to the auld chaos."

"I should not be surprised," continued the master, apparently heedless of Malcolm's consternation, "if the day should come when well-meaning men, excellent in the commonplace, but of dwarfed imagination, refused to believe in a God on the ground of apparent injustice in the very frame and constitution of things. Such would argue, that there might be either an omnipotent being who did not care, or a good being who could not help; but that there could not be a being both all-good and omnipotent, for such would never have suffered things to be as they are."

"What wad the clergy say to hear ye, sir?" said Malcolm, himself almost trembling at the words of his master.

"Nothing to the purpose, I fear. They would never face the question. I know what they would do if they could,—burn me, as their spiritual ancestor, Calvin, would have done—whose shoe-latchet they are yet not worthy to unloose. But mind, my boy, you've not heard me speak *my* thought on the matter at all."

"But wadna 't be better to believe in twa Gods nor nane ava'?" propounded Malcolm; "ane a' guid, duin' the best for 's he cud, the ither a' ill, but as pooerfu' as the guid ane—an' forever an' aye a fecht

God should come into the world—thief-babies, say! human parasites, with no choice but feed on the social body!"

"I wonder what God thinks about it all! It's enough to make you ask whether he cares or not," said Malcolm gloomily.

"It is," responded Mr Graham solemnly.

"Do *you* allow that, sir?" returned Malcolm aghast. "That sounds as if all creation were rushing together back to the old chaos."

"I should not be surprised," continued the master, apparently heedless of Malcolm's consternation, "if the day should come when well-meaning men, excellent in the commonplace, but of dwarfed imagination, refused to believe in a God on the ground of apparent injustice in the very frame and constitution of things. Such would argue, that there might be either an omnipotent being who did not care, or a good being who could not help; but that there could not be a being both all-good and omnipotent, for such would never have suffered things to be as they are."

"What would the clergy say to hear you, sir?" said Malcolm, himself almost trembling at the words of his master.

"Nothing to the purpose, I fear. They would never face the question. I know what they would do if they could,—burn me, as their spiritual ancestor, Calvin, would have done—whose shoe-latchet they are yet not worthy to unloose. But mind, my boy, you've not heard me speak *my* thought on the matter at all."

"But wouldn't it be better to believe in two Gods than none at all?" propounded Malcolm; "one all good, doing the best he could for us, the other all bad, but as powerful as the good one—and ever and always atween them, whiles ane getting' the warst o' 't, an whiles the ither? It wad quaiet yer hert ony gait, an' the battle o' Armageddon wad gang on as gran' 's ever."

"Two Gods there could not be," said Mr Graham. "Of the two beings supposed, the evil one must be called *devil* were he ten times the more powerful."

"Wi' a' my hert!" responded Malcolm.

"But I agree with you," the master went on, that "Manicheism is unspeakably better than atheism, and *unthinkably* better than believing in an unjust God. But I am not driven to such a theory."

"Hae ye ane o' yer ain 'at 'll fit, sir?"

"If I knew of a theory in which was never an uncompleted arch or turret, in whose circling wall was never a ragged breach, that theory I should know but to avoid: such gaps are the eternal windows through which the dawn shall look in. A complete theory is a vault of stone around the theorist—whose very being yet depends on room to grow."

"Weel, I wad like to hear what ye hae agane Manicheism!"

"The main objection of theologians would be, I presume, that it did not present a God perfect in power as in goodness; but I think it a far more objectionable point that it presents evil as possessing power in itself. My chief objection, however, would be a far deeper one—namely, that its good being cannot be absolutely good; for, if he knew himself unable to insure the well-being of his creatures, if he could not avoid exposing them to such foreign attack, had he a right to create them? Would he have chosen such a doubtful existence for one whom he meant to love

a fight between them, neither having the upper hand for long? It would quiet your heart anyway, and the battle of Armageddon would go on as grand as ever."

"Two Gods there could not be," said Mr Graham. "Of the two beings supposed, the evil one must be called *devil* were he ten times the more powerful."

"With all my heart!" responded Malcolm.

"But I agree with you," the master went on, that "Manicheism is unspeakably better than atheism, and *unthinkably* better than believing in an unjust God. But I am not driven to such a theory."

"Have you one of your own that'll fit, sir?"

"If I knew of a theory in which was never an uncompleted arch or turret, in whose circling wall was never a ragged breach, that theory I should know but to avoid: such gaps are the eternal windows through which the dawn shall look in. A complete theory is a vault of stone around the theorist—whose very being yet depends on room to grow."

"Well, I would like to hear what you have against Manicheism!"

"The main objection of theologians would be, I presume, that it did not present a God perfect in power as in goodness; but I think it a far more objectionable point that it presents evil as possessing power in itself. My chief objection, however, would be a far deeper one—namely, that its good being cannot be absolutely good; for, if he knew himself unable to insure the well-being of his creatures, if he could not avoid exposing them to such foreign attack, had he a right to create them? Would he have chosen such a doubtful existence for one whom he meant to love absolutely?—Either, then, he did not love like a God, or he would not have created."

"He micht ken himsel' sure to win i' the lang rin."

"Grant the same to the God of the Bible, and we come back to where we were before."

"Does that satisfee yersel', Maister Graham?" asked Malcolm, looking deep into the eyes of his teacher.

"Not at all," answered the master.

"Does onything?"

"Yes: but I will not say more on the subject now. The time may come when I shall have to speak that which I have learned, but it is not yet. All I will say now is, that I am at peace concerning the question. Indeed, so utterly do I feel myself the offspring of the One, that it would be enough for my peace now—I don't say it would have been always—to know my mind troubled on a matter: what troubled me would trouble God: my trouble at the seeming wrong must have its being in the right existent in him. In him, supposing I could find none I should yet say there *must* lie a lucent, harmonious, eternal, not merely consoling, but absolutely satisfying solution."

"Winna ye tell me a' 'at 's in yer hert aboot it, sir?"

"Not now, my boy. You have got one thing to mind now—before all other things—namely, that you give this woman—whatever she be—fair play: if she be your mother, *as* such you must take her, that is, as such you must treat her."

"Ye're richt, sir," returned Malcolm, and rose.

"Come back to me," said Mr Graham, "with whatever news you gather."

absolutely?—Either, then, he did not love like a God, or he would not have created."

"He might know himself sure to win in the long run."

"Grant the same to the God of the Bible, and we come back to where we were before."

"Does that satisfy you, Mister Graham?" asked Malcolm, looking deep into the eyes of his teacher.

"Not at all," answered the master.

"Does anything?"

"Yes: but I will not say more on the subject now. The time may come when I shall have to speak that which I have learned, but it is not yet. All I will say now is, that I am at peace concerning the question. Indeed, so utterly do I feel myself the offspring of the One, that it would be enough for my peace now—I don't say it would have been always—to know my mind troubled on a matter: what troubled me would trouble God: my trouble at the seeming wrong must have its being in the right existent in him. In him, supposing I could find none I should yet say there *must* lie a lucent, harmonious, eternal, not merely consoling, but absolutely satisfying solution."

"Won't you tell me all that's in your heart about it, sir?"

"Not now, my boy. You have got one thing to mind now—before all other things—namely, that you give this woman—whatever she be—fair play: if she be your mother, *as* such you must take her, that is, as such you must treat her."

"You're right, sir," returned Malcolm, and rose.

"Come back to me," said Mr Graham, "with whatever news you gather."

"I will, sir," answered Malcolm, and went to find Miss Horn. He was shown into the little parlour, which, for all the grander things he had been amongst of late, had lost nothing of its first charm. There sat Miss Horn.

"Sit doon, Ma'colm," she said gruffly.

"Hae ye h'ard onything, mem?" asked Malcolm, standing.

"Ay, ower muckle," answered Miss Horn, with all but a scowl. "Ye been ower to Gersefell, I reckon."

"Forbid it!" answered Malcolm. "Never till this hoor—or at maist it 's nae twa sin' I h'ard the first cheep o' 't, an' that was frae Meg Partan. To nae human sowl hae I made mention o' 't yet 'cep' Maister Graham: to him I gaed direck."

"Ye cudna hae dune better," said the grim woman, with relaxing visage.

"An' here I am the noo, straucht frae him, to beg o' you, Miss Horn, to tell me the trowth o' the maitter."

"What ken I aboot it?" she returned angrily. "What *sud* I ken?"

"Ye micht ken whether the wuman's been sayin' 't or no."

"Wha has ony doobt aboot that?"

"Mistress Stewart *has* been sayin' she's my mither, than?"

"Ay—what for no?" returned Miss Horn, with a piercing *glower* at the youth.

"Guid forfen'!" exclaimed Malcolm.

"Say ye that, laddie?" cried Miss Horn, and, starting up, she grasped his arm and stood gazing in his face.

"What ither sud I say?" rejoined Malcolm, surprised.

"God be laudit!" exclaimed Miss Horn. "The limmer may say 'at she likes noo."

"I will, sir," answered Malcolm, and went to find Miss Horn. He was shown into the little parlour, which, for all the grander things he had been amongst of late, had lost nothing of its first charm. There sat Miss Horn.

"Sit down, Malcolm," she said gruffly.

"Have you heard anything, ma'am?" asked Malcolm, standing.

"Ay, too much," answered Miss Horn, with all but a scowl. "You've been over to Gersefell, I reckon."

"Forbid it!" answered Malcolm. "Never till this hour—or at most, it's less than two since I heard the first cheep of it, and that was from Meg Partan. I haven't mentioned it yet to living soul except Mister Graham: I went to him at once."

"You couldn't have done better," said the grim woman, with relaxing visage.

"And here I am now, straight from him, to beg of you, Miss Horn, to tell me the truth of the matter."

"What do I know of it?" she returned angrily. "What *should* I know?"

"You might know whether the woman's been saying it or not."

"Who has any doubt about that?"

"Mistress Stewart *has* been saying she's my mother, then ?"

"Ay—why not?" returned Miss Horn, with a piercing *glower* at the youth.

"Heaven forfend!" exclaimed Malcolm.

"Say you that, laddie?" cried Miss Horn, and, starting up, she grasped his arm and stood gazing in his face.

"What else should I say?" rejoined Malcolm, surprised.

"God be praised!" exclaimed Miss Horn. "The hussy may say what she likes now."

"*Ye* dinna believe 't than, mem?" cried Malcolm. "Tell me ye dinna, an' haud me ohn curst like a cadger."

"I dinna believe ae word o' 't, laddie," answered Miss Horn eagerly. "Wha *cud* believe sic a fine laad come o' sic a fause mither?"

"She micht be ony body's mither, an' fause tu," said Malcolm gloomily.

"That's true laddie; and the mair mither the fauser! There's a warl' o' witness i' your face 'at gien she be yer mither, the markis, an no puir honest hen-peckit John Stewart, was the father o' ye.—The Lord forgie' me! what am I sayin'!" adjected Miss Horn, with a cry of self-accusation, when she saw the pallor that overspread the countenance of the youth, and his head drop upon his bosom: the last arrow had sunk to the feather. "It's a' havers, ony gait," she quickly resumed. "I div not believe ye hae ae drap o' her bluid i' the body o' ye, man. But," she hurried on, as if eager to obliterate the scoring impression of her late words—"that she's been sayin' 't, there can be no mainner o' doot. I saw her mysel' rinnin' aboot the toon, frae ane till anither, wi' her lang hair doon the lang back o' her, an' fleein' i' the win', like a body dementit. The only question is, whether or no she believes 't hersel'."

"What cud gar her say 't gien she didna believe 't?"

"Fowk says she expecs that w'y to get a grip o' things oot o' the han's o' the puir laird's trustees: ye wad be a son o' her ain, cawpable o' mainagin' them. But ye dinna tell me she's never been at yersel' aboot it?"

"Never a blink o' the ee has passed atween's sin' that day I gaed till Gersefell, as I tellt ye, wi' a letter frae the markis. I thoucht I was ower mony for her than: I wonner she daur be at me again."

"*You* don't believe it then, ma'am?" cried Malcolm. "Tell me you don't, and keep me from cursing!"

"I don't believe one word of it, laddie," answered Miss Horn eagerly. "Who *could* believe such a fine lad come of such a false mother?"

"She might be anyone's mother, and false too," said Malcolm gloomily.

"That's true laddie; and the more mother the falser! There's a world of witness in your face that if she be your mother, the marquis, and not poor honest hen-pecked John Stewart, was the father of you.— The Lord forgive me! what am I saying!" adjected Miss Horn, with a cry of self-accusation, when she saw the pallor that overspread the countenance of the youth, and his head drop upon his bosom: the last arrow had sunk to the feather. "It's all nonsense, anyway," she quickly resumed. "I don't believe you have one drop of her blood in your body, man. But," she hurried on, as if eager to obliterate the scoring impression of her late words—"that she's been saying it, there can be no manner of doubt. I saw her myself running about the town, from one to another, with her long hair down the long back of her, and flying in the wind, like one demented. The only question is, whether or not she believes it herself."

"What could make her say it if she didn't believe it?"

"Folk say she'd use it to snatch things out of the hands of the poor laird's trustees: you would be a son of her own, capable of managing them. But you don't mean to say she's never been to you about it?"

"Never a blink of the eye has passed between us since that day I went to Gersefell, as I told you, with a letter from the marquis. I thought I was too much for her then: I wonder she dares be at me again."

"She's daurt her God er' noo, an' may weel daur you.—But what says yer gran'father till 't, no?"

"He hasna hard a chuckie's cheep o' 't."

"What are we haverin' at than! Canna he sattle the maitter aff han'?"

Miss Horn eyed him keenly as she spoke.

"He kens nae mair aboot whaur I come frae, mem, nor your Jean, wha 's hearkenin' at the keyhole this verra meenute."

The quick ear of Malcolm had caught a slight sound of the handle, whose proximity to the keyhole was no doubt often troublesome to Jean.

Miss Horn seemed to reach the door with one *spang*. Jean was ascending the last step of the stair with a message on her lips concerning butter and eggs. Miss Horn received it, and went back to Malcolm.

"Na; Jean wadna du that," she said quietly.

But she was wrong, for, hearing Malcolm's words, Jean had retreated one step down the stair, and turned.

"But what's this ye tell me aboot yer gran'father, honest man?" Miss Horn continued.

"Duncan MacPhail's nae bluid o' mine—the mair's the pity!" said Malcolm sadly—and told her all he knew.

Miss Horn's visage went through wonderful changes as he spoke.

"Weel, it *is* a mercy I hae nae feelin's!" she said when he had done.

"Ony wuman can lay a claim till me 'at likes, ye see," said Malcolm.

"She may lay 'at she likes, but it 's no ilka egg laid has a chuckie intill 't," answered Miss Horn sententiously. "Jist ye gang hame to auld Duncan, an' tell him to turn the thing ower in 's min' till he's

"She's dared her God ere now, and may well dare you.—But what says your grandfather to it, now?

"He hasn't heard a word of it."

"What are we jawing about then! Can't he settle the matter off hand?"

Miss Horn eyed him keenly as she spoke.

"He knows no more about where I come from, ma'am, than your Jean, who's listening at the keyhole this very minute."

The quick ear of Malcolm had caught a slight sound of the handle, whose proximity to the keyhole was no doubt often troublesome to Jean.

Miss Horn seemed to reach the door with one spring. Jean was ascending the last step of the stair with a message on her lips concerning butter and eggs. Miss Horn received it, and went back to Malcolm.

"Na; Jean wouldn't do that," she said quietly.

But she was wrong, for, hearing Malcolm's words, Jean had retreated one step down the stair, and turned.

"But what's this you tell me about your grandfather, honest man?" Miss Horn continued.

"Duncan MacPhail's no blood of mine—the more's the pity!" said Malcolm sadly—and told her all he knew.

Miss Horn's visage went through wonderful changes as he spoke.

"Well, it *is* a mercy I have no feelings!" she said when he had done.

"Any woman that likes can lay a claim to me, you see," said Malcolm.

"She may say what she likes, but it's not every egg laid that has a chicken in it," answered Miss Horn sententiously. "Just you go home to old Duncan, and tell him to turn it over in his mind till he's able to able to sweir to the verra nicht he fan' the bairn in 's lap. But no ae word maun he say to leevin' sowl aboot it afore it 's requiret o' 'im."

"I wad be the son o' the puirest fisher-wife i' the Seaton raither nor hers," said Malcolm gloomily.

"An' it shaws ye better bred," said Miss Horn. "But she'll be at ye or lang—an' tak ye tent what ye say. Dinna flee in her face; lat her jaw awa', an' mark her words. She may lat a streak o' licht oot o' her dirk lantren oonawaurs."

swear to the very night he found the child in his lap. But not one word must he say to living soul about it before it's required of him."

"I would be the son of the poorest fisher-wife in the Seaton rather than hers," said Malcolm gloomily.

"And it shows you better bred," said Miss Horn. "But she won't let you alone for long—and be careful what you say. Don't fly in her face; let her talk, and mark her words. She may let a streak of light out of her dark lantern unawares."

Malcolm returned to Mr Graham. They agreed there was nothing for it but to wait. He went next to his grandfather and gave him Miss Horn's message. The old man fell a thinking, but could not be certain even of the year in which he had left his home. The clouds hung very black around Malcolm's horizon.

Since the adventure in the Baillies' Barn, Lady Florimel had been on a visit in Morayshire: she heard nothing of the report until she returned.

"So you're a gentleman after all, Malcolm!" she said, the next time she saw him.

The expression in her eyes appeared to him different from any he had encountered there before. The blood rushed to his face; he dropped his head, and saying merely, "It maun be a' as it maun," (It must be all as it must,) pursued the occupation of the moment.

But her words sent a new wind blowing into the fog. *A gentleman* she had said! Gentlemen married ladies! Could it be that a glory it was madness to dream of, was yet a possibility? One moment, and his honest heart recoiled from the thought: not even for Lady Florimel could he *consent* to be the son of that woman! Yet the thought, especially in Lady Florimel's presence, would return, would linger, would whisper, would tempt.

In Florimel's mind also, a small demon of romance was at work. Uncorrupted as yet by social influences, it would not have seemed to her absurd that an heiress of rank should marry a poor country gentleman; but the thought of marriage never entered her head: she only felt that the discovery justified a nearer approach from both sides. She had nothing, not even a flirtation in view. Flirt she might, likely enough, but she did not foremean it.

Had Malcolm been a schemer, he would have tried to make something of his position. But even the growth of his love for his young mistress was held in check by the fear of what that love tempted him to desire.

Lady Florimel had by this time got so used to his tone and dialect, hearing it on all sides of her, that its quaintness had ceased to affect her, and its coarseness had begun to influence her repulsively. There were still to be found in Scotland old fashioned gentlefolk speaking the language of the country with purity and refinement; but Florimel had never met any of them, or she might possibly have been a little less repelled by Malcolm's speech.

Within a day or two of her return, Mrs Stewart called at Lossie House, and had a long talk with her, in the course of which she found no difficulty in gaining her to promise her influence with Malcolm. From his behaviour on the occasion of their sole interview, she stood in a vague awe of him, and indeed could not recall it without a feeling of rebuke—a feeling which must either turn her aside from her purpose or render her the more anxious to secure his favour. Hence it came that she had not yet sought him: she would have the certainty first that he was kindly disposed towards her claim—a thing she would never have doubted but for the glimpse she had had of him.

One Saturday afternoon, about this time, Mr Stewart put his head in at the door of the schoolroom, as he had done so often already, and seeing the master seated alone at his desk, walked in, saying once more, with a polite bow,

"I dinna ken whaur I cam frae: I want to come to the school."

"I don't know where I came from: I want to come to the school."

Mr Graham assured him of welcome as cordially as if it had been the first time he came with the request, and yet again offered him a chair; but the laird as usual declined it, and walked down the room to find a seat with his companion-scholars. He stopped midway, however, and returned to the desk, where, standing on tiptoe, he whispered in the master's ear: "I canna come upo' the door." ("I can't find the door.") Then turning away again, he crept dejectedly to a seat where some of the girls had made room for him. There he took a slate, and began drawing what might seem an attempt at a door; but ever as he drew he blotted out, and nothing that could be called a door was the result. Meantime, Mr Graham was pondering at intervals what he had said.

School being over, the laird was modestly leaving with the rest, when the master gently called him, and requested the favour of a moment more of his company. As soon as they were alone, he took a Bible from his desk, and read the words:

"I am the door: by me if any man enter in, he shall be saved, and shall go in and out, and find pasture."

Without comment, he closed the book, and put it away. Mr Stewart stood staring up at him for a moment, then turned, and gently murmuring, "I canna win at the door," walked from the schoolhouse.

Without comment, he closed the book, and put it away. Mr Stewart stood staring up at him for a moment, then turned, and gently murmuring, "I can't get at the door," walked from the schoolhouse.

It was refuge the poor fellow sought—whether from temporal or spiritual foes will matter little to him who believes that the only shelter from the one is the only shelter from the other also.

CHAPTER XLVIII

THE BAILLIES' BARN AGAIN

It began to be whispered about Portlossie, that the marquis had been present at one of the fishermen's meetings—a report which variously affected the minds of those in the habit of composing them. Some regarded it as an act of espial, and much foolish talk arose about the covenanters and persecution and martyrdom. Others, especially the less worthy of those capable of public utterance, who were by this time, in virtue of that sole gift, gaining an influence of which they were altogether unworthy, attributed it to the spreading renown of the preaching and praying members of the community, and each longed for an opportunity of exercising his individual gift upon the conscience of the marquis. The soberer portion took it for an act of mere curiosity, unlikely to be repeated.

Malcolm saw that the only way of setting things right was that the marquis should go again—openly, but it was with much difficulty that he persuaded him to present himself in the assembly. Again accompanied by his daughter and Malcolm, he did, however, once more cross the links to the Baillies' Barn. Being early they had a choice of seats, and Florimel placed herself beside a pretty young woman of gentle and troubled countenance, who sat leaning against the side of the cavern.

The preacher on this occasion was the sickly young student—more pale and haggard than ever, and halfway nearer the grave since his first sermon. He still set himself to frighten the sheep into the fold by wolfish cries; but it must be allowed that, in this sermon at least, his representations of the miseries of the lost were not by any means so gross as those usually favoured by preachers of his kind. His imagination was sensitive enough to be roused by the words of Scripture themselves, and was not dependent for stimulus upon those of Virgil, Dante, or Milton. Having taken for his text the fourteenth verse of the fifty-ninth psalm, "And at evening let them return; and let them make a noise like a dog, and go round about the city," he dwelt first upon the condition and character of the eastern dog as contrasted with those of our dogs; pointing out to his hearers, that so far from being valued for use or beauty or rarity, they were, except swine, of all animals the most despised by the Jews—the vile outcasts of the border-land separating animals domestic and ferine—filthy, dangerous, and hated; then associating with his text that passage in the Revelation, "Blessed are they that do his commandments, that they may have right to the tree of life, and may enter in through the gates into the city; for without are dogs," he propounded, or rather asserted, that it described one variety of the many punishments of the wicked, showing at least a portion of them condemned to rush howling for ever about the walls of the New Jerusalem, haunting the gates they durst not enter.

"See them through the fog steaming up from the shores of their Phlegethon!" he cried, warming into eloquence; "see the horrid troop, afar from the crystal walls!—if indeed ye stand on those heights of glory, and course not around them with the dogs!—hear them howl and bark as they scour along! Gaze at them more earnestly as they draw nigher; see upon the dog-heads of them the signs and symbols of rank and authority which they wore when they walked erect, men—ay, women too, among men and women! see the crown jewels flash over the hanging ears, the tiara tower thrice circled over the hungry eyes! see the plumes and the coronets, the hoods and the veils!"

Here, unhappily for his eloquence, he slid off into the catalogue of women's finery given by the prophet Isaiah, at the close of which he naturally found the oratorical impulse gone, and had to sit down in the mud of an anticlimax. Presently, however, he recovered himself, and, spreading his wings, once more swung himself aloft into the empyrean of an eloquence, which, whatever else it might or might not be, was at least genuine.

"Could they but surmount those walls, whose inherent radiance is the artillery of their defence, those walls high-uplifted, whose lowest foundations are such stones as make the glory of earthly crowns; could they overleap those gates of pearl, and enter the golden streets, what think ye they would do there? Think ye they would rage hither and thither at will, making horrid havoc amongst the white-robed inhabitants of the sinless capital? Nay, verily; for, in the gold transparent as glass, they would see their own vile forms in truth-telling reflex, and, turning in agony, would rush yelling back, out again into the darkness—the outer darkness—to go round and round the city again and for evermore, tenfold tortured henceforth with the memory of their visioned selves."

Here the girl beside Lady Florimel gave a loud cry, and fell backwards from her seat. On all sides arose noises, loud or suppressed, mingled with murmurs of expostulation. Even Lady Florimel, invaded by shrieks, had to bite her lips hard to keep herself from responding with like outcry; for scream will call forth scream, as vibrant string from its neighbour will draw the answering tone.

"Deep calleth unto deep! The wind is blowing on the slain! The Spirit is breathing on the dry bones!" shouted the preacher in an ecstacy. But one who rose from behind Lizzy Findlay, had arrived at another theory regarding the origin of the commotion—and doubtless had a right to her theory, in as much as she was a woman of experience, being no other than Mrs Catanach.

At the sound of her voice seeking to soothe the girl, Malcolm shuddered; but the next moment, from one of those freaks of suggestion which defy analysis, he burst into laughter: he had a glimpse of a she-dog, in Mrs Catanach's Sunday bonnet, bringing up the rear of the preacher's canine company, and his horror of the woman found relief in an involuntary outbreak that did not spring altogether from merriment.

It attracted no attention. The cries increased; for the preacher continued to play on the harp-nerves of his hearers, in the firm belief that the Spirit was being poured out upon them. The marquis, looking very pale, for he could never endure the cry of a woman even in a play, rose, and taking Florimel by the arm, turned to leave the place. Malcolm hurried to the front to make way for them. But the preacher caught sight of the movement, and, filled with a fury which seemed to him sacred, rushed to the rescue of souls.

"Stop!" he shouted. "Go not hence, I charge you. On your lives I charge you! Turn ye, turn ye: why will ye die? There is no fleeing from Satan. You must resist the devil. He that flies is lost. If you turn your backs upon Apollyon, he will never slacken pace until he has driven you into the troop of his dogs, to go howling about the walls of the city. Stop them, friends of the cross, ere they step beyond the sound of mercy; for, alas! the voice of him who is sent cannot reach beyond the particle of time wherein he speaks: now, this one solitary moment, gleaming out of the eternity before us only to be lost in the eternity behind us—this *now* is the accepted time; *this* NOW and no other is the moment of salvation!"

Most of the men recognized the marquis; some near the entrance saw only Malcolm clearing the way: marquis or fisher, it was all the same when souls were at stake: they crowded with one consent to oppose their exit: yet another chance they must have, whether they would or not. These men were in the mood to give—not their own—but those other men's bodies to be burnt on the poorest chance of saving their souls from the everlasting burnings.

Malcolm would have been ready enough for a fight, had he and the marquis been alone, but the presence of Lady Florimel put it out of the question. Looking round, he sought the eye of his master.

Had Lord Lossie been wise, he would at once have yielded, and sat down to endure to the end. But he jumped on the form next him, and appealed to the common sense of the assembly.

"Don't you see the man is mad?" he said, pointing to the preacher. "He is foaming at the mouth. For God's sake look after your women: he will have them all in hysterics in another five minutes. I wonder any man of sense would countenance such things!"

As to *hysterics*, the fisher folk had never heard of them; and though the words of the preacher were not those of soberness, they yet believed them the words of truth, and himself a far saner man than the marquis.

<table>
<tr>
<td>

"Gien a body comes to oor meetin'," cried one of them, a fine specimen of the *argle-bargling* Scotchman—a creature known and detested over the habitable globe—"he maun just du as we du, an' sit it oot. It's for yer sowl's guid."

</td>
<td>

"If anyone comes to our meeting," cried one of them, a fine specimen of the *argle-bargling* Scotchman—a creature known and detested over the habitable globe—"he must just do as we do, and sit it out. It's for your soul's good."

</td>
</tr>
</table>

The preacher, checked in full career, was standing with open mouth, ready to burst forth in a fresh flood of oratory so soon as the open channels of hearing ears should be again granted him; but all were now intent on the duel between the marquis and Jamie Ladle.

"If, the next time you came, you found the entrance barricaded," said the marquis, "what would you say to that?"

"Ow, we wad jist tak doon the sticks," answered Ladle.

"You would call it *persecution*, wouldn't you?"

"Ay; it wad be that."

"And what do you call it now, when you prevent a man from going his own way, after he has had enough of your foolery?"

"Ow, we ca' 't dissiplene!" answered the fellow.

The marquis got down, annoyed, but laughing at his own discomfiture. "I've stopped the screaming, anyhow," he said.

Ere the preacher, the tap of whose eloquence presently began to yield again, but at first ran very slow, had gathered way enough to carry his audience with him, a woman rushed up to the mouth of the cave, the borders of her cap flapping, and her grey hair flying like an old Maenad's. Brandishing in her hand a *spurtle* with which she had been making the porridge for supper, she cried in a voice that reached every ear:

"What's this I hear o' 't! Come oot o' that, Lizzy, ye limmer! Ir ye gauin' frae ill to waur, i' the deevil's name!"

It was Meg Partan. She sent the congregation right and left from her, as a ship before the wind sends a wave from each

---

The preacher, checked in full career, was standing with open mouth, ready to burst forth in a fresh flood of oratory so soon as the open channels of hearing ears should be again granted him; but all were now intent on the duel between the marquis and Jamie Ladle.

"If, the next time you came, you found the entrance barricaded," said the marquis, "what would you say to that?"

"Oh, we would just take down the sticks," answered Ladle.

"You would call it *persecution*, wouldn't you?"

"Ay; it would be that."

"And what do you call it now, when you prevent a man from going his own way, after he has had enough of your foolery?"

"Oh, we call it discipline!" answered the fellow.

The marquis got down, annoyed, but laughing at his own discomfiture. "I've stopped the screaming, anyhow," he said.

Ere the preacher, the tap of whose eloquence presently began to yield again, but at first ran very slow, had gathered way enough to carry his audience with him, a woman rushed up to the mouth of the cave, the borders of her cap flapping, and her grey hair flying like an old Maenad's. Brandishing in her hand a *spurtle* with which she had been making the porridge for supper, she cried in a voice that reached every ear:

"What's this I hear of it! Come out of that, Lizzy, you jade! Are you going from bad to worse, in the devil's name!"

It was Meg Partan. She sent the congregation right and left from her, as a ship before the wind sends a wave from each side of her bows. Men and women gave place to her, and she went surging into the midst of the assembly.

"Whaur's that lass o' mine?" she cried, looking about her in aggravated wrath at failing to pounce right upon her.

"She's no verra weel, Mrs Findlay," cried Mrs Catanach, in a loud whisper, laden with an insinuating tone of intercession. "She'll be better in a meenute. The minister's jist *ower* pooerfu' the nicht."

side of her bows. Men and women gave place to her, and she went surging into the midst of the assembly.

"Where's that lass of mine?" she cried, looking about her in aggravated wrath at failing to pounce right upon her.

"She's not very well, Mrs Findlay," cried Mrs Catanach, in a loud whisper, laden with an insinuating tone of intercession. "She'll be better in a minute. The minister's just *too* powerful tonight."

Mrs Findlay made a long reach, caught Lizzy by the arm, and dragged her forth, looking scared and white, with a red spot upon one cheek. No one dared to bar Meg's exit with her prize; and the marquis, with Lady Florimel and Malcolm, took advantage of the opening she made, and following in her wake soon reached the open air.

Mrs Findlay was one of the few of the fisher women who did not approve of conventicles, being a great stickler for every authority in the country except that of husbands, in which she declared she did not believe: a report had reached her that Lizzy was one of the lawless that evening, and in hot haste she had left the porridge on the fire to drag her home.

"This is the second predicament you have got us into, MacPhail," said his lordship, as they walked along the Boar's Tail—the name by which some designated the dune, taking the name of the rock at the end of it to be the Boar's Craig, and the last word to mean, as it often does, not *Crag*, but *Neck*, like the German *kragen*, and perhaps the English *scrag*.

"I'm sorry for't, my lord," said Malcolm; "but I'm sure yer lordship had the worth o' 't in fun."

"I can't deny that," returned the marquis.

"And *I* can't get that horrid shriek out of my ears," said Lady Florimel.

"Which of them?" said her father. "There was no end to the shrieking. It nearly drove me wild."

"I mean the poor girl's who sat beside us, papa. Such a pretty nice-looking creature too! And that horrid woman close behind us all the time! I hope you won't go

"This is the second predicament you have got us into, MacPhail," said his lordship, as they walked along the Boar's Tail—the name by which some designated the dune, taking the name of the rock at the end of it to be the Boar's Craig, and the last word to mean, as it often does, not *Crag*, but *Neck*, like the German *kragen*, and perhaps the English *scrag*.

"I'm sorry for it, my lord," said Malcolm; "but I'm sure your lordship had the worth of it in fun."

"I can't deny that," returned the marquis.

"And *I* can't get that horrid shriek out of my ears," said Lady Florimel.

"Which of them?" said her father. "There was no end to the shrieking. It nearly drove me wild."

"I mean the poor girl's who sat beside us, papa. Such a pretty nice-looking creature too! And that horrid woman close behind us all the time! I hope you won't go again papa. They'll convert you if you do, and never ask your leave. You wouldn't like that, *I* know."

"What do you say to shutting up the place altogether?"

"*Do*, papa. It's shocking. Vulgar and horrid!"

"I wad think twise, my lord, afore I wad sair them as ill as they saired me."

"Did I ask your advice?" said the marquis sternly.

"It's nane the waur 'at it 's gien oonsoucht," said Malcolm. "It's the richt thing ony gait."

"You presume on this foolish report about you, I suppose, MacPhail," said his lordship; "but that won't do."

"God forgie ye, my lord, for I hae ill duin' 't!" said Malcolm.

again papa. They'll convert you if you do, and never ask your leave. You wouldn't like that, *I* know."

"What do you say to shutting up the place altogether?"

"*Do*, papa. It's shocking. Vulgar and horrid!"

"I would think twice, my lord, before I would serve them as ill as they served me."

"Did I ask your advice?" said the marquis sternly.

"It's none the worse that it's given unsought," said Malcolm. "It's the right thing anyway."

"You presume on this foolish report about you, I suppose, MacPhail," said his lordship; "but that won't do."

"God forgive you my lord, for I don't know how I'm to do it!" said Malcolm.

He left them and walked down to the foamy lip of the tide, which was just waking up from its faint recession. A cold glimmer, which seemed to come from nothing but its wetness, was all the sea had to say for itself.

But the marquis smiled, and turned his face towards the wind which was blowing from the south.

In a few moments Malcolm came back, but to follow behind them, and say nothing more that night.

The marquis did not interfere with the fishermen. Having heard of their rudeness, Mr Cairns called again, and pressed him to end the whole thing; but he said they would only be after something worse, and refused.

The turn things had taken that night determined their after course. Cryings out and faintings grew common, and fits began to appear. A few laid claim to visions,—bearing, it must be remarked, a strong resemblance to the similitudes, metaphors, and more extended poetic figures, employed by the young preacher, becoming at length a little more original and a good deal more grotesque. They took to dancing at last, not by any means the least healthful mode of working off their excitement. It was, however, hardly more than a dull beating of time to the monotonous chanting of a few religious phrases, rendered painfully commonplace by senseless repetition.

I would not be supposed to deny the genuineness of the emotion, or even of the religion, in many who thus gave show to their feelings. But neither those who were good before nor those who were excited now were much the better for this and like modes of playing off the mental electricity generated by the revolving cylinder of intercourse.

Naturally, such men as Joseph Mair now grew shy of the assemblies they had helped to originate, and withdrew—at least into the background; the reins slipped from the hands of the first leaders, and such windbags as Ladle got up to drive the chariot of the gospel—with the results that could not fail to follow. At the same time it must be granted that the improvement of their habits, in so far as strong drink was concerned, continued: it became almost a test of faith with them, whether or not a man was a total abstainer. Hence their moral manners, so to say, improved greatly; there were no more public-house orgies, no fighting in the streets, very little of what they called breaking of the Sabbath, and altogether there was a marked improvement in the look of things along a good many miles of that northern shore.

Strange as it may seem, however, morality in the deeper sense, remained very much at the same low ebb as before. It is much easier to persuade men that God cares for certain observances, than that he cares for simple honesty and truth and gentleness and loving-kindness. The man who would shudder at the idea of a rough word of the description commonly called swearing, will not even have a twinge of conscience after a whole morning of ill-tempered sullenness, capricious scolding, villainously unfair animadversion, or surly cross-grained treatment generally of wife and children! Such a man will omit neither family worship nor a sneer at his neighbour. He will neither milk his cow on the first day of the week without a Sabbath mask on his face, nor remove it while he waters the milk for his customers. Yet he may not be an absolute hypocrite. What can be done for him, however, hell itself may have to determine.

Notwithstanding their spiritual experiences, it was, for instance, no easier to get them to pay their debts than heretofore. Of course there were, and had always been, thoroughly honest men and women amongst them; but there were others who took prominent part in their observances, who seemed to have no remotest suspicion that religion had anything to do with money or money's worth—not to know that God cared whether a child of his met his obligations or not. Such fulfilled the injunction to owe nothing by acknowledging nothing. One man, when pressed, gave as a reason for his refusal, that Christ had paid all his debts. Possibly this contemptible state of feeling had been fostered by an old superstition that it was unlucky to pay up everything, whence they had always been in the habit of leaving at least a few shillings of their shop-bills to be carried forward to the settlement after the next fishing season. But when a widow whose husband had left property, would acknowledge no obligation to discharge his debts, it came to be rather more than a whim. Evidently the religion of many of them was as yet of a poor sort—precisely like that of the negroes, whose devotion so far outstrips their morality.

If there had but been some one of themselves to teach that the true outlet and sedative of overstrained feeling is right action! that the performance of an unpleasant duty, say the paying of their debts, was a far more effectual as well as more specially religious mode of working off their excitement than dancing! that feeling is but the servant of character until it becomes its child! or rather, that feeling is but a mere vapour until condensed into character! that the *only* process through which it can be thus consolidated is well-doing—the putting forth of the right thing according to the conscience universal and individual! and that thus, and thus only, can the veil be withdrawn from between the man and his God, and the man be saved in beholding the face of his Father!

"But have patience—give them time," said Mr Graham, who had watched the whole thing from the beginning. "If their religion is religion, it will work till it purifies; if it is not, it will show itself for what it is, by plunging them into open vice. The mere excitement and its extravagance—the mode in which their gladness breaks out—means nothing either way. *The man* is the willing, performing being, not the feeling shouting singing being: in the latter there may be no individuality—nothing more than receptivity of the movement of the mass. But when a man gets up and goes out and discharges an obligation, he is an individual; to him God has spoken, and he has opened his ears to hear: God and that man are henceforth in communion."

These doings, however, gave—how should they fail to give?—a strong handle to the grasp of those who cared for nothing in religion but its respectability—who went to church Sunday after Sunday, "for the sake of example" as they said—the most arrogant of Pharisaical reasons! Many a screeching, dancing fisher-lass in the Seaton was far nearer the kingdom of heaven than the most respectable of such respectable people! I would unspeakably rather dance with the wildest of fanatics rejoicing over a change in their own spirits, than sit in the seat of the dull of heart, to whom the old story is an outworn tale.

CHAPTER XLIX

MOUNT PISGAH

The intercourse between Florimel and Malcolm grew gradually more familiar, until at length it was often hardly to be distinguished from such as takes place between equals, and Florimel was by degrees forgetting the present condition in the possible future of the young man. But Malcolm, on the other hand, as often as the thought of that possible future arose in her presence, flung it from him in horror, lest the wild dream of winning her should make him for a moment desire its realization.

The claim that hung over him haunted his very life, turning the currents of his thought into channels of speculation unknown before. Imagine a young fisherman meditating—as he wandered with bent head through the wilder woods on the steep banks of the burn, or the little green levels which it overflowed in winter—of all possible subjects what analogy there might be betwixt the body and the soul in respect of derivation—whether the soul was *traduced* as well as the body?—as his material form came from the forms of his father and mother, did his soul come from their souls? or did the Maker, as at the first he breathed his breath into the form of Adam, still, at some crisis unknown in its creation, breathe into each form the breath of individual being? If the latter theory were the true, then, be his earthly origin what it might, he had but to shuffle off this mortal coil to walk forth a clean thing, as a prince might cast off the rags of an enforced disguise, and set out for the land of his birth. If the former were the true, then the wellspring of his being was polluted, nor might he by any death fling aside his degradation, or show himself other than defiled in the eyes of the old dwellers in "those high countries," where all things seem as they are, and are as they seem.

One day when, these questions fighting in his heart, he had for the hundredth time arrived thus far, all at once it seemed as if a soundless voice in the depth of his soul replied,

"Even then—should the well-spring of thy life be polluted with vilest horrors such as, in Persian legends, the lips of the lost are doomed to drink with loathings inconceivable— the well is but the utterance of the water, not the source of its existence; the rain is its father, and comes from the sweet heavens. Thy soul, however it became known to itself, is from the pure heart of God, whose thought of thee is older than thy being—is its first and eldest cause. Thy essence cannot be defiled, for in him it is eternal."

Even with the thought, the horizon of his life began to clear; a light came out on the far edge of its ocean—a dull and sombre yellow, it is true, and the clouds hung yet heavy over sea and land, while miles of vapour hid the sky; but he could now believe there might be a blue beyond, in which the sun lorded it with majesty.

He had been rambling on the waste hill in which the grounds of Lossie House, as it were, dissipated. It had a far outlook, but he had beheld neither sky or ocean. The Soutars of Cromarty had all the time sat on their stools large in his view; the hills of Sutherland had invited his gaze, rising faint and clear over the darkened water at their base, less solid than the sky in which they were set, and less a fact than the clouds that crossed their breasts; the land of Caithness had lain lowly and afar, as if, weary of great things, it had crept away in tired humility to the rigours of the north; and east and west his own rugged shore had gone lengthening out, fringed with the white burst of the dark sea; but none of all these things had he noted.

Lady Florimel suddenly encountered him on his way home, and was startled by his look.

"Where *have* you been, Malcolm?" she exclaimed.	"Where *have* you been, Malcolm?" she exclaimed.
"I hardly ken, my leddy: somewhaur aboot the feet o' Mount Pisgah, I'm thinkin', if no freely upo' the heid o' 't."	"I hardly know, my lady: somewhere about the feet of Mount Pisgah, I'm thinking, if not quite upon the head of it."
"That's not the name of the hill up there!"	"That's not the name of the hill up there!"
"Ow na; yon's the Binn."	"Oh na; that's the Binn."
"What have you been about? Looking at things in general, I suppose."	"What have you been about? Looking at things in general, I suppose."
"Na; they've been luikin' at me, I daursay; but I didna heed them, an' they didna fash me."	"Na; they've been looking at me, I daresay; but I didn't heed them, and they didn't bother me."
"You look so strangely bright!" she said, "as if you had seen something both marvellous and beautiful!"	"You look so strangely bright!" she said, "as if you had seen something both marvellous and beautiful!"

The words revealed a quality of insight not hitherto manifested by Florimel. In truth, Malcolm's whole being was irradiated by the flash of inward peace that had visited him—a statement intelligible and therefore credible enough to the mind accustomed to look over the battlements of the walls that clasp the fair windows of the senses. But Florimel's insight had reached its limit, and her judgment, vainly endeavouring to penetrate farther, fell floundering in the mud.

"I know!" she went on: "You've been to see your lady mother!"

Malcolm's face turned white as if blasted with leprosy. The same scourge that had maddened the poor laird fell hissing on his soul, and its knotted sting was the same word *mother*. He turned and walked slowly away, fighting a tyrannous impulse to thrust his fingers in his ears and run and shriek.

"Where are your manners?" cried the girl after him, but he never stayed his slow foot or turned his bowed head, and Florimel wondered.

For the moment, his new-found peace had vanished. Even if the old nobility of heaven might regard him without a shadow of condescension—that self-righteous form of contempt—what could he do with a mother whom he could neither honour or love? Love! If he could but cease to hate her! There was no question yet of loving.

But might she not repent? Ah, then, indeed! And might he not help her to repent?—He would not avoid her. How was it that she had never yet sought him?

As he brooded thus, on his way to Duncan's cottage, and, heedless of the sound of coming wheels, was crossing the road which went along the bottom of the glen, he was nearly run over by a carriage coming round the corner of a high bank at a fast trot. Catching one glimpse of the face of its occupant, as it passed within a yard of his own, he turned and fled back through the woods, with again a horrible impulse to howl to the winds the cry of the mad laird: "I dinna ken whaur I cam frae!" When he came to himself, he found his hands pressed hard on his ears, and for a moment felt a sickening certainty that he too was a son of the lady of Gersefell.

When he returned at length to the House, Mrs Courthope informed him that Mrs Stewart had called, and seen both the marquis and Lady Florimel.

Meantime he had grown again a little anxious about the laird, but as Phemy plainly avoided him, had concluded that he had found another concealment, and that the child preferred not being questioned concerning it.

With the library of Lossie House at his disposal, and almost nothing to do, it might now have been a grand time for Malcolm's studies; but alas! he too often found it all but impossible to keep his thoughts on the track of a thought through a single sentence of any length.

The autumn now hung over the verge of its grave. Hoar frost, thick on the fields, made its mornings look as if they had turned gray with fear. But when the sun arose, grayness and fear vanished; the back-thrown smile of the departing glory was enough to turn old age into a memory of youth. Summer was indeed gone, and winter was nigh with its storms and its fogs and its rotting rains and its drifting snows, but the sun was yet in the heavens, and, changed as was his manner towards her, would yet have many a half smile for the poor old earth—enough to keep her alive until he returned, bringing her youth with him. To the man who believes that the winter is but for the sake of the summer; exists only in virtue of the summer at its heart, no winter, outside or in, can be unendurable. But Malcolm sorely missed the ministrations of compulsion: he lacked labour—the most helpful and most healing of all God's holy things, of which we so often lose the heavenly benefit by labouring inordinately that we may rise above the earthly need of it. How many sighs are wasted over the toil of the sickly—a toil which perhaps lifts off half the weight of their sickness, elevates their inner life, and makes the outer pass with tenfold rapidity. Of those who honestly pity such, many would themselves be far less pitiable were they compelled to share in the toil they behold with compassion. They are unaware of the healing virtue which the thing they would not pity at all were it a matter of choice, gains from the compulsion of necessity.

All over the house big fires were glowing and blazing. Nothing pleased the marquis worse than the least appearance of stinting the consumption of coal. In the library two huge gratefuls were burning from dawn to midnight—well for the books anyhow, if their owner seldom showed his face amongst them. There were days during which, except the servant whose duty it was to attend to the fires, not a creature entered the room but Malcolm. To him it was as the cave of Aladdin to the worshipper of Mammon, and yet now he would often sit down indifferent to its hoarded splendours, and gather no jewels.

But one morning, as he sat there alone, in an oriel looking seawards, there lay on a table before him a thin folio, containing the chief works of Sir Thomas Brown—amongst the rest his well known Religio Medici, from which he had just read the following passage:

"When I take a full view and circle of myself, without this reasonable moderatour, and equall piece of justice, Death, I doe conceive my self the most miserablest person extant; were there not another life that I hoped for, all the vanities of this world should not intreat a moment's breath from me; could the Devil work my belief to imagine I could never die, I would not outlive that very thought: I have so abject a conceit of this common way of existence, this retaining to the Sun and elements, I cannot think this is to be a man, or to live according to the dignity of humanity. In expectation of a better, I can with patience embrace this life, yet in my best meditations do often desire death; I honour any man that contemnes it, nor can I highly love any that is afraid of it: this makes me naturally love a Soldier, and honour those tatter'd and contemptible Regiments that will die at the command of a Sergeant."

These words so fell in with the prevailing mood of his mind, that having gathered them, they grew upon him, and as he pondered them, he sat gazing out on the bright blowing autumn day. The sky was dimmed with a clear pallor, across which small white clouds were driving; the yellow leaves that yet clave to the twigs were few, and the wind swept through the branches with a hiss. The far-off sea was alive with multitudinous white—the rush of the jubilant over-sea across the blue plain. All without was merry, healthy, radiant, strong; in his mind brooded a single haunting thought that already had almost filled his horizon, threatening by exclusion to become madness! Why should he not leave the place, and the horrors of his history with it? Then the hideous hydra might unfold itself as it pleased; he would find at least a better fortune than his birth had endowed him withal.

Lady Florimel entered in search of something to read: to her surprise, for she had heard of no arrival, in one of the windows sat a Highland gentleman, looking out on the landscape. She was on the point of retiring again, when a slight movement revealed Malcolm.

The explanation was, that the marquis, their seafaring over, had at length persuaded Malcolm to don the highland attire: it was an old custom of the house of Lossie that its lord's henchman should be thus distinguished, and the marquis himself wore the kilt when on his western estates in the summer, also as often as he went to court,—would indeed have worn it always but that he was no longer hardy enough. He would not have succeeded with Malcolm, however, but for the youth's love to Duncan, the fervent heat of which vaporized the dark heavy stone of obligation into the purple vapour of gratitude, and enhanced the desire of pleasing him until it became almost a passion. Obligation is a ponderous roll of canvas which Love spreads aloft into a tent wherein he delights to dwell.

This was his first appearance in the garments of Duncan's race.

It was no little trial to him to assume them in the changed aspect of his circumstances; for alas! he wore them in right of service only, not of birth, and the tartan of his lord's family was all he could claim.

He had not heard Lady Florimel enter. She went softly up behind him, and laid her hand on his shoulder. He started to his feet.

"A penny for your thoughts," she said, retreating a step or two.

"I wad gie twa to be rid o' them," he returned, shaking his bushy head as if to scare the invisible ravens hovering about it.

"How fine you are!" Florimel went on, regarding him with an approbation too open to be altogether gratifying. "The dress suits you thoroughly. I didn't know you at first. I thought it must be some friend of papa's. Now I remember he said once you must wear the proper dress for a henchman. How do you like it?"

"It's a' ane to me," said Malcolm. "I dinna care what I weir.—Gien only I had a richt till 't!" he added with a sigh.

"It is too bad of you, Malcolm!" rejoined Florimel in a tone of rebuke. "The moment fortune offers you favour, you fall out with her—won't give her a single smile. You don't deserve your good luck."

Malcolm was silent.

"There's something on your mind," Florimel went on, partly from willingness to serve Mrs Stewart, partly enticed by the romance of being Malcolm's comforter, or perhaps confessor.

"Ay is there, my leddy."

"What is it? Tell me. You can trust me!"

"I could trust ye, but I canna tell ye. I daurna—I maunna."

"A penny for your thoughts," she said, retreating a step or two.

"I would give two to be rid of them," he returned, shaking his bushy head as if to scare the invisible ravens hovering about it.

"How fine you are!" Florimel went on, regarding him with an approbation too open to be altogether gratifying. "The dress suits you thoroughly. I didn't know you at first. I thought it must be some friend of papa's. Now I remember he said once you must wear the proper dress for a henchman. How do you like it?"

"It's all one to me," said Malcolm. "I don't care what I wear.—If only I had a right to it!" he added with a sigh.

"It is too bad of you, Malcolm!" rejoined Florimel in a tone of rebuke. "The moment fortune offers you favour, you fall out with her—won't give her a single smile. You don't deserve your good luck."

Malcolm was silent.

"There's something on your mind," Florimel went on, partly from willingness to serve Mrs Stewart, partly enticed by the romance of being Malcolm's comforter, or perhaps confessor.

"Ay there is, my lady."

"What is it? Tell me. You can trust me!"

"I could trust you, but I can't tell you. I daren't—I mustn't."

"I see you will not trust me," said Florimel, with a half pretended, half real offence.

"I wad lay doon my life—what there is o' 't—for ye, my leddy; but the verra natur o' my trouble winna be tauld. I maun beir 't my lane."

"I would lay down my life—what there is of it—for you, my lady; but the very nature of my trouble won't be told. I must bear it alone."

It flashed across Lady Florimel's brain, that the cause of his misery, the thing he dared not confess, was love of herself. Now, Malcolm, standing before her in his present dress, and interpreted by the knowledge she believed she had of his history, was a very different person indeed from the former Malcolm in the guise of fisherman or sailor, and she felt as well as saw the difference: if she was the cause of his misery, why should she not comfort him a little? why should she not be kind to him? Of course anything more was out of the question; but a little confession and consolation would hurt neither of them. Besides, Mrs Stewart had begged her influence, and this would open a new channel for its exercise. Indeed, if he was unhappy through her, she ought to do what she might for him. A gentle word or two would cost her nothing, and might help to heal a broken heart! She was hardly aware, however, how little she wanted it healed—all at once.

For the potency of a thought it is perhaps even better that it should not be logically displayed to the intellect; anyhow the germ of all this, undeveloped into the definite forms I have given, sufficed to the determining of Florimel's behaviour. I do not mean that she had more than the natural tendency of womankind to enjoy the emotions of which she was the object; but besides the one in the fable, there are many women with a tendency to mousing; and the idea of deriving pleasure from the sufferings of a handsome youth was not quite so repulsive to her as it ought to have been. At the same time, as there cannot be many cats capable of understanding the agonies of the mice within reach of their waving whiskers, probably many cat-women are not quite so cruel as they seem.

"*Can't* you trust me, Malcolm?" she said, looking in his eyes very sweetly, and bending a little towards him; "*Can't you trust me?*"

"*Can't* you trust me, Malcolm?" she said, looking in his eyes very sweetly, and bending a little towards him; "*Can't you trust me?*"

At the words and the look it seemed as if his frame melted to ether. He dropped on his knees, and, his heart half stifled in the confluence of the tides of love and misery, sighed out between the pulses in his throat:

At the words and the look it seemed as if his frame melted to ether. He dropped on his knees, and, his heart half stifled in the confluence of the tides of love and misery, sighed out between the pulses in his throat:

"There's naething I could na tell ye 'at ever I thoucht or did i' my life, my leddy; but it 's ither fowk, my leddy! It's like to burn a hole i' my hert, an' yet I daurna open my mou'."

"There's nothing I couldn't tell you that ever I thought or did in my life, my lady; but it's other folk, my lady! It's like to burn a hole in my heart, and yet I daren't open my mouth."

There was a half angelic, half dog-like entreaty in his up-looking hazel eyes that seemed to draw hers down into his: she must put a stop to that.

"Get up, Malcolm," she said kindly, "what would my father or Mrs Courthope think?"

"I dinna ken, an' I maist dinna care; atween ae thing an' anither, I'm near han' distrackit," answered Malcolm, rising slowly, but not taking his eyes from her face. "An' there's my daddy!" he went on, "maist won ower to the enemy—an' I daurna tell even him what for I canna bide it!—*Ye* haena been sayin' onything till him—hiv ye, my leddy?"

"I don't quite understand you," returned Florimel, rather guiltily, for she had spoken on the subject to Duncan. "Saying anything to your grandfather? About what?"

"Aboot—aboot—*her*, ye ken, my leddy."

"What her?" asked Florimel.

"Her 'at—The leddy o' Gersefell."

"And why? What of her? Why, Malcolm! what can have possessed you? You seem actually to dislike her!"

"I canna bide her," said Malcolm, with the calm earnestness of one who is merely stating an incontrovertible fact, and for a moment his eyes, at once troubled and solemn, kept looking wistfully in hers, as if searching for a comfort too good to be found, then slowly sank and sought the floor at her feet.

"And why?"

"I canna tell ye."

She supposed it an unreasoned antipathy.

"But that is very wrong," she said, almost as if rebuking a child. "You ought to be ashamed of yourself. What!—dislike your own mother?"

There was a half angelic, half dog-like entreaty in his up-looking hazel eyes that seemed to draw hers down into his: she must put a stop to that.

"Get up, Malcolm," she said kindly, "what would my father or Mrs Courthope think?"

"I don't know, and I hardly care; between one thing and another, I'm near hand distracted," answered Malcolm, rising slowly, but not taking his eyes from her face. "And there's my daddy!" he went on, "all but won over to the enemy—and I daren't tell even him why I can't endure it!—*You* haven't been saying anything to him—have you, my lady?"

"I don't quite understand you," returned Florimel, rather guiltily, for she had spoken on the subject to Duncan. "Saying anything to your grandfather? About what?"

"About—about—*her*, you know, my lady."

"What her?" asked Florimel.

"Her that—the lady of Gersefell."

"And why? What of her? Why, Malcolm! what can have possessed you? You seem actually to dislike her!"

"I can't stand her," said Malcolm, with the calm earnestness of one who is merely stating an incontrovertible fact, and for a moment his eyes, at once troubled and solemn, kept looking wistfully in hers, as if searching for a comfort too good to be found, then slowly sank and sought the floor at her feet.

"And why?"

"I can't tell you."

She supposed it an unreasoned antipathy.

"But that is very wrong," she said, almost as if rebuking a child. "You ought to be ashamed of yourself. What!—dislike your own mother?"

"Dinna say the word, my leddy," cried Malcolm in a tone of agony, "or ye'll gar me skirl an' rin like the mad laird. He's no a hair madder nor I wad be wi' sic a mither."

He would have passed her to leave the room.

But Lady Florimel could not bear defeat. In any contest she must win or be shamed in her own eyes, and was she to gain absolutely nothing in such a passage with a fisher lad? Was the billow of her persuasion to fall back from such a rock, self-beaten into poorest foam? She would, she must subdue him! Perhaps she did not know how much the sides of her intent were pricked by the nettling discovery that she was not the cause of his unhappiness.

"You're not going to leave me so!" she exclaimed, in a tone of injury.

"I'll gang or bide as ye wull, my leddy," answered Malcolm resignedly.

"Bide then," she returned. "I haven't half done with you yet."

"Ye mauna jist tear my hert oot," he rejoined—with a sad half smile, and another of his dog-like looks.

"That's what you would do to your mother!" said Florimel severely.

"Say nae ill o' my mither!" cried Malcolm, suddenly changing almost to fierceness.

"Why, Malcolm!" said Florimel, bewildered, "what ill was I saying of her?"

"It's naething less than an in*sult* to my mither to ca' yon wuman by her name," he replied with set teeth.

It was to him an offence against the idea of motherhood—against the mother he had so often imagined luminous against the dull blank of memory, to call such a woman his mother.

"Don't say the word, my lady," cried Malcolm in a tone of agony, "or you'll make me scream and run like the mad laird. He's not a hair madder than I would be with such a mother."

He would have passed her to leave the room.

But Lady Florimel could not bear defeat. In any contest she must win or be shamed in her own eyes, and was she to gain absolutely nothing in such a passage with a fisher lad? Was the billow of her persuasion to fall back from such a rock, self-beaten into poorest foam? She would, she must subdue him! Perhaps she did not know how much the sides of her intent were pricked by the nettling discovery that she was not the cause of his unhappiness.

"You're not going to leave me so!" she exclaimed, in a tone of injury.

"I'll go or stay as you will, my lady," answered Malcolm resignedly.

"Stay then," she returned. "I haven't half done with you yet."

"You mustn't quite tear my heart out," he rejoined—with a sad half smile, and another of his dog-like looks.

"That's what you would do to your mother!" said Florimel severely.

"Speak no ill of my mother!" cried Malcolm, suddenly changing almost to fierceness.

"Why, Malcolm!" said Florimel, bewildered, "what ill was I speaking of her?"

"It's nothing less than an in*sult* to my mother to call that woman by her name," he replied with set teeth.

It was to him an offence against the idea of motherhood—against the mother he had so often imagined luminous against the dull blank of memory, to call such a woman his mother.

"She's a very ladylike, handsome woman—handsome enough to be *your* mother even, Mr Malcolm Stewart."

Florimel could not have dared the words but for the distance between them; but, then, neither would she have said them while the distance was greater! They were lost on Malcolm though, for never in his life having started the question whether he was handsome or not, he merely supposed her making game of him, and drew himself together in silence, with the air of one bracing himself to hear and endure the worst.

"Even if she should not be your mother," his tormentor resumed, "to show such a dislike to any woman is nothing less than cruelty."

"She maun pruv' 't," murmured Malcolm—not the less emphatically that the words were but just audible.

"Of course she will do that; she has abundance of proof. She gave me a whole hour of proof."

"Lang's no strang," returned Malcolm: "there's comfort i' that! Gang on my leddy."

"Poor woman! it was hard enough to lose her son; but to find him again such as you seem likely to turn out, I should think ten times worse."

"Nae doobt! nae doobt!—But there's ae thing waur."

"What is that?"

"To come upon a mither 'at—"

He stopped abruptly; his eyes went wandering about the room, and the muscles of his face worked convulsively.

Florimel saw that she had been driving against a stone wall. She paused a moment, and then resumed.

"Anyhow, if she *is* your mother," she said, "nothing you can do will alter it."

"She's a very ladylike, handsome woman—handsome enough to be *your* mother even, Mr Malcolm Stewart."

Florimel could not have dared the words but for the distance between them; but, then, neither would she have said them while the distance was greater! They were lost on Malcolm though, for never in his life having started the question whether he was handsome or not, he merely supposed her making game of him, and drew himself together in silence, with the air of one bracing himself to hear and endure the worst.

"Even if she should not be your mother," his tormentor resumed, "to show such a dislike to any woman is nothing less than cruelty."

"She must prove it," murmured Malcolm—not the less emphatically that the words were but just audible.

"Of course she will do that; she has abundance of proof. She gave me a whole hour of proof."

"Long's not strong," returned Malcolm: "there's comfort in that! Go on my lady."

"Poor woman! it was hard enough to lose her son; but to find him again such as you seem likely to turn out, I should think ten times worse."

"No doubt! no doubt!—But there's one thing worse."

"What is that?"

"To come upon a mother that—"

He stopped abruptly; his eyes went wandering about the room, and the muscles of his face worked convulsively.

Florimel saw that she had been driving against a stone wall. She paused a moment, and then resumed.

"Anyhow, if she *is* your mother," she said, "nothing you can do will alter it."

"She maun pruv' 't," was all Malcolm's dogged reply.

"Just so; and if she can't," said Florimel, "you'll be no worse than you were before—and no better," she added with a sigh.

Malcolm lifted his questioning to her searching eyes.

"She must prove it," was all Malcolm's dogged reply.

"Just so; and if she can't," said Florimel, "you'll be no worse than you were before—and no better," she added with a sigh.

Malcolm lifted his questioning to her searching eyes.

"Don't you see," she went on, very softly, and lowering her look, from the half-conscious shame of half-unconscious falseness, "I can't be all my life here at Lossie? We shall have to say goodbye to each other—never to meet again most likely. But if you should turn out to be of good family, you know,—"

Florimel saw neither the paling of his brown cheek nor the great surge of red that followed, but, glancing up to spy the effect of her argument, did see the lightning that broke from the darkened hazel of his eyes, and again cast down her own.

"—then there might be some chance," she went on, "of our meeting somewhere—in London, or perhaps in Edinburgh, and I could ask you to my house—after I was married you know."

Heaven and earth seemed to close with a snap around his brain. The next moment, they had receded an immeasurable distance, and in limitless wastes of exhausted being he stood alone. What time had passed when he came to himself he had not an idea; it might have been hours for anything his consciousness was able to tell him. But, although he recalled nothing of what she had been urging, he grew aware that Lady Florimel's voice, which was now in his ears, had been sounding in them all the time. He was standing before her like a marble statue with a dumb thrill in its helpless heart of stone. He must end this! Parting was bad enough, but an endless parting was unendurable! To know that measureless impassable leagues lay between them, and yet to be for ever in the shroud of a cold leave-taking! To look in her eyes, and know that she was not there! A parting that never broke the bodily presence—that was the form of agony which the infinite moment assumed. As to the possibility she would bribe him with—it was not even the promise of a glimpse of Abraham's bosom from the heart of hell. With such an effort as breaks the bonds of a nightmare dream, he turned from her, and, heedless of her recall, went slowly, steadily, out of the house.

While she was talking, his eyes had been resting with glassy gaze upon the far off waters: the moment he stepped into the open air, and felt the wind on his face, he knew that their turmoil was the travailing of sympathy, and that the ocean had been drawing him all the time. He walked straight to his little boat, lying dead on the sands of the harbour, launched it alive on the smooth water within the piers, rove his halliard, stepped his mast, hoisted a few inches of sail, pulled beyond the sheltering sea-walls, and was tossing amidst the torn waters whose jagged edges were twisted in the loose-flying threads of the northern gale. A moment more, and he was sitting on the windward gunwale of his spoon of a boat, with the tiller in one hand and the sheet in the other, as she danced like a cork over the broken tops of the waves. For help in his sore need, instinct had led him to danger.

Half way to the point of Scaurnose, he came round on the other tack, and stood for the Death Head.

Glancing from the wallowing floor beneath him, and the one wing that bore him skimming over its million deaths, away to the House of Lossie, where it stood steady in its woods, he distinguished the very window whence, hardly an hour ago, from the centre of the calm companionship of books, he had gazed out upon the wind-swept waste as upon a dream.

"How strange," he thought, "to find myself now in the midst of what I then but saw! This reeling ocean was but a picture to me then—a picture framed in the window; it is now alive and I toss like a toy on its wild commotion. Then I but saw from afar the flashing of the white out of the blue water, and the blue sky overhead, which no winds can rend into pallid pains; now I have to keep eye and hand together in one consent to shun death; I meet wind and wave on their own terms, and humour the one into an evasion of the other. The wind that then revealed itself only in white blots and streaks now lashes my hair into my eyes, and only the lift of my bows is betwixt me and the throat that swallows the whales and the krakens.

"Will it be so with death? It looks strange and far off now, but it draws nigh noiselessly, and one day I meet it face to face in the grapple: shall I rejoice in that wrestle as I rejoice in this? Will not my heart grow sick within me? Shall I not be faint and fearful? And yet I could almost wish it were at hand!

"I wonder how death and this wan water here look to God! To him is it like a dream—a picture? Water cannot wet him; death cannot touch him. Yet Jesus could have let the water wet him; and he granted power to death when he bowed his head and gave up the ghost. God knows how things look to us both far off and near; he also can see them so when he pleases. What they look to him is what they are: we cannot see them so, but we see them as he meant us to see them, therefore truly, according to the measure of the created. Made in the image of God, we see things in the image of his sight."

Thoughts like these, only in yet cruder forms, swept through the mind of Malcolm as he tossed on that autumn sea. But what we call crude forms are often in reality germinal forms; and one or other of these flowered at once into the practical conclusion that God must know all his trouble, and would work for him a worthy peace. Ere he turned again towards the harbour, he had reascended the cloud-haunted Pisgah whence the words of Lady Florimel had hurled him.

CHAPTER L

LIZZY FINDLAY

Leaving his boat again on the dry sand that sloped steep into the harbour, Malcolm took his way homeward along the shore. Presently he spied, at some little distance in front of him, a woman sitting on the sand, with her head bowed upon her knees. She had no shawl, though the wind was cold and strong, blowing her hair about wildly. Her attitude and whole appearance were the very picture of misery. He drew near and recognized her.

"What on earth's gane wrang wi' ye, Lizzy?" he asked.

"Ow naething," she murmured, without lifting her head. The brief reply was broken by a sob.

"That canna be," persisted Malcolm, trouble of whose own had never yet rendered him indifferent to that of another. "Is 't onything 'at a body cun stan' by ye in?"

Another sob was the only answer.

"I'm in a peck o' troubles mysel'," said Malcolm. "I wad fain help a body gien I cud."

"Naebody can help me," returned the girl, with an agonized burst, as if the words were driven from her by a convulsion of her inner world, and therewith she gave way, weeping and sobbing aloud. "I doobt I'll hae to droon mysel'," she added with a wail, as he stood in compassionate silence, until the gust should blow over; and as she said it she lifted a face tear-stained, and all white, save where five fingers had branded their shapes in red. Her eyes scarcely encountered his; again she buried her face in her hands, and rocked herself to and fro, moaning in fresh agony.

"What on earth's gone wrong with you, Lizzy?" he asked.

"Oh nothing," she murmured, without lifting her head. The brief reply was broken by a sob.

"That can't be," persisted Malcolm, trouble of whose own had never yet rendered him indifferent to that of another. "Is it anything that a body could stand by you in?"

Another sob was the only answer.

"I'm in a peck of troubles myself," said Malcolm. "I would fain help a body if I could."

"Nobody can help me," returned the girl, with an agonized burst, as if the words were driven from her by a convulsion of her inner world, and therewith she gave way, weeping and sobbing aloud. "I think I'll have to drown myself," she added with a wail, as he stood in compassionate silence, until the gust should blow over; and as she said it she lifted a face tear-stained, and all white, save where five fingers had branded their shapes in red. Her eyes scarcely encountered his; again she buried her face in her hands, and rocked herself to and fro, moaning in fresh agony.

"Yer mither's been sair upo' ye, I doobt!" he said. "But it'll sune blaw ower. She cuils as fest 's she heats."

As he spoke he set himself down on the sand beside her. But Lizzy started to her feet, crying,

"Dinna come near me, Ma'colm. I'm no fit for honest man to come nigh me. Stan' awa'; I hae the plague."

She laughed, but it was a pitiful laugh, and she looked wildly about, as if for some place to run to.

"I wad na be sorry to tak it mysel', Lizzy. At ony rate I'm ower auld a freen' to be driven frae ye that gait," said Malcolm, who could not bear the thought of leaving her on the border of the solitary sea, with the waves barking at her all the cold winterly gloamin'. Who could tell what she might do after the dark came down? He rose and would have taken her hand to draw it from her face; but she turned her back quickly, saying in a hard forced voice:

"A man canna help a wuman—'cep it be till her grave." Then turning suddenly, she laid her hands on his shoulders, and cried: "For the love o' God, Ma'colm, lea' me this moment. Gien I cud tell ony man what ailed me, I wad tell you; but I canna, I canna! Rin laddie; rin' an' lea' me."

It was impossible to resist her anguished entreaty and agonized look. Sore at heart and puzzled in brain, Malcolm yielding turned from her, and with eyes on the ground, thoughtfully pursued his slow walk towards the Seaton.

At the corner of the first house in the village stood three women, whom he saluted as he passed. The tone of their reply struck him a little, but, not having observed how they watched him as he

"Your mother's been hard upon you, I expect!" he said. "But it'll soon blow over. She cools as fast as she heats."

As he spoke he set himself down on the sand beside her. But Lizzy started to her feet, crying,

"Don't come near me, Malcolm. I'm not fit for honest man to come nigh me. Stand back; I have the plague."

She laughed, but it was a pitiful laugh, and she looked wildly about, as if for some place to run to.

"I wouldn't be sorry to catch it myself, Lizzy. At any rate I'm too old a friend to be driven from you like that," said Malcolm, who could not bear the thought of leaving her on the border of the solitary sea, with the waves barking at her all the cold winterly gloamin'. Who could tell what she might do after the dark came down? He rose and would have taken her hand to draw it from her face; but she turned her back quickly, saying in a hard forced voice:

"A man can't help a woman—except it be to her grave." Then turning suddenly, she laid her hands on his shoulders, and cried: "For the love of God, Malcolm, leave me this moment. If I could tell any man my sorrow, I would tell you; but I can't, I can't! Run laddie; run and leave me."

It was impossible to resist her anguished entreaty and agonized look. Sore at heart and puzzled in brain, Malcolm yielding turned from her, and with eyes on the ground, thoughtfully pursued his slow walk towards the Seaton.

At the corner of the first house in the village stood three women, whom he saluted as he passed. The tone of their reply struck him a little, but, not having observed how they watched him as he

Her attitude and whole appearance were the very picture of misery.

approached, he presently forgot it. The moment his back was turned to them, they turned to each other and interchanged looks.

"Fine feathers mak fine birds," said one of them.

"Ay, but he luiks booed doon," said another.

"An' weel he may! What 'll his leddy mither say to sic a ploy? she'll no sawvour bein' made a granny o' efter sic a fashion 's yon," said the third.

"'Deed, lass, there's feow oucht to think less o' 't," returned the first.

approached, he presently forgot it. The moment his back was turned to them, they turned to each other and interchanged looks.

"Fine feathers make fine birds," said one of them.

"Ay, but he looks bowed down," said another.

"And well he may! What'll his lady mother say to such a ploy? she won't relish being made a granny of in that manner," said the third.

"Indeed, lass, there's few ought to think less of it," returned the first.

Although they took little pains to lower their voices, Malcolm was far too much preoccupied to hear what they said. Perceiving plainly enough that the girl's trouble was much greater than a passing quarrel with her mother would account for, and knowing that any intercession on his part would only rouse to loftier flames the coal-pits of maternal wrath, he resolved at length to take counsel with Blue Peter and his wife, and therefore, passing the sea-gate, continued his walk along the shore, and up the red path to the village of Scaurnose.

He found them sitting at their afternoon meal of tea and oatcake. A peat fire smouldered hot upon the hearth; a large kettle hung from a chain over it—fountain of plenty, whence the great china teapot, splendid in red flowers and green leaves, had just been filled; the mantelpiece was crowded with the gayest of crockery, including the never-absent half-shaved poodles, and the rarer Gothic castle, from the topmost story of whose keep bloomed a few late autumn flowers. Phemy too was at the table: she rose as if to leave the room, but apparently changed her mind, for she sat down again instantly.

"Man ye're unco braw the day—i' yer kilt an' tartan hose!" remarked Mair as he welcomed him.

"I pat them on to please my daddy an' the markis," said Malcolm, with a half shamed-faced laugh.

"Are na ye some cauld aboot the k-nees?" asked the guidwife.

"Nae that cauld! I ken 'at they're there; but I'll sune be used till 't."

"Weel, sit ye doon an' tak a cup o' tay wi' 's."

"Man, you're mighty fine today—in your kilt and tartan hose!" remarked Mair as he welcomed him.

"I put them on to please my daddy and the marquis," said Malcolm, with a half shamed-faced laugh.

"Aren't you pretty cold about the knees?" asked the goodwife.

"Not that cold! I know that they're there; but I'll soon be used to it."

"Well, have a seat and take a cup of tea with us."

"I haena muckle time to spare," said Malcolm; "but I'll tak a cup o' tay wi' ye. Gien 't warna for wee bit luggies I wad fain spier yer advice aboot ane 'at wants a wuman-freen', I'm thinkin'."

Phemy, who had been regarding him with compressed lips and suspended operations, deposited her bread and butter on the table, and slipped from her chair.

"Whaur are ye gaein', Phemy?" said her mother.

"Takin' awa' my lugs," returned Phemy.

"Ye cratur!" exclaimed Malcolm, "ye're ower wise. Wha wad hae thoucht ye sae gleg at the uptak!"

"Whan fowk winna lippen to me—" said Phemy and ceased.

"What can ye expec," returned Malcolm, while father and mother listened with amused faces, "whan ye winna lippen to fowk? Phemy, whaur's the mad laird?"

A light flush rose to her cheeks, but whether from embarrassment or anger could not be told from her reply.

"I ken nane o' that name," she said.

"Whaur's the laird o' Kirkbyres, than?"

"Whar ye s' never lay han' upo' 'im!" returned the child, her cheeks now rosy red, and her eyes flashing.

"*Me* lay han' upo' 'im!" cried Malcolm, surprised at her behaviour.

"Gien 't hadna been for you, naebody wad hae fun' oot the w'y intil the cave," she rejoined, her gray eyes, blue with the fire of anger, looking straight into his.

"Phemy! Phemy!" said her mother. "For shame!"

"There's nae shame intill 't," protested the child indignantly.

"But there *is* shame intill 't," said Malcolm quietly, "for ye wrang an honest man."

"I haven't much time to spare," said Malcolm; "but I'll take a cup of tea with you. If it weren't for little ones' ears I'd be glad of your advice about one that wants a woman-friend, I'm thinking."

Phemy, who had been regarding him with compressed lips and suspended operations, deposited her bread and butter on the table, and slipped from her chair.

"Where are you going, Phemy?" said her mother.

"Taking away my ears," returned Phemy.

"What a lassie!" exclaimed Malcolm, "you're too clever. Who'd have thought you so quick at the uptake!"

"When folk won't trust me—" said Phemy and ceased.

"What can you expect," returned Malcolm, while father and mother listened with amused faces, "when you won't trust other folk? Phemy, where's the mad laird?"

A light flush rose to her cheeks, but whether from embarrassment or anger could not be told from her reply.

"I know none of that name," she said.

"Where's the laird of Kirkbyres, then?"

"Where you'll never lay hand upon him!" returned the child, her cheeks now rosy red, and her eyes flashing.

"*Me* lay hand upon him!" cried Malcolm, surprised at her behaviour.

"If it hadn't been for you, nobody would have found out the way into the cave," she rejoined, her gray eyes, blue with the fire of anger, looking straight into his.

"Phemy! Phemy!" said her mother. "For shame!"

"There's no shame in it," protested the child indignantly.

"But there *is* shame in it," said Malcolm quietly, "for you wrong an honest man."

"Weel, ye canna deny," persisted Phemy, in mood to brave the evil one himself, "'at ye was ower at Kirkbyres on ane o' the markis's mears, an' heild a lang confab wi' the laird's mither!"

"I gaed upo' my maister's eeran'," answered Malcolm.

"Ow, ay! I daursay!—But wha kens—wi' sic a mither!"

She burst out crying, and ran into the street.

Malcolm understood it now.

"She's like a' the lave!" he said sadly, turning to her mother.

"I'm jist affrontit wi' the bairn!" she replied, with manifest annoyance in her flushed face.

"She's true to *him*," said Malcolm, "gien she binna fair to *me*. Sayna a word to the lassie. she'll ken me better or lang. An' noo for my story."

Mrs Mair said nothing while he told how he had come upon Lizzy, the state she was in, and what had passed between them; but he had scarcely finished, when she rose, leaving a cup of tea untasted, and took her bonnet and shawl from a nail in the back of the door. Her husband rose also.

"I'll jist gang as far 's the Boar's Craig wi' ye mysel', Annie," he said.

"I'm thinkin' ye'll fin' the puir lassie whaur I left her," remarked Malcolm. "I doobt she daured na gang hame."

That night it was all over the town, that Lizzy Findlay was in a woman's worst trouble, and that Malcolm was the cause of it.

"Well, you can't deny," persisted Phemy, in mood to brave the evil one himself, "that you were over at Kirkbyres on one of the marquis's mares, and held a long talk with the laird's mother!"

"I went upon my master's errand," answered Malcolm.

"Oh, ay! I daresay!—But who knows—with such a mother!"

She burst out crying, and ran into the street.

Malcolm understood it now.

"She's like all the rest!" he said sadly, turning to her mother.

"I'm just affronted with the child!" she replied, with manifest annoyance in her flushed face.

"She's true to *him*," said Malcolm, "though she's less than fair to *me*. Don't say a word to the lassie. She'll know me better soon. And now for my story."

Mrs Mair said nothing while he told how he had come upon Lizzy, the state she was in, and what had passed between them; but he had scarcely finished, when she rose, leaving a cup of tea untasted, and took her bonnet and shawl from a nail in the back of the door. Her husband rose also.

"I'll just go as far as the Bored Craig with you myself, Annie," he said.

"I'm thinking you'll find the poor lassie where I left her," remarked Malcolm. "I expect she was too scared to go home."

That night it was all over the town, that Lizzy Findlay was in a woman's worst trouble, and that Malcolm was the cause of it.

CHAPTER LI

THE LAIRD'S BURROW

Annie Mair had a brother, a carpenter, who, following her to Scaurnose, had there rented a small building next door to her cottage, and made of it a workshop. It had a rude loft, one end of which was loosely floored, while the remaining part showed the couples through the bare joists, except where some planks of oak and mahogany, with an old door, a boat's rudder, and other things that might come in handy, were laid across them in store. There also, during the winter, hung the cumulus clouds of Blue Peter's herring-nets; for his cottage, having a garret above, did not afford the customary place for them in the roof.

When the cave proved to be no longer a secret from the laird's enemies, Phemy, knowing that her father's garret could never afford him a sufficing sense of security, turned the matter over in her active little brain until pondering produced plans, and she betook herself to her uncle, with whom she was a great favourite. Him she found no difficulty in persuading to grant the hunted man a refuge in the loft. In a few days he had put up a partition between the part which was floored and that which was open, and so made for him a little room, accessible from the shop by a ladder and a trap-door. He had just taken down an old window-frame to glaze for it, when the laird coming in and seeing what he was about, scrambled up the ladder, and, a moment after, all but tumbled down again in his eagerness to put a stop to it: the window was in the gable, looking to the south, and he would not have it glazed.

In blessed compensation for much of the misery of his lot, the laird was gifted with an inborn delicate delight in nature and her ministrations such as few poets even possess; and this faculty was supplemented with a physical hardiness which, in association with his weakness and liability to certain appalling attacks, was truly astonishing. Though a rough hand might cause him exquisite pain, he could sleep soundly on the hardest floor; a hot room would induce a fit, but he would lie under an open window in the sharpest night without injury; a rude word would make him droop like a flower in frost, but he might go all day wet to the skin without taking cold. To all kinds of what are called hardships, he had readily become inured, without which it would have been impossible for his love of nature to receive such a full development. For hence he grew capable of communion with her in all her moods, undisabled either by the deadening effects of present, or the aversion consequent on past suffering. All the range of earth's shows, from the grandeurs of sunrise or thunderstorm down to the soft unfolding of a daisy or the babbling birth of a spring, was to him an open book. It is true, the delight of these things was constantly mingled with, not unfrequently broken, indeed, by the troublous question of his origin; but it was only on occasions of jarring contact with his fellows, that it was accompanied by such agonies as my story has represented. Sometimes he would sit on a rock, murmuring the words over and over, and dabbling his bare feet, small and delicately formed, in the translucent green of a tide-abandoned pool. But oftener in a soft dusky wind, he might have been heard uttering them gently and coaxingly, as if he would wile from the evening zephyr the secret of his birth—which surely mother Nature must know. The confinement of such a man would have been in the highest degree cruel, and must speedily have ended in death. Even Malcolm did not know how absolute was the laird's need, not simply of air and freedom, but of all things accompanying the enjoyment of them.

There was nothing then of insanity in his preference of a windowless bedroom;—it was that airs and odours, birds and sunlight—the sound of flapping wing, of breaking wave, and quivering throat, might be free to enter. Cool clean air he must breathe, or die; with that, the partial confinement to which he was subjected was not unendurable; besides, the welcome rain would then visit him sometimes, alighting from the slant wing of the flying blast; while the sun would pour in his rays full and mighty and generous, unsifted by the presumptuous glass—green and gray and crowded with distorting lines; and the sharp flap of pigeon's wing would be mimic thunder to the flash which leapt from its whiteness as it shot by.

He not only loved but understood all the creatures, divining by an operation in which neither the sympathy nor the watchfulness was the less perfect that both were but half conscious, the emotions and desires informing their inarticulate language. Many of them seemed to know him in return—either recognizing his person, and from experience deducing safety, or reading his countenance sufficiently to perceive that his interest prognosticated no injury. The maternal bird would keep her seat in her nursery, and give back his gaze; the rabbit peeping from his burrow would not even draw in his head at his approach; the rooks about Scaurnose never took to their wings until he was within a yard or two of them: the laird, in his half-acted utterance, indicated that they took him for a scarecrow and *therefore* were not afraid of him. Even Mrs Catanach's cur had never offered him a bite in return for a caress. He could make a bird's nest, of any sort common in the neighbourhood, so as deceive the most cunning of the nest-harrying youths of the parish.[19]

Hardly was he an hour in his new abode ere the sparrows and robins began to visit him. Even strange birds of passage flying in at his hospitable window, would espy him unscared, and sometimes partake of the food he had always at hand to offer them. He relied, indeed, for the pleasures of social intercourse with the animal world, on stray visits alone; he had no pets—dog nor cat nor bird; for his wandering and danger-haunted life did not allow such companionship.

---

[19] See article *Martin Féreol,* in *St. Paul's Magazine* vol. iv. generally.

He insisted on occupying his new quarters at once. In vain Phemy and her uncle showed reason against it. He did not want a bed; he much preferred a heap of *spales*, that is, wood shavings. Indeed, he would not have a bed; and whatever he did want he would get for himself. Having by word and gesture made this much plain, he suddenly darted up the ladder, threw down the trap-door, and, lo! like a hermit-crab, he had taken possession. Wisely they left him alone.

For a full fortnight he allowed neither to enter the little chamber. As often as they called him, he answered cheerfully, but never showed himself except when Phemy brought him food, which, at his urgent request, was only once in the twenty-four hours— after nightfall, the last thing before she went to bed; then he would slide down the ladder, take what she had brought him, and hurry up again. Phemy was perplexed, and at last a good deal distressed, for he had always been glad of her company before.

At length, one day, hearing her voice in the shop, and having peeped through a hole in the floor to see that no stranger was present, he invited her to go up, and lifted the trap-door.

"Come, come," he said hurriedly, when her head appeared and came no farther.

He stood holding the trap-door, eager to close it again as soon as she should step clear of it, and surprise was retarding her ascent.

Before hearing his mind, the carpenter had already made for him, by way of bedstead, a simple frame of wood, crossed with laths in the form of lattice work: this the laird had taken and set up on its side, opposite the window, about two feet from it, so that, with abundant passage for air, it served as a screen. Fixing it firmly to the floor, he had placed on the top of it a large pot of the favourite cottage plant there called *Humility*, and trained its long pendent runners over it. On the floor between it and the window, he had ranged a row of flower pots—one of them with an ivy-plant, which also he had begun to train against the trellis; and already the humility and the ivy had begun to intermingle.

At one side of the room, where the sloping roof met the floor, was his bed of fresh pine-shavings, amongst which, their resinous half-aromatic odour apparently not sweet enough to content him, he had scattered a quantity of dried rose-leaves. A thick tartan plaid, for sole covering, lay upon the heap.

"I wad hae likit hay better," he said, pointing to this lair rather than couch, "but it's some ill to get, an' the spales they're at han', an' they smell unco clean."

At the opposite side of the room lay a corresponding heap, differing not a little, however, in appearance and suggestion. As far as visible form and material could make it one, it was a grave—rather a short one, but abundantly long for the laird. It was in reality a heap of mould, about a foot and a half high, covered with the most delicate grass, and bespangled with daisies.

"I would have liked hay better," he said, pointing to this lair rather than couch, "but it's hard to get, and the spales are at hand, and they smell so clean."

At the opposite side of the room lay a corresponding heap, differing not a little, however, in appearance and suggestion. As far as visible form and material could make it one, it was a grave—rather a short one, but abundantly long for the laird. It was in reality a heap of mould, about a foot and a half high, covered with the most delicate grass, and bespangled with daisies.

"Laird!" said Phemy, half reproachfully, as she stood gazing at the marvel, "ye hae been oot at nicht!"

"Aye—a' nicht whiles, whan naebody was aboot 'cep' the win'"—he pronounced the word with a long drawn imitative sough—"an' the cloods an' the splash o' the watter."

"Laird!" said Phemy, half reproachfully, as she stood gazing at the marvel, "you've been out at night!"

"Aye—all night sometimes, when nobody was about except the wind"—he pronounced the word with a long drawn imitative sough[20]—"and the clouds and the splash of the water."

Pining under the closer imprisonment in his garret, which the discovery of his subterranean refuge had brought upon him, the laird would often have made his escape at night but for the fear of disturbing the Mairs; and now that there was no one to disturb, the temptation to spend his nights in the open air was the more irresistible that he had conceived the notion of enticing nature herself into his very chamber. Abroad then he had gone, as soon as the first midnight closed around his new dwelling, and in the fields had with careful discrimination begun to collect the mould for his mound, a handful here and a handful there. This took him several nights, and when it was finished, he was yet more choice in his selection of turf, taking it from the natural grass growing along the roads and on the earthen dykes, or walls, the outer sides of which feed the portionless cows of that country. Searching for miles in the moonlight, he had, with eye and hand, chosen out patches of this grass, the shortest and thickest he could find, and with a pocket knife, often in pieces of only a few inches, removed the best of it and carried it home, to be fitted on the heap, and with every ministration and blandishment enticed to flourish. He pressed it down with soft firm hands, and beshowered it with water first warmed a little in his mouth; when the air was soft, he guided the wind to blow upon it; and as the sun could not reach it where it lay, he gathered a marvellous heap of all the bright sherds he could find—of crockery and glass and mirror, so arranging them in the window, that each threw its tiny reflex upon the turf. With this last contrivance, Phemy was specially delighted; and the laird, happy as a child in beholding her delight, threw himself in an ecstasy on the mound and clasped it in his arms. I can hardly doubt that he regarded it as representing his own grave, to which in his happier moods he certainly looked forward as a place of final and impregnable refuge.

As he lay thus, foreshadowing his burial, or rather his resurrection, a young canary which had flown from one of the cottages, flitted in with a golden shiver and flash, and alighted on his head. He took it gently in his hand and committed it to Phemy to carry home, with many injunctions against disclosing how it had been captured.

His lonely days were spent in sleep, in tending his plants, or in contriving defences; but in all weathers he wandered out at midnight, and roamed or rested among fields or rocks till the first signs of the breaking day, when he hurried like a wild creature to his den.

---

20 SOUGH (Scots): a sigh, or sighing noise, as of the wind

Before long he had contrived an ingenious trap, or man-spider-web, for the catching of any human insect that might seek entrance at his window: the moment the invading body should reach a certain point, a number of lines would drop about him, in making his way through which he would straightway be caught by the barbs of countless fishhooks—the whole strong enough at least to detain him until its inventor should have opened the trapdoor and fled.

CHAPTER LII

CREAM OR SCUM?

Of the new evil report abroad concerning him, nothing had as yet reached
Malcolm. He read, and pondered, and wrestled with difficulties of every kind;
saw only a little of Lady Florimel, who, he thought, avoided him; saw less of
the marquis; and, as the evenings grew longer, spent still larger portions of them with
Duncan—now and then reading to him, but oftener listening to his music or taking
a lesson in the piper's art. He went seldom into the Seaton, for the faces there were
changed towards him. Attributing this to the reports concerning his parentage, and not
seeing why he should receive such treatment because of them, hateful though they might
well be to himself, he began to feel some bitterness towards his early world, and would
now and then repeat to himself a misanthropical thing he had read, fancying he too
had come to that conclusion. But there was not much danger of such a mood growing
habitual with one who knew Duncan MacPhail, Blue Peter, and the schoolmaster—not
to mention Miss Horn. To know one person who is positively to be trusted, will do more
for a man's moral nature—yes, for his spiritual nature—than all the sermons he has ever
heard or ever can hear.

One evening, Malcolm thought he would pay Joseph a visit, but when he reached
Scaurnose, he found it nearly deserted: he had forgotten that this was one of the nights
of meeting in the Baillies' Barn. Phemy indeed had not gone with her father and mother,
but she was spending the evening with the laird. Lifting the latch, and seeing no one in
the house, he was on the point of withdrawing when he caught sight of an eye peeping
through an inch-opening of the door of the bed-closet, which the same moment was hur-
riedly closed. He called, but received no reply, and left the cottage wondering. He had not
heard that Mrs Mair had given Lizzy Findlay shelter for a season. And now a neighbour
had observed and put her own construction on the visit, her report of which strengthened
the general conviction of his unworthiness.

Descending from the promontory, and wandering slowly along the shore, he met the
Scaurnose part of the congregation returning home. The few salutations dropped him as
he passed were distant, and bore an expression of disapproval. Mrs Mair only, who was
walking with a friend, gave him a kind nod. Blue Peter, who followed at a little distance,
turned and walked back with him.

"I'm exerceesed i' my min'," he said, as soon as they were clear of the stragglers, "aboot the turn things hae taen, doon by at the Barn."

"They tell me there's some gey queer customers taen to haudin' furth," returned Malcolm.

"It's a fac'," answered Peter. "The fowk 'll hardly hear a word noo frae ony o' the aulder an' soberer Christians. They haena the gift o' the Speerit, they say. But in place o' steerin' them up to tak hold upo' their Maker, thir new lichts set them up to luik doon upo' ither fowk, propheseein' an' denuncin', as gien the Lord had committit jeedgment into their han's."

"What is 't they tak haud o' to misca' them for?"

"It's no sae muckle," answered Peter, "for onything they du, as for what they believe or dinna believe. There's an 'uman frae Clamrock was o' their pairty the nicht. She stude up an' spak weel, an' weel oot, but no to muckle profit, as 't seemed to me; only maybe I'm no a fair jeedge, for I cudna be rid o' the notion 'at she was lattin' at mysel' a' the time. I dinna ken what for. An' I cudna help wonnerin' gien she kent what fowk used to say aboot hersel' whan she was a lass; for gien the sma' half o' that was true, a body micht think the new grace gien her wad hae driven her to hide her head, i' place o' exaltin' her horn on high. But maybe it was a' lees—she kens best hersel'."

"There canna be muckle worship gaein' on wi' ye by this time, than, I'm thinkin'," said Malcolm.

"I dinna like to say 't," returned Joseph; "but there's a speerit o' speeritooal pride abroad amang 's, it seems to me, 'at's no fawvourable to devotion. They hae taen 't

"I've been giving a deal of thought," he said, as soon as they were clear of the stragglers, "to the turn things have taken, down there at the Barn."

"They tell me there's some very strange customers have taken to preaching there," returned Malcolm.

"It's true," answered Peter. "The folk'll hardly hear a word now from any of the older and soberer Christians. They haven't the gift of the Spirit, they say. But instead of stirring them up to take hold upon their Maker, these new lights set them up to look down upon their fellows, prophesying and denouncing, as if the Lord had committed judgement into their hands."

"What is it they claim to be denouncing them for?" asked Malcolm.

"It's not so much," answered Peter, "for anything they do, as for what they believe or don't believe. A woman from Clamrock was of their party tonight. She stood up and spoke well, and clearly, but not to much profit, as it seemed to me; only maybe I'm not a fair judge, for I couldn't be rid of the notion that she was aiming her barbs at me. I don't know why. And I couldn't help wondering if she knew what folk used to say about her when she was a lass; for if even the half of that was true, you'd expect her to hang her head when she was given new grace, instead of exalting her horn on high. But maybe it was all lies—she knows best herself."

"There can't be much worship going on with you by this time, then, I'm thinking," said Malcolm.

"I don't like to say that," returned Joseph; "but there's a spirit of spiritual pride abroad among us, it seems to me, that's not favourable to devotion. They've taken it intill their heids, for ae thing—an that's what Dilse's Bess lays on at—'at 'cause they're fisher fowk, they hae a speecial mission to convert the warl'."

"What foon' they that upo'?" asked Malcolm.

"Ow, what the Saviour said to Peter an' the lave o' them 'at was fishers—to come to him, an' he would mak them fishers o' men."

"Ay, I see!—What for dinna ye bide at hame, you an' the lave o' the douce anes?"

"There ye come upo' the thing 'at 's troublin' me. Are we 'at begude it to brak it up? Or are we to stan' aside an' lat it a' gang to dirt an' green bree? Or are we to bide wi' them, an warsle aboot holy words till we tyne a' stamach for holy things?"

"Cud ye brak it up gien ye tried?" asked Malcolm.

"I doobt no. That's ane o' the considerations 'at hings some sair upo' me: see what we hae dune!"

"What for dinna ye gang ower to Maister Graham, an' speir what he thinks?"

"What for sud I gang till him? What's *he* but a fine moaral man? I never h'ard 'at he had ony discernment o' the min' o' the speerit."

"That's what Dilse's Bess frae Clamrock wad say aboot yersel', Peter."

"An' I doobt she wadna be far wrang."

"Ony gait, she kens nae mair aboot you nor ye ken aboot the maister. Ca' ye a man wha cares for naething in h'aven or in earth but the wull o' 's Creator—ca' ye sic a man no speeritual? Jist gang ye till 'im, an' maybe he'll lat in a glent upo' ye 'at 'll astonish ye."

"He's taen unco little enterest in onything 'at was gaein' on."

into their heads, for one thing—and that's what Dilse's Bess harps on at—that because they're fisher folk, they have a special mission to convert the world."

"What do they found that upon?" asked Malcolm.

"Oh, what the Saviour said to Peter and the rest of them that were fishers—to come to him, and he would make them fishers of men."

"Ay, I see!—Why don't you and the other wiser heads stay at home then?"

"There you come upon the thing that's troubling me. Are we that began it to break it up? Or are we to stand aside and let it all fall to pieces? Or are we to stay with them, and quarrel about holy words till we lose all hunger for holy things?"

"Could you break it up if you tried?" asked Malcolm.

"Very likely not. That's one of the thoughts that hangs heavy on me: see what we've done!"

"Why don't you go over to Mister Graham, and ask what he thinks?"

"Why should I go to him? What's *he* but a fine moral man? I never heard that he could discern the mind of the spirit."

"That's what Dilse's Bess from Clamrock would say about you, Peter."

"And she wouldn't be far wrong, maybe."

"Anyway, she knows no more about you than you know about the master. Call you a man who cares for nothing in heaven or in earth but his Creator's will—call you such a man unspiritual? Just you go to him, and maybe he'll give you a glint of light to astonish you."

"He's taken precious little interest in anything that's been going on."

"Arena ye some wissin' ye hadna taen muckle mair yersel, Peter?"

"'Deed am I! But gien he be giftit like that ye say, what for didna he try to haud 's richt?"

"Maybe he thoucht ye wad mak yer mistaks better wantin' him."

"Weel, ye dinna ca' that freenly!"

"What for no? I hae h'ard him say fowk canna come richt 'cep' by haein' room to gang wrang. But jist ye gang till him noo. Maybe he'll open mair een i' yer heids nor ye kent ye had."

"Weel, maybe we micht du waur. I s' mention the thing to Bow o' meal an' Jeames Gentle, an' see what *they* say— There's nae guid to be gotten o' gaein' to the minister, ye see: there's naething in him, as the saw says, but what the spune pits intill him."

"Aren't you wishing you'd taken rather less yourself, Peter?"

"Indeed I am! But if he's as gifted as you say, why didn't he try to keep us right?"

"Maybe he thought you would make your mistakes better without him."

"Well, you don't call that friendly!"

"Why not? I've heard him say folk can't come right except by having room to go wrong. But just you go to him now. Maybe he'll open more eyes in your heads than you knew you had."

"Well, maybe we might do worse. I'll mention the thing to Bow o' meal and Jeames Gentle, and see what *they* say— There's no good to be had from going to the minister, you see: there's nothing in him, as the saw says, but what the spoon puts into him."

With this somewhat unfavourable remark, Blue Peter turned homewards. Malcolm went slowly back to his room, his tallow candle, and his volume of Gibbon.

He read far into the night, and his candle was burning low in the socket. Suddenly he sat straight up in his chair, listening: he thought he heard a sound in the next room— it was impossible even to imagine of what—it was such a mere abstraction of sound. He listened with every nerve, but heard nothing more; crept to the door of the wizard's chamber, and listened again; listened until he could no longer tell whether he heard or not, and felt like a deaf man imagining sounds; then crept back to his own room and went to bed—all but satisfied that, if it was anything, it must have been some shaking window or door he had heard.

But he could not get rid of the notion that he had smelt sulphur.

CHAPTER LIII

THE SCHOOLMASTER'S COTTAGE

The following night, three of the Scaurnose fishermen—Blue Peter, Bow o' meal, and Jeames Gentle—called at the schoolmaster's cottage in the Alton, and were soon deep in earnest conversation with him around his peat-fire, in the room which served him for study, dining-room, and bed-chamber. All the summer a honeysuckle outside watched his back window for him; now it was guarded within by a few flowerless plants. It was a deep little window in a thick wall, with an air of mystery, as if thence the privileged might look into some region of strange and precious things. The front window was comparatively commonplace, with a white muslin curtain across the lower half. In the middle of the sanded floor stood a table of white deal, much stained with ink. The green painted doors of the *box-bed* opposite the hearth stood open, revealing a spotless white counterpane. On the wall beside the front window hung by red cords three shelves of books; and near the back window stood a dark, old-fashioned bureau, with pendant brass handles as bright as new, supporting a bookcase with glass doors, crowded with well-worn bindings. A few deal chairs completed the furniture.

"It's a sair vex, sir, to think o' what we a' jeedged to be the wark o' the speerit takin' sic a turn! I'm feart it 'll lie heavy at oor door," said Blue Peter, after a sketch of the state of affairs.

"I don't think they can have sunk so low as the early Corinthian Church yet," said Mr Graham, "and St. Paul never seems to have blamed himself for preaching the gospel to the Corinthians."

"Weel, maybe!" rejoined Mair. "But, meantime, the practical p'int is—are we to tyauve to set things richt again, or are we to lea' them to their ain devices?"

"What power have you to set things right?"

"It's a hard thing, sir, to think of what we all judged to be the work of the spirit taking such a turn! I'm afraid it'll lie heavy at our door," said Blue Peter, after a sketch of the state of affairs.

"I don't think they can have sunk so low as the early Corinthian Church yet," said Mr Graham, "and St. Paul never seems to have blamed himself for preaching the gospel to the Corinthians."

"Well, maybe!" rejoined Mair. "But, meantime, the practical point is—are we to struggle to set things right again, or are we to leave them to their own devices?"

"What power have you to set things right?"

"Nane, sir. The Baillies' Barn 's as free to them as to oorsel's."

"What influence have you, then?"

"Unco little," said Bow o' meal, taking the word. "They're afore the win'. An' it 's plain eneuch 'at to stan' up an' oppose them wad be but to breed strife an' debate."

"An' that micht put mony a waukent conscience soon' asleep again—maybe no to be waukent ony mair," said Blue Peter.

"Then you don't think you can either communicate or receive benefit by continuing to take a part in those meetings?"

"I dinna think it," answered all three.

"Then the natural question is—'Why should you go?'"

"We're feart for the guilt o' what the minister ca's shism," said Blue Peter.

"That might have occurred to you before you forsook the parish church," said the schoolmaster, with a smile.

"But there was nae speeritooal noorishment to be gotten i' that houff," said Jeames Gentle.

"How did you come to know the want of it?"

"Ow, that cam frae the speerit himsel'-what else?" replied Gentle.

"By what means?"

"By the readin' o' the word an' by prayer," answered Gentle.

"By his ain v'ice i' the hert," said Bow o' meal.

"Then a public assembly is not necessary for the communication of the gifts of the spirit?"

They were silent.

"Isn't it possible that the eagerness after such assemblies may have something

"None, sir. The Baillie's Barn's as free to them as to ourselves."

"What influence have you, then?"

"Very little," said Bow o' meal, taking the word. "They're before the wind. And it's plain enough that to stand up and oppose them would be but to breed strife and debate."

"And that might put many a wakened conscience sound asleep again—maybe not to be wakened any more," said Blue Peter.

"Then you don't think you can either communicate or receive benefit by continuing to take a part in those meetings?"

"I don't," answered all three.

"Then the natural question is—'Why should you go?'"

"We're afraid for the guilt of what the minister calls schism," said Blue Peter.

"That might have occurred to you before you forsook the parish church," said the schoolmaster, with a smile.

"But there was no spiritual nourishment to be had in that haunt," said Jeames Gentle.

"How did you come to know the want of it?"

"Oh, that came from the spirit himself—what else?" replied Gentle.

"By what means?"

"By the reading of the word and by prayer," answered Gentle.

"By his own voice in the heart," said Bow o' meal.

"Then a public assembly is not necessary for the communication of the gifts of the spirit?"

They were silent.

"Isn't it possible that the eagerness after such assemblies may have something to do to do with a want of confidence in what the Lord says of his kingdom—that it spreads like the hidden leaven—grows like the buried seed? My own conviction is, that if a man would but bend his energies to *live*, if he would but try to be a true, that is, a godlike man, in all his dealings with his fellows, a genuine neighbour and not a selfish unit, he would open such channels for the flow of the spirit as no amount of even honest and so-called successful preaching could."

"Wha but ane was ever fit to lead sic a life 's that?"

"All might be trying after it. In proportion as our candle burns it will give light. No talking about light will supply the lack of its presence either to the talker or the listeners."

"There's a heap made o' the preachin' o' the word i' the buik itsel'," said Peter with emphasis.

"Undoubtedly. But just look at our Lord: he never stopped living amongst his people—hasn't stopped yet; but he often refused to preach, and personally has given it up altogether now."

"Ay, but ye see he kent what he was duin'."

"And so will every man in proportion as he partakes of his spirit."

"But dinna ye believe there *is* sic a thing as gettin' a call to the preachin'?"

"I do; but even then a man's work is of worth only as it supplements his life. A network of spiritual fibres connects the two, makes one of them."

"But surely, sir, them 'at 's o' the same min' oucht to meet an' stir ane anither up? 'They that feart the Lord spak aften thegither,' ye ken."

with a want of confidence in what the Lord says of his kingdom—that it spreads like the hidden leaven—grows like the buried seed? My own conviction is, that if a man would but bend his energies to *live*, if he would but try to be a true, that is, a godlike man, in all his dealings with his fellows, a genuine neighbour and not a selfish unit, he would open such channels for the flow of the spirit as no amount of even honest and so-called successful preaching could."

"Who but one was ever fit to lead such a life as that?"

"All might be trying after it. In proportion as our candle burns it will give light. No talking about light will supply the lack of its presence either to the talker or the listeners."

"There's a lot made of the preaching of the word in the book itself," said Peter with emphasis.

"Undoubtedly. But just look at our Lord: he never stopped living amongst his people—hasn't stopped yet; but he often refused to preach, and personally has given it up altogether now."

"Ay, but you see he knew what he was doing."

"And so will every man in proportion as he partakes of his spirit."

"But don't you believe there *is* such a thing as getting a call to preach?"

"I do; but even then a man's work is of worth only as it supplements his life. A network of spiritual fibres connects the two, makes one of them."

"But surely, sir, those that are of the same mind ought to meet and stir one another up? 'They that feared the Lord spake often together,' you know."

"What should prevent them? Why should not such as delight in each other's society, meet, and talk, and pray together,—address each the others if they like? There is plenty of opportunity for that, without forsaking the church or calling public meetings. To continue your quotation—'The Lord hearkened and heard:' observe, the Lord is not here said to hearken to sermons or prayers, but to the *talk* of his people. This would have saved you from false relations with men that oppose themselves, caring nothing for the truth—perhaps eager to save their souls, nothing more at the very best."

"Sir! sir! what wad ye hae? Daur ye say it 's no a body's first duty to save his ain sowl alive?" exclaimed Bow o' meal.

"I daur't—but there's little daur intill 't!" said Mr Graham, breaking into Scotch.

Bow o' meal rose from his chair in indignation, Blue Peter made a grasp at his bonnet, and Jeames Gentle gave a loud sigh of commiseration.

"I allow it to be a very essential piece of prudence," added the schoolmaster, resuming his quieter English—"but the first duty!—no. The Catechism might have taught you better than that! To mind his chief end must surely be man's first duty; and the Catechism says—'Man's chief end is to glorify God.'"

"And to enjoy him for ever," supplemented Peter.

"That's a safe consequence. There's no fear of the second if he does the first. Anyhow he cannot enjoy him for ever this moment, and he can glorify him at once."

"Ay, but hoo?" said Bow o' meal, ready to swoop upon the master's reply.

"Just as Jesus Christ did—by doing his will—by obedience."

"What should prevent them? Why should not such as delight in each other's society, meet, and talk, and pray together,—address each the others if they like? There is plenty of opportunity for that, without forsaking the church or calling public meetings. To continue your quotation—'The Lord hearkened and heard:' observe, the Lord is not here said to hearken to sermons or prayers, but to the *talk* of his people. This would have saved you from false relations with men that oppose themselves, caring nothing for the truth—perhaps eager to save their souls, nothing more at the very best."

"Sir! sir! what would you have? Dare you say it's not a man's first duty to save his own soul alive?" exclaimed Bow o' meal.

"I daur't—but there's little daur intill 't!" said Mr Graham, breaking into Scotch.

Bow o' meal rose from his chair in indignation, Blue Peter made a grasp at his bonnet, and Jeames Gentle gave a loud sigh of commiseration.

"I allow it to be a very essential piece of prudence," added the schoolmaster, resuming his quieter English—"but the first duty!—no. The Catechism might have taught you better than that! To mind his chief end must surely be man's first duty; and the Catechism says—'Man's chief end is to glorify God.'"

"And to enjoy him for ever," supplemented Peter.

"That's a safe consequence. There's no fear of the second if he does the first. Anyhow he cannot enjoy him for ever this moment, and he can glorify him at once."

"Ay, but how?" said Bow o' meal, ready to swoop upon the master's reply.

"Just as Jesus Christ did—by doing his will—by obedience."

"That's no faith—it's works! Ye'll never save yer sowl that gait."

"No man can ever save his soul. God only can do that. You can glorify him by giving yourself up heart and soul and body and life to his Son. Then you shall *be* saved. That you must leave to *him*, and *do what he tells you.* There will be no fear of the saving then—though it's not an easy matter—even for *him*, as has been sorely proved."

"An' hoo are we to gie oorsel's up till him?—for ye see we're practical kin' o' fowk, huz fisher fowk, Maister Graham," said Bow o' meal.

The tone implied that the schoolmaster was not practical.

"I say again—In doing *his* will and not your own."

"An' what may his wull be?"

"Is he not telling you himself at this moment? Do you not know what his will is? How should *I* come between him and you! For anything I know, it may be that you pay your next door neighbour a crown you owe him, or make an apology to the one on the other side. *I* do not know: you do."

"Dinna ye think aboot savin' yer ain sowl noo, Maister Graham?" said Bow o' meal, returning on their track.

"No, I don't. I've forgotten all about that. I only desire and pray to do the will of my God—which is all in all to me."

"What say ye than aboot the sowls o' ither fowk? Wadna ye save them, no?"

"Gladly would I save them—but according to the will of God. If I were, even unwittingly, to attempt it in any other way, I should be casting stumbling blocks in their path, and separating myself from my God—doing that which is not of faith, and therefore is sin. It is only where a man is at one with God that he can do the right thing or take the right way. Whatever springs from any other source than the spirit that dwelt in Jesus, is of sin, and works to thwart the divine will. Who knows what harm may be done to a man by hurrying a spiritual process in him?"

"I doobt, sir, gien yer doctrine was to get a hearin', there wad be unco little dune for the glory o' God i' this place!"!" remarked Bow o' meal, with sententious reproof.

"But what was done would be of the right sort, and surpassingly powerful."

"Weel, to come back to the business in han'—what wad be yer advice?" said Bow o' meal.

"That's a thing none but a lawyer should give. I have shown you what seem to me the principles involved: I can do no more."

"Ye dinna ca' that neebourly, whan a body comes speirin' 't?"

"Are you prepared then to take my advice?"

"Ye wadna hae a body du that aforehan'! We micht as weel a' be Papists, an' believe as we're tauld."

"Precisely so. But you can exercise your judgment upon the principles whereon my opinion is founded, with far more benefit than upon my opinion itself—which I cannot well wish you to adopt, seeing I think it far better for a man to go wrong upon his own honest judgment, than to go right upon anybody else's judgment, however honest also."

"Ye hae a heap o' queer doctrines, sir."

"And yet you ask advice of me?"

"We haena ta'en muckle, ony gait," returned Bow o' meal rudely, and walked from the cottage.

Jeames Gentle and Blue Peter bade the master a kindly good night, and followed Bow o' meal.

The next Sunday evening Blue Peter was again at the Alton, accompanied by Gentle and another fisherman, not Bow o' meal, and had another and longer conversation with the schoolmaster. The following Sunday he went yet again; and from that time, every Sunday evening, as soon as he had had his tea, Blue Peter took down his broad bonnet, and set out to visit Mr Graham. As he went, one and another would join him as he passed, the number increasing every time, until at last ten or twelve went regularly.

But Mr Graham did not like such a forsaking of wives and children on the Sunday.

"Why shouldn't you bring Mrs Mair with you?" he said one evening, addressing Joseph first. Then turning to the rest—"I should be happy to see any of your wives who can come," he added; "and some of you have children who would be no trouble. If there is any good in gathering this way, why shouldn't we have those with us who are our best help at all other times?"

"'Deed, sir," said Joseph, "we're sae used to oor wives 'at we're ower ready to forget hoo ill we cud du wantin' them."

"Indeed, sir," said Joseph, "we're so used to our wives that we're too ready to forget how ill we could manage without them."

Mrs Mair and two other wives came the next night. A few hung back from modesty and dread of being catechized; but ere long about half a dozen went when they could.

I need hardly say that Malcolm, as soon as he learned what was going on, made one of the company. And truly, although he did not know even yet all the evil that threatened him, he stood in heavy need of the support and comfort to be derived from such truths as Mr Graham unfolded. Duncan also, although he took little interest in what passed, went sometimes, and was welcomed.

The talk of the master not unfrequently lapsed into monologue, and sometimes grew eloquent. Seized occasionally by the might of the thoughts which arose in him,—thoughts which would, to him, have lost all their splendour as well as worth, had he imagined them the offspring of his own faculty, meteors of his own atmosphere instead of phenomena of the heavenly region manifesting themselves on the hollow side of the celestial sphere of human vision,—he would break forth in grand poetic speech that roused to aspiration Malcolm's whole being, while in the same instant calming him with the summer peace of profoundest faith.

To no small proportion of his hearers some of such outbursts were altogether unintelligible—a matter of no moment; but there were of them who understood enough to misunderstand utterly: interpreting his riches by their poverty, they misinterpreted them pitifully, and misrepresented them worse. And, alas! in the little company there were three or four men who, for all their upward impulses, yet remained capable of treachery, because incapable of recognizing the temptation to it for what it was. These by and by began to confer together and form an opposition—in this at least ungenerous, that they continued to assemble at his house, and show little sign of dissension. When, however, they began at length to discover that the master did not teach that interpretation of atonement which they had derived—they little knew whence, but delivered another as the doctrine of St. Paul, St. Peter, and St. John, they judged themselves bound to take measures towards the quenching of a dangerous heresy. For the more ignorant a man is, the more capable is he of being absolutely certain of many things—with such certainty, that is, as consists in the absence of doubt. Mr Graham, in the meantime, full of love, and quiet solemn fervour, placed completest confidence in their honesty, and spoke his mind freely and faithfully.

CHAPTER LIV

ONE DAY

The winter was close at hand—indeed, in that northern region, might already have claimed entire possession; but the trailing golden fringe of the skirts of autumn was yet visible behind him, as he wandered away down the slope of the world. In the gentle sadness of the season, Malcolm could not help looking back with envy to the time when labour, adventure, and danger, stormy winds and troubled waters, would have helped him to bear the weight of the moral atmosphere which now from morning to night oppressed him. Since their last conversation, Lady Florimel's behaviour to him was altered. She hardly ever sent for him now, and when she did, gave her orders so distantly that at length, but for his grandfather's sake, he could hardly have brought himself to remain in the house even until the return of his master who was from home, and contemplated proposing to him as soon as he came back, that he should leave his service and resume his former occupation, at least until the return of summer should render it fit to launch the cutter again.

One day, a little after noon, Malcolm stepped from the house. The morning had broken gray and squally, with frequent sharp showers, and had grown into a gurly gusty day. Now and then the sun sent a dim yellow glint through the troubled atmosphere, but it was straightway swallowed up in the volumes of vapour seething and tumbling in the upper regions. As he crossed the threshold, there came a moaning wind from the west, and the water-laden branches of the trees all went bending before it, shaking their burden of heavy drops on the ground. It was dreary, dreary, outside and in. He turned and looked at the house. If he might have but one peep of the goddess far withdrawn! What did he want of her? Nothing but her favour—something acknowledged between them—some understanding of accepted worship! Alas it was all weakness, and the end thereof dismay! It was but the longing of the opium-eater or the drinker for the poison which in delight lays the foundations of torture. No; he knew where to find food—something that was neither opium nor strong drink—something that in torture sustained, and, when its fruition came, would, even in the splendours of delight, far surpass their short-lived boon! He turned towards the schoolmaster's cottage.

Under the trees, which sighed aloud in the wind, and, like earth-clouds, rained upon him as he passed, across the churchyard, bare to the gray, hopeless-looking sky, through the iron gate he went, and opened the master's outer door. Ere he reached that of his room, he heard his voice inviting him to enter.

"Come to condole with me, Malcolm?" said Mr Graham cheerily.

"What for, sir?" asked Malcolm.

"You haven't heard, then, that I'm going to be sent about my business? At least, it's more than likely."

Malcolm dropped into a seat, and stared like an idol. Could he have heard the words? In his eyes Mr Graham was the man of the place—the real person of the parish. He dismissed! The words breathed of mingled impiety and absurdity.

The schoolmaster burst out laughing at him.

"I'm feart to speyk, sir," said Malcolm. "Whatever I say, I'm bun' to mak a fule o' mysel'! What in plain words div ye mean, sir?"

"Somebody has been accusing me of teaching heresy—in the school to my scholars, and in my own house to the fisherfolk: the presbytery has taken it up, and here is my summons to appear before them and answer to the charge."

"Guid preserve 's, sir! And is this the first ye hae h'ard o't?"

"The very first."

"An' what are ye gauin' to do?"

"Appear, of course."

"An' what 'll ye say to them?"

"I shall answer their questions."

"They'll condemn ye!"

"I do not doubt it."

"An' what neist?"

"I shall have to leave Scotland, I suppose."

"Sir, it's awfu'."

The horror stricken expression of Malcolm's face drew a second merry laugh from Mr Graham.

"They can't burn me," he said: "you needn't look like that."

"But there's something terrible wrang, sir, whan sic men hae pooer ower sic a man."

"I'm afraid to speak, sir," said Malcolm. "Whatever I say, I'm bound to make a fool of myself! What in plain words do you mean, sir?"

"Somebody has been accusing me of teaching heresy—in the school to my scholars, and in my own house to the fisherfolk: the presbytery has taken it up, and here is my summons to appear before them and answer to the charge."

"Lord preserve us, sir! And is this the first you've heard of it?"

"The very first."

"And what are you going to do?"

"Appear, of course."

"And what will you say to them?"

"I shall answer their questions."

"They'll condemn you!"

"I do not doubt it."

"And what next?"

"I shall have to leave Scotland, I suppose."

"Sir, it's awful."

The horror stricken expression of Malcolm's face drew a second merry laugh from Mr Graham.

"They can't burn me," he said: "you needn't look like that."

"But there's something very wrong, sir, when such men have power over such a man."

"They have no power but what's given them. I shall accept their decision as the decree of heaven."

"It's weel to be you, sir—'at can tak a thing sae quaiet."

"You mustn't suppose I am naturally so philosophical. It stands for five and forty years of the teaching of the Son of Man in this wonderful school of his, where the clever would be destroyed but for the stupid, where the church would tear itself to pieces but for the laws of the world, and where the wicked themselves are the greatest furtherance of godliness in the good."

"But wha ever cud hae been baze eneuch to du 't!" said Malcolm, too much astounded for his usual eager attention to the words that fell from the master.

"That I would rather not inquire," answered Mr Graham. "In the meantime it would be better if the friends would meet somewhere else, for this house is mine only in virtue of my office. Will you tell them so for me?"

"Surely, sir. But will ye no mak ane?"

"Not till this is settled. I will after, so long as I may be here."

"Gien onybody had been catecheesin' the bairns, I wad surely hae h'ard o' 't!" said Malcolm, after a pause of rumination, "Poochy wad hae tellt me. I saw him thestreen.—Wha 'll ever say again a thing's no poassible!"

"Whatever doctrine I may have omitted to press in the school," said Mr Graham, "I have inculcated nothing at variance with the Confession of Faith or the Shorter Catechism."

"They have no power but what's given them. I shall accept their decision as the decree of heaven."

"It's well to be you, sir—that can take things so quietly."

"You mustn't suppose I am naturally so philosophical. It stands for five and forty years of the teaching of the Son of Man in this wonderful school of his, where the clever would be destroyed but for the stupid, where the church would tear itself to pieces but for the laws of the world, and where the wicked themselves are the greatest furtherance of godliness in the good."

"But who ever could have been base enough to do it!" said Malcolm, too much astounded for his usual eager attention to the words that fell from the master.

"That I would rather not inquire," answered Mr Graham. "In the meantime it would be better if the friends would meet somewhere else, for this house is mine only in virtue of my office. Will you tell them so for me?"

"Surely, sir. But won't you come yourself?"

"Not till this is settled. I will after, so long as I may be here."

"If anyone had been questioning the children, I would surely have heard of it!" said Malcolm, after a pause of rumination, "Poochy would have told me. I saw him last night.—Who'll ever say again that a thing's not possible!"

"Whatever doctrine I may have omitted to press in the school," said Mr Graham, "I have inculcated nothing at variance with the Confession of Faith or the Shorter Catechism."

"Hoo can ye say that, sir?" returned Malcolm, "whan, in as weel's oot o' the schuil, ye hae aye insistit 'at God 's a just God—abune a' thing likin' to gie fair play?"

"Well, does the Catechism say anything to the contrary?"

"No in sae mony words, doobtless; but it says a sicht o' things 'at wad mak God oot the maist oonrichteous tyrant 'at ever was."

"I'm not sure you can show that logically," said Mr Graham. "I will think it over, however—not that I mean to take up any defence of myself. But now I have letters to write, and must ask you to leave me. Come and see me again tomorrow."

Malcolm went from him—

"How can you say that, sir?" returned Malcolm, "when, in as well as out of school, you've always insisted that God is just—above all things liking to give fair play?"

"Well, does the Catechism say anything to the contrary?"

"Not in so many words, doubtless; but it says plenty of things that would make God out the most unrighteous tyrant that ever was."

"I'm not sure you can show that logically," said Mr Graham. "I will think it over, however—not that I mean to take up any defence of myself. But now I have letters to write, and must ask you to leave me. Come and see me again tomorrow."

Malcolm went from him—

like one that hath been stunned,
And is of sense forlorn.

Here was trouble upon trouble! But what had befallen him compared with what had come upon the schoolmaster! A man like him to be so treated! How gladly he would work for him all the rest of his days! And how welcome his grandfather would make him to his cottage! Lord Lossie would be the last to object. But he knew it was a baseless castle while he built it, for Mr Graham would assuredly provide for himself, if it were by breaking stones on the road and saying the Lord's Prayer. It all fell to pieces just as he lifted his hand to Miss Horn's knocker.

She received him with a cordiality such as even she had never shown him before. He told her what threatened Mr Graham. She heard him to the end without remark, beyond the interjection of an occasional "Eh, sirs!" then sat for a minute in troubled silence.

"There's a heap o' things an 'uman like me," she said at length, "canna un'erstan'. I divna ken whether some fowk mair nor preten' to un'erstan' them. But set Sandy Graham doon upo' ae side, an' the presbytery doon upo' the ither, an' I hae wit eneuch to ken whilk I wad tak my eternal chance wi'. Some o' the presbytery's guid eneuch men, but haena ower muckle gumption; an' some o' them has plenty o' gumption, but

"There's a heap of things that a woman like me," she said at length, "can't understand. I don't know whether some folk more than pretend to understand them. But set Sandy Graham down upon one side, and the presbytery down upon the other, and I've wit enough to know which I'd take my eternal chance with. Some of the presbytery are good enough men, but have little gumption; and some of them haena ower muckle grace, ta jeedge by the w'y 'at they glower an' rair, layin' doon the law as gien the Almichty had been driven to tak coonsel wi' them. But luik at Sandy Graham! *Ye* ken whether he has gumption or no; an' gien he be a stickit minister, he stack by the grace o' moadesty. But, haith, I winna peety him! for, o' a' things, to peety a guid man i' the richt gate is a fule's folly. Troth, I'm a hantle mair concernt about yersel', Ma'colm!"

Malcolm heard her without apprehension. His cup seemed full, and he never thought that cups sometimes run over. But perhaps he was so far the nearer to a truth: while the cup of blessing may and often does run over, I doubt if the cup of suffering is ever more than filled to the brim.

"Onything fresh, mem?" he asked, with the image of Mrs Stewart standing ghastly on the slopes of his imagination.

"I wadna be fit to tell ye, laddie, gien 't warna, as ye ken, 'at the Almichty 's been unco mercifu' to me i' the maitter o' feelin's. Yer freen's i' the Seaton, an' ower at Scaurnose, *hae* feelin's, an' that's hoo nane o' them a' has pluckit up hert to tell ye o' the waggin' o' slanderous tongues against ye."

"What are they sayin' noo?" asked Malcolm with considerable indifference.

"Naither mair nor less than that ye're the father o' an oonborn wean," answered Miss Horn.

"I dinna freely unnerstan' ye," returned Malcolm, for the unexpectedness of the disclosure was scarcely to be mastered at once.

have plenty of gumption, but have little grace, to judge by the way that they glower and roar, laying down the law as if the Almighty had been driven to take counsel with them. But look at Sandy Graham! *You* know whether he has gumption or not; and if he be a stickit minister, he stuck by the grace of modesty. But, faith, far be it from me to pity him! for, of all things, to pity a good man when he's doing right is a fool's folly. Indeed, I'm much more concerned about you, Malcolm!"

Malcolm heard her without apprehension. His cup seemed full, and he never thought that cups sometimes run over. But perhaps he was so far the nearer to a truth: while the cup of blessing may and often does run over, I doubt if the cup of suffering is ever more than filled to the brim.

"Anything fresh, ma'am?" he asked, with the image of Mrs Stewart standing ghastly on the slopes of his imagination.

"I wouldn't be fit to tell you, laddie, if it weren't, as you know, that the Almighty has been very merciful to me in the matter of feelings. Your friends in the Seaton, and over at Scaurnose, *have* feelings, and that's why none of them have plucked up the courage to tell you of the wagging of slanderous tongues against you."

"What are they saying now?" asked Malcolm with considerable indifference.

"Neither more nor less than that you're the father of an unborn child," answered Miss Horn.

"I don't quite understand you," returned Malcolm, for the unexpectedness of the disclosure was scarcely to be mastered at once.

I shall not put on record the plain form of honest speech whereby she made him at once comprehend the nature of the calumny. He started to his feet, and shouted "Wha daur say that?" so loud that the listening Jean almost fell down the stair.

"Wha *sud* say 't but the lassie hersel'?" answered Miss Horn simply. "*She* maun hae the best richt to say wha's wha."

"It wad better become *ony*body but her," said Malcolm.

"What mean ye there, laddie?" cried Miss Horn, alarmed.

"'At nane cud ken sae weel 's hersel' it was a damned lee. Wha is she?"

"Wha but Meg Partan's Lizzy!"

"Puir lassie! is that it?—Eh, but I'm sorry for her! *She* never said it was me. An' whaever said it, surely ye dinna believe 't o' me, mem?"

"*Me* believe 't! Malcolm MacPhail, wull ye daur insult a maiden wuman 'at's stude clear o' reproch till she's lang past the danger o' 't? It's been wi' unco sma' diffeeclety, I maun alloo, for I haena been led into ony temptation!"

"Eh, mem!" returned Malcolm, perceiving by the flash of her eyes and the sudden halt of her speech that she was really indignant—"I dinna ken what I hae said to anger ye!"

"Anger me! quo' he? What though I hae nae feelin's! Will he daur till imaigine 'at he wad be sittin' there, an' me haudin' him company, gien I believed him cawpable o' turnin' oot sic a meeserable, contemptible wratch! The Lord come atween me an' my wrath!"

"I beg yer pardon, mem. A body canna aye put things thegither afore he speyks. richt sair obleeged till ye for takin' my pairt."

I shall not put on record the plain form of honest speech whereby she made him at once comprehend the nature of the calumny. He started to his feet, and shouted "Who dares say that?" so loud that the listening Jean almost fell down the stair.

"Who *should* say it but the lassie herself?" answered Miss Horn simply. "*She* must have the best right to say who's who."

"It would better become *any*body but her," said Malcolm.

"What mean you by that, laddie?" cried Miss Horn, alarmed.

"That none could know as well as her it was a damned lie. Who is she?"

"Who but Meg Partan's Lizzie!"

"Poor lassie! is that it?—Eh, but I'm sorry for her! *She* never said it was me. And whoever said it, surely you don't believe it of me, ma'am?"

"*Me* believe it! Malcolm MacPhail, will you dare insult a maiden woman who's stood clear of reproach till she's long past the danger of it? It's been the less difficult, I must allow, that I haven't been led into any temptation!"

"Eh, ma'am!" returned Malcolm, perceiving by the flash of her eyes and the sudden halt of her speech that she was really indignant—"I don't know what I've said to anger you!"

"Anger me! says he? What though I have no feelings! Will he dare to imagine that he would be sitting there, and me keeping him company, if I believed him capable of turning out such a miserable, contemptible wretch! The Lord come between me and my wrath!"

"I beg your pardon, ma'am. A body can't always make sense of things before he speaks. I'm much obliged to you for taking my part."

"I tak naebody's pairt but my ain, laddie. Obleeged to me for haein' a wheen common sense—a thing 'at I was born wi'! Toots! Dinna haiver."

"Weel, mem, what wad ye hae me du? I canna sen' my auld daddie roon the toon wi' his pipes, to procleem 'at I'm no the man. I'm thinkin' I'll hae to lea' the place."

"Wad ye sen' yer daddy roun' wi' the pipes to say 'at ye *was* the man? Ye micht as weel du the tane as the tither. Mony a better man has been waur misca'd, an' gart fowk forget that ever the lee was lee'd. Na, na; never rin frae a lee. An' never say, naither, 'at ye didna du the thing, 'cept it be laid straucht to yer face. Lat a lee lie i' the dirt. Gien ye pike it up, the dirt 'll stick till ye, though ye fling the lee ower the dyke at the warl's en'. Na, na! Lat a lee lie, as ye wad the deevil's tail 'at the laird's Jock took aff wi' the edge o' 's spaud."

"A' thing 's agane me the noo!" sighed Malcolm.

"Auld Jobb ower again!" returned Miss Horn almost sarcastically. "The deil had the warst o' 't though, an' wull hae, i' the lang hinner en'. Meanwhile ye maun face him. There's nae airmour for the back aither i' the Bible or i' the Pilgrim's Progress."

"What wad ye hae me du, than, mem?"

"Du? Wha said ye was to du onything? The best duin whiles is to bide still. Lat ye the jaw gae ower ohn joukit."

"Gien I binna to du onything, I maist wiss I hadna kent," said Malcolm, whose honourable nature writhed under the imputed vileness.

"I take nobody's part but my own, laddie. Obliged to me for having a smattering of common sense—a thing I was born with! Goodness! Don't talk nonsense."

"Well, ma'am, what would you have me do? I can't send my old daddy round the town with his pipes, to proclaim my innocence. I'm thinking I'll have to leave the place."

"Would you send your daddy round with the pipes to say that you *were* the man? You might as well do the one as the other. Many a better man has been slandered worse, and made folk forget that ever the lie was spoken. Na, na; never run from a lie. And never say, either, that you didn't do the thing, except you're accused to your face. Let a lie lie in the dirt. Pick it up, and the dirt will stick to you, though you fling it over the wall at the world's end. Na, na! Let it lie, as you would the devil's tail that the laird's Jock took off with the edge of his spade."

"Everything's against me just now!" sighed Malcolm.

"Old Job over again!" returned Miss Horn almost sarcastically. "The devil had the worst of it though, and will have, at the long last. Meanwhile you must face him. There's no armour for the back either in the Bible or in the Pilgrim's Progress."

"What would you have me do, then, ma'am?"

"Do? Who said you were to do anything? The best doing sometimes is to stand still. Let the wave pass over without ducking."

"If I'm not to do anything, I almost wish I hadn't known," said Malcolm, whose honourable nature writhed under the imputed vileness.

"It's aye better to ken in what licht ye stan' wi' ither fowk. It hauds ye ohn lippent ower muckle, an' sae dune things or made remarks 'at wad be misread till ye. Ye maun haud an open ro'd, 'at the trowth whan it comes oot may have free course. The ae thing 'at spites me is, 'at the verra fowk 'at was the first to spread yer ill report, 'ill be the first to wuss ye weel whan the trowth's kent—ay, an they'll persuaud their verra sel's 'at they stuck up for ye like born brithers."

"There *maun* be some jeedgement upo' leein'!"

"The warst wuss I hae agane ony sic back-biter is that he may live to be affrontit at himsel'. Efter that he'll be guid eneuch company for me. Gang yer wa's, laddie; say yer prayers, an' haud up yer heid. Wha wadna raither be accused o' a' the sins o' the comman'ments nor be guilty o' ane o' them?"

Malcolm did hold up his head as he walked away.

"It's always better to know how you stand with other folk. It keeps you from trusting too far, and so from doing or saying things they'd read amiss. You must walk an open road, that the truth when it comes out may have free course. The one thing that vexes me is, that the very folk that first spread your ill report, will be the first to wish you well when the truth's known—ay, and they'll persuade their very selves that they stuck up for you like born brothers."

"There *must* be some judgement upon lying!"

"The worst wish I have against any such back-biter is that he may live to be ashamed of himself. After that he'll be good enough company for me. Be off now, laddie; say your prayers, and hold up your head. Who wouldn't rather be accused of all the sins of the commandments than be guilty of one of them?"

Malcolm did hold up his head as he walked away.

Not a single person was in the street. Far below, the sea was chafing and tossing—grey green broken into white. The horizon was formless with mist, hanging like thin wool from the heavens down to the face of the waters, against which the wind, which had shifted round considerably towards the north, and blew in quicker-coming and more menacing gusts, appeared powerless. He would have gone to the sands and paced the shore till nightfall, but that he would not expose himself thus to unfriendly eyes and false judgments. He turned to the right instead, and walked along the top of the cliffs eastward. Buffeted by winds without and hurrying fancies within, he wandered on until he came near Colonsay Castle, at sight of which the desire awoke in him to look again on the scene of Lady Florimel's terror. He crossed the head of the little bay and descended into the heart of the rock. Even there the wind blew dank and howling through all the cavernous hollows. As he approached the last chamber, out of the Devil's Window flew, with clanging wing, an arrow-barbed sea-gull, down to the grey-veiled tumult below, and the joy of life for a moment seized his soul. But the next, the dismay of that which is forsaken was upon him. It was not that the once lordly structure lay abandoned to the birds and the gusts, but that *she* would never think of the place without an instant assay at forgetfulness. He turned and re-ascended, feeling like a ghost that had been wandering through the forlorn chambers of an empty skull.

When he rose on the bare top of the ruin, a heavy shower from the sea was beating slant against the worn walls and gaping clefts. Myriads of such rains had, with age-long inevitableness, crumbled away the strong fortress till its threatful mass had sunk to an abject heap. Thus all-devouring Death—nay, nay! it is all-sheltering, all-restoring mother Nature, receiving again into her mighty matrix the stuff worn out in the fashioning toil of her wasteful, greedy, and slatternly children. In her genial bosom, the exhausted gathers life, the effete becomes generant, the disintegrate returns to resting and capable form. The rolling oscillating globe dips it for an aeon in growing sea, lifts it from the sinking waters of its thousand-year bath to the furnace of the sun, remodels and remoulds, turns ashes into flowers, and divides mephitis into diamonds and breath. The races of men shift and hover like shadows over her surface, while, as a woman dries her garment before the household flame, she turns it, by portions, now to and now from the sun-heart of fire. Oh joy that all the hideous lacerations and vile gatherings of refuse which the worshippers of mammon disfigure the earth withal, scoring the tale of their coming dismay on the visage of their mother, shall one day lie fathoms deep under the blessed ocean, to be cleansed and remade into holy because lovely forms! May the ghosts of the men who mar the earth, turning her sweet rivers into channels of filth, and her living air into irrespirable vapours and pestilences, haunt the desolations they have made, until they loathe the work of their hands, and turn from themselves with a divine repudiation.

It was about half tide, and the sea coming up, with the wind straight from the north, when Malcolm, having descended to the shore of the little bay, and scrambled out upon the rocks, bethought him of a certain cave which he had not visited since he was a child, and climbing over the high rocks between, took shelter there from the wind. He had forgotten how beautiful it was, and stood amazed at the richness of its colour, imagining he had come upon a cave of the serpentine marble which is found on the coast; for sides and roof and rugged floor were gorgeous with bands and spots and veins of green, and rusty red. A nearer inspection, however, showed that these hues were not of the rock itself but belonged to the garden of the ocean, and when he turned to face the sea, lo! they had all but vanished, the cave shone silvery gray, with a faint moony sparkle, and out came the lovely carving of the rodent waves. All about, its sides were fretted in exquisite curves, and fantastic yet ever-graceful knots and twists; as if a mass of gnarled and contorted roots, first washed of every roughness by some ethereal solvent, leaving only the soft lines of yet grotesque volutions, had been transformed into mingled silver and stone. Like a soldier crab that had found a shell to his mind, he gazed through the yawning mouth of the cavern at the turmoil of the rising tide, as it rushed straight towards him through a low jagged channel in the rocks. But straight with the tide came the wind, blowing right into the cave; and finding it keener than pleasant, he turned and went farther in. After a steep ascent some little way, the cavern took a sharp turn to one side, where not a breath of wind, not a glimmer of light, reached, and there he sat down upon a stone, and fell a thinking.

He must face the lie out, and he must accept any mother God had given him: but with such a mother as Mrs Stewart, and without Mr Graham, how was he to endure the altered looks of his old friends? Faces indifferent before, had grown suddenly dear to him; and opinions he would have thought valueless once, had become golden in his eyes. Had he been such as to deserve their reproaches, he would doubtless have steeled himself to despise them; but his innocence bound him to the very people who judged him guilty. And there was that awful certainty slowly but steadily drawing nearer—that period of vacant anguish, in which Lady Florimel must vanish from his sight, and the splendour of his life go with her, to return no more.

But not even yet did he *cherish* any fancy of coming nearer to her than the idea of absolute service authorized. As often as the fancy had, compelled by the lady herself, crossed the horizon of his thoughts, a repellent influence from the same source had been at hand to sweep it afar into its antenatal chaos. But his love rose ever from the earth to which the blow had hurled it, purified again, once more all devotion and no desire, careless of recognition beyond the acceptance of its offered service, and content that the be-all should be the end-all.

The cave seemed the friendliest place he had yet found. Earth herself had received him into her dark bosom, where no eye could discover him, and no voice reach him but that of the ocean, as it tossed and wallowed in the palm of God's hand. He heard its roar on the rocks around him; and the air was filled with a loud noise of broken waters, while every now and then the wind rushed with a howl into the cave, as if searching for him in its crannies; the wild raving soothed him, and he felt as if he would gladly sit there, in the dark torn with tumultuous noises, until his fate had unfolded itself.

The noises thickened around him as the tide rose; but so gradually that, although at length he could not have heard his own voice, he was unaware of the magnitude to which the mighty uproar had enlarged itself. Suddenly, something smote the rock as with the hammer of Thor, and, as suddenly, the air around him grew stifling hot. The next moment it was again cold. He started to his feet in wonder, and sought the light. As he turned the angle, the receding back of a huge green foam-spotted wave, still almost touching the roof of the cavern, was sweeping out again into the tumult. It had filled the throat of it, and so compressed the air within by the force of its entrance, as to drive out for the moment a large portion of its latent heat. Looking then at his watch, Malcolm judged it must be about high tide: brooding in the darkness, he had allowed the moments to lapse unheeded, and it was now impossible to leave the cavern until the tide had fallen. He returned into its penetral, and sitting down with the patience of a fisherman, again lost himself in reverie.

The darkness kept him from perceiving how the day went, and the rapidly increasing roar of the wind made the diminishing sound of the tide's retreat less noticeable. He thought afterwards that perhaps he had fallen asleep; anyhow, when at length he looked out, the waves were gone from the rock, and the darkness was broken only by the distant gleam of their white defeat. The wind was blowing a hurricane, and even for his practised foot, it was not easy to surmount the high, abrupt spines he must cross to regain the shore. It was so dark that he could see nothing of the castle, though it was but a few yards from him; and he resolved therefore, the path along the top of the cliffs being unsafe, to make his way across the fields, and return by the high road. The consequence was, that, what with fences and ditches, the violence of the wind, and uncertainty about his direction, it was so long before he felt the hard road under his feet that with good reason he feared the house would be closed for the night ere he reached it.

THE SAME NIGHT

When he came within sight of it, however, he perceived, by the hurried movement of lights, that instead of being folded in silence, the house was in unwonted commotion. As he hastened to the south door, the prince of the power of the air himself seemed to resist his entrance, so fiercely did the wind, eddying round the building, dispute every step he made towards it; and when at length he reached and opened it, a blast, rushing up the glen straight from the sea, burst wide the opposite one, and roared through the hall like a torrent. Lady Florimel, flitting across it at the moment, was almost blown down, and shrieked aloud for help. Malcolm was already at the north door, exerting all his strength to close it, when she spied him, and, bounding to him, with white face and dilated eyes, exclaimed—

"Oh Malcolm! what a time you have been!"

"What's wrang, my leddy?" cried Malcolm with respondent terror.

"Don't you hear it?" she answered. "The wind is blowing the house down. There's just been a terrible fall, and every moment I hear it going. If my father were only come! We shall be all blown into the burn."

"Nae fear o' that, my leddy!" returned Malcolm. "The wa's o' the auld carcass are 'maist live rock, an' 'ill stan' the warst win' 'at ever blew—this side o' the tropics, ony gait. Gien 't war ance to get its nose in, I wadna say but it micht tirr the rufe, but it winna blaw 's intil the burn, my leddy. I'll jist gang and see what's the mischeef."

"Oh Malcolm! what a time you have been!"

"What's wrong, my lady?" cried Malcolm with respondent terror.

"Don't you hear it?" she answered. "The wind is blowing the house down. There's just been a terrible fall, and every moment I hear it going. If my father were only come! We shall be all blown into the burn."

"No fear of that, my lady!" returned Malcolm. "The walls of the old carcass are mostly live rock and will stand the worst wind that ever blew—this side of the tropics, anyway. Should it once get its nose in, I wouldn't say but it might strip the roof, but it won't blow us into the burn, my lady. I'll just go and see what's the trouble."

He was moving away, but Lady Florimel stopped him. "No, no, Malcolm!" she said. "It's very silly of me, I dare say; but I've been so frightened. They're such a set of geese—Mrs Courthope, and the butler, and all of them! Don't leave me, please."

"I *maun* gang and see what's amiss, my leddy," answered Malcolm; "but ye can come wi' me gien ye like. What's fa'en, div ye think?"

"Nobody knows. It fell with a noise like thunder, and shook the whole house."

"It's far ower dark to see onything frae the ootside," rejoined Malcolm, "at least afore the mune's up. It's as dark's pick. But I can sune saitisfee mysel' whether the deil 's i' the hoose or no."

He took a candle from the hall-table, and went up the square staircase, followed by Florimel.

"What w'y is 't, my leddy, 'at the hoose is no lockit up, an' ilka body i' their beds?" he asked.

"My father is coming home tonight. Didn't you know? But I should have thought a storm like this enough to account for people not being in bed!"

"It's a fearfu' nicht for him to be sae far frae his! Whaur's he comin' frae! Ye never speyk to me noo, my leddy, an' naebody tell't me."

"He was to come from Fochabers tonight. Stoat took the bay mare to meet him yesterday."

"He wad never start in sic a win'! It's fit to blaw the saiddle aff o' the mear's back."

"He may have started before it came on to blow like this," said Lady Florimel.

He was moving away, but Lady Florimel stopped him. "No, no, Malcolm!" she said. "It's very silly of me, I dare say; but I've been so frightened. They're such a set of geese—Mrs Courthope, and the butler, and all of them! Don't leave me, please."

"I *must* go and see what's amiss, my lady," answered Malcolm; "but you can come with me if you like. What's fallen, do you think?"

"Nobody knows. It fell with a noise like thunder, and shook the whole house."

"It's far too dark to see anything from the outside," rejoined Malcolm, "at least before the moon's up. It's as dark as pitch. But I can soon satisfy myself whether the devil's in the house or not."

He took a candle from the hall-table, and went up the square staircase, followed by Florimel.

"Why is it, my lady, that the house isn't locked up, and everyone in their beds?" he asked.

"My father is coming home tonight. Didn't you know? But I should have thought a storm like this enough to account for people not being in bed!"

"It's a fearful night for him to be so far from us! Where's he coming from! You never speak to me now, my lady, and nobody told me."

"He was to come from Fochabers tonight. Stoat took the bay mare to meet him yesterday."

"He would never start in such a wind! It's fit to blow the saddle off the mare's back."

"He may have started before it came on to blow like this," said Lady Florimel.

Malcolm liked the suggestion the less because of its probability, believing, in that case, he should have arrived long ago. But he took care not to increase Florimel's alarm.

By this time Malcolm knew the whole of the accessible inside of the roof well—better far than any one else about the house. From one part to another, over the whole of it, he now led Lady Florimel. In the big-shadowed glimmer of his one candle, all parts of the garret seemed to him frowning with knitted brows over resentful memories—as if the phantom forms of all the past joys and self-renewing sorrows, all the sins and wrongs, all the disappointments and failures of the house, had floated up, generation after generation, into that abode of helpless brooding, and there hung hovering above the fast fleeting life below, which now, in its turn, was ever sending up like fumes from heart and brain, to crowd the dim, dreary, larva-haunted, dream-wallowing chaos of half-obliterated thought and feeling. To Florimel it looked a dread waste, a region deserted and forgotten, mysterious with far-reaching nooks of darkness, and now awful with the wind raving and howling over slates and leads so close to them on all sides,— as if a flying army of demons were tearing at the roof to get in and find covert from pursuit.

At length they approached Malcolm's own quarters, where they would have to pass the very door of the wizard's chamber to reach a short ladder-like stair that led up into the midst of naked rafters, when, coming upon a small storm window near the end of a long passage, Lady Florimel stopped and peeped out.

"The moon is rising," she said, and stood looking.

Malcolm glanced over her shoulder. Eastward a dim light shone up from behind the crest of a low hill. Great part of the sky was clear, but huge masses of broken cloud went sweeping across the heavens. The wind had moderated.

"Aren't we somewhere near your friend the wizard?" said Lady Florimel, with a slight tremble in the tone of mockery with which she spoke.

Malcolm answered as if he were not quite certain.

"Isn't your own room somewhere hereabouts?" asked the girl sharply.	"Isn't your own room somewhere hereabouts?" asked the girl sharply.
"We'll jist gang till ae ither queer place," observed Malcolm, pretending not to have heard her, "and gien the rufe be a' richt there, I s' no bather my heid mair aboot it till the mornin'. It's but a feow steps farther, an' syne a bit stair."	"We'll just go to one other queer place," observed Malcolm, pretending not to have heard her, "and if the roof be all right there, I won't bother my head about it till the morning. It's but a few steps farther, and then a small stair."
A fit of her not unusual obstinacy had however seized Lady Florimel.	A fit of her not unusual obstinacy had however seized Lady Florimel.
"I won't move a step," she said, "until you have told me where the wizard's chamber is."	"I won't move a step," she said, "until you have told me where the wizard's chamber is."

"Ahint ye, my leddy, gien ye wull hae 't," answered Malcolm, not unwilling to punish her a little; "—jist at the far en' o' the transe there."	"Behind you, my lady, if you must know," answered Malcolm, not unwilling to punish her a little; "—just at the far end of the passage there."

In fact the window in which she stood, lighted the whole length of the passage from which it opened.

Even as he spoke, there sounded somewhere as it were the slam of a heavy iron door, the echoes of which seemed to go searching into every cranny of the multitudinous garrets. Florimel gave a shriek, and laying hold of Malcolm, clung to him in terror. A sympathetic tremor, set in motion by her cry, went vibrating through the fisherman's powerful frame, and, almost involuntarily, he clasped her close. With wide eyes they stood staring down the long passage, of which, by the poor light they carried, they could not see a quarter of the length. Presently they heard a soft footfall along its floor, drawing slowly nearer through the darkness; and slowly out of the darkness grew the figure of a man, huge and dim, clad in a long flowing garment, and coming straight on to where they stood. They clung yet closer together. The apparition came within three yards of them, and then they recognized Lord Lossie in his dressing gown.

They started asunder. Florimel flew to her father, and Malcolm stood, expecting the last stroke of his evil fortune. The marquis looked pale, stern, and agitated. Instead of kissing his daughter on the forehead as was his custom, he put her from him with one expanded palm, but the next moment drew her to his side. Then approaching Malcolm, he lighted at his the candle he carried, which a draught had extinguished on the way.

"Go to your room, MacPhail," he said, and turned from him, his arm still round Lady Florimel.

They walked away together down the long passage, vaguely visible in flickering fits. All at once their light vanished, and with it Malcolm's eyes seemed to have left him. But a merry laugh, the silvery thread in which was certainly Florimel's, reached his ears, and brought him to himself.

CHAPTER LVI

SOMETHING FORGOTTEN

I will not trouble my reader with the thoughts that kept rising, flickering, and fading, one after another, for two or three dismal hours, as he lay with eyes closed but sleepless. At length he opened them wide, and looked out into the room. It was a bright moonlit night; the wind had sunk to rest; all the world slept in the exhaustion of the storm; he only was awake; he could lie no longer; he would go out, and discover, if possible, the mischief the tempest had done.

He crept down the little spiral stair used only by the servants, and knowing all the mysteries of lock and bar, was presently in the open air. First he sought a view of the building against the sky, but could not see that any portion was missing. He then proceeded to walk round the house, in order to find what had fallen.

There was a certain neglected spot nearly under his own window, where a wall across an interior angle formed a little court or yard; he had once peeped in at the door of it, which was always half open, and seemed incapable of being moved in either direction, but had seen nothing except a broken pail and a pile of brushwood; the flat arch over this door was broken, and the door itself half-buried in a heap of blackened stones and mortar. Here was the avalanche whose fall had so terrified the household! The formless mass had yesterday been a fair-proportioned and ornate stack of chimneys.

He scrambled to the top of the heap and sitting down on a stone carved with a plaited Celtic band, yet again fell athinking. The marquis must dismiss him in the morning; would it not be better to go away now, and spare poor old Duncan a terrible fit of rage? He would suppose he had fled from the pseudo-maternal net of Mrs Stewart; and not till he had found a place to which he could welcome him would he tell him the truth. But his nature recoiled both from the unmanliness of such a flight, and from the appearance of conscious wrong it must involve, and he dismissed the notion. Scheme after scheme for the future passed through his head, and still he sat on the heap in the light of the high-gliding moon, like a ghost on the ruins of his earthly home, and his eyes went listlessly straying like servants without a master. Suddenly he found them occupied with a low iron-studded door in the wall of the house, which he had never seen before. He descended, and found it hardly closed, for there was no notch to receive the heavy latch. Pushing it open on great rusty hinges, he saw within what in the shadow appeared a precipitous descent. His curiosity was roused; he stole back to his room and fetched his candle; and having, by the aid of his tinderbox, lighted it in the shelter of the heap, peeped again through the doorway, and saw what seemed a narrow cylindrical pit, only, far from showing a great yawning depth, it was filled with stones and rubbish nearly to the bottom of the door. The top of the door reached almost to the vaulted roof, one part of which, close to the inner side of the circular wall, was broken. Below this breach, fragments of stone projected from the wall, suggesting the remnants of a stair. With the sight came a foresight of discovery.

One foot on the end of a long stone sticking vertically from the rubbish, and another on one of the stones projecting from the wall, his head was already through the break in the roof; and in a minute more he was climbing a small, broken, but quite passable spiral staircase, almost a counterpart of that already described as going like a huge augerbore through the house from top to bottom—that indeed by which he had just descended. There was most likely more of it buried below, probably communicating with an outlet in some part of the rock towards the burn, but the portion of it which, from long neglect, had gradually given way, had fallen down the shaft, and cut off the rest with its ruins.

At the height of a storey, he came upon a built-up doorway, and again, at a similar height, upon another; but the parts filled in looked almost as old as the rest of the wall. Not until he reached the top of the stair, did he find a door. It was iron-studded, and heavily hinged, like that below. It opened outward—noiselessly he found, as if its hinges had been recently oiled, and admitted him to a small closet, the second door of which he opened hurriedly, with a beating heart. Yes! there was the check-curtained bed! it must be the wizard's chamber! Crossing to another door, he found it both locked and further secured by a large iron bolt in a strong staple. This latter he drew back, but there was no key in the lock. With scarce a doubt remaining, he shot down the one stair and flew up the other to try the key that lay in his chest. One moment and he stood in the same room, admitted by the door next his own.

Some exposure was surely not far off! Anyhow here was room for counter-plot, on the chance of baffling something underhand—villainy most likely, where Mrs Catanach was concerned!—And yet, with the control of it thus apparently given into his hands, he must depart, leaving the house at the mercy of a low woman—for the lock of the wizard's door would not exclude her long if she wished to enter and range the building! He would not go, however, without revealing all to the marquis, and would at once make some provision towards her discomfiture.

Going to the forge, and bringing thence a long bar of iron to use as a lever, he carefully drew from the door-frame the staple of the bolt, and then replaced it so, that, while it looked just as before, a good push would now send it into the middle of the room. Lastly, he slid the bolt into it, after having carefully removed all traces of disturbance, left the mysterious chamber by its own stair, and once more ascending to the passage, locked the door, and retired to his room with the key.

He had now plenty to think about beyond himself! Here certainly was some small support to the legend of the wizard earl. The stair which he had discovered, had been in common use at one time; its connection with other parts of the house had been cut off with an object; and by degrees it had come to be forgotten altogether; many villainies might have been effected by means of it. Mrs Catanach must have discovered it the same night on which he found her there, had gone away by it then, and had certainly been making use of it since. When he smelt the sulphur, she must have been lighting a match.

It was now getting towards morning, and at last he was tired. He went to bed and fell asleep. When he woke, it was late, and as he dressed, he heard the noise of hoofs and wheels in the stable yard. He was sitting at breakfast in Mrs Courthope's room, when she came in full of surprise at the sudden departure of her lord and lady. The marquis had rung for his man, and Lady Florimel for her maid, as soon as it was light; orders were sent at once to the stable; four horses were put to the travelling carriage; and they were gone, Mrs Courthope could not tell whither.

Dreary as was the house without Florimel, things had turned out a shade or two better than Malcolm had expected, and he braced himself to endure his loss.

CHAPTER LVII

THE LAIRD'S QUEST

Things were going pretty well with the laird: Phemy and he drew yet closer to each other, and as he became yet more peaceful in her company, his thoughts flowed more freely, and his utterance grew less embarrassed; until at length, in talking with her, his speech was rarely broken with even a slight impediment, and a stranger might have overheard a long conversation between them without coming to any more disparaging conclusion in regard to him than that the hunchback was peculiar in mind as well as in body. But his nocturnal excursions continuing to cause her apprehension, and his representations of the delights to be gathered from Nature while she slept, at the same time alluring her greatly, Phemy had become, both for her own pleasure and his protection, anxious in these also to be his companion.

With a vital recognition of law, and great loyalty to any utterance of either parent, she had yet been brought up in an atmosphere of such liberty, that except a thing were expressly so conditioned, or in itself appeared questionable, she never dreamed of asking permission to do it; and, accustomed as she had been to go with the laird everywhere, and to be out with him early and late, her conscience never suggested the possibility of any objection to her getting up at twelve, instead of four or five, to accompany him. It was some time, however, before the laird himself would consent; and then he would not unfrequently interpose with limitations, especially, if the night were not mild and dry, sending her always home again to bed. The mutual rule and obedience between them was something at once strange and lovely.

At midnight Phemy would enter the shop, and grope her way until she stood under the trap-door. This was the nearest she could come to the laird's chamber, for he had not only declined having the ladder stand there for his use, but had drawn a solemn promise from the carpenter that at night it should always be left slung up to the joists. For himself he had made a rope-ladder, which he could lower from beneath when he required it, invariably drew up after him, and never used for coming down.

One night Phemy made her customary signal by knocking against the trap-door with a long slip of wood: it opened, and, as usual, the body of the laird appeared, hung for a moment in the square gap, like a huge spider, by its two hands, one on each side, then dropped straight to the floor, when, without a word, he hastened forth, and Phemy followed.

The night was very still—and rather dark, for it was cloudy about the horizon, and there was no moon. Hand in hand the two made for the shore—here very rocky—a succession of promontories with little coves between. Down into one of these they went by a winding path, and stood at the lip of the sea. A violet dimness, or, rather, a semi-transparent darkness, hung over it, through which came now and then a gleam, where the slow heave of some Triton shoulder caught a shine of the sky; a hush also, as of sleep, hung over it, which not to break, the wavelets of the rising tide carefully stilled their noises; and the dimness and the hush seemed one. They sat down on a rock that rose but a foot or two from the sand and for some moments listened in silence to the inarticulate story of the night. At length the laird turned to Phemy, and taking one of her hands in both of his, very solemnly said, as if breaking to her his life's trouble,

"Phemy, I dinna ken whaur I cam frae."

"Hoot, laird! ye ken weel eneuch ye cam frae Go-od," answered Phemy, lengthening out the word with solemn utterance.

The laird did not reply, and again the night closed around them, and the sea hushed at their hearts. But a soft light air began to breathe from the south, and it waked the laird to more active thought.

"Gien he wad but come oot an' shaw himsel'!" he said. "What for disna he come oot?"

"Wha wad ye hae come oot?" asked Phemy.

"Ye ken wha, weel eneuch. They say he 's a' gait at ance: jist hearken. What for will he aye bide in, an' *never* come oot an' lat a puir body see him?"

The speech was broken into pauses, filled by the hush rather than noise of the tide, and the odour-like wandering of the soft air in the convolutions of their ears.

"The lown win' maun be his breath—sae quaiet!—He 's no hurryin' himsel' the nicht.—there's never naebody rins efter *him*.—Eh, Phemy! I jist thoucht he was gauin' to speyk!"

"Phemy, I don't know where I came from."

"Heavens, laird! you know well enough you came from Go-od," answered Phemy, lengthening out the word with solemn utterance.

The laird did not reply, and again the night closed around them, and the sea hushed at their hearts. But a soft light air began to breathe from the south, and it waked the laird to more active thought.

"If he would but come out and show himself!" he said. "Why doesn't he come out?"

"Who would you have come out?" asked Phemy.

"You know who, well enough. They say he's everywhere at once: just listen. Why will he always stay in, and *never* come out and let a poor body see him?"

The speech was broken into pauses, filled by the hush rather than noise of the tide, and the odour-like wandering of the soft air in the convolutions of their ears.

"The calm wind must be his breath—so quiet!—He's not hurrying himself tonight.—nobody ever runs after *him*.—Eh, Phemy! I just thought he was going to speak!"

This last exclamation he uttered in a whisper, as the louder gush of a larger tide-pulse died away on the shore.

"Luik, Phemy, luik!" he resumed. "Luik oot yonner! Dinna ye see something 'at micht grow to something?"

His eyes were fixed on a faint spot of steely blue, out on the sea, not far from the horizon. It was hard to account for, with such a sky overheard, wherein was no lighter part to be seen that might be reflected in the water below; but neither of the beholders was troubled about its cause: there it glimmered on in the dimness of the wide night—a cold, faint splash of blue-grey.

"I dinna think muckle o' that, sir," said Phemy.

"It micht be the mark o' the sole o' his fut, though," returned the laird. "He micht hae jist setten 't doon, an' the watter hae lowed up aboot it, an' the low no be willin' to gang oot! Luik sharp, Phemy; there may come anither at the neist stride—anither fut mark. Luik ye that gait an' I'll luik this.—What for willna he come oot? The lift maun be fu' o' 'im, an' I'm hungert for a sicht o' 'im. Gien ye see ony thing, Phemy, cry oot."

"What will I cry?" asked Phemy.

"Cry 'Father o' lichts!'" answered the laird.

"Will he hear to that—div ye think, sir?"

"Wha kens! He micht jist turn his heid; an' ae luik wad sair me for a hunner year."

"I s' cry, gien I see onything," said Phemy.

As they sat watching, by degrees the laird's thought swerved a little. His gaze had

This last exclamation he uttered in a whisper, as the louder gush of a larger tide-pulse died away on the shore.

"Look, Phemy, look!" he resumed. "Look out yonder! Don't you see something that might grow to something?"

His eyes were fixed on a faint spot of steely blue, out on the sea, not far from the horizon. It was hard to account for, with such a sky overheard, wherein was no lighter part to be seen that might be reflected in the water below; but neither of the beholders was troubled about its cause: there it glimmered on in the dimness of the wide night—a cold, faint splash of blue-grey.

"I don't think much of that, sir," said Phemy.

"It might be the mark of the sole of his foot, though," returned the laird. "He might have just set it down, and the water have flamed up about it, and the glow not be willing to go out! Look sharp, Phemy; there may come another at the next stride—another foot mark. You look that way and I'll look this.—Why will he not come out? The sky must be full of him, and I'm hungry for a sight of him. If you see anything, Phemy, cry out."

"What will I cry?" asked Phemy.

"Cry 'Father of lights!'" answered the laird.

"Will he hearken to that—do you think, sir?"

"Who knows! He might just turn his head; and one look would serve me for a hundred years."

"I'll cry, if I see anything," said Phemy.

As they sat watching, by degrees the laird's thought swerved a little. His fixed on the northern horizon, where, as if on the outer threshold of some mighty door, long low clouds, with varied suggestion of recumbent animal forms, had stretched themselves, like creatures of the chase, watching for their lord to issue.

"Maybe he's no oot o' the hoose yet," he said. "Surely it canna be but he comes oot ilka nicht! He wad never hae made sic a sicht o' bonny things to lat them lie wi'oot onybody to gaither them! An' there's nae ill fowk furth at this time o' nicht, ta mak an oogly din, or disturb him wi' the sicht o' them. He maun come oot i' the quaiet o' the nicht, or else what's 't a' for?—Ay! he keeps the nicht till himsel', an' lea's the day to hiz. That 'll be what the deep sleep fa's upo' men for, doobtless—to haud them oot o' his gait! Eh! I wuss he wad come oot whan I was by! I micht get a glimp o' 'm.—Maybe he wad tak the hump aff o' me, an' set things in order i' my heid, an' mak me like ither fowk. Eh me! that wad be gran'! Naebody wad daur to touch me syne. Eh! Michty! come oot! Father o' lichts! Father o' lichts!"

gaze had fixed on the northern horizon, where, as if on the outer threshold of some mighty door, long low clouds, with varied suggestion of recumbent animal forms, had stretched themselves, like creatures of the chase, watching for their lord to issue.

"Maybe he's yet to leave the house," he said. "Surely it can't be but he comes out every night! He would never have made such a world of bonny things to let them lie with no one to gather them! And there's no bad folk about at this time of night, to make an ugly din, or disturb him with the sight of them. He must come out in the quiet of the night, or else what's it all for?—Ay! he keeps the night to himself, and leaves the day to us. That'll be what the deep sleep falls upon men for, doubtless—to keep them out of his way! Eh! I wish he would come out when I was by! I might catch a glimpse of him.—Maybe he would take the hump off my back, and set things right in my head, and make me like other folk. Eh me! that would be grand! Nobody would dare to touch me then. Eh! Mighty! come out! Father of lights! Father of lights!"

He went on repeating the words till, growing softer and softer, his voice died away in silence, and still as his seat of stone he sat, a new Job, on the verge of the world-waters, like the old Job on his dunghill when he cried out,—

"Lo, he goeth by me, and I see him not; he passeth on also, but I perceive him not—Call thou, and I will answer; or let me speak and answer thou me.—Oh that I knew where I might find him! that I might come even to his seat!—Behold I go forward, but he is not there; and backward, but I cannot perceive him; on the left hand, where he doth work, but I cannot behold him; he hideth himself on the right hand, that I cannot see him."

At length he rose and wandered away from the shore, his head sunk upon his chest. Phemy rose also and followed him in silence. The child had little of the poetic element in her nature, but she had much of that from which everything else has to be developed—heart. When they reached the top of the brae, she joined him, and said, putting her hand in his, but not looking at, or even turning towards him,

"Maybe he 'll come oot upo' ye afore ye ken some day—whan ye're no luikin' for him."

"Maybe he'll come out upon you before you know some day—when you're not looking for him."

The laird stopped, gazed at her for a moment, shook his head, and walked on.

Grassy steeps everywhere met the stones and sands of the shore, and the grass and the sand melted, as it were, and vanished each in the other. Just where they met in the next hollow, stood a small building of stone with a tiled roof. It was now strangely visible through the darkness, for from every crevice a fire-illumined smoke was pouring. But the companions were not alarmed or even surprised. They bent their way towards it without hastening a step, and coming to a fence that enclosed a space around it, opened a little gate, and passed through. A sleepy watchman challenged them.

"It's me," said the laird.

"It's me," said the laird.

"A fine nicht, laird," returned the voice, and said no more.

"A fine night, laird," returned the voice, and said no more.

The building was divided into several compartments, each with a separate entrance. On the ground in each burned four or five little wood fires, and the place was filled with smoke and glow. The smoke escaped partly by openings above the doors, but mostly by the crannies of the tiled roof. Ere it reached these, however, it had to pass through a great multitude of pendent herrings. Hung up by the gills, layer above layer, nearly to the roof, their last tails came down as low as the laird's head. From beneath nothing was to be seen but a firmament of herring-tails. These fish were the last of the season, and were thus undergoing the process of kippering. It was a new venture in the place, and its success as yet a question.

The laird went into one of the compartments, and searching about a little amongst the multitude within his reach, took down a plump one, then cleared away the blazing wood from the top of one of the fires, and laid his choice upon the glowing embers beneath.

"What are ye duin' there, laird?" cried Phemy from without, whose nostrils the resulting odour had quickly reached. "The fish is no yours."

"What are you doing there, laird?" cried Phemy from without, whose nostrils the resulting odour had quickly reached. "The fish isn't yours."

"Ye dinna think I wad tak it wantin' leave, Phemy!" returned the laird. "Mony a supper hae I made this w'y, an' mony anither I houp to mak. It'll no be this sizzon though, for this lot's the last o' them. They're fine aitin', but I'm some feart they winna keep."

"You don't think I would take it without leave, Phemy!" returned the laird. "Many a supper I've made this way, and many another I hope to make. It won't be this season though, for this lot's the last of them. They're fine eating, but I'm afraid they won't keep."

"Wha gae ye leave, sir?" persisted Phemy showing herself the indivertible guardian of his morals as well as of his freedom.

"Who gave you leave, sir?" persisted Phemy showing herself the indivertible guardian of his morals as well as of his freedom.

"Ow, Mr Runcie himsel', of coorse!" answered the laird. "Wull I pit ane on to you?"	"Oh, Mr Runcie himself, of course!" answered the laird. "Will I put one on for you?"
"Did ye speir leave for me tu?" asked the righteous maiden.	"Did you ask leave for me too?" asked the righteous maiden.
"Ow, na; but I'll tell him the neist time I see him."	"Oh, na; but I'll tell him the next time I see him."
"I'm nae for ony," said Phemy.	"I don't want any," said Phemy.

The fish wanted little cooking. The laird turned it, and after another half-minute of the fire, took it up by the tail, sat down on a stone beside the door, spread a piece of paper on his knees, laid the fish upon it, pulled a lump of bread from his pocket, and proceeded to make his supper. Ere he began, however, he gazed all around with a look which Phemy interpreted as a renewed search for the Father of lights, whom he would fain thank for his gifts. When he had finished, he threw the remnants into one of the fires, then went down to the sea, and there washed his face and hands in a rock-pool, after which they set off again, straying yet further along the coast.

One of the peculiarities in the friendship of the strange couple was that, although so closely attached, they should maintain such a large amount of mutual independence. They never quarrelled, but would flatly disagree, with never an attempt at compromise; the whole space between midnight and morning would sometimes glide by without a word spoken between them; and the one or the other would often be lingering far behind. As, however, the ultimate goal of the night's wandering was always understood between them, there was little danger of their losing each other.

On the present occasion, the laird, still full of his quest, was the one who lingered. Every few minutes he would stop and stare, now all around the horizon, now up to the zenith, now over the wastes of sky—for, any moment, from any spot in heaven, earth, or sea, the Father of lights might show foot, or hand, or face. He had at length seated himself on a lichen-covered stone with his head buried in his hands, as if, wearied with vain search for him outside he would now look within and see if God might not be there, when suddenly a sharp exclamation from Phemy reached him. He listened.

"Rin! rin! rin!" she cried—the last word prolonged into a scream.	"Run! run! run!" she cried—the last word prolonged into a scream.

While it yet rang in his ears, the laird was halfway down the steep. In the open country he had not a chance; but, knowing every cranny in the rocks large enough to hide him, with anything like a start near enough to the shore for his short-lived speed, he was all but certain to evade his pursuers, especially in such a dark night as this.

He was not in the least anxious about Phemy, never imagining she might be less sacred in other eyes than in his, and knowing neither that her last cry of loving solitude had gathered intensity from a cruel grasp, nor that while he fled in safety, she remained a captive.

Trembling and panting like a hare just escaped from the hounds, he squeezed himself into a cleft, where he sat half covered with water until the morning began to break. Then he drew himself out and crept along the shore, from point to point, with keen circumspection, until he was right under the village and within hearing of its inhabitants, when he ascended hurriedly, and ran home. But having reached his burrow, pulled down his rope ladder, and ascended, he found, with trebled dismay, that his loft had been invaded during the night. Several of the hooked cords had been cut away, on one or two were shreds of clothing, and on the window-sill was a drop of blood.

He threw himself on the mound for a moment, then started to his feet, caught up his plaid, tumbled from the loft, and fled from Scaurnose as if a visible pestilence had been behind him.

CHAPTER LVIII

MALCOLM AND MRS STEWART

When her parents discovered that Phemy was not in her garret, it occasioned them no anxiety. When they had also discovered that neither was the laird in his loft, and were naturally seized with the dread that some evil had befallen him, his hitherto invariable habit having been to house himself with the first gleam of returning day, they supposed that Phemy, finding he had not returned, had set out to look for him. As the day wore on, however, without her appearing, they began to be a little uneasy about her as well. Still the two might be together, and the explanation of their absence a very simple and satisfactory one; for a time therefore they refused to admit importunate disquiet. But before night, anxiety, like the slow but persistent waters of a flood, had insinuated itself through their whole being—nor theirs alone, but had so mastered and possessed the whole village that at length all employment was deserted, and every person capable joined in a search along the coast, fearing to find their bodies at the foot of some cliff. The report spread to the neighbouring villages. In Portlossie Duncan went round with his pipes, arousing attention by a brief blast, and then crying the loss at every corner. As soon as Malcolm heard of it, he hurried to find Joseph, but the only explanation of their absence he was prepared to suggest was one that had already occurred to almost everybody—that the laird, namely, had been captured by the emissaries of his mother, and that, to provide against a rescue, they had carried off his companion with him—on which supposition, there was every probability that, within a few days at farthest, Phemy would be restored unhurt.

"There can be little doobt they hae gotten a grip o' 'm at last, puir fallow!" said Joseph. "But whatever 's come till him, we canna sit doon an' ait oor mait ohn kent hoo Phemy 's farin, puir wee lamb! Ye maun jist haud awa' ower to Kirkbyres, Ma'colm, an' get word o' yer mither, an' see gien onything can be made oot o' her."

The proposal fell on Malcolm like a great billow.

"There can be little doubt they've got hold of him at last, poor fellow!" said Joseph. "But whatever's become of him, we can't have bite nor sup without knowing how Phemy's faring, poor wee lamb! You must go over to Kirkbyres, Malcolm, and have a word with your mother, and see if anything can be made out of her."

The proposal fell on Malcolm like a great billow.

"Blue Peter," he said, looking him in the face, "I took it as a mark o' yer freen'ship 'at ye never spak the word to me. What richt has ony man to ca' that wuman my mither? *I* hae never allooed it!"

"I'm thinkin'," returned Joseph, the more easily nettled that his horizon also was full of trouble, "your word upo' the maitter winna gang sae far 's John o' Groat's. Ye 'll no be suppeent for *your* witness upo' the pint."

"I wad as sune gang a mile intill the mou' o' hell, as gang to Kirkbyres!" said Malcolm.

"I hae my answer," said Peter, and turned away.

"But I s' gang," Malcolm went on. "The thing 'at maun be can be.—Only I tell ye this, Peter," he added, "gien ever ye say sic a word 's yon i' my hearin' again, that is, afore the wuman has priven hersel' what she says, I s' gang by ye ever efter ohn spoken, for I'll ken 'at ye want nae mair o' *me*."

Joseph, who had been standing with his back to his friend, turned and held out his hand. Malcolm took it.

"Ae question afore I gang, Peter," he said. "What for didna ye tell me what fowk was sayin' aboot me—anent Lizzy Findlay?"

"'Cause I didna believe a word o' 't, an' I wasna gaein' to add to yer troubles."

"Lizzy never mootit sic a thing?"

"Never."

"I was sure o' that!—Noo I'll awa' to Kirkbyres—God help me! I wad raither face Sawtan an' his muckle tyke.—But dinna ye expec' ony news. Gien yon ane kens, she's a' the surer no to tell. Only ye sanna say I didna du my best for ye."

"Blue Peter," he said, looking him in the face, "I took it as a mark of your friendship that you never spoke the word to me. What right has any man to call that woman my mother? *I* have never allowed it!"

"I'm thinking," returned Joseph, the more easily nettled that his horizon also was full of trouble, "your word on the matter won't go so far as John o' Groat's. You won't be called to give *your* witness upon it."

"I would as soon go a mile into the mouth of hell, as go to Kirkbyres!" said Malcolm.

"I have my answer," said Peter, and turned away.

"But I'll go," Malcolm went on. "The thing that must be can be.—Only I tell you this, Peter," he added, "if ever you say such a word as that in my hearing again, that is, before the woman has proven herself what she says, I'll never speak to you more, for I'll know that you want no more of *me*."

Joseph, who had been standing with his back to his friend, turned and held out his hand. Malcolm took it.

"One question before I go, Peter," he said. "Why didn't you tell me what folk were saying—about me and Lizzy Findlay?"

"Because I didn't believe a word of it, and I wasn't going to add to your troubles."

"No hint of it came from Lizzy?"

"None at all."

"I was sure of that!—Now I'll be off to Kirkbyres—God help me! I would rather face Satan and his great hell-hound.—But don't expect any news. If that woman knows, she's all the surer not to tell. Only you'll never say I did less than my best for you."

It was the hardest trial of the will Malcolm had yet had to encounter. Trials of submission he had had, and tolerably severe ones: but to go and do what the whole feeling recoils from is to be weighed only against abstinence from what the whole feeling urges towards. He walked determinedly home. Stoat saddled a horse for him while he changed his dress, and once more he set out for Kirkbyres.

Had Malcolm been at the time capable of attempting an analysis of his feeling towards Mrs Stewart, he would have found it very difficult to effect. Satisfied as he was of the untruthful—even cruel nature of the woman who claimed him, and conscious of a strong repugnance to any nearer approach between them, he was yet aware of a certain indescribable fascination in her. This, however, only caused him to recoil from her the more—partly from dread lest it *might* spring from the relation asserted, and partly that, whatever might be its root, it wrought upon him in a manner he scarcely disliked the less that it certainly had nothing to do with the filial. But his feelings were too many and too active to admit of the analysis of any one of them, and ere he reached the house his mood had grown fierce.

He was shown into a room where the fire had not been many minutes lighted. It had long narrow windows, over which the ivy had grown so thick, that he was in it some moments ere he saw through the dusk that it was a library—not half the size of that at Lossie House, but far more ancient, and, although evidently neglected, more study-like.

A few minutes passed, then the door softly opened, and Mrs Stewart glided swiftly across the floor with outstretched arms.

"At last!" she said, and would have clasped him to her bosom.

But Malcolm stepped back.

"Na, na, mem!" he said; "it taks twa to that!"

"Malcolm!" she exclaimed, her voice trembling with emotion—of some kind.

"Ye may ca' me your son, mem, but I ken nae gr'un' yet for ca'in' you my—"

He could not say the word.

"That is very true, Malcolm," she returned gently; "but this interview is not of my seeking. I wish to precipitate nothing. So long as there is a single link, or half a link even, missing from the chain of which one end hangs at my heart—"

She paused, with her hand on her bosom, apparently to suppress rising emotion. Had she had the sentence ready for use?

"At last!" she said, and would have clasped him to her bosom.

But Malcolm stepped back.

"Na, na, ma'am!" he said; "that takes two!"

"Malcolm!" she exclaimed, her voice trembling with emotion—of some kind.

"You may call me your son, ma'am, but I know no grounds yet for calling you my—"

He could not say the word.

"That is very true, Malcolm," she returned gently; "but this interview is not of my seeking. I wish to precipitate nothing. So long as there is a single link, or half a link even, missing from the chain of which one end hangs at my heart—"

She paused, with her hand on her bosom, apparently to suppress rising emotion. Had she had the sentence ready for use?

"I will not subject myself," she went on, "to such treatment as it seems I must look for from you. It is hard to lose a son but it is harder yet to find him again after he has utterly ceased to be one."

Here she put her handkerchief to her eyes.

"Till the matter is settled, however," she resumed, "let us be friends—or at least not enemies.—What did you come for now? Not to insult me surely. Is there anything I can do for you?"

Malcolm felt the dignity of her behaviour, but not the less, after his own straightforward manner, answered her question to the point.

"I cam aboot naething concernin' mysel', mem, I cam to see whether ye kent onything aboot Phemy Mair."

"Is it a wo?—I don't even know who she is.—You don't mean the young woman that—?—Why do you come to me about her? Who is she?"

Malcolm hesitated a moment: if she really did not know what he meant, was there any risk in telling her? But he saw none.

"Wha is she, mem!" he returned. "I whiles think she maun be the laird's guid angel, though in shape she's but a wee bit lassie. She maks up for a heap to the laird.—Him an' her, mem, they've disappeart thegither, naebody kens whaur."

Mrs Stewart laughed a low unpleasant laugh, but made no other reply. Malcolm went on.

"An' it's no to be wonnert at gien fowk wull hae 't 'at ye maun ken something aboot it, mem."

"I will not subject myself," she went on, "to such treatment as it seems I must look for from you. It is hard to lose a son but it is harder yet to find him again after he has utterly ceased to be one."

Here she put her handkerchief to her eyes.

"Till the matter is settled, however," she resumed, "let us be friends—or at least not enemies.—What did you come for now? Not to insult me surely. Is there anything I can do for you?"

Malcolm felt the dignity of her behaviour, but not the less, after his own straightforward manner, answered her question to the point.

"I came about nothing concerning myself, ma'am, I came to see whether you knew anything about Phemy Mair."

"Is it a wo?—I don't even know who she is.—You don't mean the young woman that—?—Why do you come to me about her? Who is she?"

Malcolm hesitated a moment: if she really did not know what he meant, was there any risk in telling her? But he saw none.

"Who is she, ma'am!" he returned. "I sometimes think she must be the laird's good angel, though in shape she's but a wee lassie. She makes up for a good deal to the laird.—Him and her, ma'am, they've disappeared together, nobody knows where."

Mrs Stewart laughed a low unpleasant laugh, but made no other reply. Malcolm went on.

"And it's small wonder if folk are sure you must know something about it, ma'am."

"I know nothing whatever," she returned emphatically. "Believe me or not, as you please," she added, with heightened colour. "If I did know anything," she went on, with apparent truthfulness, "I don't know that I should feel bound to tell it. As it is, however, I can only say I know nothing of either of them. That I do say most solemnly."

Malcolm turned,—satisfied at least that he could learn no more.

"You are not going to leave me so!" the lady said, and her face grew "sad as sad could be."

"There's naething mair atween 's, mem," answered Malcolm, without turning even his face.

"You will be sorry for treating me so some day."

"Weel than, mem, I will be; but that day's no the day."

"Think what you could do for your poor witless brother, if—"

"Mem," interrupted Malcolm, turning right round and drawing himself up in anger, "priv' 'at I'm your son, an' that meenute I speir at you wha was my father."

Mrs Stewart changed colour—neither with the blush of innocence nor with the pallor of guilt, but with the gray of mingled rage and hatred. She took a step forward with the quick movement of a snake about to strike, but stopped midway, and stood looking at him with glittering eyes, teeth clenched, and lips half open.

Malcolm returned her gaze for a moment or two.

"*Ye* never was the mither, whaever was the father o' me!" he said, and walked out of the room.

"I know nothing whatever," she returned emphatically. "Believe me or not, as you please," she added, with heightened colour. "If I did know anything," she went on, with apparent truthfulness, "I don't know that I should feel bound to tell it. As it is, however, I can only say I know nothing of either of them. That I do say most solemnly."

Malcolm turned,—satisfied at least that he could learn no more.

"You are not going to leave me so!" the lady said, and her face grew "sad as sad could be."

"There's nothing more between us, ma'am," answered Malcolm, without turning even his face.

"You will be sorry for treating me so some day."

"Well then, ma'am, I will be; but that day's not today."

"Think what you could do for your poor witless brother, if—"

"Ma'am," interrupted Malcolm, turning right round and drawing himself up in anger, "prove that I'm your son, and that minute I demand of you who was my father."

Mrs Stewart changed colour—neither with the blush of innocence nor with the pallor of guilt, but with the gray of mingled rage and hatred. She took a step forward with the quick movement of a snake about to strike, but stopped midway, and stood looking at him with glittering eyes, teeth clenched, and lips half open.

Malcolm returned her gaze for a moment or two.

"*You* never were the mother, whoever was the father of me!" he said, and walked out of the room.

He had scarcely reached the door, when he heard a heavy fall, and looking round saw the lady lying motionless on the floor. Thoroughly on his guard, however, and fearful both of her hatred and her blandishments, he only made the more haste down stairs, where he found a maid, and sent her to attend to her mistress. In a minute he was mounted and trotting fast home, considerably happier than before, inasmuch as he was now almost beyond doubt convinced that Mrs Stewart was not his mother.

CHAPTER LIX

AN HONEST PLOT

Ever since the visit of condolence with which the narrative of these events opened, there had been a coolness between Mrs Mellis and Miss Horn. Mr Mellis's shop was directly opposite Miss Horn's house, and his wife's parlour was over the shop, looking into the street; hence the two neighbours could not but see each other pretty often; beyond a stiff nod, however, no sign of smouldering friendship had as yet broken out. Miss Horn was consequently a good deal surprised when, having gone into the shop to buy some trifle, Mr Mellis informed her, in all but a whisper, that his wife was very anxious to see her alone for a moment, and begged her to have the goodness to step up to the parlour. His customer gave a small snort, betraying her first impulse to resentment, but her nobler nature, which was never far from the surface, constrained her compliance.

Mrs Mellis rose hurriedly when the plumb-line figure of her neighbour appeared, ushered in by her husband, and received her with a somewhat embarrassed *empressement*, arising from the consciousness of goodwill disturbed by the fear of imputed meddlesomeness. She knew the inward justice of Miss Horn, however, and relied upon that, even while she encouraged herself by waking up the ever present conviction of her own superiority in the *petite morale* of social intercourse. Her general tendency indeed was to look down upon Miss Horn: is it not usually the less that looks down on the greater? I had almost said it must be, for that the less only *can* look down; but that would not hold absolutely in the kingdoms of this world, while in the kingdom of heaven it is all looking up.

"Sit ye doon, Miss Horn," she said; "it's a lang time sin we had a news thegither."	"Take a seat, Miss Horn," she said; "it's a long time since we've had a talk together."
Miss Horn seated herself with a begrudged acquiescence.	Miss Horn seated herself with a begrudged acquiescence.
Had Mrs Mellis been more of a tactician, she would have dug a few approaches ere she opened fire upon the fortress of her companion's fair-hearing: but instead of that, she at once discharged the imprudent question—	Had Mrs Mellis been more of a tactician, she would have dug a few approaches ere she opened fire upon the fortress of her companion's fair-hearing: but instead of that, she at once discharged the imprudent question—

"Was ye at hame last nicht, mem, atween the hoors o' aucht an' nine?"—a shot which instantly awoke in reply the whole battery of Miss Horn's indignation.

"Wha am I, to be speirt sic a queston! Wha but yersel' wad hae daurt it, Mistress Mellis?"

"Huly, huly, Miss Horn!" expostulated her questioner. "I hae nae wuss to pry intill ony secrets o' yours, or—"

"Secrets!" shouted Miss Horn.

But her consciousness of good intent, and all but assurance of final victory, upheld Mrs Mellis.

"—or Jean's aither," she went on, apparently regardless; "but I wad fain be sure ye kent a' aboot yer ain hoose 'at a body micht chance to see frae the croon o the caus'ay."

"The parlour-blind 's gane up crookit sin' ever that thoomb-fingert cratur, Watty Witherspail, made a new roller till 't. Gien 't be that ye mean, Mistress Mellis,—"

"Hoots!" returned the other. "—Hoo far can ye lippen to that Jean o' yours, mem?"

"Nae farer nor the len'th o' my nose, an' the breid o' my twa een," was the scornful answer.

Although, however, she thus manifested her resentment of Mrs Mellis's catechetical attempts in introducing her subject, Miss Horn had no desire to prevent the free outcome of her approaching communication.

"In that case, I may speyk oot," said Mrs Mellis.

"Use yer freedom."

"Weel, I will. Ye was hardly oot o' the hoose last nicht, afore—"

"Were you at home last night, ma'am, between the hours of eight and nine?"—a shot which instantly awoke in reply the whole battery of Miss Horn's indignation.

"Who am I, to be questioned so! Who but yourself would have dared it, Mistress Mellis?"

"Calm yourself, Miss Horn!" expostulated her questioner. "I have no wish to pry into any secrets of yours, or—"

"Secrets!" shouted Miss Horn.

But her consciousness of good intent, and all but assurance of final victory, upheld Mrs Mellis.

"—or Jean's either," she went on, apparently regardless; "but I would fain be sure you knew all about your own house that a body might chance to see from the crown of the street."

"The parlour-blind's gone up crooked ever since that thumb-fingered Watty Witherspail made a new roller for it. If that's what you mean, Mistress Mellis,—"

"Heavens!" returned the other. "—How far can you trust that Jean of yours, ma'am?"

"No farther than the length of my nose, and the breadth of my two eyes," was the scornful answer.

Although, however, she thus manifested her resentment of Mrs Mellis's catechetical attempts in introducing her subject, Miss Horn had no desire to prevent the free outcome of her approaching communication.

"In that case, I may speak out," said Mrs Mellis.

"Use your freedom."

"Well, I will. You were hardly out of the house last night, before—"

"Ye saw me gang oot?"

"Ay did I."

"What gart ye speir than? What for sud a body come screwin' up a straucht stair—noo the face an' noo the back o' her?"

"Weel, I nott na hae speirt. But that's naething to the p'int.—Ye hadna been gane, as I was sayin', ower a five meenutes, whan in cam a licht intill the bedroom neist the parlour, an' Jean appeart wi' a can'le in her han'. There was nae licht i' this room but the licht o' the fire, an' no muckle o' that, for 'twas maistly peat, sae I saw her weel eneuch—ohn been seen mysel'. She cam straucht to the window, and drew doon the blind, but lost hersel' a bit or she wad never hae set doon her can'le whaur it cuist a shaidow o' hersel' an' her doin's upo' the blind."

"An' what was 't she was efter, the jaud?" cried Miss Horn, without any attempt to conceal her growing interest.

"She made naething o' 't, whatever it was; for doon the street cam the schuilmaister, an' chappit at the door, an gaed in an' waitit till ye came hame."

"Weel!" said Miss Horn.

But Mrs Mellis held her peace.

"Weel!!?" repeated Miss Horn.

"Weel," returned Mrs Mellis, with a curious mixture of deference and conscious sagacity in her tone, "a' 'at I tak upo' me to say is—Think ye twice afore ye lippen to that Jean o' yours."

"I lippen naething till her! I wad as sune lippen to the dottle o' a pipe amo' dry strae. What saw ye, Mistress Mellis?"

"Ye needna speyk like that," returned Mrs Mellis, for Miss Horn's tone was threatening: "I'm no Jean."

"You saw me go out?"

"Ay, I did."

"Why did you ask me then? Why should a body come screwing up a straight stair—now the face and now the back of her?"

"Well, I needn't have asked. But that's nothing to the point.—You hadn't been gone, as I was saying, more than five minutes, when in came a light into the bedroom next the parlour, and Jean appeared with a candle in her hand. There was no light in this room but the light of the fire, and little of that, for it was mostly peat, so I saw her well enough—without being seen myself. She came straight to the window, and drew down the blind, but lost herself a bit or she would never have set down her candle where it cast a shadow of herself and her doings on the blind."

"And what was it she was after, the jade?" cried Miss Horn, without any attempt to conceal her growing interest.

"She made nothing of it, whatever it was; for down the street came the schoolmaster, and knocked at the door, and went in and waited till you came home."

"Well!" said Miss Horn.

But Mrs Mellis held her peace.

"Well!!?" repeated Miss Horn.

"Well," returned Mrs Mellis, with a curious mixture of deference and conscious sagacity in her tone, "All that I venture to say is—Think twice before trusting to that Jean of yours."

"I trust her not a whit! I would as soon trust to the dottle of a pipe among dry straw. What saw you, Mistress Mellis?"

"You needn't speak like that," returned Mrs Mellis, for Miss Horn's tone was threatening: "I'm not Jean."

"What saw ye?" repeated Miss Horn, more gently, but not less eagerly.

"Whause is that kist o' mahogany drawers i' that bedroom, gien I may preshume ta spier?"

"Whause but mine?"

"They're no Jean's?"

"Jean's!"

"Ye micht hae latten her keep her bit duds i' them, for onything I kent!"

"Jean's duds i' my Grizel's drawers! A lik'ly thing!"

"Hm! They war puir Miss Cam'ell's, war they?"

"They war Grizell Cam'ell's drawers as lang's she had use for ony; but what for ye sud say *puir* till her, I dinna ken, 'cep' it be 'at she's gane whaur they haena muckle 'at needs layin' in drawers. That's neither here nor there.—Div ye tell me 'at Jean was intromittin' wi thae drawers? They're a' lockit, ilk ane o' them—an' they're guid locks."

"No ower guid to hae keyes to them—are they?"

"The keyes are i' my pooch," said Miss Horn, clapping her hand to the skirt of her dress. "They're aye i' my pooch, though I haena had the feelin's to mak use o' them sin' she left me."

"Are ye sure they war there last nicht, mem?"

Miss Horn seemed struck.

"I had on my black silk last nicht," she answered vaguely, and was here silent, pondering doubtfully.

"Weel, mem, jist ye put on yer black silk again the morn's nicht, an' come ower aboot aucht o'clock; an' ye'll be able to jeedge by her ongang when ye're no i' the hoose, gien there be onything amiss wi' Jean. There canna be muckle ill dune yet—that's a comfort!"

"What saw you?" repeated Miss Horn, more gently, but not less eagerly.

"Whose is the mahogany chest of drawers in that bedroom, if I may presume to ask?"

"Whose but mine?"

"They're not Jean's?"

"Jean's!"

"You might have let her keep her cloths in them, for anything I knew!"

"Jean's cloths in my Grizel's drawers! A likely thing!"

"Hm! They were poor Miss Campbell's, were they?"

"They were Grizell Campbell's drawers as long as she had use for any; but why you should tack a *poor* to her name, I don't know, except perhaps that she's gone where there's little to be laid in drawers. But that's neither here nor there.—Do you tell me that Jean was meddling with those drawers? They're all locked, every one of them—and they're good locks."

"Not too good to have keys to them—are they?"

"The keys are in my pocket," said Miss Horn, clapping her hand to the skirt of her dress. "They're always there, though I haven't had the feelings to make use of them since she left me."

"Are you sure they were there last night, ma'am?"

Miss Horn seemed struck.

"I had on my black silk last night," she answered vaguely, and was here silent, pondering doubtfully.

"Well, ma'am, just you put on your black silk again tomorrow night, and come over about eight o'clock; and you'll be able to judge by her behaviour when you're away, whether there be anything amiss with Jean. There can't be much harm done yet—that's a comfort!"

"What ill, by meddlin' wi' what doesna concern her, cud the wuman du?" said Miss Horn, with attempted confidence.

"That ye sud ken best yersel', mem. But Jean's an awfu' gossip, an' a lady like yer cousin micht hae left dockiments ahint her 'at she wadna jist like to hear procleemt frae the hoose-tap. No 'at *she*'ll ever hear onything mair, puir thing!"

"What mean ye?" cried Miss Horn, half frightened, half angry.

"Jist what I say—neither mair nor less," returned Mrs Mellis. "Miss Cam'ell may weel hae left letters for enstance, an' hoo wad they fare in Jean's han's?"

"Whan *I* never had the hert to open her drawers!" exclaimed Miss Horn, enraged at the very notion of the crime. "I hae *nae* feelin's, thank God for the furnishin' o' me!"

"I doobt Jean has her full share o' a' feelin's belangin' to fallen human natur'," said Mrs Mellis, with a slow horizontal oscillation of the head. "But ye jist come an' see wi' yer ain een, an' syne jeedge for yersel': it's nae business o' mine."

"I'll come the nicht, Mrs Mellis. Only lat it be atween 's twa."

"I can haud my tongue, mem,—that is, frae a' but ane. Sae lang 's married fowk sleeps in ae bed, it 's ill to haud onything till a body's sel'."

"Mr Mellis is a douce man, an' I carena what he kens," answered Miss Horn.

She descended to the shop, and having bought bulk enough to account to Jean for her lengthened stay, for she had beyond a doubt been watching the door of the shop, she crossed the street, went up to

"What harm, besides meddling with what doesn't concern her, could the woman do?" said Miss Horn, with attempted confidence.

"That you should know best yourself, ma'am. But Jean's an awful gossip, and a lady like your cousin might have left documents behind her that she wouldn't just like to hear shouted from the house-top. Not that *she*'ll ever hear anything more, poor thing!"

"What d'ye mean?" cried Miss Horn, half frightened, half angry.

"Just what I say—neither more nor less," returned Mrs Mellis. "Miss Campbell may well have left letters for instance, and how would they fare in Jean's hands?"

"When *I* never had the heart to open her drawers!" exclaimed Miss Horn, enraged at the very notion of the crime. "I have *no* feelings, thank God for my furnishing!"

"I suspect Jean has her full share, though—of all the feelings belonging to fallen man," said Mrs Mellis, with a slow horizontal oscillation of the head. "But just you come and see with your own eyes, and then judge for yourself: it's no business of mine."

"I'll come tonight, Mrs Mellis. Only let it be kept between the two of us."

"I can hold my tongue, ma'am,—that is, from all but one. So long as married folk sleep in the same bed, it's ill for either to keep secrets."

"Mr Mellis is a man of sense, and I don't care what he knows," answered Miss Horn.

She descended to the shop, and having bought bulk enough to account to Jean for her lengthened stay, for she had beyond a doubt been watching the door of the shop, she crossed the street, went up to her parlour, and rang the bell. The same moment Jean's head was popped in at the door: she had her reasons for always answering the bell like a bullet.

"Mem?" said Jean.

"Jean, I'm gaein' oot the nicht. The minister oucht to be spoken till aboot the schuilmaister, honest man. Tak the lantren wi' ye to the manse aboot ten o'clock. That 'll be time eneuch."

"Verra weel, mem. But I'm thinkin' there's a mune the nicht."

"Naething but the doup o' ane, Jean. It's no to ca' a mune. It's a mercy we hae lantrens, an' sic a sicht o' cairds aboot."

"Ay, a lantren lats them see whaur ye are, an' haud oot o' yer gait," said Jean, who happened not to relish going out that night.

"Troth, wuman, ye're richt there!" returned her mistress, with cheerful assent. "The mair they see o' ye, the less they 'll meddle wi' ye—caird or cadger. Haud ye the licht upo' yer ain face, lass, an' there's feow 'll hae the hert to luik again."

"Haith, mem, there's twa sic like o' 's!" returned Jean bitterly, and bounced from the room.

"That's true tu," said her mistress—adding after the door was shut, "It's a peety we cudna haud on thegither."

"I'm gaein' noo, Jean," she called into the kitchen as she crossed the threshold at eight o'clock.

her parlour, and rang the bell. The same moment Jean's head was popped in at the door: she had her reasons for always answering the bell like a bullet.

"Ma'am?" said Jean.

"Jean, I'm going out tonight. The minister ought to be spoken to about the schoolmaster, honest man. Take the lantern with you to the manse about ten o'clock. That'll be time enough."

"Very well, ma'am. But I'm thinking there's a moon tonight."

"The tail-end of one at most, Jean. It's no moon to speak of. It's a mercy we have lanterns, with so many tramps about."

"Ay, a lantern lets them see where you are, and keep out of your way," said Jean, who happened not to relish going out that night.

"You're right there, woman!" returned her mistress, with cheerful assent. "The more they see of you, the less they'll meddle with you—tramp or tinker. Hold the light to your own face, lass, and there's few'll have the heart to look again."

"Faith ma'am, there's two of us the same, then!" returned Jean bitterly, and bounced from the room.

"That's true too," said her mistress—adding after the door was shut, "It's a pity we're soon to part."

"I'm going now, Jean," she called into the kitchen as she crossed the threshold at eight o'clock.

She turned towards the head of the street, in the direction of the manse; but, out of the range of Jean's vision, made a circuit, and entered Mr Mellis's house by the garden at the back.

In the parlour she found a supper prepared to celebrate the renewal of old goodwill. The clear crystal on the table; the new loaf so brown without and so white within; the rich, clear-complexioned butter, undebased with a particle of salt; the self-satisfied hum of the kettle in attendance for the guidman's toddy; the bright fire, the golden glow of the brass fender in its red light, and the dish of boiled potatoes set down before it, under a snowy cloth; the pink eggs, the yellow haddock, and the crimson strawberry jam; all combined their influences—each with its private pleasure wondrously heightened by the zest of a secret watch and the hope of discomfitted mischief—to draw into a friendship what had hitherto been but a somewhat insecure neighbourship. From below came the sound of the shutters which Mr Mellis was putting up a few minutes earlier than usual; and when presently they sat down to the table, and, after prologue judged suitable, proceeded to enjoy the good things before them, an outside observer would have thought they had a pleasant evening, if not Time himself, by the forelock.

But Miss Horn was uneasy. The thought of what Jean might have already discovered had haunted her all day long; for her reluctance to open her cousin's drawers had arisen mainly from the dread of finding justified a certain painful suspicion which had haunted the whole of her intercourse with Grizell Campbell—namely, that the worm of a secret had been lying at the root of her life, the cause of all her illness, and of her death at last. She had fought with, out-argued, and banished the suspicion a thousand times while she was with her, but evermore it had returned; and now since her death, when again and again on the point of turning over her things, she had been always deterred by the fear, not so much of finding what would pain herself as of discovering what Grizell would not wish her to know. Never was there a greater contrast between form and reality, between person and being, between manner and nature, than existed in Margaret Horn: the shell was rough, the kernel absolute delicacy. Not for a moment had her suspicion altered her behaviour to the gentle suffering creature towards whom she had adopted the relation of an elder and stronger sister. To herself, when most satisfied of the existence of a secret, she steadily excused her cousin's withholdment of confidence, on the ground of her own lack of feelings: how could she unbosom herself to such as she! And now the thought of eyes like Jean's exploring Grizell's forsaken treasures, made her so indignant and restless that she could hardly even pretend to enjoy her friend's hospitality.

Mrs Mellis had so arranged the table and their places, that she and her guest had only to lift their eyes to see the window of their watch, while she punished her husband for the virile claim to greater freedom from curiosity by seating him with his back to it, which made him every now and then cast a fidgety look over his shoulder— not greatly to the detriment of his supper, however. Their plan was, to extinguish their own the moment Jean's light should appear, and so watch without the risk of counter-discovery.

"There she comes!" cried Mrs Mellis; and her husband and Miss Horn made such haste to blow out the candle, that they knocked their heads together, blew in each other's face, and the first time missed it. Jean approached the window with hers in her hand, and pulled down the blind. But, alas, beyond the form of a close bent elbow moving now and then across a corner of the white field, no shadow appeared upon it!

Miss Horn rose.

"Sit doon, mem, sit doon; ye hae naething to gang upo' yet," exclaimed Mr Mellis, who, being a bailie, was an authority.

"I can sit nae langer, Mr Mellis," returned Miss Horn. "I hae eneuch to gang upo' as lang 's I hae my ain flure aneth my feet: the wuman has nae business there. I'll jist slip across an' gang in, as quaiet as a sowl intill a boady; but I s' warran' I s' mak a din afore I come oot again!"

"Sit down, ma'am, sit down; you've nothing to go upon yet," exclaimed Mr Mellis, who, being a bailie, was an authority.

"I can sit no longer, Mr Mellis," returned Miss Horn. "I've enough to go upon while my own floor's beneath my feet: the woman has no business there. I'll just slip across and go in, as quiet as a soul into a body; but you can be sure I'll make a din before I come out again!"

With a grim diagonal nod she left the room.

Although it was now quite dark, she yet deemed it prudent to go by the garden-gate into the back lane, and so cross the street lower down. Opening her own door noiselessly, thanks to Jean, who kept the lock well oiled for reasons of Mrs Catanach's, she closed it as silently, and, long-boned as she was, crept up the stair like a cat. The light was shining from the room; the door was ajar. She listened at it for a moment, and could distinguish nothing; then fancying she heard the rustle of paper, could bear it no longer, pushed the door open, and entered. There stood Jean, staring at her with fear-blanched face, a deep top-drawer open before her, and her hands full of things she was in the act of replacing. Her terror culminated, and its spell broke in a shriek, when her mistress sprang upon her like a tigress.

The watchers in the opposite house heard no cry, and only saw a heave of two inter-mingled black shadows across the blind, after which they neither heard nor saw anything more. The light went on burning until its final struggle with the darkness began, when it died with many a flickering throb. Unable at last to endure the suspense, now growing to fear, any longer, they stole across the street, opened the door, and went in. Over the kitchen fire, like an evil spirit of the squabby order, crouched Mrs Catanach, waiting for Jean; no one else was to be found.

About ten o'clock the same evening, as Mr Graham sat by his peat fire, some one lifted the latch of the outer door and knocked at the inner. His invitation to enter was answered by the appearance of Miss Horn, gaunt and grim as usual, but with more than the wonted fire gleaming from the shadowy cavern of her bonnet. She made no apology for the lateness of her visit, but seated herself at the other side of the deal table, and laid upon it a paper parcel, which she proceeded to open with much deliberation and suppressed plenitude. Having at length untied the string with the long fingers of a hand which, not-withstanding its evident strength, trembled so as almost to defeat the attempt, she took from the parcel a packet of old letters sealed with spangled wax, and pushed it across the table to the schoolmaster, saying—

"Hae, Sandy Graham! Naebody but yersel' has a richt to say what's to be dune wi' *them*."

"There, Sandy Graham! Nobody but you has a right to say what's to be done with *them*."

He put out his hand and took them gently, with a look of sadness but no surprise.

"Dinna think I hae been readin' them, Sandy Graham. Na, na! I wad read nae honest man's letters, be they written to wha they micht."

Mr Graham was silent.

"Ye're a guid man, Sandy Graham," Miss Horn resumed, "gien God ever took the pains to mak ane. Dinna think onything atween you an' her wad hae brocht me at this time o' nicht to disturb ye in yer ain chaumer. Na, na! Whatever was atween you twa had an honest man intill 't, an' I wad hae taen my time to gie ye back yer dockiments. But there's some o' anither mark here."

As she spoke, she drew from the parcel a small cardboard box, broken at the sides, and tied with a bit of tape. This she undid and, turning the box upside down, tumbled its contents out on the table before him.

"What mak ye o' sic like as thae?" she said.

"Do you want me to—?" asked the schoolmaster with trembling voice.

"I jist div," she answered.

They were a number of little notes—some of them but a word or two, and signed with initials; others longer, and signed in full. Mr Graham took up one of them reluctantly, and unfolded it softly. He had hardly looked at it when he started and exclaimed,—

"God have mercy! What can be the date of this!"

There was no date to it. He held it in his hand for a minute, his eyes fixed on the fire, and his features almost convulsed with his efforts at composure; then laid it gently on the table, and said but without turning his eyes to Miss Horn,—

He put out his hand and took them gently, with a look of sadness but no surprise.

"Don't think I have been reading them, Sandy Graham. Na, na! I would read no honest man's letters, be they written to who they might."

Mr Graham was silent.

"You're a good man, Sandy Graham," Miss Horn resumed, "if ever God made one. Don't think anything between you and her would have brought me at this late hour to disturb you in your own room. Na, na! Whatever was between you two had an honest man in it, and I would have taken my time to give you back your documents. But there's some of another mark here."

As she spoke, she drew from the parcel a small cardboard box, broken at the sides, and tied with a bit of tape. This she undid and, turning the box upside down, tumbled its contents out on the table before him.

"What make you of these ones?" she said.

"Do you want me to—?" asked the schoolmaster with trembling voice.

"Exactly that," she answered.

They were a number of little notes—some of them but a word or two, and signed with initials; others longer, and signed in full. Mr Graham took up one of them reluctantly, and unfolded it softly. He had hardly looked at it when he started and exclaimed,—

"God have mercy! What can be the date of this!"

There was no date to it. He held it in his hand for a minute, his eyes fixed on the fire, and his features almost convulsed with his efforts at composure; then laid it gently on the table, and said but without turning his eyes to Miss Horn,—

"I cannot read this. You must not ask me. It refers doubtless to the time when Miss Campbell was governess to Lady Annabel. I see no end to be answered by *my* reading one of these letters."

"I daursay! Wha ever saw 'at wadna luik?" returned Miss Horn, with a glance keen as an eagle's into the thoughtful eyes of her friend.

"Why not do by the writer of these as you have done by me? Why not take them to him?" suggested Mr Graham.

"That wad be but thoomb-fingert wark—to lat gang the en' o' yer hank!" exclaimed Miss Horn.

"I do not understand you, ma'am."

"Weel, I maun gar ye un'erstan' me. There's things whiles, Sandy Graham, 'at 's no easy to speyk aboot—but I hae nae feelin's, an' we'll a' be deid or lang, an' that's a comfort. Man 'at ye are, ye're the only human bein' I wad open my moo' till aboot this maitter, an' that's 'cause ye lo'e the memory o' my puir lassie, Grizell Cam'ell."

"It is not her memory, it is herself I love," said the schoolmaster with trembling voice. "Tell me what you please: you may trust me."

"Gien I needit you to tell me that, I wad trust ye as I wad the black dog wi' butter!—Hearken, Sandy Graham."

"I cannot read this. You must not ask me. It refers doubtless to the time when Miss Campbell was governess to Lady Annabel. I see no end to be answered by *my* reading one of these letters."

"I daresay! Who ever saw that wouldn't look?" returned Miss Horn, with a glance keen as an eagle's into the thoughtful eyes of her friend.

"Why not do by the writer of these as you have done by me? Why not take them to him?" suggested Mr Graham.

"That would be but clumsy work—to let go the end of your hank!" exclaimed Miss Horn.

"I do not understand you, ma'am."

"Well, I must make you understand me. Sometimes there are things, Sandy Graham, that aren't easy to speak about—but I have no feelings, and we'll all be dead ere long, and that's a comfort. Man that you are, you're the only human being I would open my mouth to about this matter, and that's because you love the memory of my poor lassie, Grizell Campbell."

"It is not her memory, it is herself I love," said the schoolmaster with trembling voice. "Tell me what you please: you may trust me."

"If I needed you to tell me that, I would trust you as I would the black dog with butter!—Listen, Sandy Graham."

The result of her communication and their following conference was, that she returned about midnight with a journey before her, the object of which was to place the letters in the safe keeping of a lawyer friend in the neighbouring county town.

Long before she reached home, Mrs Catanach had left—not without communication with her ally, in spite of a certain precaution adopted by her mistress, the first thing the latter did when she entered being to take the key of the cellar stairs from her pocket, and release Jean, who issued crestfallen and miserable, and was sternly dismissed to bed. The next day, however, for reasons of her own, Miss Horn permitted her to resume her duties about the house without remark, as if nothing had happened serious enough to render further measures necessary.

CHAPTER LX

THE SACRAMENT

Abandoning all her remaining effects to Jean's curiosity, if indeed it were no worse demon that possessed her, Miss Horn, carrying a large reticule, betook herself to the Lossie Arms, to await the arrival of the mail coach from the west, on which she was pretty sure of a vacant seat.

It was a still, frosty, finger-pinching dawn, and the rime lay thick wherever it could lie; but Miss Horn's red nose was carried in front of her in a manner that suggested nothing but defiance to the fiercest attacks of cold. Declining the offered shelter of the landlady's parlour, she planted herself on the steps of the inn, and there stood until the sound of the guard's horn came crackling through the frosty air, heralding the apparition of a flaming chariot, fit for the sun-god himself, who was now lifting his red radiance above the horizon. Having none inside, the guard gallantly offered his one lady-passenger a place in the heart of his vehicle, but she declined the attention—to him, on the ground of preferring the outside,—for herself, on the ground of uncertainty whether he had a right to bestow the privilege. But there was such a fire in her heart that no frost could chill her; such a bright bow in her west, that the sun now rising in the world's east was but a reflex of its splendour. True, the cloud against which it glowed was very dark with bygone wrong and suffering, but so much the more brilliant seemed the hope now arching the entrance of the future. Still, although she never felt the cold, and the journey was but of a few miles, it seemed long and wearisome to her active spirit, which would gladly have sent her tall person striding along, to relieve both by the discharge of the excessive generation of muscle-working electricity.

At length the coach drove into the town, and stopped at the Duff Arms. Miss Horn descended, straightened her long back with some difficulty, shook her feet, loosened her knees, and after a douceur to the guard more liberal than was customary, in acknowledgment of the kindness she had been unable to accept, marched off with the stride of a grenadier to find her lawyer.

Their interview did not relieve her of much of the time, which now hung upon her like a cloak of lead, and the earliness of the hour would not have deterred her from at once commencing a round of visits to the friends she had in the place; but the gates of the lovely environs of Fife House stood open, and although there were no flowers now, and the trees were leafless, waiting in poverty and patience for their coming riches, they drew her with the offer of a plentiful loneliness and room. She accepted it, entered, and for two hours wandered about their woods and walks.

Entering with her the well known domain, the thought meets me: what would be the effect on us men of such a periodical alternation between nothing and abundance as these woods undergo? Perhaps in the endless variety of worlds there may be one in which that is among the means whereby its dwellers are saved from self and lifted into life; a world in which during the one half of the year they walk in state, in splendour, in bounty, and during the other are plunged in penury and labour.

Such speculations were not in Miss Horn's way; but she was better than the loftiest of speculations, and we will follow her. By and by she came out of the woods, and found herself on the banks of the Wan Water, a broad, fine river, here talking in wide-rippled innocence from bank to bank, there lying silent and motionless and gloomy, as if all the secrets of the drowned since the creation of the world lay dim-floating in its shadowy bosom. In great sweeps it sought the ocean, and the trees stood back from its borders, leaving a broad margin of grass between, as if the better to see it go. Just outside the grounds and before reaching the sea, it passed under a long bridge of many arches—then, trees and grass and flowers and all greenery left behind, rushed through a waste of storm-heaped pebbles into the world-water. Miss Horn followed it out of the grounds and on to the beach.

Here its channel was constantly changing. Even while she stood gazing at its rapid rush, its bank of pebbles and sand fell almost from under her feet. But her thoughts were so busy that she scarcely observed even what she saw, and hence it was not strange that she should be unaware of having been followed and watched all the way. Now from behind a tree, now from a corner of the mausoleum, now from behind a rock, now over the parapet of the bridge, the mad laird had watched her. From a heap of shingle on the opposite side of the Wan Water, he was watching her now. Again and again he had made a sudden movement as if to run and accost her, but had always drawn back again and concealed himself more carefully than before.

At length she turned in the direction of the town. It was a quaint old place—a royal burgh for five centuries, with streets irregular and houses of much individuality. Most of the latter were humble in appearance, bare and hard in form, and gray in hue; but there were curious corners, low archways, uncompromising gables, some with corbel-steps—now and then an outside stair, a delicious little dormer window, or a gothic doorway, sometimes with a bit of carving over it.

With the bent head of the climber, Miss Horn was walking up a certain street, called from its precipitousness the Strait, that is *Difficult*, Path—an absolute Hill of Difficulty, when she was accosted by an elderly man, who stood in the doorway of one of the houses.

"Ken ye wha's yon watchin' ye frae the tap o' the brae, mem?" he said.

Miss Horn looked up: there was no one there.

"That's it! he's awa' again! That's the w'y he's been duin' this last hoor, at least, to *my* knowledge. I saw him watchin' ilka mov' ye made, mem, a' the time ye was doon upo' the shore—an' there he is noo, or was a meenute ago, at the heid o' the brae, glowerin' the een oot o' 's heid at ye, mem!"

"Div ye ken him?" asked Miss Horn.

"No, mem—'cep' by sicht o' ee; he hasna been lang aboot the toon. Some fowk say he's dementit; but he's unco quaiet, speyks to nobody, an' gien onybody speyk to him, jist rins. Cud he be kennin' you, no? ye're a stranger here, mem."

"No sic a stranger, John!" returned Miss Horn, calling the man by his name, for she recognized him as the beadle of the parish church. "What 's the body like?"

"A puir, wee, hump-backit cratur, wi' the face o' a gentleman."

"I ken him weel," said Miss Horn. "He *is* a gentleman—gien ever God made ane. But he 's sair afflickit. Whaur does he lie at nicht—can ye tell me?"

"I ken naething aboot him, mem, by what comes o' seein' him sic like 's the day, an' ance teetin in at the door o' the kirk. I wad hae weised him till a seat, but the moment I luikit at him, awa' he ran. He's unco cheenged though, sin' the first time I saw him."

"Do you know who that is, watching you from the top of the hill, ma'am?" he said.

Miss Horn looked up: there was no one there.

"That's it! he's away again! He's been at the same game this last hour, at least, to *my* knowledge. I saw him watching every move you made, ma'am, all the time you were down upon the shore—and there he is now, or was a minute ago, on the brow of the hill, glowering the eyes out of his head at you, ma'am!"

"Do you know him?" asked Miss Horn.

"No, ma'am—except to look at; he hasn't been long about the town. Some folk say he's demented; but he's very quiet, speaks to no one, and if anyone speaks to him, just runs. Is it possible he knows you? you're a stranger here, ma'am."

"Not such a stranger, John!" returned Miss Horn, calling the man by his name, for she recognized him as the beadle of the parish church. "What's the fellow like?"

"A poor, wee, hump-backed creature, with the face of a gentleman."

"I know him well," said Miss Horn. "He *is* a gentleman—if ever God made one. But he's sore afflicted. Where does he sleep at night—can you tell me?"

"I know nothing more of him, ma'am, than what comes of seeing him on days like today, and once peering in at the door of the church. I would have shown him to a seat, but the moment I looked at him, off he shot. He's much changed though, since the first time I saw him."

Since he lost Phemy, fear had been slaying him. No one knew where he slept; but in the daytime he haunted the streets, judging them safer than the fields or woods. The moment any one accosted him, however, he fled like the wind. He had "no art to find the mind's construction in the face;" and not knowing whom to trust, he distrusted all.

Humanity was good in his eyes, but there was no man. The vision of Miss Horn was like the dayspring from on high to him; with her near, the hosts of the Lord seemed to encamp around him; but the one word he had heard her utter about his back, had caused in him an invincible repugnance to appearing before her, and hence it was that at a distance he had haunted her steps without nearer approach.

There was indeed a change upon him! His clothes hung about him—not from their own ragged condition only, but also from the state of skin and bone to which he was reduced, his hump showing like a great peg over which they had been carelessly cast. Half the round of his eyes stood out from his face, whose pallor betokened the ever-recurring rush of the faintly sallying troops back to the citadel of the heart. He had always been ready to run, but now he looked as if nothing but weakness and weariness kept him from running always. Miss Horn had presently an opportunity of marking the sad alteration.

For ere she reached the head of the Strait Path, she heard sounds as of boys at play, and coming out on the level of the High Street, saw a crowd, mostly of little boys, in the angle made by a garden wall with a house whose gable stood half-way across the pavement. It being Saturday, they had just left school in all the exuberance of spirits to which a half-holiday gives occasion. In most of them the animal nature was, for the time at least, far wider awake than the human, and their proclivity towards the sport of the persecutor was strong. To them any living thing that looked at once odd and helpless was an outlaw—a creature to be tormented, or at best hunted beyond the visible world. A meagre cat, an overfed pet spaniel, a ditchless frog, a horse whose days hung over the verge of the knacker's yard—each was theirs in virtue of the amusement latent in it, which it was their business to draw out; but of all such property an idiot would yield the most, and a hunchback idiot, such as was the laird in their eyes, was absolutely invaluable—beyond comparison the best game in the known universe. When he left Portlossie, the laird knew pretty well what risks he ran, although he preferred even them to the dangers he hoped by his flight to avoid. It was he whom the crowd in question surrounded.

They had begun by rough teasing, to which he had responded with smiles—a result which did not at all gratify them, their chief object being to enrage him. They had therefore proceeded to small torments, and were ready to go on to worse, their object being with the laird hard to compass. Unhappily, there were amongst them two or three bigger boys.

The moment Miss Horn descried what they were about, she rushed into the midst of them, like a long bolt from a catapult, and scattering them right and left from their victim, turned and stood in front of him, regarding his persecutors with defiance in her flaming eye, and vengeance in her indignant nose. But there was about Miss Horn herself enough of the peculiar to mark her also, to the superficial observer, as the natural prey of boys; and the moment the first billow of consternation had passed and sunk, beginning to regard her as she stood, the vain imagination awoke in these young lords of misrule. They commenced their attack upon her by resuming it upon her protégé. She spread out her skirts, far from voluminous, to protect him as he cowered behind them, and so long as she was successful in shielding him, her wrath smouldered—but powerfully. At length one of the bigger boys, creeping slyly up behind the front row of smaller ones, succeeded in poking a piece of iron rod past her, and drawing a cry from the laird. Out blazed the lurking flame. The boy had risen, and was now attempting to prosecute like an ape, what he had commenced like a snake. Inspired by the God of armies—the Lord of hosts, she rushed upon him, and struck him into the gutter. He fell in the very spot where he had found his weapon, and there he lay. The Christian Amazon turned to the laird; overflowing with compassion she stooped and kissed his forehead, then took him by the hand to lead him away. But most of the enemy had gathered around their fallen comrade, and seized with some anxiety as to his condition, Miss Horn approached the group: the instant she turned towards it, the laird snatched his hand from hers, darted away like a hunting spider, and shot down the Strait Path to the low street: by the time his protectress had looked over the heads of the group, seen that the young miscreant was not seriously injured, and requested him to take that for meddling with a helpless inno-cent, the object of her solicitude, whom she supposed standing behind her, was nowhere to be seen. Twenty voices, now obsequious, were lifted to acquaint her with the direction in which he had gone; but it was vain to attempt following him, and she pursued her way, somewhat sore at his want of faith in her, to the house of a certain relative, a dressmaker, whom she visited as often as she went to Duff Harbour.

Now Miss Forsyth was one of a small sect of worshippers which had, not many years before, built a chapel in the town—a quiet, sober, devout company, differing from their neighbours in nothing deeply touching the welfare of humanity. Their chief fault was, that, attributing to comparative trifles a hugely disproportionate value, they would tear the garment in pieces rather than yield their notion of the right way of wrapping it together.

It so happened that, the next morning, a minister famous in the community was to preach to them, on which ground Miss Forsyth persuaded her relative to stop over the Sunday, and go with her to their chapel. Bethinking herself next that her minister had no sermon to prepare, she took Miss Horn to call upon him.

Mr Bigg was one of those men whose faculty is always underestimated by their acquaintances and overestimated by their friends; to overvalue him was impossible. He was not merely of the salt of the earth, but of the leaven of the kingdom, contributing more to the true life of the world than many a thousand far more widely-known and hon-oured. Such as this man are the chief springs of thought, feeling, inquiry, action, in their neighbourhood; they radiate help and breathe comfort; they reprove, they counsel, they sympathize; in a word, they are doorkeepers of the house of God. Constantly upon its threshold, and every moment pushing the door to peep in, they let out radiance enough to keep the hearts of men believing in the light. They make an atmosphere about them in which spiritual things can thrive, and out of their school often come men who do greater things, better they cannot do, than they.

Although a separatist as to externals, he was in heart a most catholic man—would have found himself far too catholic for the community over which he presided, had its members been capable of understanding him. Indeed, he had with many, although such was the force of his character that no one dared a word to that effect in his hearing, the reputation of being lax in his ideas of what constituted a saving faith; and most of the sect being very narrow-minded, if not small-hearted, in their limitations of the company fitly partaking of the last supper of our Lord—requiring proof of intellectual accord with themselves as to the *how* and *why* of many things, especially in regard of what they called the plan of salvation, he was generally judged to be misled by the deceitful kindliness of the depraved human heart in requiring as the ground of communion only such an uplook to Jesus as, when on earth, Jesus himself had responded to with healing. He was larger-hearted, and *therefore* larger-minded, than his people.

In the course of their conversation, Miss Forsyth recounted, with some humour, her visitor's prowess on behalf of the laird—much to honest Mr Bigg's delight.

"What ither cud I du?" said Miss Horn apologetically. "But I doobt I strack ower sair. Maybe ye wadna objec', sir, to gang and speir efter the laddie, an' gie him some guid advice?"

"I'll do that," returned Mr Bigg.—"Are we to have the pleasure of your company in our conventicle tomorrow?" he added, after a little pause. "Dr Blare is going to preach."

"Will ye hae me, Mr Bigg?"

"Most willingly, ma'am; and we'll be still better pleased if you'll sit down with us to the Lord's table afterwards."

"I gang to the perris kirk, ye ken," said Miss Horn, supposing the good man unaware of the fact.

"Oh! I know that, ma'am. But don't you think, as we shall, I trust, sit down together to his heavenly supper it would be a good preparation to sit down together, once at least, to his earthly supper first?"

"I didna ken 'at ye wad hae ony but yer ain fowk! I hae aften thoucht mysel', it was jist the ae thing ony Christian sud be ready to du wi' ony ither. Is 't a new thing wi' ye to haud open hoose this gait, sir,—gien I may tak the leeberty to speir?"

"What else could I do?" said Miss Horn apologetically. "But I'm afraid I struck too hard. Maybe you wouldn't object, sir, to go and ask after the laddie, and give him some good advice?"

"I'll do that," returned Mr Bigg.—"Are we to have the pleasure of your company in our conventicle tomorrow?" he added, after a little pause. "Dr Blare is going to preach."

"Will you have me, Mr Bigg?"

"Most willingly, ma'am; and we'll be still better pleased if you'll sit down with us to the Lord's table afterwards."

"I go to the parish church, you know," said Miss Horn, supposing the good man unaware of the fact.

"Oh! I know that, ma'am. But don't you think, as we shall, I trust, sit down together to his heavenly supper it would be a good preparation to sit down together, once at least, to his earthly supper first?"

"I didn't know that you would have any but your own folk! I have often thought myself, it was just the one thing any Christian should be ready to do with any other. Is it a new thing with you to keep open house that way, sir,—if I may take the liberty to ask?"

"We don't exactly keep open house. We wouldn't like to have any one with us who would count it poor fare. But still less would we like to exclude one of the Lord's friends. If that is a new thing, it ought to be an old one.—You believe in Jesus Christ—don't you, ma'am?"

"I dinna ken whether I believe in him as ye wad ca' believin' or no—there's sic a heap o' things broucht to the fore noo-adays 'at I canna richtly say I un'erstan'. But as he dee'd for me, I wad dee for him. Raither nor say I didna ken him, I wad hing aside him. Peter an' a', I canna say less."

Mr Bigg's eyes began to smart, and he turned away his head.

"Gien that 'll du wi' ye," Miss Horn went on, "an' ye mean nae desertion o' the kirk o' my father an' his fathers afore him, I wad willin'ly partak wi' ye."

"You'll be welcome, Miss Horn—as welcome, as any of my own flock."

"Weel, noo, that I ca' Christ-ian," said Miss Horn, rising. "An' 'deed I cud wuss," she added, "'at in oor ain kirk we had mair opportunity, for ance i' the twalmonth 's no verra aften to tak up the thouchts 'at belang to the holy ordnance."

The next day, after a powerful sermon from a man who, although in high esteem, was not for moral worth or heavenly insight to be compared with him whose place he took, they proceeded to the celebration of the Lord's supper, after the fashion of that portion of the church universal.

The communicants sat in several long pews facing the communion table, which was at the foot of the pulpit. After the reading of St Paul's account of the institution of the Lord's Supper, accompanied by prayers and addresses, the deacons carried the bread to the people, handing a slice to the first in each pew; each person in turn broke off a portion, and handed what remained to the next: thus they divided it among themselves.

It so happened that, in moving up to the communion seats, Miss Forsyth and Miss Horn were the last to enter one of them, and Miss Horn, very needlessly insisting on her custom of having her more capable ear towards her friend, occupied the place next the passage.

The service had hardly commenced, when she caught sight of the face of the mad laird peeping in at the door, which was in the side of the building, near where she sat. Their eyes met. With a half-repentant, half-apologetic look, he crept in, and, apparently to get as near his protectress as he could, sat down in the entrance of an empty pew, just opposite the one in which she was seated, on the other side of the narrow passage. His presence attracted little notice, for it was quite usual for individuals of the congregation who were not members of the church to linger on the outskirts of the company as spectators.

By the time the piece of bread reached Miss Horn from the other end, it was but a fragment. She broke it in two, and, reserving one part for herself, in place of handing the remnant to the deacon who stood ready to take it, stretched her arm across the passage, and gave it to Mr Stewart, who had been watching the proceedings intently. He received it from her hand, bent his head over it devoutly, and ate it, unconscious of the scandalized looks of the deacon, who knew nothing of the miserable object thus accepting rather than claiming a share in the common hope of men.

When the cup followed, the deacon was on the alert, ready to take it at once from the hands of Miss Horn. But as it left her lips she rose, grasping it in both hands, and with the dignity of a messenger of the Most High, before which the deacon drew back, bore it to the laird, and having made him drink the little that was left, yielded it to the conservator of holy privileges, with the words:

"Hoots, man! the puir body never had a taste o' the balm o' Gilead in a' 's persecutit life afore!"	"Heavens, man! the poor body never had a taste of the balm of Gilead in all his persecuted life before!"

The liberality of Mr Bigg had not been lost upon her: freely she had received—freely she gave. What was good must, because it was good, be divided with her neighbour. It was a lawless act.

As soon as the benediction was spoken, the laird slipped away, but as he left the seat, Miss Horn heard him murmur—"Eh, the bonny man! the bonny man!" He could hardly have meant the deacon. He might have meant Mr Bigg, who had concluded the observance with a simple and loving exhortation.

CHAPTER LXI

MISS HORN AND THE PIPER

When Miss Horn bethought herself that night, in prospect of returning home the next day, that she had been twice in the company of the laird and had not even thought of asking him about Phemy, she reproached herself not a little; and it was with shame that she set out, immediately on her arrival, to tell Malcolm that she had seen him. No one at the House being able to inform her where he was at the moment, she went on to Duncan's cottage. There she found the piper, who could not tell her where his boy was, but gave her a hearty welcome, and offered her a cup of tea, which, as it was now late in the afternoon, Miss Horn gladly accepted. As he bustled about to prepare it, refusing all assistance from his guest, he began to open his mind to her on a subject much in his thoughts—namely, Malcolm's inexplicable aversion to Mrs Stewart.

"Ta nem of Stewart will pe a nople worrt, mem," he said.

"Ta name of Stewart will be a noble wort, mem," he said.

"It's guid eneuch to ken a body by," answered Miss Horn.

"It's good enough to know a body by," answered Miss Horn.

"If ta poy will pe a Stewart," he went on, heedless of the indifference of her remark, "who'll pe knowing put he'll may pe of ta plood royal!"

"If ta boy will be a Stewart," he went on, heedless of the indifference of her remark, "who'll be knowing but he'll may be of ta blood royal!"

"There didna leuk to be muckle royalty aboot auld John, honest man, wha cudna rule a wife, though he had but ane!" returned Miss Horn.

"There was little sign of royalty about old John, honest man, who couldn't rule a wife, though he had but one!" returned Miss Horn.

"If you'll please, mem, ton't you'll pe too sherp on ta poor man whose wife will not pe ta coot wife. If ta wife will pe ta paad wife, she will pe ta paad wife however, and ta poor man will pe hafing ta paad wife and ta paad plame of it too, and tat will pe more as 'll pe fair, mem."

"If you'll please, mem, ton't you'll be too sharp on ta poor man whose wife will not be ta coot wife. If ta wife will be ta baad wife, she will be ta baad wife however, and ta poor man will be hafing ta baad wife and ta baad blame of it too, and tat will be more as (than) 'll be fair, mem."

"'Deed ye never said a truer word, Maister MacPhail!" assented Miss Horn. "It's a mercy 'at a lone wuman like me, wha has a maisterfu' temper o' her ain, an' nae feelin's, was never putten to the temptation o' occkypeein' sic a perilous position. I doobt gien auld John had been married upo' me, I micht hae putten on the wrang claes some mornin' mysel', an' may be had ill gettin' o' them aff again."

The old man was silent, and Miss Horn resumed the main subject of their conversation.

"But though he michtna objec' till a father 'at he wasna jist Hector or Golia' o' Gath," she said, "ye canna wonner at the yoong laad no carin' to hae sic a mither."

"And what would pe ta harm with ta mother? Will she not pe a coot woman, and a coot letty more to ta bargain?"

"Ye ken what fowk says till her guideship o' her son?"

"Yes; put tat will pe ta lies of ta peoples. Ta peoples wass always telling lies."

"Weel, allooin', it's a peety ye sudna ken, supposin' him to be hers, hoo sma' fowk hauds the chance o' his bein' a Stewart, for a' that!"

"She'll not pe comprestanding you," said Duncan, bewildered.

"He's a wise son 'at kens his ain faither!" remarked Miss Horn, with more point than originality. "The leddy never bore the best o' characters, as far 's my memory taks me,—an' that's back afore John an' her was married ony gait. Na, na; John Stewart never took a dwaum 'cause Ma'colm MacPhail was upo' the ro'd."

"Indeed you never said a truer word, Mister MacPhail!" assented Miss Horn. "It's a mercy that a lone woman like me, who has a masterful temper of her own, and no feelings, was never put to the test of occupying such a perilous post. I suspect if old John had been married to me, I might have put the wrong clothes on some morning, and had a hard job getting them off again."

The old man was silent, and Miss Horn resumed the main subject of their conversation.

"But though he might not object to a father because he wasn't quite Hector or Goliath of Gath," she said, "you can't wonder at the young lad not caring to have such a mother."

"And what would pe ta harm with ta mother? Will she not be a coot woman, and a coot letty more to ta bargain?"

"You know the rumours about how she's treated her son?"

"Yes; but tat will be ta lies of ta peoples. Ta peoples wass always telling lies."

"Well, granting what you say, you ought to know, supposing him to be hers, what long odds folk lay against his being a Stewart, for all that!"

"She'll not be comprestanding you," said Duncan, bewildered.

"He's a wise son that knows his own father!" remarked Miss Horn, with more point than originality. "The lady never bore the best of characters, as far as my memory takes me,—and that's back before John and she were married anyway. Na, na; John Stewart never turned faint because Malcolm MacPhail was on the way."

Miss Horn was sufficiently enigmatical; but her meaning had at length, more through his own reflection than her exposition, dawned upon Duncan. He leaped up with a Gaelic explosion of concentrated force, and cried,

"Ta woman is not pe no mothers to Tuncan's poy!"

"Huly, huly, Mr MacPhail!" interposed Miss Horn, with good-natured revenge; "it may be naething but fowk's lees, ye ken."

"Ta woman tat ta peoples will pe telling lies of her, wass not pe ta mother of her poy Malcolm. Why tidn't ta poy tell her ta why tat he wouldn't pe hafing her?"

"Ye wadna hae him spread an ill report o' his ain mither?"

"Put she'll not pe his mother, and you'll not pelieve it, mem."

"Ye canna priv that—you nor him aither."

"It will pe more as would kill her poy to haf a woman like tat to ta mother of him."

"It wad be near han' as ill as haein' her for a wife," assented Miss Horn; "but no freely," she added.

The old man sought the door, as if for a breath of air; but as he went, he blundered, and felt about as if he had just been struck blind; ordinarily he walked in his own house at least, as if he saw every inch of the way. Presently he returned and resumed his seat.

"Was the bairn laid mither-nakit intill yer han's, Maister MacPhail?" asked Miss Horn, who had been meditating.

"Och! no; he wass his clo'es on," answered Duncan.

"Hae ye ony o' them left?" she asked again.

Miss Horn was sufficiently enigmatical; but her meaning had at length, more through his own reflection than her exposition, dawned upon Duncan. He leaped up with a Gaelic explosion of concentrated force, and cried,

"Ta woman is not be no mothers to Tuncan's boy!"

"Softly, now, Mr MacPhail!" interposed Miss Horn, with good-natured revenge; "it may be nothing but folk's lies, you know."

"Ta woman tat ta peoples will be telling lies of her, wass not be ta mother of her boy Malcolm. Why tidn't ta boy tell her ta why tat he wouldn't be hafing her?"

"You wouldn't have him spread an ill report of his own mother?"

"But she'll not be his mother, and you'll not believe it, mem."

"You can't prove that—and nor can he."

"It will be more as would kill her boy to haf a woman like tat for ta mother of him."

"It would be nearly as bad as having her for a wife," assented Miss Horn; "but not quite," she added.

The old man sought the door, as if for a breath of air; but as he went, he blundered, and felt about as if he had just been struck blind; ordinarily he walked in his own house at least, as if he saw every inch of the way. Presently he returned and resumed his seat.

"Was the child laid mother-naked into your hands, Mister MacPhail?" asked Miss Horn, who had been meditating.

"Och! no; he wass his clo'es on," answered Duncan.

"Have you any of them left?" she asked again.

"Inteet not," answered Duncan. "Yes, inteet not."

"Ye lay at the Salmon, didna ye?"

"Yes, mem, and they wass coot to her."

"Wha drest the bairn till ye?"

"Och! She'll trest him herself," said Duncan, still jealous of the women who had nursed the child.

"But no aye?" suggested Miss Horn.

"Mistress Partan will pe toing a coot teal of tressing him, sometimes. Mistress Partan is a coot 'oman when she'll pe coot—fery coot when she'll pe coot."

Here Malcolm entered, and Miss Horn told him what she had seen of the laird, and gathered concerning him.

"That luiks ill for Phemy," remarked Malcolm, when she had described his forlorn condition. "She canna be wi' 'im, or he wadna be like that. Hae ye onything by w'y o' coonsel, mem?"

"I wad coonsel a word wi' the laird himsel'—gien 't be to be gotten. He mayna ken what 's happent her, but he may tell ye the last he saw o' her, an' that maun be mair nor ye ken."

"He 's taen sic a doobt o' me 'at I'm feart it 'll be hard to come at him, an' still harder to come at speech o' 'im, for whan he 's frichtit he can hardly muv is jawbane—no to say speyk. I maun try though and du my best. Ye think he's lurkin' aboot Fife Hoose, div ye, mem?"

"He's been seen thereawa' this while—aff an' on."

"Weel, I s' jist gang an' put on my fisher-claes, an set oot at ance. I maun haud ower to Scaurnose first, though, to lat them ken 'at he 's been gotten sicht o'. It 'll be but sma' comfort, I doobt."

"Inteet not," answered Duncan. "Yes, inteet not."

"You stayed at the Salmon, didn't you?"

"Yes, mem, and they wass coot to her."

"Who dressed the babe for you?"

"Och! She'll trest him herself," said Duncan, still jealous of the women who had nursed the child.

"But not always?" suggested Miss Horn.

"Mistress Partan will pe toing a coot teal of tressing him, sometimes. Mistress Partan is a coot 'oman when she'll pe coot—fery coot when she'll pe coot."

Here Malcolm entered, and Miss Horn told him what she had seen of the laird, and gathered concerning him.

"That looks bad for Phemy," remarked Malcolm, when she had described his forlorn condition. "She can't be with him, or he wouldn't be like that. Have you anything by way of advice, ma'am?"

"I would advise a word with the laird himself—if it's to be had. He may not know what's become of her, but he may tell you the last he saw of her, and that must be more than you know."

"He's grown so suspicious of me that I'm afraid it'll be hard to come at him, and still harder to come to speech with him, for when he's frightened he can hardly move his jaw—not to say speak. I must try though and do my best. You think he's lurking about Fife House, do you, ma'am?"

"He's been seen in those parts this while—off and on."

"Well, I'll just go and put on my fisher-clothes, and set out at once. I must go in past Scaurnose first, though, to let them know he's been seen. It'll be but small comfort, I expect."

"Malcolm, my son," interjected Duncan, who had been watching for the conversation to afford him an opening, "if you'll pe meeting any one will caal you ta son of tat woman, gif him a coot plow in ta face, for you'll pe no son of hers, efen if she'll proof it—no more as hersel. If you'll pe her son, old Tuncan will pe tisown you for efer, and efermore, amen."

"What's broucht you to this, daddie?" asked Malcolm, who, ill as he liked the least allusion to the matter, could not help feeling curious, and indeed almost amused.

"Nefer you mind. Miss Horn will pe hafing coot reasons tat Mistress Stewart 'll not can pe your mother."

Malcolm turned to Miss Horn.

"I've said naething to Maister MacPhail but what I've said mair nor ance to yersel', laddie," she replied to the eager questioning of his eyes. "Gang yer wa's. The trowth maun cow the lee i' the lang rin. Aff wi' ye to Blue Peter!"

"Malcolm, my son," interjected Duncan, who had been watching for the conversation to afford him an opening, "if you'll be meeting any one will caal you ta son of tat woman, gif him a coot blow in ta face, for you'll be no son of hers, efen if she'll proof it—no more as hersel. If you'll be her son, old Tuncan will be tisown you for efer, and efermore, amen."

"What's brought you to this, daddy?" asked Malcolm, who, ill as he liked the least allusion to the matter, could not help feeling curious, and indeed almost amused.

"Nefer you mind. Miss Horn will be hafing coot reasons tat Mistress Stewart 'll not can be your mother."

Malcolm turned to Miss Horn.

"I've said nothing to Mister MacPhail but what I've said more than once to yourself, laddie," she replied to the eager questioning of his eyes. "On your way, now. The truth must cow the lie in the long run. Off with you to Blue Peter!"

When Malcolm reached Scaurnose he found Phemy's parents in a sad state. Joseph had returned that morning from a fruitless search in a fresh direction, and reiterated disappointment seemed to have at length overcome Annie's endurance, for she had taken to her bed. Joseph was sitting before the fire on a three-legged stool rocking himself to and fro in a dull agony. When he heard Malcolm's voice, he jumped to his feet, and a flash of hope shot from his eyes: but when he had heard all, he sat down again without a word, and began rocking himself as before. Mrs Mair was lying in the darkened closet, where, the door being partly open, she had been listening with all her might, and was now weeping afresh. Joseph was the first to speak: still rocking himself with hopeless oscillation, he said, in a strange muffled tone which seemed to come from somewhere else—

"Gien I kent she was weel deid I wadna care. It's no like a father to be sittin' here, but whaur 'll I gang neist? The wife thinks I micht be duin' something: I kenna what to du. This last news is waur nor nane. I hae maist nae faith left. Ma'colm, man!" and with a bitter cry he started to his feet—"I maist dinna believe there's a God ava'. It disna luik like it—dis 't noo?"

"If I knew she was well dead I wouldn't care. It's not like a father to be sitting here, but where am I to go next? The wife thinks I might be doing something: I don't know what to do. This last news is worse than none. My faith is almost gone. Malcolm, man!" and with a bitter cry he started to his feet—"I hardly believe there's a God at all. It doesn't look like it—does it now?"

There came an answering cry from the closet; Annie rushed out, half undressed, and threw her arms about her husband.

"Joseph! Joseph!" she said, in a voice hard with agony—almost more dreadful than a scream—"gien ye speyk like that, ye'll drive me mad. Lat the lassie gang, but lea' me my God!" Joseph pushed her gently away; turned from her, fell on his knees, and moaned out—"O God, gien thoo has her, we s' neither greit nor grum'le: but dinna tak the faith frae 's."

He remained on his knees silent, with his head against the chimney-jamb. His wife crept away to her closet.

"Peter," said Malcolm, "I'm gaein' aff the nicht to luik for the laird, and see gien he can tell 's onything aboot her: wadna ye better come wi' me?"

There came an answering cry from the closet; Annie rushed out, half undressed, and threw her arms about her husband.

"Joseph! Joseph!" she said, in a voice hard with agony—almost more dreadful than a scream—"if you speak like that, you'll drive me mad. Let the lassie go, but leave me my God!" Joseph pushed her gently away; turned from her, fell on his knees, and moaned out—"O God, if thou has her, we shall neither cry nor grumble: but don't take our faith from us."

He remained on his knees silent, with his head against the chimney-jamb. His wife crept away to her closet.

"Peter," said Malcolm, "I'm going off tonight to look for the laird, and see if he can tell us anything about her: hadn't you better come with me?"

To the heart of the father it was as the hope of the resurrection of the world. The same moment he was on his feet and taking down his bonnet; the next he disappeared in the closet, and Malcolm heard the tinkling of the money in the lidless teapot; then out he came with a tear on his face and a glimmer in his eyes.

The sun was down, and a bone-piercing chill, incarnate in the vague mist that haunted the ground, assailed them as they left the cottage. The sea moaned drearily. A smoke seemed to ascend from the horizon halfway to the zenith, something too thin for cloud, too black for vapour; above that the stars were beginning to shine. Joseph shivered and struck his hands against his shoulders.

"Care's cauldrife," he said, and strode on.

"Care chills," he said, and strode on.

Almost in silence they walked together to the county town, put up at a little inn near the river, and at once began to make inquiries. Not a few persons had seen the laird at different times, but none knew where he slept or chiefly haunted. There was nothing for it but to set out in the morning, and stray hither and thither, on the chance of somewhere finding him.

CHAPTER LXII

THE CUTTLE FISH AND THE CRAB

Although the better portion of the original assembly had forsaken the Baillies' Barn, there was still a regular gathering in it as before, and if possible even a greater manifestation of zeal for the conversion of sinners. True, it might not be clear to an outsider that they always made a difference between being converted and joining their company, so ready were they to mix up the two in their utterances; and the results of what they counted conversion were sometimes such as the opponents of their proceedings would have had them: the arrogant became yet more arrogant, and the greedy more greedy; the tongues of the talkative went yet faster, and the gad-abouts were yet seldomer at home, while there was such a superabundance of private judgment that it overflowed the cisterns of their own concerns, and invaded the walled gardens of other people's motives: yet, notwithstanding, the good people got good, if the other sort got evil; for the meek shall inherit the earth, even when the priest ascends the throne of Augustus. No worst thing ever done in the name of Christianity, no vilest corruption of the Church, can destroy the eternal fact that the core of it is in the heart of Jesus. Branches innumerable may have to be lopped off and cast into the fire, yet the word *I am the vine* remaineth.

The demagogues had gloried in the expulsion of such men as Jeames Gentle and Blue Peter, and were soon rejoiced by the return of Bow o' meal—after a season of backsliding to the fleshpots of Egypt, as they called the services of the parish church—to the bosom of the Barn, where he soon was again one of the chief amongst them. Meantime the circles of their emanating influence continued to spread, until at length they reached the lower classes of the upper town, of whom a few began to go to Barn. Amongst them, for reasons best known to herself, though they might be surmised by such as really knew her, was Mrs Catanach. I do not know that she ever professed repentance and conversion, but for a while she attended pretty often. Possibly business considerations had something to do with it. Assuredly the young preacher, though he still continued to exhort, did so with failing strength, and it was plain to see that he was going rapidly: the exercise of the second of her twin callings might be required. She could not, however, have been drawn by any large expectations as to the honorarium. Still, she would gain what she prized even more—a position for the moment at the heart of affairs, with its excelling chances of hearing and overhearing. Never had lover of old books half the delight in fitting together a rare volume from scattered portions picked up in his travels, than Mrs Catanach found in vitalizing stray remarks, arranging odds and ends of news, and cementing the many fragments, with the help of the babblings of gossip, into a plausible whole; intellectually considered, her special pursuit was inasmuch the nobler as the faculties it brought into exercise were more delicate and various; and if her devotion to the minutia of biography had no high end in view, it never caused her to lose sight of what ends she had, by involving her in opinions, prejudices, or disputes: however she might break out at times, her general policy was to avoid quarrelling. There was a strong natural antagonism between her and the Partaness, but she had never shown the least dislike to her, and that although Mrs Findlay had never lost an opportunity of manifesting hers to the midwife. Indeed, having gained a pretext by her ministrations to Lizzy when overcome by the suggestions of the dog-sermon, Mrs Catanach had assayed an approach to her mother, and not without success. After the discovery of the physical cause of Lizzy's ailment, however, Mrs Findlay had sought, by might of rude resolve, to break loose from the encroaching acquaintanceship, but had found, as yet, that the hard-shelled crab was not a match for the glutinous cuttlefish.

On the evening of the Sunday following the events related in the last chapter, Mrs Catanach had, not without difficulty, persuaded Mrs Findlay to accompany her to the Baillies' Barn, with the promise of a wonderful sermon from a new preacher—a ploughman on an inland farm. That she had an object in desiring her company that night, may seem probable from the conversation which arose as they plodded their way thither along the sands.

"I h'ard a queer tale aboot Meg Horn at Duff Harbour the ither day," said the midwife, speaking thus disrespectfully both to ease her own heart and to call forth the feelings of her companion, who also, she knew, disliked Miss Horn.

"Ay! an' what micht that be?"

"But she's maybe a freen' o' yours, Mrs Findlay? Some fowk likes her, though I canna say I'm ane o' them."

"Freen' o' mine!" exclaimed the Partaness. "We gree like twa bills i' the same park!"

"I wadna wonner!—for they tellt me 'at saw her fechtin' i' the High Street wi' a muckle loon, near-han' as big 's hersel'! an' haith, but Meg had the best o' 't, an' flang him intil the gutter, an' maist fellt him! An' that's Meg Horn!"

"She had been at the drink! But I never h'ard it laid till her afore."

"Didna ye than? Weel, I'm no sayin' onything—that's what I h'ard."

"Ow, it 's like eneuch! She was bulliraggin' at me nae langer ago nor thestreen; but I doobt I sent her awa' wi' a flech in her lug!"

"Whaten a craw had she to pluck wi' *you*, no?"

"Ow fegs! ye wad hae ta'en her for a thief-catcher, and me for the thief! She wad threpe 'at I bude to hae keepit some o' the duds 'at happit Ma'colm MacPhail the reprobat, whan first he cam to the Seaton—a puir scraichin' brat, as reid 's a bilet lobster. Wae 's me 'at ever he was creatit! It jist drives me horn daft to think 'at ever he got the breast o' me. 'At *he* sud sair me sae! But I s' hae a grip o' 'im yet, or my name 's no—what they ca' me."

"It's the w'y o' the warl', Mistress Findlay. What cud ye expec' o' ane born in sin an' broucht furth in ineequity?"—a stock phrase of Mrs Catanach's, glancing at her profession, and embracing nearly the whole of her belief.

"It's a true word. The mair 's the peety he sud hae hed the milk o' an honest wuman upo' the tap o' that!"

"But what cud the auld runt be efter? What was *her* business wi' 't? *She* never did onything for the bairn."

"Na, no *she*! She never had the chance, guid or ill—Ow! doobtless it wad be anent what they ca' the eedentryfeein' o' 'im to the leddy o Gersefell. *She* had sent her. She micht hae waled a mair welcome messenger, an' sent her a better eeran! But she made little o' me."

"*Ye* had naething o' the kin', I s' wad."

"She had been at the drink! But I never heard it laid to her before."

"Didn't you then? Well, I'm saying nothing—that's what I heard."

"Oh, I don't doubt it! She was bullyragging at me only last night; but I think I sent her packing with a flea in her ear!"

"What kind of crow had she to pluck with *you*, now?"

"Oh! you would have thought her a thief-catcher, and me the thief! By her way of it, I must have kept some of the clothes that swaddled that reprobate Malcolm MacPhail, when first he came to the Seaton—a poor screeching brat, as red as a boiled lobster. Woe's me that he was ever created! It just drives me mad to think that ever I gave him suck. That *he* should serve me so! But I'll get a grip of him yet, or my name's not—what they call me!"

"It's the way of the world, Mistress Findlay. What could you expect of one born in sin and brought forth in iniquity?"—a stock phrase of Mrs Catanach's, glancing at her profession, and embracing nearly the whole of her belief.

"It's a true word. The more's the pity he should have had the milk of an honest woman to boot!"

"But what could the old runt be after? What makes it *her* business? *She* never did anything for the child."

"Na, not *she*! She never had the chance, good or ill—Oh! doubtless it would be to do with what they call the identifying of him to the lady of Gersefell. *She* had sent her. She might have chosen a more welcome messenger, and sent her a better errand! But she made little of me."

"*You* had nothing of the kind, I'll wager."

"Never a threid. There *was* a twal-hunner shift upo' the bairn, rowt roon 'im like deid-claes:—gien 't had been but the Lord's wull! It gart me wonner at the time, for that wasna hoo a bairn 'at had been caret for sud be cled."

"Was there name or mark upo' 't?" asked cuttlefish.

"Nane; there was but the place whaur the reid ingrain had been pykit oot," answered crab.

"An what cam o' the shift?"

"Ow, I jist made it doon for a bit sark to the bairn whan he grew to be rinnin' aboot. 'At ever I sud hae ta'en steik in claith for sic a deil's buckie! To *me* 'at was a mither till 'im! The Lord haud me ohn gane mad whan I think o' 't!"

"An' syne for Lizzy!—" began Mrs Catanach, prefacing fresh remark.

But at her name the mother flew into such a rage that, fearful of scandal, seeing it was the Sabbath and they were on their way to public worship, her companion would have exerted all her powers of oiliest persuasion to appease her. But if there was one thing Mrs Catanach did not understand it was the heart of a mother.

"Hoots, Mistress Findlay! Fowk 'll hear ye. Haud yer tongue, I beg. She may dee i' the strae for me. I s' never put han' to the savin' o' her, or her bairn aither," said the midwife, thinking thus to pacify her.

"Not a thread. There *was* a twelve-hundred shift on the babe, wrapped round him like dead-clothes:—had it been but the Lord's will! It made me wonder at the time, for that wasn't how a baby that had been cared for should be clothed."

"Was there name or mark upon it?" asked cuttlefish.

"None; there was but the place where the red ingrain had been picked out," answered crab.

"And what came of the shift?"

"Oh, I just turned it into a shirt for the child when he grew to be running about. That ever I should have put stitch in cloth for such a snake! To *me* that was a mother to him! The Lord keep me sane when I think of it!"

"And then for Lizzy!—" began Mrs Catanach, prefacing fresh remark.

But at her name the mother flew into such a rage that, fearful of scandal, seeing it was the Sabbath and they were on their way to public worship, her companion would have exerted all her powers of oiliest persuasion to appease her. But if there was one thing Mrs Catanach did not understand it was the heart of a mother.

"Heavens, Mistress Findlay! Folk'll hear you. Hold your tongue, I beg. She may die in the straw for me. I'll never put hand to the saving of her, or her child either," said the midwife, thinking thus to pacify her.

Then, like the eruption following mere volcanic unrest, out brake the sore-hearted woman's wrath. And now at length the crustacean was too much for the mollusk. She raved and scolded and abused Mrs Catanach, till at last she was driven to that final resource—the airs of an injured woman. She turned and walked back to the upper town, while Mrs Findlay went on to take what share she might in the worship of the congregation.

Mrs Mair had that evening gone once more to the Baillies' Barn in her husband's absence; for the words of unbelief he had uttered in the Job-like agony of his soul, had haunted the heart of his spouse, until she too felt as if she could hardly believe in a God.

Few know what a poor thing their faith is till the trial comes. And in the weakness consequent on protracted suffering, she had begun to fancy that the loss of Phemy was a punishment upon them for deserting the conventicle. Also the schoolmaster was under an interdict, and that looked like a judgment too! She must find some prop for the faith that was now shaking like a reed in the wind. So to the Baillies' Barn she had gone.

The tempest which had convulsed Mrs Findlay's atmosphere, had swept its vapours with it as it passed away; and when she entered the cavern, it was with an unwonted inclination to be friendly all round. As fate would have it, she unwittingly took her place by Mrs Mair, whom she had not seen since she gave Lizzy shelter. When she discovered who her neighbour was, she started away, and stared; but she had had enough of quarrelling for the evening, and besides had not had time to bar her door against the angel Pity, who suddenly stepped across the threshhold of her heart with the sight of Mrs Mair's pale thin cheeks and tear-reddened eyes. As suddenly, however, an indwelling demon of her own house, whose name was Envy, arose from the ashes of her hearth to meet the white-robed visitant: Phemy, poor little harmless thing, was safe enough! who would harm a hair of her? but Lizzy! And this woman had taken in the fugitive from honest chastisement! She would yet have sought another seat but the congregation rose to sing; and her neighbour's offer of the use in common of her psalm book, was enough to quiet for the moment the gaseous brain of the turbulent woman. She accepted the kindness, and, the singing over, did not refuse to look on the same holy page with her daughter's friend, while the ploughman read, with fitting simplicity, the parable of the Prodigal Son. It touched something in both, but a different something in each. Strange to say, neither applied it to her own case, but each to her neighbour's. As the reader uttered the words "was lost and is found" and ceased, each turned to the other with a whisper. Mrs Mair persisted in hers; and the other, which was odd enough, yielded and listened.

"Wad the tale haud wi' lassies as weel 's laddies, Mistress Findlay, div ye think?" said Mrs Mair.

"Ow, surely!" was the response; "it maun du that. There no respec' o' persons wi' *him*. There's no a doobt but yer Phemy 'ill come hame to ye safe an' soon'."

"I was thinkin' aboot Lizzy," said the other, a little astonished; and then the prayer began, and they had to be silent.

The sermon of the ploughman was both dull and sensible,—an excellent variety where few of the sermons were either; but it made little impression on Mrs Findlay or Mrs Mair.

"Would the tale hold true for lassies as well's laddies, Mistress Findlay, think you?" said Mrs Mair.

"Oh, surely!" was the response; "it must do that. There's no respect of persons with *him*. Your Phemy will surely come home to you safe and sound."

"I was thinking about Lizzy," said the other, a little astonished; and then the prayer began, and they had to be silent.

The sermon of the ploughman was both dull and sensible,—an excellent variety where few of the sermons were either; but it made little impression on Mrs Findlay or Mrs Mair.

As they left the cave together in the crowd of issuing worshippers, Mrs Mair whispered again:

"I wad invete ye ower, but ye wad be wantin' Lizzy hame, an' I can ill spare the comfort o' her the noo," she said, with the cunning of a dove.

"An' what comes o' *me?*" rejoined Mrs Findlay, her claws out in a moment where her personal consequence was touched.

"Ye wadna surely tak her frae me a' at ance!" pleaded Mrs Mair. "Ye micht lat her bide—jist till Phemy comes hame; an' syne—"

But there she broke down; and the tempest of sobs that followed quite overcame the heart of Mrs Findlay. She was, in truth, a woman like another; only being of the crustacean order, she had not yet swallowed her skeleton, as all of us have to do more or less, sooner or later, the idea of that scaffolding being that it should be out of sight. With the best commonplaces at her command she sought to comfort her companion; walked with her to the foot of the red path; found her much more to her mind than Mrs Catanach: seemed inclined to go with her all the way, but suddenly stopped, bade her goodnight, and left her.

As they left the cave together in the crowd of issuing worshippers, Mrs Mair whispered again:

"I would invite you over, but you'd be wanting Lizzy home, and I can ill spare her comfort just now," she said, with the cunning of a dove.

"And what of *me?*" rejoined Mrs Findlay, her claws out in a moment where her personal consequence was touched.

"You wouldn't surely take her from me all at once!" pleaded Mrs Mair. "You might let her stay—just till Phemy comes home; and then—"

But there she broke down; and the tempest of sobs that followed quite overcame the heart of Mrs Findlay. She was, in truth, a woman like another; only being of the crustacean order, she had not yet swallowed her skeleton, as all of us have to do more or less, sooner or later, the idea of that scaffolding being that it should be out of sight. With the best commonplaces at her command she sought to comfort her companion; walked with her to the foot of the red path; found her much more to her mind than Mrs Catanach: seemed inclined to go with her all the way, but suddenly stopped, bade her goodnight, and left her.

CHAPTER LXIII

MISS HORN AND LORD LOSSIE

Notwithstanding the quarrel, Mrs Catanach did not return without having gained something; she had learned that Miss Horn had been foiled in what she had no doubt was an attempt to obtain proof that Malcolm was not the son of Mrs Stewart. The discovery was a grateful one; for who could have told but there might be something in existence to connect him with another origin than she and Mrs Stewart would assign him?

The next day the marquis returned. Almost his first word was the desire that Malcolm should be sent to him. But nobody knew more than that he was missing; whereupon he sent for Duncan. The old man explained his boy's absence, and as soon as he was dismissed, took his way to the town, and called upon Miss Horn. In half an hour, the good lady started on foot for Duff Harbour. It was already growing dark; but there was one feeling Miss Horn had certainly been created without, and that was *fear*.

As she approached her destination, tramping eagerly along, in a half-cloudy, half star-lit night, with a damp east wind blowing cold from the German Ocean, she was startled by the swift rush of something dark across the road before her. It came out of a small wood on the left towards the sea, and bolted through a hedge on the right.

"Is that you, laird?" she cried; but there came no answer.

She walked straight to the house of her lawyer-friend, and, after an hour's rest, the same night set out again for Portlossie, which she reached in safety by her bedtime.

Lord Lossie was very accessible. Like Shakspere's Prince Hal, he was so much interested in the varieties of the outcome of human character, that he would not willingly lose a chance of seeing "more man." If the individual proved a bore, he would get rid of him without remorse; if amusing, he would contrive to prolong the interview. There was a great deal of undeveloped humanity somewhere in his lordship, one of whose indications was this spectacular interest in his kind. As to their bygone history, how they fared out of his sight, or what might become of them, he never gave a thought to anything of the kind—never felt the pull of one of the bonds of brotherhood, laughed at them the moment they were gone, or, if a woman's story had touched him, wiped his eyes with an oath, and thought himself too good a fellow for this world.

Since his retirement from the more indolent life of the metropolis to the quieter and more active pursuits of the country, his character had bettered a little—inasmuch as it was a shade more accessible to spiritual influences; the hard soil had in a few places cracked a hair's-breadth, and lay thus far open to the search of those sun-rays which, when they find the human germ, that is, the conscience, straightway begin to sting it into life. To this betterment the company of his daughter had chiefly contributed; for if she was little more developed in the right direction than himself she was far less developed in the wrong, and the play of affection between them was the divinest influence that could as yet be brought to bear upon either; but certain circumstances of late occurrence had had a share in it, occasioning a revival of old memories which had a considerably sobering effect upon him.

As he sat at breakfast, about eleven o'clock on the morning after his return, one of his English servants entered with the message that a person, calling herself Miss Horn, and refusing to explain her business desired to see his lordship for a few minutes.

"Who is she?" asked the marquis.

The man did not know.

"What is she like?"

"An odd-looking old lady, my lord, and very oddly dressed."

"Show her into the next room. I shall be with her directly."

Finishing his cup of coffee and pea-fowl's egg with deliberation, while he tried his best to recall in what connection he could have heard the name before, the marquis at length sauntered into the morning room in his dressing-gown, with the *Times* of the day before yesterday, just arrived, in his hand. There stood his visitor waiting for him, such as my reader knows her, black and gaunt and grim, in a bay window, whose light almost surrounded her, so that there was scarcely a shadow about her, and yet to the eyes of the marquis she seemed wrapped in shadows. Mysterious as some sybil, whose being held secrets the first whisper of which had turned her old, but made her immortal, she towered before him, with her eyes fixed upon him, and neither spoke nor moved.

"To what am I indebted—?" began his lordship; but Miss Horn speedily interrupted his courtesy.

"Own to nae debt, my lord, till ye ken what it 's for," she said, without a tone or inflection to indicate a pleasantry.

"Good!" returned his lordship, and waited with a smile. She promised amusement, and he was ready for it—but it hardly came.

"Ken ye that han' o' wreet, my lord?" she inquired, sternly advancing a step, and holding out a scrap of paper at arm's length, as if presenting a pistol.

"To what am I indebted—?" began his lordship; but Miss Horn speedily interrupted his courtesy.

"Own to no debt, my lord, till you know what it's for," she said, without a tone or inflection to indicate a pleasantry.

"Good!" returned his lordship, and waited with a smile. She promised amusement, and he was ready for it—but it hardly came.

"Do you know that handwriting, my lord?" she inquired, sternly advancing a step, and holding out a scrap of paper at arm's length, as if presenting a pistol.

The marquis took it. In his countenance curiosity had mingled with the expectation. He glanced at it. A shadow swept over his face but vanished instantly: the mask of impervious non-expression which a man of his breeding always knows how to assume, was already on his visage.

"Where did you get this?" he said quietly, with just the slightest catch in his voice.

"I got it, my lord, whaur there's mair like it."

"Show me them."

"I hae shawn ye plenty for a swatch, my lord."

"You refuse?" said the marquis; and the tone of the question was like the first cold puff that indicates a change of weather.

"I div, my lord," she answered imperturbably.

"If they are not my property, why do you bring me this?"

"Are they your property, my lord?"

"This is my handwriting."

"Ye alloo that?"

"Certainly, my good woman. You did not expect me to deny it?"

"God forbid, my lord! But will ye uphaud yersel' the lawfu' heir to the deceased? It lies 'atween yer lordship an' mysel'—i' the meantime."

He sat down, holding the scrap of paper between his finger and thumb.

"I will buy them of you," he said coolly, after a moment's thought, and as he spoke he looked keenly at her.

The form of reply which first arose in Miss Horn's indignant soul never reached her lips.

The marquis took it. In his countenance curiosity had mingled with the expectation. He glanced at it. A shadow swept over his face but vanished instantly: the mask of impervious non-expression which a man of his breeding always knows how to assume, was already on his visage.

"Where did you get this?" he said quietly, with just the slightest catch in his voice.

"I got it, my lord, where there's more like it."

"Show me them."

"I have shown you plenty for a pattern, my lord."

"You refuse?" said the marquis; and the tone of the question was like the first cold puff that indicates a change of weather.

"I do, my lord," she answered imperturbably.

"If they are not my property, why do you bring me this?"

"Are they your property, my lord?"

"This is my handwriting."

"You allow that?"

"Certainly, my good woman. You did not expect me to deny it?"

"God forbid, my lord! But will you own yourself the lawful heir to the deceased? It lies between your lordship and myself—in the meantime."

He sat down, holding the scrap of paper between his finger and thumb.

"I will buy them of you," he said coolly, after a moment's thought, and as he spoke he looked keenly at her.

The form of reply which first arose in Miss Horn's indignant soul never reached her lips.

"It's no my trade," she answered, with the coldness of suppressed wrath. "I dinna deal in sic waurs."

"What do you deal in then?" asked the marquis.

"In trouth an' fair play, my lord," she answered, and was again silent.

So was the marquis for some moments, but was the first to resume.

"If you think the papers to which you refer of the least value, allow me to tell you it is an entire mistake."

"There was ane thoucht them o' vailue," replied Miss Horn—and her voice trembled a little, but she hemmed away her emotion—"for a time at least, my lord; an' for her sake they're o' vailue to me, be they what they may to yer lordship. But wha can tell? Scots law may put life intill them yet, an' gie them a vailue to somebody forbye me."

"What I mean, my good woman, is, that if you think the possession of those papers gives you any hold over me which you can turn to your advantage, you are mistaken."

"Guid forgie ye, my lord! *My* advantage! I thoucht yer lordship had been mair o' a gentleman by this time, or I wad hae sent a lawyer till ye, in place o' comin' mysel'."

"What do you mean by that?"

"It's plain ye cudna hae been muckle o' a gentleman ance, my lord; an' it seems ye're no muckle mair o' ane yet, for a' ye maun hae come throu' i' the meantime."

"I trust you have discovered nothing in those letters to afford ground for such a harsh judgment," said the marquis seriously.

"It's not my trade," she answered, with the coldness of suppressed wrath. "I don't deal in such wares."

"What do you deal in then?" asked the marquis.

"In truth and fair play, my lord," she answered, and was again silent.

So was the marquis for some moments, but was the first to resume.

"If you think the papers to which you refer of the least value, allow me to tell you it is an entire mistake."

"There was one thought them of value," replied Miss Horn—and her voice trembled a little, but she hemmed away her emotion—"for a time at least, my lord; and for her sake they're of value to me, be they what they may to your lordship. But who can tell? Scots law may put life into them yet, and give them a value to someone besides me."

"What I mean, my good woman, is, that if you think the possession of those papers gives you any hold over me which you can turn to your advantage, you are mistaken."

"God forgive you, my lord! *My* advantage! I thought your lordship had been more of a gentleman by this time, or I would have sent a lawyer to you, instead of coming myself."

"What do you mean by that?"

"It's plain you couldn't have been much of a gentleman once, my lord; and it seems you're not much more of one yet, for all you must have come through in the meantime."

"I trust you have discovered nothing in those letters to afford ground for such a harsh judgment," said the marquis seriously.

"Na, no a word i' them, but the mair oot o' them. Ye winna threep upo' me 'at a man wha lea's a wuman, lat alane his wife—or ane 'at he ca's his wife—to a' the pains o' a mither, an' a' the penalties o' an oonmerried ane, ohn ever speirt hoo she wan throu' them, preserves the richt he was born till o' bein' coontit a gentleman? Ony gait, a maiden wuman like mysel' wha *has* nae feelin's will *not* alloo him the teetle—Guid forbid it!"

"You are plain-spoken."

"I'm plain-made, my lord. I ken guid frae ill, an' little forbye, but aye fand that eneuch to sare my turn. Aither thae letters o' yer lordship's are ilk ane o' them a lee, or ye desertit yer wife an' bairn."

"Alas!" interrupted the marquis with some emotion—"she deserted me—and took the child with her!"

"Wha ever daurt sic a lee upo' my Grizel?" shouted Miss Horn, clenching and shaking her bony fist at the world in general. "It was but a fortnicht or three weeks, as near as I can judge, efter the birth o' your bairn, that Grizel Cam'ell—"

"Were you with her then?" again interrupted the marquis, in a tone of sorrowful interest.

"No, my lord, I was not. Gien I had been, I wadna be upo' sic an eeran' this day. For nigh twenty lang years 'at her 'an me keepit hoose thegither, till she dee'd i' my airms, never a day was she oot o' my sicht, or ance—"

The marquis leaped rather than started to his feet, exclaiming, "What in the name of God do you mean, woman?"

"I kenna what *ye* mean, my lord. I ken 'at I'm but tellin' ye the trouth whan I tell ye 'at Grizel Cam'ell, up to that day, an' that's little ower sax month sin' syne,—"

"Na, not a word in them, but the more out of them. Am I to be told, sir, that a man who leaves a woman, let alone his wife—or one that he calls his wife—to all the pains of a mother, and all the penalties of an unmarried one, without once asking how she won through them, preserves the right he was born to of being counted a gentleman? Anyway, a maiden woman like me who *has* no feelings *won't* allow him the title—God forbid it!"

"You are plain-spoken."

"I'm plain-made, my lord. I know good from ill, and little besides, but it was always enough to serve my turn. Either those letters of your lordship's are every one a lie, or you deserted your wife and child."

"Alas!" interrupted the marquis with some emotion—"she deserted me—and took the child with her!"

"Who ever dared such a lie against my Grizel?" shouted Miss Horn, clenching and shaking her bony fist at the world in general. "It was but a fortnight or three weeks, as near as I can judge, after the birth of your child, that Grizell Campbell—"

"Were you with her then?" again interrupted the marquis, in a tone of sorrowful interest.

"No, my lord, I was not. If I had been, I wouldn't be upon such an errand today. For nigh twenty long years that we kept house together, till the hour she died in my arms, never a day was she out of my sight, until—"

The marquis leaped rather than started to his feet, exclaiming, "What in the name of God do you mean, woman?"

"I don't know what *you* mean, my lord. I know I'm but telling you the truth when I say that Grizel Campbell, up to that day, and that's little over six months ago,—"

"Good God!" cried the marquis; "and here have I—Woman! are you speaking the truth? If—," he added threateningly, and paused.

"Leein' 's what I never cud bide, my lord, an' I'm no likly to tak till 't at my age, wi' the lang to-come afore me."

The marquis strode several times up and down the floor. "I'll give you a thousand pounds for those letters," he said, suddenly stopping in front of Miss Horn.

"They're o' nae sic worth, my lord—I hae yer ain word for 't. But I carena the leg o' a spin-maggie! Pairt wi' them I will not, 'cep' to him 'at pruves himsel' the richtfu' heir to them."

"A husband inherits from his wife."

"Or maybe her son micht claim first—I dinna ken. But there's lawyers, my lord, to redd the doot."

"Her son! You don't mean—"

"I div mean Ma'colm MacPhail, my lord."

"God in heaven!"

"His name 's mair i' yer mou' nor i' yer hert, I'm doobtin', my lord! Ye a' cry oot upo' *him*—the men o' ye—whan ye're in ony tribble, or want to gar women believe ye! But I'm thinkin' he peys but little heed to sic prayers."

Thus Miss Horn; but Lord Lossie was striding up and down the room, heedless of her remarks, his eyes on the ground, his arms straight by his sides, and his hands clenched.

"Can you prove what you say?" he asked at length, half stopping, and casting an almost wild look at Miss Horn, then resuming his hurried walk. His voice sounded hollow, as if sent from the heart of a gulf of pain.

"Good God!" cried the marquis; "and here have I—Woman! are you speaking the truth? If—," he added threateningly, and paused.

"Lying's what I never could stand, my lord, and I'm not likely to take to it at my age, with eternity stretched out before me."

The marquis strode several times up and down the floor. "I'll give you a thousand pounds for those letters," he said, suddenly stopping in front of Miss Horn.

"They're not worth such a sum, my lord—I have your own word for it. But I don't care a straw! Part with them I shall not, except to him that proves himself the rightful heir to them."

"A husband inherits from his wife."

"Or maybe her son might claim first—I don't know. But there's lawyers, my lord, to clear the doubt."

"Her son! You don't mean—"

"I do mean Malcolm MacPhail, my lord."

"God in heaven!"

"His name's more in your mouth than in your heart, I think, my lord! You all call out upon *him*—you men—when you're in any trouble, or want to make women believe you! But I'm thinking he pays little heed to such prayers."

Thus Miss Horn; but Lord Lossie was striding up and down the room, heedless of her remarks, his eyes on the ground, his arms straight by his sides, and his hands clenched.

"Can you prove what you say?" he asked at length, half stopping, and casting an almost wild look at Miss Horn, then resuming his hurried walk. His voice sounded hollow, as if sent from the heart of a gulf of pain.

"No, my lord," answered Miss Horn.

"Then what the devil," roared the marquis, "do you mean by coming to me with such a cock-and-bull story."

"There's naither cock-craw nor bill-rair intill 't my lord. I cum to you wi' 't i' the houp ye 'll help to redd it up, for I dinna weel ken what we can du wantin' ye. There's but ane kens a' the truth o' 't, an' she's the awfu'est leear oot o' purgatory—no 'at I believe in purgatory, but it 's the langer an' lichter word to mak' use o'."

"Who is she?"

"By name she's Bauby Cat'nach, an' by natur' she's what I tell ye—an' gien I had her 'atween my twa een, it 's what I wad say to the face o' her."

"It can't be MacPhail! Mrs Stewart says he is *her* son, and the woman Catanach is her chief witness in support of the claim."

"The deevil has a better to the twa o' them, my lord, as they 'll ken some day. *His* claim 'll want nae supportin'. Dinna ye believe a word Mistress Stewart or Bauby Catanach aither wad say to ye.—Gien he be Mistress Stewart's, wha was his father?"

"You think he resembles my late brother: he has a look of him, I confess."

"He has, my lord. But onybody 'at kent the mither o' 'im, as you an' me did, my lord, wad see anither lik'ness as weel."

"I grant nothing."

"Ye grant Grizel Cam'ell yer wife, my lord, whan ye own to that wreet. Gien 't war naething but a written promise an' a bairn to follow, it wad be merriage eneuch i' this cuintry, though it mayna be in cuintries no sae ceevileest."

"No, my lord," answered Miss Horn.

"Then what the devil," roared the marquis, "do you mean by coming to me with such a cock-and-bull story."

"There's neither cock-crow nor bull-roar about it, my lord. I'm come to you hoping you'll help clear it up, for I don't well know what we can do without you. There's but one knows all the truth of it, and she's the worst liar out of purgatory—not that I believe in purgatory, but it's the longer and the lighter word to use."

"Who is she?"

"By name she's Bauby Catanach, and by nature she's what I tell you—and if I had her between these two eyes, I'd say it to her face."

"It can't be MacPhail! Mrs Stewart says he is *her* son, and the woman Catanach is her chief witness in support of the claim."

"The devil has a better to the two of them, my lord, as they'll know some day. *His* claim will want no supporting. Don't you believe a word Mistress Stewart or Bauby Catanach either would say to you.—If he be Mistress Stewart's, who was his father?"

"You think he resembles my late brother: he has a look of him, I confess."

"He has, my lord. But anyone that knew his mother, as you and I did, my lord, would see another likeness as well."

"I grant nothing."

"You grant Grizell Campbell your wife, my lord, when you own to that writing. If it were nothing but a written promise and a child to follow, it would be marriage enough in this country, though it mightn't be in countries less civilised."

"But all that is nothing as to the child. Why do you fix on this young fellow? You say you can't prove it."

"But *ye* cud, my lord, gien ye war as set upo' justice as I am. Gien ye winna muv i' the maitter, we s' manage to hirple throu' wantin ye, though, wi' the Lord's help."

The marquis, who had all this time continued his walk up and down the floor, stood still, raised his head as if about to speak, dropped it again on his chest, strode to the other window, turned, strode back, and said,

"This is a very serious matter."

"It's a' that, my lord," replied Miss Horn.

"You must give me a little time to turn it over," said the marquis.

"Isna twenty year time eneuch, my lord?" rejoined Miss Horn.

"I swear to you that till this moment I believed her twenty years in her grave. My brother sent me word that she died in childbed, and the child with her. I was then in Brussels with the Duke."

Miss Horn made three great strides, caught the marquis's hand in both hers, and said, "I praise God ye're an honest man, my lord."

"I hope so," said the marquis, and seized the advantage:— "You'll hold your tongue about this?" he added, half inquiring, half requesting.

"As lang as I see rizzon, my lord, nae langer," answered Miss Horn, dropping his hand. "Richt maun be dune."

"Yes—if you can tell what right is, and avoid wrong to others."

"Richt 's richt, my lord," persisted Miss Horn. "I'll hae nae modifi-qualifications!"

"But all that is nothing as to the child. Why do you fix on this young fellow? You say you can't prove it."

"But *you* could, my lord, if you were as set upon justice as I am. If you won't move in the matter, we'll manage to hobble through without you, though, with the Lord's help."

The marquis, who had all this time continued his walk up and down the floor, stood still, raised his head as if about to speak, dropped it again on his chest, strode to the other window, turned, strode back, and said,

"This is a very serious matter."

"It certainly is, my lord," replied Miss Horn.

"You must give me a little time to turn it over," said the marquis.

"Isn't twenty years time enough, my lord?" rejoined Miss Horn.

"I swear to you that till this moment I believed her twenty years in her grave. My brother sent me word that she died in childbed, and the child with her. I was then in Brussels with the Duke."

Miss Horn made three great strides, caught the marquis's hand in both hers, and said, "I praise God you're an honest man, my lord."

"I hope so," said the marquis, and seized the advantage:— "You'll hold your tongue about this?" he added, half inquiring, half requesting.

"As long as I see reason, my lord, no longer," answered Miss Horn, dropping his hand. "Right must be done."

"Yes—if you can tell what right is, and avoid wrong to others."

"Right's right, my lord," persisted Miss Horn. "I'll have no modifi-qualifications!"

His lordship once more began to walk up and down the room, every now and then taking a stolen glance at Miss Horn, a glance of uneasy anxious questioning. She stood rigid—a very Lot's wife of immobility, her eyes on the ground, waiting what he would say next.

"I wish I knew whether I could trust her," he said at length, as if talking aloud to himself.

Miss Horn took no notice.

"Why don't you speak, woman?" cried the marquis with irritation. How he hated perplexity!

"Ye speired nae queston, my lord; an' gien ye had, my word has ower little weicht to answer wi'."

"Can I trust you, woman—I want to know," said his lordship angrily.

"No far'er, my lord, nor to du what I think 's richt."

"I want to be certain that you will do nothing with those letters until you hear from me?" said the marquis, heedless of her reply.

"I'll du naething afore the morn. Far'er nor that I winna pledge mysel'," answered Miss Horn, and with the words moved towards the door.

"Hadn't you better take this with you?" said the marquis, offering the little note, which he had carried all the time between his finger and thumb.

"There's nae occasion. I hae plenty wantin' that. Only dinna lea' 't lyin' aboot."

"There's small danger of that," said the marquis, and rang the bell.

His lordship once more began to walk up and down the room, every now and then taking a stolen glance at Miss Horn, a glance of uneasy anxious questioning. She stood rigid—a very Lot's wife of immobility, her eyes on the ground, waiting what he would say next.

"I wish I knew whether I could trust her," he said at length, as if talking aloud to himself.

Miss Horn took no notice.

"Why don't you speak, woman?" cried the marquis with irritation. How he hated perplexity!

"You asked no question, my lord; and if you had, my word has too little weight to answer with."

"Can I trust you, woman—I want to know," said his lordship angrily.

"No farther, my lord, than to do what I think's right."

"I want to be certain that you will do nothing with those letters until you hear from me?" said the marquis, heedless of her reply.

"I'll do nothing before tomorrow. Farther than that I'll make no promises." answered Miss Horn, and with the words moved towards the door.

"Hadn't you better take this with you?" said the marquis, offering the little note, which he had carried all the time between his finger and thumb.

"There's no occasion. I have plenty of others. Only don't leave it lying about."

"There's small danger of that," said the marquis, and rang the bell.

The moment she was out of the way, he went up to his own room, and, flinging the door to, sat down at the table, and laid his arms and head upon it. The acrid vapour of tears that should have been wept long since, rose to his eyes: he dashed his hand across them, as if ashamed that he was not even yet out of sight of the kingdom of heaven. His own handwriting, of a period when all former sins and defilements seemed about to be burned clean from his soul by the fire of an honest and virtuous love, had moved him; for genuine had been his affection for the girl who had risked and lost so much for him. It was with no evil intent, for her influence had rendered him for the time incapable of playing her false, but in part from reasons of prudence, as he persuaded himself, for both their sakes, and in part led astray by the zest which minds of a certain cast derive from the secrecy of pleasure, that he had persuaded her to the unequal yoking of honesty and secrecy. But, suddenly called away and sent by the Prince on a private mission, soon after their marriage, and before there was any special reason to apprehend consequences that must lead to discovery, he had, in the difficulties of the case and the hope of a speedy return, left her without any arrangement for correspondence and all he had ever heard of her more was from his brother, then the marquis—a cynical account of the discovery of her condition, followed almost immediately by a circumstantial one of her death and that of her infant. He was deeply stung; and the thought of her sufferings in the false position where his selfishness had placed her, haunted him for a time beyond his endurance—for of all things he hated suffering, and of all sufferings remorse is the worst. Hence, where a wiser man might have repented, he rushed into dissipation, whose scorching wind swept away not only the healing dews of his sorrow, but the tender buds of new life that had begun to mottle the withering tree of his nature. The desire after better things which had, under his wife's genial influence, begun to pass into effort, not only vanished utterly in the shameless round of evil distraction, but its memory became a mockery to the cynical spirit that arose behind the vanishing angel of repentance; and he was soon in the condition of the man from whom the exorcised demon had gone but to find his seven worse companions.

Reduced at length to straits—almost to want, he had married the mother of Florimel, to whom for a time he endeavoured to conduct himself in some measure like a gentleman. For this he had been rewarded by a decrease in the rate of his spiritual submergence, but his bedraggled nature could no longer walk without treading on its own plumes; and the poor lady who had bartered herself for a lofty alliance, speedily found her mistake a sad one and her life uninteresting, took to repining and tears, alienated her husband utterly, and died of a sorrow almost too selfish to afford even a suggestion of purifying efficacy. But Florimel had not inherited immediately from her mother, so far as disposition was concerned; in these latter days she had grown very dear to him, and his love had once more turned his face a little towards the path of righteousness. Ah! when would he move one step to set his feet in it?

And now, after his whirlwind harvest of evil knowledge, bitter disappointment, and fading passion, in the gathering mists of gray hopelessness, and the far worse mephitic air of indifference, he had come all of a sudden upon the ghastly discovery that, while overwhelmed with remorse for the vanished past, the present and the future had been calling him, but had now also—that present and that future—glided from him, and folded their wings of gloom in the land of shadows. All the fierce time he might have been blessedly growing better, instead of heaping sin upon sin until the weight was too heavy for repentance; for, while he had been bemoaning a dead wife, that wife had been loving a renegade husband! And the blame of it all he did not fail to cast upon that Providence in which until now he had professed not to believe: such faith as he was yet capable of, awoke in the form of resentment! He judged himself hardly done by; and the few admonitory sermons he had happened to hear, especially that in the cave about the dogs going round the walls of the New Jerusalem, returned upon him, not as warnings, but as old threats now rapidly approaching fulfilment.

Lovely still peered the dim face of his girl-wife upon him, through the dusty lattice of his memory; and a mighty corroboration of Malcolm's asserted birth lay in the look upon his face as he hurried aghast from the hermit's cell; for not on his first had the marquis seen that look and in those very circumstances! And the youth was one to be proud of—one among a million! But there were other and terrible considerations.

Incapable as he naturally was of doing justice to a woman of Miss Horn's inflexibility in right, he could yet more than surmise the absoluteness of that inflexibility—partly because it was hostile to himself, and he was in the mood to believe in opposition and harshness, and deny—not providence, but goodness. Convenient half-measures would, he more than feared, find no favour with her. But she had declared her inability to prove Malcolm his son without the testimony of Mrs Catanach, and the latter was even now representing him as the son of Mrs Stewart! That Mrs Catanach at the same time could not be ignorant of what had become of the child born to him, he was all but certain; for, on that night when Malcolm and he found her in the wizard's chamber, had she not proved her strange story—of having been carried to that very room blindfolded, and, after sole attendance on the birth of a child, whose mother's features, even in her worst pains, she had not once seen, in like manner carried away again,—had she not proved the story true by handing him the ring she had drawn from the lady's finger, and sewn, for the sake of future identification, into the lower edge of one of the bed curtains—which ring was a diamond he had given his wife from his own finger when they parted? She probably believed the lady to have been Mrs Stewart, and the late marquis the father of the child. Should he see Mrs Catanach? And what then?

He found no difficulty in divining the reasons which must have induced his brother to provide for the secret accouchement of his wife in the wizard's chamber, and for the abduction of the child—if indeed his existence was not owing to Mrs Catanach's love of intrigue. The elder had judged the younger brother unlikely to live long, and had expected his own daughter to succeed himself. But now the younger might any day marry the governess, and legalize the child; and the elder had therefore secured the disappearance of the latter, and the belief of his brother in the death of both.

Lord Lossie was roused from his reverie by a tap at the door, which he knew for Malcolm's, and answered with admission.

When he entered, his master saw that a change had passed upon him, and for a moment believed Miss Horn had already broken faith with him and found communication with Malcolm. He was soon satisfied of the contrary, however, but would have found it hard indeed to understand, had it been represented to him, that the contentment, almost elation, of the youth's countenance had its source in the conviction that he was not the son of Mrs Stewart.

"So here you are at last!" said the marquis.

"Ay, my lord."

"Did you find Stewart?"

"Ay did we at last, my lord; but we made naething by 't, for he kent noucht aboot the lassie, an 'maist lost his wuts at the news."

"No great loss, that!" said the marquis. "Go and send Stoat here."

"Is there ony hurry aboot Sto't, my lord?" asked Malcolm, hesitating. "I had a word to say to yer lordship mysel'."

"Make haste then."

"I'm some fain to gang back to the fishin', my lord," said Malcolm. "This is ower easy a life for me. The deil wins in for the liftin' o' the sneck. Forbye, my lord, a life wi'oot aither danger or wark 's some wersh-like; it wants saut, my lord. But a' that's naither here nor there, I ken, sae lang's ye want me oot o' the hoose, my lord."

"Who told you I wanted you out of the house? By Jove! I should have made shorter work of it. What put that in your head? Why should I?"

"Gien yer lordship kens nane, sma' occasion hae I to haud a rizzon to yer han'. I thoucht—but the thoucht itsel's impidence."

"You young fool! You thought, because I came upon you as I did in the garret the other night—Bah!—You damned ape! As if I could not trust—! Pshaw!"

"So here you are at last!" said the marquis.

"Ay, my lord."

"Did you find Stewart?"

"Ay, we did at last, my lord; but he couldn't help us, for he knew nothing about the lassie, and almost lost his wits at the news."

"No great loss, that!" said the marquis. "Go and send Stoat here."

"Is there any hurry about Stoat, my lord?" asked Malcolm, hesitating. "I had a word to say to your lordship myself."

"Make haste then."

"I've a good mind to go back to the fishing, my lord," said Malcolm. "This is too easy a life for me. The devil gets in for the lifting of the latch. Besides, my lord, a life without either danger or work has little relish; it wants salt, my lord. But all that's neither here nor there, I know, so long as you want me out of the house, my lord."

"Who told you I wanted you out of the house? By Jove! I should have made shorter work of it. What put that in your head? Why should I?"

"If your lordship knows none, I've small cause to give you a reason. I thought—but the thought itself is impudence."

"You young fool! You thought, because I came upon you as I did in the garret the other night—Bah!—You damned ape! As if I could not trust—! Pshaw!"

For the moment Malcolm forgot how angry his master had certainly been, although, for Florimel's sake doubtless, he had restrained himself; and fancied that, in the faint light of the one candle, he had seen little to annoy him, and had taken the storm and its results, which were indeed the sole reason, as a sufficient one for their being alone together. Everything seemed about to come right again. But his master remained silent.

"I houp my leddy's weel," ventured Malcolm at length.

"Quite well. She's with Lady Bellair, in Edinburgh."

Lady Bellair was the bold-faced countess.

"I dinna like her," said Malcolm.

"Who the devil asked you to like her?" said the marquis. But he laughed as he said it.

"I beg yer lordship's pardon," returned Malcolm. "I said it or I kent. It was nane o' my business wha my leddy was wi'."

"Certainly not. But I don't mind confessing that Lady Bellair is not one I should choose to give authority over Lady Florimel. You have some regard for your young mistress, I know, Malcolm."

"I wad dee for her, my lord."

"That's a common assertion," said the marquis.

"No wi' fisher fowk. I kenna hoo it may be wi' your fowk, my lord."

"Well, even with us it means something. It implies at least that he who uses it would risk his life for her whom he wishes to believe it. But perhaps it may mean more than that in the mouth of a fisherman? Do you fancy there is such a thing as devotion—real devotion, I mean—self sacrifice, you know?"

For the moment Malcolm forgot how angry his master had certainly been, although, for Florimel's sake doubtless, he had restrained himself; and fancied that, in the faint light of the one candle, he had seen little to annoy him, and had taken the storm and its results, which were indeed the sole reason, as a sufficient one for their being alone together. Everything seemed about to come right again. But his master remained silent.

"I hope my lady's well," ventured Malcolm at length.

"Quite well. She's with Lady Bellair, in Edinburgh."

Lady Bellair was the bold-faced countess.

"I don't like her," said Malcolm.

"Who the devil asked you to like her?" said the marquis. But he laughed as he said it.

"I beg your lordship's pardon," returned Malcolm. "I said it before I knew. It was none of my business who my lady was with."

"Certainly not. But I don't mind confessing that Lady Bellair is not one I should choose to give authority over Lady Florimel. You have some regard for your young mistress, I know, Malcolm."

"I would die for her, my lord."

"That's a common assertion," said the marquis.

"Not with fisher folk. I don't know how it may be with your own folk, my lord."

"Well, even with us it means something. It implies at least that he who uses it would risk his life for her whom he wishes to believe it. But perhaps it may mean more than that in the mouth of a fisherman? Do you fancy there is such a thing as devotion—real devotion, I mean—self sacrifice, you know?"

"I daurna doobt it, my lord."

"Without fee or hope of reward?"

"There maun be some cawpable o' 't, my lord, or what for sud the warl' be? What ither sud haud it ohn been destroyt as Sodom was for the want o' the ten richteous? There maun be saut whaur corruption hasna the thing a' its ain gait."

"You certainly have pretty high notions of things, MacPhail. For my part, I can easily enough imagine a man risking his life; but devoting it!—that's another thing altogether."

"There maun be 'at wad du a' 't cud be dune, my lord."

"What, for instance, would you do for Lady Florimel, now? You say you would die for her: what does dying mean on a fisherman's tongue?"

"It means a' thing, my lord—short o' ill. I wad sterve for her, but I wadna steal. I wad fecht for her, but I wadna lee."

"Would you be her servant all your days? Come, now."

"Mair nor willin'ly, my lord—gien she wad only hae me, an' keep me."

"But supposing you came to inherit the Kirkbyres property?"

"My lord," said Malcolm solemnly, "that's a puir test to put me till. It gangs for naething. I wad raither clean my leddie's butes frae mornin' to nicht, nor be the son o' that wuman, gien she war a born duchess. Try me wi' something worth yer lordship's mou'."

But the marquis seemed to think he had gone far enough for the present. With gleaming eyes he rose, took his withered love-letter from the table, put it in his waistcoat pocket, and saying—

"I daren't doubt it, my lord."

"Without fee or hope of reward?"

"There must be some such men, my lord, or why should the world be? What else should keep it from being destroyed like Sodom for the want of the ten righteous? There must be salt where corruption hasn't taken over the whole concern."

"You certainly have pretty high notions of things, MacPhail. For my part, I can easily enough imagine a man risking his life; but devoting it!—that's another thing altogether."

"There must be those that would do all they could, my lord."

"What, for instance, would you do for Lady Florimel, now? You say you would die for her: what does dying mean on a fisherman's tongue?"

"It means everything, my lord—short of wrong. I would starve for her, but I wouldn't steal. I would fight for her, but I wouldn't lie."

"Would you be her servant all your days? Come, now."

"More than willingly, my lord—if she would only have me, and keep me."

"But supposing you came to inherit the Kirkbyres property?"

"My lord," said Malcolm solemnly, "that's a poor test to put me to. It goes for nothing. I would rather clean my lady's boots from morning to night, than be the son of that woman, if she were a born duchess. Try me with something worth your lordship's mouth."

But the marquis seemed to think he had gone far enough for the present. With gleaming eyes he rose, took his withered love-letter from the table, put it in his waistcoat pocket, and saying—

"Well, find out for me what this is they're about with the school-master," walked to the door.

"I ken a' aboot that, my lord," answered Malcolm, "ohn speirt at onybody."

Lord Lossie turned from the door, ordered him to bring his riding coat and boots, and, ringing the bell, sent a message to Stoat to saddle the bay mare.

"Well, find out for me what this is they're about with the school-master," walked to the door.

"I know all about that, my lord," answered Malcolm, "without the trouble of asking."

Lord Lossie turned from the door, ordered him to bring his riding coat and boots, and, ringing the bell, sent a message to Stoat to saddle the bay mare.

CHAPTER LXIV

THE LAIRD AND HIS MOTHER

When Malcolm and Joseph set out from Duff Harbour to find the laird, they could hardly be said to have gone in search of him: all in their power was to seek the parts where he was occasionally seen in the hope of chancing upon him; and they wandered in vain about the woods of Fife House all that week, returning disconsolate every evening to the little inn on the banks of the Wan Water. Sunday came and went without yielding a trace of him; and, almost in despair, they resolved, if unsuccessful the next day, to get assistance and organize a search for him. Monday passed like the days that had preceded it, and they were returning dejectedly down the left bank of the Wan Water, in the gloamin', and nearing a part where it is hemmed in by precipitous rocks, and is very narrow and deep, crawling slow and black under the lofty arch of an ancient bridge that spans it at one leap, when suddenly they caught sight of a head peering over the parapet. They dared not run for fear of terrifying him, if it should be the laird, and hurried quietly to the spot. But when they reached the end of the bridge its round back was bare from end to end. On the other side of the river, the trees came close up, and pursuit was hopeless in the gathering darkness.

"Laird, laird! they've taen awa' Phemy, an' we dinna ken whaur to luik for her," cried the poor father aloud.

"Laird, laird! they've taken away our Phemy, and we don't know where to look for her," cried the poor father aloud.

Almost the same instant, and as if he had issued from the ground, the laird stood before them. The men started back with astonishment—soon changed into pity, for there was light enough to see how miserable the poor fellow looked. Neither exposure nor privation had thus wrought upon him: he was simply dying of fear. Having greeted Joseph with embarrassment, he kept glancing doubtfully at Malcolm, as if ready to run on his least movement. In a few words Joseph explained their quest, with trembling voice and tears that would not be denied enforcing the tale. Ere he had done, the laird's jaw had fallen, and further speech was impossible to him. But by gestures sad and plain enough, he indicated that he knew nothing of her, and had supposed her safe at home with her parents. In vain they tried to persuade him to go back with them, promising every protection: for sole answer he shook his head mournfully.

There came a sudden gust of wind among the branches. Joseph, little used to trees and their ways with the wind, turned towards the sound, and Malcolm unconsciously followed his movement. When they turned again, the laird had vanished, and they took their way homeward in sadness.

What passed next with the laird, can be but conjectured. It came to be well enough known afterwards where he had been hiding; and had it not been dusk as they came down the riverbank, the two men might, looking up to the bridge from below, have had it suggested to them. For in the half spandrel-wall between the first arch and the bank, they might have spied a small window, looking down on the sullen, silent gloom, foam-flecked with past commotion, that crept languidly away from beneath. It belonged to a little vaulted chamber in the bridge, devised by some banished lord as a kind of sum-mer-house—long neglected, but having in it yet a mouldering table, a broken chair or two, and a rough bench. A little path led steep from the end of the parapet down to its hidden door. It was now used only by the gamekeepers for traps and fishing-gear, and odds and ends of things, and was generally supposed to be locked up. The laird had, how-ever, found it open, and his refuge in it had been connived at by one of the men, who, as they heard afterwards, had given him the key, and assisted him in carrying out a plan he had devised for barricading the door. It was from this place he had so suddenly risen at the call of Blue Peter, and to it he had as suddenly withdrawn again—to pass in silence and loneliness through his last purgatorial pain.[21]

Mrs Stewart was sitting in her drawing-room alone: she seldom had visitors at Kirk-byres—not that she liked being alone, or indeed being there at all, for she would have lived on the Continent, but that her son's trustees, partly to indulge their own aversion to her, taking upon them a larger discretionary power than rightly belonged to them, kept her too straitened, which no doubt in the recoil had its share in poor Stephen's misery. It was only after scraping for a whole year that she could escape to Paris or Hamburg, where she was at home. There her sojourn was determined by her good or ill fortune at faro.

What she meditated over her knitting by the fire-light,—she had put out her can-dles,—it would be hard to say, perhaps unwholesome to think:—there are souls to look into which is, to our dim eyes, like gazing down from the verge of one of the Swedenbor-gian pits.

But much of the evil done by human beings is as the evil of evil beasts: they know not what they do—an excuse which, except in regard of the past, no man can make for him-self, seeing the very making of it must testify its falsehood.

She looked up, gave a cry, and started to her feet: Stephen stood before her, halfway between her and the door. Revealed in a flicker of flame from the fire, he vanished in the

---

[21] *Com'io fui dentro, in un bogliente vetro*
Gittato mi sarci per rinfrescarmi,
Tant' era ivi lo 'ncendio senza metro.
[Del Purgatoria, xxvii. 49.]

following shade, and for a moment she stood in doubt of her seeing sense. But when the coal flashed again, there was her son, regarding her out of great eyes that looked as if they had seen death. A ghastly air hung about him as if he had just come back from Hades, but in his silent bearing there was a sanity, even dignity, which strangely impressed her. He came forward a pace or two, stopped, and said—

"Dinna be frichtit, mem. I'm come. Sen' the lassie hame, an' du wi' me as ye like. I canna haud aff o' me. But I think I'm deein', an ye needna misguide me."

"Don't be afraid, ma'am. I'm come. Send the lassie home, and do with me as you like. I can't defend myself. But I think I'm dying, so you needn't hurt me."

His voice, although it trembled a little, was clear and unimpeded, and though weak, in its modulation manly.

Something in the woman's heart responded. Was it motherhood— or the deeper godhead? Was it pity for the dignity housed in the crumbling clay, or repentance for the son of her womb? Or was it that sickness gave hope, and she could afford to be kind?

"I don't know what you mean, Stephen," she said, more gently than he had ever heard her speak.

Was it an agony of mind or of body, or was it but a flickering of the shadows upon his face? A moment, and he gave a half-choked shriek, and fell on the floor. His mother turned from him with disgust, and rang the bell.

"Send Tom here," she said.

An elderly, hard-featured man came.

"Stephen is in one of his fits," she said.

The man looked about him: he could see no one in the room but his mistress.

"There he is," she continued, pointing to the floor. "Take him away. Get him up to the loft and lay him in the hay."

The man lifted his master like an unwieldy log, and carried him convulsed from the room.

Stephen's mother sat down again by the fire, and resumed her knitting.

CHAPTER LXV

THE LAIRD'S VISION

Malcolm had just seen his master set out for his solitary ride, when one of the maids informed him that a man from Kirkbyres wanted him. Hiding his reluctance, he went with her and found Tom, who was Mrs Stewart's grieve, and had been about the place all his days.

"Mr Stephen's come hame, sir," he said, touching his bonnet, a civility for which Malcolm was not grateful.

"It's no possible!" returned Malcolm. "I saw him last nicht."

"He cam about ten o'clock, sir, an' hed a turn o' the fa'in' sickness o' the spot. He's verra ill the noo, an' the mistress sent me ower to speir gien ye wad obleege her by gaein' to see him."

"Has he ta'en till 's bed?" asked Malcolm.

"We pat him till 't, sir. He 's ravin' mad, an' I'm thinkin' he 's no far frae his hin'er en'."

"I'll gang wi' ye direckly," said Malcolm.

In a few minutes they were riding fast along the road to Kirkbyres, neither with much to say to the other, for Malcolm distrusted every one about the place, and Tom was by nature taciturn.

"What garred them sen' for me—div ye ken?" asked Malcolm at length, when they had gone about halfway.

"He cried oot upo' ye i' the nicht," answered Tom.

"Mr Stephen's come home, sir," he said, touching his bonnet, a civility for which Malcolm was not grateful.

"It's not possible!" returned Malcolm. "I saw him last night."

"He came about ten o'clock, sir, and had a turn of the falling sickness on the spot. He's very ill just now, and the mistress sent me over to ask if you would oblige her by going to see him."

"Has he taken to his bed?" asked Malcolm.

"We put him to it, sir. He's raving mad, and I think his time must be running short."

"I'll go with you at once," said Malcolm.

In a few minutes they were riding fast along the road to Kirkbyres, neither with much to say to the other, for Malcolm distrusted every one about the place, and Tom was by nature taciturn.

"What made them send for me—do you know?" asked Malcolm at length, when they had gone about halfway.

"He called your name in the night," answered Tom.

When they arrived, Malcolm was shown into the drawing room, where Mrs Stewart met him with red eyes.

"Will you come and see my poor boy?" she said.

"I wull du that, mem. Is he verra ill?"

"Very. I'm afraid he is in a bad way."

She led him to a dark old fashioned chamber, rich and gloomy. There, sunk in the down of a huge bed with carved ebony posts, lay the laird, far too ill to be incommoded by the luxury to which he was unaccustomed. His head kept tossing from side to side, and his eyes seemed searching in vacancy.

"Has the doctor been to see 'im, mem?" asked Malcolm.

"Yes; but he says he can't do anything for him."

"Wha waits upon 'im, mem?"

"One of the maids and myself."

"I'll jist bide wi' 'im."

"That will be very kind of you."

"I s' bide wi' 'im till I see 'im oot o' this, ae w'y or ither," added Malcolm, and sat down by the bedside of his poor distrustful friend. There Mrs Stewart left him.

The laird was wandering in the thorny thickets and slimy marshes which, haunted by the thousand mis-shapen horrors of delirium, beset the gates of life. That one so near the light, and slowly drifting into it, should lie tossing in hopeless darkness! Is it that the delirium falls, a veil of love, to hide other and more real terrors?

His eyes would now and then meet those of Malcolm, as they gazed tenderly upon him, but the living thing that looked out of the windows was darkened, and saw

When they arrived, Malcolm was shown into the drawing room, where Mrs Stewart met him with red eyes.

"Will you come and see my poor boy?" she said.

"I'll do that, ma'am. Is he very ill?"

"Very. I'm afraid he is in a bad way."

She led him to a dark old fashioned chamber, rich and gloomy. There, sunk in the down of a huge bed with carved ebony posts, lay the laird, far too ill to be incommoded by the luxury to which he was unaccustomed. His head kept tossing from side to side, and his eyes seemed searching in vacancy.

"Has the doctor been to see him, ma'am?" asked Malcolm.

"Yes; but he says he can't do anything for him."

"Who waits upon him, ma'am?"

"One of the maids and myself."

"I'll just stay with him."

"That will be very kind of you."

"I'll stay with him till I see him out of this, one way or other," added Malcolm, and sat down by the bedside of his poor distrustful friend. There Mrs Stewart left him.

The laird was wandering in the thorny thickets and slimy marshes which, haunted by the thousand mis-shapen horrors of delirium, beset the gates of life. That one so near the light, and slowly drifting into it, should lie tossing in hopeless darkness! Is it that the delirium falls, a veil of love, to hide other and more real terrors?

His eyes would now and then meet those of Malcolm, as they gazed tenderly upon him, but the living thing that looked out of the windows was darkened, and him not. Occasionally a word would fall from him, or a murmur of half-articulation float up, like the sound of a river of souls; but whether Malcolm heard, or only seemed to hear, something like this, he could not tell, for he could not be certain that he had not himself shaped the words by receiving the babble into the moulds of the laird's customary thought and speech.

"I dinna ken whaur I cam frae!—I kenna whaur I'm gaein' till.—Eh, gien he wad but come oot an' shaw himsel'!—O Lord! tak the deevil aff o' my puir back.—O Father o' lichts! gar him tak the hump wi' him. I hae nae fawvour for 't, though it 's been my constant companion this mony a lang."

But in general, he only moaned, and after the words thus heard or fashioned by Malcolm, lay silent and nearly still for an hour.

All the waning afternoon Malcolm sat by his side, and neither mother, maid, nor doctor came near them.

"Dark wa's an' no a breath!" he murmured or seemed to murmur again. "Nae gerse, nor flooers, nor bees!—I hae na room for my hump, an' I canna lie upo' 't, for that wad kill me!—Wull I *ever* ken whaur I cam frae?—The wine 's unco guid. Gie me a drap mair, gien ye please, Lady Horn.—I thought the grave was a better place. I hae lain safter afore I dee'd!— Phemy! Phemy! Rin, Phemy, rin! I s' bide wi' them this time. Ye rin, Phemy!"

As it grew dark, the air turned very chill, and snow began to fall thick and fast. Malcolm laid a few sticks on the smouldering peat-fire, but they were damp and did not catch. All at once the laird gave a

saw him not. Occasionally a word would fall from him, or a murmur of half-articulation float up, like the sound of a river of souls; but whether Malcolm heard, or only seemed to hear, something like this, he could not tell, for he could not be certain that he had not himself shaped the words by receiving the babble into the moulds of the laird's customary thought and speech.

"I don't know where I came from!—I don't know where I'm going to.—Eh, if he would but come out and show himself!—O Lord! take the devil off my poor back.—O Father of lights! make him take the hump with him. I have no liking for it, though it's been my constant companion this many a day."

But in general, he only moaned, and after the words thus heard or fashioned by Malcolm, lay silent and nearly still for an hour.

All the waning afternoon Malcolm sat by his side, and neither mother, maid, nor doctor came near them.

"Dark walls and no wind!" he murmured or seemed to murmur again. "No grass, nor flowers, nor bees!—I haven't room for my hump, and I can't lie upon it, for that would kill me!—Will I *ever* know where I came from?—The wine's very good. Give me another drop, if you please, Lady Horn.—I thought the grave was a better place. I have lain softer before I died!— Phemy! Phemy! Run, Phemy, run! I'll stay with them this time. You run, Phemy!"

As it grew dark, the air turned very chill, and snow began to fall thick and fast. Malcolm laid a few sticks on the smouldering peat-fire, but they were damp and did not catch. All at once the laird gave a shriek, and crying out, "Mither, mither!" fell into a fit so violent that the heavy bed shook with his convulsions. Malcolm held his wrists and called aloud. No one came, and bethinking himself that none could help, he waited in silence, for what would follow.

The fit passed quickly, and he lay quiet. The sticks had meantime dried, and suddenly they caught fire and blazed up. The laird turned his face towards the flame; a smile came over it; his eyes opened wide, and with such an expression of seeing gazed beyond Malcolm, that he turned his in the same direction.

"Eh, the bonny man! The bonny man!" murmured the laird.

But Malcolm saw nothing, and turned again to the laird: his jaw had fallen, and the light was fading out of his face like the last of a sunset. He was dead.

Malcolm rang the bell, told the woman who answered it what had taken place, and hurried from the house, glad at heart that his friend was at rest.

He had ridden but a short distance when he was overtaken by a boy on a fast pony, who pulled up as he neared him.

"Whaur are ye for?" asked Malcolm.

"I'm gaein' for Mistress Cat'nach," answered the boy.

"Gang yer wa's than, an' dinna haud the deid waitin'," said Malcolm, with a shudder.

The boy cast a look of dismay behind him, and galloped off.

The snow still fell, and the night was dark. Malcolm spent nearly two hours on the way, and met the boy returning, who told him that Mrs Catanach was not to be found.

shriek, and crying out, "Mother, mother!" fell into a fit so violent that the heavy bed shook with his convulsions. Malcolm held his wrists and called aloud. No one came, and bethinking himself that none could help, he waited in silence, for what would follow.

The fit passed quickly, and he lay quiet. The sticks had meantime dried, and suddenly they caught fire and blazed up. The laird turned his face towards the flame; a smile came over it; his eyes opened wide, and with such an expression of seeing gazed beyond Malcolm, that he turned his in the same direction.

"Eh, the bonny man! The bonny man!" murmured the laird.

But Malcolm saw nothing, and turned again to the laird: his jaw had fallen, and the light was fading out of his face like the last of a sunset. He was dead.

Malcolm rang the bell, told the woman who answered it what had taken place, and hurried from the house, glad at heart that his friend was at rest.

He had ridden but a short distance when he was overtaken by a boy on a fast pony, who pulled up as he neared him.

"Where are you headed?" asked Malcolm.

"I'm going for Mistress Catanach," answered the boy.

"Be off then, and don't keep the dead waiting," said Malcolm, with a shudder.

The boy cast a look of dismay behind him, and galloped off.

The snow still fell, and the night was dark. Malcolm spent nearly two hours on the way, and met the boy returning, who told him that Mrs Catanach was not to be found.

His road lay down the glen, past Duncan's cottage, at whose door he dismounted, but he did not find him. Taking the bridle on his arm he walked by his horse the rest of the way. It was about nine o'clock, and the night very dark. As he neared the house, he heard Duncan's voice.

"Malcolm, my son! Will it pe your own self?" it said.

"It wull that, daddy," answered Malcolm.

The piper was sitting on a fallen tree, with the snow settling softly upon him.

"But it 's ower cauld for ye to be sittin' there i' the snaw, an' the mirk tu!" added Malcolm.

"Ta tarkness will not be ketting to ta inside of her," returned the seer. "Ah, my poy! where ta light kets in, ta tarkness will pe ketting in too. Tis now, your whole pody will pe full of tarkness, as ta piple will say, and Tuncan's pody—tat will pe full of ta light." Then with suddenly changed tone he said "Listen, Malcolm, my son! she'll pe fery uneasy till you 'll wass pe come home."

"What's the maitter noo, daddy?" returned Malcolm. "Ony thing wrang aboot the hoose?"

"Someting will pe wrong, yes, put she'll not can tell where. No, her pody will not pe full of light! For town here in ta curset Lowlands, ta sight has peen almost cone from her, my son. It will now pe no more as a co creeping troo' her, and she'll nefer see plain no more till she'll pe cone pack to her own mountains."

"The puir laird's gane back to his," said Malcolm. "I won'er gien he kens yet, or gien he gangs speirin' at ilk ane he meets gien he can tell him whaur he cam frae. He's mad nae mair, ony gait."

"How? Will he pe not tead? Ta poor lairt! Ta poor maad lairt!"

His road lay down the glen, past Duncan's cottage, at whose door he dismounted, but he did not find him. Taking the bridle on his arm he walked by his horse the rest of the way. It was about nine o'clock, and the night very dark. As he neared the house, he heard Duncan's voice.

"Malcolm, my son! Will it be your own self?" it said.

"It will that, daddy," answered Malcolm.

The piper was sitting on a fallen tree, with the snow settling softly upon him.

"But it's too cold for you to be sitting there in the snow, and the dark too!" added Malcolm.

"Ta tarkness will not be ketting to ta inside of her," returned the seer. "Ah, my boy! where ta light kets in, ta tarkness will pe ketting in too. Tis now, your whole pody will be full of tarkness, as ta bible will say, and Tuncan's body—tat will be full of ta light." Then with suddenly changed tone he said "Listen, Malcolm, my son! she'll be fery uneasy till you 'll wass pe come home."

"What's the matter now, daddy?" returned Malcolm. "Anything wrong about the house?"

"Someting will be wrong, yes, but she'll not can tell where. No, her body will not be full of light! For town here in ta cursed Lowlands, ta sight has been almost cone from her, my son. It will now be no more as a co creeping troo' her, and she'll nefer see plain no more till she'll be cone back to her own mountains."

"The poor laird's gone back to his," said Malcolm. "I wonder if he knows yet, or if he goes asking everyone he meets if he can tell him where he came from. He's mad no more, anyway."

"How? Will he be not tead? Ta poor lairt! Ta poor maad lairt!"

"Ay, he's deid: maybe that's what 'll be troublin' yer sicht, daddy."

"No, my son. Ta maad lairt was not fery maad, and if he was maad he was not paad, and it was not to ta plame of him; he wass coot always however."

"He was that, daddy."

"But it will pe something fery paad, and it will pe troubling her speerit. When she'll pe take ta pipes, to pe amusing herself, and will plow *Till an crodh a' Dhonnachaidh (Turn the cows, Duncan)*, out will pe come *Cumhadh an fhir mhoir (The Lament of the Big Man)*. All is not well, my son."

"Weel, dinna distress yersel', daddy. Lat come what wull come. Foreseein' 's no forefen'in'. Ye ken yersel' 'at mony 's the time the seer has broucht the thing on by tryin' to haud it aff."

"It will pe true, my son. Put it would aalways haf come."

"Nae doobt; sae ye jist come in wi' me, daddy, an' sit doon by the ha' fire, an' I'll come to ye as sune 's I've been to see 'at the maister disna want me. But ye'll better come up wi' me to my room first," he went on, "for the maister disna like to see me in onything but the kilt."

"And why will he no pe in ta kilts aal as now?"

"I hae been ridin', ye ken, daddy, an' the trews fits the saiddle better nor the kilts."

"She'll not pe knowing tat. Old Allister, your creat—her own crandfather, was ta pest horseman ta worrlt efer saw, and he'll nefer pe hafing ta trews to his own lecks nor ta saddle to his horse's pack. He'll chust make his men pe strap on an old plaid, and he 'll pe kive a chump, and away they wass, horse and man, one peast, aal two of tem poth together."

"Ay, he's dead: maybe that's what'll be troubling your sight, daddy."

"No, my son. Ta maad lairt was not fery maad, and if he was maad he was not baad, and it was not to ta blame of him; he wass coot always however."

"He was that, daddy."

"But it will be something fery baad, and it will be troubling her speerit. When she'll be take ta pipes, to be amusing herself, and will blow *Till an crodh a' Dhonnachaidh (Turn the cows, Duncan)*, out will be come *Cumhadh an fhir mhoir (The Lament of the Big Man)*. All is not well, my son."

"Well, don't distress yourself, daddy. Let come what will come. Foreseeing's not forfending. You know yourself that many's the time the seer has brought the thing on by trying to prevent it."

"It will pe true, my son. But it would aalways haf come."

"No doubt; so you just come in with me, daddy, and sit down by the hall fire, and I'll come to you as soon as I've made sure the master doesn't want me. But you'd better come up with me to my room first," he went on, "for the master doesn't like to see me in anything but the kilt."

"And why will he no be in ta kilts aal as now?"

"I have been riding, you know, daddy, and the trews fit the saddle better than the kilt."

"She'll not be knowing tat. Old Allister, your creat—her own crandfather, was ta best horseman ta worrlt efer saw, and he'll nefer be hafing ta trews to his own lecks nor ta saddle to his horse's back. He'll chust make his men be strap on an old plaid, and he'll be give a chump, and away they wass, horse and man, one beast, aal two of tem both together."

Thus chatting they went to the stable, and from the stable to the house, where they met no one, and went straight up to Malcolm's room—the old man making as little of the long ascent as Malcolm himself.

Thus chatting they went to the stable, and from the stable to the house, where they met no one, and went straight up to Malcolm's room—the old man making as little of the long ascent as Malcolm himself.

CHAPTER LXVI

THE CRY FROM THE CHAMBER

Brooding, if a man of his temperament may ever be said to brood, over the sad history of his young wife and the prospects of his daughter, the marquis rode over fields and through gates—he never had been one to jump a fence in cold blood—till the darkness began to fall; and the bearings of his perplexed position came plainly before him.

First of all, Malcolm acknowledged, and the date of his mother's death known, what would Florimel be in the eyes of the world? Supposing the world deceived by the statement that his mother died when he was born, where yet was the future he had marked out for her? He had no money to leave her, and she must be helplessly dependent on her brother.

Malcolm, on the other hand, might make a good match, or, with the advantages he could secure him, in the army, still better in the navy, well enough push his way in the world.

Miss Horn could produce no testimony; and Mrs Catanach had asserted him the son of Mrs Stewart. He had seen enough, however, to make him dread certain possible results if Malcolm were acknowledged as the laird of Kirkbyres. No; there was but one hopeful measure, one which he had even already approached in a tentative way—an appeal, namely, to Malcolm himself—in which, acknowledging his probable rights, but representing in the strongest manner the difficulty of proving them, he would set forth, in their full dismay, the consequences to Florimel of their public recognition, and offer, upon the pledge of his word to a certain line of conduct, to start him in any path he chose to follow.

Having thought the thing out pretty thoroughly, as he fancied, and resolved at the same time to feel his way towards negotiations with Mrs Catanach, he turned and rode home.

After a tolerable dinner, he was sitting over a bottle of the port which he prized beyond anything else his succession had brought him, when the door of the dining-room opened suddenly, and the butler appeared, pale with terror.

"My lord! my lord!" he stammered, as he closed the door behind him.

"Well? What the devil's the matter now? Whose cow's dead?"

"Your lordship didn't hear it then?" faltered the butler.

"You've been drinking, Bings," said the marquis, lifting his seventh glass of port.

"I didn't say I heard it, my lord."

"Heard what—in the name of Beelzebub?"

"The ghost, my lord."

"The what?" shouted the marquis.

"That's what they call it, my lord. It's all along of having that wizard's chamber in the house, my lord."

"You're a set of fools," said the marquis, "the whole kit of you!"

"That's what I say, my lord. I don't know what to do with them, stericking and screaming. Mrs Courthope is trying her best with them; but it's my belief she's about as bad herself."

The marquis finished his glass of wine, poured out and drank another, then walked to the door. When the butler opened it, a strange sight met his eyes. All the servants in the house, men and women, Duncan and Malcolm alone excepted, had crowded after the butler, every one afraid of being left behind; and there gleamed the crowd of ghastly faces in the light of the great hall-fire. Demon stood in front, his mane bristling, and his eyes flaming. Such was the silence that the marquis heard the low howl of the waking wind, and the snow like the patting of soft hands against the windows. He stood for a moment, more than half enjoying their terror, when from somewhere in the building a far-off shriek, shrill and piercing, rang in every ear. Some of the men drew in their breath with a gasping sob, but most of the women screamed outright, and that set the marquis cursing.

Duncan and Malcolm had but just entered the bedroom of the latter, when the shriek rent the air close beside, and for a moment deafened them. So agonized, so shrill, so full of dismal terror was it, that Malcolm stood aghast, and Duncan started to his feet with responsive outcry. But Malcolm at once recovered himself.

"Bide here till I come back," he whispered, and hurried noiselessly out.

In a few minutes he returned—during which all had been still.

"Noo, daddy," he said, "I'm gaein' to drive in the door o' the neist room. there's some deevilry at wark there. Stan' ye i' the door, an' ghaist or deevil 'at wad win by ye, grip it, an' haud on like Demon the dog."

"She will so, she will so!" muttered Duncan in a strange tone. "Ochone! that she'll not pe hafing her turk with her! Ochone! Ochone!"

"Wait here till I come back," he whispered, and hurried noiselessly out.

In a few minutes he returned—during which all had been still.

"Now, daddy," he said, "I'm going to drive in the door of the next room. There's some devilry at work there. Just you stand in the door, and ghost or devil that would go by you, grip it, and hold on like Demon the dog."

"She will so, she will so!" muttered Duncan in a strange tone. "Alas! that she'll not pe hafing her dirk with her! Alas! Alas!"

Malcolm took the key of the wizard's chamber from his chest, and his candle from the table, which he set down in the passage. In a moment he had unlocked the door, put his shoulder to it, and burst it open. A light was extinguished, and a shapeless figure went gliding away through the gloom. It was no shadow, however, for, dashing itself against a door at the other side of the chamber, it staggered back with an imprecation of fury and fear, pressed two hands to its head, and, turning at bay, revealed the face of Mrs Catanach.

In the door stood the blind piper, with outstretched arms, and hands ready to clutch, the fingers curved like claws, his knees and haunches bent, leaning forward like a rampant beast prepared to spring. In his face was wrath, hatred, vengeance, disgust—an enmity of all mingled kinds.

Malcolm was busied with something in the bed, and when she turned, Mrs Catanach saw only the white face of hatred gleaming through the darkness.

"Ye auld donnert deevil!" she cried, with an addition too coarse to be set down, and threw herself upon him.

"You daft old devil!" she cried, with an addition too coarse to be set down, and threw herself upon him.

The old man said never a word, but with indrawn breath hissing through his clenched teeth, clutched her, and down they went together in the passage, the piper undermost. He had her by the throat, it is true, but she had her fingers in his eyes, and kneeling on his chest, kept him down with a vigour of hostile effort that drew the very picture of murder. It lasted but a moment, however, for the old man, spurred by torture as well as hate, gathered what survived of a most sinewy strength into one huge heave, threw her back into the room, and rose, with the blood streaming from his eyes—just as the marquis came round the near end of the passage, followed by Mrs Courthope, the butler, Stoat, and two of the footmen. Heartily enjoying a *row*, he stopped instantly, and signing a halt to his followers, stood listening to the mud-geyser that now burst from Mrs Catanach's throat.

"Ye blin' abortion o' Sawtan's soo!" she cried, "didna I tak ye to du wi' ye as I likit. An' that deil's tripe ye ca' yer oye—he! he!—*him* yer gran'son! He's naething but ane o' yer hatit Cawm'ells!"

"You blind abortion of Satan's sow!" she cried, "didn't I take you for a tool to my hand? And that devil's tripe you call your grandson—he! he!—*him* your grandson! He's nothing but one of your hated Campbells!"

"A teanga a' diabhuil mhoir, tha thu ag deanamh breug (*O tongue of the great devil thou art making a lie*)!" screamed Duncan, speaking for the first time.

"A teanga a' diabhuil mhoir, tha thu ag deanamh breug (*O tongue of the great devil thou art making a lie*)!" screamed Duncan, speaking for the first time.

"God lay me deid i' my sins gien he be onything but a bastard Cawm'ell!" she asseverated with a laugh of demoniacal scorn. "Yer dautit Ma'colm 's naething but the dyke-side brat o' the late Grizel Cawm'ell, 'at the fowk tuik for a sant 'cause she grat an'

"God lay me dead in my sins if he be aught but a bastard Campbell!" she asseverated with a laugh of demoniacal scorn. "Your petted Malcolm's nothing but the dyke-side brat of the late Grizel Campbell, that the folk took for a saint because she

He's nothing but one of your hated Campbells!

said naething. I laid the Cawm'ell pup i' yer boody airms wi' my ain han's, upo' the tap o' yer curst scraighin' bagpipes 'at sae aften drave the sleep frae my een. Na, ye wad nane o' me! But I ga'e ye a Cawm'ell bairn to yer hert for a' that, ye auld, hungert, weyver-leggit, worm-aten idiot!"

A torrent of Gaelic broke from Duncan, into the midst of which rushed another from Mrs Catanach, similar, but coarse in vowel and harsh in consonant sounds.

The marquis stepped into the room.

"What is the meaning of all this?" he said with dignity. The tumult of Celtic altercation ceased. The piper drew himself up to his full height, and stood silent. Mrs Catanach, red as fire with exertion and wrath, turned ashy pale. The marquis cast on her a searching and significant look.

"See here, my lord," said Malcolm.

Candle in hand, his lordship approached the bed. The same moment Mrs Catanach glided out with her usual downy step, gave a wink as of mutual intelligence to the group at the door, and vanished.

On Malcolm's arm lay the head of a young girl. Her thin, worn countenance was stained with tears, and livid with suffocation. She was recovering, but her eyes rolled stupid and visionless.

"It's Phemy, my lord—Blue Peter's lassie 'at was tint," said Malcolm.

"It begins to look serious," said the marquis. "Mrs Catanach!—Mrs Courthope!"

He turned towards the door. Mrs Courthope entered, and a head or two peeped in after her. Duncan stood as before, drawn up and stately, his visage working, but his body motionless as the statue of a sentinel.

wept to herself in silence. I laid the Campbell pup in your scarecrow arms with my own hands, upon the top of your cursed screeching bagpipes that so often drove the sleep from my eyes. Na, you would none of me! But I gave you a Campbell boy to your heart for all that, you old, starved, spider-legged, worm-eaten idiot!"

A torrent of Gaelic broke from Duncan, into the midst of which rushed another from Mrs Catanach, similar, but coarse in vowel and harsh in consonant sounds.

The marquis stepped into the room.

"What is the meaning of all this?" he said with dignity. The tumult of Celtic altercation ceased. The piper drew himself up to his full height, and stood silent. Mrs Catanach, red as fire with exertion and wrath, turned ashy pale. The marquis cast on her a searching and significant look.

"See here, my lord," said Malcolm.

Candle in hand, his lordship approached the bed. The same moment Mrs Catanach glided out with her usual downy step, gave a wink as of mutual intelligence to the group at the door, and vanished.

On Malcolm's arm lay the head of a young girl. Her thin, worn countenance was stained with tears, and livid with suffocation. She was recovering, but her eyes rolled stupid and visionless.

"It's Phemy, my lord—Blue Peter's lassie that was lost," said Malcolm.

"It begins to look serious," said the marquis. "Mrs Catanach!—Mrs Courthope!"

He turned towards the door. Mrs Courthope entered, and a head or two peeped in after her. Duncan stood as before, drawn up and stately, his visage working, but his body motionless as the statue of a sentinel.

"Where is the Catanach woman gone?" cried the marquis.

"Cone!" shouted the piper. "Cone! and her huspant will pe waiting to pe killing her! Och nan ochan!"

"Her husband!" echoed the marquis.

"Ach! she'll not can pe helping it, my lort—no more till one will pe tead—and tat should pe ta woman, for she'll pe a paad woman—ta worstest woman efer was married, my lort."

"That's saying a good deal," returned the marquis.

"Not one worrt more as enough, my lort," said Duncan. "She was only pe her next wife, put, ochone! ochone! why did she'll pe marry her? You would haf stapt her long aco, my lort, if she'll was your wife, and you was knowing the tamned fox and padger she was pe. Ochone! and she tidn't pe have her turk at her hench nor her sgian in her hose."

"Where is the Catanach woman gone?" cried the marquis.

"Cone!" shouted the piper. "Cone! and her husbant will pe waiting to pe killing her! Och nan ochan!"

"Her husband!" echoed the marquis.

"Ach! she'll not can be helping it, my lort—no more till one will be tead—and tat should be ta woman, for she'll be a baad woman—ta worstest woman efer was married, my lort."

"That's saying a good deal," returned the marquis.

"Not one worrt more as enough, my lort," said Duncan. "She was only be her next wife, but, alas! alas! why did she'll be marry her? You would haf stabbed her long ago, my lort, if she'll was your wife, and you was knowing the tamned fox and badger she was be. Alas! and she tidn't be have her dirk at her hench (hip) nor her sgian (sheath-knife) in her hose."

He shook his hands like a despairing child, then stamped and wept in the agony of frustrated rage.

Mrs Courthope took Phemy in her arms, and carried her to her own room, where she opened the window, and let the snowy wind blow full upon her. As soon as she came quite to herself Malcolm set out to bear the good tidings to her father and mother.

Only a few nights before had Phemy been taken to the room where they found her. She had been carried from place to place, and had been some time, she believed, in Mrs Catanach's own house. They had always kept her in the dark, and removed her at night, blindfolded. When asked if she had never cried out before, she said she had been too frightened; and when questioned as to what had made her do so then, she knew nothing of it: she remembered only that a horrible creature appeared by the bedside, after which all was blank. On the floor they found a hideous death-mask, doubtless the cause of the screams which Mrs Catanach had sought to stifle with the pillows and bedclothes.

When Malcolm returned, he went at once to the piper's cottage, where he found him in bed, utterly exhausted, and as utterly restless.

"Weel, daddy," he said, "I doobt I daurna come near ye noo."

"Well, daddy," he said, "I expect you won't let me near you now."

"Come to her arms, my poor poy!" faltered Duncan. "She'll pe sorry in her sore heart for her poy! Nefer you pe minding, my son; you couldn't help ta Cam'ell mother, and you'll pe her own poy however. Ochone! it will pe a plot upon you aal your tays, my son, and she'll not can help you, and it 'll pe preaking her old heart!"

"Gien God thoucht the Cam'ells worth makin', daddy, I dinna see 'at I hae ony richt to compleen 'at I cam' o' them."

"She hopes you'll pe forgifing ta plind old man, however. She couldn't see, or she would haf known at once petter."

"I dinna ken what ye're efter noo, daddy," said Malcolm.

"That she'll do you a creat wrong, and she'll be ferry sorry for it, my son."

"What wrang did ye ever du me, daddy?"

"That she was let you crow up a Cam'ell, my poy. If she tid put know ta paad plood was pe in you, she wouldn't pe tone you ta wrong as pring you up."

"That's a wrang no ill to forgi'e, daddy. But it's a pity ye didna lat me lie, for maybe syne Mistress Catanach wad hae broucht me up hersel', an' I micht hae come to something."

"Ta duvil mhor (*great*) would pe in your heart and prain and poosom, my son."

"Weel, ye see what ye hae saved me frae."

"Yes; put ta duvil will pe to pay, for she couldn't safe you from ta Cam'ell plood, my son! Malcolm, my poy," he added after a pause, and with the solemnity of a mighty hate, "ta efil woman herself will pe a Cam'ell—ta woman Catanach will pe a Cam'ell, and her nain sel' she'll not know it pefore she'll be in ta ped with the worsest Cam'ell tat ever God made—and she pecks his pardon, for she'll not pelieve he wass making ta Cam'ells."

"Come to her arms, my poor boy!" faltered Duncan. "She'll be sorry in her sore heart for her boy! Nefer you be minding, my son; you couldn't help ta Cam'ell mother, and you'll be her own boy however. Alas! it will be a blot upon you aal your days, my son, and she'll not can help you, and it'll be breaking her old heart!"

"If God thought the Campbells worth making, daddy, I don't see that I have any right to complain that I came of them."

"She hopes you'll be forgifing ta blind old man, however. She couldn't see, or she would haf known at once better."

"I don't know what you're driving at now, daddy," said Malcolm.

"That she'll do you a creat wrong, and she'll be ferry sorry for it, my son."

"What wrong did you ever do me, daddy?"

"That she was let you grow up a Cam'ell, my boy. If she tid but know ta baad blood was be in you, she wouldn't be tone you ta wrong as bring you up."

"That's a wrong it's easy to forgive, daddy. But it's a pity you didn't let me lie, for maybe then Mistress Catanach would have brought me up herself, and I might have come to something."

"Ta duvil mhor (*great devil*) would be in your heart and brain and boosom, my son."

"Well, you see what you have saved me from."

"Yes; but ta duvil will be to pay, for she couldn't safe you from ta Cam'ell blood, my son! Malcolm, my boy," he added after a pause, and with the solemnity of a mighty hate, "ta efil woman herself will be a Cam'ell—ta woman Catanach will be a Cam'ell, and her nain sel' she'll not know it before she'll be in ta bed with the worsest Cam'ell tat ever God made—and she becks his pardon, for she'll not believe he wass making ta Cam'ells."

"Divna ye think God made me, daddy?" asked Malcolm.

The old man thought for a little.

"Tat will tepend on who was pe your father, my son," he replied. "If he too will be a Cam'ell—ochone! ochone! Put tere may pe some coot plood co into you, more as enough to say God will pe make you, my son. Put don't pe asking, Malcolm. Ton't you'll pe asking."

"What am I no to ask, daddy?"

"Ton't pe asking who made you—who was ta father to you, my poy. She would rather not pe knowing, for ta man might pe a Cam'ell poth. And if she couldn't pe lofing you no more, my son, she would pe tie pefore her time, and her tays would pe long in ta land under ta crass, my son."

"Don't you think God made me, daddy?" asked Malcolm.

The old man thought for a little.

"Tat will tepend on who was be your father, my son," he replied. "If he too will be a Cam'ell—alas! alas! But tere may be some coot blood co into you, more as enough to say God will be make you, my son. But don't be asking, Malcolm. Ton't you'll be asking."

"What am I not to ask, daddy?"

"Ton't be asking who made you—who was ta father to you, my boy. She would rather not be knowing, for ta man might be a Cam'ell both. And if she couldn't be lofing you no more, my son, she would be die before her time, and her days would be long in ta land under ta crass, my son."

But the memory of the sweet face whose cold loveliness he had once kissed, was enough to outweigh with Malcolm all the prejudices of Duncan's instillation, and he was proud to take up even her shame. To pass from Mrs Stewart to her, was to escape from the clutches of a vampire demon to the arms of a sweet mother angel.

Deeply concerned for the newly-discovered misfortunes of the old man to whom he was indebted for this world's life at least, he anxiously sought to soothe him; but he had far more and far worse to torment him than Malcolm even yet knew, and with burning cheeks and bloodshot eyes, he lay tossing from side to side, now uttering terrible curses in Gaelic, and now weeping bitterly. Malcolm took his loved pipes, and with the gentlest notes he could draw from them tried to charm to rest the ruffled waters of his spirit; but his efforts were all in vain, and believing at length that he would be quieter without him, he went to the House, and to his own room.

The door of the adjoining chamber stood open, and the long forbidden room lay exposed to any eye. Little did Malcolm think as he gazed around it, that it was the room in which he had first breathed the air of the world; in which his mother had wept over her own false position and his reported death; and from which he had been carried, by Duncan's wicked wife, down the ruinous stair, and away to the lip of the sea, to find a home in the arms of the man whom he had just left on his lonely couch, torn between the conflicting emotions of a gracious love for him, and the frightful hate of her.

CHAPTER LXVII

FEET OF WOOL

The next day, Miss Horn, punctual as Fate, presented herself at Lossie House, and was shown at once into the marquis's study, as it was called. When his lordship entered, she took the lead the moment the door was shut.

"By this time, my lord, ye 'll doobtless hae made up yer min' to du what's richt?" she said.

"That's what I have always wanted to do," returned the marquis.

"Hm!" remarked Miss Horn, as plainly as inarticulately.

"In this affair," he supplemented; adding, "It's not always so easy to tell what *is* right!"

"It's no aye easy to luik for 't wi' baith yer een," said Miss Horn.

"This woman Catanach—we must get her to give credible testimony. Whatever the fact may be, we must have strong evidence. And there comes the difficulty, that she has already made an altogether different statement."

"It gangs for naething, my lord. It was never made afore a justice o' the peace."

"I wish you would go to her, and see how she is inclined."

"Me gang to Bawbie Catanach!" exclaimed Miss Horn. "I wad as sune gang an' kittle Sawtan's nose wi' the p'int o' 's tail. Na, na, my lord! Gien onybody gang till her wi' my wull, it s' be a limb o' the law. I s' hae nae cognostin' wi' her."

"By this time, my lord, you'll doubtless have made up your mind to do what's right?" she said.

"That's what I have always wanted to do," returned the marquis.

"Hm!" remarked Miss Horn, as plainly as inarticulately.

"In this affair," he supplemented; adding, "It's not always so easy to tell what *is* right!"

"It's not always easy to look for it with both your eyes," said Miss Horn.

"This woman Catanach—we must get her to give credible testimony. Whatever the fact may be, we must have strong evidence. And there comes the difficulty, that she has already made an altogether different statement."

"It goes for nothing, my lord. It was never made before a justice of the peace."

"I wish you would go to her, and see how she is inclined."

"Me go to Bawby Catanach!" exclaimed Miss Horn. "I would as soon go and tickle Satan's nose with the point of his tail. Na, na, my lord! If anyone should go to her with my will, it'll be a limb of the law. I'll have no colloguing with her."

"You would have no objection, however, to my seeing her, I presume—just to let her know that we have an inkling of the truth?" said the marquis.

Now all this was the merest talk, for of course Miss Horn could not long remain in ignorance of the declaration fury had, the night previous, forced from Mrs Catanach; but he must, he thought, put her off and keep her quiet, if possible, until he had come to an understanding with Malcolm, after which he would no doubt have his trouble with her.

"Ye can du as yer lordship likes," answered Miss Horn; "but I wadna hae 't said o' me 'at I had ony dealin's wi' her. Wha kens but she micht say ye tried to bribe her? There's naething she wad bogle at gien she thoucht it worth her while. No 'at I'm feart at her. Lat her lee! I'm no sae blate but—! Only dinna lippen till a word she says, my lord."

The marquis meditated.

"I wonder whether the real source of my perplexity occurs to you, Miss Horn," he said at length. "You know I have a daughter?"

"Weel eneuch that, my lord."

"By my second marriage."

"Nae merridge ava', my lord."

"True,—if I confess to the first."

"A' the same, whether or no, my lord."

"Then you see," the marquis went on, refusing offence, "what the admission of your story would make of my daughter?"

"That's plain eneuch, my lord."

"Now, if I have read Malcolm right, he has too much regard for his—mistress—to put her in such a false position."

"That is, my lord, ye wad hae yer lawfu' son beir the lawless name."

"You would have no objection, however, to my seeing her, I presume—just to let her know that we have an inkling of the truth?" said the marquis.

Now all this was the merest talk, for of course Miss Horn could not long remain in ignorance of the declaration fury had, the night previous, forced from Mrs Catanach; but he must, he thought, put her off and keep her quiet, if possible, until he had come to an understanding with Malcolm, after which he would no doubt have his trouble with her.

"You can do as your lordship likes," answered Miss Horn; "but I wouldn't have it said of me that I had any dealings with her. Who knows but she might say you tried to bribe her? There's nothing she'd stick at if she thought it worth her while. Not that I'm afraid of her. Let her lie! I'm not so gullible but—! Only don't trust a word she says, my lord."

The marquis meditated.

"I wonder whether the real source of my perplexity occurs to you, Miss Horn," he said at length. "You know I have a daughter?"

"Ay, well enough, my lord."

"By my second marriage."

"No marriage at all, my lord."

"True,—if I confess to the first."

"All the same, whether or not, my lord."

"Then you see," the marquis went on, refusing offence, "what the admission of your story would make of my daughter?"

"That's plain enough, my lord."

"Now, if I have read Malcolm right, he has too much regard for his—mistress—to put her in such a false position."

"That is, my lord, you would have your lawful son bear the lawless name."

"No, no; it need never come out what he is. I will provide for him—as a gentleman, of course."

"It canna be, my lord. Ye can du naething for him wi' that face o' his, but oot comes the trouth as to the father o' 'im; an' it wadna be lang afore the tale was ekit oot wi' the name o' his mither—Mistress Catanach wad see to that, gien 'twas only to spite me; an' I wunna hae my Grizel ca'd what she is not, for ony lord's dauchter i' the three kynriks."

"What *does* it matter, now she's dead and gone?" said the marquis, false to the dead in his love for the living.

"Deid an' gane, my lord! What ca' ye deid an' gane? Maybe the great anes o' the yerth get sic a forlethie o' gran'ur 'at they're for nae mair, an' wad perish like the brute beast. For onything I ken, they may hae their wuss, but for mysel', I wad warstle to haud my sowl waukin', i' the verra article o' deith, for the bare chance o' seein' my bonny Grizel again.—It's a mercy I hae nae feelin's!" she added, arresting her handkerchief on its way to her eyes, and refusing to acknowledge the single tear that ran down her cheek.

Plainly she was not like any of the women whose characters the marquis had accepted as typical of womankind.

"Then you won't leave the matter to her husband and son," he said reproachfully.

"I tellt ye, my lord, I wad du naething but what I saw to be richt. Lat this affair oot o' my han's I daurna. That laad ye micht work to onything 'at made agane himsel'. He 's jist like his puir mither there."

"If Miss Campbell *was* his mother," said the marquis.

"No, no; it need never come out what he is. I will provide for him—as a gentleman, of course."

"It can't be, my lord. You can do nothing for him with that face of his, but out comes the truth that you're the father of him; and it wouldn't be long before the tale grew to the adding of his mother's name—Mistress Catanach would see to that, if it was only to spite me; and I won't have my Grizel called what she's not, for any lord's daughter in the three kingdoms."

"What *does* it matter, now she's dead and gone?" said the marquis, false to the dead in his love for the living.

"Dead and gone, my lord! What call you dead and gone? Maybe the great ones of the earth get such a gorging of grandeur that they've no taste for more, and would perish like the brute beast. For anything I know, they may have their wish, but for myself, I would fight to keep my soul awake, in the very article of death, for the bare chance of seeing my Grizel again.—It's a mercy I have no feelings!" she added, arresting her handkerchief on its way to her eyes, and refusing to acknowledge the single tear that ran down her cheek.

Plainly she was not like any of the women whose characters the marquis had accepted as typical of womankind.

"Then you won't leave the matter to her husband and son," he said reproachfully.

"I told you, my lord, I would do nothing but what I saw to be right. I daren't let this business out of my hands. That lad you might persuade to anything that made against himself. He's just like his poor mother there."

"If Miss Campbell *was* his mother," said the marquis.

"Miss Cam'ell!" cried Miss Horn. "I'll thank yer lordship to ca' her by her ain, an' that's Lady Lossie."

What if the something ruinous heart of the marquis was habitable, was occupied by his daughter, and had no accommodation at present either for his dead wife or his living son. Once more he sat thinking in silence for a while.

"I'll make Malcolm a post captain in the navy, and give you a thousand pounds," he said at length, hardly knowing that he spoke.

Miss Horn rose to her full height, and stood like an angel of rebuke before him. Not a word did she speak, only looked at him for a moment, and turned to leave the room. The marquis saw his danger, and striding to the door, stood with his back against it.

"Think ye to scare *me*, my lord?" she asked, with a scornful laugh. "Gang an' scare the stane lion beast at yer ha' door. Haud oot o' the gait, an' lat me gang."

"Not until I know what you are going to do," said the marquis, very seriously.

"I hae naething mair to transac' wi' yer lordship. You an' me 's strangers, my lord."

"Tut! tut! I was but trying you."

"An' gien I had taen the disgrace ye offert me, ye wad hae drawn back?"

"No, certainly."

"Ye wasna tryin' me than: ye was duin' yer best to corrup' me."

"I'm no splitter of hairs."

"My lord, it 's nane but the corrup'ible wad seek to corrup'."

The marquis gnawed a nail or two in silence. Miss Horn dragged an easy chair within a couple of yards of him.

"Miss Campbell!" cried Miss Horn. "I'll thank your lordship to call her by her own, and that's Lady Lossie."

What if the something ruinous heart of the marquis was habitable, was occupied by his daughter, and had no accommodation at present either for his dead wife or his living son. Once more he sat thinking in silence for a while.

"I'll make Malcolm a post captain in the navy, and give you a thousand pounds," he said at length, hardly knowing that he spoke.

Miss Horn rose to her full height, and stood like an angel of rebuke before him. Not a word did she speak, only looked at him for a moment, and turned to leave the room. The marquis saw his danger, and striding to the door, stood with his back against it.

"Do you think to scare *me*, my lord?" she asked, with a scornful laugh. "Go and scare that stone-carved lion at your hall door. Stand back now, and let me go."

"Not until I know what you are going to do," said the marquis, very seriously.

"I have nothing more to say to your lordship. You and I are strangers, my lord."

"Tut! tut! I was but trying you."

"And if I had taken the disgrace you offered me, you would have drawn back?"

"No, certainly."

"Then you weren't trying me: you were doing your best to corrupt me."

"I'm no splitter of hairs."

"My lord, it's none but the corruptible would seek to corrupt."

The marquis gnawed a nail or two in silence. Miss Horn dragged an easy chair within a couple of yards of him.

"We'll see wha tires o' this ghem first, my lord!" she said, as she sank into its hospitable embrace.

The marquis turned to lock the door, but there was no key in it. Neither was there any chair within reach, and he was not fond of standing. Clearly his enemy had the advantage.

"Hae ye h'ard o' puir Sandy Graham—hoo they're misguidin' him, my lord?" she asked with composure.

The marquis was first astounded, and then tickled by her assurance.

"No," he answered.

"They hae turnt him oot o' hoose an' ha'—schuil, at least, an' hame," she rejoined. "I may say, they hae turnt him oot o' Scotlan'; for what presbytery wad hae him efter he had been fun' guilty o' no thinkin' like ither fowk? Ye maun stan' his guid freen', my lord."

"He shall be Malcolm's tutor," answered the marquis, not to be outdone in coolness, "and go with him to Edinburgh—or Oxford, if he prefers it."

"Never yerl o' Colonsay had a better!" said Miss Horn.

"Softly, softly, ma'am!" returned the marquis. "I did not say he should go in that style."

"He s' gang as my lord o' Colonsay, or he s' no gang at *your* expense, my lord," said his antagonist.

"Really, ma'am, one would think you were my grandmother, to hear you order my affairs for me."

"I wuss I war, my lord: I sud gar ye hear rizzon upo' baith sides o' yer heid, I s' warran'!"

The marquis laughed.

"We'll see who tires of this game first, my lord!" she said, as she sank into its hospitable embrace.

The marquis turned to lock the door, but there was no key in it. Neither was there any chair within reach, and he was not fond of standing. Clearly his enemy had the advantage.

"Have you heard of poor Sandy Graham—the shameful way they're using him, my lord?" she asked with composure.

The marquis was first astounded, and then tickled by her assurance.

"No," he answered.

"They have turned him out of house and hall—school, at least, and home," she rejoined. "I may say, they have turned him out of Scotland; for what presbytery would have him after he had been found guilty of thinking for himself? You must stand his good friend, my lord."

"He shall be Malcolm's tutor," answered the marquis, not to be outdone in coolness, "and go with him to Edinburgh—or Oxford, if he prefers it."

"Never earl of Colonsay had a better!" said Miss Horn.

"Softly, softly, ma'am!" returned the marquis. "I did not say he should go in that style."

"He shall go as my lord of Colonsay, or he shan't go at *your* expense, my lord," said his antagonist.

"Really, ma'am, one would think you were my grandmother, to hear you order my affairs for me."

"I wish I were, my lord: I should make you hear reason upon both sides of your head!"

The marquis laughed.

"Well, I can't stand here all day!" he said, impatiently swinging one leg.

"I'm weel awaur o' that, my lord," answered Miss Horn, rearranging her scanty skirt.

"How long are you going to keep me, then?"

"I wadna hae ye bide a meenute langer nor 's agreeable to yersel'. But *I'm* in nae hurry sae lang 's ye 're afore me. Ye 're nae ill to luik at—though ye maun hae been bonnier the day ye wan the hert o' my Grizzel."

The marquis uttered an oath, and left the door. Miss Horn sprang to it; but there was the marquis again.

"Miss Horn," he said, "I beg you will give me another day to think of this."

"Whaur's the use? A' the thinkin' i' the warl' canna alter a single fac'. Ye maun du richt by my laddie o' yer ain sel', or I maun gar ye."

"You would find a lawsuit heavy, Miss Horn."

"An' ye wad fin' the scandal o' 't ill to bide, my lord. It wad come sair upo' Miss—I kenna what name she has a richt till, my lord."

The marquis uttered a frightful imprecation, left the door, and sitting down, hid his face in his hands.

Miss Horn rose, but instead of securing her retreat, approached him gently, and stood by his side.

"My lord," she said, "I canna thole to see a man in tribble. Women 's born till 't, an' they tak it, an' are thankfu'; but a man never gies in till 't, an' sae it comes harder upo' him nor upo' them. Hear me, my lord: gien there be a man upo' this earth wha wad shield a wuman, that man 's Ma'colm Colonsay."

"Well, I can't stand here all day!" he said, impatiently swinging one leg.

"I'm well aware of that, my lord," answered Miss Horn, rearranging her scanty skirt.

"How long are you going to keep me, then?"

"I wouldn't have you stay a minute longer than you find agreeable. But *I'm* in no hurry so long as you remain. You're not an unpleasant study—though you must have been bonnier the day you won the heart of my Grizzel."

The marquis uttered an oath, and left the door. Miss Horn sprang to it; but there was the marquis again.

"Miss Horn," he said, "I beg you will give me another day to think of this."

"Where's the use? All the thinking in the world can't alter a single fact. You must do right by my laddie of yourself, my lord, or I must make you."

"You would find a lawsuit heavy, Miss Horn."

"And you would find the scandal of it no lighter, my lord. It would be sore too upon Miss—I don't know what name she has a right to, my lord."

The marquis uttered a frightful imprecation, left the door, and sitting down, hid his face in his hands.

Miss Horn rose, but instead of securing her retreat, approached him gently, and stood by his side.

"My lord," she said, "I can't bear to see a man in trouble. Women are born to it, and they take it, and are thankful; but a man never gives in to it, and so it comes harder upon him than upon them. Hear me, my lord: if there be a man upon this earth who would shield a woman, that man's Malcolm Colonsay."

"If only she weren't his sister!" murmured the marquis.

"An' jist bethink ye, my lord: wad it be onything less nor an imposition to lat a man merry her ohn tellt him what she was?"

"You insolent old woman!" cried the marquis, losing his temper, discretion, and manners, all together. "Go and do your worst, and be damned to you!"

So saying, he left the room, and Miss Horn found her way out of the house in a temper quite as fierce as his,—in character, however, entirely different, inasmuch as it was righteous.

At that very moment Malcolm was in search of his master; and seeing the back of him disappear in the library, to which he had gone in a half-blind rage, he followed him.

"My lord!" he said.

"What do you want?" returned his master in a rage. For some time he had been hauling on the curb rein, which had fretted his temper the more; and when he let go, the devil ran away with him.

"I thoucht yer lordship wad like to see an auld stair I cam upo' the ither day, 'at gang's frae the wizard's chaumer."

"Go to hell with your damned tom-foolery!" said the marquis. "If ever you mention that cursed hole again, I'll kick you out of the house."

"If only she weren't his sister!" murmured the marquis.

"And just bethink you, my lord: would it be anything less than an imposition to let a man marry her without telling him what she was?"

"You insolent old woman!" cried the marquis, losing his temper, discretion, and manners, all together. "Go and do your worst, and be damned to you!"

So saying, he left the room, and Miss Horn found her way out of the house in a temper quite as fierce as his,—in character, however, entirely different, inasmuch as it was righteous.

At that very moment Malcolm was in search of his master; and seeing the back of him disappear in the library, to which he had gone in a half-blind rage, he followed him.

"My lord!" he said.

"What do you want?" returned his master in a rage. For some time he had been hauling on the curb rein, which had fretted his temper the more; and when he let go, the devil ran away with him.

"I thought your lordship would like to see an old stair I came upon the other day, that goes from the wizard's chamber."

"Go to hell with your damned tom-foolery!" said the marquis. "If ever you mention that cursed hole again, I'll kick you out of the house."

Malcolm's eyes flashed, and a fierce answer rose to his lips, but he had seen that his master was in trouble, and sympathy supplanted rage. He turned and left the room in silence.

Lord Lossie paced up and down the library for a whole hour—a long time for him to be in one mood. The mood changed colour pretty frequently during the hour, however, and by degrees his wrath assuaged. But at the end of it he knew no more what he was going to do than when he left Miss Horn in the study. Then came the gnawing of his usual ennui and restlessness: he must find something to do.

The thing he always thought of first was a ride; but the only animal of horse kind about the place which he liked was the bay mare, and her he had lamed. He would go and see what the rascal had come bothering about—alone though, for he could not endure the sight of the fisher-fellow—damn him!

In a few moments he stood in the wizard's chamber, and glanced round it with a feeling of discomfort rather than sorrow—of annoyance at the trouble of which it had been for him both fountain and storehouse, rather than regret for the agony and contempt which his selfishness had brought upon the woman he loved; then spying the door in the furthest corner, he made for it, and in a moment more, his curiosity, now thoroughly roused, was slowly gyrating down the steps of the old screw stair. But Malcolm had gone to his own room, and hearing some one in the next, half suspected who it was, and went in. Seeing the closet door open, he hurried to the stair, and shouted,

"My lord! my lord! or whaever ye are! tak care hoo ye gang, or ye'll get a terrible fa'."

"My lord! my lord! or whoever you are! take care how you go, or you'll get a terrible fall."

Down a single yard the stair was quite dark, and he dared not follow fast for fear of himself falling and occasioning the accident he feared. As he descended, he kept repeating his warnings, but either his master did not hear or heeded too little, for presently Malcolm heard a rush, a dull fall, and a groan. Hurrying as fast as he dared with the risk of falling upon him, he found the marquis lying amongst the stones in the ground entrance, apparently unable to move, and white with pain. Presently, however, he got up, swore a good deal, and limped swearing into the house.

The doctor, who was sent for instantly, pronounced the knee-cap injured, and applied leeches. Inflammation set in, and another doctor and surgeon were sent for from Aberdeen. They came; applied poultices, and again leeches, and enjoined the strictest repose. The pain was severe; but to one of the marquis's temperament, the enforced quiet was worse.

CHAPTER LXVIII

HANDS OF IRON

The marquis was loved by his domestics; and his accident, with its consequences, although none more serious were anticipated, cast a gloom over Lossie House. Far apart as was his chamber from all the centres of domestic life, the pulses of his suffering beat as it were through the house, and the servants moved with hushed voice and gentle footfall.

Outside, the course of events waited upon his recovery, for Miss Horn was too generous not to delay proceedings while her adversary was ill. Besides, what she most of all desired was the marquis's free acknowledgment of his son; and after such a time of suffering and constrained reflection as he was now passing through, he could hardly fail, she thought, to be more inclined to what was just and fair.

Malcolm had of course hastened to the schoolmaster with the joy of his deliverance from Mrs Stewart; but Mr Graham had not acquainted him with the discovery Miss Horn had made, or her belief concerning his large interest therein, to which Malcolm's report of the wrath-born declaration of Mrs Catanach had now supplied the only testimony wanting, for the right of disclosure was Miss Horn's. To her he had carried Malcolm's narrative of late events, tenfold strengthening her position; but she was anxious in her turn that the revelation concerning his birth should come to him from his father. Hence Malcolm continued in ignorance of the strange dawn that had begun to break on the darkness of his origin.

Miss Horn had told Mr Graham what the marquis had said about the tutorship; but the schoolmaster only shook his head with a smile, and went on with his preparations for departure.

The hours went by; the days lengthened into weeks, and the marquis's condition did not improve. He had never known sickness and pain before, and like most of the children of this world, counted them the greatest of evils; nor was there any sign of their having as yet begun to open his eyes to what those who have seen them call truths, those who have never even boded their presence count absurdities.

More and more, however, he desired the attendance of Malcolm, who was consequently a great deal about him, serving with a love to account for which those who knew his nature would not have found it necessary to fall back on the instinct of the relation between them. The marquis had soon satisfied himself that that relation was as yet unknown to him, and was all the better pleased with his devotion and tenderness.

The inflammation continued, increased, spread, and at length the doctors determined to amputate. But the marquis was absolutely horrified at the idea,—shrank from it with invincible repugnance. The moment the first dawn of comprehension vaguely illuminated their periphrastic approaches, he blazed out in a fury, cursed them frightfully, called them all the contemptuous names in his rather limited vocabulary, and swore he would see them—uncomfortable first.

"We fear mortification, my lord," said the physician calmly.

"So do I. Keep it off," returned the marquis.

"We fear we cannot, my lord."

It had, in fact, already commenced.

"Let it mortify, then, and be damned," said his lordship.

"I trust, my lord, you will reconsider it," said the surgeon. "We should not have dreamed of suggesting a measure of such severity had we not had reason to dread that the further prosecution of gentler means would but lessen your lordship's chance of recovery."

"You mean then that my life is in danger?"

"We fear," said the physician, "that the amputation proposed is the only thing that can save it."

"What a brace of blasted bunglers you are!" cried the marquis, and turning away his face, lay silent. The two men looked at each other, and said nothing.

Malcolm was by, and a keen pang shot to his heart at the verdict. The men retired to consult. Malcolm approached the bed.

"My lord!" he said gently.

No reply came.

"Dinna lea 's oor lanes, my lord—no yet," Malcolm persisted. "What's to come o' my leddy?"

The marquis gave a gasp. Still he made no reply.

"She has naebody, ye ken, my lord, 'at ye wad like to lippen her wi'."

"You must take care of her when I am gone, Malcolm," murmured the marquis; and his voice was now gentle with sadness and broken with misery.

"Me, my lord!" returned Malcolm. "Wha wad min' me? An' what cud I du wi' her? I cudna even haud her ohn wat her feet. Her leddy's maid cud du mair wi' her—though I wad lay doon my life for her, as I tauld ye, my lord—an' she kens 't weel eneuch."

"My lord!" he said gently.

No reply came.

"Don't leave us alone, my lord—not yet," Malcolm persisted. "What's to become of my lady?"

The marquis gave a gasp. Still he made no reply.

"She has nobody, you know, my lord, that you would like to trust her with."

"You must take care of her when I am gone, Malcolm," murmured the marquis; and his voice was now gentle with sadness and broken with misery.

"Me, my lord!" returned Malcolm. "Who would mind me? And what could I do with her? I couldn't even keep her from wetting her feet. Her lady's maid could do more with her—though I would lay down my life for her, as I told you, my lord—and she knows it well enough."

Silence followed. Both men were thinking.

"Gie me a richt, my lord, an' I'll du my best," said Malcolm, at length breaking the silence.

"What do you mean?" growled the marquis, whose mood had altered.

"Gie me a legal richt, my lord, an' see gien I dinna."

"See what?"

"See gien I dinna luik weel efter my leddy."

"How am I to see? I shall be dead and damned."

"Please God, my lord, ye'll be alive an' weel—in a better place, if no here to luik efter my leddy yersel'."

"Oh, I dare say!" muttered the marquis.

"But ye'll hearken to the doctors, my lord," Malcolm went on, "an' no dee wantin' time to consider o' 't."

"Yes, yes; tomorrow I'll have another talk with them. We'll see about it. There's time enough yet. They're all cox-combs—every one of them. They never give a patient the least credit for common sense."

"I dinna ken, my lord," said Malcolm doubtfully.

After a few minutes' silence, during which Malcolm thought he had fallen asleep, the marquis resumed abruptly.

"What do you mean by giving you a legal right?" he said.

"There's some w'y o' makin' ae body guairdian till anither, sae 'at the law 'ill uphaud him—isna there, my lord?"

"Yes, surely. Well!—Rather odd—wouldn't it be?—A young fisher-lad guardian to a marchioness! Eh? They say there's nothing new under the sun; but that sounds rather like it, I think."

Silence followed. Both men were thinking.

"Give me a right, my lord, and I'll do my best," said Malcolm, at length breaking the silence.

"What do you mean?" growled the marquis, whose mood had altered.

"Give me a legal right, my lord, and see if I don't."

"See what?"

"See if I don't look well after my lady."

"How am I to see? I shall be dead and damned."

"Please God, my lord, you'll be alive and well—in a better place, if not here to look after my lady yourself."

"Oh, I dare say!" muttered the marquis.

"But you'll listen to the doctors," Malcolm went on, "and not die without time to consider it."

"Yes, yes; tomorrow I'll have another talk with them. We'll see about it. There's time enough yet. They're all cox-combs—every one of them. They never give a patient the least credit for common sense."

"I don't know, my lord," said Malcolm doubtfully.

After a few minutes' silence, during which Malcolm thought he had fallen asleep, the marquis resumed abruptly.

"What do you mean by giving you a legal right?" he said.

"There's some way of making one person guardian to another, that the law will recognise—isn't there, my lord?"

"Yes, surely. Well!—Rather odd—wouldn't it be?—A young fisher-lad guardian to a marchioness! Eh? They say there's nothing new under the sun; but that sounds rather like it, I think."

Malcolm was overjoyed to hear him speak with something like his old manner. He felt he could stand any amount of chaff from him now, and so the proposition he had made in seriousness, he went on to defend in the hope of giving amusement, yet with a secret wild delight in the dream of such full devotion to the service of Lady Florimel.

"It wad soon' queer eneuch, my lord, nae doobt; but fowk maunna min' the soon' o' a thing gien 't be a' straucht an' fair, an' strong eneuch to stan'. They cudna lauch me oot o' my richts, be they 'at they likit—Lady Bellair, or ony o' them—na, nor jaw me oot o' them aither!"

"They might do a good deal to render those rights of little use," said the marquis.

"That wad come till a trial o' brains, my lord," returned Malcolm; "an' ye dinna think I wadna hae the wit to speir advice—an' what's mair, to ken whan it was guid, an' tak it! There's lawyers, my lord."

"And their expenses?"

"Ye cud lea' sae muckle to be waured upo' the cairryin' oot o' yer lordship's wull."

"Who would see that you applied it properly?"

"My ain conscience, my lord—or Mr Graham, gien ye likit."

"And how would you live yourself?"

"Ow! lea' ye that to me, my lord. Only dinna imaigine I wad be behauden to yer lordship. I houp I hae mair pride nor that. Ilka poun'-not', shillin', an' baubee sud be laid oot for *her*, an' what was left hainet for her."

"By Jove! it's a daring proposal!" said the marquis; and, which seemed strange to Malcolm, not a single thread of ridicule ran through the tone in which he made the remark.

Malcolm was overjoyed to hear him speak with something like his old manner. He felt he could stand any amount of chaff from him now, and so the proposition he had made in seriousness, he went on to defend in the hope of giving amusement, yet with a secret wild delight in the dream of such full devotion to the service of Lady Florimel.

"It would sound queer enough, my lord, no doubt; but folk mustn't mind the sound of a thing if it be all straight and fair, and strong enough to stand. They couldn't laugh me out of my rights, be they who they liked—Lady Bellair, or any of them—na, nor jaw me out of them either!"

"They might do a good deal to render those rights of little use," said the marquis.

"That would come to a trial of brains, my lord," returned Malcolm; "and you don't think I would lack the wit to ask advice—and what's more, to know when it was good, and take it! There's lawyers, my lord."

"And their expenses?"

"You could leave enough to be spent on the carrying out of your lordship's will."

"Who would see that you applied it properly?"

"My own conscience, my lord—or Mr Graham, if you liked."

"And how would you live yourself?"

"Oh! leave that to me, my lord. Only don't imagine I'd be beholden to your lordship. I hope I have more pride than that. Every pound-note, shilling, and halfpence should be laid out for *her*, and the rest saved for her."

"By Jove! it's a daring proposal!" said the marquis; and, which seemed strange to Malcolm, not a single thread of ridicule ran through the tone in which he made the remark.

The next day came, but brought neither strength of body nor of mind with it. Again his professional attendants besought him, and he heard them more quietly, but rejected their proposition as positively as before. In a day or two he ceased to oppose it, but would not hear of preparation. Hour glided into hour, and days had gathered to a week, when they assailed him with a solemn and last appeal.

"Nonsense!" answered the marquis. "My leg is getting better. I feel no pain—in fact nothing but a little faintness. Your damned medicines, I haven't a doubt."

"You are in the greatest danger, my lord. It is all but too late even now."

"Tomorrow, then—if it must be. Today I could not endure to have my hair cut—positively; and as to having my leg off,—pooh! the thing's preposterous!"

He turned white and shuddered, for all the nonchalance of his speech.

When tomorrow came, there was not a surgeon in the land who would have taken his leg off. He looked in their faces, and seemed for the first time convinced of the necessity of the measure.

"You may do as you please," he said. "I am ready."

"Not today, my lord," replied the doctor. "Your lordship is not equal to it today."

"I understand," said the marquis, paled frightfully, and turned his head aside.

When Mrs Courthope suggested that Lady Florimel should be sent for, he flew into a frightful rage, and spoke as it is to be hoped he had never spoken to a woman before. She took it with perfect gentleness, but could not repress a tear. The marquis saw it, and his heart was touched.

"You mustn't mind a dying man's temper," he said.

"It's not for myself, my lord," she answered.

"I know: you think I'm not fit to die; and, damn it! you are right. Never one was less fit for heaven, or less willing to go to hell."

"Wouldn't you like to see a clergyman, my lord?" she suggested, sobbing.

He was on the point of breaking out in a still worse passion, but controlled himself.

"A clergyman!" he cried; "I would as soon see the undertaker. What could he do but tell me I was going to be damned—a fact I know better than he can? That is, if it's not all an invention of the cloth, as, in my soul, I believe it is! I've said so any time this forty years."

"Oh, my lord, my lord! do not fling away your last hope."

"You imagine me to have a chance then? Good soul! You don't know better!"

"The Lord is merciful."

The marquis laughed—that is, he tried, failed, and grinned.

"Mr Cairns is in the dining room, my lord."

"Bah! A low pettifogger, with the soul of a bullock! Don't let me hear the fellow's name. I've been bad enough, God knows! but I haven't sunk to the level of *his* help yet. If he's God Almighty's factor, and the saw holds—'Like master, like man!' well, I would rather have nothing to do with either."

"That is, if you had the choice, my lord," said Mrs Courthope, her temper yielding a little, though in truth his speech was not half so irreverent as it seemed to her.

"Tell him to go to hell. No, don't: set him down to a bottle of port and a great sponge-cake and you needn't tell him to go to heaven, for he'll be there already. Why, Mrs Courthope, the fellow isn't a gentleman! And yet all he cares for the cloth is, that he thinks it makes a gentleman of him—as if anything in heaven, earth, or hell could work that miracle!"

In the middle of the night, as Malcolm sat by his bed, thinking him asleep, the marquis spoke suddenly.

"You must go to Aberdeen tomorrow, Malcolm," he said.

"Verra weel, my lord."

"And bring Mr Glennie, the lawyer, back with you."

"Yes, my lord."

"Go to bed then."

"I wad raither bide, my lord. I cudna sleep a wink for wantin' to be back aside ye."

"You must go to Aberdeen tomorrow, Malcolm," he said.

"Very well, my lord."

"And bring Mr Glennie, the lawyer, back with you."

"Yes, my lord."

"Go to bed then."

"I would rather stay, my lord. I couldn't sleep a wink for wanting to be back beside you."

The marquis yielded, and Malcolm sat by him all the night through. He tossed about, would doze off and murmur strangely, then wake up and ask for brandy and water, yet be content with the lemonade Malcolm gave him.

Next day he quarrelled with every word Mrs Courthope uttered, kept forgetting he had sent Malcolm away, and was continually wanting him. His fits of pain were more severe, alternated with drowsiness, which deepened at times to stupor.

It was late before Malcolm returned. He went instantly to his bedside.

"Is Mr Glennie with you?" asked his master feebly.

"Yes, my lord."

"Tell him to come here at once."

When Malcolm returned with the lawyer, the marquis directed him to set a table and chair by the bedside, light four candles, get everything necessary for writing, and go to bed.

CHAPTER LXIX

THE MARQUIS AND THE SCHOOLMASTER

Before Malcolm was awake, his lordship had sent for him. When he re-entered the sick chamber, Mr Glennie had vanished, the table had been removed, and instead of the radiance of the wax lights, the cold gleam of a vapour-dimmed sun, with its sickly blue-white reflex from the wide-spread snow, filled the room. The marquis looked ghastly, but was sipping chocolate with a spoon.

"What w'y are ye the day, my lord?" asked Malcolm.

"Nearly well," he answered; "but those cursed carrion-crows are set upon killing me—damn their souls!"

"We'll hae Leddy Florimel sweirin' awfu', gien ye gang on that gait, my lord," said Malcolm.

The marquis laughed feebly.

"An' what 's mair," Malcolm continued, "I doobt they're some partic'lar aboot the turn o' their phrases up yonner, my lord."

The marquis looked at him keenly.

"You don't anticipate that inconvenience for me?" he said. "I'm pretty sure to have my billet where they're not so precise."

"Dinna brak my hert, my lord!" cried Malcolm, the tears rushing to his eyes.

"I should be sorry to hurt you, Malcolm," rejoined the marquis gently, almost tenderly. "I won't go there if I can help it. I shouldn't like to break any more hearts. But how the devil am I to keep out

"How are you today, my lord?" asked Malcolm.

"Nearly well," he answered; "but those cursed carrion-crows are set upon killing me—damn their souls!"

"We'll have Lady Florimel swearing like a sailor, if you go on that way, my lord," said Malcolm.

The marquis laughed feebly.

"And what's more," Malcolm continued, "I've a notion they're quite particular about the turn of their phrases up yonder, my lord."

The marquis looked at him keenly.

"You don't anticipate that inconvenience for me?" he said. "I'm pretty sure to have my billet where they're not so precise."

"Don't break my heart, my lord!" cried Malcolm, the tears rushing to his eyes.

"I should be sorry to hurt you, Malcolm," rejoined the marquis gently, almost tenderly. "I won't go there if I can help it. I shouldn't like to break any more hearts. But how the devil am I to keep out of it? Besides, there are people up there I don't want to meet; I have no fancy for being made ashamed of myself. The fact is I'm not fit for such company, and I don't believe there is any such place. But if there be, I trust in God there isn't any other, or it will go badly with your poor master, Malcolm. It doesn't look *like* true—now does it? Only such a multitude of things I thought I had done with for ever, keep coming up and grinning at me! It nearly drives me mad, Malcolm—and I would fain die like a gentleman, with a cool bow and a sharp face about."

"Wadna ye hae a word wi' somebody 'at kens, my lord?" said Malcolm, scarcely able to reply.

"No," answered the marquis fiercely. "That Cairns is a fool."

"He's a' that an' mair, my lord. I didna mean *him*."

"They're all fools together."

"Ow, na, my lord! there's a heap o' them no muckle better, it may be; but there's guid men an' true amang them, or the kirk wad hae been wi' Sodom and Gomorrha by this time. But it 's no a minister I wad hae yer lordship confar wi'."

"Who then? Mrs Courthope? Eh?"

"Ow na, my lord—no Mistress Coorthoup! she's a guid body, but she wadna believe her ain een gien onybody ca'd a minister said contrar' to them."

"Who the devil do you mean then?"

"Nae deevil, but an honest man 'at 's been his warst enemy sae lang 's I hae kent him: Maister Graham, the schuilmaister."

"Pooh!" said the marquis with a puff. "I'm too old to go to school."

"I dinna ken the man 'at isna a bairn till *him*, my lord."

of it? Besides, there are people up there I don't want to meet; I have no fancy for being made ashamed of myself. The fact is I'm not fit for such company, and I don't believe there is any such place. But if there be, I trust in God there isn't any other, or it will go badly with your poor master, Malcolm. It doesn't look *like* true—now does it? Only such a multitude of things I thought I had done with for ever, keep coming up and grinning at me! It nearly drives me mad, Malcolm—and I would fain die like a gentleman, with a cool bow and a sharp face about."

"Wouldn't you have a word with somebody that knows, my lord?" said Malcolm, scarcely able to reply.

"No," answered the marquis fiercely. "That Cairns is a fool."

"He's all that and more, my lord. I didn't mean *him*."

"They're all fools together."

"Oh, na, my lord! there's many of them little better, perhaps; but there's good men and true among them, or the church would have been with Sodom and Gomorrah by this time. But it's not a minister I was thinking of."

"Who then? Mrs Courthope? Eh?"

"Oh na, my lord—not Mistress Courthope! she's a good woman, but she wouldn't believe her own eyes if anyone called a minister disputed them."

"Who the devil do you mean then?"

"No devil, but an honest man who's been his worst enemy so long as I have known him: Mister Graham, the schoolmaster."

"Pooh!" said the marquis with a puff. "I'm too old to go to school."

"I don't know the man that isn't a child to *him*, my lord."

"In Greek and Latin?"

"I' richteousness an' trouth, my lord; in what's been an' what is to be."

"What! has he the second sight, like the piper?"

"He *has* the second sicht, my lord—but ane 'at gangs a sicht farther than my auld daddy's."

"He could tell me then what's going to become of me?"

"As weel 's ony man, my lord."

"That's not saying much, I fear."

"Maybe mair nor ye think, my lord."

"Well, take him my compliments, and tell him I should like to see him," said the marquis, after a pause.

"He'll come direckly, my lord."

"Of course he will!" said the marquis.

"Jist as readily, my lord, as he wad gang to ony tramp 'at sent for 'im at sic a time," returned Malcolm, who did not relish either the remark or its tone.

"What do you mean by that? *You* don't think it such a serious affair—do you?"

"My lord, ye haena a chance."

"In Greek and Latin?"

"In righteousness and truth, my lord; in what's been and what is to be."

"What! has he the second sight, like the piper?"

"He *has* the second sight, my lord—but one that goes a sight farther than my old daddy's."

"He could tell me then what's going to become of me?"

"As well as any man, my lord."

"That's not saying much, I fear."

"Maybe more than you think, my lord."

"Well, take him my compliments, and tell him I should like to see him," said the marquis, after a pause.

"He'll come directly, my lord."

"Of course he will!" said the marquis.

"Just as readily, my lord, as he would go to any tramp that sent for him at such a time," returned Malcolm, who did not relish either the remark or its tone.

"What do you mean by that? *You* don't think it such a serious affair—do you?"

"My lord, you haven't a chance."

The marquis was dumb. He had actually begun once more to buoy himself up with earthly hopes.

Dreading a recall of his commission, Malcolm slipped from the room, sent Mrs Courthope to take his place, and sped to the schoolmaster. The moment Mr Graham heard the marquis's message, he rose without a word, and led the way from the cottage. Hardly a sentence passed between them as they went, for they were on a solemn errand.

"Mr Graham's here, my lord," said Malcolm.

"Where? Not in the room?" returned the marquis.

"Waitin' at the door, my lord."

"Bah! You needn't have been so ready. Have you told the sexton to get a new spade? But you may let him in. And leave him alone with me."

Mr Graham walked gently up to the bedside.

"Sit down, sir," said the marquis courteously—pleased with the calm, self-possessed, unobtrusive bearing of the man. "They tell me I'm dying, Mr Graham."

"I'm sorry it seems to trouble you, my lord."

"What! wouldn't it trouble you then?"

"I don't think so, my lord."

"Ah! you're one of the elect, no doubt?"

"That's a thing I never did think about, my lord."

"What do you think about then?"

"About God."

"And when you die you'll go straight to heaven of course—"

"I don't know, my lord. That's another thing I never trouble my head about."

"Ah! you're like me then! *I* don't care much about going to heaven! What do you care about?"

"The will of God. I hope your lordship will say the same."

"No I won't. I want my own will."

"Well, that is to be had, my lord."

"How?"

"By taking his for yours, as the better of the two, which it must be every way."

"That's all moonshine."

"It *is* light, my lord."

"Well, I don't mind confessing, if I am to die, I should prefer heaven to the other place; but I trust I have no chance of either. Do you now honestly believe there are two such places?"

"I don't know, my lord."

"You don't know! And you come here to comfort a dying man!"

"Your lordship must first tell me what you mean by 'two *such* places.' And as to comfort, going by my notions, I cannot tell which you would be more or less comfortable in; and that, I presume, would be the main point with your lordship."

"And what, pray, sir, would be the main point with you?"

"To get nearer to God."

"Well—I can't say *I* want to get nearer to God. It's little he's ever done for me."

"It's a good deal he has tried to do for you, my lord."

"Well, who interfered? Who stood in his way, then?"

"Yourself, my lord."

"I wasn't aware of it. When did he ever try to do anything for me, and I stood in his way?"

"When he gave you one of the loveliest of women, my lord," said Mr Graham, with solemn, faltering voice, "and you left her to die in neglect, and the child to be brought up by strangers."

The marquis gave a cry. The unexpected answer had roused the slowly gnawing death, and made it bite deeper.

"What have *you* to do," he almost screamed, "with my affairs? It was for *me* to introduce what I chose of them. You presume."

"Pardon me, my lord: you led me to what I was bound to say. Shall I leave you, my lord?"

The marquis made no answer.

"God knows I loved her," he said after a while, with a sigh.

"You loved her, my lord!"

"I did, by God!"

"Love a woman like that, and come to this?"

"Come to this! We must all come to this, I fancy, sooner or later. Come to what, in the name of Beelzebub?"

"That, having loved a woman like her, you are content to lose her. In the name of God, have you no desire to see her again?"

"It would be an awkward meeting," said the marquis. His was an old love, alas! He had not been capable of the sort that defies change. It had faded from him until it seemed one of the things that are not! Although his being had once glowed in its light, he could now speak of a meeting as awkward!

"Because you wronged her?" suggested the schoolmaster.

"Because they lied to me, by God!"

"Which they dared not have done, had you not lied to them first."

"Sir!" shouted the marquis, with all the voice he had left. "O God, have mercy! I *cannot* punish the scoundrel."

"The scoundrel is the man who lies, my lord."

"Were I anywhere else—"

"There would be no good in telling you the truth, my lord. You showed her to the world as a woman over whom you had prevailed, and not as the honest wife she was. What *kind* of a lie was that, my lord? Not a white one, surely?"

"You are a damned coward to speak so to a man who cannot even turn on his side to curse you for a base hound. You would not dare it but that you know I cannot defend myself."

"You are right, my lord; your conduct is indefensible."

"By heaven! if I could but get this cursed leg under me, I would throw you out of the window."

"I shall go by the door, my lord. While you hold by your sins, your sins will hold by you. If you should want me again, I shall be at your lordship's command."

He rose and left the room, but had not reached his cottage before Malcolm overtook him, with a second message from his master. He turned at once, saying only, "I expected it."

"Mr Graham," said the marquis, looking ghastly, "you must have patience with a dying man. I was very rude to you, but I was in horrible pain."

"Don't mention it, my lord. It would be a poor friendship that gave way for a rough word."

"How can you call yourself my friend?"

"I should be your friend, my lord, if it were only for your wife's sake. She died loving you. I want to send you to her, my lord. You will allow that, as a gentleman, you at least owe her an apology."

"By Jove, you are right, sir! Then you really and positively believe in the place they call heaven?"

"My lord, I believe that those who open their hearts to the truth, shall see the light on their friends' faces again, and be able to set right what was wrong between them."

"It's a week too late to talk of setting right!"

"Go and tell her you are sorry, my lord,—that will be enough to her."

"Ah! but there's more than her concerned."

"You are right, my lord. There is another—one who cannot be satisfied that the fairest works of his hands, or rather the loveliest children of his heart, should be treated as you have treated women."

"But the Deity you talk of—"

"I beg your pardon, my lord: I talked of no deity; I talked of a living Love that gave us birth and calls us his children. Your deity I know nothing of."

"Call him what you please:—*he* won't be put off so easily!"

"He won't be put off one jot or one tittle. He will forgive anything, but he will pass nothing. Will your wife forgive you?"

"She will—when I explain."

"Then why should you think the forgiveness of God, which created her forgiveness, should be less?"

Whether the marquis could grasp the reasoning, may be doubtful.

"Do you really suppose God cares whether a man comes to good or ill?"

"If he did not, he could not be good himself."

"Then you don't think a good God would care to punish poor wretches like us?"

"Your lordship has not been in the habit of regarding himself as a poor wretch. And, remember, you can't call a child a poor wretch without insulting the father of it."

"That's quite another thing."

"But on the wrong side for your argument—seeing the relation between God and the poorest creature is infinitely closer than that between any father and his child."

"Then he can't be so hard on him as the parsons say."

"He will give him absolute justice, which is the only good thing. He will spare nothing to bring his children back to himself—their sole well-being. What would you do, my lord, if you saw your son strike a woman?"

"Knock him down and horsewhip him."

It was Mr Graham who broke the silence that followed.

"Are you satisfied with yourself, my lord?"

"No, by God!"

"You would like to be better?"

"I would."

"Then you are of the same mind with God."

"Yes but I'm not a fool! It won't do to say I should like to be: I must be it, and that's not so easy. It's damned hard to be good. I would have a fight for it, but there's no time. How is a poor devil to get out of such an infernal scrape?"

"Keep the commandments."

"That's it, of course; but there's no time, I tell you—at least so those cursed doctors will keep telling me."

"If there were but time to draw another breath, there would be time to begin."

"How am I to begin? Which am I to begin with?"

"There is one commandment which includes all the rest."

"Which is that?"

"To believe on the Lord Jesus Christ."

"That's cant."

"After thirty years' trial of it, it is to me the essence of wisdom. It has given me a peace which makes life or death all but indifferent to me, though I would choose the latter."

"What am I to believe about him then?"

"You are to believe *in* him, not about him."

"I don't understand."

"He is our Lord and Master, Elder Brother, King, Saviour, the divine Man, the human God: to believe in him is to give ourselves up to him in obedience, to search out his will and do it."

"But there's no time, I tell you again," the marquis almost shrieked.

"And I tell you, there is all eternity to do it in. Take him for your master, and he will demand nothing of you which you are not able to perform. This is the open door to bliss. With your last breath you can cry to him, and he will hear you, as he heard the thief on the cross who cried to him dying beside him. 'Lord, remember me when thou comest into thy kingdom.' 'Today shalt thou be with me in paradise.' It makes my heart swell to think of it, my lord! No cross-questioning of the poor fellow! No preaching to him! He just took him with him where he was going, to make a man of him."

"Well, you know something of my history: what would you have me do now? At once, I mean. What would the person you speak of have me do?"

"That is not for me to say, my lord."

"You could give me a hint."

"No. God is telling you himself. For me to presume to tell you, would be to interfere with him. What he would have a man do, he lets him know in his mind."

"But what if I had not made up my mind before the last came?"

"Then I fear he would say to you—'Depart from me, thou worker of iniquity.'"

"That would be hard when another minute might have done it."

"If another minute would have done it, you would have had it."

A paroxysm of pain followed, during which Mr Graham silently left him.

CHAPTER LXX

END OR BEGINNING?

When the fit was over, and he found Mr Graham was gone, he asked Malcolm, who had resumed his watch, how long it would take Lady Florimel to come from Edinburgh.

"Mr Crathie left wi' fower horses frae the Lossie Airms last nicht, my lord," said Malcolm; "but the ro'ds are ill, an' she winna be here afore sometime the morn."

The marquis stared aghast: they had sent for her without his orders.

"What *shall* I do?" he murmured. "If once I look in her eyes, I shall be damned. Malcolm!"

"Yes, my lord!"

"Is there a lawyer in Portlossie?"

"Yes, my lord; there's auld Maister Carmichael."

"He won't do! He was my brother's rascal. Is there no one besides?"

"No in Portlossie, my lord. There can be nane nearer than Duff Harbour, I doobt."

"Take the chariot and bring him here directly. Tell them to put four horses to. Stokes can ride one."

"I'll ride the ither, my lord."

"You'll do nothing of the kind: you're not used to the pole."

"I can tak the leader, my lord."

"Mr Crathie left with four horses from the Lossie Arms last night, my lord," said Malcolm; "but the roads are bad, and she won't be here before sometime tomorrow."

The marquis stared aghast: they had sent for her without his orders.

"What *shall* I do?" he murmured. "If once I look in her eyes, I shall be damned. Malcolm!"

"Yes, my lord!"

"Is there a lawyer in Portlossie?"

"Yes, my lord; there's old Mister Carmichael."

"He won't do! He was my brother's rascal. Is there no one besides?"

"Not in Portlossie, my lord. There can be none nearer than Duff Harbour, I expect."

"Take the chariot and bring him here directly. Tell them to put four horses to. Stokes can ride one."

"I'll ride the other, my lord."

"You'll do nothing of the kind: you're not used to the pole."

"I can take the leader, my lord."

"I tell you you're to do nothing of the kind!" cried the marquis angrily. "You're to ride inside, and bring Mr—what's his name? back with you."

"Soutar, my lord, gien ye please."

"Be off, then. Don't wait to feed. The brutes have been eating all day, and they can eat all night. You must have him here in an hour."

In an hour and a quarter, Miss Horn's friend stood by the marquis's bedside. Malcolm was dismissed, but was presently summoned again to receive more orders.

Fresh horses were put to the chariot, and he had to set out once more—this time to fetch a justice of the peace, a neighbour-laird. The distance was greater than to Duff Harbour; the roads were worse; the north wind, rising as they went, blew against them as they returned, increasing to a violent gale; and it was late before they reached Lossie House.

When Malcolm entered, he found the marquis alone.

"Is Morrison here at last?" he cried in a feeble, irritated voice.

"Yes, my lord."

"What the devil kept you so long? The bay mare would have carried me there and back in an hour and a half."

"The roads war verra heavy, my lord. An' jist hear till the win'!"

The marquis listened a moment, and a frightened expression grew over his thin, pale, anxious face.

"You don't know what depends on it," he said, "or you would have driven better. Where is Mr Soutar?"

"I dinna ken, my lord. I'm only jist come, an' I've seen naebody."

"I tell you you're to do nothing of the kind!" cried the marquis angrily. "You're to ride inside, and bring Mr—what's his name? back with you."

"Soutar, my lord, if you please."

"Be off, then. Don't wait to feed. The brutes have been eating all day, and they can eat all night. You must have him here in an hour."

In an hour and a quarter, Miss Horn's friend stood by the marquis's bedside. Malcolm was dismissed, but was presently summoned again to receive more orders.

Fresh horses were put to the chariot, and he had to set out once more—this time to fetch a justice of the peace, a neighbour-laird. The distance was greater than to Duff Harbour; the roads were worse; the north wind, rising as they went, blew against them as they returned, increasing to a violent gale; and it was late before they reached Lossie House.

When Malcolm entered, he found the marquis alone.

"Is Morrison here at last?" he cried in a feeble, irritated voice.

"Yes, my lord."

"What the devil kept you so long? The bay mare would have carried me there and back in an hour and a half."

"The roads were very heavy, my lord. And just listen to the wind!"

The marquis listened a moment, and a frightened expression grew over his thin, pale, anxious face.

"You don't know what depends on it," he said, "or you would have driven better. Where is Mr Soutar?"

"I don't know, my lord. I'm only just come, and I've seen nobody."

"Go and tell Mrs Courthope I want Soutar. You'll find her crying some-where—the old chicken! because I swore at her. What harm could that do the old goose?"

"It'll be mair for love o' yer lordship than fricht at the sweirin', my lord."

"You think so? Why should *she* care? Go and tell her I'm sorry. But really she ought to be used to me by this time! Tell her to send Soutar directly."

Mr Soutar was not to be found, the fact being that he had gone to see Miss Horn. The marquis flew into an awful rage, and began to curse and swear frightfully.

"My lord! my lord!" said Malcolm, "for God's sake, dinna gang on that gait. He canna like to hear that kin' o' speech—an' frae ane o' his ain tu!"

"Go and tell Mrs Courthope I want Soutar. You'll find her crying some-where—the old chicken! because I swore at her. What harm could that do the old goose?"

"It'll be more for love of your lordship than fright at the swearing, my lord."

"You think so? Why should *she* care? Go and tell her I'm sorry. But really she ought to be used to me by this time! Tell her to send Soutar directly."

Mr Soutar was not to be found, the fact being that he had gone to see Miss Horn. The marquis flew into an awful rage, and began to curse and swear frightfully.

"My lord! my lord!" said Malcolm, "for God's sake, don't go on that way. He can't like to hear that kind of speech—and from one of his own, too!"

The marquis stopped, aghast at his presumption, and choking with rage; but Malcolm's eyes filled with tears, and instead of breaking out again, his master turned his head away and was silent.

Mr Soutar came.

"Fetch Morrison," said the marquis, "and go to bed."

The wind howled terribly as Malcolm ascended the stairs and half felt his way, for he had no candle, through the long passages leading to his room. As he entered the last, a huge vague form came down upon him, like a deeper darkness through the dark. Instinctively he stepped aside. It passed noiselessly, with a long stride, and not even a rustle of its garments—at least Malcolm heard nothing but the roar of the wind. He turned and followed it. On and on it went, down the stair through a corridor, down the great stone turnpike stair, and through passage after passage. When it came into the more frequented and half-lighted thoroughfares of the house, it showed as a large figure in a long cloak, indistinct in outline.

It turned a corner close by the marquis's room. But when Malcolm, close at its heels, turned also, he saw nothing but a vacant lobby, the doors around which were all shut. One after another he quickly opened them, all except the marquis's, but nothing was to be seen. The conclusion was that it had entered the marquis's room. He must not disturb the conclave in the sick chamber with what might be but "a false creation, proceeding from the heat-oppressed brain," and turned back to his own room, where he threw himself on his bed and fell asleep.

About twelve Mrs Courthope called him: his master was worse, and wanted to see him.

The midnight was still, for the dark and wind had ceased. But a hush and a cloud seemed gathering in the stillness and darkness, and with them came the sense of a solemn celebration, as if the gloom were canopy as well as pall—black, but bordered and hearted with purple and gold; and the stillness seemed to tremble as with the inaudible tones of a great organ, at the close or commencement of some mighty symphony.

With beating heart he walked softly towards the room where, as on an altar, lay the vanishing form of his master, like the fuel in whose dying flame was offered the late and ill-nurtured sacrifice of his spirit.

As he went through the last corridor leading thither, Mrs Catanach, type and embodiment of the horrors that haunt the dignity of death, came walking towards him like one at home, her great round body lightly upborne on her soft foot. It was no time to challenge her presence, and yielding her the half of the narrow way, he passed without a greeting. She dropped him a courtesy with an uplook and again a vailing of her wicked eyes.

The marquis would not have the doctor come near him, and when Malcolm entered there was no one in the room but Mrs Courthope. The shadow had crept far along the dial. His face had grown ghastly, the skin had sunk to the bones, and his eyes stood out as if from much staring into the dark. They rested very mournfully on Malcolm for a few moments, and then closed softly.

"Is she come yet?" he murmured, opening them wide, with sudden stare.

"No, my lord."

The lids fell again, softly, slowly.

"Be good to her, Malcolm," he murmured.

"I wull, my lord," said Malcolm solemnly.

Then the eyes opened and looked at him; something grew in them—a light as of love, and drew up after it a tear; but the lips said nothing. The eyelids fell again, and in a minute more, Malcolm knew by his breathing that he slept.

The slow night waned. He woke sometimes, but soon dozed off again. The two watched by him till the dawn. It brought a still grey morning, without a breath of wind, and warm for the season. The marquis appeared a little revived, but was hardly able to speak. Mostly by signs he made Malcolm understand that he wanted Mr Graham, but that some one else must go for him. Mrs Courthope went.

As soon as she was out of the room, he lifted his hand with effort, laid feeble hold on Malcolm's jacket, and drawing him down, kissed him on the forehead. Malcolm burst into tears, and sank weeping by the bedside.

Mr Graham entering a little after, and seeing Malcolm on his knees, knelt also, and broke into a prayer.

"O blessed Father!" he said, "who knowest this thing, so strange to us, which we call death, breathe more life into the heart of thy dying son, that in the power of life he may front death. O Lord Christ, who diedst thyself, and in thyself knowest it all, heal this man in his sore need—heal him with strength to die."

Came a faint *Amen* from the marquis.

"Thou didst send him into the world: help him out of it. O God, we belong to thee utterly. We dying men are thy children, O living Father! Thou art such a father, that thou takest our sins from us and throwest them behind thy back. Thou cleanest our souls, as thy Son did wash our feet. We hold our hearts up to thee: make them what they must be, O Love, O Life of men, O Heart of hearts! Give thy dying child courage, and hope, and peace—the peace of him who overcame all the terrors of humanity, even death itself, and liveth for evermore, sitting at thy right hand, our God-brother, blessed to all ages—amen."

"Amen!" murmured the marquis, and slowly lifting his hand from the coverlid, he laid it on the head of Malcolm, who did not know it was the hand of his father, blessing him ere he died.

"Be good to her," said the marquis once more. But Malcolm could not answer for weeping, and the marquis was not satisfied. Gathering all his force he said again, "Be good to her."

"I wull, I wull," burst from Malcolm in sobs, and he wailed aloud.

The day wore on, and the afternoon came. Still Lady Florimel had not arrived, and still the marquis lingered.

As the gloom of the twilight was deepening into the early darkness of the winter night, he opened wide his eyes, and was evidently listening. Malcolm could hear nothing; but the light in his master's face grew, and the strain of his listening diminished. At length Malcolm became aware of the sound of wheels, which came rapidly nearer, till at last the carriage swung up to the hall door. A moment, and Lady Florimel was flitting across the room.

"Papa! papa!" she cried, and, throwing her arm over him, laid her cheek to his.

The marquis could not return her embrace; he could only receive her into the depths of his shining tearful eyes.

"Flory!" he murmured, "I'm going away. I'm going—I've got—to make an—apology. Malcolm, be good—"

The sentence remained unfinished. The light paled from his countenance—he had to carry it with him. He was dead.

Lady Florimel gave a loud cry. Mrs Courthope ran to her assistance.

"My lady's in a dead faint!" she whispered, and left the room to get help.

Malcolm lifted Lady Florimel in his great arms, and bore her tenderly to her own apartment. There he left her to the care of her women, and returned to the chamber of death.

Meantime Mr Graham and Mr Soutar had come. When Malcolm re-entered, the schoolmaster took him kindly by the arm and said:

"Malcolm, there can be neither place nor moment fitter for the solemn communication I am commissioned to make to you: I have, as in the presence of your dead father, to inform you that you are now Marquis of Lossie; and God forbid you should be less worthy as marquis than you have been as fisherman!"

Malcolm stood stupefied. For a while he seemed to himself to be turning over in his mind something he had heard read from a book, with a nebulous notion of being somehow concerned in it. The thought of his father cleared his brain. He ran to the dead body, kissed its lips, as he had once kissed the forehead of another, and falling on his knees, wept, he knew not for what. Presently, however, he recovered himself, rose, and, rejoining the two men, said—

"Gentlemen, hoo many kens this turn o' things?"

"None but Mr Morrison, Mrs Catanach, and ourselves—so far as I know," answered Mr Soutar.

"And Miss Horn," added Mr Graham. "She first brought out the truth of it, and ought to be the first to know of your recognition by your father."

"I s' tell her mysel'," returned Malcolm. "But, gentlemen, I beg o' ye, till I ken what I'm aboot an' gie ye leave, dinna open yer moo' to leevin' cratur' aboot this. There's time eneuch for the warl' to ken 't."

"Your lordship commands me," said Mr Soutar.

"Yes, Malcolm,—until you give me leave," said Mr Graham.

"Whaur's Mr Morrison?" asked Malcolm.

"He is still in the house," said Mr Soutar.

"Gang till him, sir, an' gar him promise, on the word o' a gentleman, to haud his tongue. I canna bide to hae 't blaret a' gait an' a' at ance. For Mistress Catanach, I s' deal wi' her mysel'."

"Gentlemen, how many know this turn of things?"

"None but Mr Morrison, Mrs Catanach, and ourselves—so far as I know," answered Mr Soutar.

"And Miss Horn," added Mr Graham. "She first brought out the truth of it, and ought to be the first to know of your recognition by your father."

"I shall tell her myself," returned Malcolm. "But, gentlemen, I beg of you, till I know what I'm about and give you leave, don't open your mouth to living soul about this. There's time enough for the world to know it."

"Your lordship commands me," said Mr Soutar.

"Yes, Malcolm,—until you give me leave," said Mr Graham.

"Where's Mr Morrison?" asked Malcolm.

"He is still in the house," said Mr Soutar.

"Go to him, sir, and make him promise, on the word of a gentleman, to hold his tongue. I can't bear to have it blared out everywhere and all at once. For Mistress Catanach, I'll deal with her myself."

The door opened, and, in all the conscious dignity conferred by the immunities and prerogatives of her calling, Mrs Catanach walked into the room.

"A word wi' ye, Mistress Catanach," said Malcolm.

"Certainly, my lord," answered the howdy, with mingled presumption and respect, and followed him to the dining-room.

"Weel, my lord," she began, before he had turned from shutting the door behind them, in the tone and with the air, or rather *airs*, of having conferred a great benefit, and expecting its recognition.

"Mistress Catanach," interrupted Malcolm, turning and facing her, "gien I be un'er ony obligation to you, it 's frae anither tongue I maun hear 't. But I hae an offer to mak ye: Sae lang as it disna come oot 'at I'm onything better nor a fisherman born, ye s' hae yer twinty poun' i' the year, peyed ye quarterly. But the moment fowk says wha I am, ye touch na a poun' note mair, an' I coont mysel' free to pursue onything I can pruv agane ye."

Mrs Catanach attempted a laugh of scorn, but her face was grey as putty, and its muscles declined response.

"*Ay* or *no?*" said Malcolm. "I winna gar ye sweir, for I wad lippen to yer aith no a hair."

"Ay, my lord," said the howdy, reassuming at least outward composure, and with it her natural brass, for as she spoke she held out her open palm.

"Na, na!" said Malcolm, "nae forehan payments! Three months o' tongue-haudin', an' there's yer five poun'; an' Maister Soutar o' Duff Harbour 'ill pay 't intill yer ain han'. But brak troth wi' me, an' ye s' hear o' 't; for gien ye war hangt,

The door opened, and, in all the conscious dignity conferred by the immunities and prerogatives of her calling, Mrs Catanach walked into the room.

"A word with you, Mistress Catanach," said Malcolm.

"Certainly, my lord," answered the howdy, with mingled presumption and respect, and followed him to the dining-room.

"Well, my lord," she began, before he had turned from shutting the door behind them, in the tone and with the air, or rather *airs*, of having conferred a great benefit, and expecting its recognition.

"Mistress Catanach," interrupted Malcolm, turning and facing her, "if I be under any obligation to you, it's from another tongue I must hear it. But I have an offer to make you: So long as it doesn't come out that I'm anything better than a fisherman born, you'll have your twenty pounds a year, paid down quarterly. But the moment folk say who I am, you'll get not a pound more, and I count myself free to pursue anything I can prove against you."

Mrs Catanach attempted a laugh of scorn, but her face was grey as putty, and its muscles declined response.

"*Ay* or *no?*" said Malcolm. "I won't make you swear, for I don't set your oath at a pin's fee."

"Ay, my lord," said the howdy, reassuming at least outward composure, and with it her natural brass, for as she spoke she held out her open palm.

"Na, na!" said Malcolm, "no forehand payments! Three months of tongue-holding, and there's your five pounds; and Mister Soutar of Duff Harbour will pay it into your own hand. But break troth with me, and you shall hear of it; for if you the warl' wad be but the cleaner. Noo quit the hoose, an' never lat me see ye aboot the place again. But afore ye gang, I gie ye fair warnin' 'at I mean to win at a' yer byganes."

The blood of red wrath was seething in Mrs Catanach's face; she drew herself up, and stood flaming before him, on the verge of explosion.

"Gang frae the hoose," said Malcolm, "or I'll set the muckle hun' to shaw ye the gait."

were hanged, the world would be but the cleaner. Now quit the house, and never let me see you about the place again. But before you go, I give you fair warning that I mean to sniff out all your secrets."

The blood of red wrath was seething in Mrs Catanach's face; she drew herself up, and stood flaming before him, on the verge of explosion.

"Leave the house," said Malcolm, "or I'll get the great dog to show you the way."

Her face turned the colour of ashes, and with hanging cheeks and scared but not the less wicked eyes, she turned from the room. Malcolm watched her out of the house, then following her into the town, brought Miss Horn back with him to aid in the last of earthly services, and hastened to Duncan's cottage.

But to his amazement and distress, it was forsaken, and the hearth cold. In his attendance on his father, he had not seen the piper—he could not remember for how many days; and on inquiry he found that, although he had not been missed, no one could recall having seen him later than three or four days agone. The last he could hear of him in the neighbourhood was, that, about a week before, a boy had spied him sitting on a rock in the Baillies' Barn, with his pipes in his lap. Searching the cottage, he found that his broadsword and dirk, with all his poor finery, were gone.

That same night Mrs Catanach also disappeared.

A week after, what was left of Lord Lossie was buried. Malcolm followed the hearse with the household. Miss Horn walked immediately behind him, on the arm of the schoolmaster. It was a great funeral, with a short road, for the body was laid in the church—close to the wall, just under the crusader with the Norman canopy.

Lady Florimel wept incessantly for three days; on the fourth she looked out on the sea and thought it very dreary; on the fifth she found a certain gratification in hearing herself called the marchioness; on the sixth she tried on her mourning, and was pleased; on the seventh she went with the funeral and wept again; on the eighth came Lady Bellair, who on the ninth carried her away.

To Malcolm she had not spoken once.

Mr Graham left Portlossie.

Miss Horn took to her bed for a week.

Mr Crathie removed his office to the House itself, took upon him the function of steward as well as factor, had the state rooms dismantled, and was master of the place.

Malcolm helped Stoat with the horses, and did odd jobs for Mr Crathie. From his likeness to the old marquis, as he was still called, the factor had a favour for him, firmly believing the said marquis to be his father, and Mrs Stewart his mother. Hence he allowed him a key to the library, of which Malcolm made good use.

The story of Malcolm's plans and what came of them, requires another book.

THE END.

LITERAL ENGLISH TRANSLATION OF MR GRAHAM'S POEM (CHAPTER XLII)

The water ran down from the high valley-head
With a Run, river, run;
It rippled, and waggled, and sang a screed
Of nonsense, and wouldn't cease,
With its Run, river, run.

From the heart of the world, with a swirl and a sway,
And a Run, river, run,
That water leapt clear from the dark to the day,
And singing away did spin,
With its Run, river, run.

One short mile from the high valley-head,
With a Run, river, run,
'Mong her ewes and her lambs the herd lassie stood
And she let a tear fall in,
With a Run, river, run.

From the heart of the maiden that tear-drop rose,
With a Run, river, run;
Wearily climbing up narrow ways,
There was but a drop to fall in,
So slow did that river run.

Two short miles from the high valley-head,
With a Run, river, run,
Down crept a cowering streak of red,
And melted away within,
With a Run, river, run.

From the heart of a youth came the trickling red,
With a Run, river, run;
It ran and ran till it left him dead,
And then it dried up in the wind,
And that river no more did run.

When the rippling river that from three hearts went
With a Run, river, run,
Came to the lip of the sea so broad,
It curled and shuddered with pain of sin—
But it took that river in.